BE STILL

April Joy Spring

Copyright © 2019 by April Joy Spring.

Library of Congress Control Number:		2019902149
ISBN:	Hardcover	978-1-7960-1770-0
	Softcover	978-1-7960-1769-4
	eBook	978-1-7960-1781-6

All rights reserved. No part of this book may be reproduced or transmitted in any form or by any means, electronic or mechanical, including photocopying, recording, or by any information storage and retrieval system, without permission in writing from the copyright owner.

This is a work of fiction. All of the characters, names, incidents, organizations, and dialogue in this novel are either the products of the author's imagination or are used fictitiously.

Any people depicted in stock imagery provided by Getty Images are models, and such images are being used for illustrative purposes only.
Certain stock imagery © Getty Images.

Print information available on the last page.

Rev. date: 03/01/2019

To order additional copies of this book, contact:
Xlibris
1-888-795-4274
www.Xlibris.com
Orders@Xlibris.com
775874

Book 3

Dorothy!

"Be still and know that I am God." Psalm 46:10

Dear reader, when life becomes difficult, remember to Be Still, Trust God, and Fear Not.

April Avery

CHAPTER 1

After setting off the fireworks in town, and receiving the odd text on his phone that read, "Hey, Jamie, I like your display, but check this out," Jamie drove as fast as he dared, to the abandoned oil refinery north of Alva, which appeared to be ablaze. *Why in the world would Jimmy set a fire at the oil refinery?*

The two teen boys had discussed doing something spectacular on Christmas eve, like a bonfire or explosion, back in November, at the Enlightened One's Thanksgiving dinner, but neither had committed to any particular plan at that time.

Jamie tried calling the number from the text, but to no avail. He left a message, but hadn't received a reply. *Jimmy, I hope you're okay.*

Screeching to a halt on the gravel near the blazing refinery, Jamie jumped from the idling vehicle, and ran towards the inferno, calling Jimmy's name.

"Over here!" He heard over the roar of the flames.

"Jimmy?"

"Jamie? Over here. I'm stuck!"

Jamie ran toward a pile of rubble, and found Jimmy with his leg trapped under a large beam, connected to a piece of metal roofing.

Assessing the situation, he found a metal pipe, and began prying the beam off Jimmy's leg. Between curses, grunts, and yelps of pain, Jimmy managed to extract himself from the trap. With Jamie's help, he limped towards the car.

"How did you get here?" Jamie asked, as he helped his friend onto the passenger's seat.

Gritting his teeth against the pain, Jimmy said, "I rode my bike."

Looking around the lot, and seeing nothing but smoldering piles of wood and metal, Jamie asked, "Where is it?"

Pointing to an area not far from the car, Jimmy said, "Over in those bushes."

Jamie hopped in the vehicle, drove over to the indicated spot, wrestled the bike into his trunk, and drove in the opposite direction from which he came.

As he pulled onto the road, which would take them to Jimmy's house, he could see the flashing lights, and hear the sirens of the police, emergency vehicles, and fire trucks.

Jamie was so focused on driving, he barely heard Jimmy's whispered, "Thank you."

Once they were a couple of miles down the road, Jamie relaxed his grip on the steering wheel, and unclenched his jaw. He pulled the car into Jimmy's driveway, killed the engine, and turned to face his friend.

"What were you thinking, Jimmy? What was that all about?"

Jimmy wiped his eyes, and moaned, as he turned his body to face Jamie.

"I just wanted to do something epic."

Jamie shook his head. "Well, that was certainly epic. My goodness, you could have been killed!"

Jimmy looked down, and nodded slightly.

"Yeah. But I wasn't."

"If I hadn't come along, you would still be lying there when the police and firemen, arrived."

"I almost got away, but that second explosion took me by surprise. That beam knocked me down so fast and hard, I couldn't breath for a minute. I thought I would die for sure."

Jamie ran his hands through his hair, and let out a lungful of air, and asked, "Do you think your leg is broken?"

Jimmy struggled to move the injured limb. "No. I can move it. It's beginning to swell though. I can feel my pants and shoes getting tighter."

Looking at the leg, Jamie asked, "Is it bleeding?"

"Maybe. I can't really tell. It feels weird though. Kinda tingly, and my jeans feel wet."

Turning the overhead light on, Jimmy gasped when he saw his bloody jeans, and blood stained hand.

Opening his door, Jamie said, "Let's go in, and check out that leg, then we'd better come up with a believable story as to *how* and *why* it's injured. If your dad sees you limping around, he'll wonder what happened."

Jimmy shook his head. "I doubt it. He never pays attention to me anyway."

Jamie helped his friend into his bedroom, and stood in the doorway, while Jimmy removed his jeans and examined his leg. There was a trail of blood from a puncture wound in his right thigh, to his tennis shoe.

"Man! That looks bad!" Jamie said, as he watched his friend limp to the bathroom.

"Yeah, but I don't think it's as bad as it looks. I can put weight on it, so it's not broken."

"Well, that's good, but you do have a puncture wound. Have you had a tetanus shot lately?"

"Yeah, a few years ago. I think if I put ice on it, and keep it elevated for a couple of days, it should be okay. I don't think the nail went in very far."

Jamie sighed. "You are one lucky dude."

Closing the door to the bathroom, Jimmy nodded, and said, "Don't I know it?"

While Jimmy showered, Jamie gathered the smoke and blood saturated clothes and put them in the washer. As strong as the smell was, he figured they'd have to go through a couple of washings. He watched as the water changed from clear to red and gray, as the blood and oily smoke residue was leeched from the jeans. *This is bad*, he thought. Shaking his head, he closed the washer lid, and headed for his car to unload the bicycle. Opening the trunk, he was overwhelmed by the strong smoky odor permeating his vehicle. After putting the bike in the garage, he went into the house to search for a can of air-freshener, hoping it would clear the smoky evidence from his car.

Jimmy exited the bathroom, dressed in black athletic pants, and a maroon Alva Eagles t-shirt. He hobbled to the Lazy-Boy chair in the living room, gingerly sat, and raised the foot extender.

"Hey Jamie, could you bring me a couple of ice-packs?"

Jamie brought them, and sat across from his friend. They talked about the two incidences, and what alibis they would use, if per chance, they were questioned. Jimmy then told of his near discovery at the Conger's farm house.

Shaking his head, Jamie said, "I can't believe you entered that old couple's house."

"Yeah, the old man scared me half to death! That was too close for comfort!" Jimmy said, wincing as he adjusted the ice-packs on his leg.

"So I take it you're not going back there?"

Grinning, Jimmy said, "No way! Maybe somewhere else, but not there. I think he'd shoot me first, and ask questions later!"

Nodding, and smiling, Jamie said, "You know, if you keep taking these kind of risks, you're bound to get caught."

Jimmy cocked his head. "Maybe, but you're doing the same thing. You could get caught too."

Jamie shrugged. "Possibly, but I've become kind of an expert at breaking and entering."

Nodding, Jimmy said, "True, but there's always that one possibility of getting caught."

Grinning, Jamie said, "Yeah, but that's what makes it so fun!"

Stuffing a pillow under his knee, Jimmy asked, "So, are you gonna go back to the Sander's house?"

Nodding, Jamie said, "I want to. I like that family, and like being close to them, even if they don't know I'm there. Besides, I need to return something."

"What?"

"I took a photo album." Shrugging, he added, "I wanted to get to know them better."

"Do you?"

"Do I what?"

"Know them better?"

Smiling, Jamie said, "Yeah. I wish I had a family like that."

"So, when are you gonna return it?"

Shrugging, Jamie said, "Soon. Maybe next week."

"You gonna take anything else?"

Jamie scrunched his face. "I haven't decided yet."

Jimmy moaned. "Could you bring me some pain pills? There should be some in the kitchen cabinet, by the stove. My dad has some prescription Motrin, or something like that in there."

Jamie went to the kitchen, and Jimmy heard him rummaging through the cabinet.

He called out, "I found a prescription for Tylenol with codeine and 800 milligram Ibuprofen tablets."

"Bring me the one with codeine."

Jamie returned a few minutes later, with a pill and a glass of water.

"Thanks, I hope this doesn't knock me out."

"It might," Jamie said. "One time, I took some cough syrup with codeine, and I slept for twelve hours."

"Geeze! Well, if I pass out, make sure my clothes are washed good. I don't want them smelling like smoke."

Jamie said, "They're in the wash right now. Hey, I was thinking that maybe you should call your dad, and ask him about the explosions. He may think it odd if you aren't curious. Besides, it'll take any suspicion off you."

Nodding, Jimmy said, "That's a good idea."

Jamie handed him the phone, and listened to Jimmy's side of the conversation.

The residents of Alva weren't sure what to make of the two different explosions that had just occurred. The first one, a celebration of sorts, and the second, dangerous, and destructive.

They couldn't help but wonder what the purpose was, and who was behind them—a mystery that may never be solved.

Larry Clifton, the Police Chief of Alva, gripped the steering wheel, and sat in stoney silence as he, and his deputy, Mike Owens, traveled to the burning oil refinery. It was hardly recognizable, as flames, like hungry hands, reached towards the sky, engulfing it.

Turning onto the graveled lot, and looking up at the burning inferno in awe, Mike whispered, "Oh man! I hope no one was in there."

Larry stepped out of the car, and motioned for the fire trucks to pull up beside him. Jesse McCoy, the Alva Fire Chief, and father of Jimmy, left his truck, and began barking orders. The twenty or so firemen, and volunteers, began unfurling the water hoses, connecting them to the water and chemical tankers, behind them. The chemical tanker held a foamy substance that would squelch the oil related fire, while the water took care of any wooden structure that was ablaze.

The chemical tanker, which hadn't been used since the purchase of it last summer, held a few thousand gallons, and still had that shiny, new look about it.

When Jesse had read about the tanker, and it's usefulness, he had brought it before the city council, who at first balked at the idea. Watching his men spray the foam on the oily fire, and watching the flames sizzle and die, Jesse was thankful the council had changed their collective minds, and gave the go-ahead for him to make the purchase.

Larry walked over and asked, "Hey, Jesse, do you think we need to call in help from the nearby towns?"

Jesse nodded. "I already called units from West, Waxahachi, and Milford. They should be arriving in a few minutes. If that doesn't seem to be enough, I have the Waco team on stand-by."

Larry nodded. "Mike and I are going to walk around, and see if there is any evidence of foul play left behind...or any victims."

Jesse nodded. "Yeah. Once the fire is under control, I'll do my own investigating."

Mike and Larry walked around the perimeter of the burning structure, and besides a few footprints, car tracks, and smoldering debris, they were unable to find any thing out of the ordinary. Larry let out a sigh.

Removing his hat, and wiping his brow, Larry said, "Well, thank goodness, there aren't any bodies."

Removing his own hat, and running his hand through his hair, Mike sighed, and said, "Man, three incidences in one night! And of all nights. Christmas eve. Weird. You think they're related?"

Returning his hat to his head, Larry rubbed his chin, and shrugged. "Maybe."

Once the other fire-trucks, crews, and water tankers arrived, and were situated on all four sides of the burning inferno, the men hooked the hoses up to their tankers, and began spraying.

Jesse McCoy, and three of his men, entered the structure to make an initial assessment, and confirm the absence of victims. As they were exiting, an explosion knocked the four men to the ground, covering them with debris from the few remaining smoldering beams. Realizing what had happened, the volunteers and firemen from the Alva and Milford teams, ran towards the pile of rubble, and began digging. The rest of the teams continued spraying water, in hopes of squelching the remaining flames.

Jesse, who had been closest to the entrance, was the first to be extracted. Loading the unconscious man into the awaiting ambulance, and hooking him up to a cardiac monitor, the EMTs did an initial assessment, and found the only obvious injury was a gash, and large lump on the back of his head. His vital signs were strong, and his heart rate was steady. After putting a temporary bandage on his head, the two EMTs breathed a sigh of relief, looked out the window, and silently hoped that the other fire-men had been as lucky. After strapping their patient, and themselves in, and giving the driver a nod, the flashing lights, and siren, were engaged, as the ambulance sped to the nearby hospital. The other three men were loaded into two other ambulances, which followed closely behind the one holding Jesse McCoy.

Sheriff Clifton watched the disappearing lights fade, then turned to face the inferno, which didn't seem to be dissipating as quickly as he would have thought, given the amount of water and chemicals being sprayed. Closing his eyes, he listened. Turning his head to the right, and then to the left, he heard a strange noise. Sure, there were the shouts of the men, the water and chemicals rushing through the hoses, the low rumble of the fire truck's engines, and the pop and sizzle of the fire, as it was being hit by the cold water, but under all that, he heard something else. Before he began walking around the perimeter, he asked that the engines be shut down for a few minutes. Every few feet, he would stop, close his eyes, and listen. Every now and then, a man from one of the crews would try to speak to him, but he would hold up his finger, and point to his ear, indicating that he was listening for something. They would either turn back to their job at hand, or stand with him, trying to determine what it was that he was listening for. He had almost returned to the spot from whence he began, when he heard it again.

"Did you hear that?" He asked the group of men standing around him.

Cocking their heads in the direction the sheriff had pointed, one of the men spoke.

"I did hear something. Sounded like a whine of some sort."

Turning in a circle, and cupping both ears with their hands, they continued to listen.

Another man said, "I heard a kind of whistling sound. Like air escaping from a tire."

Turning to the men, he asked, "What direction do you think the sound is coming from?'

The group pointed to their right. Larry nodded. "Yeah, me too."

Larry led a couple of the men to the east side of the burning structure.

The closer he walked to the main concentration of the fire, the louder the sound became. Holding his hand up, he motioned for the men to stop. A look of terror crossed his face, as he realized what the sound was.

Yelling for the men to follow, he ran away from the structure, waving his arms and shouting, "Run! Everybody get out of here!"

Most of the fire men didn't hear him because of the other sounds emanating from the fire and hoses, but they understood the body language, and dropping their hoses, ran away from the skeletal structure, just as a loud whoosh sounded, followed closely by a deafening boom. The men closest to the fire, were knocked off their feet. After a few minutes of disorienting chaos, men began running towards the sheriff, asking if he was okay.

Standing on shaky legs, he nodded. He couldn't hear anyone or anything, but he wasn't experiencing any pain, so he reasoned that he was indeed, okay. Rubbing his ears, shaking his head and opening and closing his mouth, he hoped to open his ear canals, and regain his hearing. He watched as men were running about, grabbing hoses and shouting orders.

The EMT men took the sheriff's hands and led him over to one of the ambulances. He sat at the back of the vehicle with an oxygen mask over his nose, watching the chaos, as his vital signs were being assessed. The EMT who was doing the testing, wrote on a notepad, that his hearing would return in a few minutes, as there was no signs of damage to his ear drums.

Meanwhile, the Emergency Room doctors, and staff, worked diligently and efficiently to assess, and determine the seriousness of the injuries of the three men, who were thrown to the ground during the first explosion. It was agreed among the medical team, that two of the men needed more care than the little hospital could offer.

After contacting the next of kin, and signing the various forms, the severely injured men were reloaded in the ambulances, and rushed to the burn unit located in Dallas Memorial Hospital.

Jesse, Alva's Fire Chief, regained consciousness, and hearing of the injured men, asked one of the ER nurses to take him to see them, before they left the building. He wasn't sure they would be aware of his presence, but he wanted to let their families know he cared, and would work night and day to discover what, or who, had started the fire. He felt helpless, and angry. Of all nights for this to happen. If his guys didn't pull through, he knew their kids would forever be traumatized. *How could one explain to a child that their daddy died on Christmas eve? A time of Santa, gifts, joy and celebration.* As he walked back to his cubicle in the Emergency room, he thought about his own life, and what would happen to his son, Jimmy, if he died. *Would my kid even miss me?*

When his wife had died five years ago, Jesse had shut down emotionally. He had thrown himself into his work, and had ignored his son. Sitting on the side of the bed, he let his mind explore the reasons for his neglect, and realized his behavior made no sense. *Just because Jimmy looks a lot like his mother, and every time I look at him, I see my wife, that doesn't give me the right to ignore or lash out at him. Was that justifiable? Of course not!* He felt his heart catch, as tears stung his eyes. Pinching the bridge of his nose to stop the flow of tears, and failing, as a few escaped anyway, and ran down his cheeks, he groaned in frustration. He had always associated tears with weakness.

"Strong men don't cry." His dad had told him time and again. Knowing why he had this new found emotion, did alleviate his frustration.

Ever since Jack and I went to that men's meeting in Dallas a couple of weeks ago...what was it called? Oh yes, Promise Keepers, I've become and emotional wreck. I used to never cry, and now, I find my eyes tearing up for the least little thing.

He knew his behavior towards his son had been wrong, and had asked God's forgiveness, right there, in his seat, surrounded by thousands of other men doing the same. He had never seen so many men break down, and cry like babies—just like Jack, and himself. They both had been guilty of emotional, verbal, and physical abuse towards their sons, and knew it was time for a change.

As he prayed for God's forgiveness, he had felt as if a heavy blanket had been lifted from his shoulders. He had also felt, or heard, he wasn't sure, God's voice saying he needed to make amends with Jimmy. He had every intention of doing so, but the days just kept passing by, and here it was, a couple of weeks later, and no resolution.

Bowing his head, he whispered, "Please forgive me, God. I will talk to Jimmy soon."

As he was being unloaded from the ambulance, Jesse's phone rang. The EMT, who was caring for the unconscious Fire Chief, dug the phone out of the uniform, and answered it.

"Hello? Dad?"

"No, this is Doug, the EMT. Is your dad the Fire Chief?"

Jimmy's breath caught. "Yeah. Why are you answering my dad's phone? Is he okay?"

"Well, Son, there was an explosion out at the old oil refinery, and your dad was injured."

Panic filled Jimmy's voice. "Injured? How? How bad? Is he going to be okay?"

"Whoa! First of all, let me tell you, he's unconscious, but his vital signs are strong, and stable. I believe he'll be okay, but we're taking him to the hospital to run a few tests, to make sure."

Jimmy felt his eyes tear-up. With a shaky voice, he asked, "Was anyone else hurt?"

The EMT cleared his throat. "Yes. There were three other men."

"Oh man! That's terrible! Nobody died, did they?"

The EMT sighed and answered, "No. Not yet."

"Not yet? What does that mean?"

"Well, at least two of the guys had to be taken to Dallas, because of burns. But, hey, you don't need to worry about that."

Jamie was silently asking what happened.

Understanding the possible consequences of his actions, Jimmy sat in stunned silence, almost dropping the phone.

Jamie grabbed it before it hit the floor, and said, "Uhm, I'll be there in a little while."

The EMT said, "It'll take a while for your dad to be admitted, so don't worry about rushing. Get here when you can."

After disconnecting, Jamie shook his friend, demanding that Jimmy tell him what happened. Jimmy did. The boys sat in silence a few minutes, as they digested the news.

Jimmy asked, "Hey, did you happen to find a lighter in the jean's pocket?"

Jamie shook his head. "Nope. Why?"

"Could you go look in your car?"

"Sure. What kind of lighter am I looking for?"

"A silver one, with the initials JM on the front."

"JM? Was that your dad's lighter?"

Jimmy nodded. I couldn't find any other one around, so I took his."

Jamie frowned. "Okay, but what if I don't find it? You don't think it fell out of your pocket when that beam fell on you, do you?"

Panic filled Jimmy's eyes. "Oh man! I hope not! Please look around for it!"

Jamie nodded, then headed out to his car. He returned a few minutes later, shaking his head. "No lighter anywhere."

Jimmy ran a hand through his hair. *Things were going from bad to worse. I just wanted to bring some excitement to Alva. I never expected this.*

Christina Sanders, and her three children, Brad, Stacey, and Nicky, and most of the residents of Alva, stood on their front lawns, watching the fire and smoke, billow up from the abandoned oil refinery, wondering what had happened to cause such an inferno.

The Sander's family had moved to Alva, Texas, Christina's home town, after the death of Christina's husband, David. Over the past few months, she had reconnected with friends, and relatives, and had been hired as an RN on the Cardiac Care Unit, or CCU, in the local hospital. The transition from Michigan to Texas had been challenging, as trial after trial had plagued the Sander's family. Their faith had been stretched and tested, as they walked through each trail, while learning lessons on trusting God, and remaining fearless, in spite of the circumstances.

"Mom?" Nicky whispered, breaking the silence.

"Yes, Nicky."

"Do you think there will be any more explosions?"

Christina sighed, and pulled him close, "I sure hope not."

Nodding, Nicky said, "Yeah, me too."

Pulling the hood of his jacket over his head, he said, "I'm cold. I think I'll go back in."

Christina felt a shiver course through her body. "Yeah, me too. I think we should all go back to bed. There's nothing else to see."

As the Sander's family ascended the stairway leading to their bedrooms, Stacy said, "I wonder if the same person set off the fireworks, and started the fire at the refinery."

Brad said, "I doubt it. They were almost simultaneous, and being so far apart, I don't see how anyone could travel that distance so quickly."

Stacy nodded. "Yeah, that would be hard, for sure, unless they had some remote control thing."

Giggling, Nicky said, "Or they were like Superman, and could fly."

Christina smiled, and shook her head. Looking at the hall clock, she said, "It's one o'clock. Off to bed you three. I'll see you later."

After hugs and kisses, they went to their separate rooms, settling in for the remaining night.

Christina, despite knowing she had to be at work in a few hours, had difficulty falling asleep as worrisome thoughts invaded her weary mind.

The Police Chief, leaning against his cruiser, watched the firemen working diligently to squelch the last of the flames. He felt a sudden chill, as the temperature dropped, and the wind increased in intensity. He reached in his car, and pulled out a stocking cap and gloves. As he donned them, he glanced up, and watched in awe, as a tornado-like funnel, sometimes referred to as a Wind Devil, picked up fire and ashes, and took them high above the refinery. *That's weird*, he thought. Looking around the lot, he realized he was the only one witnessing the strange phenomena. The wind, as if being directed, headed towards the hospital a quarter mile away. *Surely, it will burn out before it reaches the hospital,* he thought, as he watched in awe.

He breathed a sigh of relief, as the funnel disappeared, thinking everything had been resolved.

Glancing around the lot, he headed toward the Fire Chief from the Milford department.

The Chief reached out to shake Larry's hand.

"Hey, Larry, how's your hearing?"

Smiling, and doing a thumbs up sign, Larry said, "Back to normal."

Nodding, the Chief said, "That's good. Just wanted you to know that our crew is packing up. Everything seems to be under control, so we'll be heading back to the station."

Larry nodded. "Thanks for coming. Hopefully, we won't need any more assistance for a while."

Loading a toolbox behind the seat of the cab, then hoisting himself up, the Milford Fire Chief nodded, and said, "Yeah. We can hope."

Larry waved, as the truck, and its occupants left the lot, then turned and headed towards the Alva team.

Two crewmen were manning the fire hose, and directing the spray where there were still flames, or smoldering areas. The other four were walking around, kicking, and moving piles of smoking debris, to insure there would be no surprise fires re-igniting.

Stepping over hoses and debris, Larry called out, "Hey guys, how's it going?"

The crewman, whose name tag identified him as Joe Slanek, answered, "I think we're about finished here." Looking around, he added, "If it hadn't been for the Waxahachi, West, and Milford teams joining in, I'm not sure we would have been successful in dousing the flames without more casualties."

Nodding, Larry said, "Right. Y'all did a great job working together. Has anyone found any evidence of how, or where the fire started?"

Finding it difficult to hear over the flow of water from the hose, Joe patted his fellow crewman on the shoulder, indicating that he would be laying his section of the hose on the ground.

The crewman nodded, and gripped the nozzle tighter.

Slanek, and the Police Chief, walked a few yards away. Removing his helmet, mask and gloves, Joe said, "It's difficult to tell exactly where the fire began, but we're positive it didn't start on its own. There had to have been a catalyst of some sort. With all the residual oil, and piles of debris, it's no wonder it took off so quickly, and burned so intensely. I highly doubt we'll find any evidence of where, or how it started."

Larry nodded.

Running a hand through his hair, Slanek said, "I heard there was another incident in town. What was that about?"

Smiling, Larry shook his head. "Well, oddly enough, someone thought it would be cool to set off fireworks down by the courthouse. Shook most of the residents out of their beds, but no damage was done. We'll be investigating that as well." Rolling his eyes, he added, "Probably some teenagers."

Joe shook his head. "I remember doing a few questionable things as a teen, but nothing as spectacular as that. I'll have to give them credit for ingenuity."

Larry chuckled, "It was pretty ingenious. I personally would have never thought of doing something like that." Shaking his head, he added, "Kids nowadays."

Slanek asked, "Have you heard anything about the Fire Chief? How he's doing?"

Pulling his phone out to check for missed calls or messages, he said, "No. Not yet. I'll run over to the hospital in a few minutes to check on him, and the other guys. I know there was one guy complaining of chest pain. I haven't heard anything about the guys sent to Dallas."

Nodding, Slanek said, "Okay. We'll finish up here, and get a report to you as soon as possible. Let us know what you find out about the Chief, and other guys."

"Will do. I'll call the station and report in. In the mean time, I'm going to go check on the Waxahachi team."

Slanek waved, as he headed back to his teammate.

Larry walked around to the side where the Waxahachi team was packing up their equipment.

The Fire-Chief, Jason Hill, extended his hand, when he saw Larry approach.

Shaking hands, and patting him on the shoulder, Larry said, "Looks like y'all have everything under control."

"Yep. It was touch and go for a while there, but it's pretty much out." Pointing, he added," There may be a few smoldering areas left, but nothing to be concerned about. There's nothing left to burn, but ash."

Nodding, Larry said, "Good. Wouldn't want to be called out again tonight."

Chuckling, Jason said, "Ain't that the truth. We're pretty beat. Looking forward to heading back to the station, then home. A lot of these guys have little kids, so they have to get home, and put toys together for Christmas morning, which is..." glancing at his watch, "about an hour or two away."

Grimacing, Larry said, "Oh yeah, I forgot about that." Patting the Chief on his shoulder, Larry said, "Well, I won't keep you. Get your guys, and head on out. I'll talk to you tomorrow." Turning he said, "Oh, yeah. Merry Christmas!"

Jason nodded, and waved, "Merry Christmas to you!"

The Emergency Room was alive with activity, when the Police Chief entered. He stood and watched a moment, before walking over to the admissions desk. The hospital staff was busy answering phones, filling out paper work, and talking to patients, and family members—*a very unusual way to spend Christmas Eve*, he thought.

A young woman, who appeared to be in her mid-thirties, and with a name tag that read Lucy, greeted him with a grin. She was the first Lucy he had ever come across in all his thirty-nine years, besides Lucille Ball, whom she favored, with her read hair, fair skin and green eyes. *She's cute*, he thought. *I wonder if she's single?* He glanced at her wedding ring finger, which was bare, and thought, *I wonder if she has a boyfriend? Someone as cute as she is, probably does. I guess I'll have to find out. If she doesn't, maybe she would go out with me.* His rambling thoughts were interrupted, when she said, in a strong southern drawl, "Hey, Sheriff, how are you doing tonight?"

Removing his hat, and smiling, he said, "Well, I've been better. It's been a rough night."

"That's what I've heard. We've never had anything like this in all the years I've lived here. It's been crazy busy here too."

Nodding, Larry said, "Yep. It's been a wild ride tonight. First, a bomb threat at the high school, then a fire-works display, then a fire at the refinery." Shaking his head, he said, "I hope that's it for a while."

Furrowing her brow, she said, "I didn't hear about the bomb threat, and I didn't see the fire-works, but I did see the fire raging outside the windows. It was so close. You don't think it could spread to here, do you?"

Larry shook his head. "I doubt it. There were a lot of firemen working hard to keep it contained. Which reminds me, how are the guys they sent to Dallas?"

The vision of the fire and ash whirlwind, passed through his mind, and his heart skipped a beat. *I'm sure it burned out when it disappeared.* He shook his head, and dismissed the thought.

She said, "Last I heard, they were doing okay. They weren't as bad off, as it was initially thought."

Nodding, Larry said, "That's good to hear. It would be a tragedy to lose anyone on Christmas Eve."

She nodded in agreement. "Yeah, that's for sure."

"So, can I see the Fire Chief?"

Smiling, and nodding, she said, "Of course. He's in the second curtained area."

"Is he doing alright?"

Nodding, she said, "He seems to be. Just a bump and gash on the head, and some smoke inhalation, but he's alert, and ready to leave."

Larry turned to go.

Standing, she said, "Here, let me walk with you."

Smiling, he let her take the lead. It was only a few yards to the second cubicle, but she chatted the whole time. He loved her Texas twang, and felt he could listen to her prattle on for hours.

Entering the Chief's cubicle, they found him alert, and asking the attending nurse, "When can I leave? Do I need this oxygen anymore? Why is there a bandage on my head, and, oh yeah, when can I get this IV out?"

Larry said, "Hey, Jesse. Are you giving these nurses a hard time?"

Jesse smiled sheepishly. "Well, maybe a little. I just want to get out of here, and back to my crew."

Larry opened his mouth to tell Jesse that his team had packed up, when Dr. Jim Harrison walked in, carrying a chart.

"Hey, Doc. When can I get out of here?" Jesse asked.

After shaking hands with the Police Chief, Dr. Harrison walked over to Jesse's bedside.

"I have good news. I have just signed the papers for your release. The nurse will remove your IV, give you some last minute instructions, and a prescription for antibiotics."

"It's about time! I need to get back to the fire, and check on my crew."

Larry cleared his throat, and said, "Jesse, they've packed up, and left by now. The other teams had already headed out when I left, and the Alva team was finishing up it's final inspection. They're probably at the fire station now."

Jesse cursed under his breath. "Well, I'd still like to go over to the refinery, and do one final inspection."

Larry nodded. "I'll take you, when you're ready."

After listening to Jesse's heart and lungs, and checking his bandaged head wound, Dr. Harrison said, "Okay, my friend, you are good to go. I'd like to see you next week to remove those stitches." He laid the chart, and paperwork, on Jesse's bed. The nurse, who was in the process of removing the IV, nodded in acknowledgment.

"Sure thing, Doc. Thanks for taking care of me."

As the two men waited for the nurse to disconnect the IV, they discussed the night's events, and agreed that the culprits were probably young males.

Jesse said, "I guess I can understand the fireworks, but the fire at the refinery? Well, that just seems foolish. I'm surprised it stayed so well contained though, especially when the wind began kicking up."

Larry sighed, and nodded, remembering once again, the little whirlwind of smoke and ash.

As the nurse disposed of the IV equipment, she rattled off a list of do's and don'ts for the Fire Chief. "The most important thing Sir, is if your headache gets worse, or you start running a fever, get yourself back here ASAP."

Jesse nodded, saying, "Yes, Ma'am."

After signing the appropriate paper work, Jesse began removing the hospital gown, as Larry handed him the bag of clothes from under the gurney. He then stepped out of the curtained off area, as Jesse finished dressing.

Jamie helped his pal into the car once again, and drove him to the hospital to see his dad.

Walking into the cubicle, both boys were surprised to find the Fire Chief fully clothed, and sitting on the side of the bed, wrestling his foot into a boot.

Looking up, he too was shocked to see his son, and Jamie, standing there.

Jimmy limped over to his dad, and gave him a hug. Much to his surprise, his dad returned it.

"Jimmy, what are you doing here?" Jesse asked, lacing up his boot.

Looking everywhere, but into his dad's eyes, Jimmy said, "When I heard the explosion, and saw the fire, I called your phone. An EMT guy told me you were injured, and on your way to the hospital. I asked Jamie to bring me here."

Jesse looked over at Jamie, and nodded. "Huh." Looking back at his son, he asked, "Why are you limping?"

Glancing over at Jamie, who was avoiding any eye contact as well, he said, "Well, Jamie and I were out riding the 4-wheeler, and I took a curve too fast, and wiped out. The 4-wheeler landed on top of my leg."

His dad grimaced. "Bet that hurt."

Jimmy nodded. Continuing the lie that he and Jamie had concocted, he said, "Yeah. I thought I broke my leg for sure, but when I checked it out, something had poked a hole in it, and it was badly bruised." Glancing around the cubicle, he asked, "Are they letting you go already? Didn't you have a concussion, or something?"

Jesse nodded. "Well, guess my head's harder than we thought. No concussion, just a bump and a little gash."

Grimacing, Jimmy said, "Well, I'm glad you're okay. Do you want to ride back with Jamie and me?"

Shaking his head, then grimacing from the pain, Jesse said, "Nah. The Police Chief and I are heading out to the refinery, to check on things one more time, then he'll drop me off at the station. I left my truck there. I should be home after that."

Nodding, and shrugging, Jimmy said, "Well, okay. Guess we'll head back home."

Walking over to the bedside, Jamie shook the Fire Chiefs hand. "Glad you're okay, Sir. Do you know what caused the fire?"

Standing to don his jacket, the Fire Chief said, "Nah. Probably some boys looking for excitement. I'm sure we'll get to the bottom of it, though."

Jamie felt his heart skip a couple of beats, and a lump form in his throat. Swallowing hard to dislodge the lump, and appear nonplussed, he said, "Yes, Sir. I'm sure you will." Thinking, *Oh goodness, I hope not!*

Jesse walked over, and patted his son's back.

"Thanks for coming to check on me." Glancing at Jamie, he asked, "Are you staying the night, Jamie?"

Jamie nodded.

"Then I'll see you boys later."

During the ride back to Jimmy's house, Jamie said, "Wow. I didn't expect your dad to be so nice. It kind of freaked me out. I expected him to yell at you, or something. Definitely not reach out and hug you."

Shaking his head, Jimmy said, "I know. I think his head got hit a lot harder than he's letting on. What else could explain his sudden change in behavior?"

CHAPTER 2

In the intensive care unit, thirteen year old Linda sat beside her mother, Janet, gently stroking the woman's cold, limp hand, and encouraging the comatose woman to wake up. Ever since the car accident, that had landed them both in the hospital, right after Thanksgiving, Janet had been in a medically induced coma, until a couple of days ago. She had taken the brunt of the collision, and had suffered many broken bones, and internal injuries. Linda had been somewhat fortunate, in only sustaining a broken arm, and internal bleeding and bruising, from the seat belt. Dr. Carmichael, the pediatric physician, and surgeon, had set the bone, and repaired the internal injury.

Pleading, as tears rolled down her cheeks, the girl whispered, "Please, come back to me, Mom. I need you. It's Christmas day, and you've been asleep long enough. Wake up!"

Linda reached down, and lifted one of her mother's eyelids. She recoiled when she looked into the dead eyes. It was if there was no life or soul in her body—an empty shell. Linda crawled onto the bed next to her mother, and laid her head on her mother's chest, and sobbed.

"God, if you're for real, please, please, bring my mom back to me!"

Four hours after she had set it, Christina's alarm was buzzing. Reaching over to shut it off, she had an intense urgency to pray for Janet.

She had visited Janet and Linda, before leaving for home the afternoon before, and was pleased to see that the nurses had set up a cot in Janet's room, so Linda could be with her mom on Christmas day. Linda had asked if Christina thought her mom would wake up for Christmas. In childlike innocence, she had said, "Wouldn't that be an awesome gift?"

As Christina remembered this, tears stung her eyes.

"God, I bring Janet and Linda before you. Please, for both their sakes, bring Janet back, and restore them both to complete health."

The residents of Alva, who were up early because of young children excited about opening gifts—or as in Christina's case, preparing for work—were able to witness the transformation of the indigo blue sky of night to the sunny clear blue sky of day. As they prepared for the day, they were unaware of the smoldering ash, on the paint saturated tarps, on the hospital's roof, brought by the wind devil earlier that morning. The spark quickly grew into a full-fledged flame, and began devouring more and more of the tarps, causing a blackish smoke cloud to form and float upwards.

Once the tarps were consumed, the fire, like a living being, sought other food sources to devour, and began to feast on the tar stained wooden construction of the roof.

When Christina pulled her car into the back lot of the hospital, she glanced up, marveling at the clarity of the sky. Noticing something dark and shadowy in her peripheral vision, she focused in on the hospital roof. Nothing. Shrugging, and dismissing the observation as a figment of her imagination, she walked across the lot to the entrance. Glancing over to the east where the oil refinery had burned the previous night, she saw smoke continuing to waft up from the smoldering remains.

The bitter, acrid smell of the smoke still hung in the air, and she could taste it when she inhaled.   Stomping the slush from the remaining snow off her shoes, she heard someone calling her name.

"Hey, Christina! Wait up!"

It was Dr. Dawson, the attending cardiologist. She smiled as he approached.

"Good morning, Steven."

Stomping his feet, he said, "Good morning to you."

Confusion registering on her face, she asked, "What are you doing here? I thought you had the day off?"

Opening the door, and allowing her to precede him, he said, "Yeah. I do, but I have to check in on a new admission."

Removing her gloves, and tucking them into her coat pockets, she asked, "Were you here last night?"

He nodded. "Yeah."

As they walked down the hallway towards his office to drop off his outer clothing, and change into his lab coat, he explained what had occurred the previous evening.

"One of the volunteer fire men began experiencing chest pains, after being brought in for smoke inhalation. His EKG was a little off, so I admitted him, and started him on IV meds. Hopefully, the problem was stress-induced, but I want to check on him, and schedule him for a stress test, and possibly a cardiac catheterization."

Pushing the third floor button in the elevator, Christina asked, "So, there are three patients on the unit now?"

Nodding, he said, "I had so hoped to get everyone out, so they could celebrate Christmas at home, but unfortunately, Mrs. Snapka, and Mr. Russell, weren't quite ready."

Exiting the elevator on the third floor Cardiac Care Unit, Christina told Steven she'd see him in a few minutes, and headed for the nurse's lounge. Hanging up her winter coat, and donning her lab coat, she was again hit with the need to pray for Janet. Before exiting the room, she stopped, and said a quick prayer for the woman, and her daughter. She would visit them during her lunch break. Something had to be happening with Janet. Either she was getting better, or she was dying. *Why else would I be feeling such a strong urge to pray?*

Janet, completely unaware of her physical surroundings, was acutely aware of the spiritual realm she was in. Leaving her physical body, and floating toward the ceiling, she looked down at the body on the bed, as if were something foreign—unable to recognize it as her own flesh and blood. She noticed Linda crying hysterically, standing next to the prone woman, and surmised that the body must belong to her, but wondered how she could be in both places. Fascinated, she watched as nurses and doctors came and went from the room, trying to revive the being on the bed—completely unaware of her presence near the ceiling. She tried calling out to Linda, and the nurses, but realized they couldn't see or hear her.

A voice next to her said, "Come. I want to show you something."

She looked towards the voice, and saw a glowing, translucent being, holding its hand out to her. Taking the extended hand, she was immediately whisked out of the hospital to another place, more beautiful than words could ever describe. When they stopped, the being released her hand, and stepped away. They were in a meadow with every color of flower imaginable, and grass that seemed to glow green from within. Turning in circles, she realized that everything—trees, grass, flowers, rocks—had the same glow. The sky, and surrounding atmosphere, being absent of a sun, had a golden glow. Everything was bright, but not to the point of being painful. It was far from comprehensible. A line from the Wizard of Oz, when Dorothy and Toto landed in a very strange land, came to her: *We're not in Kansas anymore.*

Holding clenched fists up to her mouth, not out of fear, but reverential awe, she whispered, "Where are we?"

The being next to her smiled, and said, "Pretty amazing, huh?"

Nodding, she said, "Yeah!"

"By the way, I'm Azra, your guardian angel."

"I have a guardian angel?"

Chuckling, and nodding, he answered, "Yes. All earthly beings have guardian angels. We are assigned to you, as soon as you are conceived."

Skepticism registered on her face. "So, what happens when we humans die? Do you get a different assignment?"

Shaking his head, he answered, "No. We stay with our person for eternity."

"So what do you do all day? Sit around on clouds, playing harps?"

Azra laughed out loud. "Now that's funny! You can't even comprehend the amount of work it takes to run Heaven."

"Heaven? I'm in heaven? Am I dead?"

Smiling, Azra shook his head. "You are in between."

"In between? What does that mean?"

"Your physical body isn't dead, although it appears to be, but your soul has left temporarily."

"So I can go back to my body?"

"If you want to, but Father wants me to show you a few things first."

He pointed at a distant mountain, and said, "Look, tell me what you see."

She looked towards the mountain, and saw it as clearly as if she were standing on it.

"Oh my goodness! I can see every flower, and blade of grass, and tiniest of pebbles. How is that possible? I'm so far away from it."

"Here, everything is within touch or sight, if we so wish it. You may travel anywhere, if you just think about it."

"So, if I want to be on that mountain, I just have to think it?"

The angel smiled, and nodded. "Try it."

Janet closed her eyes, and thought of the mountain. When she opened them, she was standing at the apex, looking all around the amazing world she had just entered. Covering her mouth, she exclaimed, "Oh, my goodness! How is this even possible?"

"You aren't on Earth any more. This is God's domain."

"God? You mean like the creator of the world, God?"

Azra smiled, and nodded, "Exactly."

"Will I see Him? I have so many questions."

Reaching out to pat her arm, he said, "I know. He will see you when it's time. Right now, I will take you to meet someone."

In what seemed and instant, Janet and Azra were back down in the meadow where they had first landed.

In the middle of the field, was a large tree, with a swing attached to one of its branches.

"Where did that tree come from? It wasn't there before."

Azra ignored the question, and pointed. "What do you see?"

Janet wasn't sure what to make of the sight before her. A girl, appearing to be around six years old was there on a swing, being pushed by another older girl, who looked to be around twelve. They were both laughing.

Janet felt as if she should know the girls, and when they turned and smiled, she did know.

"Mama!" The youngest girl exclaimed, as she jumped off the swing, and ran to Janet's open arms. The older girl hung back for a moment, as mother and daughter reunited.

Janet bent down and picked up the little dark-haired, dark-skinned girl, and knew immediately it was her baby she had miscarried so long ago. *How could this be?*

Crying tears of joy, she held her tightly, as she spun around. Her daughter giggled, and squealed with delight, When she sat her down, the child ran, and grabbed the other girl's hand, and brought her to Janet.

"Mama, this is Mary, your sister."

Memories flooded Janet's mind as she relived the moment Mary was taken from her in the tornado. Janet sat in the cool grass, as Mary came, and put her arms around her sister's neck.

Looking up at Azra, Janet asked, "How? How can this be?" The angel smiled, but didn't answer.

The three females embraced for quite some time, before Azra said, "It's time to move on."

Janet looked at him pleadingly, as tears ran down her face.

"Please, can't I stay? I have so many questions I need answered."

When she looked back to where the girls had just been standing, they were gone, as well as the tree. Taking Azra's extended hand, she stood.

"I must leave you for a little while. I cannot go where you are going, but I will be waiting for you, when you return."

Before she could ask, "What do you mean?" She was whisked by unseen hands into a dark tunnel, and landed in what seemed to be a pit. The darkness was absolute. She touched her face to see if her eyes were open. They were, but they were useless. She crinkled her nose, as a foul stench, like rotten garbage, and animal feces, permeated the air.

She stood, and reached out, touching something cold, and slimy. *A wall?* Withdrawing her hand, she called out, "Hello? Is anyone there? Azra, where are you?" She could hear whispering voices, but couldn't make out any distinct words.

She sensed that someone was in the pit with her.

"Hello? Who's there?"

She felt something brush past her, and she recoiled, putting up her hands in defense. The rancid odor was making her gag. Never in her life on earth, had she smelled something so nauseatingly horrible.

"Azra, please help me! I can't see, and I'm scared!"

She heard a vile, mocking voice, "Oh, you're blind, and scared? Well boo hoo for you! There's no one here to help you."

She then heard what sounded like hundreds of voices, laughing, and mocking her.

She fell to her knees, and cried.

"Please, help me! I want to go home! I don't want to be here any more!"

One of the voices whispered in her ear, "Sorry Honey, there's no going back from here!"

Again, she heard laughter. This mocking torture seemed to go on for quite some time.

"This must be hell." She whispered.

She knew this was where she belonged, but she didn't want to be here. She curled up in the fetal position on the slimy floor, sobbing. Holding her hands over her ears, to block out the incessant mocking, she thought of her grandmother.

"Wait! What?" She yelled at the voices to shut up. Her grandmother was trying to tell her something.

What was it? Then as if she had been transported, to a sweeter, more innocent time of childhood, she remembered what her grandmother had said. *"When you don't know what to say, or how to pray, just say, Jesus. His name will calm your fears, and help you be brave."*

Janet sat up, wiped her eyes, and took a cleansing breath. At first, she whispered the name. She heard the beings hiss, and felt them recoil. Feeling bolder, she said it louder. "Jesus!"

The beings screamed, and she could feel them leaving the area. She stood, and yelled as loudly as possible. "Jesus!"

The first time she said the name of Jesus, she saw a tiny spark of light in the distance. As she repeated the name, it grew in intensity, as it descended towards her. By the third time, she could discern the shape of a man. She recognized him. It was the same man, from a dream she had before the accident. The one who had given her a drink of water, when she was alone in the desert. He had told her to stop running from him. *Was this Jesus?*

He reached out His hand, and she took it, looking into His kind, loving eyes.

"Jesus?" She whispered.

Smiling, he said, "I am He. Come."

As they ascended out of the pit, she asked, "Was that hell?"

When they landed on the bright green grass, He reached out, and waved a hand over the entrance, closing the gaping hole. Janet could hear voices screaming, and cursing, as the gaping hole was sealed.

Taking her hand, and guiding her to a large boulder on which to sit, He said, "Janet, you have seen, and tasted both heaven and hell. It is time to choose. If you choose to believe in Me, you will be with Me forever in Heaven. If however, you choose to ignore Me, then you will spend eternity away from Me. I have given you a free will. It is up to you now."

"But Jesus, why do I have to choose? I'm a good person. Aren't my good deeds enough to get me into Heaven?"

His compassionate eyes looked into hers, and she saw her life flash before her. All the good, and the bad she had experienced, or done. She was definitely not as good as she had thought.

She broke eye contact, and buried her face in her hands, and wept. He reached out His hand, and she felt a warmth she had never experienced before. It was as if she were being cleansed from the inside out with a warm bath.

Looking up into His face, she said, "I'm so sorry. I'll understand if You don't want me in Heaven."

"Janet, it's not that I don't want you here, because I want all of my children to spend eternity with Me. The choice has to be yours. Do you want to spend eternity with Me?"

Wiping her eyes, she said, "Yes! I do! I'll do anything You want me to. I never want to go back into that pit. He reached out, and pulled her into an embrace. She felt her anxieties drain from her being. With her head resting on His chest, she whispered, "Can I stay here, now?"

Smiling, he said, "I have a few more tasks for you to complete on Earth, before I will call you home."

Nodding, and sighing, she said, "Okay. When will I see You again?"

He whispered, "In heavenly time, but a moment."

The instant He spoke those words, she was miraculously back in her earthly body.

Opening her eyes, she was surprised to see a sheet over her face. She could hear voices, and someone next to the bed was crying.

She tried speaking, but couldn't make a sound, because her throat was raw and swollen, from the bronchial tube that had been present for several days.

She felt her body being lifted, and groaned when her back hit the gurney. Angela, one of the ICU nurses jumped back, when she heard Janet's moan. She pulled the sheet back, and was surprised to see Janet's open eyes.

"Janet!" She cried, and looked to the foot of the bed, where Carla stood in shocked silence.

Carla and Angela put Janet back in her bed, and Carla ran out to call Dr. Harrison.

Angela re-attached the cardiac monitor, and put an oxygen tube in Janet's nose. She had never had a patient return from the dead, and realized she was a bit frightened, and not sure what to do. Her hands were shaking, as she checked Janet's blood pressure and pulse. Janet tried to speak, but Angela put her hand up to silence her.

Linda, realizing that her mom had returned from the dead, stood in shocked silence by the door.

She was frightened by the choking noises her mom was making, as she tried to clear her throat to speak.

Angela, noticing the girl's distress, said, "It's okay, Honey. Your mom's throat is just irritated from the breathing tube. She'll be fine in a moment or two."

Janet made hand signs that indicated she wanted to sit up. Linda pushed the button on the remote control, and the head of the bed rose.

Dr. Harrison entered the room, surprise registering on his face.

Janet was not only fully conscience, she sitting up, smiling, and trying to speak. She had so much to say, but all that came out of her mouth were laryngitis-like whispers.

Patting his patient on the arm, Dr. Harrison said, "Well, well. Welcome back, Janet."

She smiled, and did a thumbs-up sign.

Whispering, she said, "Thanks. It's nice to be back. Every inch of me hurts like crazy though."

Nodding, he said, "I will order some morphine for you. You have quite extensive injuries, and I will tell you about them later, but first I want to check your vital signs."

Reaching for the blood pressure cuff hanging on the wall, he said, "You left us for quite a while. I've never had a patient return after such a long absence."

"How long was I gone?" She whispered.

Holding a finger up to indicate he'd answer after taking her blood pressure, he inflated the arm band, laid his stethoscope on the crook of her elbow, and listened for the heart beats. Everyone remained silent, as he repeated the process on the opposite arm. Removing the cuff, he announced, "Your blood pressure is within normal parameters, given the trauma your body has suffered."

He then bent and listened to her chest, asking her to take as deep a breath as possible, checked her pupil reaction time, and examined her wounds and bandages. When he completed his examination, he patted her arm, and said, "Now, back to your question about how long you were gone. From the time your heart stopped, 'till now, it's been a good forty-five minutes."

Janet gasped. *How in the world could I have been gone that long, and still be able to return?*

He then added, "In fact, the nurses were taking you down to the morgue."

Janet shook her head in disbelief. She looked over to where Linda was still standing by the door. The girl was chewing on a fingernail, as tears streamed down her face. Janet tried raising her hand to motion her over, but it felt so heavy. All she could manage was a wiggle of her finger.

Linda noticed this, but was too frightened to accept the invitation. She shook her head, and chose another nail to chew on.

Janet whispered, "It's okay, Honey. You can come over here."

Linda shook her head. She had finally accepted the fact that her mom had died, and now, she was alive again. She needed a few more minutes to process this. *What if this was just a dream, and she'd wake up in a minute, and her mom would be truly dead? Or, what if her mom's heart would stop again?*

Janet nodded, and grimaced, as a shock-wave of pain coursed through her head and neck, all the way down to her toes.

Dr. Harrison frowned. "Janet where are you hurting?"

Squeezing her eyes shut, she whispered, "From the top of my head all the way down to my toes"

Nodding, he turned, and asked the nurse to go ahead and prepare the morphine. While waiting for the nurse to return, Dr. Harrison asked, "Janet, do remember what happened?"

Shaking her head, she whispered, "Not really. It must have been an awful accident, for me to be in such bad shape."

Nodding, he said, "Yes, it was."

Smiling, she said, "When my voice returns, I have the most amazing story to tell you all."

Patting her arm, Dr. Harrison said, "I'll look forward to hearing it. In the meantime, you rest and let your body heal. And, again, welcome back, and Merry Christmas."

Nodding, and smiling, she whispered, "It's Christmas?"

After administering the Morphine via her IV line, everyone left Janet's room, leaving mother and child alone. Janet patted the spot on the bed next to her, and Linda, finally convinced that her mother was truly alive, crawled up, and laid her head once again, on her mother's chest. It was so nice listening to her mother's heart beat, and rhythmic breathing without the whoosh and whir of the machine.

Janet stared at the ceiling, thinking about her encounter with the angel, Jesus, the two little girls, and the horrible pit. *Was it real? It sure felt real. If the experience was indeed real, and what Jesus said was true, then I need to think seriously about the direction in which my life is headed. Maybe I do need to make some changes. Where do I start?* Christina Sander's name came to mind, as she drifted off into a morphine induced sleep.

After visiting the three cardiac patients, Dr. Steven Dawson, stood at the counter, making the necessary changes in medication, ordering lab tests, and scheduling procedures, before leaving the third floor cardiac care unit.

He listened in as two aides, pausing on their way down the hallway, discussed the previous night's events. Not recognizing the women as the regular CCU aides, he glanced at their name tags.

Retrieving a piece of paper from the counter, Cara said, "Hey, Dr. Dawson. Merry Christmas."

He returned the greeting. He then overheard her asking the other aide, Brenda, "Why in the world would someone set off fireworks? What was the purpose? To scare the daylights out of folks?"

Shaking her head, Brenda said, "Well, it certainly scared us out of bed. I had just dropped off to sleep, because I knew I had to come in today. Seemed like it took me forever to get back to sleep!" Giggling, she added, "I almost threw the alarm across the room when it went off."

Nodding, Cara said, "I know. I thought a bomb had gone off somewhere! I might have gotten three hours of sleep. I had to leave my poor husband to deal with the kids today. Hopefully, for him, they slept in."

Turning to walk away, Brenda said, "It's a good thing we only have three patients today. I don't think I could handle any more stress."

Steven smiled, and shook his head. He had a feeling the whole town would be buzzing about last night's events. Christina approached the counter with two cups of coffee.

Handing him one, she asked, "You okay?"

Taking a sip from the cup, he said, "Thanks. I'm just tired like everyone else."

Sitting, she said, "I sure hope there aren't any more surprises today. I'm feeling a bit edgy."

Leaning on the counter, he nodded, and said, "Yeah. Me too. I thought it was because of last night's events, and it may be residual effects, but it's almost like my nerves are vibrating. Like something isn't right in the atmosphere, and my sub conscience knows it."

Sipping her coffee, she leaned back in the chair, and nodded. "Exactly. You think we may have more surprises coming?"

Shrugging, he shook his head. "I hope not." Downing the last few drops of coffee, he set the mug on the counter, and said, "Well, I'm going to head on home. Call me if anything changes."

Standing, she reached out, and touched his arm, "Steven, you want to come by the house this evening for dinner? Say around six?"

Raising his eyebrows in surprise, he smiled, and said, "I'd love to. It's been a while since I've seen the kids. Want me to bring something?"

Shaking her head, she said, "Just yourself."

"Alright. I'll see y'all at six."

She watched as he departed, and boarded the elevator. Her heart was doing a tap dance in her chest. *I hadn't planned to invite him over, but I'm glad I did. I think I'll order pizza and a salad from Pizza Hut.*

"Mrs. Sanders?"

Looking up, she saw Brenda at the counter.

"Yes?"

"Mr. Jonas, the firefighter in room four, says he has a headache, and wants an aspirin or something."

"Thanks, Brenda. I'll check his chart to see what he has ordered."

Brenda turned to go. "Hey, Brenda." Christina called out, "Thanks for coming in today."

Brenda smiled. "No problem."

"Oh, and Merry Christmas."

"You too, Mrs. Sanders."

"Christina."

"Excuse me?"

"You may call me Christina. Mrs. Sanders sounds so formal."

Smiling, and nodding, Brenda said, "Yes, Ma'am. Christina, it is."

Christina watched Brenda's departure. She looked to be in her mid-forties. Tall and lean with long, thick, salt and pepper hair. Christina had never met Brenda before, nor had she seen her at the hospital. *I'll have to have a one-on-one with her.*

Cara, the other aide, in her mid thirties, had worked on the cardiac unit one previous time, but Christina didn't know her well either.

Christina stood, stretched, and took in a lungful of air. Releasing it, she made a face.

The acrid smoke smell was more prevalent. She looked up and down the hallways, but didn't detect any smoke, and the alarms hadn't sounded, indicating a fire.

Shrugging, she thought, *the smell must be coming from the refinery, but why would it smell stronger, and how could it permeate an almost air-tight building? I'll take Mr. Jonas his medication, then I'm going to walk around. Maybe I should call Larry, or the Fire Chief.*

Christina retrieved Mr. Jonas' chart, and read that he could have Morphine for chest pain, or Tylenol for other aches and pains. She took the Tylenol to him.

Walking into his room, she was surprised to see him standing at the window.

"Mr. Jonas?"

Turning, he said, "Yes, Ma'am?"

"The aide informed me that you have a headache?"

"Yes, Ma'am."

"Are you having any other discomfort?"

"No, Ma'am. Just a headache."

"Do you mind if I take your blood pressure?"

Walking over to the bed, he sat on the edge, and extended his arm.

According to his chart, his name was Noah Jonas, forty-five years old, married, with two children, and no history of any cardiac anomalies. He was a big, muscular man, standing a little over six feet, and weighing in at two-hundred and fifty pounds. He had graying, black hair, intense blue eyes, and an engaging smile, complete with a dimple in his right cheek. He had a mild-mannered disposition, but she sensed an underlying strength of character, and nobility. She felt he would be a good ally in any kind of confrontation.

After taking his blood pressure, and finding it within normal parameters, she checked his IV, noting that his Heparin bag was almost empty. She asked him to lie down, and she ran a short EKG. Smiling, she said, "Everything seems to be fine. Did you sleep well?"

Shaking his head, he said, "Not really. I kept having dreams about fires, and being unable to reach people."

Nodding, she said, "I guess that's normal, given last night's circumstances." She handed him the Tylenol, and poured him a cup of water. He took both with a nod. "Thanks."

"I was looking out at what's left of the refinery. There seems to be several smoldering pockets left. It might be my imagination, but I keep smelling smoke. I'm wondering if it's coming in through the outside vents on the roof."

"Funny you should say that. I was thinking the same thing. I'm planning to take a walk around the unit, to see if anything is amiss. I was also thinking I should call the Fire Chief and have him come take a look around, but I hate to bother him after such a late night, and because it's Christmas day."

Shaking his head, he said, "Well, I'd rather err on the side of caution. I'll call him, and explain our concern. Let me know if you find anything."

Nodding, she asked, "Is there anything else I can get you?"

Shaking his head, and looking at his watch, he said, "My wife and kids should be here in a little while."

"I'm sorry you're missing Christmas day at home with them."

He smiled, and said, "Yeah. It would be worse if my kids were little, but they're in their teens now, so it's not as crucial for me to be there." Adjusting the sheets and blanket, he asked, "Do you have kids?"

Christina smiled, and nodded. "Yes. Three. Boy, girl, boy."

"What are their ages?"

"Brad is sixteen, Stacey is twelve and Nicky is ten."

"Too bad you're having to work."

Shaking her head, she said, "It's okay. We celebrated last week when my in-laws were here, and we'll open the remaining gifts tonight. I'm sure they'll enjoy sleeping in, and just laying around today."

"Is your husband home today?"

"I'm widowed. My husband died a couple of years ago."

"Oh, I'm sorry. This must be a difficult time for you."

Nodding, she said, "The first Christmas was difficult for all of us, but this year isn't as bad. I'm sure it'll get easier as time passes."

He nodded, as if he understood.

Sighing, and turning to exit, she said, "Well, I'd better get going."

"When my wife gets here, I'd like to introduce you two."

Smiling, Christina said, "I'd like that."

Before taking a walk around the unit, she returned to the desk, and wrote the pertinent medical information in Mr. Jonas' chart. As she was placing it back in the chart holder, her cell-phone buzzed in her pocket. Pulling it out, she saw that the call was from Brad.

"Hey, Brad," she said, as she put the phone to her ear.

"Hey, Mom. Merry Christmas. How's your day going?"

"Merry Christmas to you! It's quiet so far. There's only three patients on the floor. Should be an easy day."

"Good. I'm the only one up. I just checked on Stacey, and Nicky, and they're both sawing logs." Smiling, she said, "After last night, I'm not surprised. So what are your plans for the day?"

"I'll probably lay around, watch TV, and call Eric later to see if he'd like to come over." Eric was Brad's best friend.

"Sounds like a good plan. I'll see y'all around four thirty. I invited Dr. Dawson over for dinner. How does pizza, and salad sound?"

"That sounds great. Want me to do anything special?"

"Nope. I'll call in the order before I leave for home. Oh, yeah, just make sure the house is clean."

Brad chuckled, "Right."

After disconnecting, Christina found Brenda and Cara changing the bedding in Mrs. Snapka's room, and informed them that she'd be walking around the unit if they needed her for anything.

The CCU was designed, so that the nurse's station was in the middle, and the six patient rooms surrounded it. A utility closet containing cleaning supplies and linen, nurses' locker room, and a medication and supply room, were all situated at one end, close to the elevators. The hallway by the elevator, continued west to the medical-surgical unit, which she rarely visited.

She decided that if she didn't find anything out of the ordinary in her area, she'd go over to the Med-Surg unit, and check there. If nothing was amiss, she'd assume everything was okay, and dismiss the uneasiness she felt, as left over adrenaline from the previous night.

Exiting the first room, she heard the ding of the elevator announcing an arrival. She watched as a woman and two teens—a boy and girl—exited, and made a bee-line for Mr. Jonas' room. She would give them a few minutes of privacy, before entering, and introducing herself.

Christina was standing with her hand on the doorknob to the utility room, when Mrs. Jonas flagged her down. Abandoning the investigation for the time-being, she went to meet the Jonas' family.

Cindy woke with a start. Her phone was ringing. Glancing at the clock, she moaned as she pulled herself from the warm covers, and ran across the cold wooden floor to the dresser, where her phone rang and buzzed.

Scurrying back to the bed, and burying herself under the covers, she said, "Good morning, Ed. merry Christmas!"

Ed said, "Well, good morning, and merry Christmas to you, Beautiful!"

Cindy giggled. "If you could see me, you wouldn't think I was so beautiful."

"Darlin' you'd be beautiful covered in mud!"

Cindy laughed.

He cleared his throat, and asked, "Has everything settled down there in Alva?"

"I think so. I haven't heard any sirens, or explosions since last night."

When the explosions occurred around midnight, Cindy had called Ed to inform him. He was four hours away, at his mother's house in Lamesa, celebrating Christmas with his sisters, and their families.

"So, when will you be here?" She asked, after they had chatted a few minutes.

"I plan to leave here around noon, so I should be there between four and five."

Nodding, she said, "Okay. Tell your mom and sisters, hi for me. And Ed, please be careful."

Before disconnecting, he said, "I plan to. I'm anxious to see my girls."

Cindy grabbed her thick, red robe at the foot of her bed, donned her slippers and headed to the kitchen for a hot cup of coffee. When she passed her daughter's bedroom door, she heard their little Shitsu dog, Sasha, whimpering. She opened the door and Sasha ran out, jumping and yipping at Cindy's feet.

"Okay, Baby. I'll let you out."

Cindy prepared her coffee, while Sasha finished her business outside. She noted the time. Eleven o'clock. Opening the door to let the dog in, she mumbled, "Man, I didn't mean to sleep in so late."

Pulling the curtains aside, she marveled at the beautiful, clear blue sky. Grabbing the latest magazine off the coffee table, she settled onto the couch, as Sasha curled up on her lap. An hour later, her fourteen year old daughter, Samara, joined her.

"Mornin', Mom." She said, as she plopped down on the couch, next to her mother.

Cindy reached out, and pulled Samara into a hug. Kissing the top of her head, she said, "Mornin' Babe. Did you sleep okay?"

Samara nodded, then stretched and yawned. "Yeah. It took me a long time to fall back to sleep though. I kept expecting another explosion."

Sasha left Cindy's lap in favor of Samara's, and began to lick her young mistresses' face.

Giggling, Samara asked, "Is Ed coming over today?"

Smiling, Cindy nodded. "I just talked to him. He said he'd be here around four or five."

Scratching Sasha behind the ears, Samara said, "Oh, by the way, merry Christmas!"

Cindy acted surprised, "Oh, yes. It is Christmas day, isn't it?"

Samara rolled her eyes, "As if you didn't remember." Glancing at the pile of gifts under the tree, Samara asked, "Can we open our gifts, or do we have to wait on Ed?"

Cindy thought for a moment, then said, "Well, how about we open one gift each, then save the rest for when Ed arrives?"

Disappointment showing on her face, Samara asked, "Just one?"

Cindy sighed, "Oh, alright. You can open two, but I'll only open one."

Giggling, and clapping her hands together, then setting Sasha back on her mom's lap, Samara went to the tree, and began moving packages around.

Cindy shook her head, and smiled. She was glad Samara still got excited about Christmas. She knew there would come a time, all too soon, when she wouldn't. In the past year, Cindy had noticed that as Samara was developing into a young woman, she was beginning to put her childhood toys and interests away, in favor of girlfriends, phone time, studies and practicing the piano. Samara seemed to be much more secure in her person-hood, and didn't crave male attention, or constant accolades as Cindy had at her age. Cindy watched her daughter, and thought, *I sure hope she continues on this path. I don't want her to experience all the ups and downs, hurts, rejections, and guilt, that I did.*

Samara held up the largest, and smallest boxes.

"Okay. I think I'll open these two. You want me to pick one for you?"

Cindy nodded. "That'd be great!"

After chatting with the Jonas family, Christina headed back down the hallway towards the utility room. Thinking about the encounter, and how much she liked the family, she didn't notice the small tendril of smoke creeping out from under the utility room door. She pulled the door open, and was met with a blast of heat, smoke and fire, which threw her against the opposite wall. Losing consciousness for just a moment, she slid down the wall, and landed in a heap on the floor. The fire, relishing the fresh oxygen, immediately left the confined area of the utility room, and began making its way along the ceiling tiles of the corridor, like a spider stalking its prey. When Christina recovered, she looked up at the ceiling, watching in horror as the fire spread. She stood, felt a wave of dizziness, and calling out to Brenda and Cara, stumbled to the fire alarm, a few feet down the hall. After pushing the alarm button, she slumped down to the floor, and succumbed to the darkness once again.

The two aides, who were in a patient's room changing the bed, didn't hear Christina's call. They did, however, hear the clanging of the fire alarm bell, and stepped out to see what had caused it. When they saw Christina slumped on the floor, under the alarm, they dropped their linens, and ran to her aid.. Brenda was the first to notice the spread of the fire, and felt in her pocket.. No phone. *I left it at the desk*, she thought.

Feeling a rise of panic within, she shouted, "Cara, call 911!"

Cara, who was bent over Christina, trying to revive her, looked up, saw the fire, and immediately reached in her pocket, which did have a phone, and dialed.

Christina opened her eyes, and said, "Get the patients out! I'll be okay."

Brenda helped Christina to her feet, and noticed a trickle of blood on the back of her neck.

"Christina, you're bleeding. Let me look."

Christina reached up, and touched the back of her head, feeling stickiness on her fingers. Examining her fingers that were covered with bright red blood, she said, "I must have hit that wall harder than I thought. I think I'll be okay."

Pulling Christina's hair back and examining the wound, Brenda made a face, and said, "I don't know. I think you're going to need a few stitches."

"That bad, huh?"

Brenda nodded. "Let me at least put a pressure bandage on it until you can get it looked at."

"Okay. I'll have it checked out later. In the mean time, we need to get the patients to another area."

Pausing by the desk, while Brenda applied the bandage, Christina said, "I'm going to run down the hall, and let the surgical wing know we'll be bringing our patients over."

As Brenda and Cara helped Mr. Jonas into a wheelchair, he asked, "Is there anything I can do?" Cara said, "I don't think so. Right now, I'd like for you, your wife, and children, to head on over to the Med-Surg unit across the hall. Mrs. Sanders has informed them of your impending arrival."

Brenda said, "We'll be bringing the other two patients over there as well."

As his wife pushed the wheelchair into the hallway, he asked, "Where is the fire, and how fast is it spreading?"

Cara answered, "It's on the other side of the station. It looks like it started in the utility room, and is spreading across the ceiling tiles."

"Can you take me to see?"

"I'd rather not, Sir. The smoke is getting pretty thick. I need to get you to safety first."

Nodding, but sounding frustrated, he said, "Okay."

Brenda called, "Hey, Cara. I need your help."

"Sorry, I have to go. Y'all get to the Med-Surg unit, and we'll see you in a few minutes."

As the Jonas family passed the elevators, heading to the Medical-Surgical wing, Christina was making her way back to the CCU.

She reached out, and patted her patient's shoulder.

"Mr. and Mrs. Jonas, I'm glad y'all are okay. I'll see you in a few minutes. The nurses at the station will get you settled in."

By the time they had the second patient ready for transport, the fire department team arrived.

Christina, so focused on getting her patients to safety, was barely aware of the cacophony of sounds, and activity, going on around her, as the firemen worked frantically to get the fire under control.

Larry and Jesse walked around the burned out oil refinery, checking for any remaining hot spots, and possible clues as to how the fire had started. Alva was a small enough town, that the instigators of something of this magnitude, wouldn't be hidden for long. Someone was bound to let something slip, and the truth would come out. One thing Larry knew for sure, the truth always came out—eventually.

As Jesse walked around, he thought about his near neath experience, when the building collapsed on him, and his men. He remembered, that right before he blacked out, he saw his wife telling him he needed to mend his relationship with Jimmy. *How did she know that?*

When Jimmy and Jamie had come to visit him in the hospital, it had touched a place in his heart—a place that he had unconsciously boarded up—causing an influx of long lost, and forgotten feelings. In spite of his mistreatment of the boy, it was obvious that the kid still loved him, and wanted his love in return. He vowed, that he would talk to Jimmy, when he returned home.

"Hey, Jesse, come here. I think I found something."

Jesse joined the sheriff, who was squatting, and moving pieces of debris. Picking up an object, he stood, and showed it to Jesse. It was a lighter with the initials JM engraved on the side. His lighter. Given to him by his wife the Christmas before she died. *How did my lighter end up here?*

Carefully moving the pile of debris, Larry said, "I think I found something else." He held up a nail pierced board, containing a piece of denim, and a few drops of blood.

Jesse took it, and his heart began doing a tap dance in his chest. The pieces were falling into place, and he didn't like the implications. *Didn't Jimmy say something had poked him in the leg? But he said it was from the four-wheeler* accident. Was it a coincidence, or could Jimmy and Jamie be involved in the arson? If so, how and why?

Larry stood, and noticing Jesse's far away look, asked, "Hey, Jesse. You okay?"

Jesse shook his head, to clear away the images prancing in front of his mind's eye.

"Sorry. I was just imagining what may have taken place."

Larry said, "Well, I think we've got a couple of good clues here. Looks like the person was trying to escape, and this pile of rubble fell on him. I'll send in the wood with the nail and blood, and see what the blood type is. If it's a common one like O positive, it may be a problem. If it is a rarer type, we can start eliminating suspects quicker."

Jesse nodded in agreement, even though talons of fear gripped his heart. *What if the blood type matched Jimmy's? AB negative isn't all that common.*

"So, Larry," he said, as they continued walking the perimeter, "What happens when you catch the arsonist?"

Larry stopped, removed his hat, scratched his head, returned the hat, looked around at the fire damage, crossed his arms, then said, "Well, it depends on a few factors. Whether this is a first offense or not, and if it involves physical injury, or death. Fortunately, no one has died, so that's off the table. The age of the perpetrator, or perpetrators, will be taken into account as well. I'm still thinking they were teens."

"Why do you think they were teens?" Jesse asked, looking around the area.

Larry sighed. "I can't say for sure. It's just a gut feeling. We've never had an incident like this before, but it just seems to fit the M O of a teen-age-boy. Kinda like the fire bombings at that mall in Waco."

"I read that the police caught the culprits."

Larry nodded. "Yep. Four teen boys, and a girl, just looking for some excitement, and fame."

Jesse shook his head. "A girl was involved?"

Shaking his head, Larry said, "Yeah. She was the sister of one of the boys. Only thirteen, so she'll get off pretty easy. Her attorney will probably plead coercion, because of her age."

Nodding, Jesse asked, "How old were the boys?"

"Between the ages of fourteen and sixteen. This was a first offense for each, so they'll probably do some community service, and be on probation for a year. They all seemed remorseful, so hopefully, they won't do anything like that again."

Jesse nodded. "Well, good. Too bad some people have to learn their lessons the hard way."   Nodding in agreement, Larry said, "Wouldn't it be nice if folks would just realize that somewhere down the line, they're probably gonna get caught. Even most cold cases get solved, eventually."

Grimacing, Jesse thought, *If Jimmy and Jamie were involved, their sentencing would be more severe, as they would be tried as adults. They may even do some jail time.* His heart did a triple beat.

Nodding, and resuming his walk around the perimeter, Larry chuckled, and said, "If everyone played by the rules, we'd be out of jobs."

As the men turned the last corner of the burned out refinery, both their cell phones rang.

"That's odd." Larry said, as he pulled his phone from his pocket.

"Yeah," agreed Jesse. Hearing the message on the other end of the lines, both men reacted by turning, and running to the squad car.

As Larry drove, Jesse barked orders over the phone. They arrived in the hospital parking lot within five minutes, and before Larry could stop the car, the Fire Chief was out the door, and running to the hospital entrance.

Dr. Steven Dawson had just stepped out of the shower, when he heard the fire alarms and sirens, announcing another emergency somewhere in town.

Wrapping a towel around his waist, he walked over to his patio window and looked out. His back yard was adjacent to a field, and he had a clear view of the hospital, and surrounding area. Thinking perhaps there was another fire at the refinery, he was surprised to see smoke billowing from the hospital rooftop—right over the CCU. *Christina!*

Throwing on a pair of jeans, a sweater, and tennis shoes, he grabbed a jacket, and was out of his house, and on his way in five minutes. Pulling into the parking lot, he threw his car into park, jumped out, and ran to the back entrance, and up the back staircase to the third floor, arriving winded, and drenched in sweat. Looking around the unit, he saw fire, smoke, firemen, and policemen—but no Christina.

Noticing him, one of the firemen approached.

"Excuse me, Sir. You can't be here."

Taking a few breaths to calm his racing heart, Steven said, "I'm Dr. Steven Dawson, the cardiologist. This is my unit. Do you know where my patients, and nursing staff are?"

The Fire Chief approached, removed a glove and extended his hand.

"Dr. Dawson, I'm the Fire Chief, Jesse McCoy. Your patients have been moved over to the Med-Surg unit next door. If we can't get this fire under control, we'll probably have to move them down stairs."

After shaking the Fire Chief's hand, Steven asked, "What about the nurses? Are they okay?"

Nodding, the chief said, "They went next door with the patients."

Looking around at the mess, Dr. Dawson shook his head, thinking, *It'll take a long time to get this back in order.* Sighing, he said, "I'm going to head over to the other unit, and check on my patients and staff." Looking back over his shoulder, he thought, *I sure hope the medical equipment can be salvaged.*

As the Med-Surg nurses, and CCU aides, settled the three patients into rooms, Christina stood at the counter, and went over the protocols, and nursing needs of her patients. Occasionally, she'd rub her forehead, in an effort to squelch the headache trying to invade it.

Jean, the nurse in charge, who was going over the information with Christina, noticed this, and asked, "Are you okay?"

Smiling, and not wanting to admit any weakness, she answered, "Oh, yeah. Just a headache coming on. I bumped my head earlier."

Noticing the blood drops on Christina's white lab coat, she pointed, and said, "I think you should get that checked out."

Christina reached up, touching the back of her head, and was surprised to see blood on her fingers. "Huh. I thought that had quit bleeding. Guess not."

Jean handed her a tissue, and said "Here, let me look at that."

Christina turned around, and winced, when Jean lifted the bandage, and probed the area.

Shaking her head as she wiped the blood on a tissue, and spritzing alcohol on her hands, Jean said, "Yep, you're gonna need a stitch or two."

Christina sighed heavily. "I will go to the ER, once everything is settled here."

As Christina turned to leave, she bumped into Dr. Dawson, who had just approached the desk.

"Oh hey, Christina. Sorry." Noticing the fresh blood on the back of her collar, he asked, "You okay? What happened?"

She put her hand up to where he was looking. "Oh, that. When I opened the utility room door, the explosion knocked me into the wall." Nodding at the nurse behind the counter, she added, "According to Jean, there's a nice little gash, that will probably need a couple of stitches."

"Explosion?" He turned her head, and looked at the wound. "Christina, you need to go get that looked at. Now. It looks deep, and it's still oozing blood."

Sighing, she said, "I know. I'm heading down to ER right now. I just wanted to make sure the patients were taken care of first."

Glancing over at Jean, who was nodding, Steven said, "Well, they are. Now go."

Nodding, and half-smiling, she said, "Yes, Sir."

Because of the fire, she couldn't use the elevator, so by the time she reached the ER on the first floor, she was winded, and dizzy. Putting her hand out to the wall to steady herself, she approached the counter. "Are you okay, Ma'am?"

Assuring her that she was indeed okay, she gave the receptionist the pertinent information, and was immediately escorted into an examination cubicle.

She removed her lab coat, sat on a gurney, and was fitted with a blood pressure cuff, an oxygen monitor on her finger, and a thermometer under her tongue. The aide smiled as she wrote down the findings, and assured Christina that all her readings were normal.

Before exiting, and pulling the curtain closed behind her, she said, "Dr. Briggs will be in to see you in just a moment."

Christina jumped off the gurney, and sat in a nearby chair. She had just picked up a magazine, which was missing it's front cover, when she heard a commotion on the other side of the curtain.

She returned the magazine to the nearby table, and hopped back up on the gurney. The curtain was pulled back, and a young twenty-something looking Dr., with sandy blonde hair, green eyes, and fair skin, approached her. He introduced himself, and did an initial evaluation.

He said, "Mrs. Sanders, your chart says you sustained this wound when you were thrown into the wall, after an explosion?" She nodded. "Was this up on the third floor?"

She nodded, and explained the incident.

After poking, and prodding the wound, he said, "Well, it looks like you're going to need a few stitches. The aide will have to shave a small area around the wound. I'll go ahead and inject it with Novocaine, and let that take affect, while she preps the area."

Christina grimaced, and nodded.

As an unfamiliar aide, who's name tag read, Bev, donned a pair of gloves, she inquired about the extent of the fire up on the third floor. Holding a comb and a tiny pair of scissors, she began separating, and cutting, Christina's hair around the wound. Setting the scissors down, she then took a small razor, and shaved the area.

Christina sighed heavily. "It's a mess. It's gonna take a long time to get everything repaired, and back in order."

As she worked, Bev asked, "Do they know where, and how the fire started?"

Christina could hear the scissors snipping away at her hair, but because of the Novocaine, she felt nothing.

"I overheard the Fire Chief say it began on the roof, so I'm assuming a spark from the oil refinery fire blew over, and somehow started the fire."

Removing the gloves, and wrapping the hair and equipment in a disposable bag, Bev said, "Man, I hope this is the end of this fiasco, and those responsible will be caught."

Christina nodded. "Me too. I think we've had enough excitement for quite a while."

Dr. Briggs reappeared, donned gloves, and began stitching the one-inch gash on the back of Christina's head. As he worked, she asked where he was from, and if he had been at the hospital long.

Picking up a pad of gauze, she felt him pat the injured area, but no pain followed.

"I'm from the Waco area, and I've only been here a couple of weeks." She felt a tug, as he pulled the needle and thread through her skin.

"I'm in the residency program out of Baylor University, and I'm doing a semester in ER medicine."

"Why are you here, and not at the Baylor hospital?"

Smiling, he said, "During the week, I am at Baylor, but the weekends and holidays, I choose to come here. This hospital is small, with less chaos, and close to my folks who live here in Alva. Plus, I get free room and board while I'm working."

Christina smiled. "Well, that is a plus. How long will you be here?"

"I'm on the schedule until my next semester, which starts in February, then back to Baylor to finish out my residency."

"I don't mean to be nosy, but how old are you?"

He laughed. "I'm twenty-four. This is my second year in Med School. I went to Baylor University for my pre-lims."

"Well, I hope you enjoy your stint here. The staff is amazing. I've been working here about five months, and I really love the people, and the atmosphere. Like you said, it's small compared to the other major hospitals in the area, but big enough to handle most medical emergencies."

Nodding, and smiling, while tying off the last stitch, he said, "I've been quite impressed so far." After applying a gauze pad over the wound, and adhering it with tape, he removed his gloves, and said, "Well, I think that does it. Do you have a primary care doctor?"

She nodded.

"Why don't you make an appointment with him in a week or so, and get the stitches removed?"

"I'll do that." Standing, she turned and said, "Thanks. It was nice chatting with you."

Glancing at her watch, and noting that it was close to noon, she decided to go visit Janet and Linda, then grab some lunch. She pulled out her cell-phone, and called Brenda.

When the aide answered after the second ring, Christina asked, "How are our patients?"

Brenda informed her that all was well, and quiet, on the Med-Surg unit.

Christina, relieved to hear this, informed Brenda of her lunch plans.

Before disconnecting, Christina asked, "Is the fire under control?"

Brenda sighed. "Well, it's hard to tell. The doors are still shut, and I hear a lot of commotion, and yelling back and forth."

Nodding, Christina said, "We haven't had any more alarms or warnings, so I guess that's good."

Chuckling, Brenda agreed.

After disconnecting, Christina walked down the hallway to the ICU.

The Fire Chief, opening the double doors by the elevators, and closing them rapidly to keep the smoke laden air confined, removed his mask, hat, and gloves, and took in a lungful of clean air. He dug in his pocket for a handkerchief, and wiped his sweat-drenched face and head, soaking the thin material. Stuffing it back in his pocket, he sighed. He was hot, and sweaty all over, and wished he could strip down to his underwear—but that would have to wait. Massaging his forehead, and temples, where a headache had taken up residence, he thought about the past twenty-four hours, and how unexpected, and strange, the sequence of events had been.

The bomb threat at the high-school had definitely been a diversion, so whoever set off the fire-works could get away. The fire at the oil refinery, however, was a mystery. There didn't seem to be any rhyme or reason for that. And, how in the world did the fire begin here at the hospital? There must have been smoldering ash, that somehow was picked up by the wind, and brought here. That doesn't seem possible, since there was very little wind to speak of. It's a quarter of a mile away, for goodness sakes! How could ash stay volatile for that distance?

Thinking these thoughts, made his headache intensify.

"I desperately need some aspirin," he mumbled, as he turned, and headed to the Med-Surg unit.

Stopping at the counter, he asked the nurse in charge if he could have something for his killer headache.

"Is Advil okay?" She asked.

"Got anything stronger?"

Shaking her head, she said, "Sorry."

"What's the biggest dose I can take?"

"Well, I know there's a prescription dose for 800 milligrams, so I'd say no more than that."

He took four pills, popped them into his mouth, and guzzled down the cup of water the nurse handed him. Nodding, and donning his hat and gloves once again, he said, "Thanks."

"So, how's it going over there?" She asked, before he attached the breathing mask.

Sighing, and shaking his head, he said, "Not as well as I had hoped. Seems we find one pocket of fire, and take care of that, when another one pops up somewhere else. It's almost like the fire has a mind of its own. Weird."

"Do you think it'll make its way over here?"

Shaking his head, he said, "Highly doubtful. It seems to be confined to the CCU. We'll do our best to keep it there, and under control."

"And hopefully out, soon." She added.

Nodding, he said, "Yes, that too."

Donning his mask, he turned, and headed back to help his men slay the fire dragon.

Samara squealed with delight, as she opened the small box, and found a "mood ring" that changed colors when her body temperature changed, indicating what kind of "mood" she was in. An enclosed pamphlet explained what the colors meant. She immediately put it on, and watched as it turned from black to aqua green—indicating that she was happy—which she was.

Hugging her mother, she said, "Thanks Mom. I love it!"

Cindy smiled. "You're welcome. Now open the other gift."

Samara unwrapped the larger box, and pulled out a royal blue cashmere sweater.

Holding it up, she said, "Oh, Mom, this is beautiful!"

Cindy smiled, and said. "I love the color too. So, can I borrow it sometime?"

Samara gave her a look that said, "No way," but she said, "Uhm, I guess."

Cindy giggled. "I'm kidding. I don't think it would fit me very well. Besides, I liked yours so much, I bought a red one for myself."

Samara raised her eyebrows, and asked, "So, can I borrow yours sometime?"

Cindy smiled, and shook her head, "Nope." She knew there was another box under the tree, containing a red sweater for Samara.

Opening her gift, Cindy found a silver bracelet, with two charms on it. One was a C and the other was an S.

Holding it up, she said, "Oh Sweetie, this is beautiful! Can you help me put it on?"

Samara smiled, and scooted over to help her mom.

"I thought it was pretty cool. You can add other charms to it too."

Cindy reached out, and hugged her. "I always wanted a charm bracelet, but never got around to getting one. Thanks for getting it for me."

After cleaning up the discarded wrapping paper and boxes, Samara headed to the bathroom to take a shower. Cindy said, "I'm gonna call Christina, and wish her merry Christmas, then I'll make us breakfast."

Christina walked into Janet's room, and was surprised to see her sitting up.

"Janet!" She exclaimed, "You're awake."

Janet smiled and nodded, whispering, "Yes. Pretty amazing, huh?"

"Wow! I didn't expect to see you so alert." She walked over, and gave Janet a hug. Amazingly, Janet hugged back. Not like the last time, when she felt stiff as a board. *Maybe the accident did a number on her brain. Maybe she forgot how much she dislikes me.*

Glancing over, she saw Linda sitting on a cot next to her mother's bed. Reaching out, Christina pulled her into a hug as well.

"How are you doing, Honey?"

Linda sighed, and shrugging her shoulders, said, "I'm okay. I'm still pretty sore, and my arm aches."

"I'm sure the nurse can give you something for the pain."

Linda nodded, "Yeah, I already took something, but it hasn't kicked in yet."

Christina patted her shoulder. "It usually takes about fifteen minutes before you feel the effects."

Linda nodded. "It's only been about five."

Looking over at Janet, Christina asked, "So, how long have you been awake?"

Because her throat was still raw from the intubation tube, she whispered, "Well, after being dead for about forty-five minutes, I came to about half an hour ago."

Christina inhaled sharply, "What? You were dead?"

Linda limped over to the bed, and took her mother's hand, saying, "Yeah, it was weird. Her heart stopped, and the Dr. and nurses worked on her a while, but it wouldn't start, so they quit, and were getting ready to take her to the morgue, when she suddenly woke up!"

Christina, unable to hide her surprise and shock, looked from mother to daughter, and back again, not sure what to say.

"Wow!" Was what came out.

"Yeah, right?" Agreed Linda.

"I'm not sure what to say. I guess, welcome back?"

Smiling, Janet nodded in agreement. Whispering, she said, "It's good to be back, although I'm in a lot of pain. The meds help, but there's this deep throbbing pain all over my body, that the meds just aren't touching. Plus, my throat feels like I swallowed broken glass."

Christina nodded. "Bless your heart! Considering the extent of your injuries, and how long you had that tube in, it's no wonder you're miserable. Hopefully, they'll get the discomfort under control, and you can rest."

Janet nodded. Noticing the bandage on Christina's head, she asked, "What happened to you?"

Christina reached up, and touched the bandage. "Oh that. A wall and I had a little confrontation. It won."

"How?" Janet whispered.

Christina told her about the fire, and how she ended up with stitches.

Janet gasped. "There's a fire in the hospital?"

"There is, but it's up on the third floor, and the firemen have it pretty well contained. I highly doubt it'll get this far. Y'all are safe for now."

Janet sighed. "Okay. Sounds like you've had quite a night, and day, of drama."

Christina laughed. "It's been crazy, but not as crazy as your experience."

Janet nodded, then winced. "I'm afraid to look in a mirror. I must look hideous."

Christina shook her head. "Not hideous. Just battered, and bruised."

Janet gave a crooked smile. "Well, I guess that's better."

Linda stood by her mother's head. "Mom, it doesn't matter how you look. I'm just glad you're still here, and you finally woke up."

Janet reached out for Linda's hand, and began to cry. "I'm so sorry, Baby. I should have been paying closer attention. I never meant to hurt you."

Linda began crying as well. "It's okay, Mom. I'll be okay."

Christina's eyes filled with tears. "You'll both be okay, but it's gonna take a while."

Janet looked down at her broken body.

"According to Dr. Harrison, I don't have very many intact bones. He said most of my major bones were broken." Sighing, she said, "No wonder I feel like I've been hit, and dragged by a train."

Christina wiped her eyes, and gave a crooked smile. "Janet, I want you to know that we'll be happy to have Linda stay with us, when she gets released, and while you're recuperating."

Linda frowned. "No! I don't want to leave my mom!"

Janet furrowed her brow. She hadn't had time to think about that. "Thanks, Christina. We'll discuss that later."

Christina nodded. "I just wanted to put that out there."

Feeling her eyes begin to droop, Janet nodded slightly, and said, "I think my pain meds just kicked in. I need to sleep."

Christina patted Janet's hand, and hugged Linda. "I'll see you both later."

The Fire Chief looked down the third floor CCU corridor, assessing the damage done by the fire. He watched as his men ripped out ceiling tiles and dry wall, to stay ahead of the fire. Even if they cleaned up the debris from the floor, there would be no electrical, or water, as all wiring and plastic pipes were gone. It would be a major renovation for sure.

Shaking his head, he thought about how much worse it could have been. He was thankful that no one had been injured, or died, and they didn't have to evacuate the hospital. *Where would they have put the patients? Not outside, for* sure. *Thank goodness, there were only three on this unit to deal with.* Removing his mask, and gloves, he wiped the sweat from his brow, and thought, *I should talk to the hospital administrators about a plan of action, in case we ever do have to evacuate the hospital. Of all nights and days to have so much disaster rain down on this little town. I sure hope we can find the culprits behind this. I sure hope it's not Jimmy and Jamie.*

Walking down the hallway, he called out for his guys.

After dropping the Fire Chief off at the hospital, and realizing he wasn't needed, the Police Chief, went back to the police station to catch up on some paper work, and think things through. The station was abandoned, as everyone was at home or elsewhere spending Christmas day with loved ones. He had no one to go home to, as his wife chose to live with her mother, instead of him. He would be glad when the divorce was finalized, and he could close the book on that chapter of his life.

Yawning, and rubbing his eyes, he glanced over at the couch, which was his bed of late. Sighing, he decided that if he laid down, his mind wouldn't let him sleep. He was too wired from all the coffee he had ingested over the past several hours, and all the information racing around his brain. Stretching, he walked over to his desk chair, and sat.

Staring at the computer, he wondered why so many crazy things were happening in his little town. The break-ins, the fire at the middle-school, Janet and Linda's accident, the high-school bomb threat, the fire-work display, the oil-refinery fire, and now the fire at the hospital. It seemed like his town was under some kind of invisible siege.

Pinching the bridge of his nose, and squeezing his eyes shut, he thought, *I wonder what else is going to happen?* Not being a religious man, he rarely thought of praying, but at this moment, because he felt so helpless in protecting his town and its occupants, he decided it couldn't hurt to ask the Almighty for a bit of help. He bowed his head.

As Ed drove towards Alva, he thought about the events of the past several months, and how they had affected so many people—not only in his family, circle of friends, and co-workers, but also around the USA, and the world.

Why weren't the terrorists discovered sooner? So many lost lives. It made his heart hurt, and anger burn within.

Why did God allow such evil to persist? Why did some people think it was okay to kill other people? Was there more to come? If so, how could they, meaning the government and military, *be ready to defend their people? Could all the events occurring in Alva be related somehow?*

He knew he was only one piece in the whole scheme of things, but he was willing to do anything to protect his country, and those he loved—even if it meant sacrificing his life. He clenched his fist, and hit the steering wheel. "God," he pleaded, "please help us!"

His cell-phone rang. Retrieving it from the front passenger seat, he answered.

"Hey, Ed, it's Tom. Just wanted to wish you a merry Christmas!"

Ed smiled. Tom was not only his partner on most investigations of the ATO, or Anti-Terrorist Organization, but he was also a good friend. He had met Tom when they were in training at Quantico many years ago. Tom, recently divorced from Eleanor, shared custody of their five-year-old son, Tommy.

"Tom! Thanks, and merry Christmas to you. What are you up to today?"

"Well, I'm at Eleanor's parents house in Alva. Tommy just opened all his gifts, and we're about ready to sit down for a big ole' breakfast. What are you up to?"

"I'm headed to Alva, to spend the day with Cindy, and Samara."

"Oh, yes, I remember you went out to your mom's. When will you be back?"

"I think around five. What's up?" Ed asked, as he passed a semi.

"I was just thinking, that maybe we can get together later for dinner, or desert."

"That sounds good. I'll check with Cindy, and see what we can arrange. I'm sure they'd like to see y'all. So, did you hear about the excitement during the night in Alva?"

"What? There was excitement in Alva?"

Ed brought Tom up to date on the events in Alva. Because Eleanor's parents home was about five miles out of town, they were unaware of the fireworks, and refinery fire.

Tom said, "We were all in bed by ten, because we knew Tommy would be up early to open gifts, so we didn't hear a thing. I guess everyone will hear about it today, though. Eleanor and her folks will be shocked to know all that happened during the night."

Ed chuckled, "Yeah, Cindy said the noise of the fireworks display practically knocked her, and Samara, out of bed. She said she thought a plane had crashed, or something."

Tom asked, "Don't they live a few blocks from town?"

"Yes. The noise had to be ground shaking, for sure."

"So, someone burned the old oil refinery down too? Interesting."

"I'll say. Cindy didn't have a lot of details on that, so I'll go by, and talk to the sheriff later on. If I can catch him."

"So where are you now?" Tom asked, motioning to Tommy that he'd be off the phone in a moment.

Ed said, "I'm on highway 180 coming east. I just passed through Snyder, so I've got a ways to go yet."

"Okay. I've gotta go, so let me know when you get into town."

The men disconnected, and Ed's phone rang immediately. It was Cindy.

"Ed, you won't believe what I just heard!" She said excitedly.

She informed him of the fire at the hospital.

"I just talked to Christina. She said it pretty much destroyed the Cardiac Care Unit."

Ed shook his head. *Unbelievable!*

Turning his blinker on to switch lanes, he asked, "Is she okay? Was anyone hurt?"

"She hit her head, and had to have a few stitches, but she's okay."

"What? How'd that happen?"

"When she opened the utility closet door, the fire exploded out, and knocked her into a wall!"

As he passed a semi carrying the latest edition of cars, he asked, "Was anyone else hurt?"

"No. She said they got the patients out, and so far the fire is confined to the CCU."

Sighing, Ed said, "Goodness, does it ever end?"

"I know, right? Seems like we jump from one crisis to the next! Where are you?"

"I just passed through Snyder, so about three more hours before I get there. Hey, on a brighter note, I just talked to Tom. He said he, Eleanor and Tommy, are at her folks house, and asked if we wanted to get together this evening."

"Well, I guess it depends on when you get here, and when we open our gifts, and such."

"If you don't want to, I'll understand."

Hearing the disappointment in his voice, she quickly said, "Oh, no, it's not that. I'm thinking it may be late though. Let's just play it by ear."

Nodding, he said, "Sounds good. I'll see you girls in a while."

"Please drive carefully."

"I plan to."

After checking on her patients, writing pertinent information in their charts, and informing the evening shift on the condition of her patients, Christina prepared to leave the Med-Surg unit, confident that everything would be handled properly. As she, and the two aides entered the elevator, her phone rang.

It was Brad.

As soon as she answered, he said, "Mom, I just saw on the news that there was a fire at the hospital. Are you okay? Why didn't you call me?"

"Oh, Honey, everything is okay. The fire is under control, and I'm leaving right now. I'll be home in a few minutes, and fill you in on the details. I need to pick up the pizza and salad first."

Sighing, he said, "Alright, I'll see you in a few minutes."

Cara asked, "Was that one of your kids?"

Nodding, Christina said, "Yes. My oldest son. I didn't realize the fire had made the afternoon news. He saw the report, and was concerned."

Cara cocked her head, "Really? Alva is becoming famous overnight, it seems. With the fireworks, oil-refinery fire, and now the hospital fire, the reporters are having a field day."

Brenda said, "I wonder if they'll be camped outside the hospital? If so, be ready to be bombarded."

"Oh, my," responded Christina, "I didn't think of that. I parked in the back, so maybe I'll miss them, if they are out front."

"Unfortunately," Cara said, rolling her eyes, "Brenda and I parked in the front lot. If we're lucky, they'll be gone."

When the women exited the elevator, and looked out the front door, they shook their heads. There were several reporters, and cameramen, standing in the parking lot.

Cara said, "Oh man! I wish I had parked out back!"

Brenda agreed. "Me too. Let's just plow through and say 'No comment' like they do on TV."

Nodding, Cara sighed, and arm in arm, the two women headed for the door.

Christina grimaced, and said, "Good luck," then turned, and headed to the rear exit, hoping no reporters had camped out there. She opened the door slowly, and peeked out. No one was in the parking lot. She ran to her van, started the engine, and pulled up to the exit. Glancing in her rear view mirror, she caught a glimpse of Brenda and Cara being followed to their cars, by a mob of reporters and cameramen. *Poor gals*, she thought as she turned her vehicle onto the road that would take her to Pizza Hut. She smiled, as she recalled inviting Steven over for food and fun. Brad had picked up a card game called Sequence, that he wanted to play. From his description, it sounded like a game everyone could enjoy.

Pulling into the garage, and exiting the van, she was surprised when all three kids met her at the back door.

"Mom! We're so glad you're home!" Stacey said, as she and her brothers, hugged their mother.

Brad took the pizza and salad boxes from his mom, setting them on the counter.

"Merry Christmas!" Nicky said, when he disengaged.

"Merry Christmas to y'all!" Christina said, removing her coat and hat.

Noticing the bandage on her mother's head, Stacey exclaimed, "Mom! What happened to your head!"

Christina put her hand up to the bandaged area, "Oh that. I bumped my head, and had to have a few stitches."

Frowning, Brad asked, "And how did that happen?"

"Let me grab a glass of tea, and I'll tell you all about it."

When Ed reached the Dallas city limits, he called Sheriff Clifton, and was informed of the events of the past twenty-four hours.

"So, Larry, I plan to be in Alva for a couple of days. Can I come by sometime tomorrow, and go over this more thoroughly?"

"Sure, how about after lunch? Say one-o'clock?"

Nodding, Ed said, "Okay. See you then."

He pulled into Cindy's driveway right at five o'clock. She and Samara must have been watching for him, for as soon as he killed the engine, they both came running out to greet him. Smiling, he grabbed the presents on the passenger seat, and exited the car. They almost knocked him down with their exuberant hugs.

Embracing them both, he said, "It's great to see y'all too!"

Disengaging, Cindy said, "I'm so glad you made it safe and sound."

"Me too!" Samara said, as she removed the packages from his hands.

Putting his arms around both women, and walking towards the house, he said, "I was lucky there wasn't a lot of traffic, and I didn't have to stop often because of construction."

Holding up the packages, Samara asked, "Can we open presents when we get inside?"

"Samara!" Cindy said, "Let's give him a few minutes to rest, and grab a bite to eat before we bombard him with that."

Samara made a face, and sighed. "Alright. I guess I can wait a while longer."

Ed laughed. "You know what? I think it'd be a good idea to go ahead and open gifts, then get a bite to eat. I don't feel all that tired, or hungry, right now."

Samara squealed with delight.

Ed winked at Cindy, who shook her head. She knew he was lying.

They spent the next hour or so, opening gifts, and oohing and ahhing over each one. When Cindy opened the envelope containing a gift card for a spa-day, for her and Samara, she squealed with delight.

Reaching out to hug Ed, she said, "Oh my goodness, Ed! I always wanted a spa day, but could never afford it. I've heard this particular place is amazing! Samara and I will certainly enjoy it, that's for sure!"

Samara said, "I'm so excited! One of my friends from school, said she and her mom went a while ago, and it was awesome! She said, she wished she could go every week!"

Reaching out to hug him, she said, "Thanks, Ed. You're the greatest!"

Looking at the pile of gifts, she added, "And thanks for all this other stuff. Your mom and sisters didn't have to get us stuff too." Smiling, she added, "That was so nice of them."

Cindy nodded in agreement. "Yeah, and so unexpected. Wish I had been so thoughtful."

Ed said, "I've talked so much about you two, they feel like they know you. They are so anxious to meet you."

Cindy smiled. "I'd like to meet them all someday, too."

Grinning, Ed asked, "How about New Year's day?"

"What?"

"New Year's day. We could drive out to Lamesa next Saturday, and spend the weekend. Y'all can meet the family, and I could show you around the area, then we could come back Sunday night, or Monday."

Clasping her hands together, Samara said, "That sounds awesome! Can we Mom?"

Ed asked, "Samara, when do you have to be back for school?"

"School starts back up on Wednesday. It'll be a half day."

"So, we could come back Monday or Tuesday evening." Looking at Cindy, he asked, "So, what do you think Cindy? Want to meet the family?"

Pursing her lips, Cindy said, "Let me think about that." Little did she know that Ed had other plans as well.

As Cindy was preparing dinner, Samara asked Ed to help her put on the necklace and bracelet his mom, and sisters, had given her.

"These are so beautiful," she said, as he fastened the clasp on each.

"I'm glad you like them." Leaning in, he whispered, "I sure hope your mom agrees to go next weekend."

Crossing her fingers, she whispered back, "Me too."

When they finished their dinner of beef stew, Ed's phone rang. It was Tom.

"Oh, hey, Tom. I'm sorry I forgot to call you when I got in. We got caught up in opening gifts, then eating dinner."

"That's okay. Just wondered if y'all still want to meet for desert somewhere?"

"Let me ask."

He put his hand over the phone, and asked. Cindy and Samara both said they'd love to.

"So, where do you want to meet?" Ed asked.

"Eleanor suggested we meet at that Desert Palace, out by the outlet mall."

"Will it be open on Christmas Day?"

"She already called to make sure. They will be open until ten tonight."

"Okay. You want to meet, say in a half hour?"

"Sounds good. We'll see you there."

Ed disconnected, and relayed the message.

Jamie took Jimmy home, and helped him into the house. Jimmy was sweating, and complained of feeling nauseous.

Groaning, as he sat and elevated his leg, he said, "Man, my leg feels like it's on fire."

Jamie said, "Let's take a look at it."

Jimmy struggled to pull his sweat pant leg up above his knee.

Jamie gasped, "Oh, Jimmy, that looks awful! I need to take you back to the hospital."

Jimmy raised his leg an inch or so, and was shocked at what he saw. His leg from the knee down to his ankle, had swollen to double its size. The puncture wound, and surrounding tissue had turned a dark purple, and was oozing a pinkish liquid that had saturated the bandages, and was running down into his sock and shoe.

Jimmy whispered, "That does look bad. Maybe that nail went in further than I thought."

Jamie asked, "When was your last tetanus shot?"

Jimmy shrugged, "I think when I was ten. I stepped on a nail, and mom rushed me to the ER."

Jamie shook his head, "Man, you need to get that looked at. You could end up with lock jaw, if you haven't had a tetanus shot in the past couple of years."

Jimmy began to cry. Burying his face in his hands, his shoulders shook with the silent sobs. *This whole night has turned into a royal fiasco. Not at all the way I had planned. How can I talk my way out of this?*

Jamie wasn't sure what to do. He'd never seen his buddy cry before. He patted Jimmy on the shoulder and said, "We'll get through this. We just have to make sure our stories match, and stick to them no matter what." He went to the bathroom, returning with a wad of tissues.

Jimmy blew his nose, and regained control over his emotions.

"Thanks. Besides the pain in my leg, which is almost unbearable, this whole night...well, it certainly didn't go the way I planned."

Jamie nodded. "Nope. But we have to try and make the best of it. So let's start going over our story. We already told your dad that you got injured on the 4-wheeler, so I need to go out, and make it look like we used it."

"How so?"

"I guess getting some mud, and putting it on the tires and such."

Jimmy slapped his forehead. "Oh man, my dad is gonna know we're lying."

"What do you mean?"

"The 4-wheeler doesn't have any spark plugs, and hasn't run for quite some time. He's gonna wonder how we got it going."

Jamie sighed. "I wish you'd told me that before we came up with the story in the first place."

He began pacing around the room. "Does your dad have any extra spark plugs laying around?"

Jimmy rubbed his head. "Geeze, I don't know."

"I'm going out to the shed, and see if I can find any. If so, I'll put them in, and start the engine. Maybe I can run it around the yard, to get dirt in the wheels and such."

Jimmy nodded. "Okay, but before you go, can you get me a few more aspirin or something? The pain is killing me!"

Jamie nodded, and headed to the kitchen, returning with two extra strength Excedrin, a glass of water, and an ice-pack.

Tears were streaming down Jimmy's cheeks, but he wasn't sobbing. Trying desperately to control his shaking voice, he said, "Please hurry, Jamie. I think you're right about going back to the hospital."

Jamie patted his friend's shoulder, and said, "I'll do my best. It may take a while though. Hopefully, the pills and ice-pack will help 'till I can get back."

Gritting his teeth, Jimmy said, "Yeah."

Jamie ran out the back door to the shed. He found the 4-wheeler under a tarp. The engine was exposed, and he could see exactly where the spark plugs were missing.

Glancing around, it wasn't obvious as to where spare plugs would be kept. The small building was full of engine parts, tools, jars of nails, screws and bolts of various sizes, boxes containing discarded items, cabinets, and a work bench. He started looking there. He searched the counter top, to no avail, then moved to the many drawers and cabinets. He was sweating profusely, and had about given up, when he spotted a metal cabinet in the back of the building. He opened the doors, and was surprised to see unopened boxes of spark-plugs, light bulbs, and other items that he deduced would be used in the four-wheeler.

"Yes!" He yelled, and did a fist pump.

He found the appropriate tools to install the plugs, and was ready to start the engine in a matter of minutes. He sighed heavily, and crossed his fingers. "Okay, this had better work."

The engine turned over after a couple of tries, and he laughed out loud. He opened the shed doors, and drove the vehicle out, and around the yard. He then deliberately went through a couple of ditches and mud puddles to make sure there would be evidence of his and Jimmy's adventure. By the time he returned the 4-wheeler to the shed, it looked sufficiently covered in mud, to make their story believable. As he closed the building's doors, he sighed in relief. *Maybe tonight can be salvaged, after all.*

Walking in the back door, he called out, "Hey, Jimmy! It's all taken care of."

Rounding the corner, he almost bumped into Jimmy's dad, who was bending over his son.

Jamie gasped. "Mr. McCoy! I didn't hear you come in."

Jesse McCoy stood to his full height—all six foot-four inches—which made Jamie take a step back. The man reminded him of a bear. A huge, two-hundred pound bear.

Cocking his head, Jesse asked, "What's taken care of, Son?"

Jamie's mind was whirling, and his heart was racing.

Jimmy spoke up.

"He was putting the 4-wheeler away. We'd left it out back, when we got the word about your accident."

Not taking his gaze off Jamie, Jesse asked, "Is that right, Son?"

Jamie nodded, realizing his mouth had gone dry. "Yes, Sir. It's covered in mud, so I can come back tomorrow, and wash it up, if you want. I doubt Jimmy will be doing much for a while, with his hurt leg and all."

Jesse nodded slowly. The boys had covered their bases. He hoped for their sake, they weren't brought in for questioning regarding the night's events. He could tell they were both nervous, and scared. They could easily break under intense scrutiny.

Jamie cleared his throat. "Mr. McCoy, I think Jimmy needs to go back to the hospital, and have that leg checked out. It looks really bad."

Jesse nodded. "I was thinking the same thing. Why don't you head on home, and I'll take my boy back to the ER. I'm sure he'll call you tomorrow, and let you know how he's doing."

Jamie began backing up slowly, calling out, "Hey, Jimmy, I hope everything goes okay!"

Jimmy, raised his hand. "Thanks for your help. I'll call you tomorrow."

Jamie wanted to run to his car, and get as far away from Jimmy and his dad, as quickly as possible. The man scared him. Not just because he was huge, he had an intense almost expressionless way of talking. He seemed too calm, and too controlled. Like he knew the truth, but wanted him and Jimmy to tangle themselves up in their lies. Instead, Jamie ambled out to his car, and took his time pulling out of the driveway. As he turned onto the road, he saw Mr. McCoy helping his son into his pick-up truck.

Jamie felt cold and clammy, and began to shake. He turned the heat on full blast, but didn't feel it's effects, until he was almost home. He needed to go to bed. He'd been up nearly twenty-four hours, and was beginning to feel exhaustion overtake him. He hoped his dad was either asleep, or not at home. He didn't have the energy to deal with him.

Jesse McCoy glanced at his son in the passenger seat. The boy's eyes were closed, and he was silent, except for an occasional moan, when the pick-up hit a bump on the road. Sweat was pouring down the boy's face, even though the outside temperature gauge read 32 degrees. He cranked the heat up another few degrees inside the cab. He noticed that Jimmy's skin had an ashen tint, and his body was shaking uncontrollably. Jesse reached over, and touched his son's hand, which felt hot. Jesse pressed the accelerator pedal down. The hospital was only ten minutes away, but he made it there in five. He was glad there were no state patrolmen out and about. As he pulled the truck into the emergency entrance, he left it idling, as he jumped out, and ran around to the passenger's side to open the door. He was helping Jimmy out, when a man with thinning gray hair, wearing a white lab coat that had VOLUNTEER stitched in red above the left breast pocket, met him with a wheelchair. Because Jimmy couldn't put any weight on his leg, Jesse had to lift him out of the cab, and together, the two men helped Jimmy hobble into the chair. As the attendant pushed Jimmy into the waiting room, Jesse parked his truck.

By the time Jesse returned, his son had been whisked into a triage room, where he was being stripped down, and assessed.

"Mr. McCoy?" Called one of the nurses behind the registration counter.

He turned to face her, worry etched on his face.

"Yes?"

"I need to ask you a few questions, and have you sign a few forms."

Jesse pulled out his wallet, and searched through it for Jimmy's health insurance card, then handed it to the middle-aged looking woman, wearing blue scrubs. He turned back towards the triage room, when he heard Jimmy cry out in pain.

"Mr. McCoy, why did you bring your son in?"

Jesse told her the story the boys had told him, even though he, himself, didn't believe it to be true.

Pushing her glasses up on her nose, the nurse looked up at him, and asked, "So he has a puncture wound on his right thigh?"

Jesse nodded, "Yes, Ma'am. As I said, he got it when the four-wheeler tipped over, and he landed on something sharp."

She nodded, and wrote down his words. "Okay, Mr. McCoy. Do you know when Jimmy's last tetanus booster was?"

Jesse said, "I think about seven years ago. He stepped on a nail."

Nodding, she said, "Okay, if you'll sign these forms, you can go back, and be with your son."

Jesse scribbled his signature on the four pages, then turned. In three large strides, he arrived at Jimmy's cubicle.

He pulled back the curtain, and entered. Jimmy had an IV in his arm, and was wearing a hospital gown, moaning, as a young looking doctor was bent over, examining his leg. Jesse cleared his throat, to let his presence be known.

The Dr. looked up, acknowledging Jesse's presence, then focused back on the injured leg.

"So, Jimmy," He said, "Do you have any idea what punctured your leg?"

Jimmy moaned, and said, "No sir. It all happened pretty fast. Jamie and I were so focused on getting the four-wheeler back up, I hardly noticed the injury, until we went back inside. It didn't hurt that much when it happened, so I thought it wasn't so bad, but it's gotten worse since then."

The Dr. nodded. "Well, I'd like to get an x-ray, and do some blood-work. I'm going to admit you for the night. The nurses will get everything ready for you."

Jimmy nodded. The Dr. motioned with his head, for Jesse to follow him out into the hall.

He extended his hand, "Hello Mr. McCoy, my name is Dr. Nathan Briggs."

Jesse shook his hand, and noticed that Dr. Briggs didn't look much older than Jimmy.

"So, as I told your son, I'd like to keep him over night, and begin some IV antibiotics and analgesics, to bring his temperature down, and relieve some of the discomfort. Once the blood-work is back, we'll have a better idea of what kind of bug we're dealing with."

Jesse nodded. "What do you mean, bug?"

"Jimmy's running a 103 degree temperature, and his leg is very hot to the touch. I'm sure there is some kind of infection brewing. Probably staph, but we need to be sure."

Jesse frowned. "So, will the antibiotics you're giving him stop the infection?"

"That's what we're hoping for, but if it doesn't completely wipe it out, we need to know what other antibiotic to use."

Nodding, Jesse said, "That makes sense. Thanks, Dr. Briggs." As he reached out to shake hands once more, the nurse pulled back the curtain, and wheeled Jimmy's bed out.

"Mr. McCoy, I'll be taking Jimmy to the x-ray department. His room assignment will be 204 on the second floor, if you'd like to wait there. I'll bring him there, as soon as he's finished."

Jesse nodded, and headed to the elevator that would take him up to the second floor, wondering how he was going to approach the subject of his pocket lighter, being found at the refinery.

Janet's eyes flew open, and she gasped, as she felt a cold hand touch her face.

"Mama?"

It took her a few seconds to get her bearings.

She turned her head, to look into her daughter's teary eyes. "I'm sorry, Mom. I didn't mean to scare you. You were calling out for someone named James."

Janet closed her eyes, and nodded. It was time to tell her daughter the truth.

Linda made a face. "I thought about everyone we know, and I don't remember a James. Except maybe that young guy from church. But I think his name is Jamie. Which, by the way, a couple of ladies came by to visit you, but you were still sleeping, so they said to tell you they were thinking about you, and sending positive energy your way." Pointing at the vases of flowers in the window sill, she added, "They also left those flowers for you." She paused a second, then asked, "You want me to read the cards to you?"

Janet whispered, "Yes."

Janet felt her heart skip beat. *Jamie.* She had forgotten about him. She patted the empty spot next to her on the bed, and Linda crawled in, holding the cards up for her mother to see, as she read the names.

"So, mom. Who is James?"

Janet took a deep breath, and released it. *Where do I start? I guess I might as well tell her everything. If for some reason I don't survive, she needs to know she has family elsewhere.*

After taking a sip of water, she began.

"You know how I always avoided talking about my childhood, and things that happened in my past?"

Linda nodded.

"Well, I never wanted to talk about that stuff, because it was so painful, and sad, and I didn't want to burden you with any of it." She cleared her throat, which still felt raw, and motioned for another sip of water, which Linda provided.

Once Linda was settled, Janet continued. "I believe you are old enough to understand everything now."

Linda looked her mother in the eyes, and with as much seriousness as a thirteen-year-old could muster, nodded, and said, "I am."

Janet smiled, and patted her daughter's arm, wincing with the effort.

Janet told her of her migrant farm working parents, her brothers, and how her mother had died giving birth to her little sister, Mary.

After another sip of water, she continued. "Up until that time, we were pretty happy. Poor as church mice, but happy."

Tears escaped her eyes, and ran down her cheeks, as she told of Mary's death, due to a tornado.

Linda patted her arm, and said, "It's okay, Mom. You don't have to keep talking, if it hurts too much."

Janet regained control of her emotions, and continued her story. She owed it to her daughter to finish what she had started. Every now and then, she had to pause, and take a sip of water, or wipe away tears. She then told of her father's death, and how her brothers had been shipped off, so to speak, to her relatives, out in west Texas.

"So, you were the oldest?"

Janet nodded.

"So, which one was James?"

"I was the oldest, then Randy, James and Mary. We were all about two years apart, except Mary, she was six years younger than James."

Linda was silent for a moment, then asked, "So, where are Randy and James now?"

Janet sighed. "I'm not one-hundred-percent sure. The last I heard, they were in the Lubbock area. We kinda lost touch when they went out west."

Linda sat up. "How come? If I had brothers or sisters, I'd want to keep in touch."

Janet shook her head slightly. "It's complicated."

"So, uncomplicate it."

Janet reached up, and pinched the bridge of her nose. "I'm not sure I can. In the beginning, after the boys left, I wrote at least once a week, and never heard back from them. Finally after a few months, my aunt, whom I never liked, told me to quit writing, because the boys had a new life, and didn't need me anymore."

Linda gasped. "Well, that was mean."

Janet nodded, then grimaced and clenched her teeth, as pain shot through her body.

"Mom? You okay?"

Janet patted Linda's hand. "Just a little pain."

Concern etching her face, Linda asked, "You want me to call the nurse?"

"Maybe in a minute. Let me see if the pain eases up first."

Linda laid back down beside her mother, and rested her head once again on her mother's chest. It was comforting hearing her mother's heartbeat, even though it sounded kinda weird—like it was having trouble finding a right beating pattern. It would beat evenly for a while, then skip or flutter, then go really fast.

"So, Mom, when you get out of the hospital, will you promise to try and find your brothers?"

Janet didn't respond for a moment. Linda sat up and looked at her mother. "Mom?"

Janet's eyes were closed.

"Mom? Wake up!" Linda began shaking her mother's limp body, and getting no response, began crying and yelling at her. "No, no, no, Mom, don't do this again! It's Christmas! We have to open our gifts! Mom!"

When Janet didn't respond, Linda thought maybe she had fallen into a deep sleep, but then the heart monitor began buzzing, and beeping, and soon the ICU nurses, Carla and Angela, were running into the room.

They began assessing the situation, and knew they had to act quickly. Janet's heart was fibrillating, and needed immediate attention.

Approaching the bed, Angela, said, "Linda, honey, you need to get off the bed. We need to take care of your mom now."

Linda, on the verge of hysteria said, "No! She's just sleeping! We need to wake her up!"

Angela helped the girl off the bed, and sat her on her cot. "Stay right there, Sweetie, while we try to wake your mama."

Linda nodded, curled up in a ball, closed her eyes, and stuck her fingers in her ears to keep from hearing all the voices, and awful noises filling the room.

She heard a man's voice. Opening her eyes, she saw Dr. Harrison.

"What happened?" He asked.

Angela told him, and he began talking and telling the nurses to hand him things, and do stuff that confused, and frightened Linda, because she had no idea what he was talking about. All she knew was that her mother was very sick, and hurt, and it seemed like they were hurting her more.

She jumped off the cot, and started screaming for them to stop, and began throwing punches at Dr. Harrison.

Dr. Harrison almost dropped the syringe he was holding, when he heard the child scream. He hadn't realized she was on the cot next to the bed.

Clenching his teeth, he said, "Angela, please restrain that child!"

Angela, also shocked by the sudden outburst, grabbed Linda, and calmly pulled her away from the bedside, and out the door.

Looking at the cardiac monitor, Dr. Harrison said, "Could one of you call Dr. Dawson?"

Carla said, "Yes, Sir. I'll call him."

Taking the hysterical girl by the shoulders, Angela firmly, but calmly said, "Linda! Linda! You need to stop! This behavior is not helping your mother!"

As they stood outside the door, Dr. Dawson rushed past.

Linda seemed to come out of her fear induced hysteria, and looked into Angela's eyes. Shaking, and continuing to cry more quietly, she seemed to melt in the nurse's arms. Angela grabbed her before she hit the floor, and helped walk her to a nearby chair. Kneeling in front of Linda, she said, "I know you're scared, but Dr. Harrison, Dr. Dawson, and the other nurses are doing their best to help your mama. I need you to sit here, while we do our jobs. Can I count on you to do that?"

Linda nodded.

"If you get tired, and want to lie down, the arms of these two chairs fold down to make a bench. You can stretch out there. I'll bring your pillow and blanket off your bed. Is that okay?"

Linda wiped her eyes and nose, with the hem of her gown, then nodded.

"I'll get you some tissues too." No one noticed when Angela retrieved the pillow, blanket, and a box of tissues from the crowded room, and took them to the waiting child. Entering Janet's room once again, she stood by the doorway, listening, as the doctors discussed the options, and grim prognosis of their badly broken patient. Dr. Steven Dawson said, "Her heart is so weak, and damaged, I don't think she'd survive a trip over to Dallas."

"What if we med-vac'd her there?" Dr. Harrison asked. "The chopper could be here in a half hour, and they could have her there in that amount of time, as opposed to an hour or more by ambulance. Their ICU is much better equipped to handle a case as severe as hers."

Dr. Dawson pinched the bridge of his nose. Sighing, he said, "Well, she's not going to survive the next twenty-four hours here, so I guess we don't have anything to lose. She's got a fifty-fifty chance, either way." Shaking his head, he said, "It'll take a miracle, if she even makes it that far. Twenty-twenty hindsight says we should have sent her there right from the accident."

Nodding, and blowing air through his lips, Dr, Harrison said, "You could be right, but I was hoping, because of her age, and health, her body would be strong enough to heal itself, given time."

Steven said, "Well, it is what it is. We have to do what we can now, and let nature take its course."

Dr. Harrison turned to Angela. "Will you please call Dallas General, and explain the situation, and have them send a chopper ASAP?" Looking at Carla, he said, "Will you get the paperwork ready?"

Both women nodded, and turned to go. Angela asked, "What are we to do with the girl?"

Dr. Harrison shook his head, and sighed. "Oh man. Does she have any other family around?"

Angela shook her head. "No Sir."

Pinching the bridge of his nose, he asked, "Is there anyone who can watch after her?"

Angela shook her head, "Afraid not, Sir. We can keep her here for a while longer, then I guess she could go up to the pediatric unit until we can get Social Services, or Child Welfare involved."

Dr. Harrison shook his head. "I'm not sure what we can do."

Dr. Dawson, who had been listening, said, "Christina Sanders said she would be glad to take Linda while her mother recuperated. I think she may have mentioned it to Janet. Maybe we should ask Christina if she's still willing."

Everyone looked at him, and began speaking as one. "Yes. What a great idea!"

Steven smiled, and nodded. "I think we'd all agree that staying with Christina beats going into the foster care system. Right?"

Everyone in the room nodded.

Angela asked, "Should we call Sheriff Clifton, and ask him about it. I'd hate it if we did something illegal, and Linda got taken away permanently."

Dr. Harrison nodded. "Thank you Angela. I didn't even think of that. I can give him a call and explain the situation. In the meantime, Steven, if you can talk to Christina, and have her get back to me? I'll talk to Dr. Carmichael, and let him know of our plans. As the child's pediatrician, he needs to be aware of her physical, and emotional reaction, to this plan of action. She may need to be sedated before we can transfer her mother. I don't think she'll be very cooperative, if we try to take her mother from her."

Steven called Christina, and informed her he would be later than he had anticipated. He explained that as he was leaving, Dr. Harrison had called him back in, to check on Janet who was having heart irregularities. He also told of their decision to send Janet to Dallas, and asked about Christina's willingness to be Linda's guardian, of sorts.

He explained, "Dr. Harrison said he would call Larry, and see what legal papers, if any, needed to be drawn up to keep Linda out of the foster care network, if possible."

Christina said, "I just mentioned to Janet today that I'd be glad to take Linda, while she recuperated. She didn't say yes or no. Only that we could discuss that at a later date. Guess it's out of our hands now, huh?"

Steven sighed. "Yeah. We can only do so much. Do you know if Janet has other relatives?"

"Sorry, no. We weren't close friends, so we didn't talk much about personal stuff." After a moment of silence, she said, "So, Steven, do you know how long you'll be? Should we just plan for another time?"

"I should be finished here in the next half hour, then if it's not too late, I can be at your house in about an hour or so?"

Christina thought for a moment, then said, "That'll be fine. I got a couple orders of bread-sticks, so the kids can munch on those, if they're starving, and just can't wait."

"Sounds good. I'll see y'all soon."

Dr. Aaron Carmichael, the pediatrician on staff, met Dr. Harrison in his office.

The men shook hands, and Dr. Harrison explained the situation with Janet, and his concern for Linda.

Aaron nodded, and said, "I'll go talk to the girl, and explain what needs to take place. If she becomes too hysterical, I'll administer a tranquilizer. I hope I can avoid that, but for her safety, it may be necessary. When are you planning to move her mother?"

"As soon as the helicopter arrives." Looking at his watch, he said, "Should be in about twenty minutes."

Dr. Carmichael nodded, and stood. "Well, I'd better go talk to Linda."

Because her mother had to be put back on the respirator, and more IV's and cardiac monitor wires were attached, Linda couldn't lay on the bed next to her, so she stood beside the bed, holding her mother's hand, begging her to wake up.

Dr. Carmichael approached, and laid his hand on Linda's shoulder. She inhaled sharply, and turned to face him.

"Dr. Carmichael! I didn't hear you come in. You scared me!"

"Sorry, Linda. I didn't mean to startle you, but we need to talk. Will you please follow me into the hallway?"

She nodded, and laid her mother's hand down on the bed, covering it with the sheet.

Dr. Carmichael motioned to the two chairs in the hallway, and they both sat.

Taking Linda's hand in his, he said, "Linda, you do understand that your mother was injured very badly in the car accident?"

Linda nodded.

"Well, because she was injured so badly, her body is having a really hard time healing itself. Dr. Harrison, and the nurses here have done everything they know to do to help her, but she isn't getting any better. Dr. Harrison has decided that your mother will have a better chance of healing, if she's in a hospital that specializes in her kind of injuries."

"Are they sending her somewhere else?"

Dr. Carmichael nodded. "Yes. They want to send her to a hospital in Dallas. It's one of the best trauma hospitals in Texas. Your mom will get excellent care there."

"Can I go with her?"

Dr. Carmichael shook his head. "I'm sorry, Honey, but you have to stay here a while longer. You need to get stronger yourself."

Linda pulled her hand free, and crossed her arms. Frowning, she asked, "How long do I have to stay here? If my mom is in the hospital in Dallas, where am I going to go? Do I just stay here, or what?"

"Mrs. Sanders has volunteered to take you to her house when you're released. You can stay with her until your mom is released."

Linda sighed. With tears streaming down her face, she asked, "Is my mom gonna die?"

Dr. Carmichael paused for a moment before answering. *Should I tell her the truth?* Rubbing his forehead, he reached out, and took her hand. Looking into her tear-rimmed eyes, he said, "I don't know. I do know, that everyone is doing everything they can, to help your mom survive. That's why she is being transferred to Dallas, where they have better equipment, and a medical staff that is more experienced in handling someone as badly injured as your mom. She has a lot of broken bones, and internal injuries that will take time, and special care to heal properly."

Linda nodded, then removed her hand to wipe her eyes. Dr. Carmichael looked around for a tissue, and spotted a box on the counter of the nursing station. He stood, and retrieved it. Handing it to Linda, he said, "I know this is scary, not knowing what is going to happen, but as soon as you are well enough to travel, I'm sure Mrs. Sanders will be happy to take you to see your mom."

Frowning, she asked, "So how long will I have to wait?"

Shaking his head, Aaron said, "Well, I can't say exactly, but if you continue to improve, I'm guessing sometime in the next couple of weeks."

"Cool! Wait! School starts in two weeks. Will I be able to go back then?"

Smiling, Aaron said, "We'll see. Let's just take a day at a time for now."

Linda nodded, and gave him a crooked smile.

One of the ICU nurses exited Janet's room, and headed over to Dr. Carmichael, and Linda.

"Linda, the helicopter just arrived, so why don't you go see your mom again, before we have to take her?"

Linda stood, wincing with the effort, and limped to the room that was suddenly bustling with people, and activity. When Dr. Harrison saw Linda, he put his hand up, and said to everyone, "Why don't we give Linda, and her mom, a few minutes? The transfer crew will be here shortly."

Dr. Harrison, the nurses and a few other folks Linda didn't recognize, left the room. Dr. Carmichael stood in the doorway, watching his young patient approach her mother, concern and compassion filling his heart.

Linda approached the bed, speaking softly to her mother.

"Mom? It's me, Linda." Tears streamed down her face, once again, as she held her mother's hand, explaining the transfer plan. "They are going to take you away for a while, to another hospital, so you'll get better quicker. I have to stay here, but I'll come see you as soon as I can."

As she watched her mother's chest rise and fall, she knew, that in spite of her appearance, her mother was still fighting to stay connected to this world. To her.

"So mom, if you wake up in the helicopter, look outside, and you can see all the Christmas lights. I'm sure they'll look amazing from that high up."

Dr. Harrison, re-entered the room, and patted Linda's shoulder.

"Honey, the transfer team is here to take your mom. You need to step out of the room."

Linda hobbled over to Dr. Carmichael, wrapping her arms around his waist. He led her out to the hallway, where they stood silently watching, as Janet was wheeled out of the room, to the helicopter pad outside. Linda followed behind, and waved as the helicopter rose into the crystal clear black sky.

Looking up at Dr. Carmichael, she said, "I'm tired. I'd like to go to my room now."

Aaron nodded, put his arm around Linda's shoulders, and led her back to Janet's former room, where she gathered up her belongings. Looking around the room, she asked, "Can I have the flowers for my room?"

"Of course. I will ask one of the nurses to bring them up to you."

She nodded, and wiped her eyes. *These stupid tears won't stop coming*, she thought, as she turned to join Dr. Carmichael by the door.

As they exited the room, Aaron asked, "Would you like to ride in a wheelchair, or do you feel up to walking?"

"I can walk. It's not that far, right?"

Aaron shook his head. They both entered the elevator, and silently rode it up to the children's ward. Standing by the nurses' station, she began to cry silently, as Dr. Carmichael, and the nurses, filled out the necessary paperwork, which allowed her to stay on the ward without a parent or guardian. Realizing she was the only child there, Linda felt utterly alone. Wiping her eyes and nose, on the hem of her gown, she followed the head nurse, named Caroline, and Dr. Carmichael to a room directly across from the station.

Caroline explained the procedures, and rules of the ward, as Linda climbed onto the bed.

Smiling, she added, "Since you're the only one here, you have our complete attention, so don't hesitate to call us, or come ask us for anything."

Cocking her head, Linda asked, "How many nurses are here? I only saw you when we entered."

Caroline nodded, and smiled. "I'm the only nurse right now, and there is one aide. She's getting towels, and toiletries for you. She'll be right in."

As soon as she said this, a twenty-something woman entered, carrying towels, and a bag of bathroom essentials.

Caroline said, "This is Amanda."

Amanda smiled, and said, "Hi, Linda. I'll put these things in the bathroom, but if you find you need something else, don't hesitate to call me."

Linda nodded. Crawling under the covers, Linda yawned, and said, "Right not, I just want to go to sleep."

The two ladies nodded, and Caroline said, "Sure thing, Honey, but I need to give you your meds first."

Dr. Carmichael stood by the bed, and asked if he could listen to her heart and breathing. She agreed, and when he finished, he patted her arm and said, "Sweet dreams. I'll see you tomorrow."

She reached up to hug him. "Thanks, Dr. Carmichael. You have sweet dreams, too."

He smiled, and nodded. Entering the hallway, he wiped his eyes, for it was difficult to see where he was going, with so much moisture forming in them. He went to his office, and laid his head on the desk.

"God," he began, "I don't know what Your plans are for Janet and Linda, but for the child's sake, I ask You to please heal Janet, so they may be reunited soon. If you choose to take Janet, please take care of Linda, as only You can."

Looking at his watch, he decided it wasn't too late to make a phone call.

Steven arrived at Christina's house a little after seven. He was greeted at the door by her youngest son, Nicky, who, grabbing his hand, yelled, "Yeah, you're here! I'm starving!"

Steven chuckled.

"Nicky!" Christina scolded. "That's kind of a rude way to greet someone."

Nicky made a face. "Sorry, Dr. Dawson."

Steven patted the boy's shoulder. "It's okay. I'm starving too."

"Dr. Dawson!" Stacey said, as she entered the room. "Glad you're here. What do you want to drink?"

Steven thought for a moment. "I think I'd like a Dr. Pepper if you have one."

Stacey smiled. "Are you kidding? We always have Dr. Pepper."

Smiling at Steven, Christina shook her head. "Y'all go ahead and pick a seat. I'll get the salad and dressings."

Brad bounded down the stairs, greeting Steven as he entered the room, and plopped down in the nearest chair.

Christina and Stacey entered, carrying the rest of the food and drinks.

Amidst laughter, chatter, and munching sounds, the pizza, salad, and bread-sticks were devoured in a matter of minutes. Christina heard her phone ringing in the family room.

"Excuse me, I need to go answer that."

Picking up the phone, she heard a roar of laughter from the dining room. Chuckling, she answered. It was Aaron. Her heart did a double beat.

A few minutes later, she re-entered the dining room, much more somber than when she had left.

Noticing the change in his mom, Nicky asked, "What's wrong, Mom?"

Everyone grew silent, as she sat, and explained the situation with Janet and Linda.

Looking at her children, she said, "Steven told me earlier about them sending Janet to Dallas, but according to Aaron, her prognosis is pretty grim. He told Linda that I, or we, could keep her until her mother recovers, or...."

Nicky whispered, "Or she dies."

"Poor Linda!" Stacey said, as tears filled her eyes.

Christina cleared her throat. "So, I guess I should ask if it's okay with y'all if Linda comes here for a while? And I don't know how long a while is, so...."

Brad shrugged. "Fine with me."

Stacey, and Nicky, nodded. "Yep. Fine with us."

Stacey frowned, and said, "Does that mean I have to share my room with her?"

Christina thought for a moment before answering. "I was thinking, we could make the upstairs sun room into her room."

Stacey made a face. "Are you sure that's warm enough? It gets a bit chilly in the winter."

Christina nodded. "I'm sure we can work something out."

Steven spoke up. "We could put plastic over the windows, and bring in one of those electrical baseboard heaters." Christina cocked her head, and smiled at Steven, thinking, *he said, "we."*

Stacey smiled, and said, "Yeah, and we could put a bigger rug in there too!"

Nicky asked, "What about a bed and dresser? We don't have any extra lying around here, do we?"

Christina thought for a moment, before answering. "If Linda has a twin sized bed, and small dresser, we could move them here, until she goes back home. If not, we may have to ask around, or go to the resale shop in town, and get them. They seem to always have bedroom items."

"*If* she gets to go back home." Nicky mumbled.

Christina shook her head, not even wanting to think of that outcome....at least not yet. They'd cross that bridge, if, or when, the time came.

Stacey looked up, and asked, "What about a closet? There's not one in that room."

Christina bit her bottom lip, and shook her head. "I didn't think of that. Well, maybe we can get one of those portable racks or something." Sighing, she said, "So much to think about, and plan for. I'll talk to Linda tomorrow when I go to see her, and we can start sorting out the details."

"Can I come too?" Asked Stacey, scraping a melted hunk of cheese off the bottom of the pizza box, and stuffing it in her mouth.

Christina nodded. "Sure. I'm sure she'd like to see you. I don't think she's had any visitors so far."

Brad wiped pizza sauce off his lips, and asked, "Didn't they attend some kind of group meetings on Sundays? If I remember right, it isn't your typical church."

He and Steven gathered the paper plates, and began stacking them. "I've heard some kids at school refer to it as a cult." Carrying the plates to the kitchen for disposal, he added, "Seems like somebody from there should have come by."

Stacey nodded. "Oh yeah. I remember Linda telling me a little about it. I think they call themselves The Lighted Ones?"

Brad chuckled, and said, "The Enlightened Ones."

"Oh yeah, that sounds right. She said they learn how to cast spells, and use the Earth's elements for magic." Making a face, and shaking her head, she added, "It kinda sounded creepy to me."

Standing to gather the remaining dirty dishes, Christina said, "Well, maybe it will be good for Linda to come stay with us. She can attend your youth group meetings, and learn about the *creator* of the Earth's elements, and hopefully make new friends."

Returning to the table, Christina asked, "Y'all ready to play a new game?"

Jamie entered the small two-bedroom house, intending on heading straight to bed. Passing the kitchen, he saw a strange light emanating from behind the door. Curiosity getting the upper hand, he backed up, and slowly pushed open the door. He jumped when he saw the body of a man sitting in a chair, slumped over with his head resting on the table. *Is he dead?* He silently crept over to where the man was sitting, realized it was his dad, and that, no, he wasn't dead, but appeared to be sleeping. Glancing around the room, to see where the strange light was coming from, he saw a small illuminated Christmas tree on the counter. Under it was a neatly wrapped box. Jamie inched closer. There was a name tag on it—JAMIE—written in bold black letters.

What is this? His mind screamed, as he stepped back, bumping the table and jarring his sleeping dad from his slumber.

Sitting up, and rubbing his face, Jack Simmons, looked up at his son, and smiled.

"Jamie! You're finally home."

Jamie, still in shock that there was a Christmas tree, and a present that had his name on it, looked blankly at this smiling stranger, masquerading as his dad. *Had aliens come and inhabited his body? I saw a movie once where that had happened.*

His real dad hadn't put up a Christmas tree since Jamie's mom had left five years earlier. Nor had he participated in any gift exchanges with his son since then—no Christmas, birthdays, anniversaries, or any other gift exchanging occasions. Something in his dad had so completely shut down after his mom left, that it was as if Jamie and he had died, and all that remained were these walking, talking, breathing shells, masquerading as human beings.

The man stood, towering over Jamie. Jamie backed away, towards the counter.

Chuckling, Jack said, "Jamie? What's wrong, Son?"

The man laughed! I haven't heard my dad laugh for five years! Who is this person?

Jamie was dumbstruck, and terrified. *If aliens had come and taken over my dad's body, will I be next?*

Jack held out his hands, as if in surrender, when he saw the terrified look on his son's face.

"Jamie? What's wrong? Are you okay?"

Jamie, full of terror, ran out the back door, hopped in his car, and sped away, leaving his dad standing, speechless in the kitchen.

Shaking his head, he said, "Now, what in the world got into that boy? I finally come to my senses, and decide to celebrate Christmas, and he takes off like I was some kind of monster, planning on eating him!"

Walking over to the window, and looking out at the empty street, he realized his son would not return any time soon. Sighing, he headed to his bedroom. Stripping off his work clothes, he entered the bathroom, and reached in to turn on the hot water to the shower. Passing by the bathroom mirror, he hardly recognized his reflection. Gone were the scowl, the furrowed brows, and the generally angry expression that he had worn for the past five years. In their place was a softer, more peaceful looking face. One that could smile—or laugh. *No wonder Jamie ran,* he thought. *He probably thinks I've been over-taken by an alien.*

Chuckling, he said to his reflection, "In a way, I have. I've got to talk to him and explain."

Jamie drove to the Pizza Hut parking lot, pulled into a space, and killed the engine. *What in the world is going on? First Jimmy's dad is nice to him, then my dad is smiling and laughing? Something weird is going on for sure. I need to talk to Jimmy.*

Calling Jimmy's phone, and having it go to voice mail, he left a message: "Hey Jimmy. Call me when you get a chance. Something weird is going on! Please call me as soon as possible."

Once Jimmy was settled into his room, Dr. Carmichael walked in, carrying a stack of papers.

"Mr. McCoy, some of Jimmy's blood work has come back, and it shows that his white blood cell count is extremely high."

"What does that mean?" Asked Jesse.

"It means your son has a systemic infection. As of yet, the only culprit found is Staph, but I wouldn't be surprised if something else turns up. It takes about twenty-four hours for the blood cultures to show bacterial growth."

"So, are you still going to give him antibiotics?"

Nodding, Aaron said, "We've already started him on a broad-spectrum antibiotic through his IV. That alone may do the trick, and bring everything under control."

"What if he gets worse?'

"We'll cross that bridge when we get there."

Clearing his throat, Jesse asked, "So, you should know more by tomorrow morning?"

"Well, yes and no. If the antibiotics we're giving him work, then we can assume it was caused by staph, or an antibiotic sensitive bacteria. If no improvements are seen, we'll have to wait and see what else we're dealing with, and go from there."

Reaching out his hand, Jesse said, "Well, thanks Doc. I know he's in good hands here."

Aaron smiled, and nodded, thinking, *Don't thank me yet, your boy isn't out of the woods.*

Noticing how tired Jesse looked, Aaron said, "Why don't you go home, and rest. I know you've had a tough twenty-four hours."

"Thanks, but I'd rather stay here with my boy."

Aaron nodded, and said, "I'll ask the nurse to set up a cot."

Jesse sat by the bed, and took his son's hand. It was painfully hot. He remembered a time when Jimmy's whole body had felt this hot. He had been six years old, and had contracted Strep throat from one of his cousins. When his fever had spiked to 105 degrees in the middle of the night, his wife had insisted they take him to the emergency room. He had been admitted, and spent the next twenty-four hours hooked up to IV's. He and his wife had both been terrified of losing him, but he had bounced back after a couple of days, and was never that sick again. This time was different. This infection wasn't confined to one place—it was throughout his body. His boy was gravely ill, and Jesse feared the worst. He had been a lousy husband, then after his wife had died, a lousy dad, shutting down all feelings because of his own anger. *How can I repair this mess I've created?*

Watching his sleeping son, he began his confession.

"I'm so sorry Jimmy for being so angry with you, and blaming you for your mother's death. It wasn't your fault. I knew that, but I was just so mad. Mad that she left us, and mad that she left you for me to take care of. I didn't know how to care for you. My own dad wasn't around much, and when he was, he drank, and hit on us kids. He taught us that if we showed emotion, we were weak, and stupid. I knew I didn't want to be that way, but I just didn't know how to be a dad." Tears streamed down his face, and his shoulders shook, as all the bottled up emotions came pouring out.

Wiping his nose and eyes on his shirt sleeve, he continued, "Jimmy, I promise to be a better dad from now on. I just hope it's not too late."

Jimmy lay on his side, facing away from his dad, pretending to sleep, as he listened to the heart-wrenching confession. He was thankful for the shivering from the fever, as it covered his own silent sobs.

Jimmy's phone, which was in the pocket of his sweat pants, in a bag, in the closet, rang several times before going to voice-mail. No one heard it.

CHAPTER 3

Jamie woke around noon, the day after Christmas, after being up for nearly twenty-four hours the day before. Stumbling to the bathroom, he took care of his morning business. He smelled the familiar aromas of coffee, bacon and eggs. *How can that be?* he wondered, as he finished drying his hands. Peeking around the corner of the hallway, he was surprised to see his dad standing in front of the stove, and humming along with the radio. Jamie shook his head, thinking he might still be asleep, and having some kind of weird dream. His dad rarely cooked. Sure, he could heat things up, or make grilled cheese sandwiches, but to actually cook from scratch—no. Since his mom left them several years before, Jamie had taken over the cooking. Needless to say, they ate a lot of mac and cheese, sandwiches, cereal, and fast food—just about anything that didn't require a lot of time or concentration. Turning, because his bed was calling, he stopped when he heard his dad call his name.

What's going on? First, my dad is cooking breakfast, then he's calling me by my name, instead of "hey, Boy."

Turning back to face the man, Jamie said, "Yeah?"

"I cooked some eggs, and bacon. Would you like some pancakes to go with them?"

Shrugging, he answered, "Uh, yeah, I guess."

Grinning, his dad said, "Well, don't just stand there, come on in, and sit down."

Jamie walked cautiously to the table, pulled out a chair, and sat—never taking his eyes off his dad.

Turning to face his son, and glancing at the clock on the wall, his dad asked, "Did you have a good night's sleep?"

Jamie nodded.

"Jimmy's dad called last night, and told me about the accident. Says his son is very sick. I'm assuming you were with Jimmy most of yesterday?"

Jamie nodded again.

"Huh. He also asked how you were doing."

Jamie looked down at his hands. He found it difficult to meet his dad's gaze. After a minute or so of silence, his dad asked, "So, are you doing okay?" Jamie nodded again.

Mixing pancake batter in a bowl, Jack asked, "How many pancakes would you like?'

"A couple, I guess." Jamie whispered.

Jack slid the pancakes on a plate that held the eggs and bacon. Jamie sat in shocked silence, until his dad said, "Eat up, before everything gets cold."

Jamie stuffed forks full of food into his mouth. *Who is this man? Sure he looks and sounds like my dad, but he's certainly not acting like my dad. Jimmy's dad is acting weird too.*

Clearing his throat, Jack said, "Sorry I missed Christmas with you. I had to work a double shift, so some of the other guys could spend time with their families." Standing, he reached over to the kitchen counter, and retrieved a wrapped package from under the small Christmas tree. Handing it to Jamie, he said, "I know this won't make up for all the years of treating you badly, but hopefully, it'll help make your future better."

Jamie took the package, and began tearing the paper from it.

Jack said, "Son, I do want to apologize for the way I've treated you in the past. I'm really going to make an effort to change, and be the dad I should be."

Jamie could feel his blood pressure rising, and his heart accelerating.

Pulling out an envelope containing a cashier's check for five-hundred dollars, Jamie looked up at his dad, who was smiling. Anger welled up inside of Jamie, and much to his dad's amazement, the boy stood, and threw the check at him.

Like a dam, that had burst open, angry words spewed out of Jamie's mouth.

"Do you think, after five years of ignoring, belittling, and abusing me, you can just cover it over with money?"

Jack looked at his son in shocked silence.

Jamie continued, as all the years of repressing his true feelings came to the surface.

"Do you know how much it hurt to know that my mom didn't love me enough to stick around, and then after she left, when I needed you most, you abandoned me emotionally. I lost both my parents. It would have been easier, if you two had just died in a car accident together. At least I could have gone to a family that truly loved, and cared for me. Instead, I get left with you, because you're my dad."

Tears streamed down Jack's cheeks. "I'm sorry, Son."

"Sorry?" Jamie paced around the small kitchen. He wanted to hit his dad. He pictured himself pounding on his father, as years of abuse, and neglect, surfaced in his mind. Instead, he took the plate of food and threw it at the wall. The sound, and sight of it shattering, and watching the pieces of plate and food being scattered across the room, brought a strange sort of pleasure to Jamie. That's how his heart and emotions felt—broken and scattered.

Looking back at his dad, with a scowl on his face, he said, "Don't you dare call me 'Son', because I won't call you 'Dad'. You gave that title up when you abandoned me. For what? Work, drinking, women? All that stuff was more important to you, than your own flesh and blood?" Jamie couldn't stop talking. Part of him knew he should just walk away, but there was more venom needing to be released.

Leaning over, and through clenched teeth, whispered in his dad's ear, "I hate you. I did love you at one time, and I thought maybe I was the reason mom left, but after living with you all this time, I can see why she left. You only care about yourself."

The truth hit Jack like a bolt of lightning. He didn't expect that kind of reaction, but there it was. His boy's words cut through his heart like a two-edged sword. How could he convince his son that he was a changed man? All the anger, that he had been holding on to for so many years, was gone. His mind and body were at peace. All he could do at this point, was to just nod and say he was sorry.

Jamie stormed out of the kitchen. He heard his dad's apology, but said under his breath, "It's a little too late for that."

Jack sighed heavily, stood, and began picking up shards of the broken plate, and pieces of food that had scattered about the kitchen. Tears kept blurring his vision. Once the kitchen was back in order, he sat at the table, and resting his head in his hands, began to cry and pray, asking for wisdom in restoring his and Jamie's relationship.

The process would be difficult, and probably drawn out—after all, it had taken about five years to get where it was now. He vowed to mend this relationship before it was too late.

Cindy forced her eyes open, as she rolled over, and glanced at the bedside clock. 10:00.

"Oh, no! I can't believe I slept so late!"

Sitting up quickly, she felt a nauseating wave of dizziness pass through her. Lying back down, and gently touching the spot on her head where she had obtained stitches after slipping and falling on the ice a month earlier, she mumbled, "Geeze, I better take it a little slower." The area on her head still felt quite tender, and she wondered when it would feel normal again.

Lying quietly, as her head reset its equilibrium, she heard Samara and Ed discussing what to have for lunch. *Lunch? I haven't even had breakfast yet.*

Rising slowly, she slipped off her pajamas, and replaced them with a jogging suit, thinking, *I really need to go for a walk sometime today. I feel so sluggish and weak. Maybe I can convince Ed and Samara to go with me.*

Peeking out her bedroom door, to make sure Ed wasn't around, she tiptoed to the bathroom, to finish dressing for the day.

As she was gargling with mouthwash, she heard a knock at the door. Spitting into the sink, she answered, "Yes?"

"Mom, breakfast is ready."

"Okay, Honey, I'll be out in a minute."

Checking herself one last time in the bathroom mirror, she turned, and felt another wave of dizziness overwhelm her. *What is going on?* Reaching out for the counter top, she steadied herself, and walked over to the toilet and sat, lowering her head between her knees.

After a few seconds, the dizziness passed. *Maybe I should rethink my idea of taking a walk.*

Standing slowly, to get her bearings, she held on to the counter as she made her way to the door, all the while saying to herself, "You're okay. You've got this. Slow and easy."

Before exiting, she took a deep breath, released it slowly, stood erect, put on a happy face, and joined her two favorite people in the kitchen.

After consuming a tasty meal consisting of a vegetable omelet, and fruit crepes, Ed stood, and began clearing the table.

Cindy touched his arm, and said, "Thanks, Ed, but I'll take care of the dishes. After all, you prepared this wonderful feast."

Samara said, "Yeah Ed, we have this rule, that whoever fixes a meal, doesn't have to do the cleaning up."

Nodding, Ed said, "Well, that's a good rule, but today, we're gonna bypass that rule. As my gift to you both, I will do the dishes."

Cindy began to protest. Holding up his hand, he said, "Now, if one of you ladies would like to dry the dishes, and put them away, I suppose, I will allow that."

Cindy smiled, and looked at Samara, who said, "I need to let Sasha out."

Cindy said, "Fine. It's settled. I'll help Ed."

Samara bent down to pick up the wiggling ball of fur, and headed to the back door.

When Ed turned his back, Cindy stood slowly and cautiously, fearing another dizzying attack. What she felt was only a slight shift in her vision. When her eyes settled, she finished clearing the table, and grabbed a fresh towel out of the cabinet drawer.

"Okay, Mister, let's conquer those dishes. Ed turned and pulling her into a full body hug, swept her off her feet. Then he kissed her, and said, "Have I told you lately, that I really love, and appreciate you?"

Pulling back, and looking into those deep dark eyes, she said, "Hmm. The love part, every time you see me, the appreciate part, not so much."

He smiled, and kissed her again. "Well, Darlin' I appreciate you as much, if not more, than I love you. If that's possible."

He set her feet back on the floor, but didn't release her from the hug. Laying her head on his chest, she said, "Oh, Ed.. I love, and appreciate you too."

He kissed the top of her head, and held her close, until Samara came in, carrying Sasha.

Seeing them, she said, "Oh. Oops, sorry."

Pulling apart, both Ed and Cindy said, "It's okay. We were just having a moment."

Nodding, and smiling, Samara said, "I can see that. If you want to continue, I'll just go to my room."

Laughing, Ed said, "I think we're done. We need to focus on the dishes now."

Cindy, smiling sheepishly, nodded in agreement.

Setting Sasha down, Samara grabbed the dog's bowls, and began filling them with food and water.

Ed and Cindy glanced at each other, and smiled, each thinking, *It's going to be a great day.*

When the dishes were washed, dried, and put away, Ed turned to Cindy and said, "I talked to Larry yesterday, and we made plans to meet at the station around one. Is that okay?"

"Sure. I don't have any plans, except that I'd like to go for a walk sometime today."

"Okay. The meeting shouldn't take long. I just want an update on the investigation of the Christmas incidences. We can take a walk when I get back."

"Okay. So what do you want to do in the meantime?"

Samara walked in, and said, "I know. How about a game of Scrabble?"
Cindy and Ed exchanged looks, and said, "Sure."

Even though his body was exhausted, Larry couldn't turn his mind off. Lying on his back, with his hands under his head, Larry let his mind explore each incident over the past several months: the fire at the middle-school, the break ins, the bomb threat at the high school, the fireworks display, the fires at the oil refinery and hospital, and the mystery involving Janet Wash burn's phone messages. No matter how often he visited the incidences in his mind, he felt as if he were missing something. An important piece of the puzzle, but for the life of him, couldn't find it.

Were any of those events connected? Possibly. Were they committed by the same person? Doubtful. What was Janet's role in all of this? Not sure yet. Did she hire someone to break into Christina's house? The texts from her phone indicate the possibility. If so, why? Revenge? For what? I need to find valid answers to these questions, or I may never sleep again.

Standing and stretching, he cringed when he heard, and felt, the pop of joints, either going in or out of place. *Hopefully in. I don't have time to deal with any dysfunctional joints.*

Folding the sheet and blanket, he placed them on his office couch. *I'd be better off if I slept in my own bed at home, but not yet,* he thought, as he placed his pillow on top of the pile. The last time he went home, the house felt cold and empty, as if no warm-blooded creature had crossed the thresh hold in a very long time.

When his wife left around Thanksgiving, he hadn't given the emptiness much thought. She had left before, and always came back after a cooling off period, which could last anywhere from a day to a couple of weeks. This time, however, it was different. She had not come back. In fact, she had made it very clear that she wouldn't be returning, when he was handed the divorce papers from her lawyer. It seemed that no matter how hard he tried, he just wasn't husband material. He lacked something, but he wasn't quite sure what it was. *Compassion? Empathy? Respect? Passion? Time?* Each woman he had been in a relationship with, said he lacked one or more of those traits. He tried to be the man they had expected, but always fell short.

Well, I am who I am, he thought, as he poured a cup of coffee.

Opening the curtains, he stood sipping his coffee, watching the traffic—foot and vehicle—pass by, wondering where everyone was going. Closing his eyes, he felt the warmth of the sun, and thanked God for the beautiful day. *It is going to be a nice day, barring any unforeseen incidences,* he thought, as he took in a lungful of air, held it for a few seconds, then released it with an audible "ahh."

The weather man said the temperatures in central Texas would be in the mid fifties, and no rain, snow, or ice was predicted for the next week or so. Not so, for their neighbors up north. They were being blasted with a winter vortex, leaving many without electricity, and stranded, as high winds and record snowfalls besieged them. Larry was thankful he didn't live there. He preferred being warm, although fifty wasn't exactly a heat-wave.

He jumped, when the phone rang, causing hot coffee to splash on his hand, as it made its way to the floor.

"Shoot!" He said, as he set the coffee on his desk, and reached for a paper towel.

Inspecting his hand where the coffee had spilled, he answered the phone.

"Alva police station, Sheriff Clifton, speaking."

"Hey, Larry. It's Ed. Was wondering if we're still on for today?"

"Sure, we're still on. If you want, we can meet now. I was thinking of going to McDonald's for breakfast. We could meet there, say in the next half hour?"

"Do you think that will be private enough? I was hoping we could discuss the events that have occurred over the past several months. I have some ideas I'd like to share."

"Well, I guess you're right. It would be more convenient to meet here, where all that information is compiled. I still need to grab a bite to eat, however, so how about...around eleven?"

"Sounds good. I'll be there." Ed said, as he disconnected.

Larry grabbed his hat and car keys, jumped in the police cruiser, and headed to McDonald's for breakfast.

While Ed was on the phone with the sheriff, Cindy and Samara put the Scrabble pieces back in the box. Cindy said, "That was fun. I'm glad you suggested it."

Samara nodded. "Yes, it was, especially since I beat the socks off you and Ed."

"Well, I guess you can have bragging rights this time, but next time, you had better hold on to *your* socks!"

Samara giggled.

Returning his phone to his pocket, Ed announced, "Change of plans."

Raising her eyebrows, Cindy asked, "How so?"

"I'll be meeting Larry at eleven instead of one." Glancing at the clock on the wall, he added, "That gives me enough time to hop in the shower."

"Okay. You want to go for a walk when you get back?"

"Sounds good. Any place in particular you want to walk?"

Shaking her head, she said, "No, I just feel restless, and need to do something, besides sit around here."

Before closing the bathroom door, he said, "Okay. See you in a few."

Samara, who had disappeared into her room, after receiving a call from her friend Becky, opened her bedroom door, and called, "Hey, Mom?"

"Yes," answered Cindy from her spot on the couch.

"Becky asked if I could come to her house for a sleep-over."

Cindy said, "Sure. What time do you need to be there?"

She could hear Samara asking Becky the same question.

Cindy walked to the door, so they wouldn't have to yell back and forth.

"Becky said anytime. Can you, or Ed, drop me off there in a little while?"

Nodding, Cindy said, "Ed has to see Larry around eleven, so he could probably drop you off on his way."

Samara squealed in delight, and said into the phone, "I'll see you around eleven, Becky."

Cindy returned to her spot on the couch, and was joined by Sasha, who insinuated herself onto Cindy's lap, under the newspaper she was attempting to read.

Scratching the dog's ears, Cindy said, "Sasha, it's a good thing you're so cute!"

Sasha replied, by licking Cindy's hand.

Cindy looked up to see Ed exiting the shower, rubbing his head with a towel, and looking so fresh and clean. She could smell his after shave from across the room, and it made her breath catch.

Every ounce of her being wanted to be held in those massive arms, and be kissed by those full lips. Her inner voice said, *'Someday, Cindy. Someday. But not yet.'* It took all the willpower she could muster, to not jump up, and throw herself on him.

She reigned in her emotions. Feeling her eyes on him, he looked over, and she could see that same desire in his eyes. *Geeze, oh Pete!* If they started something, she was pretty sure they wouldn't be able to stop. They both knew it wasn't the right time to go there.

Releasing the pent-up air in her lungs, she looked away. Thank goodness, the spell was broken.

Samara, exiting her room, and carrying a backpack, bumped into Ed.

"Hey, Ed. Are you finished in the bathroom?"

Nodding, he said, "Yep, it's all yours."

"Thanks," she said, leaving her backpack in the hallway, as she closed the door behind her.

Holding the damp towel up, he asked, "Hey, Babe, where do you want me to put this?"

Gesturing towards the laundry room, she said, "On the washer. I've got a couple of loads to do today. Guess I'll do them while you're gone."

Moving out from under Sasha, Cindy stood, and stretched.

"Oh, by the way, could you drop Samara off at her friend's house on your way to town?"

"Sure. Where does this friend live?"

"A couple of streets over. Not too far out of your way."

Knocking on the bathroom door, Ed said, "Hey, Samara, are you about ready to go?"

He heard the toilet flush, then her reply.

"Yes, almost ready."

Grabbing the backpack, which felt like it held everything, plus the kitchen sink, he said, "Tell her I've got this."

Cindy nodded. When Ed opened the front door, Sasha made a bee-line for it, slipping between Ed's feet, and out the door.

"Sasha! Get back in here!" Cindy called after the escapee.

Ed smiled, and shook his head. "I forgot she was in there. Sorry. I'll get her."

He waited for her to finish sniffing all the bushes, before returning her to Cindy's waiting arms.

Cindy scolded the little dog, who apologized by licking her face.

Samara joined them by the car, and gave her mom, and Sasha, a hug and kiss.

Taking in a lung full of fresh air, and releasing it, Samara said, "If the weather is as nice as today, I can walk home tomorrow."

Placing a hand on Samara's shoulder, Cindy said, "That's fine, but don't forget to call me before you leave."

"Mom! It's only a couple of blocks over."

Nodding, Cindy said, "I know that, but a lot can happen in two blocks."

Samara rolled her eyes. "Nothing happens in Alva."

Raising her eyebrows, Cindy said, "Really? Have you forgotten so quickly, the incident with Christina's son? Or the fireworks, and fire at the refinery and hospital?"

Sighing heavily, Samara said, "Yeah. Alright. I'll call you."

"Thank you." Cindy said, as she reached out, and pulled Samara into another hug.

Ed gave Cindy a wink, and said, "I'll see you in a little while."

When Jamie left his dad sitting at the kitchen table, wondering what had just happened, he was in such a blind rage, that when he backed his car out of the driveway, black streaks were left on the cement. Throwing his car into drive, and accelerating on the road, bits of gravel and dirt went flying in all directions. He pointed the car in the direction of the hospital, in hopes of seeing Jimmy. *Maybe he can help me make sense of all this.*

Tears stung his eyes, as he pounded the steering wheel. A small voice inside his head asked, *All these years, you have craved your dad's attention and love, and now that he's trying to make things right, you reject his efforts. Why?*

Gripping the steering wheel so tightly his knuckles were white, he answered the voice by saying, "I don't know why I'm so mad. Maybe, all those years of holding in my anger have come to the surface, and I just can't repress it anymore. I love, and hate him, at the same time!"

Driving through town, on his way to the hospital, he passed by the spot where he had set off the fireworks. *Had it really been two nights ago?* He slowed the vehicle, and noticed a couple of men in uniforms scouring the area he had used for his midnight surprise. Fear gripped his heart. *Oh man, I hope they don't find anything. I'm sure I cleaned up any evidence of my involvement.*

Driving past the post office, it occurred to him, that he had never picked up the money from the last job had had done. The lady on the phone said she would leave fifty dollars in his post office box. That had been a couple of weeks ago. *Man, I could use that money now,* he thought, as he made a u-turn, and pulled into the post office parking lot.

There were several cars in the lot, as well as a crowd of people in the lobby, either ordering stamps, mailing items, or opening their own mail boxes. He didn't recognize any of them, which was a good thing, as he wasn't in the mood to speak to anyone right now.

He found his box, dialed the appropriate combination, opened it, and pulled out the envelope. Hearing a tinkling bell sound, he looked around and thought, *What was that?* He looked into the box, and seeing nothing, shook his head. Looking around the room, it was apparent that no one else heard the tinkling sound, as they all continued their transactions. Shaking his head, he closed the box, and tore open the envelope, smiling as he pulled out a fifty-dollar bill.

Tucking the bill into his wallet, he mumbled, "Thanks, Lady, whoever you are."

Little did he know, that someone had heard the bell, and was in the process of calling the police.

Jamie, oblivious of the invisible net closing in around him, continued on his trek to see Jimmy.

Feeling somewhat calmer, he turned the radio on, and sang along with a song about an Achy Breaky Heart.

Larry had just emptied his tray into the garbage receptacle, and had his hand on the door to leave McDonald's, when his phone buzzed.

"Hello? Sheriff Clifton speaking."

"Hello, Sheriff. This is Kristy from the post office."

"Yes, Kristy. What can I help you with?"

"Well, remember when you told us to let you know when someone came to claim the envelope in a certain box?"

"Yes, Ma'am."

"To help us know when someone had been in that box, we put a little bell in it. That way, if we were busy, we could at least hear it, and know that person was getting the envelope out of the box."

Nodding, Larry said, "Yes?"

"Well, a few minutes ago, I was walking by the boxes, when I heard the jingle of a bell. At first, I didn't recognize it, but then, I remembered the bell in the box!"

Larry hurried out to his cruiser, and brought it to life, as Kristy kept talking. He hoped he could make it to the post office, before his suspect disappeared.

"That's great, Kristy. Did you get a look at him? His car?"

Sighing heavily, Kristy said, "I'm sorry, Sheriff. By the time I got to the counter to take a look-see, he was gone. I have no idea what kind of car he drove, either. I asked everyone else in the lobby if they had seen him, and they all said, 'no' except a little five-year-old boy, who said the car was a small blue one. I'm sorry, Sheriff. If we hadn't been so busy with the after Christmas mob, I'm sure we would have been more helpful."

"That's okay, Kristy. The post office has a camera doesn't it?"

"Why, yes it does! I forgot all about that. I'll have to call my boss to come open the office, so we can get to the tape. Hopefully you'll be able to make out something."

"Kristy, is the little boy still there?"

"No Sir, but I know his mama. I can call and see if she'd be willing to come back here."

"I'd appreciate if you'd do that for me, Kristy. I'll be there in a few minutes."

Larry lifted his foot from the accelerator. No use rushing to find a culprit, when he wouldn't be there. As he drove, his mind tried to organize the information he had about the break-ins. Janet, the texts, the money, and the boy or young man involved, flitted through his mind. So far, he kept coming up short. If he could get the make of the car, maybe with Ed's help, he could narrow down his suspect list. Alva wasn't all that big, and assuming the culprit was in High School, or attending the junior college, the odds of them finding the car seemed pretty likely. Larry smiled. *It's about time we got a break,* he thought, as he pulled into the post office parking lot.

Putting the car in park, he saw a woman and small boy enter the front door. He did not pass a small blue car, nor did he see one in the parking lot. Entering the building, just as Kristy was explaining to the little boy how important it was to tell the sheriff about the car he saw, Larry cleared his throat, bringing the attention of the small group up to him.

After introductions, Larry squatted in front of the child, bringing them eye to eye. It was apparent that the boy was frightened, as he clung to his mother's side.

Larry removed his hat, and reached out his hand for the child to shake. He never thought about how large his hands were, until he took the boy's hand in his.

"Hi, Billy. I heard that you could help with my investigation."

Billy nodded, never taking his blue eyes from the sheriff's gaze.

"Why don't you tell me all about what you saw?"

Billy nodded, looked up at his mother, who also nodded, then took a deep breath, releasing it before speaking.

"I saw a guy go to a mailbox, over there." He pointed to the mailbox section.

Larry nodded. "Then what?"

"Well, when he took his mail out, there was this tinkling sound. He looked around, and I guess he couldn't find what had made that sound, then, he turned to go out to his car."

"Did he have a lot of mail?" Larry asked, as he felt a twinge in his lower back and knees. His body could only squat for so long, without protesting.

Billy shook his head. "It looked like one letter, or something. He threw a white paper into the garbage can."

Nodding, Larry said, "So, he got his mail, then what?"

Shrugging, and frowning in concentration, Billy continued. "Well, he saw me staring at him, then he nodded and winked at me."

"He winked? Did you see what color his hair or eyes were?"

Billy nodded. "He had a baseball cap on, so I couldn't see his hair, but he had blue eyes like me."

"How tall was he?'

Billy shrugged. "I guess about as tall as my mom."

"What kind of vehicle did he get into?"

Scrunching his face, and biting his bottom lip as he tried to remember, he finally said, "It was a small blue one. I think a Chevette, or something like that."

"A Chevette?" Larry asked, looking up into the mother's face.

Placing her hand on Billy's shoulder, she said, "Billy is really into cars, and can name just about every make and model. It amazes me. I guess he knows, because his daddy is a mechanic, and they both enjoy looking through books, and magazines, with cars and trucks in them."

Larry nodded, and stood, groaning a bit as his knees popped, and his low back protested with shooting pains.

Stretching to untangle the knot in his back, Larry then reached out to shake Billy's hand once more.

"Thanks, Billy. The information you gave me was very helpful. Maybe, when you grow up, you could be a policeman."

Shaking his head, Billy said, "No, Sir. When I grow up, I want to work on cars, like my daddy."

Nodding, Larry said, "Well, if you ever change your mind, I can help you get into the police academy."

"Thanks, Sheriff, but I don't think I will."

Smiling, Larry looked at the boy's mom. Reaching out his hand, he said, "Thank you for bringing Billy back. He has provided me with some information I didn't have before."

"Are you looking for the people who set off the fireworks, and set the oil refinery on fire?"

Nodding, Larry said, "Yes, Ma'am."

"Well, good luck with that." As mother and child exited the building, Billy turned and waved at the sheriff one last time. Larry touched the rim of his hat, and nodded. *Cute kid,* he thought as he turned to face the cashier.

Taking her hand, he said, "Kristy, thanks so much for your help. I have a better idea of who we're looking for."

As Jamie drove to the hospital, the incident with his dad continued to play through his mind, like a scratched record, unable to get past that one irritating spot. *What in the world had gotten into him? Did he find religion or something?* As much as Jamie had ached for a relationship with his dad, he had finally come to the conclusion that he would never have one. Then BAM, his dad pulls this whole 'dad thing', saying he's sorry, and wants to start over. *What? Start over?* Jamie heard a small voice in his head asking the same questions as before. *"Isn't that what you want? What you've yearned for all these years? Why are you so angry and reluctant now?"*

He said to the voice, "Well, yeah, but I didn't really expect it to happen. I just don't understand why it's happening now."

The voice continued. *"You'll be graduating soon, and leaving home. Wouldn't it be nice to leave on good terms? Aren't you tired of all the anger and resentment?"*

Jamie *was* tired of the anger, and frustration of unmet expectations. He could hardly wait for graduation. He and Jimmy had made plans to move out of their dad's homes, and find an apartment together, as far away from Alva as possible.

Pulling into the hospital parking lot, Jamie thought, *Geeze, I hope Jimmy is okay. I need to tell him about my dad, and his peculiar behavior.*

Christina woke at her usual time of 5:30. Moaning, she groggily made her way to the bathroom, as Benji followed her in. He lay down on the little oval rug in front of the tub, watching as she washed her face, and rinsed her mouth. Looking in the mirror, and noticing the dark circles under her eyes, she tried rubbing them away, to no avail. Lifting her wrist to look at her watch, which had the day and date, she remembered it was her day off. Leaning on the sink counter, she whispered, "Thank goodness. I'm exhausted." Shuffling back to her bed room, she said, "Come on Benji, let's go back to bed." Crawling in under her still warm covers, she was back in dreamland, before Benji had settled down by her feet.

When she woke again, it was almost noon. She sat up in bed, and stretched. Benji jumped to the floor, and did his own stretching. After a few minutes of trying to decide whether to get up, or go back to sleep, her body made the decision for her. Mother Nature was ringing the bell for her, and Benji. The dog began whimpering, and scratching the door, begging to be released. Throwing on her robe, she said, "Alright Benji, I'm hurrying."

When the door opened, Benji, ran down the stairs, and made a beeline to the back door, where he sat whimpering, until Christina appeared, and let him out.

When she walked into the kitchen, Brad greeted her with a cup of coffee.

"Good morning. I mean, afternoon, Mom. Did you sleep well?"

Taking the coffee, and adding cream and sugar to it, she nodded, and said, "Yes, but I feel like I could go right back to sleep."

"It's okay if you do, Mom. You've had a rough week. By the way, how's your head?"

Touching the bandaged area, she said, "It's still pretty sore. I think I'll remove the bandage today and let it air out."

Nodding, Brad asked, "Are you hungry?"

"Yes, but I want to enjoy my coffee first."

"Okay. I can whip you up some scrambled eggs, and some toast if you'd like."

Smiling, she said, "That would be very appreciated. Thanks."

"Go sit down, and I'll bring it to you when it's done."

Patting her son's arm as she walked by, she said, "You never cease to amaze me."

Nicky and Stacey paused the video game they were playing, when Christina entered the family room.

"Hi, Mom." They said in unison.

"Hey, you two. What are you playing?"

Nicky spoke first. "It's called Treasure Hunt. Our characters are on an expedition, and we have to avoid attacks by pirates, and wild animals, as we go through different landscapes, and acquire treasures."

"Treasures? What kind of treasures?"

Stacey said, "Well, they're different for each change of scenery. Like if we're on a ship we have to get a pot of gold or something, before the pirates kill us, or if we're on land, we have to find different items before a wild animal gets us."

Christina made a face. "Is this one of the games that came with your x-box?"

Nicky smiled. "No, Danny and I exchanged games. He gave me this one, and I gave him a car racing one."

Nodding, Christina said, "So, who's winning?"

"Nicky said, "I am."

Stacey punched him on the arm. "That's because you've already played this before, and this is my first time."

Christina said, "I'm sure the more you play it, the better you'll get."

They gave her a look that said, "Well, duh."

Nodding, she said, "I'm just going to sit here, and enjoy my coffee. You two go on with your game." She heard Benji bark to be let in, and opened the side door, before settling in her chair.

Elijah, the old gray and black long haired cat the Sanders family had inherited from Ellie Sterling, when she passed on a few weeks earlier, sauntered in, and jumped up to settle onto Christina's lap. She almost spilled her coffee, as he purred and nuzzled her hand. His actions surprised, and amused her.

Setting her coffee on the end table, Christina rubbed the cat's ears, while she talked to him.

"Elijah! You old kitty. What brings you in here?" The cat rarely left his favorite spot on a chair by the window in the front room, or behind the couch in the family room. Every now and then, when she had to get up in the night, she would see him curled up on one of the stair treads.

When she had agreed to take Elijah, she was concerned that he, and Stacey's cat, Chloe, would fight, but after their initial meeting, involving some hissing, growling, spitting, and swatting, they had stayed out of each others way. They were both like ghost cats—only coming out when they wanted food, or attention, unlike their dog, Benji, who was always within petting distance of someone.

Stroking the cat from head to tail, Christina asked, "Nicky, do the cats need more litter or food?"

"I just changed the litter yesterday, and we have enough for a couple more times, but their food is getting low. I think there's about three cans left."

"Okay. I'll put that on my grocery list."

Benji, feeling a bit jealous, jumped up, and after nuzzling the cat, who hissed, and swatted at him, settled on the opposite side of Christina. She scooted to the middle of the chair to accommodate both animals.

Brad brought her a tray with scrambled eggs, toast and bacon, and she shooed the animals off her lap.

Sitting up straighter in her chair, she said, "Thanks, Brad. This looks yummy."

As she was enjoying the meal, her phone buzzed in her pocket. Setting the tray on the table next to her chair, she pulled the phone out, just as it quit ringing. Looking at the caller ID, she didn't recognize the number. She reasoned that if it was important, the person would call back, or leave a message. After a minute, she heard a beep indicating that a message had been left. She punched in the number that brought up the voice-mail.

"Mrs. Sanders, this is Linda. I was wondering if you and Stacey could come see me today."

Christina's heart ached, as she continued listening. "They took my mom to a different hospital, and I'm so lonely." She heard the child sniffle, and blow her nose before she continued. "I don't like being here, alone. Please come."

Christina tried calling the number back, but it went to a busy signal.

"Hey, Stacey, you up to going to the hospital to see Linda?"

Not taking her eyes off the game, Stacey said, "Sure. When?"

"How about in an hour. I need to shower and dress."

"Can I come too?" Nicky asked.

"Sure."

Brad walked in to retrieve Christina's tray of dishes, and asked, "Go where?"

Christina said, "I just got a message from Linda saying she wants visitors. Would you like to come too?"

Nodding, and shrugging, he said, "Sure. I don't have anything else planned for the day."

Extracting herself from the chair, Christina said, "Allrighty then, let's be ready to leave in an hour."

"Hey, Mom."

"Yes, Stacey."

"I want to take Linda her Christmas present, and maybe a few other things. Got any ideas?"

"I'm not sure. Maybe some drawing, or coloring items?"

"How about some candy?" Nicky asked.

Nodding, Christina said, "She'd probably like that too. Why don't you look around and whatever you'd like, I'm pretty sure she'd like."

Stacey nodded, then said, "Yeah. I can do that." Setting the game controller down, she said, "I'm done, Nicky. You won...again."

Nicky did a fist pump, and said, "Yes!"

Christina called over her shoulder, "I'll be back down in a while. You two go get dressed."

Linda replaced the phone receiver, and let out a big sigh.

Noticing the distressed child, the housekeeping aide asked, "You okay, Honey?"

Linda shook her head. "Not really. They took my mom to a hospital in Dallas, and I'm all alone." Tears ran down her face, faster than she could wipe them away.

"Oh, Honey. I'm so sorry to hear that." Grabbing a box of tissues off her cart, the aide brought it to Linda. "Don't you have any family around here?" Sitting on the edge of the bed, she opened the box, and handed a wad of tissues to Linda.

"No, Ma'am. I do have a friend that might come visit me though."

Patting Linda's hand, the older woman said, "Well, that's somethin'. Some folks don't have anyone at all. No family, no friends, no home. It's a sad, sad thing to have no one at all."

Linda looked into the dark eyes of the woman sitting beside her, and felt love, and compassion radiating from them.

"Yes, Ma'am. I guess I should be thankful that I do have a mom, friends, and a house to go home to someday."

"I know this is a terrible time to be in the hospital, and now separated from your mama, but one day you'll look back on all of this, and have a better understanding as to why it happened the way it did."

Linda frowned, and asked, "Do you think everything happens for a reason?"

"Why, yes, Child. The Good Lord allows things to happen, so we can grow into better human beings."

Cocking her head, Linda asked, "Why would a good, loving God let His creatures suffer? If I had kids, I'd protect them from hurts." Blowing her nose, she shook her head and said, "I wouldn't stand by, and let them get hurt."

"Oh, I know that sounds like the right thing to do, and most of the time it is, but every once in a while, the only way we will learn a lesson, is to suffer through the consequence. As hard as it is to watch one's child suffer, in the long run, it really is best."

"Like when a mom tells her kid to not touch the stove because it's hot, and the kid touches it anyway, and gets burned?"

Grinning, the aide said, "Exactly. Sometimes lessons learned the hard way, are the ones that protect us in the long run."

Chewing her bottom lip as she pondered this, Linda asked, "So, what if there's really no obvious reason why something happens?"

"Well, sometimes we can't see the end, because we're too busy living in the middle."

Cocking her head, Linda said, "Huh?"

Placing a finger on her lips, and closing her eyes, the older woman said, "Let me see if I can make this clearer."

Linda waited patiently. She decided if she could choose a grandma, this lady would be her. She was dark skinned, with curly white hair, small boned, and even though her eyes were dark, there was a twinkle in them—like she knew a secret, and was just waiting for you to guess it. She had dazzling white teeth, and a smile that could melt the hardest of hearts. Yep. This woman was definitely grandma material. She glanced at her name tag: Mattie.

After a moment, Mattie opened her eyes, and smiled. Holding both of Linda's hands in hers, she said, "I'm thinkin' we need to start at the beginnin'. Now feel free to interrupt if you have a question or comment."

Linda nodded. "Okay."

For the next half hour or so, Mattie, kept Linda enthralled, as she told about God, His creation, the downfall of man, the redemption of man through Jesus' death and resurrection, and some of what was predicted for the future. Occasionally, Linda would interrupt with a question, but mostly she listened. Some of the information she knew from talking to Stacey, but most of it was foreign. Her mother hadn't taught her about God, or Jesus, because she believed in the power of the created things, instead of the Creator of those things. As Mattie continued telling story after story, Linda felt herself beginning to drift away. Noticing this, Mattie said, "Goodness, Child! I've talked on and on. Your ears must be exhausted."

Linda said, "Sorry. I just can't help it. I need to go to sleep for a little bit."

Patting Linda's hand, the elderly woman stood, and said, "Tell you what, I'll come back tomorrow, after you've had a nice rest, and we can continue where we left off, or if you have other questions, we can address those."

Linda nodded, and said, "Thank you, Miss Mattie, for telling me all that. I'll see you tomorrow."

Mattie left Linda's room, and stopped by the nurses' station.

Addressing the nurse behind the counter, she asked, "How long is that child going to be here?"

"You mean Linda?"

"Why, yes. Isn't she the only child here?"

Shaking her head, and smiling, the nurse, who's name-tag read Jane Dodge, said, "Yes. I haven't been here for a couple of days, and I'm still thinking there are more, but they went home yesterday. I wish Linda could have gone as well."

"Did her doctor say when she could leave?"

Looking at Linda's chart, Jane said, "Dr. Carmichael says maybe in another day or two. She is still running a low-grade fever, and he wants to make sure she's well enough to send home."

"Home?" Mattie asked. "She said she doesn't have anyone around here."

Nodding, the nurse said, "Right. From what I understand, Christina Sanders, the nurse up on the Cardiac floor, has asked to take Linda home with her, until her mother is able to be discharged."

Nodding, Mattie said, "Yes, that's what Linda said." Pondering this for a moment, she said, "I don't know Mrs. Sanders. Do you?"

Shaking her head, Jane said, "No. Not personally. I've seen her around, and hear she's a nice lady. I'd hate to think Linda had to go home with someone with a bad reputation."

Mattie said, "Well, I'm sure it will all work out for the best." Turning, she said, "I told Linda I'd be back tomorrow. Will you be here as well?"

"Yes. I'll be here from seven till three."

"Good. I hope to see you then, Jane."

Jane watched as Mattie pushed her cleaning cart down the hall, and disappear around the corner. She then went to check on Linda, who was sound asleep. She pulled the covers up, and was tempted to lean down, and kiss her on the forehead, like she did with her own sleeping children. Instead, she whispered the words she said to her own kids, "Sleep well, little one. May God's angels give you sweet dreams."

She knew Linda wasn't little—like most of the children who passed through the pediatric unit doors—she was thirteen after all. She did look small and vulnerable, however, curled up on her side with her hair draped over her face.

Jimmy turned on his right side, and was surprised, and pleased, that his leg wasn't throbbing with pain like it had when he was admitted to the hospital. Now it was more like a dull ache, which he could tolerate. His dad was lightly snoring on the cot next to his bed. Jimmy lay there a while, watching his dad sleep, and thought about the confession he had verbalized the previous night.

Jimmy hadn't seen or heard his dad express any emotion in the past five years, following his mother's funeral. During her service and internment, his dad held himself together, but that night, Jimmy heard his gut-wrenching sobs through his bedroom wall. It was after that time of grieving that Jesse had seemingly shut down emotionally, and began building a wall between himself and his son. Jimmy wasn't sure what to make of this sudden change in character. *Was it because he had come close to death, and he wanted to get his affairs in order?* Whatever the reason, Jimmy was glad. He too had put up walls to protect himself from his dad's apathy, and sometimes undeserved angry outbursts.

As Jesse struggled to pull himself out of the grip of sleep, Jimmy lay motionless, debating what he should do. *Should I turn over, and pretend sleep, or do I stay here, and talk to my dad?*

The decision didn't need to be addressed at that time, because his dad woke, and sat up when he heard a knock on the door.

Jimmy called out, "Come in."

He was relieved to see Jamie walk in the door. His greatest fear was that the sheriff would conclude that he was the one who started the fire at the refinery, and would come take him away.

Jamie walked in, first addressing Mr. McCoy, then Jimmy.

"Hey, Jimmy, you look better than yesterday. How's your leg?"

Sitting up in the bed, Jimmy felt a twinge of pain in his leg, and inhaled sharply.

Jesse, fully awake now, heard his son's groan, and volunteered to raise the head of the bed so he could sit more comfortably.

"Thanks, Dad." Jimmy said through clenched teeth.

Jesse patted Jimmy's hand, and said, "I'm going to go get some breakfast. Do you need anything, Son?"

Jimmy shook his head. "No, but thanks."

Nodding, he left the room, and headed towards the cafeteria, which was on the same floor, but in a different wing. As he walked, he thought about the confession he had made the previous night, and wondered if Jimmy had heard any of it. He felt an urgency to set things right with his son. He vowed, in his heart, that when they had a few private moments together, he would approach the subject of the confession, as well as the oil refinery fire. He had a gut feeling the two boys were responsible for the Christmas night fiasco. He didn't want the boys to do jail time, but being a public servant, he felt it his duty to expose the truth, if, in fact, his intuition was right.

Jamie walked over to the bed, and gave Jimmy a high five.

"I'm glad to see you're awake. I was really scared when you and your dad left for the hospital. I thought you were a gonner, for sure."

"Yeah. Me too. My leg hurt so badly, I wanted the Doc to just cut it off." Patting his leg, he added, "I'm glad he didn't though."

Jamie smiled. "Yeah."

An awkward silence filled the room, until Jamie said, "You won't believe what just happened this morning."

Jimmy cocked his head, and asked, "What happened?"

Jamie sat in a nearby chair, and told his pal about the encounter with his dad.

When he finished telling the story, Jimmy said, "My dad is acting weird too. What's going on?"

Jamie shrugged. "Not sure. I don't think I handled it very well, though. I think I should have reacted more calmly, but doggone it, the man has hardly talked to me since my mom left, and now, he wants to be friends? All that anger, and resentment, just burst out like a broken dam, and I just couldn't stop myself."

Nodding in agreement, Jimmy said, "My old man gave quite a confession last night as well. He apologized for treating me so badly these past few years, and promised to be a better Dad. He sounded sincere, and I'll admit that I like the idea of us having a relationship. Before my mom died, we were like best friends. When she died, I think a part of him died too."

Nodding, and looking down at his hands, Jamie said, "Yeah. When my mom left, dad was so angry, that instead of lashing out at me all the time, he just sorta closed that door of his heart, and wouldn't let anyone in—especially me. He said every time he looks at me, he sees my mom."

Jimmy sighed. "Maybe we should put aside our hurt and anger, and reach out to them."

Jamie furrowed his brow "I'm not sure I'm ready for that just yet. I think I'll give it a little time, and see if he really has changed, or if this is some sort of manipulative behavior."

"Well, you do what you want, but I think I'm gonna give my old man a chance."

After a few moments of quiet consideration, Jamie said, "Do you think your dad suspects us of the...well, you know." Lowering his voice to a whisper, he said, "I don't want to say it out loud for fear of someone listening."

Jimmy nodded, then shrugged. "I don't know." He whispered back. "My gut says he suspects we were involved somehow, but he hasn't come out, and said anything. Maybe he's waiting 'till I get better. I'll admit that I'm a bit afraid of what will happen, if I am charged with arson."

"Yeah. Now that you're seventeen, you could be charged as an adult."

Tears filled Jimmy's eyes, and he wiped them away before they broke free, and cascaded down his face.

"I just wanted to do something spectacular. I had no idea that there would be so much damage done. That wasn't my intention."

Nodding, Jamie said, "I know. Me too. Now that I look back on the whole night, I'm thinkin' that we really didn't plan very well. Maybe we should have talked more about our plans to each other, and somehow avoided all the backlash."

"You're probably right, but we can't go back, and change that now. I feel so stupid!"

Jamie reached out, and patted Jimmy's leg. "Yep. Twenty-twenty hindsight, my mom used to say."

Jimmy sighed. "Well, I guess we'll just have to stick to our story, and hope for the best."

Nodding, Jamie said, "Yep, I guess so."

After a moment of silence, Jamie said, "I remember my mom used to say that the truth always comes out. No matter how much you try to cover it up, it always finds a way to expose itself."

Jimmy could feel his heart accelerate.

"If that's true, then maybe we should confess. Maybe the sheriff will give us a break." Pinching the bridge of his nose, he added, "I don't know what to do."

"Me neither." Jamie said, as he rubbed the back of his neck.

Shifting his weight in bed, Jimmy felt an electric-shock-like pain shoot down his leg.

"Man! This pain is getting worse again. I think I'm gonna have to get some Morphine or something." Reaching for the call button, he asked for more pain medicine.

"I'll be right in Mr. McCoy."

Jamie smirked. "Mr. McCoy?"

Jimmy grinned. "Yeah. Sounds weird. I keep thinking they're talking to my dad."

A few minutes later, an older woman, wearing blue scrubs, entered the room and injected a syringe full of medication into Jimmy's IV line.

"There you go. You'll start feeling much better in a few minutes." Looking around the room, she asked, "Is there anything else I can do for you? Do you want a snack or juice?"

Shaking his head, Jimmy said, "No thanks. I'm good for now."

When the nurse left the room, Jimmy said, "Say, Jamie, I was wondering if you or your dad have heard anything from your mom since she disappeared."

Jamie shook his head. "Not according to my dad. It was like she walked out the door, and disappeared. He says he tried finding her several times over the years, but never did locate her. I overheard him say to the sheriff, a couple of years ago, that he suspects she either changed her name and left the country, or she's lying dead in a grave somewhere." Sighing, he added, "Personally, I hope she's dead. It hurts to believe she chose to leave me, and never contact me again, or at least come back and get me."

Feeling his eyes getting blurry, and his body going numb, Jimmy said, "I think the Morphine has kicked in. I'm feeling all dizzy and dopey. Can you come back later?"

Jamie stood, and said, "Sure. I'll see you around dinner time?"

Jimmy nodded, and tried to raise his hand for a high five, but couldn't muster the strength.

Jamie chuckled. "Man, you are wasted. See you later."

Pulling the door open to exit, he almost bumped into Jimmy's dad.

"Oh, hey, Mr. McCoy. Sorry."

"It's okay, Son. No harm done. How's my boy?"

"He's sleeping right now. The nurse came in, and gave him some morphine, and it knocked him right out."

Nodding, Jesse said, "Well, that's good. I have to go to the fire station, and check on my men, and such. You want to come along?"

The request caught Jamie off guard. "Uh, no, but thanks. I have to take care of some business as well."

"Well, okay then. Guess I'll see you around."

"Yes, Sir. I'll be back around dinnertime to see Jimmy."

Jesse reached out to shake Jamie's hand. Jamie reciprocated, thinking it was kinda weird. Mr. McCoy had barely acknowledged him over the years. *Maybe he is a changed man,* he thought as he exited the hospital

On his way back home, Jamie stopped in at Pizza Hut, and asked his manager, Curtis Shaffer, if he needed any help.

"Thanks, Jamie, but it's been pretty slow these past couple of days. Business should pick up over the weekend, however, and we could use your help then."

Jamie looked at the work schedule tacked up on the bulletin board, and said, "I'm working Friday through Sunday, so I'll be back tomorrow afternoon."

"Great! Look forward to having you back. It seems you've been gone for a lot longer than three days."

Jamie smiled and nodded. "Yeah. It feels that way to me too." Turning to go, he called over his shoulder, "See you tomorrow."

His boss called out, "Hey, how's your car running?"

"It's great!" Jamie said, smiling. "Thanks again for giving it to me."

His boss put his hand up in a wave, and said, "I'm happy to have done it."

So focused was he on getting back home, that Jamie didn't see the patrol car enter the Pizza Hut parking lot, then turn around. By the time the deputy was able to get back on the road, Jamie's car had disappeared around the corner, and the Deputy didn't see it anywhere.

He called the sheriff, and explained the situation.

Larry asked, "Did you see which street or road he disappeared on?"

"After he left Pizza Hut, he turned right on Pecan Street. I drove up and down that street, and the ones that turn onto it, but I couldn't find that little blue car."

Larry let out a big sigh. "It's okay Ralph. Did you get a look at the driver?"

"Yes, Sir. It appeared to be a young male, but it happened so fast, I didn't get anything other than that, and the fact that the car was blue and small."

"The little kid at the post office said it looked like a Chevette, but wasn't that car discontinued some time ago?"

"Yes Sir, back in '87, but if they are well maintained, it's not unusual to see a few of those around today."

"Huh. Well, I guess we'd better keep looking. How are things going around town?"

"All's quiet, so far." The deputy said, turning into a gas station.

"Good. I'll see you later then."

"Hey, Sheriff. I need to stop for some gas. I'll be back in the station in a few minutes."

"Could you run in, and get me a two liter of Dr. Pepper?"

"Sure thing, Sheriff. Need anything else?"

"Nah. I'm just having a craving for an ice cold Dr, Pepper."

The two men disconnected, and Larry, leaning back in his chair, thought about what his deputy had said.

He stood when Ed walked into the outer office. Both men greeted each other with a handshake, then entered the sheriff's office, closing the door behind them.

After a few minutes of making small talk, Larry opened his desk drawer, and brought out several files.

He laid the stack of manilla folders on his desk, then picked up the top one, and opened it.

Ed reached for it, and said, "Whew! This is one thick and heavy file."

Nodding, Larry said, "Yes, it is. It's all the information I have collected on a woman named Janet Washburn."

Cocking his head, Ed said, "I know that name. Isn't she the nurse that works with Christina?"

Larry nodded.

"Weren't she and her little girl in an accident right before Christmas?"

"Yep."

"How are they doing?"

Larry leaned forward, and rested his arms on the desk. "Well, Janet has been taken to Dallas to a trauma care facility, and the girl is still in the hospital. I think Christina will take her in, until her mama is back home."

Nodding, Ed said, "So why do you have so much information on her?"

"I thought at one time, that she had something to do with Christina's mishaps, and break-ins, but I never had any substantial evidence to tie her to any of it, until I found a phone in her purse that suggested otherwise."

Raising his eyebrows in surprise, Ed said, "Explain."

Larry went on to tell how he had gained access to Janet's purse when she was admitted to the hospital, after the car accident.

"I was going through it to see if there were any numbers of relatives I could call, or any medical information or medications that needed to be given to the Doctors treating her. I noticed there were two phones. I checked both for texts and numbers listed, and one just held a few phone numbers, but the other one just contained text messages. You can see the printout of the texts on the top page in the folder."

Ed retrieved the page, and read the messages. "Interesting. Did you find out who she was texting?"

Shaking his head, Larry said, "No, but I was wondering if you could help with that? We just don't have the equipment to do that sort of investigation. I know you're connected to government facilities that can track down phone numbers, and owners, and such."

Nodding, Ed said, "Yeah. It shouldn't be that difficult to track down the recipient of these texts. What else is in this file?"

"After discovering the phone, I decided to do a thorough background check on Janet. It's a bit sketchy in some areas, but I have a good impression of who she is. Seems she's the oldest daughter of a couple of migrant workers with the last name of Davis. Her mother died giving birth to Janet's younger sister, who later ended up dying during a tornado back in '72."

"I remember hearing about that when I was a kid. It tore about a mile-wide swath through Alva, and the surrounding countryside. A lot of people were hurt or killed."

"Yeah, that was an awful time. I was just a kid myself when that went through. My folks and three brothers were living on the outskirts of Alva at the time. As soon as those black clouds formed, my dad took us to the storm cellar, which I believe saved our lives. When the storm was over, and we came out, our house had pretty-much collapsed in on itself. Everyone in town pitched in to help each other dig out and rebuild, but it took a couple of years for Alva to return to normal, except for those who lost loved ones. Their lives took on a new kind of normal."

Nodding, Ed said, "Tornadoes can certainly be unpredictable, and devastating, that's for sure."

Leaning back in his chair again, Larry asked, "Have you or your family experienced a tornado?"

Shaking his head, Ed said, "Fortunately for us, no, but because we lived out on the Texas plains, we would get dust storms. When we would see an orange colored cloud heading our way from miles off, we knew we only had a short time before it would hit our area. We kids helped get the livestock in, and close up the barn and house the best we could. Sometimes we only had minutes before it hit, and mom would tie wet bandanas around our noses and mouths so we wouldn't have to breath the dust. When it would finally pass over, there would be so much dust, sand and silt left behind on our furniture, we could write our names in it, but we, and our livestock, survived unscathed. So, even though those storms weren't classified as tornadoes, they could leave just as much damage as a regular tornado, if you didn't have a survivable plan."

"Did very many folks lose their lives during those storms?"

"Unfortunately, yes. Some of the older folks who couldn't get in a safe place, or couldn't seal up their homes in time, suffered physically. A lot of babies suffered asthma and lung related illnesses, which would, at times take their lives. Sometimes, a farmer who was new to the area, and hadn't been informed on how to survive a dust storm, would lose an animal or two. Now, most homes have better sealing windows, and filter systems, so there aren't as many negative effects. I've even seen some fancy barns where special windows and doors are put in to protect livestock. Out in our little town of Lamesa, there are sirens installed around the town to warn of approaching sand storms, or other kinds of storms."

Larry said, "Even here in Alva, we get residual effects from those sand storms that start out in west Texas. Fortunately for us, the sand has pretty much dissipated by the time it reaches here, but the dust left behind can be quite annoying."

"I imagine so." Ed said, as he pulled papers from the file, and began perusing them. Looking up at Larry, he asked, "Aren't computers great? Years ago, it would have been almost impossible to gather this much information on a person."

Chuckling, Larry said, "Yes, that is true. As much as I dislike most of technology, I am thankful when it makes my life easier."

Setting the papers down, Ed asked, "Is it okay if I take this file with me, so I can read through it?"

Nodding, Larry said, "Sure. Why don't you take the rest of these as well. I could use fresh eyes, and ideas. To be quite honest, I'm a bit tired of reading, and re-reading these pages. I would love to start the new year with a clean slate, and put all this turmoil behind us."

Standing, and stretching, Ed reached out, and took the files.

"I'll get these back to you in a couple of days. I'm not sure how much help I can be, or if I'll find anything you've missed, but I am curious to see what you have so far."

Larry stood as well. "As I said, fresh eyes, and ideas."

The men shook hands, and parted company.

Pulling into the driveway, Jamie was surprised to see his dad's truck parked in front of the garage. He almost turned around and left, but his dad must have heard the car, because he stepped out of the garage, and waved at him.

"Shoot!" Jamie said angrily, as he put the car in park. *I was really hoping to avoid him a while longer.* He unfastened the seat belt, and removed the keys from the ignition.

Walking towards the car, Jack said, "Hey, Jamie, come here. I want to show you something."

Now what? Rolling his eyes, and sighing loudly in frustration, he opened the car door, and sauntered over to where his dad stood. Jack put his arm around Jamie's shoulder, and the boy tensed at the physical contact, and moved away from it.

Nodding, because he understood his son's reaction, Jack motioned with his head towards the garage, and said, "Come inside."

Like an obedient child, Jamie followed his dad into the garage. Jack walked over to the corner, and lifted a tarp that was covering a crate of some kind. At first Jamie didn't know what he was looking at, but as his eyes adjusted to the dimness of the garage, he could see a small black and white dog curled around a litter of puppies.

Jamie bent down to get a better look. The little dog shivered, and whimpered, when Jamie reached out his hand to pet her. Looking up at his dad, he asked, "When did you find them?"

Squatting next to his son, he said, "This morning, after you left. I had to come out here to get a wrench to tighten up a pipe under the kitchen sink, when I heard a strange noise. I looked around and followed the sound, 'till I found this little lady with her puppies. They can't be more than a day or two old."

"I wonder how she got in here," Jamie said, looking around the garage.

"I wondered too, but I discovered a hole in the back corner. Looks like she came in there."

Sitting cross legged on the cold, cement floor, Jamie asked, "Do you think she belongs to anybody around here?"

Shaking his head, Jack said, "I haven't seen her before today. She may have been dropped off. Sometimes folks, who don't want a female dog, especially a pregnant one, will just drop them off at a farm, or in front of a store. Sometimes, they just shoot them."

Jamie picked up one of the pups who's eyes were still sealed shut. The mama dog whimpered, but didn't growl.

He reached down with his free hand, and scratched behind her ears.

Bringing the pup up to his face, he said, "It's okay, little lady. I'll put your baby right back." She responded by licking his hand.

Jamie counted four pups, and picked each one up to determine its sex. Looking at his dad who was also picking up the pups, he couldn't help but grin, when he said, "Two girls and two boys."

Jack smiled too, and said, "Now what are we gonna do?"

Looking around the crowded, cold garage, Jamie asked, "Is it okay if we bring them in the house? It's pretty cold out here."

Standing, and nodding, Jack said, "Yes. That's a great idea. Would you like to keep them in your room?"

After returning the pups to their mother, Jamie stood, and said, "Absolutely! I've always wanted a dog, and now I have five!"

Before he realized what he was doing, Jamie reached out, and hugged his dad. It had been so long since either one had shown any affection towards the other, it was a bit awkward. Pulling away, Jamie said, "Sorry."

His dad smiled, and patted his son's shoulder. "It's okay."

It was as if an invisible wall between them had begun to crumble.

Jack said, "Why don't you go fix them a spot in your bedroom, then I'll bring them in. Once they are settled, I'll run to the store, and get a couple dog bowls and food."

Jamie grinned, and said, "I'll be right back."

Jack sat on the floor by the dogs, and let out a sigh. He was so thankful that the little mama dog decided to have her pups in his garage. He had racked his brain all morning, trying to come up with a way to reach his son. *Who would have imagined a few pups would be that answer? Hopefully, having the dogs will lessen the pain of what I have to tell him.*

A few minutes later, Jamie returned, and both men carried the pups in as their mama followed at their heels. Jamie had a nice soft comforter folded in one corner of his room.

"So, Dad, what should we name the mama?"

Jack thought for a moment, then said, "How about Little Lady? It just seems to fit her."

Jamie grinned. "Little Lady. I like the sound of that." Turning to the dog, he asked, "How do you like the name, Little Lady?" She thumped her tail, and he could have sworn she smiled up at him.

Nodding, he said, "Little Lady, it is then."

Jack said, "Well, I'll head on to town. Do you need anything?"

Jamie shook his head. "Nope. I'll just sit here, and watch the pups 'till you get back."

When he heard the truck leave the driveway, Jamie curled up on the floor next to his dogs, and dozed off.

About an hour or so later, Jack returned with several bags of dog food, and a few different sized dog bowls.

Jamie woke when he heard his dad come in the back door. Rubbing the sleep out of his eyes as he walked in the kitchen, he was surprised to see the plethora of dog items.

"Jimminy, Dad. How many bowls do you think these little dogs will need? Surely not that many! And what is it with all these bags of dog food?"

Jack made a face, and said, "Well, I wasn't sure which dog food was the best, and the bowls will come in handy when the pups get bigger, so...yeah, I got a little carried away."

Jamie shook his head. "So where are we going to store all this stuff?"

Jack looked around the small kitchen, and said, "How about in your room?"

Jamie rolled his eyes. "And where in the world would I put this stuff? Did you not see how crowded my room is?"

Jack grinned. "I was just kidding. We can put it in the cabinet on the back porch. I'll have to clean it out, of course, but most of the stuff in there needs to be moved to the garage, or thrown out." Jamie gave him a skeptical look.

Shrugging, Jack said, "We'll figure it out."

Jamie looked at the wall clock. "I told Jimmy that I'd be back to visit him around five. You want to come with me?"

Jack considered this, then said, "I'd like to, but I think I should stay, and help Little Lady settle in."

Jamie nodded. "Okay. By the way, I have to work this weekend."

Leaning against the kitchen counter, Jack said, "Yeah, me too. I think the pups will be okay while we're gone, don't you?"

Jamie shrugged. "I would think so. Little Lady seems to have settled in quite nicely. As long as she has food and water, and I take her out before I leave, and one of us takes her out when we get home, she should be fine."

Jack nodded. "Yeah, you're right. She'll be fine.

Picking up a can of dog food, and reading the label, Jamie asked, "What kind of dog do you think she is?"

"She must have some Chihuahua in her because she's so little, but she has longish fur, and I've never seen a black and white Chihuahua, so, I think she's pure bred mutt."

Jamie chuckled. "I like that. Pure bred mutt. I'm thinking I should take her, and the pups, to the vet on Monday, and get them checked out. I'll ask him about shots and de-worming, and anything else that needs to be done. Not ever having a dog, I'm not sure what they need."

Jack smiled. "I can't help you with anything either, as I never had a dog... or any pet for that matter."

Jamie looked shocked. "You never had a dog? Even as a kid?"

Jack shook his head. "Nope. My old man didn't believe in dogs as pets. He said it was unnatural."

"Unnatural?" Jamie asked, puzzled.

Shaking his head, Jack said, "Your grandpa was a mean old goat. Let me just leave it at that."

Jamie nodded, and thought, *kind of like you've been these past few years. The nut didn't fall far from the tree in that department.*

When Ed returned to Cindy's house, she met him at the door wearing a pink jogging suit, tennis shoes, and a head band.

"So, I take it you're ready to go for that walk, or jog, around the neighborhood?"

"Yep, but I'll wait for you to change into something more appropriate for walking."

"You mean my dress shoes, khaki pants, and long sleeve sweater, aren't appropriate wear?"

She giggled. "Well, you're certainly welcome to wear them, but we'd better take a few band-aids for the blisters those shoes will probably cause."

Looking down at his foot attire, he shrugged.

She continued, "Sure, they're fine for strolling along, but jogging, well..."

Nodding, and chuckling, he said, "You're right, I think I would last about fifty feet in this outfit. I'll change."

As Cindy waited for Ed, she did a few stretching exercises to limber up. *I wonder what Christina is up to today. I'll call her when we get back.*

Quietly exiting the bathroom, Ed snuck up behind Cindy, and grabbed her around the waist, causing her to squeal in surprise.

"Gracious! You scared me!" She said through giggles, as she reached up, and slapped his shoulder playfully.

Exiting the house, Ed asked, "So which way are we going?"

"I was thinking we could jog down to the park, then head back up through town, then stop at the drugstore for a root beer float."

"A root beer float? Doesn't that kinda defeat the purpose of jogging? All those calories you just burned off, will be for nothing."

Rolling her eyes, she said, "Okay, you're right. Maybe we can get something a little less loaded with calories, but man, a root beer float sure sounds good!"

Nodding, he said, "It does, doesn't it? But remember, no pain, no gain."

She punched his arm, and took off in the direction of the park.

Linda had just awoken from a short, refreshing nap, when she heard a light rapping on her hospital room door.

"Come in." She called, as she sat up in bed.

Stacey was the first one to enter the room, and headed to the bed to give Linda a hug.

"Oh my goodness! It's so good to see you!" Stacey said, as she hugged her friend.

Linda returned the hug, and was pleased when the rest of the Sanders family walked in.

Releasing Stacey, she said with a grin, "I see you brought the rest of your clan."

Giggling, Stacey said, "Well, I kinda had to. You know, not being able to drive myself, and all."

Nicky, Brad and Christina walked over, and gave Linda a hug as well.

Patting the bed, Linda said, "I only have a couple of chairs as you can see, so Stacey, why don't you and Nicky sit on my bed, and your mom, and Brad can have the chairs?"

Christina asked, "So, how are you doing, Linda?"

"You mean besides being stuck here in the hospital with a broken arm, sore belly from the surgery, and missing my mom, I guess I'm okay."

A sympathetic look passed over Christina's face. "I'm sorry, Honey. I know this is a really difficult time for you. Does Dr. Carmichael say when you might be released?"

Linda shook her head. "He says I'm still running a fever, so he won't let me leave 'till that's gone."

"When you're released, would you like to come stay with us, until your mom comes home?"

Linda's face lit up, as she looked at Stacey, who was nodding and grinning.

"Really? You'd let me stay? What if it's a long time?"

"Oh, Honey," Christina said, "You will be welcomed, no matter how long it takes."

"Can I go back home, and get my stuff?"

Nodding, Christina said, "Of course. You can get whatever you want."

Stacey stood and said, "Hey, I have something for you." She reached for the gift bag sitting on the floor next to her mom. Handing it to Linda, she said, "Sorry this is late, but so much has happened these past few weeks, that I just sorta forgot to get it to you."

Reaching for the bag, Linda grinned, and said, "Oh, thanks, Stacey."

Nicky said, "It's not just from Stacey. We all put something in the bag for you."

"Nicky!" Christina chided.

"Well, I just wanted her to know that it's from all of us."

Linda smiled. "It's okay, Mrs. Sanders." Looking at Nicky, Linda said, "Thanks for letting me know. Now I can thank all of you, and not just Stacey."

Stacey gave her a friendship necklace, which matched the one around her own neck. Nicky gave her a drawing pad, and a box of colored pencils, and Brad gave her the candy he had received in his Christmas stocking.

"Oh, y'all are so sweet! I love each thing here." Stacey gathered the torn wrapping paper, and deposited it in the trash container. After the gifts were set aside, they sat and talked about what was going on around Alva.

Nicky asked, "Did you get to see the fireworks, or the fire at the oil refinery on Christmas day?"

Linda shook her head. "No, but I heard about it. There was talk about evacuating the hospital when the fire broke out on the third floor."

Looking at Christina, she asked, "How's your head, Mrs. Sanders?"

Touching the sore area, Christina said, "It's healing nicely. Thanks for asking."

"How'd you know about my mom's head?" Nicky asked.

"She came to visit my mom, soon after it happened. She wanted to make sure we were okay. That was right after my mom woke up."

Linda looked down at her hands, and sighed. "I hope she wakes up again."

Stacey patted her friend's hand, and said, "I bet she will."

Christina said, "She's in one of the best trauma hospitals now, and I've heard of miracles occurring there."

Linda looked up into Christina's face, and asked, "What kind of miracles?"

"People waking up from long time comas, people walking when no one thought they'd ever walk again, and I just recently read of a man who learned to read, and write again after a severe head trauma. I'm sure there are other amazing stories, but I just don't know them right now."

Linda nodded. "Who knows, maybe my mom will end up in one of those articles about miracles."

Brad, who had been silent up 'till then said, "We can hope, and ask God to intervene on your mom's behalf."

Linda cocked her head, and nodded.

There was a knock on the door, as an aide from the kitchen brought a tray of food in for Linda.

"Thanks." She said to the aide. "I didn't realize it was dinnertime. I am pretty hungry." Lifting the lid off the plate of food, she smiled. "A grilled cheese sandwich, and tomato soup. Hope it's as good as my mom always made."

Standing, Christina said, "Well kids, why don't we go, and let Linda eat in peace?"

"Oh, y'all don't have to go. I can eat this later."

"No, you need to eat it while it's hot. Besides, we need to go get something to eat ourselves."

Everyone gave Linda a hug before leaving.

Stacey said, "We'll be back tomorrow, and if you're still here New Year's Eve, we'll be here to celebrate with you. Right, Mom?"

Christina nodded.

Linda stood, and walked with them to the door, saying, "Hopefully, I'll be out by then."

"Yeah, hopefully," agreed Stacey.

Christina said, "If you kids don't mind, I'd like to go to the cardiac unit, and see how much damage has been done."

Brad looked at his siblings, who were nodding, and said, "Sure. We'd like to see also."

Arriving on the third floor, Christina said, "I'd like to go check on the patient's first."

She approached the nurses' station, and asked an aide who was leaning on the counter, if she could speak to the head nurse. A minute later, the nurse approached.

"Christina! It's good to see you!" Reaching up, and turning Christina's head, she asked, "How's your head doing?"

Christina said, "It's good to see you too, Libby, and my head is just fine, thank you."

"What brings you up here on your day off?"

"I was visiting one of Stacey's friends down on pediatrics, and thought I'd drop by, and check on my patients."

"Is that the young girl who was in that awful car accident a couple weeks ago?"

Christina nodded.

"Poor kid. Being in the hospital during Christmas break has got to be awful."

Putting her hands on her hips, and in an offended tone, Libby said, "So, you don't think we'd take good care of your patients?"

Christina heard her kids snicker.

"Well, they're not surgical patients, so...I'm not sure you'd know how to handle them."

Shaking her head, Libby said, "You are still as sassy as you were in high school." Christina smiled, and said, "And so are you."

Libby glanced over to where the Sanders kids were standing, as if she just saw them, and asked,

"Are these your kids?"

Christina nodded, and introduced them.

"Goodness, they are good looking. Must take after their dad's side of the family."

Christina smiled, and shook her head. It was fun to verbally spar with Libby. In high school, Libby was the life of the party, always having a quick come-back to less than flattering remarks, and could tell the best stories and jokes. Everyone loved her.

"Kids, Libby and I go back a long way. We were in middle, and high-school together." Glancing at Libby, she continued. "We traveled in different circles, because she was a cheerleader, and I was in the band geek crowd, but we've always gotten along."

Libby shook each child's hand, and whispered, "Your mom was very popular in her own little geek crowd."

Christina rolled her eyes, "Thanks. I think."

Libby laughed a bubbly, melodious laugh, and said, "Well, it's true, otherwise you wouldn't have been nominated as the band sweetheart three years in a row."

"You were the band sweetheart?" Nicky asked.

"Well, it wasn't that big a deal. Certainly not as impressive as being homecoming queen."

Shaking her head, Libby said, "That was so long ago. But they were good times, weren't they?"

Nodding, Christina said, "Yes, they were. Now, can you tell me how my patients are doing?"

Turning to go behind the desk, and retrieve the charts, Libby said, "The fireman, Noah Jonas, who had the cardiac catheterization this morning, is doing well. He's resting. Dr. Dawson doesn't want him moving around yet." Glancing at the clock, she added, "He's got a few more hours to go, before he can get up. The other two patients, were sent home today. So, really a light load around here. We only have three of our own patients, including a young man who was admitted last night. They're all doing well, as of now.

Taking Noah's chart, and scanning through it, Christina asked, "How's the repair work going over in the cardiac wing?"

"It's been pretty noisy, off and on, during the day. They usually quit around five, and start up again around seven in the morning."

Brad asked, "Have you been able to see how much damage was done."

Shaking her head, Libby said, "Not really. I did peek through the open door yesterday, and it looks pretty bad.

Christina asked, "Has anyone said how long it will be before we can move back in?"

Shaking her head, Libby said, "No. But I imagine it won't be until well after the new year."

Sighing, Christina asked, "Have you seen any of our aides, namely Sally Jean?"

"I think she is scheduled for this evening. Because there are so few patients, Mrs. Ferguson, hasn't scheduled the others in, unless she has them in a different area of the hospital."

Nodding, Christina said, "That's possible. Is it okay if I go see my patient?"

"That's fine. Just don't stay long. He's still a bit groggy from the catheterization."

"Okay."

Christina rapped lightly on the door, and was invited in.

Lying flat on his back on the hospital bed, and unable to sit up, Noah Jonas asked, "Who's there?"

Pulling the curtain back, Christina said, "Mr. Jonas. It's Christina Sanders, from the cardiac unit."

"I'm sorry, I can't sit up." He said, turning his head. He could make out other bodies, but because the room was dark, he couldn't discern who they were. "Are there other people with you?"

"Yes, my three kids. I was downstairs visiting another patient, when I decided I'd like to come up and check on you."

"Oh, that's nice. Can I meet your kids?"

"Sure."

Christina introduced them, and told him a little about each one. Reaching out his hand, Noah, shook each child's hand in greeting.

"Brad, you may know my daughter Chelsea Jonas? She's a sophomore."

Brad thought for a moment. "Oh, yes. She's one of the cheerleaders, right?"

Smiling, Noah said, "Yes."

"I don't know her personally, but everyone on the foot ball team knows who the cheerleaders are."

Chuckling, Noah said, "Yep, that's what kinda scares me."

Brad said, "She seems like a nice girl."

"She is, but she can be a bit sassy too."

Nodding, Brad said, "That could be a good thing. Hopefully, she won't put up with any bull from the guys."

"Oh, I think she'd put them in their place."

Looking at Nicky, he asked, "How old are you? I have a son about your age.

Nicky said, "I'm ten, but I have a birthday coming up soon. What's your son's name, and what grade is he in?"

"His name is Dean. He's thirteen, and in the eighth grade. What grade are you in?"

"I'm only in fifth. I don't think I know him."

Stacey said, "I know him. He's really nice."

"Thank you, Stacey. What grade are you in?"

"I'm in seventh."

"How do you know Dean?"

"Sometimes, the eighth grade kids come help us with our assignments. He's helped me study for my spelling exam."

"Oh, that's good to know. He's mentioned that he's helped kids with their assignments. I didn't realize you were one of them."

Smiling broadly, she said, "Yep. Because of him, I aced my spelling exam."

"Great! I'll mention that I met you. And you, Brad. Maybe we'll see y'all around sometime."

Christina reached out and patted Noah's arm. "I hope everything goes well with you. You only have a few more hours to go, before you can sit up. I know it's difficult to stay in one position for so many hours.."

"Yes it is. I'm not used to being still for so long."

Smiling, Christina said, "If it's any consolation, and all goes well, you'll be sleeping in your own bed tomorrow night."

"That would be great! It's really difficult to sleep here."

Nodding, Christina said, "Yes, I know. Can I get you anything before I leave?"

"Just send the nurse or aide in."

"Sure."

"Bye, Mr. Jonas." Nicky said, as they left the room.

"Bye. See y'all around."

Walking towards the elevator, Stacey said, "He seems like a nice guy."

Christina nodded. "He does, doesn't he?"

While waiting for the elevator's arrival, Christina said, "I'd like to take a look at the cardiac unit. Y'all want to come?"

Nodding, they all agreed.

The double doors to the unit were closed, but unlocked. Christina could hear men's voices, power tools buzzing, and hammering sounds. She quietly opened the doors, and stood in shocked silence, as she took in the disaster in front of her.

Putting her hand to her mouth, she said, "Oh my goodness! What a mess!"

Wires were hanging from the ceiling, piles of rubble containing charred wood, and ceiling tiles, were lying about on the floor, as well as some of the cardiac monitoring equipment. The nurse's station counter, held tools of every kind, and the curtains that hung in the patient's room for privacy, were lying in a pile by the door.

"Whoah!" Said Brad. "Looks like y'all aren't going to get back in here anytime soon."

Christina nodded. "Yeah, I think you're right."

Nicky looked around and asked, "What are they going to do with all this stuff?"

Christina said, "I don't know. Hopefully, the cardiac equipment can be salvaged. Replacing all of that would cost a ton of money. The curtains and linens will probably get washed down stairs."

Stacey said, "Maybe we could do a fundraiser or something to help pay for some of this stuff."

Christina looked at her daughter, and smiled. "I would have never thought of that, but that is a good idea. I'll talk to Steven, and see what he thinks."

"Dr. Dawson? What can he do?" Nicky asked.

"He's on the board of trustees, and they make the decisions on where the hospital's money should be spent. If they like the idea of a fundraiser, they could use some of the allotted money for other things."

Brad asked, "Stacey, what kind of fundraiser are you thinking about?"

Scrunching her face, she said, "I don't know. It's too cold for a car wash, or lemon aid stand. I'll have to think about it."

Christina said, "Maybe we can brainstorm, and I can present our ideas to Steven, who can present them to the board."

They were interrupted, when a man wearing a yellow jacket, and matching hard hat, came out of one of the rooms.

"Excuse me, Ma'am, but this is a restricted area."

"I know, but I'm one of the RN's that worked on the cardiac unit. I just wanted to see how things were progressing."

Nodding, and removing his hard hat, he said, "Are you Mrs. Sanders?"

Extending his hand for a shake, he said, "I'm Noah's brother, Hank. He told me a little about you."

Smiling, Christina shook his hand, and introduced herself, and the kids.

"We just came from Noah's room. I met his wife and kids, the day of the fire."

"How is my little brother? I haven't checked on him since last evening when I was leaving."

"He's antsy to get up. He had a cardiac catheterization this morning, so he has to lay flat for about twelve hours to prevent any bleeding from the puncture site."

Chuckling, Hank said, "He told me that he had that scheduled. I'm surprised he's agreed to lying flat for twelve hours, though. He was always the hyper active kid growing up."

Shaking her head, she said, "Well, he doesn't have much choice. If he were to give the nurses any trouble, they'd just have to give him a sedative."

"Yeah, I remember our mom saying, at times, she wished she could give him drugs to knock him out."

Chuckling, Christina said, "Now days they do have drugs that help calm hyperactive kids."

"Fortunately, for his wife and kids, he's kinda outgrown that hyperactivity. Don't get me wrong, he still has some of that restlessness, but he can channel it better by being a volunteer fire man, and working on the road crew."

Nodding, Christina said, "That's good. There seems to be road work going on every day." Looking to her kids, she said, "Well, I guess we'd better get going so you can get back to work."

"Yes, Ma'am. If you want to come back another time, and check how we're doing, just let my crew know, and I'll come talk to you."

"Thank you. I may take you up on that."

When the elevator doors opened, Mrs. Jonas, Chelsea and Dean stepped out.

"Oh, hi, Mrs. Sanders." Mrs. Jonas said in greeting. "The kids and I were on our way to see Noah. How's he doing?"

Smiling, Christina said, "He's in good spirits, even though he's been lying flat on his back for several hours."

"I'm sure he's chompin' at the bits to get up. He never was one to just lie around."

Chuckling, Christina said, "I can identify. If I'm still for more than ten minutes, my mind and body start twitching."

"I guess I'm the more laid-back type. Give me a good book or movie, and I could be lost for hours." Glancing in the Sanders kids direction, she asked, "Are these your children?"

Nodding, Christina introduced each one, and Mrs. Jonas did the same.

Chelsea looked at Brad, and asked, "You're one of the football players, right?"

He nodded, and grinned. "And you're one of the cheerleaders. I'm always amazed at how well you do those back-flips."

Smiling, she said, "Thanks." Glancing at her mom, she said, "Guess all those years of gymnastics paid off?"

Christina said, "I'm embarrassed to say this, but I've forgotten your name."

Smiling, Mrs. Jonas said, "I'm Veronica, but I go by Ronnie."

"Oh, yes. I remember now." Chuckling, she added, "For some reason, I have a difficult time remembering names."

Ronnie said, "I know. Me too. I can remember faces, but names, not so much."

Glancing at her watch, Ronnie said, "I guess we'd best get going. The kids and I are planning a trip to Waco, to catch dinner and a movie."

Nicky asked, "What are you going to see?"

Dean answered. "We're going to see The Lord of the Rings—The fellowship of the ring."

"Ooh, I want to see that! Nicky said, looking up at his mom.

Christina asked Ronnie, "Which theater is it showing in?"

"We're going to the one at the mid-town mall. You know, the one that had those bomb threats?

Nodding, Christina said, "Oh, yes. We were there that day. Fortunately, we left before all the chaos began."

Shaking her head, Ronnie said, "Seems like the whole world has gone crazy. With all the attacks around the country, and the events in our own little town."

Nodding, Christina agreed. "Yes, it is an unsettled time for sure. Well, we'd best let you go. Nice chatting with you."

Waving her hand as to dismiss the negative thoughts, Ronnie said, "We'll see y'all around."

Once on the elevator, Nicky asked, "Can we go to see Lord of the Rings?"

"Yeah, Mom. When can we go?" Stacey asked.

Shaking her head, Christina answered, "That reminds me. I need to stop by Mrs. Ferguson's office to check on the scheduling. With only one patient on the Med-Surg floor, I need to know how she plans to schedule our staff from the cardiac floor."

Tapping her arm, Nicky said, "Mom, you didn't answer our question."

"Let me check my schedule, then the movie theaters to find out which theaters and times the movie will be showing. I'll have a better idea as to when we can go."

"Oh, okay. If we go, can I bring Danny?"

"And can I bring Linda, if she's up to going, or Carmen? I haven't seen her at all since school let out."

"We'll see how it all works out." Looking at Brad, she said, "I suppose you'll want to bring Eric?"

Shrugging, Brad said, "Well, yeah."

Chuckling, Christina said, "It's a good thing I've got a van."

Sitting on bar-stools in Green's pharmacy, enjoying root beer floats, Ed brought up the subject of the New Year."

"So, Cindy, you want to go meet my family? I know for a fact, that they want to meet you, and Samara."

Cindy said, "I've been thinking about it since you first brought it up, and yes, I'd love to go meet your family. From all you've said about them, I can hardly wait!"

Grinning, Ed said, "Alright! I'll give my mom a call."

"Wait, a minute, Cowboy. I need to know what day you want to leave, and when you want to come back. I may need to make arrangements with Mary at the dress shop."

Nodding, Ed said, "I was thinking we could leave Saturday, and come back Monday or New Year's Day on Tuesday."

"That might work. Mary won't reopen the shop 'till Wednesday after New years. Right now, she's going through the inventory, ordering a new spring line, and setting up the sale items. I'll give her a call when we get back home."

"Sure. You call her, and I'll call my mom."

Putting her hand up for a high-five, Cindy said, "Sounds like a good plan."

After finishing their floats, Cindy and Ed walked hand-in-hand back to her house, enjoying the sunshine, and each others company. Cindy thought, *I could get used to this.*

When she opened the front door, Sasha greeted them with the exuberance of a young puppy. One would never guess she had reached the human equivalent of middle-age. Cindy picked up the wriggling bundle of fur, and was rewarded with a face full of doggy kisses.

"Goodness, Sasha, we've only been gone a couple of hours!" Of course, Sasha, having no idea of time, just knew that her people had been gone, and now they were back. *Oh what joy!*

Handing the squirming bundle to Ed, Cindy said, "Would you please take her out? I need to take care of some business."

Chuckling, Ed said, "Of course." When Ed sat Sasha down in the brown winter grass, she ran around the yard, sniffing around every bush and tree until she found the perfect spot to do her business. While she was exploring the yard, Ed took the opportunity to call his mom.

He returned the phone to his pocket, just as Sasha returned to him, bouncing up and down like she had springs on her feet.

Opening the back door, he said, "Come on, you little fur ball, I'll get you some food and water."

Christina rapped lightly on the nursing supervisor's door. She doubted the older woman would be in because of the holiday, but was surprised when she heard the familiar voice.

"Come in." Surprise registered on Emma Ferguson's face when she looked up, and saw Christina. Coming around the desk to give Christina a hug, she said, "Christina! What a pleasant surprise!"

After greeting her, and introducing her children, Christina asked about the work schedule for the next couple of weeks. She sat in a chair opposite Emma, as the children stood silently by the door.

"As you know, this whole fire incident has turned our hospital, and staff, topsy-turvy."

Christina nodded in agreement.

"Since Janet is out of the picture, and the cardiac patient is on the Med-Surg floor, I've been racking my brain as to how to get everyone scheduled. I may have to cut back some of the hours for the cardiac nurses and aides."

Christina said, "That must be quite a challenge. I can tell you though, if you need to cut back on my hours so the other nurses can keep theirs, that's okay. I know some of the gals can't afford to lose any hours because of their financial obligations, but we'll be okay if I don't work as much."

Nodding, Mrs. Ferguson said, "Well, that's a relief. I know being a single mom can be difficult, and I don't want to cause more stress for you."

"It's fine, really." She didn't want to go into detail about the money she was receiving from David's death benefits, and the government's subsidy, which the children were still unaware of.

"Whew! That will make my job easier, then. Thank you."

After a few more minutes of small talk, Christina stood, and reached out for Emma's hand.

"Thank you for taking the time out of your busy day to talk with me."

"Oh, Christina, you know my door is always open for you." Looking around at the kids, she added, "It's so nice to see your children again. You are truly a blessed woman."

Nodding, Christina said, "Don't I know it!"

On her way out, Christina turned and asked, "I hear you may be retiring soon? Do you have someone to replace you?"

"Well, I *had* planned to retire, but with all the chaos, I decided to stay a while longer, at least until some of this mess is resolved. In answer to your question, I do have a couple of gals in mind to take my place, but I haven't approached them yet. There's just too much going on right now, to even think about training someone."

Christina nodded. "I understand. I think it'll be at least another couple of months before the cardiac unit will be up and running again."

"I think you're right." Shaking her head, Emma said, "What a mess this has turned out to be."

Dr. Carmichael approached the nurses' station, and asked for Jimmy McCoy's chart.

"How's my patient doing?"

Handing the chart to Dr. Carmichael, Libby, the RN behind the desk said, "He's improving. He's more alert, and has been up a few times to use the toilet, and hasn't requested any pain meds in a while."

Nodding, Aaron said, "Good. Is his dad still here?"

Shaking her head, Libby said, "He just left. He said he had to go check on the work crew upstairs, then go talk to the sheriff after that." Retrieving a piece of paper, she said, "If you need to speak to him, I have his cell phone number."

"I'm assuming he'll be back later?'

Nodding, Libby said, "Yes. He said probably around dinnertime."

"Do you want me to come in with you?'

"No, I won't be long. Thanks, though."

Libby watched as Aaron walked down the hall to Jimmy's room, and thought, *That is one fine looking man.* She overheard one of the aides refer to him as Dr. Dreamy. Nodding, she thought that suited him well.

When Dr. Carmichael entered Jimmy's room, he was pleased to see him alert, and sitting up.

Looking up from the magazine he was reading, Jimmy said, "Oh, hey, Dr. Carmichael."

Extending his hand, Aaron said, "Good afternoon, Jimmy. I'm pleased to see you sitting up. What are you reading?"

Jimmy held up the magazine. "It's about motorcycles. I'm hoping to save enough money to get one this summer."

Aaron, nodded. I had a motorcycle when I was a teen. I had to sell it so I could get a car. Maybe someday, I'll get another one."

Jimmy nodded. "My dad had one for a while, too. He's not too keen on the idea of me getting one, however. He says they're dangerous. I told him that there are more accidents in cars than motorcycles. You know what he said?"

Aaron shook his head.

"He said, 'Well, in a car you have a better chance of surviving than on a motorcycle.'"

"There is some truth in that."

Nodding, Jimmy said, "Yeah, I know, but I can't live my life fearing what could happen."

"I understand. Life is too short to live in fear."

"Exactly. Now if I can convince my dad."

"Right. Good luck with that. How's your leg doing?"

Lifting his leg out from under the sheet, Jimmy said, "Well, it feels better. Not as much pain when I move it."

Aaron removed the bandage and inspected the wound. It wasn't as beet red as it was when he entered the ER two days ago. The red streak, from the wound to the groin's lymph gland, was not as prominent either, although the whole area was still quite warm to the touch. He opened the chart and checked the temperature graph. It showed that Jimmy was still running a low grade fever. Hovering around 101 degrees. *Not out of the woods yet*, he thought.

Aaron checked Jimmy's blood pressure, which was a little high for a teenager, listened to his heart, which was galloping, and lungs that had a slight wheezing sound.

After documenting his findings, Dr. Carmichael asked, "Have you ever been diagnosed with asthma?"

Shaking his head, Jimmy said, "No."

"Do you find yourself out of breath when you run, or exercise?"

"Yeah, a little. I don't run much, so it's hard to say. Why are you asking?"

Smiling, Aaron said, "Your lungs sound a little wheezy. I'm going to send you for a chest x-ray, and have someone from respiratory give you a breathing test. It could be nothing, but I want to make sure I'm not overlooking anything."

"What happens if you find something abnormal?"

"Depending on what is found, I may just order you an inhaler to use when you feel out of breath, or your chest feels tight."

"Okay. I see kids with inhalers all the time at school. It's no big deal if I get one, right?"

"Well, I wouldn't say it isn't a big deal, because if you need one, your lungs and bronchial tubes aren't working to their full capacity. Some kids outgrow the need for an inhaler, others have to have one for the rest of their lives. If I feel you need one, I will first order allergy testing. It might be as simple as removing the allergen from your environment."

Frowning, Jimmy asked, "What if it is allergies, and they can't be removed?'

"Then you may have to take allergy injections, along with the inhaler."

"Oh, man. That stinks!"

Nodding, Dr. Carmichael said, "I know it sounds awful, but, if we can get your symptoms under control, you'll feel so much better."

Taking a sip of water, Jimmy asked, "When can I go home?"

Standing, and putting his stethoscope around his neck, Aaron said, "I'm going to keep you a couple more days. I want to make sure the infection is completely gone."

Sighing, Jimmy said, "Alright. I'll let my dad know."

Patting Jimmy's shoulder, Aaron said, "I'm hoping we'll get all this resolved by the time you have to go back to school."

Making a face, Jimmy said, "Oh, yeah, school. I only have a few days of vacation left."

Looking around the room, he added, "This is not what I had planned to do on my days off."

Heading to the door, Dr. Carmichael turned, and said, "Sometimes, life throws a monkey wrench into our plans."

Letting out a big sigh, Jimmy said, "Yep."

When Dr. Carmichael left, Jimmy pulled out his cell-phone, and punched in a number.

He smiled when he heard the voice on the other end of the line.

The sheriff was on the phone with one of his deputies, when Ed walked in, smiling, and waving sheets of paper. He sat in a chair opposite the sheriff, and listened to his side of a conversation.

"Tell the Martins that if they don't stop threatening each other with bodily harm, I may have to arrest them both." He waited as his deputy relayed the message. Holding the phone away from his ear, so as not to have his eardrum ruptured, he heard yelling, screaming, and cursing—a lot of cursing.

"Mike! Mike!" He yelled into the phone, trying to get his deputy's attention. After a minute, the cacophony of noise grew fainter.

"Sorry, Sheriff. I had to step outside, so I can hear you. Those two are crazy as drunken grizzly bears! Mrs. Martin is scratching, screaming, hitting, and throwing things at Mr. Martin. He's yelling and pushing her away. Fortunately, he hasn't hit her yet."

"Do you know what the fight is about?"

"Something about him flirting with the waitress at the Black-eyed Pea restaurant."

"Seriously?" The sheriff asked, shaking his head in disbelief.

Sighing, and rubbing his forehead, he said, "Tell those two they'd better resolve this issue, or you're going to bring them both in, and charge them with disturbing the peace!"

Releasing a lung full of air to calm himself, he looked at Ed who was chuckling.

Smiling, the sheriff said, "Those two get into a fight at least once a month. I have no idea why they're still together."

"How long have they been married?" Ed asked.

"I think around twenty years or so. I've had to bring them both in on occasion, because the fighting became physical."

Curious, Ed asked, "Have they ever seriously hurt one another?"

Nodding, the sheriff said, "Yep. One time, Mrs. Martin, or Dinah, had to have several stitches on her head, and Mr. Martin, or Axel, had a broken arm from a baseball bat."

Shaking his head, Ed said, "Usually these types of abuse only get worse over time. One or both may end up dead, if they don't get themselves under control"

Nodding, Larry said, "Yep. That's always in the back of my mind, when I get a call to go break up a fight."

Standing, he walked over to the coffee bar. Looking at Ed, he gestured, *Do you want some?*

Ed shook his head, "No thanks. Cindy and I had root beer floats at Green's, and I'm still full from that."

After filling his cup with coffee, the sheriff returned to his chair.

"So what brings you in? I just saw you a little while ago."

Holding up the papers, Ed said, "I think I have the name of your suspect."

"For which crime?"

"The one that belongs to the blue Chevette, and possibly the phone number on Janet's phone."

Taking a sip of coffee, Larry asked, "Really? Let me see."

Ed handed the papers to the sheriff.

"How did you get this?" Larry asked, as he perused the papers.

Leaning forward, and pointing to the top of the page, Ed said, "I had a friend look up owners of blue Chevettes in the area, and he came across this name. It looks like it had a previous owner, and the title just recently got changed. I checked on the first name, and it's the owner of the Pizza Hut, out by the highway."

Leaning back in his chair, Larry said, "Hmm," as he read the name, and tried to remember why it was familiar.

Then the memory hit him like a semi-truck. Sitting forward, he said, "I know this kid. His dad works at the auto shop out on Waco drive. I took one of the police cars in for an oil change, and the kid was in there. At first I thought it was Christina's boy, Brad, and almost called out to him, but then I heard his dad call him Jamie."

Nodding, Ed said, "Yeah. I looked up his driver's license picture, and he and Brad could almost be twins, except this kid, Jamie, is older by a couple of years. They live out on Brandon Road, a little way down from the McCoys."

Standing, the sheriff asked Ed, "You want to come with me to bring him in for questioning?"

Ed stood as well, and said, "Sure. Let me call Cindy, and let her know I'll be a while."

The sheriff nodded as he walked over to the coat rack, and donned his hat and jacket.

Jessie McCoy, entered his son's room, and felt strangely emotional. His breath caught as he watched his boy sleep, reminding him of the many nights he would check in on him when he came home from work. Jimmy would usually be curled up on his side, sound asleep—like now. Guilt caused his heart to hurt. He still missed his wife, but after having the vision of her, when he was injured by the falling roof at the old refinery, and hearing her say that he needed to mend the chasm that he had constructed between him and Jimmy, he knew beyond a shadow of a doubt, that he needed to heed her warning. He walked over to the bed, and pulled the blanket up to Jimmy's chin, and placed his hand on his son's forehead. It felt hot. *Probably a temperature spike,* he thought. *Maybe I should tell the nurse and have her check it.*

Leaning down, he whispered in his son's ear, "I'll be back in a while."

Patting him on the shoulder, Jesse left the room, and headed to the nurses' station.

"Mr. McCoy," The nurse said in greeting. "How are you doing today?"

Smiling, Jesse said, "I'm fine, but I was wondering when my son's temperature was taken? He feels very warm."

"Let me check." Jesse noted that her name tag read 'Libby Rollins, RN', as she pulled a chart from the holder.

"It says here, that his temperature was taken a couple of hours ago. It was slightly elevated then." Looking up, she said, "I'll get the thermometer, and check it again. Do you want to come with me?"

"Sure," he said, as he watched her retrieve a hand held, battery operated thermometer.

After she swiped it across Jimmy's forehead, she watched as the numbers flashed. It finally stopped flashing, and beeped, once the body's temperature had been recorded. 103.4 degrees. Higher than the previous recording.

Jesse said, "That's higher than it's been in a couple of days. Right?"

Nodding, she said, "Yes. I will inform Dr. Carmichael. I don't know if you were aware, but the Dr. decided to keep Jimmy until his temperature returned to normal. I think that was wise, being that it has spiked again."

Jesse nodded, and said, "I sure hope the infection isn't coming back."

"Well, I guess that's a possibility, but he's still receiving antibiotics intravenously. Sometimes people's body temperatures rise when they're sleeping. I'll check it again, when he wakes up."

"Okay. Please let me know if anything changes. I need to run to the fire station, and check on a few things. I'll be back in a couple of hours."

Placing her hand on Jesse's arm, she said, "Sure thing, Mr. McCoy."

As Jesse drove to the station, he was thinking about the events of the past several days, when a disturbing thought broke in, and interrupted the flow. *What if the visit from my wife was an omen? What if she was telling me to mend my relationship with Jimmy because he was going to die, and she didn't want me to feel guilty for wasting all those years with him?* He felt a wave of horror wash over him so strongly, that he had to pull his truck over to the side of the road, until he could regain control over his emotions. His heart was galloping like a race horse, his whole body was shaking, and he was breathing way too fast. He was having a full on panic attack.

He pounded the steering wheel, and cried out to God. "Please don't take my son! I'll do anything you want me to, just don't take him! You can even take me instead if you want." He let the tears flow, as his whole body jerked with sobs. "I can't lose him now, God! I know I was a lousy father, but I want to change! Please. Please. I'm begging with every part of me! Let him live! I promise I'll do better!"

After what seemed like hours, but was only minutes, Jesse stopped crying, and was able to reign in his emotions. There was nothing else he could say, or do. His son's life hung in the balance. Either God would heal him, or He would take him. Jesse let out a heavy sigh, as he relinquished his son into God's hands.

A part of Jimmy knew he was dreaming, but another part of him felt he was witnessing something real. He was standing on the outskirts of a playground, leaning against a tree, watching a little dark haired boy, around five years old, play on the equipment. He saw a park bench with a group of women sitting and chatting. One of them looked familiar, but he wasn't sure who it was. She was young, with dark hair, and a sweet smile. She seemed to be watching the little boy, who was climbing the ladder on the slide. When he had reached the top, and was ready to descend, she waved, and smiled—encouraging him to let go of the rails. He did, and zipped down, landing on his bottom. She clapped, and shouted something, as he stood and dusted the sand off his shorts. He was laughing, as he waved at her, and ran around to the ladder once more. The dream continued for a while longer, and when it ended, Jimmy woke. He didn't want to wake up. He wanted to stay in the park, watching the little boy and his mother. He tried to go back into the dream, but to no avail. Realization hit him like a MAC truck, and he sat up. *I was the little boy, and the woman was my mother.* He felt the familiar stinging, as tears blurred his vision. Lying down, and curling up on his side, he let his mind conjure up more pleasant memories of his mother.

He had just begun his mental stroll through memory lane, when the nurse came in to take his blood pressure, and temperature.

Checking his IV bag, contents, and insertion site, and finding everything as it should be, she checked his leg, and noted that it still felt warm to the touch. When finished with her assessment, she asked, "So Mister McCoy, how was your nap?"

"Fine, I guess. I kept having weird dreams."

"I love hearing about people's dreams. What was yours about? If you don't mind telling me."

Shrugging, he told her about the dream with the little boy, and his mother.

"So, your mother passed when you were how old?"

"I was twelve."

Nodding, she said, "My mom passed on when I was fifteen. I still have dreams of her. They usually involve her coming in, and saying she was just on a long trip. In the beginning, I would wake and run to her room, thinking her sickness, and death, were the dream, and my dream was real. I was always disappointed, and would end up crying like a baby next to her bed."

Jimmy pushed a button on his remote control unit, and raised the head of the bed, so he could communicate better.

"I know! I would do the same thing, but then the reality of it all sank in. Now, I don't feel as sad. I guess time does heal wounds, physically, or emotionally."

"Yeah. I've heard it takes a good five years to finish grieving, and return to normal, but I guess it kinda depends on the circumstances, and the people involved."

Nodding, Jimmy said, "It's been five years this June since my mom died. My dad seems to have made a turnaround in his behavior in the past week, or so. Maybe it's because he was hurt at the refinery, or maybe because he is afraid of losing me." Shrugging, he said, "I don't know what changed. It's kinda creepy."

"Maybe he found religion?"

Frowning, Jimmy asked, "What? Religion? What do you mean?"

"Well, sometimes when people are feeling empty, confused, or sad, they reach out to God, and He reaches back."

After taking a sip of water, he said, "We already attend a church of sorts." Making quotation marks with his hands, he said, "It's called, "The Enlightened Ones." I personally don't see the purpose of going. The leaders talk about using the earth's energy and resources. It's all too weird for me."

"Hmm. That does sound strange. Sometimes people would rather worship the created things, instead of the creator of those things.

"I guess some people have called it a cult. I don't really understand all the lingo. I just go when my dad goes, mostly to hang out with my friends. We don't go consistently. I think my dad goes to talk to some of the single ladies."

Smiling, Libby asked, "Have y'all tried any of the local churches?"

Nodding, Jimmy said, "When my mom was alive, we went to the big Catholic church downtown, but when she was diagnosed with cancer, we quit going. She got sick, and died within six months. The Dr. said it was a tenacious form of uterine cancer. It was quite a shock for all of us. After that, we just never went back. A couple of years ago, however, one of dad's co-workers invited him to The Enlightened Ones meetings, and for some strange reason, he liked it. He said they didn't try to cram Jesus down his throat, or beg for money." Sighing heavily, he said, "I guess I never think about God, or Jesus, or church, or any of that stuff."

Libby said, "A lot of people don't. They get busy, and life just goes on. I have noticed, however, that when a tragedy strikes, even the most dedicated atheist will cry out to God. Usually to blame Him for the tragedy, but sometimes to ask for, or thank Him for protection. Like when the airplanes crashed into the twin towers back in September. How many folks said, "Pray for all the victims?" All of America, as well as the world, seemed to be on their knees during that time, but after a while, folks went back to their routines. It's kinda sad, really, to only talk to God when there's a crisis."

Jimmy said, "I guess I fall into that category. I only talked to God when my mom was sick. I begged Him to please heal her, but He didn't. I was so angry, that I decided to just ignore Him, like He ignored me."

Patting Jimmy's arm, Libby said, "I can understand how difficult it is to talk to, or believe in something, or someone you can't see, but that's where faith comes in. God is kinda like air. You can't see it, or feel it, but it's there, and without it, we'd die. If we ignore God because we can't see, feel, or touch Him, or because we are angry, or indifferent, our souls will die."

"What do you mean our souls will die?"

Thinking for a moment, she said, "We are made up of a body, and a soul, and some people say a spirit, but I think the soul and spirit are the same thing. Anyway, when our body dies, our soul leaves our body. There have been a lot of studies on this topic, and some scientists have actually seen an energy source of some kind, leave the body when the person dies."

Making a face, Jimmy said, "Really?"

Nodding, Libby said, "Really. So if the soul leaves, where does it go? Some people believe that it either goes to a place called Heaven, or a place called Hell. Heaven for those who have faith, and believe in God's Son, Jesus, and Hell for those who don't."

Scratching his head, Jimmy said, "I remember a little bit about that from the Catholic Church. That's why we had to go to confession, so we could keep our souls clean, so to speak."

"Yes. God sees our hearts, and intentions, and I believe that He will put people or situations in front of us, to give us a chance to reach out to Him. When we do, He's right there, reaching out to us."

Shaking his head, Jimmy said, "Wow! That's something to think about. So you think that happened to my dad?"

"I don't know. Anything is possible." Looking at her watch, Libby said, "I need to go check on my other patient, but I'll try to come back and talk to you later, if you'd like."

Smiling, Jimmy said, "Sure. I'll probably have a few questions by then."

When she exited the room, Jimmy lowered the head of the bed, turned on his left side, and thought about what Libby had said. *Maybe my dad did find religion, or God. He certainly started acting differently, after he went to that Promise Keepers thing a few weeks ago. If there is a God, I'd better ask Him to keep Jamie and me out of trouble with the law.* His pulse began to race as he considered the possible consequences of his and Jamie's actions on Christmas morning. *We could be in a heap of trouble.*

Jesse McCoy drove to the burned out oil refinery, stopped his pickup on the gravel drive on the north side, and stepped out. Leaning his back against the door, he looked up at the skeletal remains of the refinery. *What a mess!* He thought. Walking around the perimeter of the steel structure, he searched for any smoldering spots, that may have been missed, or reignited. He breathed a sigh of relief, when he didn't find any. His team of firemen had been thorough.

Once he was back in his truck, he sat a while thinking about his boy, and wondering what would happen to him, if he was convicted of arson. He knew in his gut, that he, and Jamie, were somehow involved. *How else could my lighter have ended up here?* He closed his eyes, and putting his calloused hands over his face, bowed his head, and asked God for wisdom to know what to do, and for protection for the two boys. Praying to an invisible God was strange to him, but it felt right.

When he finished praying, he turned his truck around, and headed into town to check on his team. Fortunately for everyone in Alva, the past couple of days had been uneventful. *I hope it stays that way. At least until New Years—which is only five days away.*

David, and his angelic friend, Jarrod, stood in the viewing room, and watched as Earth came into focus. When David had first been shown the viewing room by God, he was overwhelmed with awe and wonder. The room was vast, and had an uncountable number of screen-like images all around. David, being so new to Heaven, likened it to a TV show he had watched about a government agency that had satellite images from around the world, on hundreds of screens. In this particular room, all one had to do was think about a particular person, or group of people, and their images would pop up. God had explained that because human souls would understand, and accept those kind of images, He created the viewing room for their benefit.

He had said, "I don't need this sort of thing to watch my children, and my creation, but I wanted to give my spiritual children a glimpse of their families, and take comfort in knowing how they're doing."

David had asked, "How can we take comfort, if we see they are not well, or are in danger?"

"As you know, there is no sorrow, or tears, in Heaven. When you see activities on Earth that would normally cause sorrow in the physical form, you will not feel that here. Your spirit knows that I am in control, and everything works together for good to those who believe."

David said, "Forgive me for asking, but what about those who don't believe?"

Putting His hand on David's shoulder, God said, "That is not your concern. I have the final say in all things."

After watching Christina and his kids, David turned to face his assigned angel, Jarrod. "So Jarrod, have you heard any news from the outer realm?"

Jarrod shrugged and said, "Same stuff. Satan and his minions are plotting to overtake Alva, as well as a few other towns, and cities around the world. They continue to be obsessed with destroying Father's creation."

David shook his head. "I don't understand their actions. Surely they know that Father will not allow that."

Jarrod said, with a sigh, "Well, Satan is arrogant, and believes that somehow, he will win in the end. In the meantime, he wants to destroy as many bodies, and souls, as he can."

Patting Jarrod's shoulder, David said, "Let's take a walk."

Jamie drove to the hospital to see Jimmy, barely cognizant of the scenery whizzing past. His mind was occupied with thoughts of 'what ifs.' *What if the sheriff figured out he and Jimmy were the ones breaking into houses? What if the sheriff figures out he set off the fireworks? What if the sheriff figures out Jimmy had set fire to the refinery? What if they had to go to jail?*

Realizing he was gripping the steering wheel so tightly that his fingers were going numb, he relaxed them, and instantly felt the tingling dissipate.

He and Jimmy needed to discuss what their next move would be. *Maybe we should talk to our dads, and fill them in on our indiscretions. Maybe they'll have pity on us, being this is our first offense.*

He pulled into the parking lot, found a space by the entrance, and killed the motor. Thoughts and questions plagued him, as he rode the elevator to the third floor.

Jimmy heard someone enter his room, and turned onto his back to see who it was.

"Jamie! Man, am I glad to see you!"

Jamie approached the bed, and did a high five with his best friend.

"Hey, Jimmy, you're looking good. How are you feeling?"

Jimmy raised the head of the bed, and adjusted his pillow, and body, into a comfortable position.

Glancing around at all the monitoring equipment, Jamie asked, "So, when are they gonna let you out of this place?"

Jimmy shrugged. "I think when my fever goes down, and stays down."

Nodding, Jamie said, "How's your leg feeling?"

"Still hurts like I have a scorpion constantly stinging me."

Making a face, Jamie said, "That bad, huh?"

"Oh yeah. Still getting pain killers every few hours."

"I thought you said it was better when I talked to you this morning?"

Nodding, Jimmy said, "Well, it did feel better then, but, I don't know what happened. It started hurting again as the day progressed."

"Have you been up much?"

"Not a lot. I go to the bathroom, but even that causes muscle spasms in my leg, and I can barely make it back to bed."

"Bummer." Jamie said, as he removed his jacket, and laid it on the nearby chair.

"Yeah, bummer." Jimmy agreed.

"So," Jamie said, "Has your old man been by today?"

"Yeah. He left a while ago. He said he needed to go check on his men at the fire station."

Leaning forward in his chair, Jamie whispered, "Has he talked to you about the fire, or given any indication of who the sheriff suspects?"

Shaking his head, Jimmy said, "No. He's still acting weird though."

"How so?"

"I told you about him apologizing, and getting all choked up and crying, as he's confessing about what a lousy dad he's been?"

Jamie nodded, "Yeah."

"Well, before he left today, he actually bent down, and kissed my head, and told me he loved me."

Nodding, Jamie said, "That's weird alright." After a moment of silence, he perked up and said, "I have to tell you something that'll cheer you up."

"What?"

"Remember how I always wanted a dog, but my dad wouldn't let me have one, because he didn't want to bother with one?"

"Yeah."

Jamie told how his dad had discovered the dog with the puppies, and the events that followed.

"Whoa! Are you sure your dad hasn't been replaced by an alien?" Jimmy asked.

Jamie chuckled, "Well, maybe, but he seems genuinely changed."

Shaking his head, Jimmy said, "It is kinda creepy that both our dads have changed. Maybe they've found God, or religion or something. Seems like this change started after that event in Dallas a few weeks ago."

"Yeah. That Promise Keeper thing? Well, I don't know, but I'm kind digging it. I mean, he let me keep all five dogs! He would never let me do that a few months ago. I think when I get home later, I'm gonna have a sit down chat, and find out what's changed. It's just too weird."

"So what are the puppies' sexes?"

"Two girls and two boys. They are so tiny and cute. I can hardly wait for you to get out, so you can come see them."

Jimmy said, "Yeah. Maybe my dad will let me have one of the puppies." Pausing a beat, he said, "I need to use the bathroom."

"You want me to get the nurse?"

"No! I can do this by myself. I'll be out in a minute."

Putting his hand up, Jamie said, "Alright. I'll be right here."

After a minute or two, Jimmy opened the bathroom door. He looked pale, and drenched in sweat. Jamie jumped up, and went to help his friend.

"Hey, are you alright? You don't look so good."

Leaning on his friend, and feeling his body shake, he said, "I don't feel so good."

Jamie felt him go limp, and it took all his strength to keep him from hitting the floor.

Jamie called out. "Hey, I could use some help in here!"

Within seconds, a nurse appeared, and between the two of them, wrestled Jimmy back into bed. The nurse asked, "So what happened?"

"He had to go to the bathroom, and when he came out, he was all sweaty, and white as a sheet, then he passed out."

Nodding, she said, "Well, I'm glad you were here to help him. He could have hit his head or something."

"Yeah. Is he going to be okay?"

"I think so. Why don't you sit down, while I take his vital signs, and check him over?"

Nodding, Jamie said, "Okay."

After checking Jimmy's heart rate, blood pressure, IV's, and wound area, she stood, and breathed a sigh of relief.

"He seems to be okay. It may take a few minutes for him to come around, however." Wrapping the stethoscope around her neck, she turned, and said, "By the way, my name is Sonia. You must be Jamie."

Nodding, Jamie said, "Yeah. That's me."

"If you don't mind, Jamie, could you please stay here, while I go call Dr. Carmichael, and let him know about Jimmy's incident."

"Sure. I'll wait right here."

He stood, and walked to the window to look out. The sun was setting, and the town of Alva was preparing for the approaching darkness by turning on lights. First the street lights lit up, then the businesses by the highway, then the homes indoor, and outdoor lights, began to add their illumination. He turned, when he heard the bed creak. "Hey, Jimmy. Welcome back."

Jimmy rubbed his eyes. "What? What happened?"

"You passed out, Man."

Confusion crossed Jimmy's face. "I passed out?"

Jamie approached the bed. "Yeah, Man. You've been out for about ten minutes."

"That's so weird. I remember going into the bathroom, but nothing after that. Did I pee on myself?"

Jamie smiled, and said, "Oh, yeah. You made a royal mess."

Jimmy's face flushed. "I did? Did anyone see me?"

Jimmy laughed. "Just kidding. You didn't pee on yourself. But you almost hit the floor. It's a good thing I was there to catch you."

Running a hand through his hair, Jimmy said, "Thanks. Where's the nurse?"

"She went to call Dr. Carmichael."

Jamie walked to the door, and looked down the hallway. He heard the elevator ding, and saw Mr. McCoy step out.

"Hey, Jimmy. Your dad's here."

Jesse McCoy entered his son's hospital room, carrying a sack of food from McDonald's.

"Hey Dad."

"Hey Son. Hi Jamie."

Jamie nodded, and said, "Hi Mr. McCoy."

Holding the bag up, he said, "If I'd known you were going to be here Jamie, I would have brought you something. As it is, I only brought food for Jimmy."

Shrugging, Jamie said, "That's okay, Mr. McCoy. I ate earlier."

Jimmy took the bag from his dad and opened it. "Wow! A big-mac, fries and a pie. Thanks, Dad."

Nodding, Jesse said, "You're welcome."

Jamie headed towards the door. "I'll see you tomorrow. I have to go run a couple of errands."

Waving, Jimmy said, "Okay. See you tomorrow. And thanks for helping me."

Jamie nodded, and waved one last time before exiting the hospital room.

Pulling a chair up to his son's bed, Jesse asked, "Helped you with what?"

Unwrapping the hamburger, Jimmy said, "Oh, I had to go to the bathroom earlier, and I just passed out. It was quite embarrassing, really. If Jamie hadn't been there to catch me, I would have hit the floor for sure."

"You passed out?"

Taking a bite of the burger, he moaned, and said, "This is so good! I really hate the hospital's food."

"Jimmy. You said you passed out. Why?"

Shaking his head, Jimmy said, "I don't know. Guess I was just weaker than I thought."

Jesse stood and said, "I'm going to talk to the nurse."

When he reached the door, he almost collided with Dr. Carmichael.

"Oh, hey, Doc. I was just heading out to the nurses' station."

Reaching out a hand, Dr. Carmichael said, "Glad you're here, Mr. McCoy. I wanted to talk to you, and Jimmy, together."

"Sounds ominous, Doc."

Jesse returned to his son's bedside. Jimmy had finished the hamburger, and was putting the paper in the garbage. "Dr. Carmichael, what are you doing here?"

"The nurse called, and told me you had passed out in the bathroom. I decided to come and check on you."

"It was no big deal, Doc. I must be weaker than I thought."

"Well, there's a reason for that." Holding a piece of paper up for them to see, he said, "I just got the results from you latest blood work, and it shows some interesting things."

Jimmy and Jesse glanced at each other, exchanging worried looks. Jimmy swallowed, and asked, "Like what?"

"Your red blood count is a little lower than expected, and your white blood count is quite elevated."

Jesse asked, "What does that mean, Doc?"

"It means Jimmy may still have some bleeding going on, and the infection is still present." Lifting the sheet off Jimmy's leg, and removing the bandage, Dr. Carmichael asked, "How does your leg feel?"

Jimmy shrugged, and said, "Still hurts like crazy, and when I stand it feels weird, like it's heavy. It sometimes feels tingly, like when it falls asleep, and it's trying to wake up."

Dr. Carmichael pulled a small tape measure from his pocket, and measured the circumference of each leg—first the thigh, then the calf. He then checked the pulse in each foot, and palpated the injured right leg, from the thigh to the foot.

Jimmy, and his dad, sat in silence, both worried about what all this attention might mean.

When finished with his assessment, Dr. Carmichael sighed, and sat on the edge of the bed.

"I'm glad you're both here." Taking a pen from his pocket, he began drawing on the piece of paper he held.

"Jimmy, what you have going on in your leg is a term called, compartment syndrome. It happens sometimes when a person breaks a bone, or hemorrhaging occurs in an inclosed space. The blood ends up pooling in that area, and can't escape, so pressure builds up causing damage to surrounding tissue, blood vessels, and nerves. That's why you feel the tingling, and the heaviness in your leg."

Running his fingers through his hair, Jesse asked, "How could that have happened, Doc?"

"Usually when something like this happens, it's because of a break in a bone. Since Jimmy's leg wasn't broken, I'm thinking maybe the object that punctured it, may have nicked the bone. That didn't show up on an x-ray because the nick may have been too small, or in a different area than was x-rayed. What did you say punctured your leg?"

Jimmy felt his pulse kick up a notch, and felt his face redden. He had told his dad it was a branch or stick, but now with this new development, he wondered if he should break down, and tell the truth.

He asked, almost in a whisper, "Does it matter what punctured it?"

His dad gave him a questioning look. He suspected the injury wasn't caused by a branch, but by a nail, there at the oil refinery, but he wanted to give Jimmy a chance to confess to the truth.

Dr. Carmichael said, "Well, if it was a stick, there may be splinters I need to look for, but if it was a nail, or something metal, I won't have to look for foreign debris."

Jimmy clenched his teeth. He was between a rock, and a hard place. He didn't want to betray Jamie, but he felt the truth needed to be said.

Taking a deep breath, he said, "First of all, I need to apologize to my dad for lying to him. I told him it was a branch, but it was a nail. A very long nail."

Dr. Carmichael patted his leg. "It's okay, Jimmy. You and your dad can work out the details later, but I'm going to need to get you into surgery."

"Surgery?" Jesse asked.

"Yes. I need to relieve the pressure in his leg, and patch up whatever is causing the bleed. I figure it's either a bone fragment, or a nicked artery, or blood vessel. I will have the nurse come in, and give you the paper work, and prep Jimmy for surgery." Dr. Carmichael stood, and walked out of the room.

Jimmy was speechless. *How had such a simple idea turned out so badly? I didn't mean for the fire to be so big, and get out of control so quickly, and how was I to know a beam with a nail in it would fall on my leg, and I would end up in the hospital?*

Tears stung his eyes, as he shook his head in disbelief.

His dad patted his leg, "Jimmy?"

Jimmy exhaled a lungful of air, and looked at his dad. *Are those tears in his eyes?* He wondered, as he said, "Yeah?"

"It's okay, Son. Whatever you did to get that injury, I just want you to know that it's okay to tell me. I won't freak out, or get mad."

A tear escaped down the boy's face. He wiped it away, and clenched his teeth, so as not to allow any emotion to escape. He wanted to tell his dad everything. Just open his mouth, and let the words fall where they may. He nodded, and began to speak, when a nurse, and an aide, came in. The nurse named Sonya, handed his dad a clipboard with a few papers for him to sign, the aide laid a bundle on the bed. Her name-tag read Sally Jean.

Trying to appear nonplussed, Jimmy asked, "So, what are you planning to do there, Sally Jean?"

She smiled, and his heart skipped a beat. "Well, Mr. McCoy, I'm going to shave your leg all the way from your groin to your knee."

"What? Why?"

"The Doc doesn't want to be concerned with hair getting into the incision area. Hair contains a lot of bacteria, and if it gets into a wound, it can cause an infection."

"Huh. I guess I never thought of that."

"If you don't mind, could you take your leg out from under the covers? I'll spread a protective sheet down so your bed won't get wet."

He did as he was asked, and Sally went to work prepping his leg for the shaving.

He tried not to appear embarrassed, when she tucked the protective sheet under his underwear, but the heat on his neck and face gave away his true feelings. Trying to mask his embarrassment, he asked, "So, Sally Jean, how long have you been working here?"

Intent on the task at hand, she didn't look up, as she asked, "Here, in this area, or at this hospital?"

"I guess in this area."

Nodding, and smiling, she said, "I've only been here a couple of times. I usually work on the cardiac care unit, but that's closed because of the fire, so I'm working wherever I'm needed."

Laying the shaver, foam and a container of sterile water on the bed between Jimmy's legs, she donned a pair of latex gloves.

"Okay, Mr. McCoy, I'm going to start shaving. If you feel uncomfortable, just let me know, and I'll try to fix whatever it is that's causing you discomfort."

He smiled, and nodded. "I guess I do have a question before you start. Have you done this before?"

With a smile, and a head shake, she said, "Nope. You're the first male I've had to shave."

Jimmy's eyes widened. "Really?"

She winked, and chuckled. "No. I'm just messing with you."

Jimmy breathed a sigh of relief, and laid his head back, too embarrassed to watch, and too concerned that she might cut him.

When the task was done, Sally Jean said, "Well, good luck with your surgery. I may see you again before you leave—if I'm put on this floor again."

Nodding, Jimmy said, "Thanks. I hope I do see you again."

After a finger wave, Sally left the room, carrying her wad of used shaving equipment, and bed pads.

Jesse, having finished the paper work, ran a hand through his hair. The nurse took the clipboard, and informed the two men that she would return in a few moments with a few pre-surgery drugs.

Jesse knew he didn't have a lot of time with his son before the nurse, or aide, or whomever, would come whisk him away. He cleared his throat, and asked, "Jimmy I need you to answer a couple of questions, please."

Jimmy looked at his dad, fear registering on his face. Swallowing hard, he said, "Okay."

"Son, did you and Jamie set the fire at the oil refinery?"

Jimmy shook his head, "No, Sir. Jamie had nothing to do with it."

Sonya returned with a small bag of liquid, and a syringe full of another liquid. She attached the bag to the one already hanging, then inserted the syringe and unloaded its contents into the IV.

"You should feel the effects of the medication in a few minutes." After checking the IV, she left the room.

Jesse asked, "So did you start the fire?"

Jimmy, nodded slightly, clearing his throat to dislodge the lump that had formed in it.

"Dad, you have to understand that I just wanted to bring some excitement to Alva. I never intended for it to get as bad as it got."

Jesse nodded. He did understand the intent, but how would they handle the consequences?

"Mr. McCoy? A male voice asked, wheeling a gurney into the room.

"Yes," both McCoys answered.

The male aide looked at the clipboard in his hand. "Mr. James McCoy?"

"Yes," Jimmy answered, "that's me."

Checking the wristband, the attendant said, "I'm going to need you to slide over to the gurney."

Jimmy did as he was told.

"Okay. Off we go."

Jimmy looked at his dad, who put up his hand for a high five.

"See you later, Son."

Jimmy nodded. He was feeling the effects of the medication, and decided it was too difficult to keep his eyes open. He was vaguely aware of the transfer from the gurney, to the surgical table.

The next few hours Jesse McCoy struggled with what he should do. There was a part of him that wanted to grab his son, and run away, while his saner, more rational side, said he needed to face this problem head on. *How will I go about telling the sheriff? Should I just pretend my his son wasn't involved, and let things play out? Letting the incident become a mystery – a problem never solved? And what about Jamie? Jimmy said he wasn't involved in the fire, but he was involved somehow. Do I confront him?* Jesse played scenario after scenario in his head, and he came to the conclusion that this was not going to end well for the boys.

Exiting the van, Christina heard her phone ring.

"Brad, could you unlock the door? I'll be in in a moment."

Nodding, Brad reached for the house key, as Christina said, "Hello?" into the phone.

"Hey, Christina, it's Cindy."

Gathering her purse, and a small bag of garbage, Christina walked to the back door.

"Hey yourself. How are you doing?" She entered the house, disposed of the garbage, made her way to the den, and sat in her easy chair.

"I'm great! We haven't talked in a few days, so I thought I'd give you a call."

The two women told of their week, Christmas, the fireworks, fire, and what was going on with Janet and Linda.

"Oh, poor girl," Cindy said, after Christina told of Janet's transfer to Dallas.

"I know. Right? It'll be interesting to have another child in the house, but I have a feeling Linda won't be any trouble. She is naturally quiet, and reserved."

Changing the subject, Cindy asked, "Have you heard from Lisa regarding the adoption?"

Christina shook her head, and said, "No. I haven't even thought about that. I sure hope all goes well. I think they flew to Guatemala, to meet with the kids and officials, right?"

"Yes. They should all be returning in the next week or so."

"I can hardly wait to meet Elliana and Rico. Their pictures are adorable."

The friends chatted a while longer, before Cindy was interrupted by Ed's return from town. The two friends disconnected.

"Mom?" Brad said, as he entered the den.

"Yes? What is it, Brad?"

"I just got off the phone with Eric. He asked if I could come over to spend the night. Their family is going to spend the day at that super mall in Waco tomorrow, and he asked if I could go too. I told him I'd ask you, then call him back."

Christina said, "I think that would be fun. Ask what time they want you there today, and what time will they plan on returning tomorrow."

Brad hugged his mom, and said, "Thanks. I'll find out the details."

Christina sat, and remembered the scene from the mall right before Christmas. It had been a scary time, but once again, God had protected them. She closed her eyes, and leaned her head back on the chair. The next thing she knew, Brad was saying, "Mom?"

Shaking her head, as she opened her eyes, she said, "Sorry. I must have dozed off. So what did Eric say?"

"He said, I could come over any time, but they're having dinner at six, if I want to join them."

Nodding, Christina said, "Okay. What time is it now?"

"It's five o'clock."

"Okay. Do you have your stuff ready?'

"Yep."

"Tell your brother and sister to get ready to leave in fifteen minutes. I have a couple of things to do before we go."

Brad said, "Okay," and proceeded to yell up the stairs, "Stacey and Nicky, we're going to leave in fifteen minutes."

She heard their replies, "Why? Where are we going?"

Brad yelled again, "Mom is taking me to Eric's house."

"Okay," they both said, almost in unison.

Almost two hours after Jimmy had been wheeled into surgery, he was back in his bed, in his hospital room. Jesse watched as the surgical techs lifted his limp, and almost lifeless son, from the gurney onto the bed. The techs, one blond male, and one brown-haired female, checked the IV lines, as each hung two fresh bags of liquid—one clear, and one yellow—on the pole at the head of the bed. Making sure their patient was settled, the male turned to Jesse, and said, "The surgery went well, but Dr. Carmichael will be in shortly to speak with you."

Jesse nodded, and said, "Thanks." When they left, he read the labels on the bags. The clear one was Saline with electrolytes, and the other was an antibiotic.

Turning his attention to his son, he whispered, "Oh Jimmy, what have you gotten yourself into?"

Dr. Carmichael arrived as the techs were maneuvering the gurney out into the hall.

Reaching his hand out for a shake, Jesse said, "So, how did the surgery go? Is my boy going to be alright?"

Smiling, and nodding, as he returned the handshake, Aaron said, "The surgery went without a hitch. The bleeding was due to a pinpoint nick in the femoral artery."

"Is that why it took so long for his leg to swell up? Because it was a slow leak?" Jesse asked, trying to understand what the Dr. was saying.

"Yes, I believe so. If the nail had gone all the way through the artery, Jimmy would have been in a lot worse shape. It was fortunate for him, that only the nail tip touched the artery." Sighing, he added, "Personally, I'm baffled that the pinprick didn't grow bigger, causing a more serious bleed."

"Why would it grow bigger?" Jesse asked, troubled by what he was hearing.

Running his hand through his hair, Aaron said, "Because there is such pressure in the femoral artery, it's a miracle that it didn't balloon out, or rupture. I've seen similar injuries, and it almost always ended badly for the victim."

"So, I should be thanking our lucky stars, it wasn't worse?"

"Well, I personally would thank the Creator, but you can thank the stars if you like."

Nodding, Jesse said, "Right. I should thank the Creator."

Aaron checked Jimmy's vital signs, then said, "He'll probably be out for the rest of the night. If you want to go home, and sleep in your own bed, feel free to leave. The nurses will contact you if anything changes."

Frowning, Jesse asked, "Changes?"

"Well, Mr. McCoy, with any surgery, there's always a possibility of bleeding. I don't think anything like that will happen. When I closed up the incision, there was no bleeding present, and I thoroughly checked for that."

Rubbing his forehead, Jesse said, "I would like to go sleep in my own bed. It feels like I haven't been home in a week. With the fires, and all."

Nodding, Aaron said, "Ah, yes. You must be exhausted. As a Doctor, I highly recommend that you go home, and get a good night's sleep. And please, don't worry about Jimmy. He'll be fine."

"Thanks, Doc. I'd like to spend a few minutes with my boy, then I'll take your advise, and go home for a while."

Dr. Carmichael put out his hand, and was surprised when Jesse grabbed him, and pulled him into a bear hug. "Thanks again, Doc, for taking care of my boy."

Aaron patted Jesse on the back, and pulled free. "I'll see you sometime tomorrow."

"Right." Jesse said, as he stepped back from Aaron.

When the room was quiet once again, Jesse pulled a chair beside the bed, and picked up Jimmy's hand. "I don't know if you can hear me, but I just want to say that I'm proud of you, and am so thankful you're my son. I hope it isn't too late to make amends. I love you son." When Jesse finished talking, he squeezed the bridge of his nose to keep the tears that were forming, at bay. He felt movement, and when he opened his eyes, he was looking directly into his son's big brown unfocused eyes.

"Dad?" He whispered.

"Yes, Son."

"I'm sorry." Because he was still feeling the effects of the medication, his words were slurred.

"It's okay, Son. We'll talk about stuff when you are fully awake."

"Okay." He said as his eyes shut, and he was back to sleep.

Jesse stood, wiped his eyes, and headed towards the door. He stopped at the nurses' station, and informed them of his plans to go home, and get a little shut-eye. He'd be back tomorrow.

Sonia, the nurse behind the desk, said, "That's fine, Mr. McCoy, we'll keep a close watch on your son, and if anything changes, someone will call you."

Nodding, Jesse said, "I'd appreciate that."

Before leaving the hospital, he walked across to the CCU, to see what progress was being done there.

CHAPTER 4

Friday arrived, with clear blue skies, and warmer temperatures. Any snow or ice that had been hanging around, was quickly melted by the sun, and gentle breeze.

Christina woke to sunlight sneaking around the window shades. She stretched, yawned, rubbed her eyes, and threw the covers back—right on top of Benji, who had been sleeping soundly at the foot of her bed. He crawled out from under the covers, and slunk off the bed, reminding Christina of a slinky going down a step. She couldn't help but chuckle. He looked up at her, wagged his tail, then stretched. After stepping into her slippers, and robe, Christina went to the windows, and pulled up the shades.

"Oh, look Benji. It is a beautiful, sunny day!" Benji didn't seem the least bit interested. Instead, he went to the door, and scratched at it with his paw. All he wanted, was to go outside and relieve himself.

"Okay, Benji. I'll let you out."

Christina looked at the clock beside her bed. 7:30. Mrs. Ferguson had called her the previous evening, and asked if she would be interested in working on the Med-Surg floor, for the afternoon shift.

She had said, "Yes."

While Benji was out doing his business, she made coffee, then took a hot, steamy cup, and sat in her reclining easy chair. A few minutes later, Benji barked to come in. She settled back into her chair, when Benji jumped up, and promptly curled up in her lap. She massaged his ears, as she thought about the events of the past few days, and what her plans for the day, and weekend were. She had promised Nicky, she would look up the show times for the movie, The Lord of the Rings. She picked up a pen and pad of paper, and began making a list of all the things she planned to accomplish over the weekend, and following week.

Mrs. Ferguson had her working afternoon shifts on Monday and Wednesday, of the following week. The kids were to return to school on Wednesday, which they were already dreading.

She would have to get the spare room ready for Linda. Aaron said he would release her when her fever broke, which would be soon, he predicted. She had talked to Larry about any legal limits concerning her being Linda's guardian. He was supposed to get back with her today. She also needed to call the lawyer, Mark Taylor, regarding the money being deposited in the bank for her, and the children. She laid the paper and pen down, as her mind played back the events of the day she had met with Mr. Taylor, and the FBI men.

She had been informed of David's involvement with an anti-terrorist group, or ATO, and had died while under their employment. Because of David's association with the government, the powers that be, had felt it was their duty to help compensate Christina, and the children, for his absence. Christina had been in shock, because she had been unaware of David's involvement in the ATO, or that his death had not been a mere car accident. He had been deliberately killed, because of his dealings with the ATO. Although she was grateful for the generous financial compensation, she would gladly return it, if she could have David instead. The pain, grief, and loneliness, had ebbed somewhat during the past year, because of the move to Texas, helping her children adjust to the new environment, working at the hospital, and reconnecting with her friends, but every once in a while, she would get slammed with an emotional trigger—like now. She felt her eyes sting, and her heart ache. Pinching the bridge of her nose, and taking a few cleansing breaths, she decided to push those emotions back into their box, and return to the task at hand.

Looking around the room, she noticed the few Christmas items remaining, and added to her list, the removal and packing away of said items, as well as sorting through the Christmas cards. She needed to respond to a few of those. She reached over the dog, and grabbed the stack of cards. The one on top was from her Michigan friend, Linda. She re-read it once again, before tucking it back into the envelope. *Maybe I'll call her later today, or tomorrow,* she thought. She then picked up the envelope that had been addressed to Nicky. It was from Lulu, or Ruby, as she liked to be called.

It was an odd relationship that had occurred after Nicky's kidnapping by the mentally ill woman. She wasn't sure how she felt about that. Part of her wanted the woman completely out of their lives, but another part thought this was a good learning experience for Nicky. He seemed okay with corresponding with his former kidnapper. As long as she was in the mental facility, Christina wouldn't worry. According to Larry, Ruby would be in there for many years, and possibly her whole life. Setting that card and envelope aside, she closed her eyes, and contemplated what else to add to the list.

Nicky walked in, rubbing his eyes.

"Hey, Buddy. How are you doing?"

Yawning, he said, "Okay."

"You want to come over here, and snuggle a minute?"

Looking at Benji, who had filled the space between his mom, and the chair arm, he said, "There doesn't seem to be any room in the chair."

"I can push Benji off, and you can take his place. It's been a long time since we've snuggled."

Nodding, Nicky waited for the dog to reluctantly slink off the chair, then settled into the empty space. Christina put her arm around her son, and kissed the top of his head. She knew, as he aged, there would be less and less moments like this. He was growing by leaps and bounds, and they wouldn't be able to sit comfortably together in her chair much longer.

"What are you doing, Mom?"

"I'm making a list of the things I need to do for today, and next week."

"Next week. Ugh. I have to go back to school on Wednesday."

"You love school. Why the 'ugh?'"

Sighing, he said, "I really like being home, and hanging out with everyone. When I go to school, we don't have as much time to just hang out."

Nodding, Christina said, "True. I think we'll have to work harder to make time."

Pulling back, and looking at his mom face to face, he asked, "When do you have to work again?"

"Mrs. Ferguson called last night, and asked if I could work the afternoon shift today. I am scheduled to work Monday, Wednesday, and Friday of next week, as well."

"If you work afternoons, we won't see you very much."

"It's only for the three days. The Nurse who usually works those shifts will be on vacation that week. I will ask Mrs. Ferguson to reschedule me for the morning shifts after that. I can see you for a few minutes in the morning, then I'll be home after school."

Nodding, Nicky said, "Okay. I just wish you didn't have to work at all. Then you'd be here all the time."

Sighing, Christina thought, *I could, in reality, stop working. The notion does have an appeal,* but what she said was, "Well, I'll consider that option. It's just that I enjoy working. It's nice being with my coworkers, whom I wouldn't normally associate with, if I didn't work."

Nicky laid his head on her chest. "I know. I just like having you around all the time."

Christina squeezed his shoulder, and kissed the top of his head again. "I love being with y'all too, but when I work, I feel like that's where I belong as well. At least for now. Besides, I'll be home tomorrow, and Sunday. We can plan something fun to do then."

Nicky saw the stack of cards and envelopes, and asked to see them. Christina handed them to him, and they looked through them together.

Pulling a card out, and reading it, Nicky said, "Sometimes, I really miss Michigan, and all our friends there."

"Yeah. Me too. I'm still hoping we can go up in February when y'all have your mid-winter break."

"Oh, yeah. I remember talking about that when Grandma and Grandpa were here."

Holding the card up, he asked, "Who are Carl and Maggie Jennings?"

Christina took the card and said, "They are your great Aunt and Uncle, on my mom's side. They live in Milford."

Scrunching his face, he asked, "Have I ever met them?"

Shaking her head, Christina said, "No, not yet. I'm hoping to have a summer bar-b-q, and invite some of my family I haven't seen in a long while, and of course, all our friends we've met these past few months."

Nicky smiled, and said, "A reunion of sorts."

"Yeah. A reunion of friends, and family."

For the next hour or so, they discussed the events over the past several months, people they had met, and what they wanted to accomplish the next year. They were still sitting together, when Stacey walked in.

"Good morning, Sleepy Head."

Stacey yawned, and stretched. "Good morning, Mom. And Nicky."

Plopping down on the couch, and pulling a blanket around her feet, Stacey asked, "Mom, do you have to work today?"

Nodding, Christina said, "Yes, but I don't have to leave 'till around two-thirty."

Scratching her head, then adjusting the blanket to cover her whole body, Stacey asked, "Did you find out when that movie, The Lord of the Rings, is showing?"

"Not yet, but it's on my To Do list."

Nodding, Stacey said, "Good."

Nicky said, "Yeah! Danny's family went to see it, and he said it was awesome."

"I was thinking," Christina said, "If we go tomorrow, you may each choose a friend to take."

The siblings looked at each other, and in unison, said, "Awesome!"

Nicky disengaged himself from the chair, and headed into the kitchen.

"I need to get something to eat."

Stacey said, "Me too. I'm starving!"

Christina sat up, and asked, "Y'all want me to fix pancakes?"

After consulting with her brother, Stacey said, "That's okay, Mom. We'll just eat cereal."

Christina was relieved, because she wanted to get started on her work list.

Jamie woke to whimpering sounds, and at first, didn't recognize what they were. When he became fully awake, he realized the puppies were making the noise, as their mother licked, and cleaned each one.

He laid on his side, and watched them for a while. His heart felt like it would burst with the love he felt for the mother dog, and her babies.

Realizing her new master was awake, Little Lady looked up at him, then over to her food bowl.

He chuckled, and said, "So you're telling me your food bowl is empty?"

She thumped her tail in response. Crawling out of bed, Jamie retrieved the bowl, and headed to the back porch, where the bags of dog food were kept. As he filled the bowl, he heard his dad in the bathroom. He was so noisy in the morning, with his coughing, and nose blowing. Jamie shook his head. *I hope I don't sound like that when I'm his age.* Walking through the hallway on his way back to his room, he almost bumped into his dad, who was exiting the bathroom.

"Mornin', Son. How are the pups doing?"

Smiling, Jamie said, "They're fine. Little Lady is taking good care of them."

"Mind if I take a peek at them?"

Shaking his head, Jamie said, "No. Come on in."

Jack and Jamie sat side by side on the edge of the bed, watching Little Lady, and her pups. She was a very attentive mother, but after feeding them, and making sure they were satiated, she rose from the bed, and went to the food.

She was a very dainty eater, taking one nugget at a time, always conscious of her pups. If one whimpered, she would go lick it, as if reassuring it that she was still there. Jamie felt his eyes tear, as he remembered his mom's kisses when he would have an injury, or if he was sad, or afraid. Times like this, he felt a deep ache within his heart. He so wished she was here to share in this special moment.

Looking at his dad, he asked, "Dad, what happened to Mom? Why did she leave us?"

Taking a deep breath, and releasing it slowly, Jack nodded slightly, and said, "I've wanted to talk to you about your mother for quite a while, but never had any clear answers to why she left us, and where she went."

Jamie scooted over, so he could see his dad, face to face.

"You have some news about Mom?"

Clearing his throat, Jack began his story.

"Your mom left a note that I never shared with you. She said she needed some time away, but she'd eventually come back, when things in her mind settled."

"Did she say where she was going?"

Jack shook his head. "No. I figured she went to her sister's house down in Houston, but after a week went by, and I hadn't heard from her, I called your Aunt Carol. She said your mom had been there for a few days, then told her she was coming back to us. She said that your mom was supposed to call her when she arrived at home, but never did. She figured she just forgot, so she never pursued it. She and your mom were never very close, anyway. They would go for months without talking."

Jamie chewed on a hangnail, as his dad continued.

"Any way, I began calling your mom's friends, and none of them knew anything about her taking off like she did. After another week or so, I called the sheriff, and he did some investigating, but to no avail. It was like your mom, and her car vanished from the face of the Earth. We concluded that she would either return in her own time, or she wouldn't. The sheriff said he would keep an eye, and ear open, to any news concerning any unidentified women that may turn up."

"So, Mom never contacted you?"

Shaking his head, Jack said, "Like I said, when she walked out that day, that was the last time she had any contact with us."

"So, you said you have something else to tell me?" Jamie asked hesitantly, not sure he wanted to hear what his dad had to say. He had a sinking feeling it wouldn't be good news.

"About a week ago, the sheriff called, and said he had a possible lead on your mom. There was a car found in a ravine east of Houston, on one of the back roads. It had been buried in mud and water, so it wasn't visible to the traffic on the road above. Inside the car was a lady's body. After checking the car's registration number, and finding it matched your mom's, the sheriff called me."

Jamie's eyes grew large, as the realization hit him. Almost in a whisper, he asked, "Was it Mom?"

Nodding, Jack said, "The sheriff had DNA samples, and dental records from you mom, and they matched the woman in the car. The woman was your mom."

Jamie felt anger building inside. "How come they just now found her? Good grief, it's been five years!"

Nodding, Jack said, "I know. I asked the same question. The sheriff said the ravine was deep, and the mud was like quicksand, so her car sunk to the bottom, and couldn't be seen. When a road crew started digging out that ravine, to make it ready for widening the road, the backhoe hit something solid. The crew went to investigate, and they found the car."

"So, they're absolutely positive the body was Mom's?"

Nodding, Jack said, "Yes."

"She didn't abandon us? She was on her way back home?"

"Yep. Seems that way. The sheriff seems to think she fell asleep, and lost control of her car."

Jamie felt tears stream down his face, and wiped them away.

"All these years I thought maybe *I* had done something to make her hate me. I loved her with as much love, as a twelve year old could."

Jack whispered, "I know. I knew she wouldn't leave you, that's why I kept looking for her. I figured she had been kidnapped, or was lying dead somewhere. I'm so sorry. If I had been a better husband, she wouldn't have felt the need to leave in the first place."

Jamie stood abruptly. With venom in his voice, he pointed his finger at his dad, and said, "You! You caused her to leave! Oh my gosh! All this time, you knew, but wouldn't tell me it was your fault. Then you had the audacity to blame me!"

Jack put his hands up. "Yes, Jamie, I did blame you, because I didn't want to believe she left me, because of my behavior. I rationalized my behavior, and I was *so* angry. I just internalized it, and just sorta shut down emotionally. I know I was cruel to you, but I just didn't care anymore. To be honest, I just wanted to curl up, and die. I knew I shouldn't kill myself because it wouldn't be fair to you. You were still young enough, that you would have gone into the foster care system, and believe it or not, in my warped sense, I still loved, and cared about you. I just couldn't bring myself to express it."

"So, now you can? What changed, Dad? Why now?"

Jack sighed, and bowed his head "Jamie, you're seventeen. Almost an adult. I figured you are mature enough to make it on your own, if you had to."

"Yeah, so why does that make a difference?"

Pinching the bridge of his nose, and taking a cleansing breath, Jack continued.

"I went to the Doctor last week, because I have this cough I can't seem to get rid of. He did a chest x-ray, and saw a shadow. He was concerned, it might be cancer...given my history of smoking."

Jamie's eyes grew big. "What? Lung cancer?"

Rubbing his forehead, and returning to sit on the side of the bed, Jamie shook his head in disbelief. In his biology class they had studied the effects of smoking on a healthy lung. He had decided then and there, he would never pick up a cigarette. Now his dad was telling him he was probably going to die, because of stupid cigarettes!

"So, what is the Doctor going to do about this?"

Looking into his son's deep blue eyes, Jack said, "I'm scheduled for a lung biopsy next week?"

"When, next week?"

"On Wednesday."

"That's the day we start back to school." Jamie thought for a moment, then said, "I'll just skip it, so I can come to the hospital with you."

Jack's eyes teared. "Thanks, Son. I hope skipping out will not be a problem for you."

Jamie shook his head. "Nah. I'll explain the situation to Mr. Neal, the principal."

Jack nodded, then said, "I'd appreciate that. I was thinking if you weren't available, or willing, I'd find someone else to take me."

Jamie nodded, and chewed the inside of his cheek. "Man, this week just gets worse, and worse."

"Yeah. It's been quite a week, that's for sure."

Jamie and Jack sat silently, side by side, on the edge of the bed, watching Little Lady and her pups. Each lost in thought. Jamie let out a sigh, and said,

"Dad, since we're having confession time, I have something else to tell you, but first you have to promise you won't freak out."

Jack frowned, but nodded, wondering what in the world his boy had done.

When Samara returned home from her friend's house, Cindy reminded her of the plan to leave for LaMesa in a couple of hours.

Picking up her little Shitsu, Samara asked, "Can we take Sasha?"

Cindy looked at Ed, who was nodding. "Yes. I'll ask my mom to put her cats in the basement when we arrive. They are very spoiled, and territorial. I'm concerned they'd attack Sasha."

"How many cats are you talking about?" Samara asked, as she kissed Sasha on the head.

"Only two, but they are huge and temperamental. I was petting one once, and he was purring, when out of the blue, he not only had my hand in his mouth, he had a death grip on it with his claws."

Samara's eyes grew big. "What happened next?"

"I was able to extract him with my other hand, and he jumped down, and ran to the basement." Shaking his head, he added, "I'd be okay if I never saw him again." Shuddering, he added, "I've never been a cat person. Give me a dog any ol'e day."

"Did his bite and claws leave a mark?" Cindy asked.

Putting his hand out, and pointing to a small scar on his wrist, he said, "Yep. It was almost deep enough for stitches, but I just put some of those butterfly band-aids on it."

Cindy touched the scar, and said, "Oh, poor thing. When did this happen?"

Ed looked down, and mumbled, "Last year."

"What?"

"Last year." He said more clearly.

Cindy giggled. "Sorry, I was just trying to imagine a big man like you in an altercation with a cat."

Ed shook his head, and said, "He was a big cat. Almost the size of a lion cub."

Cindy giggled again. "Right."

Shaking his head, he said, "You'll see, when we get to my mom's house."

"How can I see, if he'll be locked in the basement?"

"Well, I'll just have to go get him, and bring him up."

Cindy said, "I thought you were afraid of him."

"I didn't say I was afraid. I said, I don't like him."

Cindy looked unconvinced. "Right."

Ed put his hands up in surrender. "Can we just change the subject?"

Samara stood in the doorway, watching the interaction between her mom and Ed. She bit her bottom lip, as she tried to hold in the laughter. Setting Sasha on the floor, she interrupted their verbal sparring with a question. "How long will we be there? Didn't you say 'till Tuesday evening?"

Ed looked her way, and said, "'till Sunday. We decided to be back here Sunday evening."

Nodding, Samara said, "Good. I'd like to enjoy a couple more days at home before I have to go back to school."

Looking at her watch, Cindy said, "Why don't you go pack your bag? We'll plan on leaving around one."

Samara nodded, and headed to her room.

Frowning, Cindy rubbed her forehead.

Ed asked, "What's wrong, Babe? You got a headache?"

Shaking her head, Cindy said, "A little. I just felt dizzy for a minute. I'm okay, now. Just weird."

Ed drew her into an embrace, resting his chin on the top of her head, as she wrapped her arms around his waist, and laid her head on his chest. *We fit together so well,* he thought. She was a good head shorter, and small boned. Even though she looked delicate, she had a tenacity, that at times amazed him. All that she had gone through before, and even after he had met her, and how she had come through them with her spirit still intact, made his spirit desire even more so meld with hers.

Always, in the back of his mind, was his first wife's memory, and that ache of missing her, but he knew that he had to move on. He couldn't, and wouldn't deny himself of happiness any longer. Knowing that Celina would want that for him, he felt he could at last open his heart, and let someone else in. Cindy was that Someone, and he longed for the time they could truly become one, as he and Celina had. He sensed Cindy desired that unity as well. The looks she gave him, the tenderness in her kisses, the closeness they shared—like now—made his mind, and body, yearn for more.

He pulled back. *This is not the right time, or place, for my body to dictate my true feelings.*

Cindy pulled back as well. She too was allowing her mind to travel to unresolvable places.

Smiling up at him, she said, "Well, I guess I should go get my bags packed."

Nodding, Ed said, "Right. Good idea."

Grinning, she turned away, and headed to her room.

As the gals packed, Ed called Tom to check in with him, and let his partner know of his plans.

The phone rang several times, and went to voice-mail.

"Hey, Tom. It's Ed. Just letting you know that the girls and I are heading out to LaMesa to see my family. We'll be back on Sunday. Give me a call when you can, so I know you got this message."

He was putting his phone back in his pocket, when Cindy and Samara walked out of their rooms, dragging suitcases that looked full enough for a week. He cocked his head, and frowned, as he eyed them, thinking, *Good grief! We're only going to be gone for a couple of days! Why in the world do they need so much stuff?* What he said was, "Okay. You girls ready?" Both nodded, as he grabbed both bags, and headed to the car.

Samara said, "You go on out, Mom, I have to grab Sasha, and a few of her things, then I'll be out."

"Okay, Babe. Just make sure the door is locked."

Hearing Ed grunt, as he put the suitcases in the trunk, she walked around to the back, and heard him muttering. Unaware of her presence, he said, "I don't understand why women have to pack so much stuff!"

Cindy giggled, then opened the passenger side door, and sat. Lowering the window to let in a light breeze, and adjusting her sunglasses, she laid her head back on the headrest, closed her eyes, and waited for her two favorite people, and dog, to settle in as well. She had never been to LaMesa, and was curious, and a bit nervous about the trip. They weren't just going to visit the town and area, they were going to see Ed's family. Meeting someone's family was a big deal. Her mind began bombarding her with questions. *What if they don't like me? What if I don't like them? Worse, yet, what if they don't like Samara? Of course, how could anyone not like Samara? She is beautiful, talented, sociable, kind, and considerate. If they don't like her, or me, then I'm not sure what to do about that. I love Ed, and don't want to end our relationship, but when two people get married, they also marry into a family. Geeze, oh Pete!*

Ed leaned down, and looked in the window. Noticing that Cindy was chewing on her bottom lip, and mumbling to herself, he asked, "You okay, Babe?"

She jumped, when she heard his voice. She had been so lost in her thoughts, she hadn't heard him approach her side of the car.

Removing her sunglasses, she looked up. "I think so. I was just thinking about meeting your family, and was beginning to feel anxious."

Cocking his head, Ed asked, "Anxious? Why?"

Shaking her head, she said, "I'm just worried that they may not like me, or Samara."

Ed shook his head, "Cindy, they will love you and Samara. It'll be fine. Don't you worry your pretty little head about anything."

Shaking her head, she said, "I know. It's silly. Just my insecurities rising to the surface."

Patting her shoulder, he said, "I'm going to check in on Samara."

As he approached the door, Samara, with Sasha under one arm, a blanket, and bag of food under the other, and a leash in her mouth, was backing out, trying to close the front door with one free hand.

Ed reached around, and grabbed the door handle. "Here, let me get that."

Grabbing the leash out of her mouth, she said, "Thanks."

Once everyone was settled in, Ed grinned, and said, "We're off!"

Which reminded Samara of the tune, "We're off to see the Wizard," which she began singing, as her mom, and Sasha, who added her howling to the slightly off-key duet, joined in.

Ed shook his head. Smiling, he said, "Ya'll could go on one of those talent shows on TV."

Samara giggled, and said, "Yeah, as an off-key trio. I'm sure that would go well."

"Hey," he said, "I've seen, and heard worse on those shows."

Cindy nodded, "If we added your voice, Ed, we could make it a quartet."

Shaking his head vigorously, Ed said, "Uh, no. Never gonna happen."

Trying hard not to laugh, Cindy turned to face Samara, and said, "And I was looking so forward to traveling around the country as a quartet." Sigh. "Guess we'll just have to let that dream crash and burn for now."

Samara giggled. "Yep. Guess so."

Putting her ear buds in, and turning on her Ipod, she closed her eyes, and laid her head back.

Ed reached over and took Cindy's hand, bringing it up to his lips.

This is gonna be a great weekend, he thought, as he glanced over, and smiled. Cindy returned the smile, then turned her head to look out the side window. He then glanced in the rear-view mirror to see Samara adjust her seat belt, so she could lie down.

Sasha whimpered, as she curled up close to Samara, who put an arm around the dog, and spoke softly to her. This was Sasha's first long distance car ride, and she was nervous. With her family close by, however, she soon relaxed, and drifted off to sleep, joined quickly, by the other two females in the car.

Ed let out a sigh. He could get used to this. He let his mind explore what it might be like to have Cindy, Samara, and even Sasha, become a permanent part of his life. He knew he was probably seeing the future through rosy colored glasses, but he truly liked what he was imagining.

God, he thought, *please let these thoughts become a reality. I know I haven't known Cindy for very long, but everything feels so right. I know we aren't supposed to let our feelings rule, but I just can't imagine living the rest of my life without her and Samara. I do believe You set everything in motion, when I first saw Cindy in Christina's house, so I trust that You have been directing the events following that encounter. Please help me become the man that You want me to be, and they deserve.*

Cindy stirred from her slumber, and stretched.

"Where are we?" She asked, as she sat up, and adjusted her glasses.

"We just went through a little town called Albany. Did you have a nice nap?"

Nodding, and covering a yawn with her hand, she said, "Yeah. I didn't expect to sleep so much. Sorry. I was planning on keeping you company." Glancing in the backseat, she saw Sasha and Samara sleeping soundly. "I guess we're not such great traveling companions."

"It's okay. Y'all must have needed the extra z's. I doubt if Samara got much sleep over at her friend's house, and you had a headache, so your bodies said it was time to shut down for a while."

Nodding, Cindy said, "Probably so."

"So, is your headache gone?"

Moving her head around, she said, "Seems to be. How much further?"

"About two more hours."

"Can we make a pit stop soon? I need to stretch my legs, and we should let Sasha out."

Nodding, Ed said, "Yep. The next town is about twenty minutes from here. If there is something sooner, I'll pull over."

Samara sat up, stretched, and yawned. "I didn't think I'd fall asleep, but I don't remember anything after going through Ft. Worth. Where are we, Ed?"

Looking in the mirror to see her, he said, "Just a couple hours away. I'm going to stop in a little while so you can let Sasha out."

"And make a pit stop." Added Cindy.

After stopping at a rest area for a few minutes, everyone returned to the car, fully refreshed.

Ed looked over at Cindy, and reached for her hand, which she gladly gave him.

"My family is going to love you, and Samara."

Cindy smiled, and said, "Think so?"

"Absolutely!"

Nodding, and wanting to change the subject, she asked him about the town of LaMesa.

Jamie ran his hands through his hair, then held them clenched together in a fist on his lap.

He took a shaky breath, and released it. He wasn't sure how his dad was going to react to his confession, and his nerves were buzzing with fear.

Jack reached out, and patted Jamie's shoulder.

"It's okay, Son. Just go ahead, and get it off your chest."

Jamie nodded, then told his dad about the fireworks display, and why he did it. He didn't tell him of the home invasions, and wouldn't, unless forced somehow. For some strange reason, he didn't want to add more disappointment to his dad's perception of him.

Jack clenched his jaw, and his hands, as he listened. He wanted to take his son's shoulders, and give them a good shake. He would have, too, if he was still that angry guy....but he wasn't him. Not any more. When Jamie finished his story, Jack took a deep breath, and released it. Amazingly, he felt calm. It was if his wife had her hand on his shoulder, telling him it was going to be okay.

Rubbing his forehead, he said, "Jamie. We need to go to the sheriff about this."

Jamie shot up from the bed, and began pacing around the room.

"No! I can't go to the sheriff."

Jack looked confused. "Why? Don't you think telling him might lessen your sentence?"

"Sentence? What does that mean?" He asked, in a panic.

Jack patted the area next to him. "Come. Sit. Let's talk this out."

Jamie shook his head, and felt tears begging to be released. He wiped his eyes before they escaped. "Alright."

Taking a seat next to his dad, he said, "I'm scared, Dad."

Jack patted his son's shoulder. "I know, Son."

The two of them talked for a while, and finally agreed that Jamie had to go to the sheriff. Jack told him, "Son, you have to understand that the truth will eventually come out. Do you want this to hang over you? Always wondering if your actions will ever be discovered? I personally wouldn't want that. If you cover it up, you will be haunted for the rest of your life. Fortunately, no one was injured, or died, so the sheriff may go easy on you."

Jamie pinched the bridge of his nose. "I have something else to tell you."

Jack looked warily at him. "Okay. What else is there?"

Jamie sighed, "Okay, here goes." He proceeded to tell his dad about the fire at the refinery, and hospital, Jimmy's injury, and subsequent hospitalization, and the cover-up story they had concocted.

Jack shook his head, ran a hand through his hair, and sighed heavily.

"Oh, Man. I'm not sure what to say about that, except Jimmy is responsible for his own actions, and consequences. However, since you two lied, and tried to cover it up, you both may get a heavier sentencing."

Jamie stood again, and began pacing once more. "Oh, Man! I was just helping Jimmy, Dad!"

"I know, Son. I don't know how the sheriff will handle this, but as I said, the truth will come out, and the sooner you get ahead of this, the better."

Jamie said, "I need to talk to Jimmy about this. We both need to be on the same page. If I confess, and he doesn't, and I get punished, and he doesn't, I'm thinkin' that will ruin our friendship."

Cocking his head, Jack asked, "Why do you think it would ruin your friendship?"

"Because, Dad, I would be afraid of saying anything around him. What if I slipped, and said something, and someone overheard us, and told the sheriff? Plus, I would be angry that I was being punished, and he wasn't. Especially, since my actions didn't damage anything, or hurt anyone, and his did."

Jack nodded. "I can see where that would be quite a dilemma. Why don't you go talk to Jimmy, and work this out?"

Standing, Jamie said, "Thanks, Dad. I'm glad we can talk now. I didn't realize how much I missed that, 'till now."

Jack nodded. "Yeah. Me too, Son.

Working the afternoon shift on the Med-Surg unit proved to be much less strenuous than Christina had anticipated. She had two cardiac patients on the floor, whom she was totally responsible for, and one Med-Surg patient.

One of the cardiac patients, Noah Jonas, the firefighter who had come in to the ER, presenting with chest pains, was released that afternoon. Dr. Dawson had ordered various tests, including a cardiac catheterization, which Noah had passed with flying colors. He had been dismissed that morning, but his wife couldn't come get him until the afternoon. Christina spent a few moments of her time talking to him, and getting to know him better.

Yes, she thought, *I do love this job. I love meeting people, and getting to know them, and I love helping heal them, or helping them transition to the other side.*

Walking out of Noah's room, she almost bumped into her friend, Libby, who was carrying a tray of medications.

"Oops! Sorry, Libby. Can I help you?"

Smiling, Libby said, "Did I tell you about the time when I was in nursing school, and backed out of a room, and into the path of the RN, who had a tray of medication?"

Shaking her head, Christina, said, "Oh no! Don't tell me you knocked the tray out of her hands!"

Nodding, Libby said, "Oh, yes! The medications went flying, and she went backwards, trying to regain her balance, which caused her to crash into one of the Doctors, who was making rounds.

"Needless to say, she was pretty ticked off at me, and I tried really hard to avoid her the times I had to be on her floor. When that wasn't possible, I just wouldn't make eye contact."

"What happened, next?"

"Well, the Doctor caught the nurse, before she hit the floor, and he laughed."

"He laughed? I don't think I ever remember any Doctor who laughed. All the ones I've ever worked with, besides Dr. Dawson, and Dr. Carmichael, have always been quite stern."

"I know! I wanted to laugh too, but the nurse wasn't in the laughing mood. I believe she was not only embarrassed, she was angry that she would have to go re-fill the cups, and document the incident."

"Did she ever get over that?"

Nodding, Libby said, "Eventually. On our last day on the Med-Surg unit, she pulled me aside, and apologized for her behavior towards me. She actually asked for my forgiveness! My forgiveness! I was the one that messed up her day, but she said she understood, and we should let by-gones be by-gones."

"Aww, I'm so glad it turned out well. Did you ever bump into her after that?"

Shaking her head, and rolling her eyes, Libby said, "No. To be quite honest, I can't remember her name either, or I'd look her up. You know how the staff comes and goes, in any big hospital."

Christina cocked her head, and asked, "Please refresh my memory. What university and hospital did you train at?"

"I went to Baylor University, so our hospital experience was at Baylor Medical Hospital. Our class did go visit Scott and White Hospital in Temple as a day trip. That place is huge!"

Nodding, Christina said, "I know! That hospital seemed so big when we were students. When I took the kids on a trip this summer, to see my old Alma Mater, Mary-Hardin-Baylor, in Belton, and Scott and White hospital in Temple, I was amazed at the growth of both. I hardly recognized either."

"It's amazing! Nothing stays the same for long. I mean, look at this place." She said, as she waved her hand around. "Who would have pictured it like this twenty years ago?"

Nodding, Christina glanced at the wall clock. "I know you need to get those meds delivered, so I'll let you go. I need to do some paper work. It's been fun chatting. We'll have to meet after our shift or something, so we can get caught up on events."

Entering the room of her first patient, Libby said, "That sounds great! I'll see you in a while."

Returning to the desk, and retrieving a chart from the rack, Christina had just begun writing, when she sensed a presence. Looking up, she was surprised to see Dr. Carmichael standing on the other side of the counter.

"Doctor Carmichael. What brings you to this floor?"

"Hi, Christina. I have a patient here. The young man named James McCoy, in room 204?"

"Oh, yes. Jimmy. I am assigned to him today. Anything I need to know, or be aware of?"

Nodding, Dr. Carmichael said, "As you know, I had to go in, and clean out a puncture wound that had become compartmentalized, and infected."

"Yes, I read that in the chart. How did the surgery go?"

"It was interesting. The object he says was a nail, nicked the femoral artery. The puncture was so small, the leak wasn't discovered until a couple of days after the accident. I thought we were just dealing with a severe sepsis, but obviously, when his symptoms didn't resolve, and in fact, were becoming worse, I had to do further investigation. I ordered an MRI, and it showed the culprit. The tiny puncture."

Christina stood, hanging on every word. "I am amazed at the technology we have available today. A few years ago, something like that wouldn't have been detected, and the patient would either lose a limb or die."

Nodding, Aaron said, "I agree. I thank God every day for the advances in modern medicine, and for the advances that are being worked on, as we speak." He smiled, and Christina's heart skipped a beat. "It's mind boggling, sometimes," he added.

Trying to focus on his eyes, instead of his beautiful white teeth, and full lips, she said, "Yes. Yes, it is."

Cocking his head, he grinned. She was exhibiting the same reaction of many of the female nurses and doctors he had dealings with. He was a bit surprised, and flattered. If she had been free of any involvement, with Steven, he would, no doubt, ask her out. As it was, he could only admire her as a fellow employee of the hospital. *But*, he thought, *I can keep that door open. She has no ring on her finger, and no sign of any real commitment to Steven, so why not continue to pursue her?*

He asked, "Christina, I haven't had the time to talk with you about your family, and all that's going on around here. Are you free after work?"

The invitation caught her by surprise. "Uhm. Not tonight. It will be pretty late, and I have a big day with the kids planned for tomorrow. Maybe next week? I can check my schedule."

Nodding, he said, "Okay. Once you know when you're free, I can make arrangements for the sitter to watch Sammie."

"How's Sammie doing?"

Smiling, and nodding, Aaron said, "She is amazing! I'm not being the least bit prejudiced when I say this, but she is undoubtedly the smartest kid in her kindergarten class."

Christina grinned, and giggled. "Spoken like a true parent! I feel the same way. No kid in any of the schools are as intelligent, or wonderful, as my three are. And, I'm not being prejudicial either!"

Aaron laughed out loud. "No, I'm sure you're not!"

Libby walked up, and asked, "Hey, what's the joke? I need a good laugh too."

Christina, looking at Aaron, who nodded, said, "We were just saying how amazing our children are, and of course, we're not the least bit prejudiced either."

Libby grinned. "I totally disagree with both of you. *My* kids are the smartest, and most adorable children on the planet."

Christina blew out some air. "Well, Doctor Carmichael, I think she's got us beat. I was just comparing mine to the kids at school, but...if hers are the best on the *planet*, then I guess her proclamation trumps ours."

Sighing heavily, Aaron said, "Yes, I believe you're right." Turning to go, then turning back, he said, "I guess I'll have to say that Sammie is the brightest, and best kid, of all the five-year-olds in the universe."

Both ladies looked at each other, and burst out laughing. "Touche' Doctor Carmichael!" Libby said.

When he had left their presence, Libby turned to Christina, and with a mischievous smile on her face, said, "So, you and Doctor Carmichael seem like friends."

Christina smiled, "Well, I guess you could say we're friends. I have never gone out with him, if that's what you're getting at."

Libby put her hand to her chest. "Really, Christina. I didn't mean to pry."

Smirking, Christina nodded, and said, "Sure, you didn't." As she walked away, Libby called out, "You never really explained your relationship."

Christina did a finger wave over her shoulder, as she entered Jimmy McCoy's room.

Janet opened her eyes, and was aware of two things: the beeping sound of a machine she couldn't identify, and the whooshing sound of another machine she didn't recognize, until she tried to take a breath, and couldn't. She was then hyper aware of everything. She tried moving her arms, but realized they were tethered to the bed. Panic overwhelmed her, as she tried desperately to call out, but couldn't because of the tube in her mouth, and throat. When the machine inflated her lungs again, she began thrashing as much as her body was able to. A nurse came running in, speaking in a calm voice, "Mrs. Washburn, you need to calm down. Let the respirator do its work."

Janet gave her a panicked look.

The nurse patted her hand, as she injected something into the IV line. A second later, Janet felt herself falling into darkness, as she left the conscious world.

The nurse on duty at the time, named Charlotte Ray, checked Janet's vital signs, recorded everything, then went back to the station to make a call to Janet's primary Doctor, Jeffery Knorr.

Dr. Knorr appeared several minutes later, and headed straight to Janet's room.

Charlotte followed him in.

"So, I'm to understand she woke, and tried to communicate?"

"Yes." Charlotte said, handing him Janet's chart. He sat in a nearby chair, and read the entries.

"Well, I'm surprised, to say the least. With her injuries, and history, I didn't expect her to regain consciousness for quite some time." Stroking the goatee on his chin, he said, "I think we should remove the ventilator, and see if she can breath on her own. If so, that'll be a sign she's improving."

Charlotte nodded in agreement. She had worked the past twenty years in different intensive care units, and from her experience, a patient who became conscious after being in a coma for a while, usually had a good survival rate.

"Could you please get the equipment to remove the tube?" Dr. Knorr asked, as he took Janet's blood pressure.

"Sure. I'll be right back," Charlotte said, leaving the room.

Taking Janet's hand, he said, "Well, Janet, it's up to you, now."

Charlotte returned, and assisted Dr. Knorr in removing Janet's ventilator tube. They waited patiently for Janet to take a breath on her own. After what seemed like minutes of silence, but in reality were just seconds, she inhaled sharply. Dr. Knorr nodded, and smiled. Charlotte exhaled, unaware that she had been holding her breath.

Patting Janet's hand, Dr. Knorr said, "Way to go, Janet. Now you just have to keep on breathing."

The nurse moved the ventilator machine to a corner of the room, for easy access, if Janet needed it again. She would send an aid in to clean it thoroughly.

Janet felt as if she were floating in a pool of black water, surrounded by a black sky, being ever so gently caressed by invisible hands. For the most part, she could see, and feel nothing. Occasionally, however, she would be conscious of hands lifting her body to change positions, or hear voices, encouraging her to wake up. She tried moving a body part, or calling out to them, to let them know she was still in there, but to no avail, until a few minutes ago. When she was able to finally break free of the void engulfing her, and make her way to the conscious world, panic, and pain, met her there. She was relieved to be sent back to the void. Floating around in peace, and free from pain, was quite comforting. If she could, she would stay in the void, instead of returning. She didn't want to do battle with pain, and panic again.

This must be what it's like inside the womb. No wonder babies cry when they are forced out of their safe, warm, and peaceful place.

After Dr. Knorr left Janet's room, he made his way to the conference room, down the hall, to speak with a group of specialists involved in Janet's care.

Surrounding the table were; a cardiologist, internist, neurologist, orthopedist, hematologist, and pulmonologist. After Dr. Knorr gave his latest assessment of Janet's condition, each doctor present expressed their own opinions, questions, and protocol. Concerning Janet's overall care, and prognosis, each felt it was wise to give her another week of deep sleep, to allow her body to continue its healing process.

As Ed pulled the car into the driveway of his mother's home, he chuckled, as he watched the screen door fly open, and several women emerge.

Turning to Cindy and Samara, who's eyes were wide with fear, he said, "Ladies, be prepared for an onslaught of hugs, kisses, and questions."

Cindy swallowed hard, and gave Ed a panicked look. He reached over, and took her hand. Bringing it up to his lips, he said, "It'll be alright."

With a tremulous voice, she said, "If you say so."

Turning to Samara, Ed said, reassuringly, "Just be yourselves. They're gonna love you both."

Reaching for the door handle, Samara said, "Well, here we go."

By the time Ed had walked around the car, and helped Cindy out, the women were already giving Samara hugs, and commenting on how cute Sasha was.

As Cindy exited the car, Ed's mother was standing there with arms outstretched. Cindy glanced at Ed, who nodded slightly. She walked into the arms, and was treated to a warm Texas hug. She couldn't help but smile, as Ed's sisters did the same with her, and Ed.

He introduced his siblings, and mother, and Cindy felt as if she knew them already, from his detailed descriptions earlier.

All the chatter reminded her of a chicken coop at feeding time. She was a bit overwhelmed, but found herself laughing, as she answered the many questions that were bombarding her. At one point, she gave Ed a desperate look. He said, "Mom! Girls! Let Cindy at least step away from the car. We can continue getting to know one another, once we're inside the house."

They giggled, and began helping gather the suitcases, and other items that needed to be transferred from the car to the house. Ed's mom linked arms with Cindy, and in what some folks would call a stage whisper, said, "Pardon our behavior. It's just that Ed has spoken so highly of you, and Samara, that we are beside ourselves with excitement at finally getting to meet y'all."

Cindy nodded, and said, "We're so happy to be here."

"How was your ride out here?"

"Not too bad," Cindy replied.

Ed's mom introduced herself, and the sister who had remained inside.

Patting Cindy's hand, she said, "I'll have the girls introduce their husbands and kids, when they all come in. In the meantime, I could use a little help in the kitchen."

Cindy nodded, as she followed Ed's mom, Gwen, and two of his sisters into the kitchen.

Cindy said, "Please forgive me if I have to ask your names over and over. I've never been good at remembering names."

Gwen chuckled and said, "It's fine, Honey. Sometimes I too have a difficult time remembering names. My mind isn't as sharp as it used to be."

"Yeah," Nicole said. "Sometimes mom names the other sisters, and granddaughters before she finally gets to my name. And I'm the oldest! You'd think she'd remember me, being the first one, and all!"

Gwen shook her head, and pointed a finger. "You just wait, young lady. One of these days you'll find yourself in the same pickle." Cocking her head, and putting a finger to her bottom lip, she said, "Oh, wait, you already do call your kids by their siblings' names!"

Cindy had a difficult time keeping her giggle in. Nicole gave her mother a look, and pointed her finger. "At least I only call them by their sibling's names. I don't go through the whole family album."

Nadine walked in about that time, and burst out laughing. "I couldn't help but overhear the squabbling. Y'all are hilarious!" Pretending to whisper, she said, "Just remember, we do have guests, and we don't want them to think we're a bunch of crazy folk."

Gwen mumbled under her breath, "I think it's a bit too late for that."

Cindy put her hand over her mouth, and thought, *I love this family.*

Samara found herself surrounded by Ed's nieces, and nephews. It was all a bit overwhelming, but flattering as well. She had never felt such love, and acceptance, by a group of strangers.

Sasha was excited as well, yipping and running in circles, as the children ran after her, taking turns getting their faces cleaned by her little tongue.

Stephanie, Ed's youngest sister, walked in, and said, "I wish I had a video camera! The kids and the dog are so adorable!"

"Wait! Andy has one." Said Nicole, Ed's older sister, as she went to the den to get her husband.

"Hey," Ed said, "Where are the guys?"

Shaking her head, Nadine, Ed's middle sister, said, "Glued in front of the TV, watching some kind of sport show."

Glancing towards the den, Ed smiled as the three brothers-in-law came sauntering out, looking a bit sheepish. Grabbing Ed's hand, each one shook it, and gave him a manly hug, then ended with a punch to the shoulder.

"Ow!" Ed said after each punch.

They all laughed. Putting his arm around Ed's shoulder, Wayne, married to Nadine, said, "What's wrong, Bro? Getting soft in your old age?"

Ed reacted by grabbing him, and throwing him to the floor. The women put their hands to their mouths, and gasped. They weren't sure if they should laugh, or offer assistance.

The other two brothers-in-law, grabbed Ed, and tried to wrestle him to the floor, but he surprised them as well, by throwing them down first.

The men gave a hearty laugh, then stood, reaching out to Ed for a handshake, who said, "Uh uh. You think I trust y'all?"

"Hey, no hard feelings? Right?" Andy said, as he threw an arm around Ed's shoulder.

Ed relaxed his defensive stance, and was caught off guard by the other two men, who managed to knock him down, and sit on him.

Ed threw them off.

"Alright, Boys!" Ed's mother admonished. "No more shenanigans. Someone is liable to get hurt."

The words were barely out of her mouth, as seven of the nine nieces and nephews piled on top of Ed. He laughed as he tickled the girls, and wrestled with the boys.

Ed's mom shook her head. "Kids."

Cindy laughed, as she followed the older woman back into the kitchen, and stole a glance over her shoulder. Ed was on his hands and knees, as a group of kids piled on top of his back, begging for a 'horsey' ride. Her heart swelled with love, and affection.

As the women entered the kitchen, Cindy was handed an apron, and asked to help set the table. She had never seen such a long table. There were seventeen place settings, and a high chair. Ed's mom, and sisters, bombarded her with questions about her family, as they set plates, flatware, glasses, and napkins. She relaxed, and began to feel like a part of the family, especially when Stephanie trusted her with her baby boy.

"Can you hold him for a minute while I go call the kids, and guys in?" She asked, as she passed the tiny child into Cindy's waiting arms.

"Sure," said Cindy. "I can't tell you how long it's been since I've held such a tiny baby." Looking down at the sleeping infant, she asked, "How old is he?"

"He's three weeks old. He was a few weeks early."

Cindy nodded. "Goodness! No wonder he's so tiny. Samara weighed eight pounds. How much does he weigh?"

"He weighed in at five and a half pounds. All our babies have been small. I think Nicole had one of the biggest, and he was only seven pounds. Most were around six pounds."

"What's his name?" Cindy asked, as she wrapped the blanket around him.

"His name is Timothy Owen. Named after my dad, and Jason's dad."

Looking down, Cindy was surprised to see the baby staring up at her.

"Well, hello little Timothy Owen."

After close scrutiny, the baby realized she wasn't his mom, and began to cry. Cindy stood, and positioning the baby so that his head was facing behind her, began humming, and patting his back. He stopped crying, and she could feel his little body relax, but when Stephanie walked in, and he heard his mother's voice, he began to wail once again.

"Thanks, Cindy. He's quite attached to me right now." Stephanie said, as she took the baby.

Handing the baby back to his mother, Cindy said, "He's so precious. I've never seen such big blue eyes on a baby."

Stephanie chuckled. "Yes, he gets those from his dad's side of the family. As you can see, this family has brown or hazel eyes."

Cindy nodded. "Funny how genes can change from child to child, and generation to generation."

Nodding, Stephanie said, "Isn't that the truth! My husband's aunt, from two generations back, married a black man, and had twins with him. When they came out, one was fair-skinned with bright red hair, and big blue eyes, like her mom, and the other had dark skin, black curly hair, and big brown eyes, like her dad."

"Oh, goodness!" Cindy remarked. "I bet that caused a bit of an uproar when they went to school."

"Well, in the beginning, but from what Jason's mom says, the aunt, I think her name was Matilda, and everyone called her Mattie, raised the girls with proper etiquette, and everyone in town loved them. Another funny thing is, the fair-skinned girl married a black man, and the dark-skinned girl married a man with the same coloring as her sister."

Furrowing her brow, Cindy said, "So, if genetics skip a generation or two, there could be any number of racial combinations."

Nodding, Stephanie said, "Yes. And there have been. I'll have to show you the family album one of these days."

"I'm so glad there isn't as much stigma placed on one's race, as there was a couple of generations ago."

Shaking her head, Stephanie said, "Well, in some parts of the south, there still are. Can you believe that there are Ku Klux Klan groups still scattered around?"

Cindy said, "Really? I figured those went out back in the 60's when Black people were finally recognized as humans, and not slaves."

"Well, I think a lot of them did phase out, but according to Jason, who works with the Police force in Lubbock, there are still groups that are active. Every now and then, they take the law into their own hands, and burn crosses in front of people's houses, or do damage to their property. Sometimes black folks go missing, and are either found dead and mutilated, or are never found at all."

Shaking her head, Cindy whispered, "That's sad."

Sighing heavily, Stephanie said, "Yes. Yes, it is."

Jason walked into the dining room, and planted a kiss on his wife's head.

"You two look like you just heard some bad news. Why the grim faces?'

Stephanie perked up. "We're fine. We were just discussing the issue of prejudice."

Nodding, Jason said, "Right. Well, hopefully, you two have some great ideas on how to avoid that."

Shaking their heads, the women said, almost in unison, "Nope."

Noticing that his infant son was asleep, Jason whispered, "Why don't I take the munchkin into the bedroom, before the kids all come in, and wake him up?"

Nodding, Stephanie said, "That'd be great, Hon. Check on Abigail as well. She is probably awake by now."

Cindy asked, "You have another child?"

Stephanie nodded, and grinned. "Yes. Abigail is nine-teen months."

"Wow!" Cindy said, "You really have your hands full!"

"Yeah, I hadn't really planned on having them so close, but sometimes, God, and nature, have their own timing. Having them so close has its advantages as well, from what I hear. When the baby gets bigger, I'm hoping they'll enjoy each others company." Shrugging, she added, "Guess we'll just have to wait and see."

Once everyone was in, and found a place to sit, Gwen asked Ed to say the blessing.

Cindy was amazed how quiet it was, as he gave thanks for the family, and the food.

When he said, "Amen," however, bedlam reigned once more.

Cindy glanced at Samara, who was heaping mashed potatoes onto the children's plates. She seemed to be enjoying herself. Cindy looked around the table. Nicole and Andy had four children with names all beginning with M. Marissa, Mark, Melissa, and Mason.

Nadine and Wayne had three children; Nico, Adam, and Josh.

Stephanie and Jason, being the youngest couple, had the youngest children; Abigail and Timothy.

Cindy looked across the table at Ed, who must have felt her gaze, as he looked up, and gave her a smile and wink, before being bombarded with plates needing to be filled with the sliced turkey, and ham. She couldn't help but grin. He seemed to be in his element. She yearned to be a part if this family. It was friendly, loving and kind. Even the children, as rambunctious as they were at times, were enjoying their time together.

The food was savory, and the conversations light. There was no talk of politics, religion, or crimes during the meal. There were, however jokes, and hilarious stories told. Cindy felt certain that some of the stories about Ed were geared to embarrass him, as well as poke fun. He took it all in stride, and gave back, as much as was given. She and Samara were at times shocked, but mostly entertained.

When dinner was finished, everyone, including the children, took their plates to the kitchen, emptied and scraped them, and put them on the counter next to the sink.

Stephanie said, "Hey Jason, could you take Abigail with you, while we finish up in here?"

Jason, said, "Sure, Babe," as he wiped Abigail's hands, and face, with a napkin he had dunked in a glass of water. The little girl squealed with delight, as he played peek-a-boo with the napkin.

The men retired to the front porch, and kept an eye on the kids, as they ran around the yard playing tag. The women, including Cindy and Samara, finished clearing the table. Nicole and Nadine rinsed the remaining debris off the dishes before stacking them in the dishwasher, as Stephanie, Cindy and Samara put the remaining food in bags and containers. There was endless banter, as the women worked together. As the last dish was put in the washer, baby Timothy could be heard protesting that he was alone, and probably hungry, and wet.

Removing her apron, Stephanie said, "Excuse me, Ladies, but I need to attend to Prince Timothy, before he gets any louder."

Ed sat in one of the rockers on his mom's spacious porch, listening, as his three brothers-in-law talked about work, and home repairs. He let his mind wander, as he envisioned a life with Cindy and Samara. It wouldn't be as noisy or rambunctious as his sister's homes were, that was for certain, but it would be warm, and cozy. He knew his feelings for Cindy were strong and true, and could hardly wait to begin a life with her, and of course, Samara. He wasn't sure how that was going to work. He'd never had kids of his own, and certainly not a teenage girl. She was a beauty, like her mom, and that concerned him. He knew, in a couple of years, she would be dating, and he dreaded that. He was pretty sure he'd want to do a background check on any potential date. *Well*, he thought, *they'd cross that bridge when that time came.* His thoughts were interrupted by Andy, Nicole's husband.

"So, Ed, have you asked Cindy to marry you, yet?"

"Yeah, Ed, what's the story? It's obvious you two are an item." Wayne asked, as he tossed a wayward ball back to his youngest son, Josh.

Ed nodded, then said, almost in a whisper, "Well, I was planning on asking her to marry me on New Year's eve."

"That's awesome!" Jason said as he reached over, and punched Ed's shoulder.

Leaning forward in his rocker, so he could see Ed, Andy asked, "You think she'll say yes?"

Nodding, Ed said, "Well, I certainly hope so."

Shaking his head, Wayne said, "I don't know. When she finds out that you snore loud enough to wake an elephant, she may have second thoughts."

Ed gave Wayne a shocked look. "I don't snore!"

The other two in-laws nodded, and shook their heads. Andy said, "Sorry to tell you this, but yeah, you do. Big time."

"And how, exactly, do you know this?" Ed asked, feeling defensive.

Andy said, "Well, you remember last Christmas, when we all stayed here?"

Ed nodded.

"Nicole and I stayed in the room next to yours, and man, you snored so loud, we had to get earplugs."

"What! How come you never mentioned it, until now?"

Andy shrugged, "It didn't seem all that important, then. But now?" Sighing, he said, "You've got another person to consider."

Ed looked at the other two men, who were nodding their heads.

Cindy walked out on the porch, as Ed was about to respond.

"Hey, guys. Y'all look serious. Did I interrupt something?"

Ed shook his head, then asked, "Do I snore?"

Cindy said, "What?"

"Do I snore? When I've slept over on your couch, did I snore?"

Smiling, she asked, "Is that what y'all were discussing? Whether or not Ed snores?"

All four men nodded, and looked at her for an answer. She felt a bit embarrassed.

The other women made their way to the porch, catching the tail-end of the question.

"What are y'all talking about?" Stephanie asked, as she sat in a rocker, holding her nursing baby.

"Ed just asked Cindy if he snores."

Shaking her head, Stephanie said, "Oh goodness! I'm anxious to know the answer."

Sighing, and looking at Ed, Cindy said, "The few times you've slept on my couch, I have not heard you snore. Of course, I'm a pretty sound sleeper, so I'm not totally sure if you do or not."

Nadine said, "Guess you'll find out for sure when y'all get married."

"Uhm," Cindy said, not sure how to address that statement, since Ed hadn't asked her to marry him...yet.

Noticing Cindy's embarrassment, Nadine put her hand to her mouth, and said, "Oh, I'm sorry. I didn't mean to put you on the spot."

Cindy glanced at Ed, who suddenly seemed quite interested in his watch, and watchband.

Smiling, she said, "It's okay. We just haven't come to that point in our relationship."

Ed pressed his lips together to keep a smile from reaching them.

Maybe, I can ask her to marry me while we're here, with the whole family present, he thought as he wrestled with the idea. Digging the engagement ring out of his pocket, he made his decision. *The sooner I ask her to marry me, the sooner we can follow through with our plans.*

Clearing his throat, he stood, and said in an authoritative voice, "May I have everyone's attention, please."

The adults stopped mid-sentence, and the children halted their play, making their way onto the porch, to either sit on a parent's lap, or stand close by them.

Ed waited as everyone settled, then walked over to Cindy, who was sitting in a rocker by then, looking nervous, and confused. He squatted, and took a knee.

The women inhaled sharply. Giggling, they realized what was about to happen.

Cindy put her hand to her mouth, and felt tears burning her eyes.

Ed took a deep breath, then said, "Cindy, I know we haven't known each other very long, and some folks would call this a whirlwind romance, but I want you to know that I love you, and Samara, and want to spend the rest of my earthly life with you two."

Samara, who was standing behind her mom, put both of her hands on Cindy's shoulders. She knew of the plan, but was surprised that Ed didn't wait 'till New Years. *Oh well, what's a few days anyway?*

Ed continued, as everyone held their breaths, wondering, *Would Cindy say yes?*

Ed, locking eyes with Cindy, continued. "Cindy, will you please marry me?

Cindy wiped a stray tear off her cheek, and leaned forward wrapping her arms around Ed's neck.

"Yes! Yes! I will!"

Ed looked up at Samara, who was wiping away escaping tears as well, and asked, "Samara, will you accept me as your step-dad?"

Samara rolled her eyes, let out a sigh, and pretended to be annoyed, said, "Oh, I guess so."

Ed stood, pulling Cindy up as well.

Samara left her spot behind her mom, came around the chair, and gave Ed a hug. Ed wrapped one arm around Samara, and the other around Cindy. Before they knew it, the whole family made a hugging circle around them.

"Group hug!" One of the children yelled.

After getting congratulations, hugs, kisses and pats on the back, the parents began gathering their children, to either leave for home, or stay the night.

Before retreating into the house, Ed's mom came up to him, and as he leaned down, she kissed his cheek, and whispered, "I like her. She's a good choice for you, Son."

Ed pulled her off her feet, and swung her around, all the while ignoring her protests. When he finally set her down, she was giggling.

Looking over to Cindy, who was talking to Nicole, she said, "I'll shoo everyone away so you two, or three, can have some privacy. I'll get the bedding for the couch in the front room. You can sleep there."

Kissing his mom on the cheek, he said, "Thanks. I don't think we'll be long. It's getting a bit chilly out here."

"If I didn't already have Nadine and her family in the den, I'd suggest that y'all sit in there. You can sit at the kitchen table, if you want to talk some more."

"That's fine, Mom. We'll figure it out. You go on to bed. I know you must be bone-weary."

Nodding, and letting out a sigh, she said, "Yes, I am tired, but in a good way. Wasn't it just a marvelous day, with the whole family here? I just wish your dad could be here as well. He would have loved all the grand babies."

Nodding, Ed said, "Yes, he would have."

"Well, I'm going to head off to bed. Please turn off any extra lighting."

"Sure thing, Mom."

Nicole gave Cindy a hug, and said, "Well, I'd better go help Andy get the little monkeys to bed."

Samara, gave her mom, and Ed, another hug, saying, "I can hardly wait to have you as a step-dad."

Ed grinned, and said, "You say that now, but wait until you start dating. You know, I'll do a background check on all your dates, right?"

Making a face, she said, "Mom! You won't let him do that, right?"

Cindy shook her head, "I don't know, Babe. Depends on who you bring home. I've seen some of those guys at school, and they look pretty shady to me."

Samara gave an exasperated sigh, and pointed a finger at both.

"Ugh!" She said, as she stormed off, trying to make stomping noises—which wasn't very effective, as she was wearing tennis shoes.

Cindy and Ed laughed. He pulled her into an embrace, her head resting on his chest, and her arms wrapped around his middle. He felt his heart swell.

Goodness I love this woman! He never thought he could love another, after losing Celina, but here he was. Ready to take the plunge into marriage, again.

Cindy pulled away first, and looked up into his dark eyes. Such love and gentleness there. Holding her hand up to look at the engagement ring, she said, "This is beautiful, Ed. How'd you know my ring size?'

"When you went to the store the other day, I snuck in, and borrowed one of your rings."

Taking her hand in his, he said, "Do you like the style? That, I wasn't sure of, but my sisters approved, so I thought it was a good choice."

Cindy chuckled, "Well, how can I dispute the three sisters? They are, after all, quite opinionated. I'm surprised they all agreed, considering how they bicker back and forth, which is quite entertaining, I must say."

Ed said, "You never answered my question."

Turning her back to him, she held her hand up, pretending to look at the ring from every angle.

"Well...," she finally said, "Not too gaudy. I love that the diamond is protected by being incorporated in the ring's overall shape. I don't like the possibility of snagging it on anything...especially the dresses at the shop.

Ed nodded. "I like that feature as well."

Looking up at him, with her head cocked, she asked, "What does the wedding band look like?"

"I'll have to show you a picture of it. I think you'll like it too. The two rings are designed to fit together, so it looks like one ring."

Cindy smiled, and stood on her toes to kiss his lips. He leaned down, grabbed her up and swung her around. "Thank you for saying, 'yes.'"

Still being held in his arms, she pulled her head back and asked, "You were worried I'd say no?"

"Not really, but I guess my insecurity got the better of me."

"Silly, Man. I love you to the moon and back."

"And I love you to infinity and beyond!"

They both chuckled, as he set her down.

CHAPTER 5

Christina woke with a start. At first, she wasn't sure what had awakened her, but then she heard the distinct sound of wind rattling the old windows, like it was trying desperately to get inside. She lay still for a moment, and listened. Soon, she heard rain pelting the roof, and sides of the house. It was comforting. She turned on her side, facing away from the door, and let her mind and body relax. Within minutes, she was asleep.

David and Jarrod stood by her bedside. In human time, David hadn't visited Christina as often as he had in the beginning of his departure from the Earthly realm. Father had kept him, and his angelic companion, Jarrod, busy with other lost, and lonely souls. David's assignment after entering the heavenly realm, was to travel back to Earth, and encourage, and guide the souls that were experiencing confusion, loneliness, and self-loathing. Jarrod was to fight the demons, if there were any, and David would gently remind the person of their purpose in life, and the fact that they had a Father in Heaven who loved them, more than any earthly being ever could. Usually, the recipient of such counsel would perk up, and find the strength to turn from the negativity, and continue on in their daily activities. Sometimes, because of their free will, all the encouragement, and intervention wasn't enough, and the human would succumb to an unfulfilled life, or death by their own hands.

Because the human souls, and angelic beings, were outside of time, their work was never done. Their ethereal forms never required food or rest, so they were well equipped to carry on the Father's work.

"Isn't she lovely?" David asked, as he stroked Christina's hair.

"Yes. She certainly is."

"You know, I don't miss the earthly life like I thought I would, but I do miss her, and my kids, and can hardly wait to be reunited with them. I want them to experience the magnificence of our Father's house. I never fully understood the words of Jesus when he said, "I go to prepare a place for you." Until now.

Nodding, Jarrod said, "Yes. If more people could truly grasp those words, I doubt there would be so many lost souls."

David reached down and touched Christina's cheek one more time, before he and Jarrod left in a blink, ready to take on new assignments.

Steven woke from a fitful sleep, minutes before his bedside alarm sounded. Sitting on the side of the bed, he let his mind check off his schedule for the day. No surgeries were scheduled, but a couple of stress tests, and three consultations, were on the agenda. He didn't usually work on Saturdays, but because these particular patients had met their insurance deductibles for the year, and wanted to take advantage of their "free" service, he had agreed to meet with them. It wasn't as if he had anything else planned for the day.

His mind continued to wander from one subject to the next, as he dressed, and ate breakfast. All the events that had occurred the past few months seemed to revolve around Christina, and her family. He couldn't help but wonder why. He began naming the incidences off in his mind.

It all began when they had moved to town—the break-ins, the death threats, aimed at Christina and Nicky, the illnesses that had plagued them—namely Stacey's appendicitis, and Brad's meningitis. Even Cindy's concussion, and Janet's car accident were tied to Christina. And yeah, the fire at the hospital. It just happened to be on the same floor as Christina. Okay, maybe the fireworks display, and the fire at the oil refinery didn't involve her or the kids, but the aftermath did. It's as if she's a magnet to bad Karma.

Looking up at the wall clock, and realizing he needed to leave in the next fifteen minutes, he drained his coffee cup, put his breakfast dishes in the sink, quickly brushed his teeth, grabbed his jacket and keys, and headed out the door. It was a good thing he only lived a couple of minutes from the hospital.

During those few moments, thoughts of Christina, and her kids, kept dancing around his mind. He had enjoyed spending time with them the other night when they had shared a meal of pizza and salad, and had played a game of Sequence. He was impressed with how intelligent Christina's kids were. Smiling, he found himself desiring to spend more time with them.

Pulling into the parking lot at the back of the hospital, he was surprised to see his aunt, pull into a spot next to him. Getting out of their cars at the same time, he asked, "What are you doing here today? I thought you had Saturday's off."

Nodding, and smiling, she said, "Well, good morning to you too, Steven."

Shaking his head, he said, "Sorry, Auntie. Good morning. I didn't mean for my question to come out so accusatory."

Shaking her head as she gathered her purse, and a stack of papers from the front seat, she said, "Normally, I do have Saturday's off, but I need to organize some paperwork, before the New Year comes rolling in."

Steven walked around the car, and said, "Here, let me take those papers for you."

Looking up at her nephew, she asked, "So, Steven, how have you been lately? Seems like I haven't seen or talked to you in a while. Even though we were together at Christmas, I didn't get to spend any alone time with you, as there was so much chaos, and you were busy with the rest of the family."

Smiling at the memory, he said, "Being together with my cousins, and their kids, was such fun. I haven't laughed that hard in a long time."

"Yes. I enjoyed it as well. By the way, what are *you* doing here? I figured you'd be taking advantage of the holiday."

Holding the back door as she entered, he said, "I'm here to see a couple of patients. It's at the end of the year, so several have decided that they want to take advantage of their insurance, before the new year kicks in, and they have to start over meeting the deductibles."

Nodding, she said, "Ah, yes. I've done that a few times, myself. Gotta save money one way or another."

Stopping in front of her office door, he said, "Well, here we are."

Before entering, she held a finger up, and said, "Wait a second. How are things going between you and Christina?"

Shaking his head, and smiling, he said, "I was wondering if you were going to approach that subject."

She cocked her head, and said, "Well?"

Chuckling, he answered, "Our relationship is going along just fine and dandy."

Still looking up at him, she asked, "So....any future together?"

Opening the door for her, he said, "We'll see."

Smiling like a Cheshire cat, she nodded, and entered her office.

"Thanks, Steven. Hope you have a great day."

"You too, Auntie."

He couldn't help but wonder if he and Christina did have a future together. They certainly enjoyed each others company, and had many mutual interests. He liked her kids, and they seemed to like him.

Approaching his office door, he noticed a couple standing in the hallway. *Ah, yes. My first consultation.*

The day had started out rainy and cold, but by ten-o'clock, the sun was shining, and the sky was a clear, crystal blue. Christina had enjoyed sleeping in until seven-thirty. As much as she wanted to take advantage of sleeping in later, her internal alarm clock woke her up at six o'clock sharp. She dozed off and on, until Benji decided she needed to get up, and let him out. Try as she might, she couldn't ignore his whining.

As soon as the bedroom door was open, he bound down the stairs like his tail was on fire, and made a bee-line to the back door, prancing and running in circles, as she made her way there.

The frantic dog ran to the back of the property to do his morning business. She took that time to start the coffee maker. By the time he was barking to come in, she had her first cup of the fortifying brew in her hand.

Settling down in her recliner, with Benji by her side, resting his head on her lap, she grabbed the stack of mail on the table next to her chair, and began perusing through it. Mostly ads and fliers, advertising the 'after Christmas sales,' and great bargains she could get, if she brought in a special coupon. Most of those ended up in the small trashcan beside her chair. Inside one of the fliers, however, she found an envelope from the law offices of Taylor, Marshall, and Campbell, in Dallas. She tore open the envelope, and found a note from Mark Taylor, the lawyer whom she had dealings with regarding David's death benefits, to her and the children.

It read:

Dear Mrs. Sanders,

I hope you had a pleasant Christmas celebration, and are looking forward to a new year of blessings, and adventures.

I just wanted to touch base with you regarding the money transfer to the savings accounts we discussed. Since I haven't heard from you, I'm assuming everything has transpired according to the plan we outlined. The money will continue to be distributed to the four accounts on a monthly basis as requested.

If you have any questions regarding these accounts, please feel free to call our office.

Wishing you a healthy and prosperous new year.

Mark Taylor

Returning the letter to the envelope, she set it aside, and let her mind wander back to the day she met Mark Taylor. She had been so nervous. Mr. Taylor had set up the meeting without giving the true agenda behind it. All she knew was that it involved David, and some kind of financial business. She had been shocked to see Ed Florres there as well.

It was then, she had been informed that David's death wasn't accidental, but an act of revenge from one of the sleeper terrorist cells located somewhere in Michigan. She had no idea of David's involvement with the government, and was shocked to learn of that as well.

She had always believed that David and she had an open, no secrets, kind of relationship. Her first reaction was one of shock, but also betrayal. *How could he keep something so important from me? Especially if it put him, or our family at risk.*

Ed's boss, Henry Steil, had shown her the document David had signed, promising to never discuss his involvement with the Anti-terrorist Organization, or ATO, as it was referred to. His job had been to translate information from known terrorists, and their cells, operating in the Detroit area. The agency was just as shocked as she was by his sudden death. Mr. Steil promised the perpetrators would eventually be brought to justice, and reassured her, that she, and the children, were safe.

She thought about that for a moment, recalling all that she and her children had been through since moving to Alva. *How safe was safe? And how can anyone guarantee anyone else's safety? Just because most of the things that had happened to her and the kids were not terrorist related, didn't mean there weren't evil forces out there, ready to destroy them.*

As one of her friends once said, "The only things guaranteed in life, are death, and taxes."

Taxes. Who in the world am I going to get to do my taxes? David had always taken care of that, and the past couple of years, she had had a friend, who was a CPA in Michigan, do them for her. *I'll have to ask one of my girlfriends about that.* She grabbed a pen and notepad, and jotted that down.

She laid her head back, and let her mind carry her to thoughts of each of her close friends. "The Fab Four" they had called themselves.

Cindy and she had been best friends since Kindergarten. The other gals, Donna, and Lisa, had joined the ranks in seventh grade, when the three elementary schools graduated their sixth-graders into the one middle school.

She thought it was interesting that Alva had three elementary schools, but one middle, and one high school. Maybe because Alva was spread across so many miles, with several different housing communities, the planning board thought it better for the younger children to attend school closer to their homes. Fortunately for her, and her kids, they lived within walking distance of each school.

She made a note to call Donna to discuss the plans concerning the introduction party Lisa and Tom were planning to have, when they arrived home form Guatemala with their newly adopted son, and daughter. Thinking about how excited Lisa had been, made Christina smile. She and David had talked about either adopting, or foster parenting one or more children. Maybe they would have somewhere down the line, if he hadn't died. The thought of all the 'what ifs' made her sad. *I wonder how different our lives would have been, if David hadn't died, and we hadn't moved to Texas.*

Because she didn't have the gift of prophesying the future, she had to live each day in faith. She had always been skeptical of people who said they could see the future, because many of their predictions were false, but there were those few who truly seemed to have a gift for discerning future events. She wasn't sure if that would be viewed as a gift or curse, especially if what lay ahead was destructive, deadly, or sad.

Was my decision to move to Alva made a bit hastily? David had been gone only a year, but the house they were living in, held too many memories. Continuing to live there would have been difficult. If her parent's house in Alva, hadn't been available, would they have moved closer to David's parents in, or around Ann Arbor? She had told her kids the move to Texas would be temporary, because she just needed to fix the house up, so it could be sold. In her heart, she knew that wasn't entirely true. She knew, and hoped, that once they were settled in, they wouldn't want to leave. It had been five months, and the kids all had new friends, and she had re-connected with her childhood friends, as well as a few relatives, she had left, when she moved to Michigan. Sighing, she thought, *I really love living here. This is where my heart and soul are rooted. Not that I didn't enjoy living in Michigan, but I always felt there was a piece of me missing. That piece was always Texas shaped.*

Nicky walked into the family room, and seeing his mom sitting in her recliner with her eyes closed, asked tentatively, "Mom?"

Opening her eyes, she smiled when she saw Nicky standing beside her chair, in his pajamas, with his hair tousled from sleep.

"Good morning. Did you sleep well?"

Nodding, and rubbing his eyes, he said, "Yeah. How about you?"

Adjusting her recliner to a sitting position, she said, "I slept like a baby, oblivious to everything."

Plopping down on the couch next to her chair, he asked, "Did you check on those show times?"

"As a matter of fact, I did. There's a showing at one o'clock. I figured we'd leave around noon."

Looking at her watch, she said, "Which gives us about an hour and a half. Why don't you go wake Stacey and Brad?"

Nodding, and stretching as he stood, he said, "Okay. I'll get dressed too."

"Maybe you can hop in the shower? No offense, but you smell a little ripe."

Making a face, he smelled under his arm, and said, "I don't smell so bad."

"When was the last time you showered?"

Scrunching his face, he said, "A couple of days ago, I think."

Christina gave him a look that said, "two days too long."

Nodding, he sighed and said, "Alright, I'll go shower."

After he left, she heard him knock on his siblings' doors, demanding they get up, so they could go to Waco to see the movie. She then heard the bathroom door close, and the shower turn on. One thing she didn't necessarily like about living in the old house, was that noise traveled through it like water through a pipe.

She stood, and stretched, and was joined by Benji, who also stretched.

On her way upstairs to get dressed, she thought about calling Donna. *Maybe she and the boys would like to join us at the movie.*

Sheriff Clifton leaned back in his desk chair, and ran his hand over his eyes, and hair. He had spent the night in his own bed, at home, and hadn't planned on coming into the office, but there was something niggling at his brain, and he couldn't sleep any longer.

His deputy, Mike Owens, had dropped in the office to retrieve the squad car keys, before heading out to drive around Alva.

He was surprised when he put the key into the doorknob, and found the door unlocked. He didn't know his boss was in the building. Being cautious, he pulled out his gun, and slowly pushed the door open, not sure what, or who he might find.

At first, he didn't see anyone, so he cautiously walked around the room, and headed towards the back of the office. He almost fired his weapon, when Sheriff Clifton walked out of the break room carrying a cup of coffee. Jumping, and spilling a bit of coffee on the floor, he said, "Good grief, Mike! What are you trying to do? Shoot me?"

Mike quickly returned his weapon to his belt. Stammering, he said, "No, Sir. I didn't know you were here, and when I saw the door ajar, I thought maybe someone had broken in."

Setting his coffee down on the desk, and grabbing a few napkins to wipe up the spill he had created, Larry asked, "And why do you think someone would break in here? And what would they find of value? An old coffee pot? Or a computer that is slow as molasses?"

Mike, looking down, and feeling quite foolish, said, "I don't know, Sir. But with all the break-ins lately, I guess my nerves are a little on edge."

Shaking his head, the sheriff said, "Aw. It's okay, Mike. Guess I'd rather you err on the side of caution, because if someone did break in to steal our coffee pot, I might want to shoot them too."

Mike tried to hide his grin. After cleaning up the spill, Larry said, "I think I know who Janet hired to break into Christina's house."

"What? Really? Who do you think it is?"

"Well, I hate to say it, but I believe it's one of our local boys. A senior named Jamie Simmons."

Leaning over Larry's shoulder to look at the computer screen, Mike asked, "What makes you think it's him?"

Larry picked up a paper from a stack the printer had just spit out, and sat behind his desk.

"According to the phone number on Janet's extra phone, Ed was able to trace it to Jamie. Plus, I talked to the owner of the Pizza Hut, Curtis Shaffer, who had given Jamie his light blue Chevette. Seems the kid didn't have transportation, except for a bicycle, and Curtis felt sorry for him, so he gave him the car. The transfer of ownership has been filed, but the final paperwork hasn't come through yet, because of the holidays."

"So the car is still in Curtis's name?"

Nodding, Larry said, "Yep. But that doesn't really matter. What matters, is that Jamie is the suspect." Rubbing his forehead, he said, "I know his dad. He works at the auto repair shop out on Waco Street."

"The one we take the police cars to?"

Nodding, Larry said, "Yep. Nice guy. His wife is the one who disappeared a few years ago, and we just recently found her body in a car, that ended up in a ditch by the side of the road."

Mike nodded. "Yes. I remember that. If the kid is responsible for the break ins, I bet it was because he was crying out for attention."

Larry gave him a confused look. "Listen to you. You sound like a psychiatrist. Attention?"

Mike shifted his weight from one foot to the other.

"Didn't you have to take a psych class at the police academy?"

Larry nodded.

Mike continued. "In the profiling class, they tell us that a lot of misdemeanor crimes committed by children, or young adults, is because of lack of parental love, guidance, or abuse. It's their way of silently screaming that they need help."

Stroking the whiskers on his chin, Larry said, "I do remember that, now that you mention it. It would make sense. The kid's mom disappears, his dad is barely functioning. I doubt his dad helped him through the grieving, as he shut down emotionally himself."

Sighing, he said, "I hate this part of our job. Having to apprehend a suspect, when he's barely out of puberty."

Mike said, "My kid brother's a senior this year. He probably knows Jamie." After a moment of silence, Mike asked, "How do you want to handle this?"

"That's what kept me awake all night. Part of me wants to just go talk to the kid. No harm, no foul. But, the policeman in me, says I have to bring him in. Breaking, and entering, is illegal."

"But you said he has no other priors, and hasn't caused any harm. The folks who reported things taken, also reported they had been returned. As you just said, no harm, no foul."

Larry shook his head. "I'm gonna have to think this through. Maybe I'll just bring the kid in for questioning, and see where it goes from there."

Nodding, Mike said, "Sounds reasonable. Do you think he may have set off the fireworks, and started the fire at the oil refinery?"

Larry shrugged. "That's possible."

Glancing at the wall clock, Mike said, "Guess I'd better head out, and make the rounds."

"Check in every now and then. I want to make sure you're not goofing off."

Mike grinned. "Right."

Larry scrolled through the information on his computer screen, once more, before shutting it down. He knew what he needed to do.

As he drove home, Jesse's mind was whirring with thoughts. Running his hand through his hair, he wondered how in the world he could have let his, and Jimmy's life, get so messed up. When his wife had died of uterine cancer five years earlier, it was as if a part of him had died along with her. He had become a shell of a man. He felt like a robot, programmed to do what it was instructed. He couldn't remember the last time he had laughed, or cried, or had a decent conversation with his son, or anyone for that matter. He was a lousy dad, and because of his actions, or in some cases, non-action, his son had resorted to this crazy attempt to "shake up Alva." Maybe it wasn't really about shaking up Alva. Maybe it was directed at him. To shake him up. Well, it had certainly shaken him up.

He and the sheriff were friends, but he didn't know if Larry would, or could help the boys get a lighter sentence. *I should call Larry, and set up a meeting time.*

Christina had been able to connect with Donna, and she agreed to meet at the movie theater. After picking up Brad's friend, Eric, Stacey's friend, Carmen, and Nicky's friend, Danny, they were able to leave Alva by a little after noon. Barring any roadwork, or accidents, Christina figured they would arrive at the theater pretty close to starting time. She would buy the tickets, and give Brad money to buy everyone popcorn and drinks. The kids who were guests, had brought their own money, and were willing to pay, but because they were on a tight time line, she decided to pay for everything, and sort out the money issue later. Donna, and her three boys, met them in the lobby, and after the food and drinks were bought, and passed around, they entered the theater just as the previews began. There weren't enough seats in one row for all of them, so a few of the kids went elsewhere, and agreed to meet in the lobby after the showing.

The movie was all it had promised to be. Afterward, the kids were so excited, their chatter could be heard all through the lobby.

"Mom?" Brad called.

"Yes?"

"Could we walk around the mall area. We kinda got interrupted the last time we were here."

Christina looked at Donna. "Do you want to hang around a while longer?"

Donna shrugged, "Sure. Why not? We didn't get to see the whole place, because of that bomb scare last time."

"Right." Nodding, Christina said to Brad, "Ya'll can go on some of the rides, but please get a buddy or buddies to hang out with. Brad, Eric, and Andy, since y'all are the three oldest, could you help keep and eye on the younger ones?"

Brad patted his jeans pocket. "Sure. We have our cell phones, if anyone gets stranded."

"Thanks." Christina said.

Donna added, "Andy, Steven, and Jason, y'all need to meet me at the theater lobby at six o'clock. We have to meet your dad for dinner at Applebees by six thirty."

The boys answered in unison, "Okay, Mom."

Andy said, "I'll set my phone to go off at five-forty-five, which will give us time to get to the meeting place."

"Thanks, Hon." Donna said, patting her son's shoulder.

As the groups started off, Christina said, "Sanders kids!"

They all stopped, and turned around.

"Please meet me back at the entrance by the theater around seven. That'll give y'all plenty of time to shop, and enjoy the rides."

Brad nodded. "See you then, Mom."

The whole group turned as one, and headed to the roller coaster.

Sighing, Christina said, "So where do you want to start?"

Donna gave a sly smile, and said, "How about Victoria's Secret? I could use some new pajamas, and they have the cutest and softest sets."

Nodding, Christina said, "It's been a long time since I've visited that store. It'll be fun to see what new items they have on sale."

After Jamie told his dad about setting off the fireworks, both sat in silence for a few minutes. Jamie crinkled his brow, and began to hit his forehead with his fist.

Noticing this odd behavior, Jack said, "Is there something you're not telling me?"

Thoughts raced through Jamie's mind, as he debated what he should do. *Should I tell him about the break ins? Maybe not yet. I still need to return the album to the Sander's family. That will be my last break in. If I'm lucky, no one will be the wiser, unless Jimmy spills the beans about it.*

Jamie shook his head, and said, "Nah. I'm just worried about all of this, and especially Jimmy."

"What's going on with Jimmy?'

"Remember, I told you about the puncture wound in his leg?"

Jack nodded,

"Well, I guess the nail nicked an artery and he had a slow bleed and his leg swelled up, and the Doc had to do surgery. I'm not sure what happened after that. I want to either go back to the hospital, or give him a call, to see how he's doing."

"I can call Jesse, if you want."

Jamie shook his head, "Nah. I'd rather talk to Jimmy, myself."

Standing, Jack said, "Son, I'm glad you told me about the fireworks, and fire. If there's ever anything else you want to talk about, or tell me, please do. I'm not going to get mad, or yell at you like I've done in the past. Those days are over. I just want us to pick up the pieces of our lives, and go on. As I've said, before, I'm so sorry it took me this long to come around."

Jamie felt tears sting his eyes, and he blinked rapidly to keep them from falling.

"Thanks, Dad."

Walking to the door, Jack said, "I'm gonna go see what I can throw together for supper. When did you want to go see Jimmy?"

Jamie stood, and set the small dog down by her puppies, who immediately began to whimper.

He smiled. "Guess I'll go after dinner. I need to get food and water for Little Lady, then I'll be in to help."

Jack nodded. "Sounds good."

As he left the room, and walked into the kitchen, Jack felt a tightness in his chest. He stopped, and leaned on the counter. Putting his fingers up to his neck, it felt as if his heart was trying to gallop right out of his chest, and neck. The pain in his chest lessened, but the sadness accompanying it, was still present.

Jamie walked past him to fill the water bowl in the sink, and noticed the pained look on his face.

"You okay, Dad?" He asked with concern, as the water ran into the bowl.

Standing straight, he said, "Yeah. I'm fine. Just trying to figure out what to fix for dinner."

Jamie asked, "How about you order a pizza, and I can pick it up on my way home from visiting Jimmy?"

Nodding, Jack said, "That's a great idea. I think I'll order a salad, too. The Doc said I need to eat healthier, because my cholesterol level is too high."

Jamie scooped a bowl of dog food into Little Lady's dish, then returned both bowls to the eagerly awaiting dog. Jumping up and down, she began running in circles around Jamie's legs.

"Alright, Girl. Here you go."

She licked his face, as he bent over, then stuck her nose into the food.

Wiping his face, he sat on the side of the bed, and watched her. Her wiry hair made her scruffy looking. He hated to admit it, but he had fallen in love with her, and her pups.

As if sensing his thoughts, she stopped eating, looked up at him with her big brown eyes, and wagged her tail. He smiled back at her, and whispered, "I love you Little Lady."

She met his eyes again for a moment, then went back to devouring her food. Once satiated, she returned to her litter, and began licking each pup from their heads to the tips of their tails.

Sighing, he left the room, grabbed his coat, hat, and gloves, said "Bye" to his dad, and headed out to the hospital, unaware that his life was about to change dramatically.

Christina and Donna had a nice visit as they walked around the mall, checking out sales, and purchasing a few necessary items. After checking in with the kids, they decided to take a break, and have a cup of coffee, while continuing their conversation.

Donna asked, "So, have you heard anything about Janet's condition?"

Christina brought her up to date.

"Oh, goodness! Poor Linda. Does she have any family around?"

"I know, right? She doesn't have any family, as far as anyone knows. I've offered to bring her to our house until Janet is back home. No one knows for sure how long that will be. Janet's injuries were extensive, and from what Steven has told me, she's in a drug-induced coma, so her body can continue to repair itself."

Donna shook her head. "I didn't realize the situation was so bad. Last I heard, she was still in the hospital in Alva, and was improving. She must have taken a turn for the worse?"

Christina nodded. "She woke up on Christmas day, and was talking, and seemed to be fine. They even removed her ventilator. Within a few hours, however, everything crashed. He heart stopped, and they had to resuscitate her, and re-insert the ventilator. It's been touch and go since. Poor Linda was witness to it all. She was hysterical for a while, and I was called in to help calm her down. Now, she's just sad, and lonely. I talked to Dr. Carmichael, and he said he would be releasing her in a few days."

"Will she be able to return to school, when it resumes?"

Shaking her head, Christina said, "I doubt it. I would imagine she'd still be pretty weak, and tired. I guess if she wants to try attending, I can let her. I'll make sure the principal knows the situation, so he can ask the teachers to keep an eye on her."

"Wow! That's quite a situation. I'm sure it'll all work out for the best."

Smiling, Christina said, "Aren't you the optimist?"

Shaking her head, and chuckling lightly, Donna said, "I just know that God isn't finished with Janet and Linda, yet."

"And how do you know this, Old Wise One?"

"I know this is going to sound weird, but I had a vision of sorts."

"A vision?"

"Yeah. I was just waking up, when I saw what appeared to be an angel at the foot of my bed. He said, "Donna, you need to pray for Janet and Linda. They are caught in the middle of a battle, and need your prayers to get them through it."

Christina sat with her mouth open, shocked at what she was hearing.

Smiling, Donna asked, "You think I'm crazy, right?"

Shaking her head, Christina said, "Uh, no. I think it's amazing that you were chosen to be an intercessor for them. I know Janet and Linda have been heavy on my heart as well, and I've been praying for them quite regularly."

"See? I know God has something amazing planned. We just have to be faithful at standing in the gap for them."

Excitement showing on her face, Christina said, "I do believe we need to pray, in expectation of a miracle. Not only for them, but for Alva, and the whole nation. After the airplane attacks, back in September, I have felt a sort of spiritual awakening."

"Me too!" Donna said, excitement building in her as well.

Christina thought for a moment, then added, "I just hope, when all this excitement dies down, and people go back to their routines, they don't forget how God, and His angels, interceded in so many instances."

Nodding, Donna said, "Yeah. Me too. That seems to happen throughout history, though. There's some kind of spiritual awakening, and revival, and people are so excited, then time passes, and they get busy, or life gets difficult, and that excitement fades...and people forget. It reminds me of a pendulum, swinging from one extreme to the next, rarely pausing in the middle."

Christina said, "A pendulum? That's a good analogy, Donna. The enemy of our souls doesn't like it when we are on fire for God. He will use whatever tactics he can, to draw us away."

"Yes. We as believers, have to constantly be on guard. There are so many activities, and things out there, that can easily draw us away. Mine is reading. I love to read! Magazines, books, the Bible, newspapers...whatever has words on it. I have to put limits on my reading time, or several hours will pass, and I haven't accomplished anything. Then I get frustrated, and usually take it out on the boys, or my husband." Shaking her head, and smiling, she added, "Not very Christ-like, that's for sure!"

Christina chuckled, and said, "I know exactly what you mean! Lately, I find myself getting caught up in cleaning, and organizing. I still have several boxes in my bedroom needing to be sorted, but between work, the kids activities, and my own needs, I find myself putting my Bible study, and quiet time with God, further down the list of activities for the day." Sighing, she added, "I just can't seem to stay consistent."

Donna reached out, and touched Christina's hand. "Honey, you and the kids have been through a lot these past couple of years. Considering what has occurred, I think you're doing an amazing job at keeping it all together. If I'd gone through half of what you've experienced, I can pretty much guarantee I'd have packed everything up, and fled back to Michigan! You've got an inner strength that I admire."

"Aww. Thanks, Donna. I certainly don't feel very strong most of the time. I feel like I'm barely putting one foot in front of the other."

Smiling, Donna said, "We're our own worst critics." As she picked up her cup to take a sip, her youngest son, Jason, along with Nicky, and Danny came running up.

Jason said, "Hi, Mom. Can we get some ice-cream?"

Donna looked at Christina, who shrugged, and said, "It's okay with me."

Donna reached into her purse, and pulled out a five dollar bill. Christina did the same, except she pulled out two fives.

She told Nicky, "You can keep the change, and get something else if you want." The boys looked at each other, and grinned.

Donna instructed her son to do the same.

"Hey, Jason." Donna called out to the retreating boys, "Have you seen any of the other kids?"

"Yeah. The girls are at some jewelry store, and the guys are in the arcade."

Nodding, Donna said, "Thanks."

The three boys took off, and were soon out of sight within seconds. Donna looked at her watch.

"Oh, shoot! I forgot to remind Jason about our leaving time. They have about forty-five minutes to kill."

Standing, Christina said, "I'm sure Andy will grab his brothers. He seems to be pretty reliable."

Donna smiled, and stood. "He is. Even though he's thirteen, and entering puberty, he's still the calmest, and most reliable of the three boys."

Depositing her coffee cup in the waste can, she added, "I hope he stays that way, because Steven, who's eleven, is going to be a challenge. He's strong-willed, and opinionated. Always testing his limits. Jason, who's nine, is still figuring out his role in the family. Being the youngest, he can be quite charming and manipulative, when he wants something."

Christina chuckled. "My three are quite different as well. I've been impressed with Brad's willingness to take on the role of oldest male. I have to remind him every now and then, that I'm still in charge, and the final decisions are mine to make. I think, because there's no man in the house, he feels the need to step into that role, and somehow protect us."

"Aww, that's sweet."

Christina smiled, and nodded. "Yes, but sometimes, I feel he is worrying about things he shouldn't, and may be missing out on just being sixteen."

Donna reached over, and patted Christina's arm. "I'm sure, when everything settles down in your lives, Brad will turn into the normal obnoxious teen that he is destined to be!"

Christina made a face. "Geeze! I hope not!"

Both women laughed out loud. Donna pointed upstairs.

"Hey, let's go look at the clothes in that store."

Christina looked up to where she was pointing. "Coldwater Creek?"

Donna nodded, and took off towards the stairs. "I love their clothes!"

Christina mumbled, "I do too, if I could only afford them." *Oh, wait, I can!* Picking up her pace, she and Donna practically ran up the stairs.

"Hey, Mike," Sheriff Clifton called out, as he walked to the squad car.

Pausing, with his hand on the door handle to the office, the deputy turned, and said, "Yeah?"

Standing by the car door, the sheriff said, "I'm going to head out to the hospital, and check on Jesse McCoy's boy. I heard he was injured, and has had a tough time."

"He was injured? How?"

Shaking his head, the sheriff said, "Not exactly sure. Some kind of puncture wound. I haven't had a chance to talk to Jesse yet. Loraine just told me what she had heard."

Nodding, and opening the door, Mike said, "Maybe I'll drop by the hospital later, after I've checked around town."

Pulling into the hospital parking lot, Larry noticed a blue Chevette, and pulled into the space next to it. Stepping out of his vehicle, he checked his surroundings to see if anyone was in, or near the vehicle. Not seeing anyone, he cupped his hands on the passenger side window, and looked in. All he saw were empty bags and boxes from various fast food places—including Pizza Hut.

Dreading what he had to do next, the sheriff entered the hospital, and asked for Jimmy McCoy's room number.

Jamie Simmons stood in front of the vending machine, trying to decide if he wanted a Dr. Pepper, or Root Beer, when he saw the sheriff walk by—heading in the direction of Jimmy's room.

"Oh, man!" he mumbled. "I wonder what he's doing here?"

Poking his head out of the doorway, he watched as the uniformed man entered Jimmy's room. Not ready for a confrontation, Jamie abandoned the soda machine, and almost ran to his car. He had just put the key in the ignition, when he heard a tap on his window.

With his heart pounding, his hands shaking, and sweat pouring out every pore, he turned to see who was standing there. It wasn't who he thought.

Releasing the breath he was holding, he rolled down the window.

"Hey, Jamie. What are you doing here?"

Smiling, he said, "Hi, Sylvia. I was just here to visit Jimmy."

Sylvia, who many had mistaken as his twin sister, because of her red hair, fair skin, and blue eyes, smiled, and said, "Me too!"

Leaning on the sheriff's car, with her arms crossed, she asked, "How's he doing?"

Not wanting to appear nervous, he clamped his hands on the steering wheel, to keep them from shaking. "Okay, I guess."

"You guess? Didn't you see him?"

"I did. He's still out of it though. He had to have surgery on his leg, because of some kind of bleeding that wouldn't stop."

Frowning, she said, "Sounds serious."

Nodding, Jamie said, "I think it was, but from what his dad says, he should be okay, soon."

Cocking her head, she asked, "Will he come back to school next week?"

Shrugging, Jamie said, "I doubt it. I don't think he'll be able to walk."

Nodding, she said, "Well, guess I'd better go see him, and deliver this card."

"Card?" Jamie asked.

Holding the card up for Jamie to see, she said, "Yeah, a few of us got together, and made it. We felt sorry for him, having to be in the hospital and all."

"That's nice." Looking around nervously, Jamie said, "I need to get going."

"Oh, yeah. Okay. See ya."

Waving, Jamie pulled out of the parking spot, as she did a finger wave.

Still feeling like his heart was trying to find a new location besides his chest, he headed for home, wondering if the sheriff knew about his, and Jimmy's escapades.

"Sheriff." Jesse McCoy said, as he stood and extended his hand.

Larry removed his hat, and shook hands with Jesse. Looking over Jesse's shoulder to the sleeping young man, he asked, "So, how's your boy doing?"

Clearing his throat, Jesse said, "The Doc says he should be coming around soon. You knew he had some kind of arterial bleed, right?"

Shaking his head, Larry said, "No. I just heard he was in here for some kind of puncture wound."

Motioning to the doorway, Jesse said, "Here, let's talk in the hallway."

Laying his hat on a nearby chair, Larry said, "Sure."

Once out of his son's hearing range, Jesse explained about the puncture wound, resulting in complications because of the arterial leak.

Shaking his head, and reaching out to pat Jesse's shoulder, Larry said, "Well, I'm glad everything is working out."

Nodding, Jesse said, "Yeah, me too."

Stroking his chin whiskers, Larry said, "You up to talking a bit?"

Looking wary, Jesse said, "Yes. Why?"

"I have a few questions that maybe you can help answer."

Glancing in the room, to see his boy was still asleep, Jesse said, "How about we go down the hall to the visitors lounge?"

Placing his hand on Jesse's shoulder, Larry said, "Okay, lead the way."

Jesse felt an icy talon of dread wrap around his heart. He had a feeling that the sheriff knew more than he was indicating. *How honest do I have to be? So far, I've been able to cover, and avoid any clues that put my son, and Jamie at risk. What if the sheriff asks me directly?*

When they reached the lounge area, Larry asked, "You want some coffee, or something?"

Jesse shook his head. "Thanks, but I've had enough caffeine for today."

Larry nodded, and headed to the vending machine. He chose a Dr. Pepper, the favorite soda of most Texans.

Pulling a chair in front of Jesse, Larry popped the top off the can of soda, and said, "So remind me again how your boy got the puncture wound."

Jesse hesitated, as his mind raced. *How can I explain it, without implicating my son?*

Exhaling, he said, "Jimmy says he and Jamie were riding the dirt bike when it fell over, and he landed on something sharp."

Larry nodded, took a sip of his soda, and said, "Interesting. So you're saying that he and Jamie weren't near the oil refinery?"

Jesse shook his head.

"If you remember, we found a board with a nail that had some blood, and denim material on it. Well, I took those to have them analyzed, and the blood type on the nail matches your son's type."

Jesse blinked rapidly, thinking. *Jimmy has AB negative, a rare type of blood. Oh man, now what am I going to say?*

Larry leaned back in his chair, and sipped his Dr. Pepper. He didn't want to be confrontational, but wanted to appear calm, and relaxed.

He continued, "Don't you find it a bit odd, that your son ends up with a puncture wound, and his blood type matches the one on the nail?"

Jesse swallowed hard. Nodding slightly, but avoiding the sheriff's eyes.

Leaning forward, Larry asked, "So, what do you really think happened the other night?"

Jesse rubbed his forehead, and sighed heavily.

Larry continued, even though seeing his friend in emotional turmoil, made him feel like a jerk.

"Look, Jesse, I don't want you to say anything that could jeopardize your son, but I need to get to the bottom of this investigation. Your son, and Jamie Simmons, are the prime suspects as of now."

Jesse asked, "Have you talked to Jamie yet?"

Shaking his head, Larry said, "No, but I plan to sometime today. The noose is tightening around these boys, and I think the sooner we get this taken care of, the sooner we can all rest in peace. If these boys are guilty of the events on Christmas morning, then I would think they'd be nervous as jackrabbits. This has got to be eating at them."

Jesse nodded. "You're right about me not wanting to say anything further. I'm going to contact a lawyer, and see what he advises."

Larry nodded. "I think that's a good idea, Jesse. We've been friends for a long time, and I don't want anything to come between that, but as an officer of the law, I have to investigate any leads that may arise, and unfortunately, that includes your son, and Jamie."

Emptying the soda can, Larry stood, and deposited it in the garbage container next to the door.

Jesse stood as well, and extending his hand, said, "Thanks, Larry. I'll get back to you as soon as I meet with our lawyer."

"Thanks, Jesse. Even if your boy, and Jamie, are involved, I will vouch for them. They are good boys, and I don't want them to be incarcerated. This would be a first offense, and they have no prior juvenile records. Hopefully, they'll get a sympathetic judge, who will take this into consideration. If they're fortunate, they'll just get a fine, and have to do some community service. They'll probably be on probation for a while, as well."

Not knowing what else to say, Jesse nodded, tight lipped, and turned to head back to his son's room.

When Larry walked to his car, he noticed the blue Chevette was gone. He wasn't surprised. The boy probably panicked, and ran, when he saw the police car next to his. Sighing, he thought, *I guess I'll have to catch him at home, or at Pizza Hut. He can't hide forever.* Starting the engine, he sat in his car a moment, thinking about his conversation with Jesse. He felt sorry for the man. He was the Fire Chief, which was a respected position, and a single dad of a boy who was in the hospital, fighting for his life. Sometimes, Larry hated what his job forced him to do. Part of him wanted to let this whole incident just fade away. Unfortunately, there had been harm. Several firefighters had been injured at the scene of the fire, then, when the fire had traveled to the hospital, Christina had been injured. The damage to the cardiac unit had been extensive, and costly, as well. The people of Alva deserved an answer as to who was responsible. It was his job, and duty, to see that the people in his town were kept safe, and the perpetrators who caused conflict, or harm, were dealt with.

Larry pulled out of the parking lot, and headed to the car repair shop, where he was hoping to find Jack Simmons, and possibly Jamie.

His mind brought up an image of Jack, sitting in the office, crying. Larry had just told him about the car, which was found in the ditch next to the highway. Poor man. He'd always wondered why his wife would leave him and Jamie.

Pulling into a spot in front of the auto repair shop, he looked around for the blue Chevette. It wasn't there. Stepping out of the car, he stretched, put on his hat, and headed into the shop.

"Hey, Sheriff." One of the guys called out. "You need your car fixed?"

Larry waved, and shook his head. "Not today, Carl. I'm here to see Jack Simmons. Is he around?"

Carl said, "Yeah. He's out back, working on a truck. Want me to get him?"

Larry nodded. "Yes, please."

Soon, Jack walked in, wiping his hands on an oily rag.

"Afternoon, Sheriff. Heard you needed to speak to me?"

Larry looked around. "Is there anywhere we can speak in private?"

"Yeah, sure," Jack said, pointing to an office across the garage. "What's this about?"

"I'll tell you once we're in the office."

Jack nodded. "Okay."

Closing the door, Jack asked, "You want anything to drink?"

Pulling a chair out to sit in, Larry said, "No, thanks."

Sitting in the only other chair, across from the sheriff, Jack asked, "So, what brings you out here?"

Larry took a deep breath, and sighed.

"I really need to speak to your son. Do you know where he might be?"

Shaking his head, Jack said, "Sorry, no. I thought he was going to visit his friend Jimmy at the hospital, then I think he has to work later today. Not sure where he is right now." Pulling out his phone, he said, "I could call him, if you want."

Larry considered this. "Sure have him come here. Don't tell him I'm here, though."

Looking confused, Jack said, "Okay."

Jamie drove home, and parked his car in the garage, then closed the door.

Paranoid, much? Entering the house, he went to his bedroom to check on Little Lady, and her pups. He smiled when he saw her lying on her side, letting her hungry brood nurse. She raised her head, whimpered a little, and thumped her tail in greeting. He knelt beside her, and scratched under her chin, and around her ears. Speaking softly, he said, "You are such a sweet girl."

He sat silently for a moment, then said, "I think I'm in big trouble, Little Lady." She looked up at him with her big brown eyes, and whimpered. *It's like she knows what I'm saying,* he thought.

When the pups were satiated, she left them curled up on top of each other, and crawled into Jamie's lap. He continued to stroke her as he spoke.

"I don't think I broke any laws when I set off the fireworks, but if the sheriff finds out I called in a false bomb threat, and have been breaking into houses, plus the fire at the middle school, I think he might arrest me." He felt tears sting his eyes. "I didn't mean to hurt anyone, on any of those occasions, I was just trying to add some excitement to our dull town."

Little Lady thumped her tail, and licked his hand, as if saying she understood, and she still loved him.

"It's been so hard without my mom. Now we find out she died five years ago. I'm glad we have closure, but I had always hoped she was alive, and would come back for me. Now there's no hope." He felt tears well up, and slide down his face. Hugging the little dog to his chest, he let the tears fall, as the sobs shook his body. Little Lady began whimpering, and he realized he was holding her too tightly. He released her, and she went straight to her puppies. He had just finished wiping his eyes and nose with the hem of his shirt, when his phone rang.

Answering, he was surprised to hear his dad's voice.

"Hey, Jamie. Can you come down to the shop for a minute?"

"Uhm. I guess. Why?"

"I just need you to come here. Can you?"

"Sure, Dad." Looking at his watch, he said, "I have to be at work in an hour."

"That's okay, Son. This won't take long."

Beginning to feel a bit uneasy, he asked, "What is this about, Dad?"

"I'll tell you when you get here. I've gotta go. See you in a few minutes?"

"Sure."

Jamie changed his shirt, pet the dog and her pups, then headed out the door. All the way to the shop, his mind whirred.

Why would Dad ask me to come to the shop? He hardly ever asks me to come there. Maybe he has a new car for me! Anything would beat this old thing. He began imagining himself in a shiny, new, royal blue Corvette. He would be the envy of all the guys at school, and the girls would go crazy, wanting to ride in his new car.

Pulling in the parking lot, he was smiling when he exited his car. He waved, and greeted Carl and Henry, the two mechanics, as he entered the shop.

"Hey, Guys! Do you know where my dad is?"

"He's in the office with the sheriff," Carl said.

Jamie stopped in his tracks. *The sheriff? Why was the sheriff here?*

He was turning on his heels, to run back to his car, when his dad called out to him.

"Jamie! Where are you going? Get in here!"

Jamie let out air like a deflating balloon. *So much for a new car*, he thought.

He walked slowly to the office. Head down, shoulders slumped. One would think he was walking to his execution. Well, maybe he was in a way.

Sheriff Clifton stood, when Jamie entered the room. He held out his hand. Jamie slowly shook it, barely looking up. Larry thought he looked downright pitiful. *Poor kid.*

"Son, Sheriff Clifton is here to ask you a few questions. If you feel uncomfortable, or don't want to answer, I can stop the questioning, and we can call a lawyer."

Jamie perked up a bit. "You mean, I don't have to answer any questions if I don't want to?"

Larry spoke up. "Well, Son, you can refuse to talk to me, and you can get a lawyer if you want, but it might be in your best interest, if you just answer some questions."

Jamie bit his bottom lip, as he thought about his options. Sighing, he said, "Okay, I'll answer some of your questions. But, I can stop if I want to?"

Nodding, Larry said, "Yes. You have the right to have an attorney present, if you want. I can't force you to talk to me."

Thinking this over, Jamie said, "Okay."

They all sat in a semi-circle as Larry pulled out his note pad, and began asking the questions he had written down. He also set a tape recorder on the desk top.

Jamie eyed it suspiciously.

Larry said, "This is so I can remember what was asked, and said, so I can write it down later."

Jamie frowned, feeling his heart begin to race. He felt nauseous, light headed, and most of all, scared..

The sheriff, noticing the boy's discomfort, said, "It's okay, Jamie. Just relax."

Jamie took in a lungful of air, and released it slowly.

"Can we begin?" Larry asked.

Nodding, Jamie said, "Okay."

Larry asked, "Do you know a lady names Janet Washburn?"

Jamie shook his head. "Oh, wait. She goes to the Enlightened Ones meetings. I know her from there."

"Okay. Good." Larry said, nodding.

"Have you ever received a phone call from Janet Washburn?"

Shaking his head, Jamie said, "No. Not that I know of."

"Is your phone number 972-555-1234?"

"Yes." Jamie answered warily. "How do you know my number?"

Larry didn't answer, but asked another question. "Have you received text messages from the number 972-555-4422?"

Jamie's hands began to sweat, and he felt like his heart was about to jump out of his chest. Swallowing hard, he said, "Yes."

Nodding, Larry said, "Thank you for being honest. Do you know who that number belongs to?"

Jamie shook his head, "No Sir."

"Why were you receiving text messages, and what were they about?"

Jamie looked at his dad, who said, "Go on, Son. Answer the questions."

Jamie shook his head, and felt tears sting his eyes. Inside, he was screaming, *"I don't want to answer the questions!"*

Noticing his discomfort, Larry leaned forward, and said in a calm, quiet tone, "I know this is difficult, Son. I already know about the text messages. All you'll be doing is confirming what I know. It has to be on record that you received the messages, and what they contained."

Jamie hung his head, squeezing his eyes to stop the tears begging to escape. *Man up!* He told himself.

Taking a moment to calm himself, he wiped his eyes, blew out a lungful of air, sat up straight in his chair, and said, "Okay, I'll tell you."

He then told Larry about the anonymous phone calls, and text messages. How he had entered the Sander's house, and taken a few objects, but always returned them later. He didn't tell him that he still had the photo album, and planned one more break-in to return it. No. He didn't know who was on the other end of the line, but he would receive cash payments in a post office box after each assignment.

Larry nodded. "Thank you, Jamie. I have a few other questions now, and I would appreciate your continued honesty."

Jamie chewed on his bottom lip, and massaged his forehead. *Well, here goes my freedom,* he thought. *How could I have been so stupid to think I'd get away with all this stuff? I'm an idiot, for sure. It was bound to catch up with me. I hope I don't have to say anything about Jimmy. I doubt we'll be in a jail cell together.*

"So, now that we established the facts concerning the break ins at the Sanders, I need to talk to you about the other night. Christmas Eve."

Looking at his dad, who nodded, and said, "Go on Son."

Looking at the sheriff, Jamie said, "I have a question to ask you."

"Okay, shoot."

"Is that Janet Washburn, the lady I was communicating with on the phone?"

Nodding, Larry said, "I believe so. We've found evidence that points in that direction,"

Clearing his throat, Jack asked, "Where is this Washburn lady?"

"Right now, she's in the trauma unit at Dallas Memorial."

Looking shocked, Jamie said, "What? What happened?"

"Yes, what happened to her?" Jack asked. He had once been infatuated with Janet, and had enjoyed her company at the Enlightened Ones' meetings.

"She, and her daughter, were in a very serious car accident the week after Thanksgiving. She ran a stop sign, and plowed into a truck."

Jack said, "I remember hearing about that, but I never heard the names of the injured people. How's the little girl?"

"She's healing nicely. She had some internal bleeding, and has a broken arm, but she should be out of the hospital soon."

"Oh man! I was wondering why I hadn't heard from the person sending the text. If it was Janet, then…" Jamie let his voice trail off.

Nodding, the sheriff said, "Yes. That would explain the absence of communication." Clearing his throat, Larry said, "I still have a few questions to ask."

"Okay." Jamie said, running his hands through his hair. He looked at his watch. "I need to leave in a few minutes, to go to work. Can we continue the questioning tomorrow?"

Larry thought for a moment. "Let me ask one more question, then I want you, and your dad, in my office, at ten-o'clock tomorrow morning."

Nodding, Jamie said, "Yes, Sir."

"Okay, then," Larry said. "Here's the next question. Where were you around midnight Christmas Eve?"

"Remember how you said I didn't have to answer questions, if I was uncomfortable?"

Larry nodded, and bit his lip to keep from smirking, as he thought, *Got you, you little snot.*

Larry said, "Yes, but let me say this. If you don't answer, then I will assume that you were somewhere you shouldn't have been, and I can arrest you for hindering an investigation." Actually, he couldn't, but the kid didn't know that.

"So, what you're saying is, I'm considered guilty of something, if I don't say where I was, and if I was to admit being somewhere I shouldn't be, I'd still be considered guilty of something? What is that something I'd be guilty of?" Jamie asked, trying to look innocent.

Nodding, Larry gave an evasive answer. "That's what we have to determine. If you weren't home at that time, and have no witnesses as to your whereabouts, you would be a suspect in an ongoing investigation."

Jamie stood, and said, "Well shoot!" Looking at his dad, he said, "I think I'd like that lawyer now."

Jack and Larry exchanged looks. Larry stood, and said, "Well, I guess we're finished for now."

Pointing a finger at Jack, he said, "I still want y'all in the office at ten-o'clock. You'd best get on the phone, and set up a meeting with your lawyer."

Nodding, Jack said, "I will."

Jamie said, "I have to go to work. Guess I'll be seeing you tomorrow, Sheriff."

Leaving the auto shop, Jamie headed to work at Pizza Hut. He knew he had flustered the sheriff, but if he was going to be in trouble anyway, he wanted a good lawyer to work at getting him a lighter sentence. *Man, I wish I could talk to Jimmy before tomorrow. Maybe he's awake now.*

Arriving a few minutes before having to check in, Jamie sat in the car, and called Jimmy's room. A groggy sounding voice answered after several rings. "Hello?"

"Hey, Jimmy. It's Jamie. How are you doing?"

"I'm okay, I guess. I've been sleeping off and on, so I'm still pretty dopey."

"Yeah. You sound drunk."

"How would you know if I sounded drunk or not? I've never been drunk."

Jamie chuckled. "You're slurring your words, and you sound like you have a wad of cotton in your mouth."

"Oh, right. I guess I do sound drunk, then. Why are you calling? I thought you were coming to visit me?"

"I did come to the hospital, but I had to leave. I gotta tell you that the sheriff is asking where I was, and what I was doing on Christmas eve. My dad is going to get a lawyer, and we have to go back to the sheriff's office tomorrow for more questioning. I'm kinda scared, Jimmy. What if he finds out the truth? We'll be put in jail for sure."

"Wow! This is too much to wrap my mind around right now. I think we'd best talk tomorrow. In the mean time, stay strong. I think we'd best tell the truth, and let the pieces fall where they may."

Blowing out a lungful of air, Jamie said, "Alright. I'll talk to you tomorrow, when you're more awake."

Exiting the car, and putting the phone in his pocket, Jamie looked up to the sky and said, "Alright, powers that be, please help."

Walking in the front door, Jamie saw his boss heading his way.

Pointing his finger at Jamie, he said, "Jamie, I'd like to see you in my office."

Jamie's heart began to gallop again. *Oh, this day just keeps getting better and better*, he thought, as he walked, slumped shouldered, towards the back office. Thinking, he was probably going to get fired, he prepared his mind and heart, for the words.

"Come in, Jamie. Please close the door behind you." Curtis Shaffer, manager of Pizza Hut said, as he walked behind his desk and sat.

Nodding, Jamie did as he was told. He couldn't look Mr. Shaffer in the eyes. Standing in front of his boss's desk, with his hands in his pockets, and his chin almost touching his chest, he shifted his weight from one foot to the other. Noticing this, Curtis sighed and said, "Jamie, have a seat."

"Yes, Sir." Jamie said, taking a seat in the chair across from the desk. He still couldn't bring himself to look Mr. Shaffer in the eyes.

Curtis watched the boy for a moment. Jamie shifted in his chair, and wrung his hands. Every now and then, he'd swipe at his nose and eyes. *Was he crying?* Jamie didn't look like the typical seventeen year old. At this moment, he looked about twelve. Compassion filled Curtis's heart.

Leaning forward, he spoke quietly.

"Jamie, look at me."

Jamie slowly raised his head, and met Mr. Shaffer, eye to eye. The boy's eyes were red rimmed.

"Jamie, why don't you tell me what happened Christmas Eve?"

"Christmas Eve?" Jamie whispered.

Nodding, Curtis said, "You know, with the fireworks, and refinery fire?"

Jamie looked down again, and pinched his bottom lip between his thumb and index finger.

Leaning back in his chair, Curtis folded his arms across his chest, and waited.

Jamie had conflicting thoughts. *How much does he know? Should I tell him the whole truth? What if I don't? Is he gonna fire me? What should I do?*

Curtis watched Jamie's eyes dart back and forth, as he fiddled with his lip. *He's trying to decide how much he should tell me*, thought Curtis.

Leaning forward, Curtis said, "Look, Jamie. I know you're struggling with what you should say, and how much you should say, but I need to tell you that the sheriff has already been here, and told me about his suspicions."

Jamie looked up with fear in his eyes.

Holding up his hands, Curtis said, "I know you must be afraid of what will happen next, but if you were involved, then you need to get that off your conscious, otherwise, it will haunt you day and night, and eat at you like a cancer."

Curtis saw Jamie shift to the edge of his seat, like he wanted to take off running.

"Jamie, I'm your boss, but I'm also your friend. Why don't you tell me what happened, then it'll be easier to tell the sheriff. I've found over the years, that the more the truth is spoken, the easier it becomes to keep speaking it. If a lie is spoken, it gets more difficult, because details get blurred, and it's harder to keep track of them."

Jamie sighed heavily. "Alright, Mr. Shaffer, I'll tell you. Maybe you can help me sort out this mess I've gotten myself into."

Leaning forward, and resting his elbows on the desk top, Curtis listened as Jamie told him the details of the Christmas Eve excitement.

Christina, and her crew, walked with Donna, and her boys, to the mall exit, and said their goodbyes. When Donna, and her boys were out of sight, Nicky asked, "Can we go on the coaster ride one more time?"

"Please!" Stacey added.

Christina rolled her eyes. "Alright. Once more, then we need to head home."

The kids took off running towards the coaster, as Brad and Eric stayed behind.

"Don't you boys want to ride the coaster one more time?" She asked.

Shaking his head, Brad said, "Nah, but we'd like to go to the arcade, and play a game or two, if that's okay."

Christina smiled, and nodded. "Alright. I just remembered that Linda asked me to find the locker with her and her mom's coats. They were here the day of the bomb threat, and were unable to get their coats from the locker. Then they were in the car accident, and never made it back. I'll go get them, then come back to this bench, and wait for y'all."

Brad nodded, and said, "Okay."

The older boys sauntered to the arcade area, and disappeared behind the large video machines.

She walked over to a map of the mall, and found the locker area. Pulling out the key Linda had given her, she found the correct locker, opened it, and saw two winter coats. She headed back to the sitting area. Someone had left a magazine on the bench, and seeing no one around to claim it, picked it up, and began perusing through it, as she sipped her bottled water. There was an article about the 911 terrorists attacks.

The whole nation, as well as the world, was in such turmoil, as fear, and paranoia seemed to rule the news media. She couldn't help but feel a bit paranoid herself. It seemed the terrorists were unrelenting in their goal to eliminate "The Great Satan," which was the United States, as well as any other infidel, who didn't believe in the Islamic religion.

The words, "fear not, trust me, and be still," echoed in her mind and spirit. She knew God was in control, and that gave her some peace, but being a single mom, she couldn't help the growing concern in her heart. and mind, for her children's lives. All it took was to be at the wrong place. at the wrong time, then boom, you're injured, or gone. She wondered how the thousands who lost loved ones, or those who were injured, back in September, were doing this first holiday season, after such a gut wrenching, tragic event. She also wondered why God would let such an event take place.

She had studied the book of Revelation, and knew that before Christ returned again, there would be increasing turmoil in the world—not only involving humans, but nature as well. Sighing, she thought, *I may not be able to control what happens around me, but I can do my best to prepare my kids for survival, physically and spiritually.*

She was so caught up in her thoughts, she didn't see the four younger kids walking towards her.

"Mom?" Nicky said, as he approached, and placed a hand on her arm.

Christina jumped, dropping her water bottle, which began to leak on the mall's tiled floor.

"Oops! Sorry, Mom." Nicky said, as he helped retrieve the bottle. Stacey ran over to one of the food counters, and grabbed a handful of napkins. Within minutes, everything was cleaned up.

"It's okay, Nicky. I was almost finished with it anyway." Looking at the group of kids, she asked, "Y'all ready to hit the road?"

She received affirmative replies.

"Nicky, would you and Danny go get your brother, and Eric. They're in the video game room."

"Sure, Mom," Nicky said, as he, and Danny, took off.

Stacey and Carmen sat on the bench next to Christina. Looking at the girls, she asked, "So did y'all have fun shopping?"

They both nodded.

"Mom, you've got to see the cute earrings Carmen and I got at that jewelry store upstairs."

The girls pulled the treasures from their bags, and showed them to Christina.

"Those are both beautiful!" She said, after inspecting each set.

Christina stood, gathering her shopping bags. Stacey asked, "What did you get, Mom?"

"I just got a few undergarments, and t-shirts."

Stacey tried to peek in the bags.

Christina pulled them closer to her side. "I'll show you when we get home," she whispered.

Stacey smiled, and nodded, then noticing the label on one of the bags, arched an eyebrow.

"Victoria's Secret?" She whispered.

Christina shrugged. "I needed some new things."

Looking up, she saw the four boys approaching.

"Okay, Gang. Let's head out to the van."

The drive home was uneventful. She enjoyed listening to the kids various topics of conversation. One, however, drew her attention.

"So, Brad," Eric said, "Did you know Sheriff Clifton might know who set off the fireworks, and the fire?"

Brad shook his head. "No. Who is it?"

"Well, according to my dad, who heard it from the sheriff's deputy, Mike Owens, they think it's that kid who works at Pizza Hut, and looks like he could be your twin."

"Jamie Simmons?" Brad asked.

Nodding, Eric said, "Yeah, that's him."

Brad considered this. "I don't know him, personally. I see him around school, though. Did your dad mention how they came to that conclusion?"

Shaking his head, Eric said, "Nah. I did hear that the sheriff is investigating the break-ins as well. According to my dad, the sheriff thinks it might be the same kid."

"Really? That's kinda weird. They're such different actions."

Holding up his hands, Eric said, "Hey, I'm just the messenger."

"Spy, is more like it."

Eric feigned innocence. "Me? A spy?" Nodding his head, he said, "Alright. I am. I actually overheard my dad, and Mike, talking the other day."

"So your dad didn't tell you those things?"

Shaking his head, Eric said, "Nope. I totally listened in."

"Well, you'd best not tell anyone else. What if Jamie is innocent? Rumors like that could ruin his reputation."

"Does he even have a reputation? From what I've heard, and observed, he's quite a loner."

Shaking his head, Brad said, "Doesn't matter. If you aren't one-hundred percent sure of something, you shouldn't say it."

Sighing, Eric said, "Yeah. You're right. I wouldn't want someone accusing me of something I didn't do."

Christina was proud of her son. Sticking up for the underdog. *Good job, Brad.*

Her mind wandered to thoughts of Linda, which then led to thoughts of Janet. Glancing at the dashboard clock, which read 8:30, she thought, *I wonder if Aaron could tell me how Linda's doing? Maybe I could call him when I get home. I don't think he'd mind, unless he's trying to put Sammie to bed.*

She pulled the van into her driveway precisely at 8:50. As she stepped out of the van, her cell-phone rang. Digging in her purse for the phone, she dropped the keys. Stacey picked them up, and whispered, "I'll go unlock the door."

Christina nodded, as she answered the phone. "Hello?"

"Christina, it's Aaron." Her heart did a triple beat.

"Oh, hi, Aaron."

"Am I catching you at a bad time?"

"No, not really. We just arrived home after going to the movies in Waco."

"You want me to call you back in a few minutes?"

"Oh, Aaron, that would be nice. I've got six kids to get in, and settled for the night."

"Okay, how about in, say, a half-hour?"

Nodding, she said, "That would be perfect."

They disconnected, and she shook her head, smiling. Her heart and mind were once again in a battle. *Aaron, or Steven? I can't have them both, that's for sure.*

True to his word, Aaron called back in thirty minutes. He asked how her day went, and she gave him a condensed version.

She said, "I was thinking about calling you tonight, but was concerned it would be too late."

"Oh. Why were you going to call?"

"I wanted to know when you were planning to release Linda, and if you'd heard how Janet was doing?"

He was silent for a moment, and she could imagine him nodding, and stroking his goatee.

"Well, I plan to release Linda either tomorrow, or Monday. She needs to be fever free, however. Today, it was slightly elevated, so I think it should continue to drop. As far as Janet, I talked to her primary Doctor this morning, and he said she's slowly improving. They removed her ventilator, and she's breathing on her own. He plans to keep her sedated for a few more days, to give her body more time to heal."

Nodding, Christina said, "I see. Well, I'll certainly keep praying for her."

"Yes. We all should."

Clearing her throat, Christina asked, "So how are the CCU repairs coming along?"

"I checked on the progress before leaving the hospital today, and most of the piles of garbage are gone. I still heard a few electric motors, probably drills, and what sounded like hammering."

Sighing, Christina said, "I'll be glad when we can get back to the unit. Caring for our patients on the Med-Surg unit, is like trying to cook a gourmet meal in the living room, when most of your equipment is still in the kitchen, which is being remodeled, and you can't get to it."

Chuckling, he said, "That's a good analogy."

There was silence for a moment, then he asked, "So when will you be back to work?"

"I'll be there Monday afternoon. Mrs. Ferguson has me working the afternoon shifts on Monday, Wednesday, and Friday of next week. Hopefully, I'll get back to my regular schedule soon."

"Are y'all planning on attending church tomorrow?" He asked.

Christina nodded, and said, "Yes. I'm not sure about Sunday School, but definitely church service. Depends if all the kids get up and dressed, and we can get there on time."

"Why don't we plan on going out to lunch after the service? I'd like to discuss the plans I have for Linda's care."

"Sure. Where would you like to go?"

"I was thinking we could go out to Zimmerman's steak house. Have you been there?"

"Yes, and it's wonderful, but I'll have six kids to feed. I'm not sure I can afford that."

Aaron chuckled. "I am treating, so no need to worry about that."

Christina chuckled, "Well, remember there are four boys that could probably eat a whole cow. The bill might be a bit expensive."

"I appreciate your concern, but I'm pretty sure I can afford whatever it may cost."

Sighing, Christina said, "Well, I'm glad it's your wallet, and not mine!"

Laughing, he said, "I'm glad to accommodate. I'll see y'all tomorrow at church, then."

"Thanks, Aaron. See you then."

She heard Sammie asking for a drink of water in the background, then Aaron's answer.

"Okay, Honey. Just one more minute, and I'll it."

Christina said, "Sounds like you have daddy duty."

"Yep. Gotta go. Have a good night." With that last statement, he disconnected.

"Mom?" She heard Nicky call from the family room.

"Yes, Nicky." She answered, setting the phone on the counter.

"We thought it'd be fun to play a game."

Nodding, she asked, "What did you have in mind?"

Stacey said, "Since there are seven of us, we decided to play Mexican Train. That way we can all play."

"That sounds like fun. Why don't y'all get it set up, and I'll go pop some popcorn."

"Hey, Mom," Brad called.

"Yeah, Brad."

"Do we have any Dr. Pepper?"

Grinning, she answered. "Do elephants have trunks?"

She heard giggling. She called out, "Brad, why don't you come get the drinks?"

"Sure, Mom." A second later, he, and Eric, joined her in the kitchen.

"Good thing I stopped for sodas on my way home from work yesterday."

As she grabbed several bags of popcorn from the cabinet, she watched as Brad handed six can of pop to Eric, who had a difficult time holding them all.

"Hey, Man! I can't carry all of these!" Eric said, shuffling the cans in his arms.

Brad closed the fridge door, and said, "Okay. I'll carry a couple." He grabbed two, and headed to the family room.

Eric groaned, as he rearranged the four cans left in his arms. Mumbling under his breath, he said, "Thanks, Man. If I drop one of these, I'm giving it to you."

Christina stifled a giggle, as she put a package of pop corn in the microwave. Three minutes later, it was done. Before emptying it in a bowl, she popped another package in.

She was vaguely aware of the noise coming from the family room, as her mind took her back to several nights before David's death. They had begun family fun night when Brad was six, and Stacey and Nicky were too young to care. As they aged, they began to participate more, adding to the chaos and fun. They had begun with simple games, then progressed to more challenging ones. Every now and then, David would bring home a new book, video, or puzzle they would all read, watch, or work on together.

The microwave dinged, and she removed the bag, and replaced it with another. She took the big bowl of popcorn into the family room, set it on the table, and watched as six sets of hands grabbed at the contents.

"Goodness! Y'all act like you haven't eaten in hours!"

"Well, actually," Nicky said, "It has been a few hours."

Christina considered this. "You're right. Guess I'd better cook up at least a dozen more bags of popcorn."

Nicky rolled his eyes. "Maybe not a dozen, but at least ten more. Please."

Christina shook her head, and went back to the kitchen. *Maybe I should make a tray with cheese, crackers, and summer sausage.* Rummaging through the fridge, she found a bag of apples and oranges. *I think I'll cut those up too,* she thought.

"Hey, Kids!" Christina called, "Go ahead and start without me. I'm gonna make up a snack tray. I'll be in in a minute."

"Okay." Stacey said, as she asked, "Anyone have a double they can start with?"

Danny said, "Oh! I do! I do!"

Christina tuned them out as she prepared the food. She didn't hear her cell phone buzzing on the counter.

Cindy closed her phone, returning it to her jacket pocket. She'd try calling Christina again before going to bed. She had to tell her about Ed's proposal. She felt giddy, and lightheaded. *Did true happiness cause that?* She wondered.

After accepting Ed's proposal, and spending a few quiet moments with him, she had slipped away to the bathroom, to call her best friend in the world—Christina. *Who, should have answered her phone, doggone it!*

There was a knock on the door. "You okay, Mom?" Samara asked, sounding worried.

"I'm fine, Honey. I'll be out in a minute."

"Okay. Stephanie and Jason are leaving, and others are getting ready to go to bed. I know you want to say good-bye."

Flushing the toilet she hadn't used, she said, "Right," and opened the door.

It was a bit chaotic the next few minutes, as family members hugged each other, and headed to their various destinations.

Cindy returned to the porch where Stephanie, holding the baby, and Jason, who was holding their toddler, were standing. Stephanie was hugging her brother.

"So what are y'all planning to do tomorrow? She asked, as she shifted the baby to her other arm.

Ed, seeing Cindy, pulled her to his side, wrapping an arm around her. "I think we'll go to church, then out to eat. I'd like to take my ladies to see all the marvelous sights in, and around LaMesa, after that."

Nodding, Stephanie said, "Sounds nice." Looking at Cindy, she said, "Seeing all the sights in, and around LaMesa, will take about five minutes."

Holding Abigail in his arms, Jason leaned over and whispered that he'd get their sleepy girl in her car seat.

Cindy shrugged, looking up at Ed. "I'm sure it will be an exciting, and educational five minutes."

"We'll see you at church, but can we tag along for lunch?"

Nodding, Ed said, "Sure. The more the merrier."

Handing the baby to Jason, Stephanie asked, "Where are y'all planning to go for lunch?"

"I'll get him strapped in, and I'll be right back," Jason whispered, not wanting to interrupt the dialogue.

Ed said, "I thought we could go to that bar-b-q place, north of town. My mouth is watering, just thinking about those juicy ribs they serve."

Stephanie nodded, and punched Ed on the arm. "Good choice, Bro."

Rubbing the assaulted arm, he said, "Ow! To be so tiny, you sure pack a wallop!"

Rolling her eyes, and crossing her arms across her chest, she said, "Seriously? You're such a wimp."

Cindy was biting her bottom lip, trying to keep a giggle in. She knew Ed was no wimp, and figured his protestations were all for show. So...she punched him on the other arm, which felt hard as a rock, making her wonder what kind of exercise regimen he was following—*lifting boxcars, perhaps?*

Once everyone had left the porch, and headed upstairs to the bedrooms prepared for them, Ed and Cindy sat on the porch swing, enjoying the quiet, cool evening.

Putting his arm around Cindy's shoulder, and pulling her close, Ed said, "Well, what do you think of my crazy family."

Cindy sighed. "Oh, Ed. I love them all! Do you think they like me?"

"Of course! They love you, and Samara."

"You're not just saying that to make me feel better, are you?"

Lifting her chin with his opposite hand, he said, "Cindy. Trust me. They love you. When you were in the bathroom, all of my sisters, and my mom, made it a point to tell me how much they love you and Samara."

"Okay. I guess I'm a little insecure. I've never had anyone's family love, and accept me, like yours has. Well, unless you count Christina."

Leaning back on the swing, he said, "Ah, yes. Christina. Have you called her yet?"

Nodding, she said, "Yeah. I tried, but she didn't answer. I'll try again later, or tomorrow."

Shivering, Cindy snuggled closer to Ed.

Feeling her shiver, Ed asked, "You getting cold?"

"Yeah," she answered, "but, I don't really want to go in yet."

Ed reached to retrieve a blanket from the rocking chair close by, and wrapped it around Cindy's shoulders.

"Thanks, Ed."

Looking at his watch, he said, "The temp is dropping pretty quickly. I heard on the radio that a few inches of snow are predicted tonight, with flurries tomorrow."

Cindy sat up. "Really? No wonder it's getting colder. We can still go to church, and all, tomorrow, right?"

Nodding, he said, "Of course. We're not gonna let a little snow stop our exciting tour of LaMesa!"

After a few more minutes of enjoying the quiet time, Cindy said, "Okay, I'm officially chilled to my bones!"

Ed nodded, and said, "Well, good. I was wondering if you were going to admit to being cold, or just sit here until we turned to popcicles."

Cindy stood, wrapping the blanket around her shoulders, and put her hands on her hips.

"Oh, I see. You won't admit you're cold, because...you're too macho?"

"No!"

Cindy raised her eyebrows, and stared at him.

He finally nodded, and said, "Alright. I was trying to be tough, and manly."

She reached out her hand, and he took it, pulling her onto his lap. She giggled.

"Ed! We need to go in, before anyone hears us."

"I know. I just want to tell you again, that I love you, and can hardly wait for you to be my wife."

He kissed her lightly, and stood up, holding her close.

Looking into his eyes, she said, "I love you too, and can hardly wait to marry you."

They kissed, and heard the front screen door open.

Pulling apart, they saw Samara standing in the opening with her arms crossed across her chest.

With obvious annoyance in her voice, she asked, "Mom? Are you coming in soon?"

Cindy said, "In a minute, Hon."

Looking up at Ed, she said, "I'll see you in the morning."

He watched, as Cindy and Samara walked through the door, disappearing into the dimly lit house.

When Jamie finished telling Mr. Shaffer about his involvement in the Christmas Eve fiasco, his boss leaned back in his chair, stroked his chin whiskers, and nodded. Silence ruled the room for several moments. Jamie sat bent over, with his head down, and his hands clasped. He just knew he was going to be fired.

Finally, Mr. Shaffer said, "Jamie. What you've told me doesn't sound so bad. Your actions didn't cause any harm to anyone, and no damage to any property. I think you should tell the sheriff what you told me. He's a pretty reasonable man, and I doubt the punishment will be severe."

Jamie nodded. "Yeah. I guess I could come clean tomorrow."

Nodding, Curtis said, "The sooner, the better."

Jamie raised his head, and asked, "Are you gonna fire me?"

Curtis smiled, and said, "No, Jamie. You're one of my best employees. However, I will give you some time off, if you need it."

Jamie nodded, and sighed heavily. "Thanks, Mr. Shaffer. I really like working here."

Curtis stood, "Well, you best get your apron on, and get to work."

Jamie stood, wiped his palms on his jeans, and reached out to shake his boss's hand.

"Thanks again, Sir."

Curtis nodded, and watched as Jamie left the room with his head high, and his shoulders squared. *He is a good kid,* he thought. *Sure hope this all works out for him.*

He sat down at his large industrial desk, and began sorting through receipts. He had a long night ahead of him, as he looked at the pile of papers before him. He had to get his finances settled before the new year, which was quickly approaching.

After leaving the boss's office, Jamie went to the restroom, splashed water on his face, and washed his hands. He felt as if a heavy mantle had been lifted off his shoulders. Looking up, he said, "Thank you God, or whoever helped. I appreciate it."

After composing himself, he joined the other team members as they took orders, and prepared pizzas. He was the chosen one to make deliveries, which he enjoyed, as it allowed him to see how other people lived.

As he drove to one of the customer's homes, he passed by the post office, which reminded him of the money he had retrieved from there, and the lady, Janet Washburn, whom he hadn't heard from because she was in the hospital in Dallas. His mind took him further on the rabbit trail, and by the time he reached the customer's home, he was planning the next break-into the Sander's home. *I have to return the album,* he thought. *It would be bad, if somehow the sheriff found it in my possession.*

On his way back to Pizza Hut, he let his mind play different scenarios as to how, and when, he would carry out his plan of returning the photo album. He finally settled on new year's eve. He figured the family would stay up late to welcome in the new year, and then they would be in their deepest sleep around three a.m., which would be an ideal time to break in. *I have to do something about the dog,* he thought. *Maybe I can sneak another dog cookie to him, when he goes out for the last time. That would mean, I'd have to be there around midnight. Knowing my dad's new interest in me, he may suggest we start the new year together. If so, I'll have to wait until he goes to sleep to take off. He's a pretty heavy sleeper, so I doubt if he'll hear my car start up.*

After playing his plans over, and over in his mind, he finally settled on one that seemed most logical, and safe. New Year's eve was a couple of days away, which was okay. *Why is the thought of entering the Sander's home causing me anxiety?*

After releasing a deep cleansing breath, and wiping his sweaty palms on his jeans, he exited the car, and entered the back door to Pizza Hut.

Grabbing the cell phone off the counter, and putting it in her pocket, Christina poured the last bag of popcorn into a bowl. Heading into the family room, she felt her phone vibrate. Pulling it out of her pocket, she realized there were two missed calls, and two messages waiting to be read. Bringing up the message page, she saw that she had a message from Cindy, and Lisa. Pushing the buttons to bring Lisa's to her screen, she read: "*Hey y'all, just wanted you to know we arrived safely back in Dallas, and have our two beautiful children with us. I'll be in touch about plans for the welcome home party.*"

"Oh, how wonderful!" Christina mumbled, as she brought up the next message.

"*Christina, I'll call you tomorrow morning. I have exciting new to share!*"

I wonder if Ed proposed to her? Glancing at the clock, which read, nine-forty-five, she decided it may be too late to call. Mumbling to herself, she said, "Guess I'll find out tomorrow."

"Find out what, tomorrow?" Stacey asked, as she passed her mother, on the way to the bathroom.

"Cindy left me a message saying she had some exciting news, but she'd call tomorrow to tell me what it is."

Stacey cocked her head. Grinning she asked, "You think Ed asked her to marry him?"

Shrugging, Christina said, "Maybe."

Clasping her hands together, and grinning from ear to ear, Stacey said, "Oh, I hope so! That would be so awesome!"

Smiling, and nodding in agreement, Christina said, "Yes, it would be."

Jesse McCoy sat by his son's bedside, chastising himself once again, as thoughts of the past five years, danced through his mind.

Rubbing his tired eyes, he rested his head on his fingertips, as he leaned forward, allowing his forehead to rest against the mattress, and silently let the tears come.

Five years worth of tears came pouring out. Tears of regret, for having wasted so many years, tears of sorrow, for losing Sheila, tears of fear, of losing his son, and tears of anger, because it had, quite literally, taken a two-by-four across his head, to wake him out of his emotional slumber.

Jimmy, still feeling groggy from the pain meds, felt his bed shaking. Opening his eyes a bit, he looked down at his dad, realizing that the shaking was due to his dad's sobbing uncontrollably. *Why is he so sad?* Lifting his hand, he laid it on his dad's shoulder.

Jesse stopped crying, rubbed his eyes, took a deep breath, released it, and felt a calm wash over him. Sitting up, he looked into the compassion filled eyes of his son.

"Dad?" He whispered.

"Yes, Son?"

"It's okay."

"What's okay, Son?"

Feeling his eyes struggling to stay open, Jimmy whispered, "Everything is okay. Mom said so."

Jesse stood, and reached down to pull his son into a hug. Whispering, he said, "Yes, it is now."

Jesse felt Jimmy go limp in his arms. He thought he had fallen asleep, and gently laid his head back down on the pillow. Tenderly brushing a damp strand of hair out of his sons eyes, he was aware of how pale he looked. Placing his hand on his son's chest, he realized he wasn't breathing. Panic filling his mind, he began shaking the boy, as he yelled, "Someone, come help!"

Within seconds, a nurse came in. Realizing the boy wasn't breathing, or reacting to stimuli, she hit the red button on the wall, and a team of hospital personnel came rushing in, bringing the cardiac resuscitation equipment.

He heard the announcement over the intercom, "Code Blue, room 301."

Soon, there were several people working on his son, and he could do nothing, but stand in the corner and watch.

As if the hospital room wasn't crowded enough, Dr. Dawson, and Dr. Carmichael entered, and began their own assessments and procedures. He was familiar with some of the medical jargon, from his fire-fighting, and rescue training, but some of the terms, and procedures, were foreign to him.

He felt a fear so powerful, it dropped him to his knees. It was the same fear he felt when Sheila lay on her hospital bed, dying. "No, no, no," He mumbled. "Please, God, spare my son. I'm sorry for being such a lousy dad. I promise, I'll do better. Please, please let him live."

It was as if he were in a box, surrounded by people, and sound, but unable to see, or understand what was happening around him. His only thought was the well-being of his son. Nothing else mattered.

After what seemed like hours, but in reality was only a few minutes, he felt a hand on his shoulder. When he felt the pressure, reality came slamming back, and it took his breath away. Good thing he was kneeling on the floor, or he would have fallen for sure.

Looking up, with tear-rimmed eyes, he saw both grim-faced doctors, standing in front of him.

Putting out a hand, Dr. Dawson helped him to his feet.

Looking over at the bed, Jesse saw his son's still, pale body.

Catching his breath, he looked at both doctors, who shook their heads.

Dr. Carmichael said, as he reached out to steady Jesse, "I'm so sorry, Jesse. We did all we could."

"What? No. You have to do more. He can't be gone!"

Clearing his throat, Dr. Dawson said, "We think he must have had a blood clot, that went to his lung, or brain. We won't know for sure, until the autopsy is done."

Jesse pushed both men aside, and went to his son. Lifting his limp body, he cradled him in his arms, weeping, and encouraging him to wake up.

Both doctors wiped their eyes. Even though they had both lost patients over the years, it was especially difficult to lose a young one. Especially someone they knew.

Both men went to Jesse, and stood by him, resting their hands on his shoulders.

The other hospital personnel quietly went about the business of cleaning the room. Jesse was totally unaware of what was going on around him. He wasn't even aware of the doctors leaving, or how the room was quiet as a tomb, until an hour or so later, when a nurse came in, and asked if she could prepare the body for transport to the autopsy room.

"What? Autopsy? They're going to cut my son up like a piece of meat? No! You can't take him. He's going to wake up any minute now." Looking down at his son, he continued stroking his face, and whispering for him to wake up.

The nurse nodded, and quietly left the room.

Soon after, the hospital chaplain entered the room.

"Mr. McCoy?"

Not taking his eyes off his son, Jesse answered, "Yes?"

"Mr. McCoy, I'm pastor Dan Jenkins."

Still not looking up, Jesse said, "Yeah? So? What are you doing here?"

Noticing the empty chair by the bed, the pastor sat, folding his hands in his lap.

He sat there in silence for a while, before Jesse acknowledged his presence. Jesse gently touched his son's face, then turned, and looked at the chaplain.

"Why are you still here?" Jesse asked, anger clouding his face.

"I don't want you to be alone." The chaplain responded, in a quiet, gentle tone.

Throwing his hands up, and with bitterness in his voice, Jesse said, "Well, I guess I'd better get used to it! First my wife, now my son? I don't need you, your religion, or your God!"

The chaplain nodded slightly, letting him rant. He understood the anger stage of grief. He had experienced it himself, when his son had died of an overdose of heroin.

With clenched teeth, Jesse said, "How do you expect me to believe in a God who has taken so much from me? He is cruel, and I hate Him!"

"Jesse." Dan said in almost a whisper, as he watched the man pace back and forth, in the small room.

"Jesse." He said again, a little louder.

"What?" Jesse yelled, as he turned to face the man, sitting in the chair. He really wanted to punch him in the face. *Well, maybe not him, but certainly God.*

"Jesse, I'm not here to speak to you about God, or religion. I'm just here, so you won't have to be alone in your grief. I know this is extremely difficult for you to accept, and honestly, I don't have any answers to why it had to happen. Just because I am a chaplain, and pastor, doesn't mean I totally understand God, and His ways. I just know, it is a little easier to deal with such horrendous grief, when someone is near by. You don't have to talk to me, unless you want to. I will be here as long as you are."

Jesse's shoulders slumped, and he placed a hand over his mouth to stifle a sob wanting to escape.

As tears ran down his cheeks, he asked, "What am I going to do? When I lost my wife, I thought I could never survive. Then I ended up shutting myself off from my son, and it's just been over the past few days, that I have worked through those issues. We were actually talking. If we had had just a little more time."

Patting a chair next to him, Dan said, "Sit."

Jesse did. Leaning forward, he buried his face in his hands, and sobbed.

Dan reached over, and patted the grieving man's back, remembering how he felt when his son had died three years ago. No words could ever be spoken, that would comfort a wound so deep. The sorrow, anger, and guilt, was unfathomable. Unless one has been through those feelings themselves, they have no clue. Yes, he would remain with this deeply wounded man, as long as he felt God's prompting to do so. He prayed that Jesse would find the strength to go on, and not allow grief to steal his life. He knew, from his own experience, that anger, and grief, would eventually turn to acceptance. He still thought of his son daily, but as time progressed, the pain, and sorrow, became less and less. He could almost feel his heart mending itself. Oh yes, there would be a huge scar, so to speak, but at least his life force wasn't continuously leaking out.

After an hour or so, the nurse, and Dr. Carmichael, came back in, and asked if she could take the body. Jesse nodded, as tears continued to run down his face.

The chaplain stood beside Jesse, as he said goodbye to his boy. Dan felt tears slip from his own eyes, not bothering to wipe them away. It was as if he was saying good-bye to his own son all over again.

Dr. Carmichael handed the signed documents to the Coroner's aides, and stood to one side of the room, watching in silence as they loaded Jimmy's limp body onto the gurney. They would take him to the Coroner's lab, where the cause of death would be determined. Dr. Carmichael felt a tightness in his chest, and a burning in his eyes, as he watched the proceedings.

CHAPTER 6

When Christina rolled over to turn off the alarm, she felt an odd sensation in her chest. Not pain, but an anxiety of sorts. Like when she had had too much caffeine. She felt her pulse on her wrist, then her neck. It was a little fast, but not so abnormal to cause concern.

"That's weird."

She crawled out of bed, and did her normal morning routine, thinking the anxiety would dissipate. It didn't. She drank her coffee, wrote a list of chores to do, then spent a few minutes reading scripture, and praying. It was a beautiful Sunday morning, and she was looking forward to attending the church service, then having lunch with Aaron and Sammie. When she heard the noise of a toilet flushing, feet walking, and murmuring voices, she began mixing up pancake batter, and putting strips of bacon in a pan to put in the oven.

As she worked, thoughts of the hospital danced across her mind. She would be so thankful when the cardiac unit would be repaired, and they could get back to a more normal schedule. It was weird being on the Med-Surg unit, especially when she had one or two cardiac patients, and a couple of surgical patients. They had different health issues to deal with, which she wasn't accustomed to. She didn't mind working the afternoon schedule while the kids were on vacation, but she didn't want this to be a permanent schedule, even if there were a few perks.

Not only was she honing her Med-Surg skills, she was renewing her friendship with Libby. They had traveled in different circles in junior-high, and high-school, but had maintained a casual friendship. She remembered being jealous of Libby, because of her beauty, outgoing personality, and the well known fact that every boy in high-school had a crush on her. Flipping a pancake in the skillet, Christina smiled, and shook her head. *How silly we were back then. Everything seemed so important, and time sensitive. If we only knew then, what we know now, it would have saved us a lot of wasted tears, and emotions.*

She knew her own kids were beginning to experience some of the teenage angst that accompanies adolescence, and hoped, and prayed, they would come through it unscathed.

Once the kids were satiated, they noisily ran up the stairs, followed closely by Benji, who was adding his own doggie noise. After a few minutes, the troupe returned, dressed and ready to head off to the church.

As soon as she pulled into a parking space in front of the familiar red brick building, the sliding door of the van opened, and the six kids exited. Christina reminded them to meet her in the sanctuary, and save two extra places for Dr. Carmichael and Sammie. Not feeling sociable, she opted to sit in the van during the Sunday school hour, and spend the time writing a letter to her Michigan friend, Linda. As she composed it, she felt a wave of homesickness wash over her heart. Linda, and her family, had been the first couple she and David had bonded with so many years ago. *I hope I can convince them to come down for a visit this summer.* Glancing around, she watched as families entered the open doors of the foyer. Tucking the letter into an envelope, she joined the throng. Even though the air had a cold nip to it, the sun felt warm on her face.

Never in all her days of attending the First Baptist church, had she seen it so packed. Maybe because it was after Christmas, and the beginning of a new year, folks were feeling nostalgic, guilt-ridden, or hopeful. Tragedies often brought about a renewed desire to worship the Creator.

There were so many unfamiliar faces, and Young families. She hoped these families would continue coming to the services, as the new year progressed. Looking around, she spotted her kids in a pew about half-way down from the back of the sanctuary. Heading in their direction, she felt a tug on her jacket, and looked down to see Sammie. Her heart did a little happy dance, when Sammie wrapped her arms around her waist. Returning the hug, Christina looked up into the smiling face of Aaron, and felt her face flush.

"Good morning. You look amazing." He said, in a stage whisper, as he grabbed his daughter's hand.

Blushing even more, and feeling self-conscious, she said, "You do too."

The pastor spoke of hope, peace, and realistic goals for the new year. Topics she had considered during her quiet times in the morning. Barring any complications, she pictured the new year to be one of settling in, and progressing in their adjustment of living in Alva, Texas.

During the benediction prayer, Christina felt Sammie take her hand, and place it into her daddy's. Christina peeked over at Aaron, who shrugged. She decided it would be rude if she disengaged her hand. The gesture was not lost on her children, who gave her a look that said, "What's going on?" Knowing how they felt about Steven, she wasn't surprised at their confusion. She was surprised as well by her fickle emotions. Holding Aaron's hand just seemed so.... comfortable. As soon as the "amen" was said, however, Aaron gave her hand a light squeeze, before releasing it.

After the church service, Eric, and Carmen, informed Christina of their need to go home. Each had some kind of family function they needed to be present for. Christina dropped the two kids off, before heading out to Zimmerman's steak house on the south side of Alva, to meet Aaron, and Sammie. Danny had permission to stay with the Sander's family for the day, and was excited about the prospect of eating the "Big Z hamburger." Christina's mouth watered, as she listened to his description of the magnificent burger.

The lunch menu, even though it supposedly had smaller portions than the dinner menu, left everyone at the table quite satiated, with plenty of left overs for at least one more meal. Everyone chuckled when Danny and Nicky moaned, and rubbed their bellies.

"Danny was right." Said Nicky, "That was the best burger ever! I feel like my belly is going to explode!"

Christina and Aaron said their good-byes, and loaded the kids into the vehicles. Aaron tooted his car horn, and he and Sammie waved, as they exited the parking lot.

The ride home was quiet, until Stacey said, "It must be difficult to be attracted to two men."

Surprised, Christina looked over at her daughter, and asked, "What do you mean?"

Stacey shrugged, and said, "Well, I know you like Dr. Dawson, and you seem to like Dr. Carmichael, too. Which I can understand. Both men being hot, and all."

Christina nodded, and bit her bottom lip. *The girl is right.* Glancing at Stacey, she said, "You're right. I do like both men. They each have characteristics I admire."

Turning to face her mom, she asked, "So, if you had to choose right now, which one would you pick?"

Christina sighed heavily, as she pondered the question.

Shaking her head, she answered, "I can't tell you the answer right now, because I don't know. As time goes by, and I get to know each one better, I'll be more equipped to give you an answer."

Stacey shrugged, and said, "Okay. Just for the record, I would have a difficult time deciding, too. They are both amazing."

When they arrived home, Christina noticed the two younger boys were asleep, reminding her of two tired puppies. *No wonder it was so quiet,* she thought. She whispered to Stacey, and Brad, to please be quiet, as she smiled, and gently closed the van door. She knew the boys would eventually wake because of the cold, or need to use the bathroom.

The rest of the day was spent in quiet solitude, as each family member retreated to their rooms for naps, or reading. Christina took the time to finish the letter to her friend in Michigan.

Aaron carried his sleeping daughter to her room, and gently laid her on the bed. She mumbled something, as she turned onto her side. He laid a soft blanket over her, and tiptoed out of the room.

Pouring himself a glass of sweet tea, he grabbed the Dallas newspaper, and sat in his recliner, intent on reading about the events around the world. He must have dozed off, because the next thing he was aware of, was Sammie tugging on his sleeve.

"Daddy?"

"Hm?" He mumbled, as his mind struggled to pull free from the grips of sleep.

"Daddy, I'm thirsty."

Forcing his eyelids open, he looked into the face of his beautiful child. She looked more and more like her mother as time passed. Glancing up at the clock, he realized two hours had passed. It seemed like minutes ago, they had arrived home.

Disengaging himself from the chair, he stood, and stretched. Picking Sammie up, he balanced her on his hip, and headed into the kitchen.

"What would you like to drink?"

"Can I have apple juice?"

"Sure thing. One apple juice coming up."

Pouring himself a cup of coffee, he leaned against the counter, forcing his mind to recall the dream he had been entrenched in, when Sammie had awakened him.

Closing his eyes, he was able to conjure up a few images. He, Sammie, Christina, and her kids were at some kind of party that had balloons. One of the balloons had floated away, and Sammie was in pursuit of it. He heard someone shout, "Sammie! Stop!"

He looked over in time to see Sammie run towards the busy intersection. Several people were running down the hill towards her. He felt like he was moving in slow motion, as he joined the throng. Right before she stepped into the lane of traffic, the dream ended. *Was this a premonition? Was God sending him a warning about Sammie?* He hoped not.

Seeing a tear trickle down her daddy's face, Sammie asked, "Daddy? Are you okay?

Wiping his eyes, Aaron said, "Of course I am. I'm still a bit sleepy from my nap."

Smiling up at him, she asked, "Can I have a cookie, too?"

Nodding, he said, "Of course, your Highness. One peanut butter cookie, and another cup of apple juice coming up."

Sammie giggled. "You're funny, Daddy."

"What would you like to do for the rest of the afternoon?"

Cocking her head, she said, "I want to color. Want to color with me?"

"I'll color one picture with you, then I have to do some reading."

"Okay. I'll go get the coloring book and crayons."

As Aaron colored a picture next to his daughter, his mind wandered to thoughts of Christina. His heart, and mind, continued to wage war with his emotions. *If I continue pursuing her, where do I imagine we'll end up? Marriage? Am I ready for that? Am I ready to take on her three kids, and be their step-dad? If I'm not ready for that possibility, then why would I want to continue in this relationship? Will I be satisfied just being friends? I wonder how she feels about me?*

CHAPTER 7

When it was time for Christina to head out to work, Monday afternoon, she called the kids into the kitchen. Smiling, she held up three piece of paper, and said, "I made a list of the few things I'd like done, while I'm at work."

The kids groaned.

"I promise it isn't a lot. I know y'all just want to relax a bit more before school starts up, but these few things need to be done." Handing each a slip of paper, she said, "First of all, I'd like y'all to make sure all your laundry is done, then put your clothes away, and clean up your rooms. Nicky, the litter boxes need to be changed, and probably washed out. They smell pretty ripe. Stacey, if you could vacuum, and dust, the downstairs, I'd appreciate it. Brad, please gather up all the garbage, and dispose of it. Also, Benji's droppings need to be cleaned up."

The Sanders kids all nodded their acknowledgment.

Reaching out to hug her mom, Stacey said, "Sure thing, Mom."

"Okay, then. Call me if you need anything. I'll be home late. Probably around eleven thirty."

Opening the back door, Brad said, "We'll be fine. Don't worry."

Nicky said, "We'll keep a light on for you!"

Chuckling, she said, "Great."

Pulling into the hospital parking lot, she heard her cell-phone ring. Pulling it out of her purse, and glancing at the clock, then the caller ID, she happily answered.

"Cindy! I got your message last night. So what's up?"

"I'm engaged!"

"What? Awesome! I want to hear all about it, but I have to go in to work now. Can I call you during my dinner break?"

"Wait. What? Dinner?"

"I'm working the afternoon shift for a couple of days. It feels weird, but guess who I'm working with?"

"Uhm...I haven't got a clue."

"Libby Rollins. Used to be Libby Scott."

There was silence for a moment, then Cindy said, "I remember her. Wasn't she a cheerleader, and homecoming queen, our senior year?"

"Yep. She's now an RN on the Med-Surg floor."

"Is she still drop dead gorgeous?"

Chuckling, Christina said, "As a matter of fact, she is."

"I take it she's married. Any kids?"

"You won't believe who she's married to."

"Well, her last name is Rollins. Wait. Is she married to Lynn Rollins?"

"Yes, Ma'am."

"Oh my goodness! Wasn't he like, the biggest nerd in school?"

Nodding, and giggling, Christina said, "Yes, but you wouldn't recognize him now. He's actually quite handsome."

"You've seen him?"

"Well, no. But she showed me a picture of her family, and I hardly recognized him. Funny how a few years can change a person."

"Yeah. Tell her hi for me."

"So, Cindy. I won't be free until around seven. Can I call you then?"

"I'll talk to you later, then."

When Christina entered the hospital, she noticed Steven heading in the opposite direction.

"Hey, Steven!" She called.

He turned at the mention of his name, and smiled, when he saw who was calling him.

He turned around, and headed in her direction.

She stood in front of the elevator doors, waiting to push the button.

Walking up to her, he unabashedly gave her a hug. She looked around nervously, hoping no one saw. Hospital gossip would be out of control, if someone saw them.

"Hey, Steven." She said, pulling free of his embrace. It wasn't that she didn't like it, or desire it, it just wasn't the right time to express their mutual affection for each other...or was it?

Why am I so concerned about what people will say? She wondered, as she pushed the elevator button.

"So, where are you headed?" She asked, as they stood, waiting for the elevator doors to open.

"I was headed to the lab, but I'd like to ride up with you, if that's okay."

Smiling, she said, "Of course it's alright with me. I've missed you. We haven't had a lot of time to talk the past few days."

Nodding, he said, "Yeah. With emergencies, and crazy schedules, it has been difficult to find time to get together."

The doors opened, and they entered. "So, you've had emergencies?"

Nodding, he said, "Yes, unfortunately."

"Do we have new cardiac patients?"

Sighing deeply, he shook his head, and said, "Last night, I was called in to try and revive a young man."

She gave him a shocked look. "Was it Jimmy McCoy?"

Lowering his head, he nodded.

Nodding, and still feeling emotionally raw, he said, "He went through the surgery fine, and everything seemed to be going as expected, but his heart just stopped, and we couldn't get it started again."

Tears welled in her eyes, as she shook her head. Steven pulled her into a hug. She wrapped her arms around his waist, and let the tears flow. She had liked the kid.

Pulling away, she wiped her eyes, and looked up into Steven's compassionate eyes.

"What does Dr. Carmichael think happened?" She asked, digging a Kleenex out of her purse.

"Well, he won't know for sure until an autopsy is done, but he thinks the kid may have had a pulmonary or brain embolism."

Nodding, she said, "Oh, that is so sad. How's his dad, Jesse, doing?"

"He took it very hard. He wouldn't release the body for several hours, because he was convinced his son would wake up. It broke my heart watching him grieve. I was reminded of how I felt when my infant daughter died, and how devastating that was. I didn't really know her, but the emotional pain was so deep. I can't imagine having a child for seventeen years, and then losing them. Or, for that matter, any amount of years. It's a parent's worse nightmare."

Nodding, Christina sighed heavily. "I agree. When we almost lost Brad, I found myself begging God to take me, instead of him. A parent, who truly loves their child, would sacrifice themselves in a heart beat, if it would save their child's life."

The elevator dinged, and the doors opened. Steven looked around, and seeing no one, he hugged Christina, and kissed the top of her head. "Want to meet for dinner?" He asked, as he put his hand out to keep the elevator doors from closing.

Feeling like a deer caught in the headlights, she stammered, "Uhm, no. Aaron and I are having dinner, so we can discuss Linda's care. He's probably going to release her on Monday, and I need to know what to expect, or do."

Nodding, he said, "Okay. Maybe later then?"

Smiling, she said, "Maybe so. I'll be here 'till eleven."

She stepped out, turned to watch the doors close, and gave a finger wave, cutting off her contact with the man she liked, admired, and cared deeply for. She wasn't sure if she could say she loved him in a romantic way, but she did love him in a dear friendship way.

As she drew near the conference room, she heard Libby telling the staff about Jimmy's death the previous night. Walking past the door, on her way to the locker room, she then heard the normal reactions of denial, and grief. Because Jimmy had been sweet, and courteous during his short stay, the nurses assigned to care for him, had become emotionally attached. It seemed he had brought out the mothering instinct in a few of the older aides, and nurses.

Donning her lab coat, Christina joined the other staff members who were getting their assignments for the day. Libby looked surprised to see her. Christina smiled when she noticed Sarah Stevens, and Sally Jean among the group receiving their patient rosters. When Libby dismissed the staff, she asked Christina to stay back for a moment.

Sally Jean, and Sarah both hugged Christina on their way out, promising to have a chat later.

When the room was empty, except for the two women, Libby said, "Let's sit."

They each took a chair across the table from each other.

Releasing a sigh, Libby said, "So, I'm surprised to see you here. Have you switched to afternoon shifts?"

Shaking her head, Christina said, "Only this week. The other nurse in charge of the cardiac patients, is home with the flu, so I'll be taking her place today, Wednesday, and Friday."

Cocking her head, Libby asked, "Have you ever done afternoons here?"

Sighing Christina said, "No. Hopefully it'll run as smoothly as the day shift."

"It should. There aren't any critical patients at this time."

Christina nodded. "Good."

"I take it you heard about Jimmy?"

Christina nodded. "Dr. Dawson told me."

Libby cocked her head. "He did? When did he tell you?"

Christina smiled, shaking her head. She knew what Libby was thinking, and she wanted to set her straight.

"Look, Libby. Dr. Dawson and I are seeing each other on occasion. We're just friends. I happened to bump into him as I was getting on the elevator. He told me about Jimmy then."

Libby smirked, "Oh, shoot! I was hoping there would be something more than friendship between you two."

Christina grinned, shaking her head. "Sorry, my friend, you'll have to get your romantic news from someone else."

Libby shook her head, not really believing there wasn't more going on between Christina and Steven. "Just friends, huh?"

Nodding, Christina said, "Yep. Just friends." Christina cleared her throat, and asked, "So what's on the agenda for the afternoon?"

Looking at a clipboard holding the patient's information, Libby said, "There are only a couple of cardiac patients you need to be responsible for. Our unit is pretty full, however. We have a few surgical patients, most of whom will be dismissed today, and the others are just sick." Looking up, and scrunching her face, she said, "Seems to be some kind of flu bug going around. Make sure you wear a mask when, or if, you go in their rooms. All we need is a sick nursing staff."

Christina nodded her agreement. "Looks like we have plenty of staff today. It must be difficult to work out a schedule for both the cardiac, and the Med-Surg unit. I'll be so glad when we can get back into our regular place, and routine."

Libby nodded. "I'll have to say, it has been kind of exciting."

"Exciting? How so?"

"Well," Libby said, "You and I have re-connected, for one, and meeting people I never would have met, if our units hadn't been combined."

Nodding, Christina smiled, and said, "Yeah. You're right. Even though it's been difficult to readjust to the surroundings and all, it has been an interesting learning experience."

Looking at her watch, and standing, Libby said, "I guess we'd better get going, even though I'd really like to sit, and chat a while."

Standing, Christina asked, "So, have you heard anything about Jimmy's autopsy?"

Shaking her head, Libby said, "No, but I did hear Dr. Carmichael tell Jesse that he's pretty sure, Jimmy had some kind of embolism."

"Yeah, that's what Steven said. Poor kid. Poor Jesse."

Walking towards the door, Libby said, "I feel so bad for him. His wife died about five years ago, and now his son." Shaking her head, and sighing, she added, "I wish there was something we could do for him."

"Yeah. I can't imagine how difficult this is for him. I sure hope he has someone he can talk to. Someone, who can help him get through this."

Libby said, as she walked to the nurses' station, "He has his fire and rescue team, plus he, and the sheriff, seem pretty buddy-buddy." Shrugging, she added, "I didn't know him on a personal level, but from what I've heard, and seen, he's got a pretty good support team."

They were interrupted by one of the new aides, who asked Libby where the room freshener was kept. One of the patients had an accident on the way to the bathroom.

Libby told her, then added, "Make sure to call housekeeping as well. The floor will have to be sanitized."

"Who's the new gal?" Christina asked, as she took the cardiac patient's charts from Libby.

"Her name is Colleen. She recently graduated from high-school, and plans to head off to Baylor next fall, when she has enough money saved to pay her tuition fees."

Opening one of the charts, Christina said, "I'm surprised Mrs. Ferguson would hire another aide. Seems like we have more workers than work."

"Yeah, me too." Shrugging, Libby added, "I think a couple of aides quit over the holiday, so maybe she's replacing them." Shaking her head, she added, "I'm sure she has her reasons. I'm always happy to have extra help."

Turning to leave, she added, "I'd love to stay and chat, but I need to get home."

Christina smiled, and nodded. "I guess I'll see you Wednesday afternoon, then."

Nodding, Libby said, "I guess I'll see you then."

Christina stood for a moment, lost in thoughts about Jesse McCoy, and his son. She said a quick prayer of peace for Jesse McCoy's mind, and spirit, as he made preparations for his son's burial. *What a strange turn of events*, she thought, as she turned and headed down the hall to check on her first patient.

Jack woke to his phone ringing. Rolling over, he glanced at the clock on the nightstand, and grabbed his phone. It was six o'clock. *Who would be calling me at this hour?*

"Hello?" He said groggily.

"Jack?" Said the voice on the other end of the line.

"Yes. Who is this?"

Hearing a strange noise in the background, he almost disconnected, thinking it was a prank call.

The disembodied voice said, "Jack, it's me, Jesse McCoy."

Jack sat up. *Why in the world would Jesse be calling at this hour?*

Clearing his throat, he said, "Hey, Jesse. What's up?"

"Jack, I lost my boy last night."

Jack thought, *What? Did I hear correctly? His son died?*

Between choked sobs, sniffling, and blowing of his nose, Jesse told him about his son.

Jack felt as if his heart would beat out of his chest.

"Oh, Jesse. I'm so sorry, Man. What can I do to help?"

Jesse blew his nose again, before speaking. "Jack, I know the boys set off the fireworks, and the fire at the refinery. I'm going to tell the sheriff that Jimmy was responsible for it all. That way Jamie won't get in trouble. I don't want your boy to be punished for anything. He deserves to have a good life. It will be hard enough when he hears about Jimmy's death. He shouldn't have to suffer the humiliation, and punishment, for a foolish prank."

Jack listened, then said, "Jesse, I appreciate you trying to protect my boy, but I don't think he'd want you to do that. He's already agreed to talk to the sheriff today, and tell of his part in the Christmas eve shenanigans." Pausing to yawn, he continued. "I'll talk to him about it, but I believe he needs to face up to his part, and deal with the consequences. Sheriff Clifton is a good man, and I doubt he'll deal with Jamie too harshly. Thanks for the offer though. I'm so sorry to hear about Jimmy. He seemed to be doing well, according to Jamie. What happened?"

Jesse told his friend about the events of the previous night.

"Jack, could you please tell Jamie for me. He and Jimmy were best friends. I'm sure it's gonna hit him hard."

Nodding, Jack said, "Sure. Let me know if there's anything we can do."

Stifling a sob, Jesse said, "I will."

The two men disconnected, and Jack sat on the side of the bed processing the news. After a few minutes, he rose, and headed to Jamie's room. When he entered, Little Lady stood to greet him, wagging her tail.

Reaching down, he picked her up, and gave her a hug and kiss, before setting her down with her puppies.

Reaching out to his son, he hesitated, wondering if he should wait 'till later to give him the news of his friend's death. *I might as well tell him now. Why put off the inevitable?*

He shook Jamie's shoulder, and said, "Jamie. Son. Wake up."

Jamie mumbled something, as he rolled over, and opened one eye.

"Dad? What are you doing in here?"

Jack said, "I have to tell you something."

Jamie became instantly awake. Sitting up, and rubbing his eyes, he asked, "Is it something about Mom?"

Jack shook his head. "No, something else." Patting the side of the bed, he asked, "May I sit?"

Jamie scooted over, to make room.

"What's going on?" Jamie asked, feeling anxious.

Pinching the bridge of his nose with his thumb, and forefinger, Jack said, "I just got a call from Jesse, Jimmy's dad."

Jamie looked at the clock. *Six-thirty. Why would he call so early? Unless....* "Oh, no! Is Jimmy alright?"

Shaking his head, and avoiding his son's frantic look, he said, "No, I'm sorry to say that Jimmy died last night."

Leaping out of bed, Jamie said, "No! That can't be! I just talked to him. He seemed fine."

Jack reached out to touch Jamie, but the boy jerked away, and began pacing the room.

"Oh my gosh! What happened?"

Sighing heavily, Jack repeated what Jesse had said.

Running his hands through his hair, Jamie cried out, "What am I going to do? Jimmy was my best friend." He fell to his knees, and began sobbing. Little Lady, not used to this behavior, began whimpering, and licking Jamie's hands, and face. She knew he was upset, but she didn't understand why. The puppies, sensing their mother's distress, began whimpering, and yelping also. Jack reached down, and picked up the shivering dog.

After several minutes of watching his son cry, and feeling quite emotional himself, Jack stood, set the mama dog down with her babies, patted his son's back, and left the room. *This is going to be a rough week,* he thought, as he entered his bedroom to get dressed for the day.

He was sitting at the kitchen table, drinking his third cup of coffee, when Jamie entered, his eyes puffy and red, and his face blotchy.

Jack started to speak, but Jamie held up a hand. Nodding, Jack sighed.

Once Jamie had consumed a cup of coffee, he said, "Dad. I really don't know what I'll do without Jimmy. We've been best friends for a long time." Rubbing his forehead, he continued.

"Poor Mr. McCoy. He and Jimmy were finally getting along. When Jimmy's mom died, his dad sorta did too. It was as if he blamed Jimmy for his wife's death."

Jack felt a catch in his heart. *Hadn't he done the same thing to Jamie?* Even though he had been angry with his wife for leaving them, he had reflected that anger towards Jamie. He hung his head in shame. *What a fool I've been. What if Jamie had been the one to die?*

Clearing his throat, he said, "I'm so sorry, Jamie."

Jamie looked at his dad, his face red with anger. He wanted to punch something. His dad's face looked like a good target. Instead, he stood abruptly, knocking his chair over, as he stormed out of the room. Jack heard the bedroom door slam.

Standing, he gathered the coffee cups, and set them in the sink. *I almost wish he would punch me. Maybe he'd feel better, and I could let go of some of the guilt I feel.*

Glancing up at the clock above the kitchen sink, he thought, *I need to get to work.*

Passing by his son's closed bedroom door, he stopped and listened. Jamie was talking to someone on the phone.

"Son? I have to go to work. If you need me, I'll be at the shop today. Oh, yeah. We also have an appointment with the sheriff at ten. I'll meet you at his office."

He didn't receive a reply, but he was pretty sure his son heard him, because he had stopped talking for a moment.

When his dad finished talking, Jamie resumed his conversation with the person on the other end of the phone line

"So, Sylvia, can you let the other kids in our class know?"

"Sure, Jamie." Pausing to blow her nose, she continued. "This is so awful! I just talked to him a couple of days ago, and he seemed fine."

"Yeah," Jamie answered.

"I know he wasn't popular, but I think most of the kids in our class knew of him. When you find out about the funeral, would you call, or text me?"

"Sure." Jamie said on a sigh.

"Well, okay. I'll talk to you later then.

"Yep. Thanks, Sylvia."

When they disconnected, Jamie laid his head back on his pillow, and let his mind wander. *Why did life have to be so hard?* Little Lady jumped up, and curled up on Jamie's abdomen, resting her head on his chest. She knew he was sad, and wanted to comfort him. He unconsciously scratched behind her ears.

He tried to imagine his life without Jimmy. Tears stung his eyes. He and Jimmy had talked about getting an apartment together, and taking road trips to explore places they'd never been—like the Alamo in San Antonio. *Well, that's never gonna happen,* he thought, as tears escaped his eyes, and ran down to his ears.

The more he thought about Jimmy, and life without him, the more the tears flowed. Turning on his side, he took a corner of the pillowcase, and wiped out the moisture that had collected in his ears. He hated that he was so sensitive. *Why can't I be tough, and not let things get to me like they do?*

Glancing at the clock, he sighed heavily, picked up his dog, and set her down with her puppies. Grabbing clean clothes out of the laundry basket, he headed for the shower. He felt as if he were walking through quick sand, his mind, and body, heavy with grief.

When Cindy woke, at seven o'clock, the house was quiet as a tomb. Sitting up, she stretched. *If I hurry, I can get in the shower, and be dressed for the day, before anyone else wakes.* She hadn't slept well, as her mind was reliving the events of the previous night. Grabbing a fresh outfit, she headed for the bathroom, hoping the noise of the shower wouldn't wake anyone.

Ed woke from a nightmare, and sat up quickly, remembering the details. He, Cindy, and Samara were in some kind of accident, involving cars, and buildings. He wasn't sure if it was a car accident, or an explosion. He just knew there was chaos, and fires, and he couldn't find Cindy, or Samara. *Was the dream a premonition, or my mind working through the fear of losing my girls? I already lost part of my heart and soul, when Celina died, and I know I'd be completely undone, if I lost Cindy and Samara. I don't want anything interfering with our plans of becoming a family.*

As he put his feet on the floor, his heart still racing, and his mind playing the dream over and over, he said a prayer of protection, as they had a long car ride ahead of them.

He cocked his head, as he heard a door closing, and water running. *Well, someone's up. Guess I'd better get the coffee brewing.* As he was measuring, and dumping the coffee grounds into the coffee filter, his mom walked in, yawning, and stretching.

"Good morning, Son. Did you sleep alright on the couch?"

Reaching down, he gave her a bear hug, and thought, *Is she shrinking?* He had forgotten how short she was, compared to his sisters, and himself.

"I slept okay, Mom. How did you sleep?"

Reaching up to retrieve a mug from the cabinet, she said, "I slept like a log. Guess I was tireder than I thought." She poured a cup of coffee before it had finished percolating.

Adding a bit of cream and sugar, she said, "I heard the shower running upstairs. I guess your ladies are up."

"I think so. Cindy is an early riser. Especially if she has plans for the day."

Nodding, as she took a sip of coffee, she said, "Yeah. I like to get up early, and have a quiet time with my thoughts, and God. I've always enjoyed those times. Even when y'all were little."

He poured a cup of the dark brew in a mug, and said, "I remember coming down, and finding you sitting in your chair with your eyes closed. I thought you were dozing, but I now know you were probably praying, or thinking. Not wanting to disturb you, I'd creep back upstairs."

Smiling, she said, "I know. I'd peek to see who had come down. You always got up before your sisters." Patting his arm, she said, "Guess you take after me in that department."

Grinning, he said, "Guess so. With my job, and crazy hours, I've learned to function on as little as an hour of sleep in a twenty-four hour day."

Shaking her head, she said, "I don't think I've had to do that. Well, there was that one time when we all had the flu. I may have been functioning on an hour or so of sleep, then."

After a moment of silence, she walked over, and turned on the oven, then asked, "So, tell me about your job, and what you've been doing lately."

Motioning to the kitchen table, he said, "Why don't we go sit, and I'll tell you what I can. There are some things I can't talk about."

"Not even with your own mother?"

Shaking his head, and putting an arm around her shoulder, "Sorry, Mom. No can do. But the secret government stuff doesn't involve you, or anyone close, so you're not missing anything."

Ed told her about the fire works, and fire in Alva.

"So, the culprits haven't been caught?"

Shaking his head, he said, "Well, not yet. I think the sheriff has a couple of leads, however."

"Who does he think is responsible?" She asked, taking a sip of coffee.

"At this point, he thinks it was a couple of teen-age boys."

Nodding, she said, "That sounds about right. I've known a few teen boys who've pulled stunts that have got them in trouble with the law."

Ed grinned. "Present company excluded?"

Chuckling, she said, "Well, yes, unless you did something I wasn't aware of."

Shaking his head, and putting his hand over his heart, he said, "I was too chicken to do anything stupid. I knew if Dad found out, there would be a trip to the woodshed, so to speak."

She smiled and nodded. "I think your dad was more growl than bite, but he would have come up with some kind of punishment, that's for sure."

"Yeah. That's what I was afraid of."

Pausing a moment to take a sip of coffee, he said, "I did have a few friends who were a lot more daring, and didn't have the fear of their dad, or God, instilled in them." Shaking his head, he added, "Amazingly, they were never caught."

His mom set her cup down, and asked, "What kind of things did they do?'

As he opened his mouth to reveal some long past secrets, Cindy walked into the kitchen, and headed to the coffee maker.

"Good morning." Ed, and his mom said together.

Smiling, Cindy said, "Good morning to you both." After walking over, and giving Ed a kiss on the top of his head, she sat in a nearby chair.

"Did you sleep well?" Ed asked, as he reached over, and took Cindy's free hand.

Nodding, and taking a sip of coffee, she said, "Pretty well. I had a difficult time turning my brain off. It kept playing, and replaying last nights events."

Ed's mom said, "I hate when that happens. Sometimes, I can't get to sleep for hours."

Nodding, Cindy said, "Yes. It happens way too often, as far as I'm concerned."

"For me too." Gwen said, standing, as she remembered the biscuits in the oven. "I've had to resort to sleep aids. Then, and only then, can I actually fall asleep, and stay asleep."

Stretching her back, and feeling her vertebrae line up like train cars, Cindy said, "I hope I don't have to resort to that, but I can't continually function on three or four hours of sleep."

Ed asked, "Are you still okay with going to church this morning?"

Cindy nodded. "What time do we have to leave here?"

"Around 10:30. Church starts at eleven."

Glancing at her watch, she nodded, and said, "We've got plenty of time to eat, and get ready. Is it okay if I wear jeans and a sweater?"

Ed nodded. "Even though some of the folks are traditionalists, and will be wearing a dressier attire, I doubt if they'll frown on you for wearing jeans. Now, if you were a regular attender, that would be a different story." Shaking his head, he said, "Old traditions, and habits are hard to break."

Sipping her coffee, Cindy said, "I didn't grow up attending church, and haven't gotten into the habit. It would be nice to begin attending some kind of church as a family." Turning to face him, she said, "I don't even know what denomination you are."

Ed said, "I grew up as a Baptist, but I'm open to attending any church that teaches the Bible."

She gave him a questioning look. "There are churches that don't teach the Bible?"

Nodding, he said, "You'd be surprised at the number of churches that don't teach from the Bible. Or, they may use the Bible as a secondary book. There are a lot of what we call cults, out there. Some are quite bizarre."

Cindy said, "You sound like you've dealt with a few of those kind of churches."

"Yes, in my line of work, we've had to do some undercover work, to make sure none of these cults are doing anything illegal."

Cocking her head, she asked, "Illegal? What kind of illegal things would a church be doing?"

Shaking his head, he drank the remainder of his coffee, and set the empty mug on the table. He then told her of a cult in Utah run by a man who convinced women and girls that he was an angel, and it was an honor to be with him. Some of the girls were as young as ten."

Cindy inhaled sharply, and covered her mouth. "Oh, my goodness! Those poor little girls."

Ed let out a deep sigh. "Yes. However, when we went to arrest the leader, all the women, and girls rallied around him, and our agents ended up using brute force. Some of the ladies ended up going to jail because they were hitting the agents with bats, iron skillets, and anything else they could get their hands on."

Cindy shook her head. "Oh, goodness! I had no idea there were groups like that. What happened to the women, once their leader was captured?"

"Most of them returned back to the compound. A couple of them did volunteer to speak against the man, when he went to trial. He's serving thirty years in prison for molesting minor girls."

"How sad for those girls. How come their mothers didn't protect them?"

"As I said, they were brainwashed into thinking it was an honor to be chosen by this man, and have their daughters chosen as well."

Cindy shook her head. "Well, I'm glad he was caught."

Nodding, Ed said, "Yes, but for every cult we dismantle, there are a dozen that continue to function. We just don't have the man power to investigate all of them."

"It must be difficult for you, knowing there are young girls being used, and not being able to help them."

"Yes, it is."

Gwen walked over, and putting a hand on each shoulder, said, "Breakfast is ready you two." She then walked to the stairway, and hollered, "Hey, Y'all! Breakfast is ready!"

Ed and Cindy heard commotion overhead, and then on the stairs, as feet scrambled to the kitchen.

She turned to Ed and whispered, "Wow! This table is as big as the one in the dining room!"

Chuckling, he whispered back, "My mom doesn't believe in separate tables. She wants the whole family sitting together." Pulling the chair out for Samara, he added, "She had this table custom made by an Amish man down the road." Cindy nodded. *How cool is that?*

Nicole and Andy, as well as their four children, seated themselves at the long table, designed to seat twenty people. Cindy and Ed greeted the family. Nicole's oldest daughter, Marissa, who was ten, reached over, and gave Cindy's arm a hug.

"I'm glad you're sitting next to me." In a whisper, she asked, "Can I see your ring?"

Cindy smiled, and held out her hand. The child looked at it from a couple of angles, and said, "That is so pretty! When I get engaged, I want a ring like that."

Chuckling, Cindy said, "Well, that would be awesome."

Gwen carried over a tray of crispy bacon, which made everyone's eyes light up.

"Mmm. Bacon." Mark, who was eight, said, as he rubbed his hands together.

"You can have as much as you want. I can fry up more, if need be." Gwen said, as she pulled out a chair, and sat.

The boy grinned from ear to ear.

Gwen looked at Ed, and said, "You want to say grace?"

He nodded, and began his prayer. He thanked God for his family, Cindy and Samara, and the food.

Cindy felt tears sting her eyes, but she batted her eyelids, and refused to let them fall. *I'm not going to cry,* she told her inner self. When the prayer was finished, the plates of food were quickly making their rounds at the table. The children were served first, then Samara and Cindy, then the remaining adults. The food was abundant, and Gwen smiled as she watched her family devour it.

"Geeze, Mom. You made enough food for Cox's army." Nicole said, as she put a couple of pancakes on her plate.

Smiling, Gwen said, "I'd rather have too much food, than not enough."

"Well, you certainly outdid yourself this morning. Not that I'm not appreciative, I just don't want to waste any."

Ed reached for the pancake platter, and said, "You really think there's going to be left overs?"

Chuckling, Nicole said, "Oh, yeah. I realize now that you haven't been served. Well, in that case, I doubt you will have any food left. I remember now. Ed eats like a starving animal."

The kids all chuckled under their breaths.

"You're right, Sis. I am starving right now, so if you want anymore food, you'd better get it quickly, or it will disappear into my belly." He said as he patted his abdomen.

As the food was consumed, there was lively conversations going on all around.

Jamie drove to the hospital, and parked his car in the front lot. He debated going in, because Jimmy wasn't there, and he wasn't sure what he could say to Mr. McCoy. Beating the steering wheel with his hands, and fists, while crying out, and yelling at God in the same breath, brought little comfort. He stopped mid-rant when he saw Mr. McCoy come stumbling out. He watched as Jimmy's dad leaned against the wall, and threw up. Jamie continued watching, as he pulled a handkerchief out of his pants pocket, and wiped his mouth, then his eyes. Jamie felt a sob building, when he saw Mr. McCoy lean against the brick wall, and begin beating it with his fist. Jamie felt hot tears stream down his own face, and knew he had to go help Jimmy's dad. He slowly exited the car, after wiping his own eyes, and nose, and walked over to Mr. McCoy. He touched the grieving man's back. When Jesse turned, and saw it was Jamie, he pulled him into a bear hug. Both began to cry anew. After what seemed hours, they pulled apart. Jesse wiped his eyes again, and blew his nose. Jamie wiped his eyes and nose on his shirt sleeve.

"Jamie. Thanks, Son, for coming. I know you and Jimmy were like brothers. I was wondering if you could help me with the funeral arrangements? You knew what he liked more than I."

Another sob escaped, and Jesse pinched the bridge of his nose, while slowly rekeasing a lungful of air, trying to reign in his emotions.

Jamie reached out, and touched Jesse's arm. "It's okay, Mr. McCoy. I'll be glad to help. There's a girl in our grade who is getting the word out. She'll help us arrange things as well."

Jesse cocked his head, looking at this boy who had spent more time with his son in the past five years, than he had. Shaking his head, and looking at the ground, he thought, *I was working to make things better. Why now? We were so close to completely reconciling.*

Unable to say anything else, Jesse hugged Jamie once more, and said, "I need to go."

Jamie nodded. He stood in front of the hospital, and looking up at the sky, asked, "Why? Why cause so much pain and heartache?" Shaking his head, because the sky didn't answer, or for that matter, any other invisible deity, he slowly walked back to his car. The day went from miserable, to unbearable in an instant. Opening the car door, he looked up once more, and saw a bright light flicker. *What is that?* he wondered, as he continued to stare. It winked a couple more times, then he heard a voice in his head say, "Jamie." He looked around thinking maybe someone had walked up, and wanted to talk to him. Not seeing anyone, he jumped in his car, completely rattled. Letting out a lungful of air, he said, "Jamie, you're losing it. Gotta get hold of yourself." After a few heartbeats, the voice spoke again.

"Jamie, I have great plans for you." Jamie stuck fingers in both ears, thinking the voice would diminish, but it spoke calmly, and clearly, as before.

"I know this is a difficult time for you, but Jimmy is with Me. All will be clearer as time passes. Just know that I am with you...always."

Jamie looked around the interior of his car, thinking this must be some kind of sick joke. Finding nothing out of the ordinary, he leaned his head back, and thought about what was said.

"Hey. You. Voice in my head." No response.

"I don't know who you are, or what kind of trick you're playing, but this is way beyond cruel. My best friend died, and you're messing with my mind? What kind of person would do something like that?" Still hearing nothing, he continued, "I'll tell you. A really sick, cruel one, that's who." Feeling a bit braver, he added, "I'm friends with the sheriff. If I find out who you are, I'm going to report you to him." He waited another heartbeat, then started his car. Even though the thermometer read thirty-two degrees, he didn't feel cold. In fact, he felt warm—as if he was wrapped snug as a bug in a rug. He hadn't thought of that description in a long time. His mom used to say it when she tucked him in at night.

He pulled out of the parking lot, and headed to Pizza Hut. He hoped his boss would give him a few days off, so he could help Mr. McCoy with the funeral arrangements.

"Thanks, Sylvia. Let me know if there's anything else I can do."

Brad disconnected from the phone call, and sat in stunned silence, as he contemplated the news he had just heard. He hadn't know Jimmy McCoy personally, but he did know about him, and recognized him at school. He seemed like a nice guy. Kinda quiet, and reserved. He knew Jimmy was Jesse McCoy's son. In fact, all of Alva knew Jesse McCoy, because he was the Fire Chief. Jimmy was so different from his dad. Brad wondered if he had been adopted. His dad was a bear of a man, and had wild red hair, and a thick mustache, and beard to match. Jimmy was on the smaller side, had dark eyes, and hair. Maybe he took after his mom's side of the family.

Brad thought about Jimmy's best friend, Jamie Simmons. Now, Jamie looked more like Mr. McCoy, with his red hair and fair skin. *Put another hundred pounds, and another foot of height, and he could easily pass as Jesse's son. Weird how genetics work*, he thought, as he slapped his hands on his thighs, and stood.

Stacey, with her nose in a book, bumped into him.

"Hey!" He said, as she walked past him.

"Sorry," she called over her shoulder, as she headed up the stairs to her room.

Stopping mid-stride, she turned and asked, "Who were you on the phone with?"

"A girl from school."

Raising her eyebrows, she asked, "Which girl?"

"Her name is Sylvia. She's a Senior."

Turning to face him with a sly grin on her face, she asked, "So, my Sophomore brother is talking to a Senior? What's up with that?"

Shaking his head, he said, "It's nothing like that. She called to tell me that one of the Senior guys died last night."

Stacey's face turned instantly into concern. "Oh, was it someone you knew?"

"No. I knew *of* him, but I didn't know him personally. His dad's the fire-chief."

"I met the fire-chief once. He came to our school to tell us about fire safety. He seemed nice. I didn't know he had a son." Sighing heavily, she said, "That's so sad. How'd he die?"

"Sylvia didn't know exactly, but she said he had just had surgery on his leg."

Sitting on the carpeted step, Stacey asked, "Why'd he have surgery on his leg?"

Shaking his head, and throwing his hands up, Brad said, "I don't know! Maybe Mom will know more."

Pulling her phone out of her jeans pocket, she asked, "Want me to call her?"

Looking at his watch, he said, "She'll be home in an hour or so. We can ask her then."

Taking a bite out of an apple, Nicky joined his siblings in the hallway, and asked, "Ask who, what?"

Stacey blurted out, "Brad just got a phone call from a Senior girl, who told him one of the Senior boys died last night."

"A guy died? What happened?"

Brad, who was leaning on the door jamb, said, "We don't know! That's why we need to ask Mom, when she gets home."

Nodding, Nicky said, "Oh. Okay." Looking at his watch, he added, "She should be home soon."

Stacey stood, turned, and finished ascending the staircase. The boys heard her bedroom door close.

Nicky looked at Brad, and asked, "So, you want to play a game or something?"

Brad shook his head. "Sorry, but I need some alone time."

Nicky shrugged. "Okay. Is it okay if I call Danny?"

Brad smiled, and reached out to tousle his brother's hair.

"It's kinda late. Maybe you should wait until tomorrow."

Nicky's shoulders slumped, as he sighed. Mumbling under his breath, he ascended the stairs.

Following Nicky up the stairs, Brad said, "He'll probably be over first thing tomorrow, anyway. He practically lives here."

Both boys entered their rooms, closing the doors behind them. Brad sat on his bed, with his back against the headboard, and closed his eyes. He felt a burning desire to pray for Jimmy's dad, and Jamie. He knew in his heart, that God wanted him to go speak to them, but he hadn't a clue as to what he should say. For the next hour or so, he read scripture, prayed, and paced around the room, having an argument of sorts, with God. He finally halted his pacing, and fell to his knees beside the bed.

"Okay, God. I remember telling You that I want to be Your servant, and ambassador. I asked You to help me feel what You feel, love like You love, and see people like You see them. I will do as you wish, and I will step out in faith, trusting that You will give me the words and actions necessary to accomplish Your will. I can do all things in Christ, who gives me strength. In Your Holy Name. Amen."

Standing, he knew without a doubt, what he needed to do. Now if he could muster up the courage.

During her drive home, Christina thought about Jesse McCoy, and remembered how close she had come to losing each one of her children, and how difficult that had been emotionally, and physically. Poor Jesse, as far as she knew, he had no close family member with whom he could share his grief. She said a prayer that someone would be there to minister to him during this most horrific time.

When she arrived home, her children came down to greet her, and bombard her with questions concerning Jimmy McCoy's death. She didn't have any new information to share with them.

"Until the coroner's report comes back, we won't know what caused his death."

After a few minutes of contemplative silence, Stacey asked, "Is there anything we can do to help Mr. McCoy?"

Shaking her head, Christina said, "I don't know. I don't know much about the man. I did hear that he's a widower, but I don't know about other family members. I imagine the fire station guys will rally around him."

Brad said, "I talked to my friend, Sylvia, and she and a bunch of seniors are going to hold a candle light ceremony in front of the high-school tomorrow evening. I'd like to go."

"Me too!" Stacey, and Nicky, said in unison.

Nodding, Christina said, "I think we should all go, to show Mr. McCoy he isn't alone in this."

After a few minutes of recounting their day's activities, Christina stood, and said, "I'm exhausted. I'm going to head on up to bed. And y'all should too, It's almost midnight."

CHAPTER 8

Jesse McCoy sat in the hospital chapel with the Chaplain. They had been there all night. Jesse didn't want to leave, and Dan was determined to stay with him.

Dan reached out to touch Jesse's arm, but decided against it, returning it to his lap. Jesse had a far off look in his eyes, as if he was having a mental argument with himself. The Chaplain sensed, that what Jesse was contemplating, wasn't good. He had seen that look in his son's eyes, a few days before he overdosed, and in his own, a while after his son's death.

"Mr. McCoy?" He asked tentatively. "Can I get you anything?"

Jesse shook his head. "No, thanks."

After a moment of silence, not turning to look at Dan, he asked, "Pastor, is there really a Heaven and Hell?"

Dan nodded. He began to speak, but was interrupted.

"Do you think my wife, and son, are there?"

Dan took in a lungful of air, and let it out slowly, before answering.

"I don't know. Only God can determine who can enter Heaven or Hell. He looks at the heart of man, not his outward appearance, and makes His judgment call based on that."

Nodding, Jesse thought, *That's what the guys at the Promise Keepers meeting said.*

Turning to look at the Chaplain, he said, "When my wife was alive, we went to church quite often. Not just Christmas, and Easter."

Dan nodded, not sure where this was going.

Jesse sighed, and sat up, leaned back in his chair, and crossing his arms across his chest, continued.

"Anyway, when she died, I tried going, but felt like everyone was talking about me, and Jimmy. We had so many folks saying how sorry they were for our loss, and asking if they could do anything. I mean, I guess, that was nice and all. It's just when I heard that, I felt angry."

Pinching the bridge of his nose, he asked, "Why would I feel angry?"

Dan said, "Anger is one of the first steps in the grieving process. Actually, it's quite common to feel angry, and want to punch people in the face."

Jesse gave a sly smile. "Yeah. I wanted to punch you in the face."

Dan smiled, and nodded. "I know. I am so glad you didn't."

Jesse smiled too. "Yeah. Me too."

The Pastor was glad Jesse could smile. "Jesse, when my son died three years ago, I wanted to die as well. He was my only boy, and I had such high hopes for him."

Jesse cocked his head, and listened. "Your son died? How old was your boy?"

"He had just turned twenty-one. We had a party for him, and invited all his high-school, college, and work friends. We didn't know at that time, he was hanging around other drug users. He hid his problem very well."

Shaking his head, he continued. "Looking back, I could see the signs. He began wearing long sleeves all the time, and he would have crazy mood swings. One minute, he was laughing and joking, and the next he was sullen, and sleeping a lot. We just ignored his behavior, making up reasons: he stayed out late, he was going through more hormonal changes, he was working too many hours, he was staying up studying." Looking up at Jesse, he said, "We were deliberately blind. We kept saying, "he would never do drugs, he's a good boy, his dad is a Pastor." He motioned with this hand indicating, that the list could go on.

Jesse shook his head. "I suppose you confronted him?"

"Yes, and of course he denied it. One evening, when we discovered he had dropped out of college, and had been fired from his job, we pleaded with him to be honest, and tell us what was going on. He became very angry, and defensive, and walked out of the house. We didn't see him again, after that incident. We got a call several days later, telling us he had died."

Jesse, leaned forward in his chair, and reached over to pat the man's shoulder.

"Man, that's tough. Now I know you do understand what I'm going through."

Nodding, and leaning back in his chair, Dan said, "It almost cost me my marriage."

"Yeah, how so?" Jesse asked.

"After the funeral, my wife withdrew. Kind of like you did. She didn't want to talk, and she didn't want to eat. She was skin and bones. Our daughters begged me to take her to the hospital. I finally did, after she passed out in the bathroom."

"What did the Docs say?"

"She was admitted for clinical depression. After several weeks of counseling, for her, and the family, she finally was able to pull herself out of that pit."

"You've been through a lot." Jesse said.

"Yeah. You want to know why she was so depressed?"

Jesse nodded.

"She was mad at me. She blamed our son's overdose on me. I was the one who insisted we have the confrontation. I was the one who got angry, and yelled at him. I was the one who told him he couldn't live with us anymore, if he was going to continue in his behavioral pattern."

Jesse leaned forward, resting his arms on his legs. Turning his body to look at Dan, he asked, "Y'all okay now?"

Nodding, and smiling, Dan said, "Yes. Finally. It wasn't an overnight transformation. We all, including my girls, had a lot to work through. I didn't realize how much this affected my girls."

"How old are your daughters?"

"They're both sixteen. Twins."

Nodding, Jesse smiled, and said, "I don't envy you. From what I hear, girls who are around sixteen, and seventeen, lose their minds, and don't find them again until they're in their twenty's."

Dan laughed. "Well, so far, mine still have their minds in tact. They are amazing, and I'm so proud to be their dad."

Jesse nodded. "You know what my son said to me, right before he died?"

"No, what did he say?"

"He said, everything is okay, Dad. Mom said so. What do you think that means?"

Dan shook his head, and asked, "It doesn't matter what I think. What do you think it means?"

Jesse sat for a moment, looking up towards the cross on the wall, thinking. He finally said, "I think it means, that everything will be okay." Shrugging he added, "I'll get through this grief, and I'll be okay." Looking over at Dan, he said, "Like you, and your family. They're okay, now?"

Nodding, Dan said, "Yes."

Jesse slapped his thighs with his hands, and stood. Dan stood as well.

He looked Jesse in the eyes, and asked, "Jesse, were you contemplating taking your life?"

Nodding slightly, he asked, "How'd you know?"

"Because, I've stood in your shoes, and I know that far off look. So, I have to ask you, are you still thinking about ending your life?"

Jesse looked down at the floor for a moment, then his eyes traveled back up to Dan's. Shaking his head, he said, "No. I think Jimmy would be disappointed if I did. He would want me to live, just like my wife did. Before she passed, she told me that I had better keep living each day to the fullest, and raise our boy to be a great man." With a catch in his voice, he said, "I failed miserably on both accounts."

Dan patted Jesse's back. "Don't let guilt rule your life. You can't undo what has happened. All the should'ofs, would'ofs, and could'ofs, don't change anything. When those thoughts come—and they will—don't dwell on them, because they will drag you down into a pit, that is quite difficult to crawl out of. From what I've heard, Jimmy was a good boy. Just keep focusing on that, and the good times you did have."

Looking at his watch, Jesse said, "It's late. I need to go to the funeral home, and make arrangements."

"Do you want me to come with you?" Dan asked, gathering up his coat, hat and gloves.

Shaking his head, and donning his own coat, Jesse said, "Nah. I think I can handle it on my own."

Reaching out to shake hands, Dan said, "If you need anything....well, you know."

Jesse nodded, then pulled the Chaplain into a hug, which caught him off guard.

"Thanks for being here with me. I feel better. Sad, and a bit angry still, but not so bogged down."

Even though the men were the same height, Dan had a much slimmer build. He had been teased about his size, when he entered middle-school, earning the nickname, "bean pole," which was shortened to "bean," when he entered high-school. He was so used to being called that, he would sometimes forget to answer to his given name. He knew Jesse could snap him like a twig, but the big man understood his strength, and surprised Dan with his gentleness. Releasing him, Jesse nodded, turned, and disappeared out the door.

Dan closed the double doors, and walked down the middle aisle to the alter. He looked up at the cross, bearing a crucified Jesus. He stared at it for a moment, and thought, *I wonder why some religions portray Jesus on the cross. Most believers know that He didn't stay on the cross. He was taken down, buried,* and rose again the third day. Maybe they portray it like that, to remind people that He did suffer unimaginable torture, and died for our sins.

He knelt, and bowed his head in prayer.

On the way to the funeral home, Jesse called Jamie, remembering the promise he had made to the boy.

When the phone buzzed in his pocket, Jamie pulled it out, and read Mr. McCoy's name. He had been wiping tables in Pizza Hut, but stepped outside for more privacy.

"Hey, Mr. McCoy." Jamie answered, as he brought the phone up to his ear.

"Hello, Jamie."

Jamie could hear the sadness in the man's voice, which touched a place in his heart.

"What can I do for you, Sir?"

Jesse explained his reason for the call.

"I'll need to clear this with my boss, but I'm pretty sure he'll let me come meet you at the funeral home. It may be a little while, however. I'll call you back if there's a problem."

He finished wiping the last two tables, took an order, and restocked the napkin dispensers. Looking around to make sure he hadn't forgotten anything, he nodded, then went to knock on his boss's door.

A male voice said, "Come on in."

Jamie entered, and explained the situation to his boss, who, much to Jamie's relief, agreed to let him off early. As he drove through town, thoughts of Jimmy brought tears to his eyes. *Hopefully, I'll be all cried out by the time I meet Mr. McCoy. I don't want to lose it in front of him. The poor man is suffering enough without having to worry about me.*

The street in front of the funeral office was crowded, and Jamie had to walk about a block to get there. He wished he had brought his heavier coat, as the temperature had dropped, and the wind had picked up. The weather man had said their area was in the path of an ice storm. *Great*, he thought, *how could they bury Jimmy if it was icy? Plus, there was that candlelight vigil at the high school tomorrow night. I doubt if anyone will show up, if it's icy.*

Mr. McCoy was sitting in front of a large desk, across from the director, but stood when Jamie walked in. Jesse pulled the boy in for a hug. The gesture caught Jamie by surprise, but he went with it, and patted the man on the back.

The man behind the desk reached out his hand, which Jamie shook, and said, My name is Harold Kingsley" He motioned for Jamie to sit in the chair next to Jesse's.

"I will be handling Mr. McCoy's arrangements. First off, thank you for coming. Next, I'll tell you what we usually do for funerals, and you can give me your input."

Looking at Jesse, Jamie whispered, "What kind of input?"

Jesse shrugged. "Not sure."

The director pushed a brochure across the table for Jesse and Jamie to look through.

"The caskets with the check marks are the ones we have here, but if you want something different, I can order it, and have it here by tomorrow. You'll notice that the prices are listed as well."

Jesse felt his breath catch, as the reality of the situation hit him squarely in the chest. He swallowed, and took a cleansing breath to calm his nerves. Glancing at Jamie, he pulled the information packet closer, so they could both see the available items. Jesse knew he didn't have a huge amount of money in his savings account, so he was inclined to choose the cheapest casket. *After all,* he reasoned, *Jimmy won't know, or care, and no one would see it after it was lowered into the ground.*

Even though the one he chose for his son was the least expensive, it still looked better than the pine boxes his great grand parents had been buried in. That thought brought a smile to his lips. *I wonder when these fancy coffins came into being, and why is it important for them to look nice? The dead person doesn't care, and I doubt if anyone else pays that much attention to the casket.*

Jesse pointed to the picture, and looked at Jamie, who shrugged, and nodded. Once that decision was made, and a check was written, and handed over, the three men went over the order of the ceremony.

The memory of his wife's funeral came tearing through Jesse's mind like a freight train. He had forgotten how tedious the tasks of deciding on the music, who was going to talk, what was going to be said, the viewing, plus the task of getting pictures together to make a memory board, and the after funeral dinner. Jesse pinched the bridge of his nose, trying to ward off the forming headache.

Jamie reached out, and touched Jesse's arm.

"Mr. McCoy?"

Jesse looked up, into Jamie's tear-rimmed eyes. "What, Son."

"If you want, I can pick the music, and go through the pictures. There's a girl from school who said she'd be glad to help."

Jesse nodded. "Thanks, Jamie. I'm not so sure I could do any of that right now."

"I know, Sir. I can follow you home, and gather up the pictures, then Sylvia, and I, can go through them this evening."

The funeral director was nodding his approval.

"So, Jesse, when would you like to have the funeral? Today is New Year's eve, so I was thinking this Thursday?"

Jesse thought for a moment, then nodded. "I guess that's okay. That'll give us a few days to get everything ready."

Mr. Kingsley wrote the date down in his notebook. Looking up at Jamie, he said, "If you can get the music list, cds, and picture board to me as soon as possible, we'll get it all together, and have it ready by Thursday. I'll also submit an announcement to the newspaper. You should have plenty of time to inform any out of town guests, and whomever else needs to be informed."

Jamie glanced up at the clock on the wall, realizing he had forgotten the meeting with the sheriff. When Jesse and Jamie had finished their business with the funeral director, Jamie walked to his car, and pulled out his cell-phone.

His dad answered on the first ring.

"Hey, Jamie. Did you forget about the meeting with the sheriff, this morning? I tried calling, but your phone went to voice mail."

"Yeah. Sorry Dad. I had my ringer off. I dropped by work, and Mr. Shaffer asked if I could stay and help for a while, then Mr. McCoy wanted me to come help him with the funeral arrangements."

Nodding in understanding, Jack said, "Okay. Sounds like your missing the meeting wasn't deliberate. I'll call the sheriff, and set up another time. Will you be free tomorrow?"

Jamie thought for a minute before answering, "Yeah, that should be okay. Tomorrow's New Year's day, so Pizza Hut won't be open."

"Oh, yes. It is New Year's. I've been so caught up in stuff, I forgot about it. I'll talk to the sheriff. He might be okay with tomorrow, but if not, we'll set it for another day this week,"

"Thanks." Jamie almost disconnected, then said, "Hey, Dad. Jimmy's funeral will be this Thursday."

Jack was silent for a moment. "Okay. I'll make sure I'm available."

After disconnecting with his son, Jack leaned back in the chair he was occupying, closed his eyes, and let his mind meander through the memories of the last several weeks. Since the twin tower incident, the world in general, and his world in particular, had been turned topsy-turvy.

He didn't consider himself to be a religious man, but he was a law-abiding citizen, and was considerate of others. Lately, though, he had begun to question if "being good" was enough. *How good is good enough? Who set the standard? Man? God?* He had asked the leader of the Enlightened Ones, and had been given a vague answer. "Everyone has to decide in their own hearts what was good, and act on it." *Did that even make sense? What if my idea of good is opposite of someone else's? Are we both right? Or wrong? Are we our own judge and jury? Why does it even matter if we're good or bad if there's nothing after this life? For that matter, is there even an after life? A Heaven or Hell, like some people think?*

When he and Jesse, along with thousands of other men attended the Promise Keepers meeting a few weeks back, because of an invitation from Scott, one of the guys at the shop, he had been enthralled by the music, testimonies, and sermon. When the invitation to accept Christ as Savior had been given, he had taken a step of faith. He, along with Jesse, and Scott, bowed their heads, and had opened their hearts and minds to Christ. When he had prayed, he knew something inside of him had broken, and been released, because he had felt lighter, and happier. It was as if an elephant had been lifted off his back. He felt incredibly free. He had talked to Jesse, and Scott on the trip back from Dallas, and they had assured him that what he was feeling must be genuine, because they felt the same way. God had indeed released him from his burdens, and he was a new man. *So why do I still have so many questions?*

His rambling thoughts were interrupted by a knock on the door.

Scott stuck his head in.

"Jack, there's a guy out here asking about our services, prices, and such. You want to come talk to him?"

Jack nodded, and extricated himself from the chair. He would continue his train of thought later, when he had another quiet time.

"Hey, Scott." He called after the mechanic.

Turning, Scott said, "Yeah?"

"Can you come by the office after work? I have a few things I'd like to discuss."

"Sure. Six, okay?"

Jack nodded. "See you then."

Ed, Cindy, and Samara, arrived safely back home late Sunday night, exhausted from their weekend of travel, and visiting with Ed's family. Ed woke to the sound of whimpering, and scratching at Samara's bedroom door, and realized it was Sasha wanting out. Samara was in such a deep sleep, she didn't hear her beloved pet. Ed threw the covers off, and quietly as possible, retrieved the dog, and took her outside.

As she sniffed around the yard, searching for the right place to eliminate, Ed took those few moments to enjoy the bright sunshine, and clear blue sky. He breathed in the cool, crisp air, and said a prayer of thanksgiving. He had many things to be thankful for. He would soon be married to an amazing woman, and become a dad to a beautiful young lady. That realization made him happy, but anxious at the same time. Having never had children, he was unsure of his parenting skills—especially with a fourteen year old girl. He had heard that teenage girls could be quite moody, and stubborn at times. *Well, shoot, so could boys.* He knew, because he had been one. He fast forwarded his mind to when Samara would begin dating. *Lord, have mercy on any boy that showed interest in her.* If he had his way, she would just stay at the age she is now. Still sweet, obedient, and happy—well, most of the time.

Sasha ran up to him, and began jumping, and yipping.

"All right, girl. I'll let you in. It is getting a bit chilly out here."

Opening the door, she ran in, heading straight to her food bowl, which was empty. With her little black nose, she began scooting it toward Ed.

Whispering, he said, "I'll get you food in a minute." Picking up the bowl, he headed to the cupboard, and withdrew an almost empty bag of dog food.

"Looks like we're gonna have to go get you some food today."

Sasha looked up, wagging her tail, anxious to fill her belly.

Setting the bowl down, he picked up the water bowl, and after rinsing it, filled it as well. Setting it beside the food bowl, he reached out, and patted Sasha on the head. Not being a pet person, he admitted to himself, that she was pretty cute. If he was planning on having Cindy and Samara as part of his family, he'd have to take Sasha as well. *At least she's not a Great Dane, or other huge dog. The amount of food and excrement would be mind-boggling.*

"Is it okay if I make my coffee now?" He asked the kibble eating, fluffy ball of fur.

She replied by looking up, and wagging her tail.

He took his cup of coffee to enjoy, as he sat on the couch, and read the Sunday edition of the Dallas Times Herald.

He had just begun to read through the sports section, when he heard Cindy's bedroom door open, and the bathroom door close. Smiling, he thought, *It won't be long until we can wake up together.*

As Cindy showered, she began making plans for her future wedding. When she had married Stan so many years ago, it had been a very small wedding which included his family, and her mom. *This time,* she thought, *I want a big church wedding, with all the trimmings.* Her heart began to race at the thought. *I should run this past Ed.* Rinsing her hair, she smiled, knowing in her heart, that he wouldn't care what kind of wedding she wanted.

Stepping from the shower, she bent over to grab the towel that had fallen off the shower rod, wrapped it around her body, and promptly hit the floor.

Ed heard the strange sound, and thought Cindy had dropped something, but when there wasn't any further noise, he went to investigate.

"Cindy?" He called, as he knocked on the door. No answer.

"Cindy, are you alright?" No answer.

Turning the knob, and finding it unlocked, he wondered if he should enter.

Opening the door a crack, he called once again, "Cindy?"

Pushing the door further in, he met some resistance. Peeking through the gap, he saw Cindy lying in a heap on the floor.

"Cindy!" He called, as he reached in, and moved her legs out of the path of the door.

Bending down, he checked the pulse in her neck. Fast, but steady. Lifting her head, he pulled her eyelids back, and looked into blank eyes. Laying her down gently, he went to Samara's door, and knocked loudly, as he took out his phone, and dialed 911.

He heard a muffled response behind the bedroom door, the same time an operator came on the phone line. He gave the woman the address, as he continued knocking on Samara's door.

"What?" Came the angry reply.

"Samara, get your clothes on. We have to take your mom to the hospital."

The door opened, and she stuck her head out. "What? My mom has to go to the hospital? Why?"

Ed said, with impatience, "She passed out in the bathroom. I called 911, and they should be here in a minute. Please get dressed."

"Okay." She closed the door, and within minutes, was standing in front of the bathroom door, looking in at her prone mother.

"What happened?" She asked, chewing on a thumb nail.

Ed started to say something, but the ambulance crew had arrived. He led them to Cindy, who remained unconscious.

Samara, stood by Ed, who put a comforting arm around her shoulders. He led her to the living room, and they sat on the edge of the couch, as the EMT men loaded Cindy onto a gurney.

One of the crew came over, and handed a clip board to Ed, asking him to sign a document, stating that he would be the responsible party.

He said, "You two can follow us to the hospital, if you'd like."

"Thanks." Ed said, as he helped Samara into her coat, and donned his own jacket.

Fortunately for everyone, the hospital was only a few miles away. The ambulance driver didn't bother turning on the siren.

During the car ride to the hospital, Samara sat staring out the window, lost in thought, when she felt Ed reach over, and pat her arm. "It'll be okay, Honey. Your mom's a fighter."

Samara nodded, and wiped away a tear that had cascaded down her cheek.

"I hope so." She whispered.

Jesse McCoy woke with a start. Sitting up in bed, and rubbing his eyes, which felt like sand was embedded in them, he turned to put his feet on the floor. He dreaded today. He had to go look at the casket he had chosen from a brochure, for his son. His boy. His reason for getting up, and going to work everyday. He wanted to crawl back under the covers, and never get up again. He had no one. His wife was gone, and now his son. *How am I supposed to go on living? Why should I go on living?* He buried his face in his hands, crying out to God, and mentally shaking his fist at Him.

"Why? Why my boy? We were just reconnecting! Why now? Why not me? If You're a God of love, why would You want to hurt me so deeply? What did I do to deserve such harsh treatment? I've tried to live a good life. Sure, I've smoked, drank, and did some things I'm not proud of, but I've always tried to be kind and fair with people. Are You even listening? Do You hear me? Do You care?"

All he received was silence. He had no idea that his guardian angel, Liam, was present. The angel knew Father was listening, but chose to work in other ways to meet Jesse's emotional, and spiritual needs. Reaching out his hand, Liam touched Jesse's shoulder. Jesse stopped his ranting. Shuddering, he looked around the room. Rubbing the area that had been touched, he muttered, "What was that?"

Liam smiled. Jesse stopped crying, wiped his eyes with a tissue he had grabbed from a box on the night stand, stood, and made his way to the bathroom, wondering why he felt as if a ton of bricks had been lifted from his shoulders, and a blanket of peace had taken its place.

Christina was hanging her coat up in the nurses' lounge, when she heard her phone ring. Retrieving it from her purse, she frowned when she read the caller ID. Ed.

Grabbing her white lab coat, she answered.

"Hey, Ed. What's up?"

"Christina, Cindy passed out in the bathroom, and we're on our way to the hospital. Could you meet us in the ER?"

Bringing her hand to her mouth, she said, "Oh, no! Is she okay?"

"We don't know. I'm not sure why she fainted, but she wasn't conscious when the EMT guys arrived. I have Samara with me. We're pulling in the lot now. I'll see you in a while."

"Okay. I have to check in with the night staff, but I'll be down as soon as I'm available."

Not expecting Christina until Wednesday evening, Libby gave her a surprised look. Christina took the chair next to her friend, and whispered, "Mrs. Ferguson called last night, and asked if I could come in today."

Libby nodded. "I see."

When the reports from the previous night were discussed, and protocols were listed, Christina explained the situation to Libby, then headed to the elevators.

Since there were only two cardiac patients on the floor, and two aides to care for them, Christina felt confident her presence would not be missed.

After informing the aides of her plans to head down to the ER, she told them to feel free to text, or call her, if there was an emergency.

Heading to the elevator, she said, "I'll try not to be gone for long."

Sally Jean, and Brenda, did a finger wave.

Brenda said, "You stay as long as you need to. We've got it covered here."

On her ride down, Christina prayed for her friend. *This is going to be a busy day,* she thought as she ran through the list in her head.

After work, she was planning to get Linda, take her to her house to get a few things, and move her into the upstairs bedroom. Now with Cindy's physical crisis, she wasn't sure if bringing Linda to her house would be feasible. Her plans depended on Cindy's diagnosis.

When Cindy had slipped on the ice back in December, and bumped her head, her blood test had indicated that she was anemic. She was supposed to have gone back for more tests, but knowing Cindy, she probably put it off because she was felling better. *I know I would have,* she thought as the elevator bell rang, and the doors opened to the first floor, which was busy with activity.

She made a bee-line to the ER. Stopping at the desk, she asked of Cindy's whereabouts.

"She's in room three." The receptionist said.

Glancing around the waiting room, to see if Ed or Samara were there, and not seeing them, she turned, and headed for room three.

Knocking lightly on the door, she heard, "Come in."

Ed was sitting in a chair, and Samara was standing by the narrow rectangle window. No Cindy.

"Where's Cindy?" She asked, as she headed over to Ed and have him a hug.

Ed said, "They took her to get x-rays to make sure she didn't crack her head when she hit the floor. They may do an MRI as well."

"What happened?" Christina asked, as she leaned against the wall.

Ed told how he had found her.

"Have any blood results come back yet?" She asked.

Shaking his head, Ed said, "Not yet. But she looks so pale, I can't help but wonder if she's still anemic."

Nodding, Christina said, "Yeah. I was thinking that. Do you know if she ever made an appointment to get her blood-work done?"

Shaking his head, "Ed said, "I don't think so." Looking at Samara, who's back was turned to them, as she gazed out the window, he asked, "Samara, do you know if your mom went back to the Doctor?"

Samara turned, and shaking her head, said, "I don't think so. If she did, she never told me."

Walking over to the girl, Christina hugged her, and said, "I need to get back upstairs."

Glancing at Ed, she asked, "Will you please call me, when she get's back, or you hear anything?"

Ed stood, "Absolutely."

Riding in the elevator back up to the third floor, Christina recalled the events involving Cindy, over the past couple of months, and thought, *I feel like I'm a bad luck magnet. Seems like anyone involved in my life, has some kind of tragedy befall them. My fault? Of course not, but, I do wonder if the enemy is attacking my friends, and family, to punish me. I know things don't happen without some purpose, but, really, why them? Why now? What's going on behind the scenes, and why is God allowing them to happen?*

No answers were forthcoming.

Sighing heavily, she shook her head, and whispered, "Okay, God. I'm trusting You in these affairs, because I certainly can't see how any of this is beneficial."

The elevator doors opened, and stepping out, she almost bumped into Steven, who had his head down, reading a chart.

"Oh, hey, Steven." She said, catching herself before she actually touched him.

Looking up from the chart, he said, "Christina! I'm so glad to see you. Libby told me about Cindy. Any word on how's she's doing?"

Shaking her head, Christina told him of her visit with Ed and Samara.

Nodding, he said, "Well, I hope she'll be okay. Keep me in the loop, please."

"Sure. Are you doing anything tonight?"

He shook his head. "Nope. No solid plans. Why?"

Smiling, she said, "I was wondering if you'd like to come over, and celebrate the coming in of the new year."

Nodding, and smiling, he said, "That would be nice. I haven't celebrated the new year coming in with anybody, in several years. It'd be nice to share that moment."

"I agree. The kids already have sparklers, and noise makers to celebrate with."

Leaning against a wall, he said, "Aaron told me you're going to be taking Linda home with you sometime this week."

Nodding, she said, "Yep. I'll get her after work today."

Cocking his head, he said, "You are amazing."

She frowned. "No, I'm not. Just doing what I would hope someone would do for my kids, if anything happened to me."

"Well, I still think you're amazing. You and Janet weren't exactly best friends. Or friends at all, from what I hear."

"Well, maybe not, but Linda and Stacey are. That counts for something. I'm not going to let that girl go into foster care, or be stranded at the hospital indefinitely. School starts back in a couple of days, and she needs to be settled somewhere."

He grinned, and shook his head. "So, you want me to come over around seven tonight?"

"That sounds great! See you then."

"Okay. How about I bring some sparkling grape juice, and we can toast in the new year?'

"That sounds like fun. Looking at her watch, she said, "I have to go. I've been gone long enough."

Smiling, she did a finger wave, entered the elevator, and arrived on the third floor.

As she approached the nurses' desk, her phone buzzed in her pocket. Pulling it out, she answered, "Ed. What's going on?"

Libby walked up, and seeing Christina on the phone, stood on the opposite side of the counter, waiting to hear about Cindy.

He said, "She's back in the ER room. Still unconscious. I'm really worried, Christina. Why would she still be unconscious? Oh, wait, she's trying to open her eyes. I'll call you back in a few minutes."

Cindy tried opening her eyes, but it felt as if the lids were glued together. The veil that seemed to cover her mind like a shroud, began to clear, and she thought, *That was the weirdest dream ever. Why would I dream I passed out, and was in the hospital?*

She heard her name being called. *Ed? Why is he trying to wake me up? I hear Samara's voice also. Am I still dreaming?*

Her mind fought against the sensation of being pulled down into an abyss. It was so exhausting. *Maybe I should just give in, and see what's down there.* She began to release her grip on consciousness, when she heard a voice saying, "Cindy. Wake up now!"

Her eyes flew open. Ed's face was directly in front of hers. She glanced around the room. *Where am I? A hospital?*

Focusing her eyes back on Ed's, he said, "Welcome back, Sweetheart."

"What happened? Why am I in the hospital?'

He explained the circumstances leading up to this moment.

Trying to sit up, she asked, "How long have I been unconscious?

Samara found the remote, and raised the head of the bed.

Cindy reached out a shaky hand, and grabbed for Samara's.

"Hey, Sweetie. You okay?'

Nodding, Samara said, "I am now. I was really scared you wouldn't wake up."

Still feeling groggy, Cindy said, "I didn't realize I was out. I thought I was still asleep, and dreaming."

A nurse walked in, and began taking Cindy's vital signs.

Surprise registering in her voice, she said, "Ms. Murray, it's nice to see you're conscious. The Doctor will be in soon, and he'll go over the test results with you."

Furrowing her eyebrows, Cindy asked, "Test result?"

Samara said, "While you were out, they took you to get an x-ray, and did some blood work."

"Did I hit my head again?" Cindy asked, as she felt around her head, and touched a fresh bandage over her left eye. Noticing the IV on her arm, she sighed, and began to cry.

Stroking her face, Ed said, "You passed out in the bathroom, and hit your head on the sink, so yes, but the Dr. didn't seem to think it was critical." Noticing the tears streaming down her face, Ed said, "Oh, Honey. It'll be okay." He sat on the edge of the bed, and pulled her into his arms, where she let the tears flow. The nurse handed Ed a box of tissues.

True to her word, Dr. Harrison walked in, as the nurse was writing down Cindy's vital statistics. Carrying a clipboard containing several papers, he placed them under his arm, freeing a hand to shake with Ed's. He then nodded a greeting to Samara.

Sitting on the edge of the bed, he began explaining the results of the various tests.

Christina was standing at the nurses' counter, when a construction crew member walked up to her.

"Excuse me, Ma'am." He said with a deep baritone voice.

She turned to face him, noticing he had removed his safety hat and goggles, and was holding them in his hands. The name embroidered on his left shirt pocket read, Chuck.

"Yes?"

"I just wanted to let you know that we're almost finished repairing, and cleaning up the Cardiac Unit. I figure by next week y'all can start moving equipment, and such, back in. It should be fully operational by the end of next week."

Christina could hardly contain her excitement. "Really? Next week?"

Nodding, and smiling, he said, "Yes, Ma'am."

Christina wanted to reach out and hug him, but instead reached out her hand for a handshake.

Looking a bit embarrassed, he took her hand in his. She noticed how big, and calloused it was. *A true, hard working laborer,* she thought.

Sally Jean approached the desk, and noticing Christina's excitement, asked, "Hey. What's going on?"

Releasing the worker's hand, Christina turned to face the young woman. "He says the Cardiac Unit should be up, and operational, by the end of next week!"

Sally said, "Well, that is good news!"

Chuck cleared his throat, and said, "Guess, I'd best head back over." Donning his hat and goggles, he turned to go.

Christina called out, "Thanks, Chuck."

Not turning, he waved a hand in the air.

Sally said, "I'm glad we'll be going back to our unit, but I will miss being here. It's been interesting, and I've made a couple of friends."

Nodding, Christina said, "Yes, it has been interesting, and a bit confusing."

Sally Jean laughed out loud. "Yes, it has."

Janet woke with a start. Trying to swallow the little bit of saliva that had collected in her mouth, she winced as her throat completed the task, feeling as if she had ingested battery acid. Her whole body ached as well. Opening her eyes, she looked around the room. *This isn't the same room I was in,* she thought, as she took in the surrounding items. The walls and curtains were a different color, light blue instead of beige, and the equipment looked foreign. *Maybe I was moved to a different unit,* she thought, as she found the remote control, and pressed the button to call a nurse.

A moment later the nurse—whom Janet didn't recognize—entered the room.

"Mrs. Washburn, you're awake!"

Janet nodded slightly. Her throat was on fire, and she didn't want to talk if she didn't have to.

"How are you feeling?"

Janet whispered, "Like I've been hit by a truck, and swallowed battery acid."

The nurse smiled, and patted Janet's arm. "Well, you kinda were hit, except, that your car hit the truck, not the other way around."

My car hit a truck? Janet winced, as she swallowed again. Rubbing her throat, she asked, "May I have a drink of water?"

"Of course, Honey," the nurse replied, picking up the pitcher, and pouring a little water in the cup. Adding a straw, she held the cup so Janet could quench her thirst.

Taking a couple of sips, Janet shook her head, indicating she had had enough..

The nurses' name tag read, Julie Hall—RN.

Janet didn't recognize the name.

"You said your throat hurts?"

Janet nodded.

"That's not unusual, after one has had a respirator tube in their throat."

Janet whispered, "How long was it in?"

"Several days. You were in a medical coma."

Janet made a face. She didn't remember any of this. It was like her mind was a blank canvas.

Julie kept talking as she took Janet's blood pressure, and temperature.

"So, because your injuries were so extensive, you were brought here."

Janet blinked several times, trying to wrap her mind around the information presented.

"Where is here?" She whispered.

Smiling, Julie said, "You're in the Trauma Intensive Care Unit, in Dallas Memorial Hospital."

"Dallas?"

Nodding, Julie said, "Yes Ma'am."

"How did I get here? What day is it?" Janet had more questions, but her throat screamed in silent protest with each whispered word.

"You arrived by helicopter a few days ago, and today is New Year's Eve."

Janet closed her eyes. *How long was I unconscious? Did I miss Christmas?* Straining against the invisible barriers in her mind, she couldn't force any memories through. A tear trickled down her cheek.

Wiping it away, with a casted hand, she looked at the petite nurse, and said, "I can't remember anything."

Patting Janet's arm, she replied, "Your memory will return the more you're awake. It's all stored in your subconscious, and has to return to your conscious mind. We see this in a lot of our trauma patients."

"What if it doesn't return?"

"I guess we'll cross that bridge if we get to it." After recording the pertinent information, Julie asked, "Is there anything else I can get you? Are you hungry?"

Janet whispered, "I just need something for this sore throat."

Julie nodded. "I'll be contacting the Doctor, and I'll mention it to him." Grabbing the water pitcher, she said, "I'll bring you some fresh water."

Janet nodded. "Thanks."

Lying prone, staring at the ceiling, Janet forced her body to relax, as she let her mind wander. Beginning with her head, she inventoried each body part, tensing and releasing the muscles surrounding each joint and extremity, as well as the muscles in her back and abdomen. Some areas were more tender than others, and she winced with awareness of each. Once the task was completed, she was left with a dull ache throughout her body.

Julie returned with a fresh pitcher of ice water, poured a glass, added a straw, and held it so Janet could take a sip.

"Thanks." Janet said appreciatively. "Could I please have something for the pain I'm feeling throughout my body?"

Nodding, Julie said, "Of course. I was planning on asking you if you needed anything."

Forcing a smile, Janet said, "I just inventoried my body, and I'm surprised to find that every inch of it hurts."

Nodding, Julie said, "Yes, Ma'am. There isn't an inch on you anywhere, that wasn't broken or bruised." Pulling a syringe out of her pocket, Julie administered a clear liquid into the IV port in Janet's hand. "There you go. You should be feeling the effects within minutes."

"Actually, I'm feeling it right now." Janet closed her eyes, and let her mind and body drift into unconsciousness.

Returning to the nurses' station, Julie was pleased to see see Dr. Knorr standing there, perusing Janet's chart.

Looking up, he asked, "So how's my patient?"

Julie informed him of Janet's progress, and asked for medication to ease her throat's discomfort.

"I'll prescribe a numbing spray for her throat."

Julie followed him into Janet's room, and stood by as he examined the sleeping woman.

Turning to Julie, he said, "I'm going to begin physical therapy this afternoon. I'd like to see her sitting up on her own, by then end of the week." Stroking his goatee, he added, "Depending on her progress, we may have her standing by the bed next week sometime. The longer she stays immobile, the weaker she will get, and it will be more difficult to retrain her brain and muscles."

Arching her eyebrows in surprise, Julie said, "Okay. When she wakes, I'll let her know."

Turning to leave, Julie asked, "Do you want me to call Physical Therapy?"

Shaking his head, he said, "No. I want to discuss the procedures, and goals, with them first. This is going to be a long, painful recovery time for Janet, and we all need to be on the same page. I have a feeling she may fight us on some of the exercises and such, because of the pain. I'll keep her on the pain meds a while longer."

Dr. Knorr handed the chart to Julie, and said, "Call me if anything out of the ordinary happens. I think Janet has made a turn for the better."

Linda gathered her meager belongings, and sat cross-legged on the bed, patiently waiting for Christina to come take her home. *Well, not my home,* she thought. Watching the second hand tic-tic-tic around the face of the clock above the TV, she felt anxiety building in her chest. *Did Mrs. Sanders forget me? Dr. Carmichael said I could be released today. Why is she so late?*

She was so ready to leave the hospital. Everyone was nice, and all, but it wasn't home. Biting a hangnail on her thumb, she thought about the accident, which led her to think about her mom. *I hope she's okay. I wonder if Mrs. Sanders will take me to see her?*

Her eyes traveled back to the clock face. Another five minutes had passed. *How long have I been here?* She knew the accident had occurred the week after Thanksgiving, and New Years day was tomorrow, so...almost two months. *Wow,* she thought, *it sure seemed longer.* It felt like several months.

She scooted to the edge of the bed, and stood, just as Christina entered the room. Linda was so happy to see her, that she wrapped her thin arms around Christina's waist.

"Oh, Honey." Christina sighed, as she returned the child's hug. "Are you ready to go?"

Nodding, she grabbed her bag of personal items from the bed, and said, "Am I ever! I hope I never have to come back here again."

Cocking her head, Christina asked, "Was it that bad?"

Smiling sheepishly, Linda said, "No. Not really. I'm just looking forward to seeing something besides hospital walls."

"Well, we've got your room all ready for you. Do you want to stop by your house to pick up clothes, school books, and such?"

Linda rolled her eyes. "Ugh, school."

Raising her eyebrows, Christina said, "I thought you loved school."

Shrugging, Linda replied, "I do. It's just I've been away for so long, and I've kinda gotten used to sleeping, eating, and watching TV anytime I want."

Putting her arm around Linda's shoulder, Christina led her out to the nurses' station. "I have to sign a couple of forms, then we can get going."

Linda watched, as two of the nurses came around the counter, and gave her hugs, and words of encouragement.

Sonya, the nurse in charge of the unit, said, "Hey, don't forget about us."

"Yeah. Come back and visit us sometime." Said another, named Caroline.

Returning the hugs, Linda said, "Thank y'all so much for taking care of me. I'll never forget you. I promise."

Sonya handed Linda an envelope. "This is a little something from all the nurses here. There's also a note from Mattie. She was sorry she couldn't be here to send you off."

Linda felt tears sting her eyes. She had so hoped to see Mattie one more time.

Turning the envelope over in her hands, she asked, "Should I open it here?"

Sonya shook her head, "Why don't you wait 'till you get home?"

"Okay." Linda said, giving hugs one more time before heading to the elevator.

Once they were in the car, and headed in the direction of Linda's house, she asked, "Mrs. Sanders, have you heard how my mom's doing?"

Smiling, and nodding, Christina said, "I was wondering when you'd ask me that. I asked Dr. Dawson to call, and check on her today, and her Doctor said she's improving. She's off the ventilator, and breathing on her own. She's even regained consciousness a couple of times."

Hope etched on her face, Linda asked, "Can I go see her soon?"

Reaching over, and patting Linda's leg, Christina said, "Of course. I'll check with the Doctor tomorrow. I'd like to see her as well."

Linda sighed heavily. "Thanks. I really miss her."

Christina said, "I know, Honey."

As the van pulled into the driveway, Linda asked, "Do you have a house-key?"

Nodding, Christina reached into her purse, and withdrew Janet's keyring.

Looking confused, Linda asked, "How did you get that?"

"The sheriff had it from the accident. When I told him I needed to bring you by to get a few things, he gave me the whole keyring, because he wasn't sure which key would open the front door."

"Oh. Okay." Holding out her hand, she said, "Here. I'll find the right key." Separating the keys, she handed the group back to Christina. As Christina opened the door, Linda sighed, and said, "It's gonna be weird going in, and not seeing my mom."

"I'll come in with you. I want to turn down the thermostats for the house, and hot water. No use wasting electricity."

Entering the warm, empty house, Christina heard Linda gasp.

"It's okay, Honey. You go get what you need. We don't have to stay long."

Making a face, Linda said, "It's just creepy. It's so...empty."

Christina felt a little uneasy herself. It always felt strange going into someone's empty house.

Glancing out the van window, as it pulled into the Sander's garage, Linda was pleased to see the Sander's siblings lined up, and ready to greet her.

Stacey ran out first, opened the van door, and practically pulled Linda out of her seat. As Linda's feet touched the concrete floor of the garage, Stacey pulled her into a hug. Releasing her, Stacey said, "I'm so glad you're here! I hope you like the room we fixed up for you. It's right next to mine."

Linda asked, "Is it the one over the porch?"

Nodding, Stacey said, "Yep."

Linda grinned. "I love that room!"

As Christina opened the back door of the van, she said, "Brad and Nicky, why don't y'all help bring these things into Linda's room?"

"Hey, Linda." Nicky called, "Do you want these bags, and stuff in the front seat?"

Linda nodded.

Grabbing a book bag, Nicky asked, "What do you have in here, a load of bricks?"

Linda giggled, "No. Just my art stuff."

Brad grabbed a couple of suit cases, and said to his mom, "I'll go put this stuff in Linda's room, then come get the rest of the stuff."

Stacey helped Linda up the back steps leading into the kitchen, past the obstacle course of abandoned shoes, laundry baskets, pet toys, and a very happy dog, who wanted desperately to lavish kisses all over Linda's face. They finally ended up in front of the couch in the family room. Linda giggled.

"Does Benji always get that excited when people come over?" She asked, as she stroked the dog's head.

Grinning, as she helped Linda sit, Stacey said, "He gets excited when we walk out of his sight for a few minutes, then return. One would think we'd been gone for hours, instead of minutes."

Shaking her head, Linda said, "Dogs are weird."

Nodding, Stacey said, "Yep, but so loveable."

Stacey, being a solicitous friend, found pillows to prop behind Linda's back, and under her casted arm, and a blanket to cover the lower half of her body.

"Is there anything else I can get you?" Stacey asked, as she watched Linda adjust her still tender and weak body, onto the couch.

Laying her head back, Linda exhaled. "Whew! That was exhausting."

Stacey grimaced. "Yeah. After I got home from having my appendix out, I immediately took a nap."

"Yeah," Linda said on a sigh. "I feel like I could take one right now."

Linda tried raising her feet so she could stretch out on the sofa, but was astounded at how weak she felt.

"I don't get it," she said, "I was able to get up and down, and walk around at the hospital, but now, I can't even raise my legs." Tears flooded her eyes, and ran down her cheeks.

Stacey bent down, and gently lifted Linda's feet onto the couch. "It's okay, Linda. Think about all you've done today. You had to get your stuff together at the hospital, then go get other stuff from your house, which included walking, bending, and lifting. It's no wonder you're tired and weak right now."

Linda wiped at the tears with her sweater sleeve.

"Here." Stacey said, handing a box of tissues to her distraught friend.

Linda wiped her eyes, and blew her nose. "I'm sorry. I'm blubbering like a baby."

Shaking her head, Stacey said, "No you're not, and you don't have to apologize for anything. I'm just glad we can be here for you."

Benji jumped on the couch, and settled himself at Linda's feet.

Once settled, Linda pulled an envelope out of her sweater pocket, and pried it open.

"What's that?" Stacey asked, as she watched Linda carefully extract the card from the envelope.

Linda said, "One of the nurses at the hospital gave it to me. I think it's a get well card."

Opening the card, and finding several ten dollar bills, she gasped. "Oh my, goodness!"

"How much is there?" Stacey asked, excitement showing on her face.

Linda counted ten bills. Putting her hand to her mouth, she whispered, "There's ten. A hundred dollars! Oh my goodness! I've never seen a hundred dollars before!"

"What does the card say?" Stacey asked, as she leaned in to get a better look.

She held it up for Stacey to see. "It basically says "Get well soon," but it has signatures, and notes of encouragement from the nurses, cleaning staff, and even Dr. Carmichael."

Christina walked in, when she heard the excitement.

Hardly able to contain her excitement, Stacey said, "Mom! The nurses gave Linda one-hundred dollars!"

Christina smiled, and nodded. "That's very generous. How sweet of them to give you such a nice gift."

Pushing Benji over, Stacey sat cross-legged at the end of the couch. "What are you going to do with it?"

Shaking her head, Linda said, "I don't know. I'd like to get a new pair of boots. The ones I have are getting too small."

Christina sat in her chair opposite the girls, and said, "When you are up to it, we can go shopping."

"Mrs. Sanders, could you help me write a thank you note to the nurses, and Mattie?"

"Of course. We can do that tomorrow. Who is Mattie?"

Linda smiled, and in a hushed, reverential tone said, "She was the most amazing lady." She told of her experience with Mattie.

Stacey said, "Maybe she was an angel, sent to make you feel better."

Linda thought for a moment, then said, "Well, it wouldn't surprise me if she was."

Christina heard the boys bounding down the stairs, sounding like a pack of dogs chasing a frightened rabbit.

"Brad?" She called.

"Yeah, Mom."

"Can you please come help me get dinner ready?"

"Sure. I'll be right in."

Nicky called out, "What are we having?"

"Spaghetti."

Rubbing his tummy as he entered the family room, Nicky asked Linda, "Have you ever had any of my mom's spaghetti?"

Shaking her head, Linda said, "No."

"Well, be prepared to eat the best spaghetti in the world!"

Stacey and Linda looked at each other, and giggled.

"The best in the world?" Linda asked. "So, you've tried other spaghetti from around the world?"

Nicky shook his head, and in all seriousness, said, "Don't need to. I just know."

The girls giggled again.

Christina heard the conversation from the kitchen, and smiled. As long as her children thought her spaghetti was the best in the world, she would gladly continue preparing it the way her mom had taught her: a jar of sauce with an added dash of this, and a pinch of that.

Brad said, "Tonight is the candlelight vigil at the high school. Do y'all still want to go?"

Stacey and Nicky said, "Of course." Linda asked if she could go too.

"Yeah. It's gonna be cold and possibly raining or snowing though." Brad said, looking at his mom.

Christina said, "Well, I can take y'all, and just wait in the van. How long do you think it'll last, Brad?"

"I'm not sure. Sylvia, the girl in charge, says she's invited our youth pastor to come lead in a few choruses, then maybe some prayers. She says it depends on how many come, and how wet and cold it is. Could be anywhere from a half-hour to two or three."

"Two or three?" Stacey asked.

Shaking his head, Brad said, "I think between a half-hour to an hour at most."

"I'm not sure I want to stay a long time." Linda said. "Maybe I should stay home. I didn't even know the guy. I'd see him at church sometimes, but we didn't talk."

Christina said, "Well, like I said, I can sit in the van, and wait. If any of you want to come back, we'll just hang out there until it's over."

Nodding, Brad said, "That sounds good. It starts at seven, so we have about an hour."

Christina said, "That'll give us time to clean up."

As Brad helped his mom load the dishwasher, she said, "That Sylvia girl sounds pretty amazing. I heard she's helping organize the funeral also."

Nodding, Brad said, "Yeah. She is amazing. She certainly has an organizational gift."

"Oh, I forgot to mention that Dr. Dawson will be here around seven-thirty to spend New-Years' eve with us. I hope the ceremony doesn't go too long. We'll be cutting it close as it is. Maybe I should call him, and ask him to come later."

Brad said, "We don't have to stay the whole time, but maybe you should let him know we may be a little late."

Nodding, she said, "Yeah. Not a bad idea."

As Christina changed the bed sheets, Wednesday morning, she thought of New Year's eve. True to his word, Steven arrived at seven-thirty, a few minutes after they had arrived home from the memorial ceremony. He surprised Christina with a bouquet of mixed flowers, and a grocery bag full of sweet and salty snacks, as well as a case of canned Dr. Pepper.

Christina was surprised, and giggled with delight.

"Steven! These flowers are beautiful! Come on in, and I'll put them in a vase."

Looking towards the den, she called, "Brad, could you please come in here and help?"

A minute later, Brad relieved Steven of the case of drinks, and bag of groceries.

Steven removed his coat, and followed Christina into the kitchen.

"Hey, Dr. Dawson." Nicky said in greeting, as he helped Brad unload the bag of snacks.

Steven reached out, and did a high-five with Nicky.

"Wow!" Nicky exclaimed as he pulled out a bag of marshmallows, graham crackers, and chocolate bars. "S'mores! Awesome!"

Brad opened the refrigerator, and re-arranged items to make room for the cans of Dr. Peppers.

Christina glanced towards the stairs, as she heard Stacey and Linda descend.

Stacey, walked over to Steven, and gave him a hug.

Steven returned the hug, and said, "Stacey, it's nice to see you again." Glancing over at Linda, he added, "It's nice to see you as well." She smiled, shyly.

Nicky asked, "Anyone want to play Spades or Scrabble, or that new game, Sequence?"

Steven said, "I haven't played any of those games in a long time. You may have to refresh my memory."

Christina placed the vase of flowers on the table in the breakfast nook.

Smiling, she said, "They look so pretty here."

"Not as pretty as you."

She shook her head, and said, "Well, I'm not so sure about that."

Opening his arms, he said, "Come here."

She did. He wrapped his arms around her, and all she could think was that he smelled terrific, and felt so warm, and strong. Sighing, she felt herself melt into him.

Stacey looked over, and spying her mom, and Dr. Dawson, nudged Linda, who nodded and grinned.

Pulling her out of her "moment," Nicky called, "Hey Mom!"

"Yes?" She said, pulling away from Steven.

"Are y'all coming or what? I've got the card table set up."

"We're coming." Taking Steven's hand, she led him into the family room.

They played a couple games of Scrabble and Sequence, and were just beginning the game of Spades, when Steven's watch beeped, indicating the new year was about to arrive. Turning the volume up on the TV, they all stood, and counted down with the crowd in New York, as the ball dropped, and heralded in a new year. Jumping, shouting, noise makers, high-fives, and hugs filled the TV screen, as well as in Christina's family room. Once the celebration ceased, they returned to the card table, and were able to finish the game of spades.

When the ball dropped in New York City, announcing the beginning of a new year, many folks in Alva, as well as around the globe, were excited and thankful. For many, it meant another chance to right some wrongs, and for others it symbolized hope—another chance to step out in faith, and begin a new adventure. For the victims, and survivors of the recent attacks on America, it held a profound sense of loss, as they stepped into a new year without a loved one.

When all the hugs, high-fives, and happy new-year wishes stopped, Christina announced it was time to clean up the den, and head off to bed.

When everything settled down, Steven announced he had a few patients to see later that morning, and should get at least a few hours of sleep.

Steven pulled Christina into a hug, at the front door, and said, "Thanks for sharing the new year celebration with me. I don't usually stay awake long enough to see the ball drop. Your kids are amazing, and fun to be around."

Christina pulled back, and looked into Steven's face.

"Thank you for coming. I know the kids enjoyed your company."

"Just the kids?" He asked.

Grinning, she said, "Oh yes. I enjoyed having you here as well."

Feigning worry, he said, "Whew! I was concerned for a minute."

She playfully punched him on the arm. He pulled her into another hug, pinning her arms to her waist.

Trying to wiggle out, she said, "Hey!"

He then leaned down, and kissed her, slowly releasing her arms. She relaxed into him, putting her arms around his neck.

When he pulled away, she lost her balance, and nearly fell.

Feeling a blush creep up her neck, and to her cheeks, she said, "Oops! I guess it could be said, that you nearly swept me off my feet!"

Laughing, he said, "I really do have to go."

Nodding, Christina said, "I know."

"You have to work today?"

"No. Not 'till Wednesday afternoon."

"Well, you best get off to bed yourself."

"That's the plan," she said, feeling a yawn creep in.

"See you soon." Steven said, as he pulled up his coat collar, and headed into the cold, gusty wind.

She closed the door, and leaned her backside on it, thinking about how fortunate she was to have such awesome kids, and friends.

"Thank you God, for loving, protecting and providing for us."

Jesse sat at his kitchen table, staring blankly at the empty beer cans sitting before him. He wasn't normally a big drinker, but after the day he had, he needed something to take the edge off his grief. He relived the past few days in his mind. Going over every minute detail. *The pain in my heart, and soul, is more than I can bear!*

His eyes stung with grief and exhaustion. He hadn't slept for more than a few hours since this whole Christmas fiasco began. Taking another sip of warm beer, he thought about Jamie.

Poor kid. He must be miserable as well. He and Jimmy were practically joined at the hip at times. I wonder how he's going to get along after all this.

Massaging his forehead, and eyes, and finding no relief, he pinched the bridge of his nose and squeezed his eyes as tight as he could, trying to keep the tears from flowing. Instead, he felt a sob begin deep in his being, and try as he might, couldn't keep it from erupting. With the sob came the tears. He stood, and knocked the empty cans off the table, turned the chair and table over, then fell to his knees, pounding his fists on the tile floor.

Sheriff Clifton knocked on Jesse's door. No one answered. Looking around, he saw the pick-up truck in the driveway. Concern filled his heart. He turned the doorknob, and finding the door unlocked, carefully opened it.

"Jesse?" He called in a stage whisper. No answer. Unsnapping his gun's holster, and keeping his hand resting on the handle of the gun, he cautiously walked through the quiet house, calling out, and checking each room. He imagined finding Jesse hanging from a fixture, or shot in the head, or some other way of ending his life. When he had talked to the grieving man that morning, he had given off an air of wanting to join his wife and son in death.

In all the years Larry had worked in law enforcement, he had only seen a couple of suicides. The one that stuck in his mind, and sometimes occupied his dreams, was a thirteen year old girl, who had slashed her wrists because she had been teased and bullied at school. She was born with a large purplish birthmark, called a Port Wine stain, over one side of her face. *Of all the places it could show up,* he wondered, *why it had to be on her face?* A few of the kids decided she was a good target for their cruelty. *Why do kids have to be so cruel?*

Finding the kitchen in disarray, and Jesse curled into a fetal position on the floor, he withdrew his gun, thinking maybe there had been a break-in. He looked around, and seeing no one, re-holstered his weapon. Walking over to Jesse, he felt for a pulse. It was strong. Spying all the empty beer cans strewn across the floor, he nodded, realizing Jesse's unconsciousness was probably caused by too much alcohol consumption, and exhaustion. He knew the man, like himself, had hardly slept since Christmas eve, when the town had been thrown into chaos, because a couple of boys, wanting to shake it up.

Pulling a chair over beside the prone man, he sat, and rubbing his temples, let his mind wander. He knew in his heart that Jimmy and Jamie had caused all the chaos. Now, he had to decide Jamie's fate.

He heard Jesse groan, and watched as he pulled himself out of an alcohol induced sleep.

Sitting up, and rubbing his eyes, he jumped when he spied the sheriff.

Cursing, he said, "Larry! You almost gave me a heart attack! What are you doing here?"

Standing, and reaching out a hand to help Jesse stand, he said, "Well, I came to check on you, for one, and I've decided what to do about Jamie."

Pulling over one of the kitchen chairs that had not been upended, he sat across from Larry.

"What do you mean you've decided what to do about Jamie?"

"Look, I know Jimmy and Jamie were responsible for all the bedlam, with the fireworks and fire."

"But how?" Jesse stuttered.

Holding a hand up, Larry said, "Let me finish."

Jesse nodded.

"I don't have a lot of evidence, besides the lighter with your initials on it, and the phone messages in Jamie's phone, but I think that's enough. I've decided not to let your son's name be tarnished with any kind of prosecution."

Jesse opened his mouth to say something, but Larry put his hand up.

"Because Jamie's been through enough punishment with losing his best friend, I have decided to be lenient with him as well. He has a clean record, so far, and I'd like to keep it that way. So, I've decided to put him on probation for a year, and he'll have to do community service."

Jesse said, "Can I speak now?"

Reaching out his hand, he said, "Thanks, Sheriff."

Nodding, and standing, Larry said, "You're welcome, and happy new year. Please, don't do any harm to yourself. I don't have that many friends, and besides, it'd ruin all the new year celebrations to come."

Jesse, couldn't help but smile. "I certainly don't want to ruin your new year's celebrations. But I have to admit, I have thought seriously about ending my life."

Nodding, Larry said, "I know. I've been there a couple of times myself. This is the worst time ever, but you do have people who care about you, and would miss you terribly if you followed through with those thoughts."

Hardly able to speak, because of the lump in his throat, Jesse said, "I know, and I'm grateful, but the pain in my chest is almost unbearable."

Larry pulled his friend into a hug, and patted his back. Words didn't need to be spoken. Both men had tears running down their cheeks, when Larry disengaged, and turned to go.

"Thanks Sheriff."

Larry couldn't speak past the lump in his throat, so he waved as he exited the house.

Jesse was alone once again. He walked to his son's room, and sat on the bed, looking around at the collection of things that defined Jimmy. He hadn't been in touch with the boy over the past five years, so some of the things he didn't recognize.

Walking over to the dresser, he thumbed through a stack of comics. Both DC and Marvel. He then picked up different cartoon figures, and examined them. *These are cool,* he thought. *I wonder when he got these?*

Smiling, he remembered watching cartoons with some of the same characters when he was a boy, and wanting the comic books, and action figures. He was never able to collect many items during his childhood, however. His dad was in the military, so when he would be reassigned, which seemed to happen every couple of years, the family would follow. As he ran a finger over the comic books, he felt a sadness in his heart, remembering how his mom would cry, as she repacked their meager belongings. When he was in grade school, the moves didn't bother him, as he would get excited about moving to a new place, and making new friends. Once he entered middle-school, then high-school, the moves became more stressful, as his friendship bonds became stronger. The summer before he was to enter his Junior year in high school, his dad was reassigned. He begged, and pleaded with his parents, to let him stay to finish out his last two years of high-school. His mom, who could see the sadness in her son, must have convinced his dad to let him stay. He ended up moving in with his best friend.

His parents were only a couple of states over, so it wasn't as if he'd never see them again. In fact, he would visit during the holidays, and over the summer. Looking back on that time, he realized the sacrifice his mother made, in letting him stay. His dad was hardly around, but his mom was always available, and involved in his life. Oh how she must have missed him, but not once did she ask him to return to her. He felt new tears, and sadness fill his being, as he thought of her, and wished he could tell her again, how much he appreciated her standing up for him.

He missed his dad too, but he didn't feel as strong a connection with him, because he was hardly around during his formative years.

He picked up different items strewn about the room, and for an instant thought, *I should get Jimmy to clean this room.*

Realizing his mistake, he swept his arm across the dresser top, and the desk that held his son's computer and books. They ended up on the floor with muffled bangs, as each item hit the wall, floor, or another object. He sat on the floor next to his son's bed, grabbed a t-shirt, wrapped his fingers in it, held it to his mouth, and screamed, and raged against God, and any other power that might be.

"*You are not alone.*" A voice seemed to say in his head.

He stopped blubbering, and inhaled sharply, as the statement felt like an arrow, hitting his center mass. *Was that the voice of God?*

"What?" He asked warily, wanting to confirm that the voice was real, and not a figment of his imagination.

"*You are not alone. I will always be with you. I have plans for you.*"

"What plans?"

He heard only silence, but felt a warm sensation wrap around his body, as if her were being enfolded in a warm blanket. *Such bliss*, he thought, as his mind, and body, relaxed into it. He felt such a profound sense of love, acceptance, and peace. After a few moments, the sensation withdrew. He knew then and there, that what he had experienced was definitely supernatural, and believed beyond a shadow of a doubt, that he had been hugged by God. The overwhelming feelings of grief, guilt, and self-loathing seemed to melt away. When he thought of his son, he was still sad, but the gut-wrenching, debilitating, grief wasn't there. *How can that be?* He wondered. *A few minutes ago, I wanted to just curl up and die, but now, it's almost like I have electricity buzzing through my body, and I can't sit still, because I know there's more I need to do. I need to talk to someone about this.* He sat for a while, mulling over the incident, and wondering who in his circle of friends, acquaintances, and colleagues, he could share this with, that wouldn't think he was crazy. The only name that popped up in his mind, was Christina Sanders.

What? He thought. *I don't even know the lady. I've only met her once when we arrived to put out the fire on the Cardiac Care Unit. How would I even approach her to talk about this? Walk up, and say 'Hey, you won't believe this, but God spoke to me, and said I need to talk to you.'*

His thoughts were interrupted by the ringing of the house phone.

He answered it on the fifth ring.

It was Jack, Jamie's dad.

After greetings, Jack said, "I just wanted to call and check up on you. I know we're not close friends, but our boys are...were."

Nodding, Jesse said, "Well, I'm doing as well as expected for a man who just lost his son." *If anyone else asks me how I'm doing, I'm afraid I might just punch them in the face.*

"If it had been Jamie, I'm sure I would feel the same." Clearing his throat, Jack continued, "I want you to know that Jamie and I are willing to do anything, to help you get through this awful time." Hearing nothing but silence, he added, "I wish I knew what to say, or do to help, but I just don't."

Jesse cleared his throat, and ran his hand over his face.

"Thanks, Jack. It means a lot to me to know that you're willing to help. Jamie has already been a great help in getting the funeral arrangements set up." Pausing, to get his emotions under control, he continued, "You've got a great son there, Jack. Please don't do as I did. Don't waste precious time blaming him for what's wrong in your life. We never know when our number is up."

Jack nodded, and wiped his eyes. He wasn't usually an emotional man, but Jimmy's death had put cracks in the barrier he had built around his emotions for the past five years.

"You're so right, Jesse."

Both men were silent for a minute, when Jack said, "Well, I guess I'll go now. Remember, if there's anything we can do, just call."

"Thanks, Jack. I'll see you around."

Setting the receiver down, Jesse thought, *As if there's anything Jack could do to help.* Heading to the garage, he thought, *I need to see if there are any empty boxes in there.*

Dr. Harrison, looking at the papers on his clip board said, "Mrs. Murray, your red blood cell count is a bit lower than it was when we ran it a couple of months ago. A normal count for a female your age should be around fifteen or sixteen. Yours is at ten. Two points lower than the previous test."

Cindy asked, "Are all the other numbers normal?"

Nodding, he said, "Yes, I'm happy to say."

Ed asked, "So where do we go from here?"

"Being this is New Year's Eve, I'll let y'all go on home, but first thing Wednesday morning, I want Cindy to call this number in Dallas, and make an appointment for a GI study, and possible, EGD."

"What is that?" Samara asked.

"It stands for esophagogastroduodenoscopy."

"What?" Cindy, Ed, and Samara asked together.

Dr. Harrison smiled. "That's why we call it an EGD. Cindy will be put to sleep, and a scope with a camera attached, will be directed down through her esophagus, into her stomach, and down to the opening to the small intestine.

During this time, the doctor will be looking at the lining of each to determine if there is an infection brewing, any kind of tear, or if there may be an ulcer which is causing the bleeding. If that proves inconclusive, then a scope of her large bowel will be ordered."

"What if that doesn't show anything?" Ed asked, concern filling his face.

Dr. Harrison stood, patting Cindy's leg. "You know what? We'll cross that bridge when, or if, we come to it. A lot of times, in instances like this, there is usually a stomach ulcer that has infringed upon a blood vessel."

Looking up, Cindy asked, "So if it's just an ulcer, what will you do?"

"It depends where it is located, and how big it is. Sometimes it can be cauterized, other times, medication, and diet, can help it heal. In the mean time, just don't eat anything spicy, or has a lot of seeds in it." Reaching out to shake Ed's hand, he said, "Happy New Year." Pointing at Cindy he said, "Let me know when your appointment with the GI doctor in Dallas is."

As he walked towards the door, Cindy said, "Hey, don't forget to sign me out."

Not turning, he nodded, and did a hand wave.

Cindy let out a sigh. "I'm sorry to have worried you two."

Ed took her hand, and kissed it, while Samara held the other hand.

"It's not like you planned this, right?" Samara said.

Cindy smiled. "Right. Doggone it! What a way to ruin a holiday, though."

Ed said, "Hey, it's not over yet. We can still make it home to watch most of the New Year Celebrations on TV."

Looking at the clock on the wall, Samara said, "Geeze, it's only eight o'clock. We've got plenty of time."

Cindy smiled. Her heart swelled with love for these two amazing people.

"Mrs. Murray?" A nurse asked, as she came into the room.

"Yes, Ma'am." Cindy answered.

"I have dismissal orders for you to sign. I can remove your IV first if you'd like."

"Sure."

Samara found the bag containing her mother's clothes, and laid them on the bed, as the nurse finished with the IV.

"Do you need me to help you, Mom?" Samara asked, as Cindy grabbed the bag, and headed to the bathroom.

"Nope. I'll be fine."

Grabbing his coat off the chair, Ed said to Samara, "I'm going to bring the car around, and get it warm."

"Good idea. We'll meet you at the entrance."

Cindy exited the bathroom, as an aide entered with a wheelchair.

"Here, Mom." Samara said, handing Cindy her coat and gloves, as she donned her own.

"I can take my mom from here," Samara said, grabbing the handles of the chair.

Shrugging, the aide said, "Okay. Just leave the chair by the entrance."

When Ed saw his ladies nearing the exit, he opened the car door. The frigid air made both women gasp.

"Jimminy Cricket! It's cold!" Squealed Samara.

Grabbing the handles of the chair, Ed said, "Get in Samara. I'll take the wheelchair back,"

"Goodness! It must have dropped another twenty degrees since we got here!" Cindy said, shivering in spite of the heater fan being on high. "I feel like I'll never be warm again!"

"I know! Me either!" Samara said from the back seat.

"According to the weather man, this is the coldest it's been in Texas on New Years eve, in years."

"I believe it!" Cindy said. "I feel the cold all the way to my bones!"

"Me too!" Added Samara.

The next morning, Cindy called Christina and informed her about Dr. Harrison's diagnosis, and plan of care.

"So," she said wearily, "I have to schedule an appointment for some kind of scope thing they put down my esophagus, to see if there may be a bleeding ulcer or something."

"Oh Cindy, I'm sorry you have to go through this, but hopefully, the Doc can get to the bottom of why you're so anemic."

Sighing, Cindy said, "Yeah, I know. It just scares me a bit."

"I know, but depending when you schedule it, I will be there. The procedure only takes about twenty minutes or so, then you wake up pretty soon after. The medication to put you under, is pretty short acting. Most folks are in and out, in a couple of hours."

"That's good. Ed said if he can, he'll take the day off to be with me. If for some reason he can't, can you be there?"

"Tell you what. Let me look at my schedule, and I'll let you know the days I'll be available. That way, I can for sure be there."

"Oh, thank you, Christina. We can do that later. By the way, happy new year."

"Happy new year to you, Ed, and Samara, as well."

Jamie sat on the bed in his room, watching Little Lady feed her whimpering puppies. Their eyes were open, and they were beginning to explore their surroundings. He smiled, as he watched her gently nudge one stray pup, who had crawled to the edge of the blanket, back to her side. Jamie chuckled as the little guy tried to find an unoccupied nursing spot. He eventually pushed one of the other pups out of the way.

Pulling the Sander's photo album from under his bed, he turned to his favorite picture of the family. David, Christina, and the three kids were at a park somewhere, probably in Michigan, in the fall, sitting on a large rock with colorful trees in the background. They looked so happy. Little did they know that their world would be shattered by David's death, in a few months. *If they had known that David would no longer be with them, would they have lived their lives differently? Maybe spent more quality time together? If he had known Jimmy would have died because of a stupid decision, would he have done something differently? Yeah. He would have told Jimmy not to follow through with his plan to burn down the refinery.*

Rubbing his eyes, which felt like someone had dumped a truck full of sand in, he returned the album to it's hiding place, and stood. He had made his decision. He would return the album tomorrow night, while everyone slept. One last visit, and he would be done exploring people's homes. He didn't want to risk getting caught. Not anymore. Who could he share that information with, now that Jimmy was gone? It wouldn't be worth the excitement, it he couldn't share with his best friend.

Suddenly, he felt an overwhelming sadness wash over him, which took his breath, and made his knees go weak. He sat back down until the feeling passed.

Grief is so weird, he thought. *One minute, I feel like I'm okay, then it rears its ugly head, and knocks the breath out of me.*

Looking around the room, he said, "Hey Buddy, if you're still hanging around, can you maybe help me out every now and then?" Hearing no reply, which didn't surprise him, he stood once again, let out a big sigh, and headed towards the kitchen, where he found his dad sitting at the table with a cup of coffee in front of him.

Janet moaned, as she tried to turn over in the narrow hospital bed. It took her a minute to remember where she was. Pushing the nurses call button, she waited patiently until someone answered.

A young woman, whom Janet didn't recognize, entered. Walking over to the chalkboard hanging directly across from Janet, she erased the previous nurse's name, and printed hers.

"Good afternoon, Mrs. Washburn. My name is Shannon. I'll be taking care of you today."

"What time is it?" Janet asked groggily.

"It is three fifteen." Walking over to turn off the call button, she asked, "So, what can I do for you?"

"First, I'd like a drink of water. My mouth doesn't seem to have any spit in it."

Shannon poured a cup of water, and handed it to Janet.

"Is there anything else?"

Swallowing the refreshing liquid, Janet asked, "Can I get up to go to the toilet?"

Shaking her head, Shannon said, "Not yet, but I can help you with the bed pan. You still have a catheter, so now that you're awake more, maybe it can be removed."

Janet frowned, and nodded.

Shannon continued, "Mrs. Washburn, you've been unconscious for almost two months. During that time, your muscles have atrophied. Plus, you have casts on both legs, and arms. They will feel very heavy, once you're up. The doctor has orders for physical therapy to begin tomorrow, to help strengthen all your muscles." Smiling, she added, "You'll be up, and back to normal before you know it."

Janet sighed heavily. "If you say so. What day is it?

Fluffing Janet's pillow, and straightening the sheets and blankets, she said, "It's Monday, new year's eve."

"New year's eve? Oh my goodness! I have been out for a while. Am I still in the hospital in Alva?"

Shaking her head, Shannon said, "No Ma'am. You are in the trauma unit at Dallas Memorial Hospital."

"Dallas? Why am I here?"

"Mrs. Washburn." Shannon began, trying not to let her irritation show, because she knew Janet had been given this information the day before.

"Call me Janet."

"Janet, you were in a terrible automobile accident."

Janet held up her hand. "What kind of automobile accident?"

"You didn't stop at an intersection, and your car plowed into a truck."

"Oh, goodness! Is the driver okay?"

Nodding, Shannon said, "Yes. His truck was a lot bigger than your car, so he wasn't injured. It did do quite a bit of damage to his passenger side door, however."

"My car?"

Shannon made a face, "Your car was totaled. It was a miracle you weren't killed."

"I don't remember that at all."

"That happens sometimes when someone is injured as severely as you were. It's kind of like your brain shuts down, to protect you from remembering the trauma."

Nodding slowly, Janet contemplated that for a moment.

"Your daughter is doing well, from what I've heard."

Janet looked surprised. "I have a daughter?"

"Yes. She's thirteen. Fortunately, her injuries were not as severe as yours, so she stayed at the Alva hospital."

Janet held up a hand. "Wait." Rubbing her forehead, she said, "It's so weird. I don't remember anything before right now."

Patting her hand, Shannon said, "That's not unusual for accident victims. Your memory should return in a few days, once all the pain medications are out of your body. They help with pain, but can really mess up ones brain function." Straightening the blanket, she asked, "Do you have any more questions?"

"So where is this daughter of mine? Is she here in this hospital?"

Shaking her head, Shannon said, "No, she's in Alva. I think she was released today, and is staying with a friend of hers."

Feeling concern for this child she didn't remember, she asked, "What injuries did she have, and who is she staying with?"

"I'm not exactly sure, but I can find out if you'd like. The doctor keeps tabs on her, so he can relay the information to you."

Nodding, Janet said, "Oh, that's nice. Maybe knowing more about her, will jog my memory."

"Maybe. Is there anything else I can do for you? Do you still need to use the toilet?"

Janet shook her head. "No. The crampy feeling has passed. Can I have something for pain. I feel like someone is sticking a knife in my back."

"I'll check."

A few minutes later, Shannon returned with a syringe full of liquid, which she squirted into the IV. The effects were almost immediate. "There you go."

Janet nodded. "I can taste it right now, and my head feels fuzzy. Can you help me turn on my side?"

"Sure. I need to grab a couple of pillows though." Finding two pillows on a chair in the corner, she laid them at the foot of the bed, while she helped Janet turn on her side. She then placed a pillow between Janet's knees and ankles.

When that task was accomplished, Janet said, "Whew. That was hard work. I actually worked up a sweat."

"That's because you haven't moved in a couple of months."

Janet felt the full effect of the Morphine within seconds of being injected into her IV port. She could hardly keep her eyes open. Through slurred speech, she said, "Thanks, Shannon."

Shannon patted Janet's hand, and said, "Sleep well, Janet."

The sheriff sat at his desk, filling out paperwork. A task he didn't enjoy, but a necessary part of his job. At least he had a computer to do it on, and for that he was thankful. One of these days, he'd have all the files transferred to discs. He and Loraine, his secretary, had been working on it sporadically over the past couple of years, and they were finally down to about a dozen files.

Leaning back in his chair to relax, he jumped when the phone on his desk rang.

Answering with his usual "Hello, this is Sheriff Clifton." He was surprised to hear a woman's voice.

"Hello, Larry." He recognized the voice as his soon-to-be ex-wife, Kathy. His heart skipped a couple of beats.

"Hi Kathy." There was more he could have said, but he couldn't get his brain, and tongue, to cooperate, and come up with something clever.

She cleared her throat, and said, "I just called to wish you a happy new year, and find out how you're doing."

"Thank you, and I'm doing okay."

"Just okay?"

Rubbing his eyes, he sighed and said, "Yeah. Got a lot of stuff going on around here, so I'm keeping busy."

There was silence for a moment.

"You know, Larry, I never meant to hurt you."

Yeah, right, he thought.

On a sigh, she said, "I just didn't think our personalities meshed well."

"So you've said." Remembering the argument they had before she walked out.

Silence reigned once again. Larry tried to think of something to say, but his heart and mind weren't in the mood.

"Thanks for signing the divorce papers, and sending them back so promptly." She said.

He was silent for a moment, before replying, "Yeah. I have to get back to my paperwork, so thanks for calling."

"Okay." She said, and disconnected.

Larry sat for a while listening to the dial tone. *Could I have said something more?* He wondered. *No. She already had her mind made-up. She doesn't want to be married to me. Plain and simple.*

He returned the phone to its cradle, and turned back to the computer. Thoughts of Kathy dissipated, as his fingers began moving across the keys.

Christina had just disconnected from Cindy, when her phone rang. The caller ID said, it was Ruth, David's mom.

"Hello, Mom. Is everything okay?"

"We're fine, Christina. I called to wish you and the children a happy new year."

"Oh, that's sweet. Happy new year to you, and Dad, as well."

"How did you celebrate it?" Ruth asked.

"Steven, the cardiologist you met when you were here for Christmas, was here to celebrate with us. We ate snacks, and played card games. We also have Linda with us. Remember me telling you about her mom and her?"

"Yes. How are they doing?"

"Janet is in a hospital in Dallas, and is slowly recovering. Linda is healing nicely."

Oh, that's nice. I'm glad Linda is with you, instead of with strangers. Steven seemed like a very nice man."

Christina smiled. *He is a nice man,* she thought, and said so to Ruth.

"What are you and Dad doing?"

"Right now, there's a blizzard blowing through, so we're staying inside until it passes."

"Oh, goodness!" Christina exclaimed, remembering the cold Michigan winters. "How much snow do you have?"

"According to the weatherman, we've got a couple of inches so far, and it's supposed to continue until noon. We may get as much as six or seven inches, but those further north may get twice that much. Of course with the wind, there will be a lot of drifting, which can get quite deep. I remember when our kids were young, they loved building snow forts in those drifts."

"Ours too! I wish I could have done that as a kid, because as an adult, it just isn't that exciting."

Ruth chuckled. "Yes! Once I was an adult, I just didn't like being out in the cold for more than a few moments. Kids, however, don't seem to mind it so much."

"I'm totally in agreement, Mom." After a pause, she said, "I'm glad that you and Dad are retired, and don't have to drive in it. I remember feeling anxious when David had to drive down to Detroit in that awful weather."

Ruth asked, "What's the weather like down your way?"

"Right now, it's chilly, but it's supposed to get up to fifty degrees."

Ruth chuckled. "I wouldn't mind fifty degrees. Even though we have a good furnace, and fireplace, this old house can get pretty cold and drafty."

"I've noticed that in this house also. I think next summer, I'm going to have new insulation, windows, and furnace put in. That should help keep the house cozy in the winter, and cooler in the summer."

Christina heard her father-in-law say something in the background.

Ruth said, "Dan asked if you had considered putting central air in as well. He said, if you get a new furnace, and duct work, the guys may be able to hook up an air-conditioner as well."

"I'll consider that. I don't like having air-conditioners hanging out the windows, so central air would be awesome."

"Well, Honey, I'll let you go. We're looking forward to seeing you all in February."

Heading towards the family room, Christina said, "Wait, Mom. The kids will want to say hi."

Christina said, "Hey kids, Grandma and Grandpa called to wish us happy new year. You want to say hi?"

All three kids, who had been watching cartoons, yelled in unison, "Hi Grandma and Grandpa! Happy new year!"

After a few more moments of chatting, they all said their good-byes.

Stacey asked, "What's the weather like in Michigan?"

"Right now, they're in the middle of a blizzard."

Linda said, "I guess living in Texas does have its advantages!"

Everyone agreed.

As he and his dad sat on opposite ends of the couch, watching the festivities going on in downtown New York, in anticipation of the dawning of a new year, all Jamie could think about was how he would sneak into the Sander's house, and return their photo album. His mind went through every scenario, and he felt this was a perfect time to act on his plan. He and Jimmy had discussed the pros and cons of such a daring mission. When they both had come to the conclusion that returning the album needed to be done as soon as possible, they had shook hands, and Jimmy promised to be the lookout guy. Jamie sighed. He'd have to conquer the mission alone.

Oh Jimmy, I wish you were here, he thought, as he shifted in his seat.

Once the ball had dropped in New York City, announcing the dawning of a new year, both males stood, and stretched.

Reaching out his hand Jack said, "Happy New Year, Son."

Jamie nodded, and returned the handshake. "You too."

Rubbing a hand through his short hair, Jack said, "Hopefully this next year will be better than this one."

Yawning, Jamie said, "Yeah."

Rubbing a hand over his face, Jack said, "Well, I'm going to bed."

Grabbing the remote, and clicking the off button, Jamie said, "Yeah. Me too."

However, Jamie wasn't going to bed. Instead, he put on a pair of black jeans, and a black sweatshirt. Stuffing a pillow under his sheets and blanket, he made it look as if he were still in it, because if his dad decided to check in on him, he would see the lump, and assume it was Jamie.

Tiptoeing into the front room to grab his jacket, he very carefully opened the front door, and stepped into the frigid cold night. He knew he couldn't start his car, for fear of waking his dad, so he pushed it to the end of the long driveway. As he jumped into the driver's seat, and turned the key, he couldn't help but shout. He was certain his dad couldn't hear the engine come to life. Little did he know, his dad was watching from his bedroom window, wondering where in the world his son was going at one in the morning.

Once Steven had gone, Christina turned off the TV, and shooed the kids upstairs.

"Get ready for bed. It's been a long day, and everyone needs their rest. Remember y'all go back to school on Wednesday."

She heard a few protests, but everyone obliged her, and headed up the stairs.

"Mrs. Sanders?" Linda asked, as they reached the second floor landing.

"Yes?"

Scrunching her face, like it hurt to even say, Linda asked, "Will I have to go back to school on Wednesday?"

Shaking her head, Christina said, "No. Dr. Carmichael wants you to wait at least another week."

"Why?"

Placing her hands on the girl's shoulders, Christina said, "He wants to make sure you're strong enough, and that your abdominal incision has healed. It would be awful if someone bumped you, and hurt your belly or arm."

Making a pouty face, which amused Christina, Linda nodded, and said, "Alright. What am I going to do when everyone is at school or work?"

"We'll discuss that tomorrow. Right now, we all need to get ready for bed." Turning to face her sons, she said, "Boys, you go first, and then the girls can."

"Aw, why do we have to go first?" Nicky asked, as he headed into the bathroom.

"Because I said so." Christina said with a smirk.

Once everyone was finished in the bathroom, Christina took her turn. As she walked past Stacey's door, she could hear the girls talking, and giggling. Returning to her room, she glanced at the clock, and called out, "Alright, Girls. Time for sleep."

Within minutes, the house was quiet, except for Benji's snoring.

She would have to go get Linda's bed, and dresser, sometime during the day. Tonight, the girls could share Stacey's double bed.

Aaron had just dropped off to sleep, when he was jolted awake by his daughter's screaming.

Jumping out of bed, he nearly tripped over his slippers he had put there, when he had retired for the evening. It had been a long grueling day with surgeries and consultations, as well as hospital visits. He wanted nothing more than to curl up in bed, and sleep for about twelve hours.

Obviously, his daughter didn't have the same agenda. Running to her room, he flipped on the overhead light.

There was a lump under the covers, right where his daughter should be. Sitting on the side of the bed, and patting the lump, he said, "Sammy? What's wrong, Honey?"

She crawled out from under the covers, and threw herself onto her daddy's lap. Wrapping her five year old arms around his neck, and burying her head under his chin, between hiccups, and sniffles, she whispered, "I had a bad dream."

Patting her back, he asked, "Do you want to talk about it?"

He could feel her head shaking a negative response.

Standing, which was awkward with her still clinging to him, he asked, "Why don't I go fix us some hot cocoa, and if you want to talk about your dream, we can. If you don't, that's okay too."

Setting her on a bar stool at the counter, he went about preparing the drinks.

"Daddy?" She asked in a hushed tone.

"Yes, Sammy?"

"Did Mommy go to heaven?"

Paralyzed, because the question caught him off guard, but also because he had a knot in his throat, and couldn't speak right away. *Why would she ask such a question? We've talked about that already.*

When the milk began to boil over, the spell of sorts was broken. Pouring the milk into mugs, and adding chocolate with marshmallows, he stirred them both, and silently asked God to help him answer the question correctly.

Taking the mug from her dad, she asked again. "Daddy? Did Mommy go to heaven when she died?"

Nodding slowly, Aaron said, "Yes, she did."

Cocking her head, as she chewed on a marshmallow, she asked, "How do you know?"

"I know because she believed that there was a God who loved her, and all of us, and she treated people as this loving God would."

"If God loved her and us so much, why would He let her die? Why would He let our hearts hurt because we miss her so much?"

Taking the empty mugs to the sink, Aaron picked up his daughter, and carried her to his big recliner. He took the blanket lying in the chair, and wrapped Sammy in it. They both sat silently for a few minutes, giving Aaron time to think how he could answer this difficult question, in terms a five year old could understand.

"Honey, I don't understand why certain things happen like they do. What I do know, is that God knows everything that is going on, and He knows who loves Him, and who doesn't. He wants everyone to believe in Him, love Him, and be obedient. Your mom was that kind of person."

The answer seemed to have satisfied her for the moment. Sitting up, and grinning, she said, "I know what obedient means. We learned it in Sunday school. It means to do what you're told to do, without complaining, or getting mad."

Squeezing her in a hug, Aaron said, "That is a good lesson to learn. I know some grown-ups who have trouble being obedient."

She laid her head back on her daddy's chest, and within minutes, she relaxed, and was breathing the deep breaths of sleep.

Aaron sat for a few minutes, enjoying the sweet smell, and warmth of his child. She was growing up so fast. It seemed like yesterday he was rocking her to sleep. He wondered why she had woken up screaming, and terrified, and why she would ask such questions. Being a new believer himself, he wasn't sure how he should have answered her. He doubted she would understand the meaning of salvation, Jesus' redemptive sacrifice on the cross, or the Holy Spirit's role in a believer's life. Glancing at the clock, he realized he only had a few hours before he would begin another day. Gently lifting Sammy, he took her to her bed, and tucked her in, leaning down for a kiss on her forehead. Turning a night light on next to her bed, he left the door ajar. Hopefully, she would sleep through the remainder of the night.

Yawning, and stretching, he headed back to his own room, thinking about his wife, and wondering what she was doing right then. Little did he know she was standing in the room with him. In fact, it was her presence that had frightened Sammy. She hadn't meant to scare the child, but little ones can see the spiritual realm a great deal more clearly than adults, and sometimes, because their minds can't always distinguish between reality, and the supernatural, they will be terrified.

Tabitha was pleased by Aaron's answer to their daughter. When she left her body behind after the car accident, she had indeed traveled to Heaven to meet with God. Even though she knew she could never return to her body, God had granted her times of visitation to her earthly family.

He granted those visitations to His newly transitioned souls, knowing that their desire to return to Earth would eventually be replaced by their desire to stay in Heaven. He told her she would know when it was time to relinquish those visits, and begin her new task as one of His servants. When her visits began frightening Sammy instead of comforting her, she knew it was time. She reached out to kiss Aaron's cheek, whispering that she loved him, and always would, then she went to Sammy's room, and leaned down to kiss her child on the forehead. Of course neither Aaron or Sammy were aware of her presence.

CHAPTER 9

When Jamie arrived at the Sander's home, he sat in his car for a few moments having an argument with himself. Part of him said this wasn't a good idea, and the other part said he needed to unload the photo album before someone—like the sheriff—decided to do a search of his room.

The house was dark, as were most of the homes up and down the block. The neighborhood was eerily quiet, which reminded him of the Christmas poem about Santa. He dug around in the glove box, and finding the house key, grasped it in his hand, as he exited the car. Holding the album under his arm, he quickly, but quietly made his way up the driveway to the back porch. Opening the screen door which led to the landing by the kitchen door, he almost dropped the album. *That's all I need,* he thought, *dropping the album, and having to chase down flying pictures.* He set the album on the concrete step, as he put the key in the door.

Concern that the dog would bark, or come greet him, he searched his pocket for the drugged dog biscuit. Slapping his hand to his forehead, he realized he had forgotten the dog treat. Sighing heavily, he thought, *Hopefully, I'll be in and out, before he even knows I'm here.*

Benji, hearing the door open downstairs, jumped off the bed, and sniffed under the door. Whimpering, he clawed at the door, waking Christina.

"Benji!" She whined, as she pulled herself out of the cozy warm bed, to let him out. The dog ran down the stairs as quickly as his little legs would carry him.

Jamie froze. *What if Mrs. Sanders comes down?* He listened intently as Benji ran down the stairs. No human footsteps were detected.

Squatting, he whispered the dog's name. He didn't want him to start barking. Benji, recognizing the intruder, wiggled up to him, and allowed the boy to scratch behind his ears. He sniffed Jamie's pockets, expecting a treat.

"Sorry," Jamie whispered, as he patted the dog, "I forgot the cookies."

Benji wagged his tail, and licked Jamie's hand as if to say, "It's okay. I'm glad you're here."

Jamie patted his pocket for a flashlight, and realized he had forgotten that as well. Fortunately, the night light in the breakfast nook, provided enough light for him to move from the kitchen to the den, without bumping into anything. He replaced the album where he had previously found it.

Noticing that the front two rooms were illuminated by the street lamp in front, he decided to explore them. After a few minutes, of looking around, he headed into the dining room, where plates of cookies, pies, and cakes were arranged on the table. Carefully pulling the plastic wrap off one of the plates, he took a peanut butter cookie with a Hershey kiss on top. His favorite. His mom used to make those when he was a little kid. Grabbing another one, he stuffed it in his jacket pocket. Knowing this was the last time he would visit the Sander's home, he decided to venture upstairs, and say "goodbye" outside each bedroom.

Entering the hallway containing the stairs, he was surprised by the absence of light. The last couple of times he had ventured upstairs, a night light in the upstairs hallway had illuminated the stairs. *A flashlight would come in handy*, he thought, as his foot landed on the first step. Carefully avoiding the second creaky step, he continued his ascent, hanging on to the railing.

He felt his way up the stairs, and right before he took the last step, his foot landed on something soft. Before he realized what it was, the thing yowled, swatted at his leg with razor sharp claws, and bit him on the ankle. Jamie lost his balance, and cursing, fell back down the stairs, snapping his ankle in the process.

Christina and Brad, hearing the cacophony of sounds, exited their bedrooms to see what had happened. Brad was armed with a baseball bat, and Christina had her cell phone at the ready. They were soon joined by the girls, who were holding on to each other.

"Mom, what's going on?" Nicky asked, joining the group at the top of the stairs.

Christina flipped the light switch, and was shocked to see a boy, or young man, who looked a lot like Brad, lying at the bottom of the stairs. She shook her head, and looked at Brad, who was heading down the stairs, holding a bat like he was ready to send a ball out of the park. The person at the bottom of the stairs, was holding his ankle, and moaning.

Approaching cautiously, and realizing who it was, Brad said, "Jamie? Is that you?"

The young man moaned. Through clenched teeth, he said, "Yes. Can you help me? I think I broke my ankle."

Brad laid his bat down, and helped Jamie sit on the second stair step. Christina went into nurse mode, and began asking questions, as she assessed the damaged ankle. "Why are you here, and how did you end up at the bottom of the stairs?"

"I stepped on a cat, and fell."

"I'm pretty sure the ankle is broken." She said, as she watched Jamie wince in pain. She didn't know what to make of this whole situation. *Why is this boy in our home?* Instead of dwelling on that, she asked Nicky to get an ice pack, while she called for an ambulance.

Through gritted teeth, Jamie moaned, "Please, don't call the sheriff. I can explain everything."

Christina patted the young man's shoulder, and said, "I've already called for an ambulance, so the sheriff will be here as well. He rarely misses an ambulance run."

"Oh, man! My dad is going to kill me!"

Resting his head in his hands, he began to cry. Christina couldn't help but feel compassion for this young man. She knew she would get the answers she needed soon enough. Right now, she had a patient to care for.

"Stacey, could you bring a box of tissues from the bathroom?"

"Sure, Mom."

Linda asked, "Is there anything I can do?"

Realizing the girl needed a task to do, she said, "Can you go turn the porch light on, and watch for the ambulance?"

"Sure."

Stacey returned with the box of tissues, handed them to Jamie, then went to stand at the door with Linda.

Remembering the cat, Christina asked Nicky to go find him, and make sure he was okay."

A few minutes later, Nicky, with tears streaming down his face, carried in a limp Elijah.

"Mom. He's dead." Nicky said between sobs.

Christina sighed. "I'm so sorry, Honey. Remember, he was a very old cat, and the trauma of being stepped on, and frightened, probably was too much for him to bear."

He sat on the floor in the hallway, stroking Elijah's fur.

With venom in his voice, he looked at Jamie and said, "It's your fault he's dead!"

Jamie nodded, and said, "I'm so sorry. I didn't know you had another cat."

Nicky scowled at him. "You have no right to be here! Why are you here, anyway?"

Jamie hung his head in shame. "I know. I'll explain it all later." Catching his breath, and wincing, he said, "Right now, I just want something for this pain. It's almost more than I can bear."

A minute later, they heard the girls announce the arrival of the ambulance. They opened the front door, and two men, dressed in EMT uniforms, entered. They were directed to the hallway.

Another minute later, the sheriff, along with his deputy, Mike Owens, came through the door.

There was so much commotion, the Sander's kids, and Linda, took seats in the front room. Nicky, still holding the dead cat said, "If Mrs. Sterling hadn't asked mom to keep Elijah, we probably would have never known that Jamie was the one breaking into our house."

Stacey nodded, and sighed. "As sad as it is, maybe this is God's way of protecting us, and maybe Jamie too."

Linda crinkled her brows. "How in the world can you believe that?"

Stacey shrugged, and said, "I believe that everything happens for a reason. Because I believe that God is in control of what happens, because He is outside of time, it only makes sense that He would orchestrate this chain of events."

Linda raised her eyebrows in surprise. "When you say God is outside of time, what do you mean?"

"I mean, He can see the past, present, and future, all at once. Nothing is a surprise to Him."

Linda furrowed her brows again, as she tried to think how to ask her questions. She had never thought about God knowing everything, much less knowing the past, present, and future, at the same time.

"So, if He knows everything, then He knew my mom would get into that car accident?"

Stacey nodded.

"Why would He allow that to happen?"

Stacey wasn't sure how to answer that, so she looked to her big brother.

Brad nodded, and said, "Linda, there are a lot of things we don't understand. Like, why would a loving God allow such tragedy to fall on certain people, while others go through life unscathed. We can't see the future, so we don't always know what the purpose is. God gives us free will, so sometimes we bring bad stuff on ourselves, other times, there are no explanations until sometime in the future. Then we say, 'Ah ha, now I understand'. Sometimes the incident isn't for us to understand, but for someone else to."

Linda shook her head. "Wow! This whole God thing is more complicated than I realized."

Concerned, Brad asked, "Does what I said make sense to you?"

Nodding, she said, "I guess so. We have free will to do whatever we want, but if God doesn't like our choice, He can zap us? Or, God uses us as puppets to do whatever He wants, and it doesn't matter what we want, think, or do."

"Hmm," Brad said, but before he could add to that, the EMT's, pulling a stretcher containing Jamie, walked through the living room, and out the door, to an awaiting ambulance.

Brad stood, and motioning to the others to stay seated, walked to the entrance of the kitchen. He could hear his mother, and the sheriff arguing.

"Christina!" The sheriff said in frustration. "For goodness sakes, the kid was found in your house, and according to him, it wasn't the first time. Why won't you press charges?"

"Larry. I know it seems like the logical thing to do, but the poor kid just lost his best friend, and according to him, he returned everything he took. It seems pointless to add to his misery."

Brad heard the sheriff blow out a lungful of air. Peeking around the corner, he watched as the man raked his fingers through his hair. Brad could feel his frustration, but knowing his mom like he did, he knew once her mind was made up about something, it would take a miracle for her to back down.

"Larry, please sit down. Would you like a cup of coffee, or something cold?"

Shaking his head, he sat across from her in the breakfast nook.

Before she took a seat, he said, "I'll take a Dr. Pepper, if you have one, because I doubt you'd have beer."

Chuckling, she said, "Nope, no beer, but Dr. Peppers we have."

Knowing she would be entering the kitchen, Brad quickly returned to the front room.

"Kids," she called from the kitchen, "I would appreciate if y'all would go back to bed."

Nicky, the first one to enter the hallway, handed her Elijah, and asked, "Can we bury him tomorrow?"

Giving her boy a hug, she said, "Sure," while thinking, *What am I to do with the dead cat right now?* Once the kids were off to their various beds, she took the cat, and laid him on the back porch. Returning to the kitchen, she washed her hands, and grabbed the drink for Larry. Handing him the cold can, Christina sat across from him,

Larry took out a note pad and opened it. "I'm going to ask you one more time, if you'd like to press charges for breaking and entering."

Shaking her head, she said, "No. I didn't change my mind, while I was in the kitchen."

Pinching the bridge of his nose, he said, "Well, alright then. Mind if I tell you what I've come up with?"

"Sure. Why not? I doubt I'll go back to sleep anyway."

Looking through his notepad, he began telling her why he believed the two boys were responsible for the break-ins, the school fire, the school bomb threat, the fireworks display, and the fire at the abandoned oil refinery, which resulted in a fire at the hospital, and eventually Jimmy's death.

"How can two boys wreak so much havoc, and do so much damage?" She asked, taking a sip of water.

"I've got a theory about that," Larry said with a sly grin. "From what I've gathered, these two boys had similar backgrounds. Both lost their moms when they were around twelve."

"How?" Christina asked, leaning forward on her elbows.

"Jamie's mom disappeared without a trace, about five years ago. A road crew just recently found a car at the bottom of a culvert, containing a woman's body. Later identified as Jamie's mom."

Christina frowned. "Why did it take so long for anyone to find her?"

"I keep asking myself the same question. I think, because of the depth of the culvert, and where it was located, no one even thought to look there." Taking a sip of his drink, he continued. "We all just thought she had found a new life somewhere else, and didn't want to be found. It really tore Jack up. It seemed a part of him died, when she wasn't found. I've heard he didn't have any kind of relationship with his boy after that."

Christina said, "Oh, how sad for Jamie. To lose both parents, at such a vulnerable time in his life."

Nodding, Larry said, "Yep."

"So tell me about Jimmy. What's the story there?"

Finishing the soda in one big gulp, Larry set the empty can on the table.

"Well, as I said, both boys lost their mothers around the same time. Jimmy's mom died of an aggressive form of uterine cancer. By the time it was diagnosed, she already had a foot in the grave."

Christina shook her head. *No way am I going to add more misery to this boys livfe, by pressing charges.*

"When Jesse's wife died, a part of him died also. He too withdrew from his son. The boy favors his mother, so I think when Jesse looked at him, he saw his wife, and it was too painful to bear."

"Oh my goodness!" Christina said, wiping tears from her eyes.

"The fortunate, or maybe not so fortunate thing is, both the men just recently found religion, and were working to make things right with their boys."

Christina asked, "What do you men they found religion?"

"Seems like someone invited both men to a men's gathering in Dallas, and somehow, they both decided to become believers in God.

Christina smiled. "Well, God does work in mysterious ways."

Nodding, Larry said, "Ain't that the truth. Before that, they both were attending that cult-like group of Enlightened Ones, out on the edge of town."

"Was that meeting the men went to called Promise Keepers?"

Nodding, Larry said, "Yes."

"I heard there was going to be a gathering in Dallas. My husband went to a couple of those in Michigan."

Feeling uncomfortable about discussing religion, he said, "Back to the story. I also found evidence that puts Janet in the middle of the mix."

Looking confused, Christina asked, "How so?"

"Remember, after the accident, I went through her purse, and found two cell-phones?"

Christina nodded.

"I had Ed take a look at them, and we discovered that the messages to the anonymous person, turned out to be Jamie Simmons. She was paying him to break into your house."

Shock, and surprise, registered on Christina's face. "What? Why?"

Larry smiled, and shook his head. "You aren't going to believe this, but, she really hated you, and all you had, and stood for. Plus, she wanted you to go back to Michigan."

Biting her bottom lip, Christina said, "Well, I'll be. I had no idea she hated me so."

Shaking his head, Larry said, "I don't know what's going on, but it seems that since you and the kids moved here, Alva hasn't been the same."

"It is weird, that's for sure. It's almost like there's a battle between good and evil. Not that I'm saying I'm so good, and Janet and others are evil, but I think the angels and demons are at war, and Alva is their battleground, and we're all their pawns."

Standing, and stretching, Larry said, "You may have something there. I've seen my share of good and evil, being in law enforcement, but I've never seen it so concentrated, in such a short amount of time." Donning his jacket, and hat, he added, "I hate to say it, but I think you are on somebody's hit list. And by somebody, I mean the Devil."

Nodding, and standing as well, she said, "I think you may be right. I know, however, that God is stronger than any demon, and He won't let anything happen to us, outside His perfect plan."

Walking towards the front door, Larry turned, and said, "I believe people can worship God, themselves, or Satan. I've seen the results of worshiping oneself, and Satan, so I'd be on team God any day."

"I'm glad to hear that, Larry. I wasn't sure where you stood on religious matters."

"Well, I wouldn't call myself religious, but I've been feeling a strange tugging on my heart to explore the whole concept of God. Something supernatural is going on, and I want to be on the right side before judgment day."

Opening the front door, Christina patted Larry's arm, and said, "Thanks for coming, and for understanding why I won't press charges."

Shaking his head, Larry said, "I didn't say I understand your position, but I do respect it."

"That's all I ask."

Christina drug her weary body up the stairs, and practically fell into bed. Benji found his spot, and both were asleep within minutes. Before dropping off, she glanced at the clock. 4:30. Fortunately, she didn't have to work that day.

Jack woke with a start, when his phone began ringing. It took a minute to orient himself, and find his phone. At first he couldn't remember why he was asleep in his recliner, but then the memory came rushing back. He had watched Jamie leave around 1 a. m., and had planned to stay awake, and confront him about his strange behavior.

The phone kept ringing. He wondered who would be calling him at four in the morning.

The caller ID said Unknown. He hoped it was a wrong number, and not someone telling him Jamie had been in an accident.

Clearing his throat, he answered. "Hello?"

"Mr. Simmons?" Asked a female voice.

"Yes."

"I'm calling to inform you that your son, Jamie, is here at the hospital emergency room."

"What? Why? Is he okay?"

"He is resting comfortably right now, but I need you to come sign some paperwork."

Standing, he said, "Sure. I'll be there in a few minutes."

After splashing cold water on his face, he headed out the door. *Jamie, what have you gotten yourself into now?*

After leaving Christina's house, the sheriff headed to the hospital, to have a chat with Jamie Simmons. He pulled into the hospital parking lot, just as Jack was exiting his vehicle. He watched as the man practically ran to the entrance. *He's going to flip out when he hears what his son has been up to.*

Exiting the police cruiser, Larry stretched, and took in a lungful of crisp, cold air. *Man, I'm tired. I feel like I could just curl up on the pavement, and fall asleep.* Pinching the bridge of his nose, he shook his head, and headed into the hospital, past the reception desk, and straight for the ER. The lady behind the counter, called out, "Good morning, Sheriff."

Larry waved a hand, and kept walking.

The ER was eerily quiet. He was glad. The last time he had been there at four in the morning, it was anything but quiet.

Walking up to the counter, he asked to see Jamie Simmons. The receptionist pointed to a curtained area, a few feet down the corridor.

Pulling the curtain aside, he entered, and was greeted by Jack, who reached out his hand.

Jamie moaned, as he shifted positions. Even with the morphine, he felt a deep throbbing pain in his ankle and leg. He had a cast from his foot to his knee, and it was suspended by some kind of contraption, so he was limited in his movement.

"Hey, Sheriff." He said in greeting.

"Jamie. How are you doing?"

"Well, not so good. As you can see, I'm pretty well confined to this bed. The pain is there, but bearable."

The sheriff took a position by Jamie's bed, to have a full view of the boy's face. During his police academy training, he had taken a class in how to read a suspects face, and body language, to discern if they were telling the truth, or lying.

"Jamie, I have a few questions I'd like you to answer. Please, tell me the truth."

Jamie nodded slightly in agreement.

"I know you told me a little about why you were in the Sander's home, but you were in such pain, I didn't press the issue. Now, however, I want some answers."

Larry heard Jack inhale sharply, and whisper, "What?"

Larry looked at Jack, and said, "Your son broke into the Sander's home tonight."

Jack looked at Jamie, and shook his head in disbelief.

"Is that true, Son?"

Jamie nodded.

"Why?" Jack asked.

Letting out a sigh, Jamie said, "I was returning a photo album I had taken a couple of weeks ago"

Jack was having trouble wrapping his mind around Jamie's confession.

Looking at the sheriff, Jamie asked, "Should I have a lawyer present?"

Jack looked at the sheriff, also. "Should he?"

"Maybe at a later date, but now, I just want Jamie to tell me again, why he was in the Sander's home. I will question him further when he isn't under the influence of drugs."

Jack nodded, and said, "Go ahead, Jamie. Tell the sheriff why you were there."

Jamie took in a lungful of air, and released it before answering.

"As I said before, I was returning a photo album I had taken a week or so ago."

"Why did you take the album in the first place?" Jack asked.

Shrugging, and looking embarrassed, he said, "Because I wanted to see what their life was like, before coming to Alva."

Jack could hardly believe what he was hearing, but he needed to know the reason behind such actions. "And why did you want to know that?"

Larry stood by, and listened to the exchange between Father and Son.

Jamie, twisting the bed sheet around his fingers, said, "Every time I saw them, they looked so happy. I guess I wanted to be that happy too, so I thought if I studied them, I could figure it out."

"Did you find out their secret to happiness?" Jack asked.

Shaking his head, he said, "No. Not really. But it was cool looking at the pictures."

Larry cleared his throat, and asked, "If you were just returning the album, why were you on the stairs?"

"This is going to sound weird, but I just wanted to be close to them. Maybe pick up some positive energy. This was going to be the last time I entered their home. I swear."

Jack sat in stunned silence. He had no idea his son had done this. Sure, Jamie had confessed to the other things he and Jimmy had done, but not the Sander's home invasion.

Larry nodded.

Jamie looked down at his hands, then over to his dad. He felt a flush begin at his neck, then travel to his face. *How much should I admit to*, he wondered.

Just as he opened his mouth to speak, a nurse walked in with a clip board, and announced that he could go home.

Jamie felt relief wash over him. The longer he could put off telling the truth, the longer he had freedom. *If I tell the sheriff everything, he won't have any choice but to arrest me. I need to go to Jimmy's funeral Thursday. I hope we can put all this on hold, 'till after the funeral.*

The nurse gave him instructions on how to take care of the newly casted ankle, as she removed his leg from the suspension pulley. "Make sure you keep this leg elevated every chance you get. It will help keep the swelling down."

Jamie nodded in understanding.

Handing him a slip of paper, she added, "If you go to the pharmacy down the hall, they have waterproof bags to put over your cast, so you can shower, and crutches you can rent or buy. Do you have any questions?"

Jamie shook his head, which made the room spin.

Looking up at the sheriff, he said, "I will tell you everything after Jimmy's funeral. Then you can decide what to do with me."

"Okay. I'll not ask again, 'till after the funeral."

"Yes, Sir."

Sliding off the bed, Jamie grabbed the bag of clothes, and limped to the bathroom, wincing as blood rushed to his ankle and foot.

Larry pulled a chair over, and sat next to Jack.

Patting the man on the back, he said, "I know this came as a shock to you, but I believe Jamie, and Jimmy have been breaking in to people's homes for the past couple of years."

Jack ran his hand over his face, and sighed.

Larry continued. "Once I get a confession, I'll have to check with the folks who have complained, and see if they want to press charges."

Jack nodded in understanding. Standing, and reaching out his hand, he said, "Thanks. I'd like to get this all resolved sooner, rather than later."

Jamie stood by the bathroom door, and waited for the sheriff to leave. He then hobbled over to the bed, and said, "I'm sorry Dad. I know this has been a shock to you, but it'll be okay."

Jack nodded. He was speechless. *How was I not aware that my son was doing these things?*

"Grabbing his coat, Jamie said, "Let's go home, Dad. I'm exhausted, and you look like you're about ready to pass out."

Again, Jack nodded without words. He felt his blood pressure rising, and clenched his fists. There was a part of him that wanted to grab his son, and shake, and punch him, until the pain of embarrassment, and disappointment, dissipated. He was afraid that if he touched Jamie right now, he'd probably maim him, so he said, and did nothing.

The ride home was in stoney silence. Jack glanced at his son every now and then. Jamie had his head laid back on the headrest, and his eyes were closed.

He felt something inside him crack like a fissure in a dam. He felt tears stream down his face. *Jamie,* he thought, *I'm so sorry I was such a lousy dad theses past few years. I will stand by you from now on, now matter the outcome. I'm pretty sure I'm guilty of pushing you into this behavior. What a way to start the new year.*

When they arrived home, Jack helped Jamie into the house. They were greeted by Little Lady, whimpering, and turning in circles. She was happy to see them, but knew something wasn't right.

Jack took Jamie to his room, and helped him wrestle the sweat pants over the cast. Little Lady jumped on the bed, and began licking Jamie's face.

Jamie picked her up, and held her at arm's length. "Hey, Girl. It's okay. I love you too."

Jack, couldn't help but smile. The puppies began whimpering, and the mama dog began squirming to be put down.

Jamie set her on the floor, and she immediately went to her pups, and began licking them, then she laid down so they could nurse.

Jamie and Jack watched for a moment, then Jack said, "Is there anything I can get you before I head off to bed?"

Jamie shook his head. "No. Thanks, though."

Jack nodded, and headed to his own bed. He was so thankful he didn't have to work later. He fell into bed, and was immediately asleep.

Jamie didn't go to sleep right away. He kept thinking about what had happened, and what he could have done differently. *For starters, I should have had a flashlight.* He thought about Jimmy, and an ache began in his chest. His funeral was in two days, and Jamie had been asked to be a casket bearer, along with a few other male relatives. Jimmy didn't have many friends in high school, so none of the guys from there had been considered. Sad. But true. He had been surprised, however, at the attendance to the candlelight ceremony in front of the high-school. There had to be at least fifty kids there in spite of the cold, wet weather. He had stood in the background, observing the activities. There had been singing, and testimonies, and prayers. Most of the people attending, hadn't even known Jimmy, yet, they were there acting like he was their best friends. Hypocrites!

Jamie considered this, and wondered if he had died instead of Jimmy, who would attend his funeral, and be his casket bearer? He knew a few students whom he considered friends, but they weren't close. Not as close as him and Jimmy. *Is there anyone who could replace Jimmy?* He wondered. *No. What am I going to do?*

He rolled over to face the wall, and promptly fell into a drug induced sleep. Worries and cares seemed to melt away.

Brad woke from a disturbing dream. He had been standing on a hill overlooking Alva, which lay in ruins. Black smoke and fire consumed the town, and neighboring subdivisions. He had felt helpless, and deeply disturbed, and had fallen to his knees, crying out to God.

He lay in bed a while, going over the dream in his mind. At least the parts he remembered. Dreams were like smoke—one could see them, but they dissipated quickly, leaving an unresolved image in one's mind. *Very frustrating*, he thought. He wasn't sure if this particular dream had any significant meaning, or if it was just a random thought process his mind chose, to work out some unresolved event in his life. Whatever it was, it had left an impression that he just couldn't shake.

Glancing at his clock, he realized the day was half over. Tomorrow, he would be returning to school. "Ugh," he mumbled. *It's going to be rather somber*, he thought. *Even though most of the kids barely knew Jimmy, his death could make one think of their own mortality, and wonder if something like that could happen to them. I wonder how many of those kids would be ready to meet their Maker?*

Just then, his cell phone rang. He grabbed it off the bed side table, and answered. He didn't recognize the number.

"Hello, Brad?" Said a man's voice.

"Yes?"

"This is Mr. McCoy. Jimmy's dad."

Brad sat up. "Yes, Mr. McCoy. What can I do for you?"

"Well, I've heard from a few of Jimmy's peers, that you would be the perfect person to give a eulogy for my son."

"Mr. McCoy, I appreciate your asking me, but I didn't know Jimmy. Sure, I'd pass him in the hall at school, but I didn't know him on a one-to-one basis."

"I understand. I've written out a few of my thoughts, and you could add or subtract from them. I just know I couldn't stand up, and eulogize my son."

"Mr. McCoy, let me think about this, and I'll call you back with an answer in a little while. My brain is still foggy from sleep."

"Oh. Okay. Why don't I drop off my list, and it may help you decide."

"Yes, Sir. That would be fine. Do you know my address?"

After exchanging address information, Brad stood, and stretched. Slipping on a pair of sweatpants, he headed downstairs. He knew his mom was up, because of the strong coffee smell, wafting it's way up the stairway.

He found her in the den, reading a magazine.

"Hey, Mom."

"Good morning, Brad. Or should I say afternoon?"

"Yeah. I was surprised myself, when I looked at the clock. I hadn't meant to sleep so late."

Nodding, Christina said, "I know. Me either. I just got up about an hour ago, myself, and that's because Benji was whimpering to go out. If not for him, I think I would have continued to sleep."

Sitting on the couch, opposite his mom, Brad said, "It's that kind of day. All cloudy, and dreary. A great way to start the new year."

"I heard on the news that we have a cold front moving in, and we may see some snow."

Brad made a face, and said, "Really? Snow? In Texas?'

Christina giggled. "Yes. Snow in Texas. Not as much as Michigan, mind you, but enough to make a snow man or two."

"Like the pitiful ones Stacey and Nicky made when Grandma and Grandpa were here?"

Nodding, she said, "Those were pretty pitiful. Nevertheless, there was enough snow to make them."

Shaking his head, Brad stood, and said, "I'm going to get a bowl of cereal, then I have something I want to discuss with you."

Christina raised her eyebrows, "Sounds serious."

Nodding, Brad said, "It kinda is. I'll be right back."

Returning with a bowl of cereal, he took a seat on the couch, across from his mom.

"I just received a weird phone call."

"From whom?" Christina asked, her interest piqued.

Taking a bite of cereal, he hastily chewed, and swallowed.

"It was from Mr. McCoy, Jimmy's dad. He wants me to give the eulogy for Jimmy."

"Why is that a problem?"

"I didn't even know the guy. What can I say about a kid I didn't even know?"

"That is interesting. Did he say why he chose you?"

"He said he heard from a few of Jimmy's peers, that I would be a good candidate for the job."

Shaking his head, he added, "He's coming by today to give me a list of things he would like me to say."

After a few minutes of silence, except for Brad chewing his cereal, Christina said, "Seems we need to pray for wisdom about this."

Brad nodded. "That's why I wanted to talk with you. Maybe this is one of God's tasks He wants me to do."

"Maybe. Just remember, that nothing happens randomly. God knows you are capable of taking on such a challenge."

Just then, the doorbell rang, which set Benji off running to the front door, barking loud enough to wake the rest of the household.

"I'll go," Brad said. "It's probably Mr. McCoy."

Sure enough, when he opened the door, Jesse McCoy was there, hunched over to avoid the cold wind. Brad invited him in, and asked if he'd like a cup of coffee to take the chill off. Nodding, and removing his heavy fire-chief coat, he sat on the sofa.

Christina walked in from the den, and introduced herself.

Standing, and reaching out his hand, he said, "Oh yes, I remember you from the hospital fire. You work on the CCU, right?"

Christina nodded. "Mr. McCoy, I'm so sorry for your loss. I can't imagine what you're going through. I know this sounds trite, and probably repetitious, but if there's anything we can do, we're here for you."

Feeling tears sting his eyes, he said, "Thank you, Mrs. Sanders. Right now, I'm just trying to put one foot in front of the other."

Christina nodded. "I do understand grief. No one truly understands, unless they've experienced it themselves."

Swiping at his eyes, Jesse nodded.

Brad walked in, carrying a tray with coffee, sugar, and creamer.

"I forgot to ask how you take your coffee, so I just brought everything." Setting the tray down on the coffee table, he took a seat opposite of his mom and Jesse.

"Thanks. I do like a bit of sugar in mine, but I have been known to drink it black."

"You don't mind if my mom is here, do you?"

"Of course not." Jesse said, taking a sip of coffee.

"Okay, so where is this list you spoke of?"

Reaching into his shirt pocket, Jesse brought out a folded piece of paper, then handed it to Brad.

Brad unfolded the paper, and was surprised. He thought it would be a page full of items, but there were only five.

"Mr. McCoy, is this the whole list?"

Nodding, and pinching the bridge of his nose, he said, "I know, it's not much. I've been a lousy dad these past few years, and I lost touch with my son. I had no idea he was such a Star Wars fan, until I began cleaning his room. He had quite a collection of books, magazines, and action figures. Eventually, I'll have to figure out what to do with all that stuff." Sighing heavily, he continued.

"I finally came to my senses a few weeks ago, when I went to a men's retreat in Dallas, called Promise Keepers. It was there, that I decided I was on the wrong track, and needed to switch directions. I never, in my worst nightmares, would have expected this. Jimmy's death was so sudden. I never got to prove to him how sorry I was, or how much I loved him."

New tears began pouring down his face, and sobs wracked his body. He tried desperately to get his emotions under control, but to no avail.

Christina handed him a box of tissues, that just happened to be close by, and patted Jesse's shoulder.

Brad didn't know what to do, so he silently prayed for peace for this broken man. After several minutes, Jesse stopped his outburst, and apologized.

Brad leaned forward, bringing his face close to Jesse's.

"Mr. McCoy, there is no need to apologize. Good grief, you lost your son! If anything, I admire you for taking care of business. Everyone grieves in their own way. There is no right or wrong, or time limit."

Jesse whispered, "Thank you, Son. I appreciate that. I'm so tired, that the least little thing sets me off. I think when I get back to work, and have something else to focus on, I won't have these emotional outbursts as often."

"I doubt anyone would judge you, if you had a few outbursts here and there."

After a moment of silence, Jesse said, "I know it's short notice, but do you think you could say a few positive things about my son?"

Nodding, Brad said, "I'll give it my best shot. I'll run it by you before Thursday."

Jesse stood, as well as Brad and Christina. He put his hand out, and Brad shook it. The man before him looked broken, and battered. Brad wondered if he had even slept, or eaten, these past several days.

Closing the front door, Brad leaned against it, and said, "Mom, I don't know where to begin with the speech he wants me to give."

Sensing his frustration, and concern, she pulled him into a hug. Stepping back, she said, "How about talking to some of his classmates. Pull some of the information from them. Even if they didn't know him well, they could at least give an impression of him. I'm sure you'll come up with something, and it will be awesome."

Shaking his head, Brad said, "Thanks for the confidence in me. Right now, I don't feel very confident."

"Why don't we pray about it? I'm sure God will grant you the words, if you ask."

Nodding, Brad said, "Okay."

They sat next to each other on the sofa, and not only prayed for wisdom, but for peace for everyone in Alva.

Ed woke to his cell-phone buzzing, on the end table by the couch. Reaching for it, he saw it was from Bill Jones, another ATO agent that helped plant bugs in Christina's house. If he was calling, there must be some kind of emergency.

"Hey, Bill. I haven't heard from you in a while. What's going on?"

"Ed, we need you back in Dallas ASAP. There's been an explosion in our office building. We got an anonymous call telling us it was going to happen, then within five minutes, the explosion rocked the building."

"Anyone hurt?" Ed asked, as he began dressing.

"A couple of maintenance men, who were in the basement. Fortunately, no one died, but there is a lot of structural damage."

"Why do you need me there?" Ed asked, pulling a sweater over his head.

"Henry wants you and Tom, to do a walk through, to determine the kind of bomb it was, and see if there are any clues left behind."

"Has anyone claimed responsibility yet?"

"No, but we have an idea who did it."

"I can call Tom. He's here in Alva, at his in-laws. We can probably come in together."

"Okay. Just get here ASAP." Bill said, as he disconnected.

"Will do."

As Ed was rummaging around for a pen and paper, Cindy walked in, rubbing her eyes.

"Hey, Babe. What are you doing?" She asked, as she walked over to give him a hug.

"Good. I'm glad you're up. I was trying to find a pen and paper to leave you a note."

"A note? Why?"

Releasing her from the hug, he said, "I've been called into work."

"Work? Why?" She asked, concern filling her voice.

"There's been an incident at our Dallas office."

Walking over to the coffee pot, she began preparing her favorite morning beverage.

"What kind of accident?" She asked, measuring coffee into the filter.

Leaning on the kitchen counter, he said, "An explosion. My boss seems to think it's terrorist related."

Nodding in understanding, she said, "Do you have to leave right away?"

"Yes, but first, I need to call Tom. We can probably ride in together."

Disappointed, she sighed, and said, "Okay. I'll wait for the coffee to brew. Should I fix you a cup to go?"

Nodding, as he punched in Tom's number on his phone, he said, "Yes. Thanks."

While he was talking to Tom, she looked around for a travel mug. Finding it in an upper cabinet, she filled it with the newly brewed beverage, adding a small amount of cream and sugar.

A few minutes later, Ed walked in, gave her a hug and kiss, grabbed the travel mug, and headed out the door.

Calling after him, she asked, "Will you be back tonight?"

Shrugging, and shaking his head, he said, "Probably not. I'll call you later."

Waving, she watched as he backed the car out. He waved one last time, before disappearing down the street.

"Well, that ruins my plans for the day." She mumbled, as she headed into the kitchen for her own cup of coffee.

She was sitting on the sofa, when Samara walked in, with Sasha at her heels.

"Mornin' Mom."

"Mornin', Babe."

Frowning, Samara asked, "Where's Ed?"

Sighing, Cindy said, "He got called into work."

"On new year's day? Why?'

Taking a sip of coffee before answering, she said, "There was an explosion at his downtown office."

"In Dallas?"

Cindy nodded, "Yep."

"Well that stinks. I thought we were planning to hang out, and play some games, and stuff."

"Yeah, me too. Guess we'll just have to make other plans."

Sasha began whimpering, as she ran in circles around Samara's feet.

"Okay, Girl, I'll let you out."

As Ed drove to the Conger's house to get Tom, he thought about the plans he and Cindy had made for the day. They were planning to watch old movies, and play table games with Samara. He hated leaving his girls, but his job came first in this instance. He knew when he signed on to be part of the ATO, or Anti-terrorist organization, he'd have to make sacrifices. He just wished it didn't have to be on new years day.

As the two men traveled to Dallas, they each recounted their Christmas experiences.

After a moment of silence, Tom said, "I've noticed that Eleanor's dad is slowly declining mentally, and physically. Sometimes, when the medication begins to wear off, he becomes disoriented and paranoid."

"How so?" Ed asked, sipping coffee from a to go cup.

"I slept on a fold out couch in their family room, and a couple of times, I've been awakened by him walking around, checking and re-checking the windows, and doors, making sure they were locked.

I tried reasoning with him, but he kept insisting that the enemy was out side, and we had to lay low, and keep silent 'till they passed by."

"What enemy was he talking about?"

Shaking his head, Tom said, "The Vietnamese, I'm guessing. He was a squadron leader back when the Vietnam war was going on. I found out the hard way, that it is best for him to just play out those dreams."

"What happened when you tried to intervene?"

Tom smiled. "I was guiding him back to his bed one night, and he spun around, and punched me in the face. Fortunately, I turned my head, when I realized what he was doing, so the blow wasn't a direct hit, but my jaw was sore for a couple of days."

Ed chuckled. "Did you get him back to bed?"

"Eventually. I had to pretend I was his Sargent, and ordered him to stand down, and return to his cot."

"If he does that a lot, it must be very hard on Eleanor's mom."

Nodding, Tom said, "She does look a little worn around the edges, but she is an amazing, gracious woman. I think she thrives on taking care of people. She sure has taken good care of us while we've been there." Patting his belly, he added, "I probably gained a few pounds. Man, that woman can cook, and bake."

Changing lanes, Ed said, "Yeah. My mom is like that too. The more people she has to feed or help, the happier she is. Me, personally, I can only handle a couple of people at a time."

Tom chuckled. "Yep. I'm right there with you. Sometimes, I don't even like being with myself, much less a crowd of people."

Ed exited the freeway, and headed to the ATO office building on the south side of Dallas. Pulling into the parking lot, they were surprised at the number of emergency vehicles. Ed had to maneuver around several, before finding a spot to park his car. Looking up at the dark smoke still rising from the wreckage, Ed let out a whistle.

"Geeze, oh Pete! What a mess!"

Exiting the vehicle, Tom said, "Yeah."

The men were approached by a Dallas Police officer, who said, "Gentlemen. This is a restricted area. May I see some ID?"

Ed and Tom reached in their pockets, and pulled out their ATO credentials. Satisfied, the officer waved them through. They had taken a couple of steps closer to the site, when Bill Jones greeted them.

"This isn't as bad as we had first thought." Bill said, waving his arm to encompass the surrounding mayhem.

"Really?" Ed said, taking in the piles of cement, cars, and other vehicles.

"I know this looks bad," Bill said, "But when we initially saw this, we thought it had done structural damage to our building, but so far, it looks solid. We're concerned that this may be a prelude of more to come."

"Has anyone claimed responsibility for this?" Tom asked, as he watched EMT men, and women extract a distraught woman from her damaged vehicle. She had blood from a gash on her forehead, running down into her eyes, and her leg was bent at an abnormal angle. She was crying, and screamed in pain as they laid her on a stretcher, then transferred her to an awaiting ambulance.

Bill shook his head. "Because it's new year's day, the office is lightly staffed. One of our guys was walking by the front desk, when the phone rang. He answered it, and someone said, 'Death to the Infidels!' and before he could say anything, the bomb went off. I could be wrong, but I'm assuming it was detonated by a fringe terrorist group here in Dallas."

"It just never ends." Ed said, rubbing his eyes. "I'm just so glad there were no fatalities."

Bill said, "Yeah. If it had been a normal work day, it would have been so much worse."

As the men began walking around the rubble, looking for clues as to where the bomb went off, and what kind it was, they were joined by the head of ATO, Henry Steils.

"Gentlemen." He said in greeting. "We just intercepted a message from the leader of the group responsible for this damage. He was bragging about how they caught us by surprise, and that they had more surprises in store for us Infidels."

"Great." Tom said. "What a way to start the new year."

Sighing, Henry said, "It's frustrating that we know who is responsible, but we don't know where they're located. They could be a local group, or they could be from anywhere in the country."

Frowning, Ed asked, "So, what's the plan? Sit around, and wait for another incident?"

Crossing his arms across his massive chest, Henry said, "Obviously, we'll continue to monitor the chatter, and we have men and women stationed around the city, keeping their eyes and ears open for any more threats. It's kinda like a cat and mouse game. An incident pops up, we investigate, they run, and pop up elsewhere."

Shaking his head, Tom said, "The instigators sure seem to enjoy keeping us on our toes."

Everyone nodded in agreement.

Clearing his throat, Henry said, "Well, I'll let you gentlemen get back to work. Keep me in the loop. Especially if you find any evidence."

Ed gave a mock salute. "Sure thing, Boss."

Bill said, "Why don't we all split up?" Pointing to the right side of the structure, he said, "Ed, you go over there. Pointing to the left side, he said, "Tom, you go there. I'll go straight down the middle."

Nodding in agreement, each man went to his appointed position.

Christina was throwing a load of laundry into the dryer, when she heard her cell-phone.

Catching it on the last ring, she answered breathlessly, but it was too late. Looking at the caller ID, she saw that it was from Lisa. She had left a message, wishing Christina a happy new year, and asking if she still wanted to help with the welcome home party for Rico and Eliana, their two adopted children from Guatemala.

Christina called her back, and the two women began planning the party.

"So, Christina, could you please call Cindy, and let her know of the plans, and I'll call Donna.

A few minutes later, Christina was on the phone with Cindy, informing her of the party plans, and being informed about the bombing in Dallas.

"Turn on the news! Ed is being interviewed."

Christina hurried to the den, found the remote, and turned on the TV. Sure enough, there was Ed, flanked by Tom, and some other man Christina didn't recognize. Ed was answering questions, and sharing what information he could. He then urged the listening audience to please call any of the law enforcement agencies, if they saw, heard, or knew anything about the bombing.

Christina, still connected to Cindy, said, "Oh my goodness, Cindy! These Islamic terrorists are relentless. They are serious about ridding the world of non-believers."

"I know! I don't understand how people can believe that taking another persons life, because they don't share the same religious belief, could possibly be right."

Christina said, "Unfortunately, our history is riddled with holy wars. I think that's why so many people don't want to be associated with any religion."

"It seems that over the past few years, conflicts have escalated." Pausing a beat, Cindy added, "Or, maybe it's because we have quicker, better access to the news as it's happening, it just seems that way."

Sighing, Christina said, "I think you're right on both accounts. Are you familiar with the books of Daniel, and Revelation, in the Bible?"

"I've heard of them, but I've never read them."

Christina cleared her throat, and explained how both of these books describe the events that will lead up to a world leader, and Christ's return." Taking a sip of water, Christina continued.

"Ever since Israel became a nation, the events that were predicted, are coming true at an alarming rate."

"Wow, Christina. I'd really like it if you'd help me understand these things. The Bible has never been one of my favorite books to read."

"That's okay, Cindy. Even though I grew up reading the Bible, there are some areas that I'm weak in too—like the prophesies of Daniel and Revelation. Maybe we could do a Bible study together."

"I'd like that." Cindy said.

"I'll look around for a good study guide for the books of Daniel and Revelation. They may have something in the church library we can use." Christina said, writing a note to herself.

After a few more minutes of chit-chat, the ladies disconnected, and Christina headed up the stairs, with a laundry basket of clothes. She could hear the girls talking and giggling. At the top of the stairs, she heard Nicky call for her, through the bathroom door.

"Mom! I don't have any clean sweatpants."

"I've got some right here for you."

Nicky opened the bathroom door, and grabbed the pants from his mom's extended hand.

"Thanks."

"You're welcome. She turned to knock on Stacey's door.

"Clean laundry!" She called. Stacey threw open her door, and she and Linda took their portions of clothes from the basket.

"Thanks, Mom."

Depositing the rest of Nicky's and Brad's laundry by their doors, she turned, and headed back downstairs. She was surprised, and cried out, when halfway down, she stepped on what she assumed was a cat's tail. She heard a loud hiss, and meow, then felt something hit her ankle.

Losing her balance, she dropped the basket, which made a loud, thumping noise as it hit each step on it's decent to the landing, and grabbed the handrail, stopping herself from following the terrified cat, and empty basket down to the first floor landing.

All of the children came out of their rooms, and simultaneously asked what happened, and if she was okay.

Laughing, she said, "I'm fine, but Stacey, you should check on your cat." She explained the incident, while pulling herself to a standing position. Stacey and Linda bounded down the stairs, in search of the missing cat.

Christina called after Stacey, "I sure hope your cat doesn't continue making the stairs her sleeping place. Someone could get seriously hurt tripping over her."

"Yeah, like that guy, Jamie." Nicky said.

"Yes." Christina said, "Like him."

Had it really been a few hours ago that Jamie Simmons had been injured on these very steps? She shuddered, thinking about the incident. *What if Elijah hadn't been on the stairs?* The thought of Jamie, or anyone else, standing outside the bedroom doors while they slept, gave her goosebumps. *No one in their right mind would do something like that. The kid's got some strange emotional issues*, she thought, as she descended the stairs.

"Why don't y'all get dressed, and I'll go whip up some biscuits and gravy?"

"I can't find Chloe," Stacey said, as she and Linda made their way back up the stairs.

Picking up the empty basket, Christina said, "I'm sure she'll show up when she gets hungry."

"Yeah. When I come down for breakfast, I'll put some food in her bowl. She always comes running when she hears that." Stacey said, as she and Linda returned to her room.

Depositing the basket by the washer on the back porch, Christina looked at the now stiff body of Elijah, and wondered if the ground was too hard to bury him in. If so, she'd have to call the local vet, and hear what he suggested they do. She didn't relish the idea of leaving him until spring.

She also didn't want him lying on the back porch. Gingerly gathering him in her arms, she carried him out to the garage, and laid him in an empty box. He could wait until tomorrow.

Returning to the kitchen, she was met by Stacey, and Linda.

"Mrs. Sanders?"

"Yes, Linda?" Christina squirted disinfectant soap on her hands, and began scrubbing.

"I was wondering if we could call my mom today? I'd like to wish her happy new year."

Nodding, Christina said, "I will try to make that happen." Glancing up at the clock, she said, "In fact, let's go in the front room, and I'll call the hospital in Dallas right now."

Linda's face brightened, as she said, "Thank you so much, Mrs. Sanders!"

After several hours, Ed, and the ATO team, left the parking garage, and headed back up to Henry Steil's office. Henry had ordered a six foot sub, and different kinds of drinks for the team. After filling their plates with food, each person found a seat at the large rectangular conference table.

"Ladies and Gentlemen," Henry began, "First, I want to thank each of you for coming in today. I'm sure many of you had plans with friends, and family, that you had to cancel or put on hold. What a way to start the new year, right?" He got a few grunts of agreement from the group.

"These are certainly troublesome times. I think it will be a long time, before we can truly relax, and enjoy our holidays, as long as there are people out there determined to destroy our country." Clearing his throat, he sat in the chair at the head of the table. Picking up a folder, he said, "Before you, you will find a folder with the information we have gathered so far." He watched as each person picked up their folder, and rifled through it.

"In it, you will find pictures, and information about our suspected bombers, and terrorists. I would like your feedback on what each of you has come up with. I'll begin with Meghan on my left, and we'll go around the table."

As each individual gave an account of their findings, Henry, as well as the other agents, took notes. By the end of the meeting, an hour or so later, the group had a better understanding of who, and what they were dealing with.

When no other information was forth coming, Henry dismissed them, and the dozen individuals left the room. He remained seated at the table, going over his notes. Smiling, he listened to the chatter, as his agents headed to the elevators. He had an amazing team working with him, and for that he was thankful. Now, if all the gathered information could end these threats and acts of terrorism, that would be a miracle. A true intervention from God. And if he was honest, he wasn't one-hundred-percent sure who's side God was on. Closing his eyes, and pinching the bridge of his nose, he thought, *I'm so tired. I could just lay my head down, and go to sleep right here.* Instead, he shook his head to dissipate the cobwebs wanting to gather there, stood, gathered his folders, and headed back to his private office. Locking the door behind him, he sat at his desk, and called the leader of the Homeland Security Agency, or HSA for short.

Ed and Tom wished their teammates a happy new year, then headed out to the parking lot. After all the commotion earlier, the men were surprised at how dark and eerily quiet the area was.

Looking around, Tom said, "Sure looks different than when we arrived."

Unlocking the car, Ed said, "Yeah. I sure hope there aren't any more surprises for a while. All this excitement is beginning to wear me down."

Entering the car, Tom said, "I agree. Seems like the whole world has gone crazy."

Before exiting the lot, both men called the ladies in their life, informing them that they'd return to Alva in about an hour or so.

The drive back was, for the most part, silent, as the men tried to process the events of the last twenty-four hours. Their nerves were strung tight, their bodies were exhausted, and their brains wouldn't stop buzzing. They couldn't help but wonder what would happen next.

Tom surprised Ed by saying, "As you know, Eleanor and I have been together a lot these past few weeks, and we've been talking, laughing, and for the first time, in a long time, have actually enjoyed each others company. A couple of nights ago, once everyone had gone to bed, we shared a bottle of wine, and really communicated. We were able to talk about the car accident, and the loss of the baby. We cried together, and the best part, is that she forgave me. She's never actually said that before. We've always danced around the subject, or didn't bring it up, which caused a lot of tension between us, and Tommy."

Smiling, Ed said, "Wow! That's great!"

"I know. Right? I feel like a ton of bricks have been lifted off my chest. I never stopped loving her, you know?"

Ed nodded, "I know."

"This has been a rough two years. I felt like I had to constantly watch what I said, or did, for fear of her shutting down, or shutting me out."

"So, what's the plan? Y'all going to move back in together, or what?"

Shaking his head, Tom said, "No. I've agreed to go to family counseling with her, and Tommy. And, we're going to start attending church again."

"Sounds like y'all are going to take it slow, and easy."

"Yep. We need to build a stronger foundation, so if anything else happens, we can weather it together."

"That is good news, Tom. I've been praying you and Eleanor would get back together."

Passing a semi-truck, he added, "It's nice to hear some good news for a change."

Nodding, Tom said, "Yeah. So what are you and Cindy planning to do?

Grinning, Ed said, "I'll let you know as soon as I know. First off, the doctors need to find out why she's so anemic. Once that is figured out, and taken care of, we can move on."

"Do you know what kind of tests the doctors are going to do?"

"She's supposed to have upper and lower GI scopes to rule out ulcers, or tumors." Shrugging, he said, "Then we'll go from there."

Nodding, Tom said, "With all the new equipment, and tests that can be performed now days, it almost seems impossible to overlook anything."

Sighing, and nodding, Ed said, "Well, whatever the cause, I hope it can be nipped in the bud."

After dropping Tom off, Ed headed to Cindy's. He quietly slipped in the door, and found Cindy asleep on the couch. He let her sleep while he prepared for bed. Lifting her in his arms, he took her to her own bed.

"Hey, Babe." She said drowsily, as he tucked the covers around her.

"Hey, yourself." Leaning down, he kissed her on the forehead, and turning on her side, she drifted back to sleep. He stood for a moment, watching as her body relaxed, and her breathing ebbed and flowed into the rhythm of sleep. An overwhelming feeling of love washed over him, and he felt his eyes sting with tears. *Is this a glimpse of how God feels when He looks at his children?*

Turning to head back to the living room, and his couch bed, he begged God to please take care of her, and help the doctors discover the root cause of her anemia.

CHAPTER 10

Wednesday morning, the second day of the new year, the Sanders family, as well as other residents of Alva, woke to alarms buzzing, parents yelling, and other methods of rousing themselves, and their offspring, out of pleasant dreams, and cozy beds. It was time to get back in the routine of school, or work, after the holiday vacation.

Christina looked at the thermometer outside the kitchen window. 36 degrees. She heard on the radio that by noon the temperature would rise to 45 degrees. Still cold, but not unbearable.

Before leaving to drop the kids off at their three schools, Christina asked, "Do y'all want to walk home, or should I come get you?"

Brad asked, how warm is it supposed to get?"

"The weather channel said forty-five degrees. Still cold enough for hats and mittens."

Nicky said, "I can walk home. It's only a couple of blocks."

Brad and Stacey agreed that they'd like to be picked up.

Christina nodded, then turned to Linda. "I'll be home in a few minutes. You sure you don't want to come with us?"

Shaking her head, Linda said, "Nah. I'll just curl up on the couch, and see what's on TV."

Everyone bid her good-bye, and piled into the van.

"Mom?" Stacey asked.

"Yes?" Christina replied, as she backed the van out of the garage.

"Are you still planning on taking Linda to see her mom on Saturday?"

Nodding, Christina said, "That's the plan. Why are you asking?"

"Are we going too?" Stacey asked.

"I'd like that, but if you don't want to go, we can make other plans for y'all."

Brad said, "I'd like to stay home, or go to Eric's."

Nicky said, "Yeah. I don't want to go either. Can I go to Danny's?"

Christina nodded. "What about you Stacey?"

"I guess I'll go, to keep Linda company there, and back. She was pretty disappointed when she didn't get to talk to her mom yesterday."

Christina sighed. "I know. My heart hurt for her."

"I heard her crying last night. This whole thing has been so hard on her." Sighing, she added, "I sure hope we can go Saturday."

Patting her daughter's leg, Christina said, "I hope so too."

Stopping the van in front of Nicky's school, Christina said, "See you later, Buddy."

Nicky hopped out of the van, and ran to meet his friend, Danny."

After dropping the other two Sanders kids off, Christina made a quick stop at the 7-11 to grab a jug of milk.

Walking into the family room, she found Linda curled up on the couch, asleep, with the TV on, and the remote in her hand.

Christina gently removed the remote, turned off the TV, and quietly left the room. Grabbing a cup of coffee, she headed for her room, with the intention of unpacking a couple of boxes she had ignored since moving in. The boxes held knick-knacks, and memorabilia she had collected over the years, so it hadn't been a priority. *What better way to start the new year than to do some sorting, and tidying up?*

Grabbing the first box, she sat cross-legged on the floor, and reached in, pulling out a tissue wrapped, hand painted vase, given to her by her grandmother, who had been a porcelain artist. Christina unwrapped it, and admired the detail of the flowers and butterflies adorning it. Smiling, she remembered the boxes of hand painted china in the basement. *Some day I will bring that up, and start using it again. No use having something, as beautiful as that, hidden away in a box.*

When they lived in Michigan, she would bring it out with each season change. Nicky once said that he felt like they were rich because they had unique, one-of-a-kind china. "We are rich," she whispered, as she re-wrapped the vase.

Linda quietly made her way up the stairs, and found Christina sitting on the floor, amidst several piles of stuff.

"Good morning, Mrs. Sanders."

Christina jumped, when she heard Linda's greeting. Turning to face her, she said, "Good morning, Linda. Did you have a nice nap?"

"I didn't mean to fall asleep, but I just couldn't help it." Looking at the piles of items, she asked, "What are you doing?"

"I'm finally going through these last few boxes."

Nodding, Linda asked, "Can I look at some of this?"

Patting a spot on the floor, Christina said, "Sit down."

After an hour or so unwrapping, reminiscing, and re-packing items, Christina closed the lid to the first box.

Standing, and stretching, Christina asked, "Why don't we take a break, and get a snack and drink?"

Linda stood as well, and said, "Sure. Can we come back, and go through some more boxes?"

Christina chuckled, "You sure you want to hear more of my rambling reminiscing?"

Linda nodded. "Yeah! I love hearing those stories."

Descending the stairs, Christina asked, "Has your mom told you stories about her childhood?"

Nodding, Linda said, "Yeah. Not until last week though. She finally told me she had two brothers and a little sister that died in a tornado, when she was two."

Christina stopped and looked at Linda. "She just recently told you?"

Nodding, the girl said, "Yeah. She was calling out for someone named James when she was sleeping. I asked her about that, and she finally told me about her family. When we go back upstairs, I'll tell you all about it."

Christina continued her descent. "Okay."

As they sat eating their BLT sandwiches, Linda asked, "What ever happened to the lady who kidnapped Nicky?"

Wiping her mouth on a napkin, Christina said, "She's in a mental facility in Dallas."

"How long will she be there?"

"I'm not sure. I think it was five years, but it could be more or less."

Popping a Frito in her mouth, Linda asked, "Do you ever hear from her?"

Nodding, Christina said, "Nicky keeps in touch with her. In fact, she sent him a Christmas card, and he sent her a care package."

Scrunching her nose, Linda said, "That's kinda weird. If that had happened to me, I would never want to see, or talk to that person again."

"I agree, but Nicky feels like he should befriend her, since she has no other friends, or family."

Shrugging, Linda said, "That is nice of him, but it's still weird."

Christina smiled.

Taking the last bite of sandwich, Linda asked, "Are we all going to the funeral tomorrow?"

Gathering up the dishes, Christina said, "Yes. Brad was asked to give a eulogy for Jimmy, and it would be a nice show of support for Mr. McCoy"

"Oh. What's a eulogy?"

Christina explained, as she cleaned up the dishes.

Nodding in understanding, Linda said, "It'll be interesting to hear what Brad says."

"Yes, it will be. You ready to head back upstairs?"

"Yes, Ma'am."

Christina was anxious to hear the story of Janet's life.

Stepping off the elevator, Dr. Steven Dawson, glanced down the hallway, and was surprised to see the doors to the CCU open. He walked over to see how much longer it would be, before the staff could re-enter the unit.

Noticing a man in coveralls, and a hard hat, standing on a ladder screwing in a light bulb, Steven walked over, and said, "Excuse me."

Turning to see who had spoken, he said, "Yes, Sir?" Recognizing Dr. Dawson, he said, "Oh, hi Dr. Dawson."

The name stitched on the coveralls read, Bob. "Hi, Bob. I just wanted to know when we can re-enter the unit?"

Nodding, as he stepped down the ladder, Bob said, "I think the boss said sometime this week. Everything has to have one final inspection, before we can allow anyone else in."

Nodding, Steven said, "I see."

Removing his hard hat, to scratch a spot on his scalp, the man said, "I'm sure you'll be one of the first to know when it will be ready for occupancy."

Steven reached out to shake the man's hand, "Thanks, Bob. We're all a bit antsy about getting back to our normal routine, in our own ward."

Nodding, and returning his hat to his head, the man said, "I can understand that."

Looking around one last time, and turning back to the entrance, Steven said, "Guess I best get going."

Bob tipped his head, and picked up his tool box.

Steven entered the Med-Surg ward, and was greeted by a familiar face.

Standing at the nurses' counter, Libby said, "Hello, Dr Dawson."

After greetings, and a brief catching up on family news, Dr. Dawson grabbed the charts for his two patients, and headed to the room of patient number one.

He heard Libby call out, "Dr. Dawson, do you need me to come along?"

Shaking his head, he said, "No. I've only got the two patients."

After signing the paperwork to dismiss both of them, Dr. Dawson headed down to his ground floor office. In the elevator, he let his mind wander back to the New Year's celebration with Christina's family. He enjoyed their company, and looked forward to spending more time with them.

He had been impressed with Brad's wisdom and intelligence, when it came to Biblical, and spiritual subjects. He also admired Brad's rock steady faith, and hoped the boy would never stray from it, like he had done over the years. He had never stopped believing in God, he just rarely thought about Him. One of his new year's resolutions was to be more consistent in church attendance, and Bible study.

Entering his office, he pulled out his cell phone, and called Christina. He knew she was scheduled to work the afternoon shift, but he just wanted to hear her voice.

Hearing the phone ring, Christina put the last object back into the "save" box, and answered it. She was pleased when she saw the caller ID.

Linda excused herself, and headed to her room, to get dressed for the day.

Steven said, "I know you'll be in later, but I just wanted to touch base, and see if you'd like to join me for dinner in the dining room."

Smiling, Christina said, "Sure. We can meet around five-thirty?"

"Sounds good. By the way, I dismissed the two cardiac patients this morning. So, I'm not sure what you'll be doing for the rest of the day."

Nodding, Christina said, "Yeah. That does present a dilemma. I wonder if I could call Mrs. Ferguson, and ask if I could just stay home."

"I think that would be a good idea. No use going to the hospital, just to stand around."

"Yes. I have several things I could do around here. Like taking down the Christmas tree."

"How's Linda settling in?" He asked, turning his chair to face the window.

"She seems to be okay physically. Mentally, and emotionally, I'm not sure. She seems subdued, and sad. We're going to Dallas on Saturday, to see her mom. I hope that will help cheer her up.

"Good. I hope it helps. The poor girl has been through a lot of struggles this past month."

"Yes, she has. I'm so glad we can have her with us for the time being."

Clearing his throat, Steven asked, "Can you let me know if you'll be at the hospital today. If not, we can make other dinner plans."

Nodding, Christina said, "Sure."

After disconnecting, Steven set the phone down, and opened his office door. His first patient had arrived.

Christina called Mrs. Ferguson, who agreed that it would be a waste of time, if she came in to work. Christina did a fist pump as she returned the phone to her pants pocket.

"Hey, Linda!" She called. "You want to help put the Christmas tree away?"

Linda met Christina in the hallway, and said, "Sure."

Grabbing several plastic bins from under the stair storage area, Christina and Linda went to tackle the job of un-decorating the tree.

They were interrupted by a buzzing sound emanating from Christina's pocket. It was an alarm, reminding her to pick up Brad and Stacey.

Donning her coat and gloves, Christina asked, "You want to stay here while I'm gone?"

Linda nodded, and said, "I can continue working on the tree."

Grabbing the keys, Chrisitna said, "Okay. Nicky should be home soon. He'll probably be glad to help you."

After picking up Stacey, Christina parked the van in front of the high-school to wait for Brad. She saw him exiting with a girl, who could easily pass as his twin sister. *This must be the girl, Sylvia, he was talking about.*

Noticing his mom, he waved in acknowledgment, and put up a finger, indicating he would be there in a moment.

Glancing over at her daughter, who was staring out the passenger side window, Christina asked, "So, how was your first day back?"

Shrugging, she said, "It was okay. We didn't do much."

After a moment, Stacey asked, "Did you see all the flowers, balloons, and stuffed animals in front of the high-school?"

Christina nodded. "I did. Jimmy must have been well liked."

Shaking her head, Stacey said, "No. That's the thing. No one seemed to even notice him when he was alive, but I think every kid in high-school, and middle school, put something on the steps as a token of...what? To make them feel better?" Sighing, she said, "It just seems so hypocritical."

Christina sighed. "I've found, over the years, that when tragedy strikes, people tend to do some introspection, and realize how fortunate they are. It is also a nice sign to Mr. McCoy."

Stacey turned in her seat, and looked at her mom.

"How is it nice for Mr. McCoy? All that outpouring of "love" is built on lies. The only person who really knew, and loved Jimmy, was his best friend, Jamie."

Christina cocked her head. "Where is all this anger coming from?"

"I just hate the whole fakeness of it all. Even girls in my school were like, "Oh, I'm so sad. Oh, poor Jimmy." Shaking her head, she added, "They even managed to shed a few tears. I asked if they knew Jimmy, and of course, they didn't. I then asked why they were pretending to be so upset."

"What did they say?"

"They shrugged, and said, 'I don't know, it's just sad.'" Crossing her arms over her chest, and making a disgusted face, she said, "Ugh!"

Nodding, Christina said, "I'm glad you don't like fakeness, but do you think you're being a bit judgmental? Some people are just naturally empathic, and feel things more strongly than others. And, sad to say, some people just like to involve themselves in the drama."

Stacey continued staring out the window for a few moments, struggling to make sense of her thoughts, and feelings. Sighing heavily, she said, "I know. Maybe I'm just cranky because I'm tired, and everything is bothering me."

"You can take a nap when we get home, if you'd like."

Nodding, Stacey said, "I think I will." Pushing a strand of hair out of her eyes, she asked, "How's Linda doing today?"

Smiling, Christina said, "She's doing okay. I kept her busy going through some boxes, and un-decorating the tree."

Turning to face her mom, Stacey said, "There's a half day of school tomorrow, because of the funeral in the afternoon."

Nodding, Christina said, "Yes. I'll pick y'all up, and we can dress, and go."

Brad entered the vehicle, and said, "The funeral tomorrow is going to be in the high-school auditorium."

"Really? That's interesting." Christina said, as she pulled the van away from the curb.

"The principal announced it over the intercom. He said because of the possible turnout, the funeral home wouldn't be large enough to accommodate the crowd."

Stacey nodded, and said, "Yeah. I forgot to mention that our principal made the same announcement."

Turning the van left at the first street, Christina asked, "So, Brad, was that Sylvia you were talking to?"

"Yeah. She wanted to go over the agenda for the funeral service. She's really great at organizing things."

Glancing in the rear-view mirror, Christina asked, "How's your eulogy coming along?"

Shaking his head, and sighing, he said, "I'm struggling, but I think I've just about got it together."

"I know it's difficult to talk about someone you didn't know, but you've been handed that responsibility for a reason. God must have thought you could handle the challenge."

Grimacing, Brad said, "If that's so, He must have a lot more faith in me, than I do."

As she drove past the elementary school, Christina saw Nicky cross the playground.

Stopping by the curb, she lowered her window and shouted, "Hey, you want a ride home?"

He waved, and nodded, then ran over ans hopped in the van.

"Thanks, Mom. I could have walked, but it is nice to be warm."

As the van entered the garage, Stacey asked, "Don't you have to work today, Mom?"

Removing the ignition key, Christina shook her head. "Nope. Mrs. Ferguson gave me the day off."

Unbuckling her seat belt, Stacey asked, "Why?"

"Because there weren't any patients for me to care for."

"That's weird."

"I know! But, I'm glad. I can get the house back in order."

Nicky asked, "Did you ever take care of Elijah?"

Shaking her head, and pointing to a box by the door, Christina said, "Not yet, but that's another thing I can get done. I think I'll take him to the vet, and let him take care of the body."

"Will they cremate him?" Nicky asked, concern filling his voice.

"Probably, but remember, he's been dead a couple of days. He won't feel anything."

Sighing, Nicky said, "I know. I was thinking we could bury him in the backyard."

"Eww!" Stacey said, "I don't want a pet cemetery in our backyard!" Remembering a movie about pets who had been buried in a certain cemetery, came back to life, and were demon possessed.

Nicky gave her a look.

Turning to face her son, Christina said, "Nicky, the ground is too hard to bury him. If you want, I can ask for the ashes."

"No. It's okay. It's not like he's been ours for a long time."

Stacey said, "Geeze Louise! It would be creepy to have a jar of cat ashes!"

Feeling offended, Nicky said, "Yeah? Let's just see how you feel when Chloe dies!"

"Well, I might just have her stuffed, or freeze dried!"

Nicky said, "That'd be great! I could use her for target practice with my BB gun."

Exasperated, Stacey said, "Mom!"

Christina chuckled. "Alright, you two. Enough. Let's go in, and check on Linda."

Dr. Aaron Carmichael sat behind the mahogany desk in his office, reading through Jimmy McCoy's chart, and coroner's report, once again. Leaning back in the chair, he rubbed his eyes, and sighed. According to the information before him, there was nothing more he, or the staff, could have done. He didn't understand why the kid had developed a blood clot. He was on blood thinners to prevent that very thing from happening.

During his time in medical school, the students were warned over and over, that just because they were planning on becoming doctors, there were certain events which would occur, that would baffle even the most educated, and dedicated of them.

One of the professors had said, "You aren't God, so don't fool yourselves into thinking you are."

In some cases, like Jimmy's, death would come unexpectedly and swift, despite heroic measures, and other times, death would be agonizingly slow, or miraculously avoided.

One of the reasons he became a pediatrician, was to challenge Death, and snatch its victims from the claws that desired to drag them down to its lair. Most of the time he succeeded, and Death would slink away. This time, however, Death won the challenge. His mind knew this, but his heart was saddened by the loss of such a promising young man. Looking at his calendar, he made sure tomorrow was clear, so he could attend the funeral.

Pushing away from the desk, he stood, and stretched. He had two patients to consult with, then he was free for the rest of the day. He'd pick Sammie up from his moms, and take her to the new mall in Waco. Christina had described it as 'an amazing place for kids of all ages.'

Seated once again, he turned to face the window behind him, and let his mind wander. One of his new years resolutions was to get to know Christina Sanders on a deeper level. As it was, he felt as if he only knew her name, rank, and serial number, so to speak. He still wasn't sure where he'd like the relationship to go, but, because he enjoyed her company, he wanted to spend more time with her. Just being around her made his heart flutter, and his face blush—like a teenage boy with a crush on a cheerleader.

Smiling at the imagery, he remembered how he felt when he had indeed had a crush on a cheerleader in high school—very much like he felt when Christina was around. He was lost in thought when he heard a knock on his door.

"Come in." He said, as he stood to greet his first patient.

As daylight turned to evening, and the sky turned from blue to orange, then to black, the residents of Alva prepared for their evening, and nighttime rituals. Another day to mark off on their calendar. Most were unaware of the emotional struggle of Jesse McCoy. The few who were, lifted him up in prayer.

Jesse sat in the dark, in his recliner, and begged for sleep to overtake him. He had been awake for at least thirty-two hours, and his body craved sleep, but his mind wouldn't let him drop off. It kept jumping from one thought to another, without giving him time to process each one. He felt jittery, and confused, and wanted nothing more than a few minutes of peace.

Because of the prayers sent up from people he barely knew, he was finally able to drop off into the black abyss of sleep, allowing his body, and mind to finally shut down.

When he woke twelve hours later, his body felt better in general, but his mind continued bombarding him with thoughts and questions. As he waited for the coffee to brew, he stretched, yawned, and rubbed his eyes.

Pouring the coffee into a mug, he went back to his recliner, and sat. Glancing at the clock, he knew he had a couple more hours before he would have to get ready for his son's funeral.

He knew his shy, sensitive son hadn't been popular, and he wondered how many attendees there would be. The principal of the high school had called to inform him that the schools would all have a half day, so the students could attend the funeral, if they chose to. In fact, the principal had said, they were to have the funeral in the high school auditorium, because of the possibility of a large attendance. Shaking his head, Jesse thought, *I highly doubt there will be more than a handful of students, and residents in attendance. How could there be more? The only person Jimmy talked to, or about, was Jamie.*

I wonder how Jamie is doing? When I finish this coffee, I'll give him a call.

Jamie woke with a start. His body ached from his head to his toes. He hadn't slept well, in spite of taking a narcotic for the pain in his ankle. His brain had felt fuzzy, but he had a difficult time dropping off, and staying asleep, and had been conscious of the clock ticking off the hours. Rolling over to his back, he lay staring up at the ceiling, thinking about what the day held for him, and the rest of Alva. He felt a catch in his breath, as a sob worked its way up, and new tears escaped, making rivulets to his ears. *How can I have any tears left?* He wondered, as he swiped them away. *I have to accept the fact that my life will never be the same. I'll always wonder if there was more I could have done. Mr. McCoy has been so nice to me, in spite of my role in Jimmy's death.*

Jamie knew he couldn't take Jimmy's place, but he told himself that he would be as close a son to Mr. McCoy as he possibly could. He would not abandon the man, like his own dad had abandoned him, when his mother had disappeared.

Little Lady, sensing Jamie's distress, jumped up on the bed, and began licking his face. Curling up on his chest, she let out a sigh, and they both dozed back to sleep. Daylight was still a couple of hours away.

Matt Kingsley, the funeral director, grabbed a cup of coffee, and a doughnut, before entering his office. He sat at his desk, and made the necessary phone calls, assuring that Jimmy McCoy's funeral service would proceed without a hitch.

An interesting thing about being a mortician, he thought, *is the ability to disengage one's feelings from the task at hand.* Usually, he could go through the preparation, and presentation of a deceased body with hardly an emotion, but when it was a young adult, child, or infant, he had a difficult time keeping the emotions in check. Sometimes, he would have to leave the room, in order to regain control of his thoughts, and feelings. He thought it interesting that he rarely felt that way about adults, and older citizens. They deserved care, reverence, and sorrow, as well, but they had lived their lives, and were, for the most part, ready to pass on to the next life. With young ones, he felt they, and their loved ones, had been cheated, and that made him sad, and angry.

He believed there was a life after death, but he could never fully wrap his mind around the fact that God, the giver and taker of life, would allow a young person's life to be snuffed out. He tried not to dwell on that thought for very long, or he would never be able to do what he felt God had called him to do. There were some things that would never have satisfactory answers until God came back, and revealed the answers to His creation. *In the meantime,* he thought, *it's up to us humans to care for one another, whether in life or death.*

Cindy woke when she heard Samara's alarm go off. Thinking Ed would be on the couch, she cracked open her door, and peeked into the empty living room. No Ed. His bedding was folded neatly on the end of the couch, with a piece of notebook paper lying on top.

She walked over to retrieve it.

Hey Babe, had to go in early to work. I'll plan to be back for the funeral, so save me a seat. If not, I'll let you know. Love you. E

"Mornin' Mom." Samara said, on her way to the bathroom.

"Mornin', Babe. Did you sleep well?"

Nodding, Samara said, "Yeah. You?"

"Like a baby."

Stopping in the bathroom doorway, Samara said, "Today is the funeral for that boy, Jimmy McCoy."

"I remember." Cindy said, heading to the kitchen to turn on the coffee maker. "It's at two. Right?"

"Yeah. We have a half day. Can you come pick me up?"

Nodding, Cindy said, "Sure. Around noon, in front of the school?"

"Yep." Looking at her watch, Samara said, "I've gotta get ready." Closing the bathroom door, she called out, "Save a cup of coffee for me."

Cindy smiled. Samara's idea of coffee was a lot like Christina's, mostly cream and sugar, with a hint of coffee flavor. There was just enough to satisfy her daughter's request.

Cindy reached up, and touched the tender spot on her head, where she and the bathroom sink had collided. She had made an appointment for the next Monday to see a gastroenterologist in Dallas, who would probably order upper and lower GI scopes. If those didn't reveal the reason she was so anemic, Dr.

Harrison said he would send her to other specialists to get to the root of the problem. She tried not to worry about her condition, but worrisome thoughts insinuated themselves anyway.

When she returned from taking Samara to school, she hopped in the shower, and dressed for the day.

As she was combing through her wet hair, her cell-phone rang. Christina.

After initial greetings, Christina asked, "Are you, Samara, and Ed, going to the funeral today?"

"Samara and I are, for sure. Ed was called into work, but he said he'd try to get back in time. Want me to save y'all seats?"

"Or, I can save y'all seats. I need to go early to give Brad his dress clothes. He's decided to just stay at school, and help get everything ready."

Pausing a beat, Christina asked, "Did I tell you that Brad was asked to do the eulogy for Jimmy?"

"No. Did he know Jimmy?"

"That's the weird thing. He didn't. Jesse McCoy said he wanted Brad to do it. I'm surprised he didn't ask Jamie Simmons. Those two were thick as thieves."

"That is kinda weird. How does Brad feel about that?"

"He has taken the task in stride, and has talked to most of the students, and faculty, to get a clearer picture of Jimmy." Sighing, she added, "This is such a sad thing to have happened. My heart aches for Jesse."

"Mine too." Agreed Cindy, as she stood in front of the mirror, applying makeup to the bruised area on her forehead.

The women chatted a while longer before disconnecting, agreeing that whoever arrived first would save seats for the other.

"Mrs Sanders?" Linda called from the top of the stairs.

"Yes, Linda?"

"I don't know what to wear."

"I'll come up in a minute, and we can decide. If you don't have anything, you could probably wear something of Stacey's."

Brad and Sylvia sat across from the principal, funeral director, and Jesse McCoy, discussing the agenda for the funeral, and addressing any concerns that may arise. Everyone wanted the event to flow smoothly, without any unforeseen glitches.

Matt Kingsley, the funeral director, looked at Brad and asked, "Brad, do you have the eulogy prepared?"

Pulling a folder out of his backpack, Brad said, "Yes, Sir. Would you like to hear it?"

Glancing at Jesse, Matt asked, "Would you like to hear it?"

Jesse shook his head. "I'm barely holding it together as it is. I don't think I could listen to it twice." Glancing at Brad, he said, "I'm sure Brad has done an excellent job, in spite of not knowing Jimmy."

Nodding, Brad said, "I hope so, Sir."

Sylvia handed each person a pamphlet containing the agenda, names of family members, speaker, singers, and a brief bio under Jimmy's senior year book picture.

Turning to face Jesse, she said, "Mr. McCoy, I'm so saddened by the loss of your son. Everyone I talked to, spoke highly of him. He may not have been one of the more popular guys, but he was always nice to everyone. I wish now that I could have known him better."

Nodding, and wiping a stray tear from his eye, Jesse said, "Thank you Sylvia, for those kind words, and for putting this all together. I haven't been in the state of mind to do any of this."

Reaching over, she patted Jess's arm. "I feel honored to have been asked to get involved."

Mr. Neal, the principal, said, "I'm anticipating a full auditorium. The local Pizza Hut manager has volunteered to provide food for after the ceremony. I called the pastors in the area, and asked if members of their congregations could provide deserts. We should be okay on food. Not everyone will eat."

Jesse nodded. "Thanks. I never even thought about that."

Placing his palms on the desk, Mr. Neal said, "If there are no further questions or information, why don't we grab a bite to eat, and meet back here in an hour or so?"

Everyone stood, shook hands, and parted company.

Brad said, "Hey, Sylvia. Want to grab some lunch over at the Eagle's nest cafe?"

Smiling, she said, "I'd love to. They make the best Frito pies around."

Brad chuckled, and shook his head. "Frito pie? I've never tried one."

Sylvia smiled. "Well, you're in for a treat, then."

As the funeral time drew nearer, the auditorium began to fill with students and families. After the lunch break, Brad, Sylvia, Mr. Neal, Mr. Kingsley, and Jesse, met once again, for one final walk through, before the ceremony began.

Mr. Kingsley, and his assistant, rolled Jimmy's casket to the area between the stage, and front row seats. They then brought in the many flowers, wreaths and plants, and hung or placed them around the casket. When they had finished, many of the students who had arrived early, came forward, and in whispered tones, paid their respect to Jimmy. Several of the girls placed long stemmed red roses on the casket, as a token of their grief. Sniffing, and sobbing, could be heard in the otherwise quiet auditorium.

Christina, and the three kids, entered the foyer of the high school, and were met by Brad. Handing her son his dress clothes, she pulled him into a hug, and whispered, "I'm so proud of you."

"Thanks, Mom. Please pray everything goes well."

"Of course. I'm sure it will. Let's meet in the cafeteria afterward."

Turning, he headed down the hall to the nearest bathroom. While changing, he took a moment to pray that everything would go well. He felt his heart rate increase, and his hands beginning to sweat. Taking a few calming breaths, he began repeating the verse, "I can do all things through Christ who strengthens me."

Exiting the bathroom, he was met by Sylvia, who reached out, and straightened his tie, then took his hand.

"You ready?"

Sighing, Brad said, "As I'm ever gonna be."

They headed to the foyer, and greeted people as they, and a few other volunteers handed out the pamphlets.

At five minutes to two, Mr. Neal came over, and whispered to Sylvia, and Brad, that it was time to begin the ceremony.

The five people in charge of the funeral arrangements, made their way to the front of the auditorium, pausing in front of the casket to pay their respects. Jesse, having held his emotions in check, lost the battle, and let them overtake him. Laying his body over the casket, he began sobbing uncontrollably. The auditorium grew eerily quiet, as if a supernatural hush had been decreed, while Jesse cried for his dead son. After a few moments, Mr. Neal, and Mr. Kingsley, took his arms, and led him to his seat in the front row. It was then, that the noise returned, as people sniffled, and blew their noses. As Brad turned, he scanned the room and was surprised at the vast number of people present. There were very few vacant seats.

Mr. Neal walked back to the podium, and introduced the girls acapella trio. They would be singing Amazing Grace. Brad, and most of the audience had never heard the trio before then, and were astounded by their performance. He and Sylvia exchanged surprised glances, and mouthed the word "wow."

When the girls had seated themselves, Mr. Neal invited audience members up to the podium to share stories involving Jimmy. He was surprised at the number of students making their way up to the stage. He knew Jimmy was a quiet, gentle young man, and had very few friends, but as he listened to story after story of how he had helped this student or that one with their math or science projects, he realized there was more to the boy than had met the eye.

As the line of students dwindled, and Brad stood to make his way to the podium to deliver the eulogy, he was surprised to see Nicky walking up the steps, then over to the microphone.

What in the world is he doing? I know for a fact that he didn't know Jimmy. Shrugging, he sat back down. Catching Nicky's eye, he gave him a thumbs up sign.

Nicky introduced himself, and informed everyone that his big brother, Brad, would be speaking after him.

He cleared his throat, and began.

"I didn't know Jimmy personally, because he was so much older than me, and he and my brother weren't friends." Looking around the room, he said, "You're probably wondering why I'm up here, if I don't have a story, or something to say about Jimmy. Well, this isn't so much about Jimmy, or for Jimmy." Looking directly at Jesse, he said, "This is for Mr. McCoy." Jesse cocked his head, and nodded, as if to say, "Okay."

Nicky cleared his throat, and began. "I had a dream last night, in which Mr. McCoy, his wife, and Jimmy, were all sitting around a campfire, next to a lake, having a grand time, when all of a sudden, out of nowhere, came a big gust of wind, that blew out the fire." Nicky made hand gestures illustrating the point. "Because it was pitch dark, Mr. McCoy quickly re-lit it the fire. Looking up, he realized his wife, and son, were gone. He ran around calling, and searching for them, but to no avail. Knowing he couldn't walk through the woods back to his car, because he didn't have a flashlight, and not having a phone, he sat on the ground, and cried, until sleep overcame him. As the sun was beginning to rise, he woke, and realized he wasn't alone. There, sitting by the campfire, cooking what looked and smelled like fish, was a man wearing camo pants, and shirt." There were a few giggles. Nicky paused a moment to catch his breath, before continuing.

"Startled, Mr. McCoy jumped up, asking the man who he was, where he came from, and if he had seen his wife, and son."

Brad looked around the auditorium, and smiled. The people seemed to be captivated by his brother's story telling. Not sure where the story was headed, he too returned his focus to his brother.

"The man held up his hand, and said, 'First we eat.' After they had filled their bellies, the man stood, and said, "Follow me."

"Why would I follow you?" Mr. McCoy asked."

"Cocking his head slightly, the man said, "I will teach you to be a fisher of men."

"Mr. McCoy stood, and with his hands crossed across his chest said, "What? Fisher of men? What does that mean?"

There were a few giggles coming from the audience because of Nicky's dramatic flair. *He is an amazing story teller,* Brad thought.

"The man turned, and continued walking. Mr. McCoy followed at a distance, not sure if he could trust this man or not, but wanting to hear what he had to say." Pausing to take a sip of water, Nicky then continued his story telling.

"Do you know where my wife, and son are?" Mr. McCoy asked more than a few times, before the man finally turned around, and said, "I do know where they are. They are in a mansion I have prepared for them. When it is time for you to go there, I will also take you."

"Mr. McCoy was a bit frightened by this declaration. He wondered, Was this man a murderer? Has he kidnapped my wife and son? Is he going to kill me also?

"Mr. McCoy stopped walking, and said, "Look, if you've killed them, or are planning to kill them or me, then just take me where they are right now."

"The man turned, and with compassion in his eyes, said, "Jesse. Do you know who I am?"

"Shaking his head vigorously, Mr. McCoy said, "No. Should I? How do you know my name?"

"Nodding, the man reached out, and touched Mr. McCoy's head. Immediately, Jesse knew. He knew he was in the presence of Jesus. God's earthly Son. He fell to his knees, and wept. Not for losing his family, but because he knew how unworthy he was to be in this man's presence.

"Jesus?" He asked in a whisper."

"The man smiled, and nodded. He then put out his hand, and helped Mr. McCoy to his feet, and they walked off together. I then woke up."

There seemed to be a collective sigh from the audience. Each person had been so caught up in the story, it was as if they had forgotten where they were.

Looking directly at Jesse again, Nicky said, "Mr. McCoy, I'm not one-hundred-percent sure what this means, but I felt I needed to tell you this. I'm sure God will reveal its true meaning in due time."

Motioning to Brad, Nicky exited the stage. Brad met him at the steps, and gave him a high-five.   Taking the microphone, he said, "That was awesome!"

Nicky gave a crooked smile, and returned to his seat.

Brad stood behind the podium and said, "That was my little brother, y'all. Pretty cool, huh?"

The people in the audience weren't sure how to react, and whispering could be heard throughout the large room. Jesse stood, and began clapping, as tears streamed down his face. He was soon joined by the rest of the audience. Motioning for Brad to hand him the microphone, Jesse turned to face the assembly.

"I just want to thank everyone for their stories, and Nicky for the dream story meant for me. I will treasure all of these. I want to applaud everyone, because I think that's what Jimmy would do."

With that, he turned, and handed the microphone back to Brad, who stood with everyone else, as they clapped their appreciation.

Once the noise ebbed, and people took their seats, Brad began his eulogy by reading the words on the pamphlet, then adding a few words of his own. He closed with prayer, and announced that food was to be served in the cafeteria. Those who wanted to go to the cemetery, were asked to line up their cars out behind the school.

The six young men chosen to bear the casket came forward, and after one last good-bye to his son, Jesse helped close the casket, and walked out with the others.

Mr. Kingsley took the microphone, and said, "If you can carpool, it'll take up less room at the cemetery."

People stood, and many of them came forward to hug Jesse, and pass on words of encouragement. Others headed to their cars, while others headed to the cafeteria. There was a hushed reverence, as everyone filed out of the auditorium.

Christina grabbed Nicky, and hugged him tightly. "I can't tell you enough how proud I am of you. I had no idea you were going to do that."

Pulling away, Nicky said, "Thanks, Mom. I wasn't sure if I was supposed to say all that or not, but I just felt this strong tugging in my…" He paused as he tried to think of the right word. "In my spirit. I knew if I didn't say anything, I'd regret it forever."

Before she could say anything else, Nicky was surrounded by a group of his peers, as well as friends of Stacey, and Brad. They were all very encouraging, and she felt her heart swell with joy and pride.

The Pizza Hut staff had not been unprepared for such a large crowd, and were beginning to panic, when Cindy, Samara, Christina, Linda, and the three Sanders kids arrived. Much to everyone's disappointment, Ed was unable to attend, otherwise, he would have donned an apron as well. They began preparations for the meal. Christina and Brad un-boxed, and sliced pizza, while Stacey, Linda and Samara, put out plates and utensils. Cindy and Nicky helped the older ladies slice up, and set out deserts.

Before heading back to the restaurant, to grab more pizza dough, the Pizza Hut owner, Curtis Shaffer, turned on the four large ovens in the kitchen. He returned with more dough, and pizza toppings, the same time the group, who had gone to the cemetery, arrived.

Jamie, who had gone to the cemetery, hobbled in, grabbed an apron, and he and Mr. Shaffer began rolling out the dough, and preparing the pizzas.

"Thanks, Jamie." His boss said, as he patted the young man's shoulder.

Sylvia had forgotten to ask for volunteers to help with kitchen duty beforehand, and began pulling classmates out of the lines. Because she had such an endearing personality, she was able to recruit enough help for preparations, serving, and clean-up. The women from the various churches brought in deserts, and salads, then added their help to the serving tables.

Once the funeral attendees had all left, the clean up crew went to work. There were a few pizza slices, salads, and deserts left, and several teens volunteered to eat them, or take them home. Sylvia had teens taking out trash, wiping down tables, sweeping, and mopping the floors, and even removing finger prints from the glass doors. After she was sure there was a job for everyone to do, she helped Mr. Shaffer in the kitchen, as he boxed, and bagged, the left over pizza items. Clean up was quick and efficient, and by the time everyone was ready to leave, the dining area, and kitchen, looked spotless.

Making one final inspection before closing, and locking the cafeteria doors, Sylvia thought, *All in all, everything worked out well.*

The five minute ride from the school, to home, was quiet. Everyone seemed to be processing the day's events. Before exiting the van at home, Christina asked everyone to meet in the den, once they had prepared for bed. She was exhausted, and knew the kids were as well. They all needed a good nights sleep, and she had no doubt they would all be off to dreamland in the next couple of hours, even though it was still considered early.

Nicky yawned, and said, "Do we have to meet downstairs? I'm so tired, I just want to go to sleep."

"Me too." Stacey added, as she yawned.

Christina sighed, and nodded. "Okay, we can talk tomorrow."

Making her way up the stairs, she thought, *One nice thing about winter, is that it gets dark early, so even if one went to bed at eight-o'clock, the mind, and body, felt it was much later.* Yawning, she entered her room, and changed into her lounging pajamas. Her feet were tired, and throbbed as she removed the black tights she had worn, and traded them for wool socks and slippers.

Putting on her winter robe, she headed downstairs, and sat in her recliner, rehashing the day's events. Her boys had certainly surprised her with their speeches.

On the way home from the funeral, Jack and Jamie rode in silence. What could they say? Nice funeral? A part of Jamie felt numb and empty. He had no words to express his misery of saying the final goodbye to his best friend. His body and mind were exhausted, and his leg and ankle throbbed in pain. All he wanted to do was to take a pain pill or two, and sleep the rest of the day, and night.

Grabbing the crutches out of the back seat, he hobbled up the sidewalk, to the front door, where he was greeted by Little Lady, who was whimpering, and prancing around. As soon as the door was opened, she ran out to take care of her business.

Entering his bedroom, Jamie was surprised to see all four puppies had their eyes open. They were standing on wobbly legs, whimpering, as they bumped into each other, trying to find their mother. He chuckled. They were so cute in their awkwardness. Laying the crutches on the bed, he reached down, and picked one up in each hand. They were warm, fat, and wiggly, as he brought them up to his face, kissing and snuggling each one.

"Dad!" He called.

"In here!" Jack called, as he opened the door for the dog, who immediately ran to her pups. Heading to his room, to change out of his suit, Jack stopped, and leaned on the door jamb of Jamie's room.

"Look!" Jamie said, as he held out the two whimpering pups.

"Their eyes are open!"

Nodding, Jack said, "You know, Jamie, we can't keep all the pups."

Jamie sighed, and said, "I know. But, we can keep them a few more weeks, right?"

Jack nodded slightly, before saying, "Yeah, but the longer we keep them, the harder it will be to let them go."

"It'll be hard whether we keep them another week, or another month. I've already become attached to them."

Jack shook his head. "Yeah. You're right." Turning, he said, "I'm gonna get out of this suit, then head over to the shop. You want to come with me?"

Jamie shook his head. "Nah. My leg and ankle are killing me. I think I'll take a pain pill, and lie down a while."

"Okay. Stopping in front of his bedroom door, Jack said, "I rescheduled the lung biopsy for next Wednesday afternoon. I asked Al if he could drive me there."

"Oh, Dad. I'm sorry. I forgot all about that. We were supposed to go yesterday, right?"

"Yeah, but..."

Jamie hung his head. "I know. I screwed everything up."

Sighing, Jack said, "Jamie. What happened to Jimmy wasn't your fault. What's done is done. We can't go back and undo it. All we can do is go forward, and hopefully, learn from the experience."

Standing in his doorway, Jamie nodded, and said, "I keep telling myself that, but it doesn't make it any easier." Pinching the bridge of his nose to squelch the tears burning the back of his eyes, he added, "Trust me, Dad, I will never do anything that foolish again."

Jack gave a crooked smile, before turning into his bedroom. "Good."

CHAPTER 11

Dr. Aaron Carmichael's alarm woke him with its annoying buzzing. Turning over to shut it off, he moaned. It felt like he had finally dropped off to sleep, and here it was, time to get up. Sitting on the side of the bed, he rubbed his face and eyes. Stumbling to the kitchen to start his coffee machine, he peeked in at his sleeping daughter, then headed to the shower.

Standing under the hot water, he rehashed his week. He still didn't understand why Jimmy McCoy had died. He had taken every precaution he could have. The Heparin he was on should have prevented the blood clot from forming. *Had it been a large enough dose? Too much, and the patient could hemorrhage, but not enough, and a clot could form. Did I miscalculate?*

Any time he lost one of his young patients, he would go through a rigorous self evaluation, until he was convinced he had done everything humanly possible to save them. Sometimes, there were no answers. Before he had begun a relationship with God, he blamed it on karma, or fate. Now, however, he understood that a power greater than any human could imagine, was in control of everything; life, death, karma, or fate.

As Brad Sanders had said in his eulogy for Jimmy, "We are all a small thread in the tapestry called life, and sometimes our thread color is only needed in a small area, while others may be woven across the whole canvas."

Aaron rested his forehead against the shower wall, enjoying the rhythmic beating of the hot water on his back, wondering what his thread would contribute to the tapestry of life.

Stepping out of the shower, he dried off quickly, and dressed for the day, before heading to the kitchen for a steaming cup of coffee. He had about an hour before he had to wake Sammie.

Sitting in front of the large east facing picture window at the back of his house, he watched as the sky turned from midnight blue to a soft salmon color, as the sun rose heavenward. The weatherman had predicted snow flurries in the afternoon or evening, which reminded him of the saying, 'Red sky in the morning, sailors take warning. Red sky at night, sailors delight.' Someone had told him that there was an actual Bible verse that said something similar to that. He had looked it up, and was surprised to read, in Matthew 16, verse 2 and 3: 'When evening comes, you say, 'It will be fair weather, for the sky is red, and in the morning, 'Today it will be stormy for the sky is red, and overcast.'

Thinking about possible snow, made his mind wander to thoughts of Christina. She had told him how cold, snowy, and long, Michigan winters had been. He was thankful he lived in Texas. A snow now and then was okay, but a winter lasting more than a few weeks, was difficult to imagine.

Christina. Just the thought of her made his pulse quicken. *What am I going to do about her?* Shaking his head, to clear his mind, he picked up the Bible next to his chair, and turned to the book of Mark. Brad had suggested he begin reading through the New Testament before the old, and had gifted him with a NIV study Bible. Having never read the Bible before meeting Brad, he was surprised how easy it was to read, and understand. He had breezed through the book of Matthew, and had been surprised by Jesus' teachings. He had just finished reading the first chapter in Mark, when Sammie came in, and crawled onto his lap. He snuggled her in the crocheted afghan his mother had given him, when Sammie was born.

"You will need this on those cold, dark nights when the baby just needs the comfort of a warm body." She had said, when she presented it to him.

How right she had been. After his wife had died, he had spent many nights holding Sammy, as she cried herself to sleep, because she missed her mother. This quiet time in the morning had been their routine since that time.

Kissing the top of her head, he whispered, "How did you sleep, Princess?"

"Good." She whispered back.

"What would you like for breakfast?"

Sitting up, she put her finger on her chin and said, "Eggo, like in that commercial."

"The one where they say, 'Leggo my Eggo?'"

Nodding vigorously, she said "Yep."

Laying her head on his chest, she said, "I love you, Daddy. You're the best daddy in the whole world."

Pulling her close, and feeling a lump in his throat, he said, "I love you too, Baby. You're the best little girl in the whole world."

After a few minutes of snuggle time, she crawled off his lap, and said, "I have to go get ready for school, and you can fix my Eggo."

Smiling, he said, "Yes, Ma'am."

Giggling, she ran to her room.

Placing his hand over his heart, he looked up at the ceiling and said, "Thank you."

Dropping Sammie off with his mother, because it was too early for school, he headed to his office in the hospital.

Focusing on the chart in his hand, as he boarded the elevator, he almost bumped into Christina.

"Aaron!" She said in surprise.

"Oops! Sorry. I didn't see you there."

Smiling, she said, "It's okay. I see you're immersed in the chart in your hand."

Closing it, he said "Yeah. A new patient. Came in this morning by ambulance. Complaining of stomach pains, and high fever. Probably appendicitis. Dr. Seltzer admitted her."

Making a face, she said, "Poor kid. How old?"

"A ten-year old girl."

Nodding, Christina remembered when she had to bring Stacey in for an emergency appendectomy. "Stacey loved Dr. Dan."

Smiling, and nodding, Aaron said, "Yeah. I haven't met a kid or parent that doesn't love him. He certainly has a gift of communication, and easing fears. He's also a great physician."

The elevator doors opened, and placing his hand to hold them open, he asked, "Are you free for dinner?"

Nodding, she said, "Yeah. What time?"

"If I have to do surgery, that'll take a couple of hours. How about five-ish? I should be free by then."

Smiling, she said, "Five-ish, it is."

Standing in the doorway, he asked, "How's it working out with Linda?'

"Good. I had to leave her at home today for a little while, but I'm pretty sure she'll be okay. She said her mom left her alone all the time. The kids should be back home in an hour or so."

"Good. She should be able to return to school in another week."

Stepping out, he couldn't help but grin. "See you later."

"Later."

Arriving on the third floor, and heading to the nurse's lounge, Christina almost collided with Sarah Stevens, the LPN from the CCU, as she opened the door.

"Sarah!" She exclaimed.

"Oh, Christina! I'm sorry. I almost knocked you down."

Reaching out for a hug, Christina said, "I was wondering when I'd see you again."

Sarah returned the hug. "I know! Mrs. Ferguson had me working all different shifts, and different areas. I guess that's one advantage of being single. I have a much more flexible schedule than those gals who have families to attend to."

Following Christina back into the lounge, Sarah said, "I did hear that the CCU should be operational by next week. They have a couple of final inspections, and are waiting for some equipment to arrive." Placing her hand over her heart, she added. "I'll be one happy nurse when everything gets back to normal."

Christina hung her outer coat in the locker, then grabbed her lab coat, and stethoscope.

"Me too! It'll be nice to work with everyone again. I miss the friendship we've developed over the past few months." As they walked towards the nurses' station, Christina asked, "So, Sarah, how are things between you and Harold?"

Sarah grinned from ear to ear. "Still dating. We get along so well."

"I'm glad. You'll have to tell me about all the fun things y'all have been doing."

Nodding, Sarah asked, "How about at dinner?"

Shaking her head, Christina said, "Not today, but maybe after work we can sit and chat a while?"

"Okay. I don't have any plans after work, so that would be fine."

After an hour or so, Christina called home to check on Linda. She was fine each time—occupying herself with reading, watching TV, or napping. Even though everything was "fine" according to Linda, Christina couldn't help but worry a bit. Linda wasn't her child, even though she had agreed to become her guardian until Janet recovered sufficiently enough to care for her, and she was barely thirteen. Although seemingly mature for her age, she was still a child. The second time she called, Brad and the other two kids were home. He was planning on making grilled cheese sandwiches for dinner.

When it was time for her dinner break, Christina excused herself, and headed to the cafeteria where she was to meet Aaron.

Motioning for her to join him in line at the salad bar, he said, "Hey, Christina. I'm so glad you could make it."

"Yeah, me too. It was a bit hectic on the third floor today. When I arrived this afternoon, there were only a dozen or so surgical and cardiac patients, but when I left for dinner, there were several more being admitted. Libby and I are the only RN's on the floor today. Thank goodness we have plenty of aides and LPN's."

Smiling, he said, "I haven't checked, but there must be a full moon."

Cocking her head as she picked up a tray and silverware, Christina asked, "What does that have to do with anything?"

Chuckling, Aaron said, "You've never heard that when the moon is full, there are more accidents and sicknesses?"

Shaking her head, she said, "No. Afraid not. So, is that an old wive's tale, or has there been evidence."

"According to some research, there is a correlation between the two. In my personal experience, however, I've never noticed any evidence of it."

Filling their salad bowls, they continued to the meat and vegetables, and filled their plates.

Once they picked their drinks, Aaron paid the cashier, and they headed to a table next to the glass wall overlooking the solarium.

Arranging their food, Christina looked down at the enclosed garden and said, "I've always loved that garden."

Aaron nodded. "It is a beautifully arranged one. Sometimes, I like to go there and eat, or read. It's very relaxing."

Nodding, Christina said, "It is! When I was a Candy Striper in High School, it was a lot smaller and not enclosed. Even then, it was beautiful and relaxing, just very hot in the summer, and very cold in the winter. I'm so glad that when the hospital was redesigned, the garden was enclosed."

Aaron nodded in agreement, then said, "I'd like to pray if you don't mind."

"Sure. I usually just bow my head, and say a silent prayer when I'm by myself."

After praying, they spent the next half hour eating, and talking about the kids, the holidays, and Jimmy's death, and funeral.

"Aaron, you do know that Jimmy's death was not your fault. Right?" Christina asked, taking a sip of iced ted.

Aaron nodded slightly, and said, "I keep telling myself that, but I can't seem to convince myself that I couldn't have done more."

Christina reached out, and laid her hand on his. "Aaron, sometimes we do everything right, and death still happens. There are things that are out of our human control."

Nodding, he said, "Yes. You're right, of course. I was so touched by what Nicky and Brad said at the funeral. You have two amazing boys...and of course, Stacey is pretty amazing as well."

Removing her hand, Christina smiled, and nodded. "They are pretty amazing aren't they?"

Wiping her lips with the napkin, she asked, "Speaking of children, how's Sammie?"

Aaron smiled broadly. "She too, is pretty amazing. Would you like to see her latest school picture?"

"Oh, yes!" Taking the picture from Aaron, she smiled. "She is so adorable!"

Looking at it once more before replacing it in his wallet, he said, "The older she gets, the more she looks like her mother."

"From what you've told me, your wife must have been a beautiful lady."

Nodding, Aaron said "Yes. She was. This may sound weird, but I'm so thankful that Sammie can carry on her beauty."

Shaking her head, Christina said, "That doesn't sound so weird. Of my three kids, Stacey favors her dad the most. She has his skin, hair, and eye coloring."

"Who does Brad favor?"

Christina chuckled. "He favors one of his great uncles. The only picture we have of him is black and white, but on the back of it, someone had written that his hair, beard and mustache were all a bright orange. I guess he was quite the anomaly at the family reunions, being everyone else had darker skin, hair and such. There must have been others like him in the gene pool, but because the only pictures we have of dead relatives are black and white, it's difficult to determine their coloring."

"I think it's interesting that your three children are all so different in looks, and coloring. The middle eastern gene pool doesn't contain much variety. Black hair, brown eyes, and tan skin are pretty much all we produce."

Christina nodded. "What if there is an anomaly? Say a child is born with different coloring?"

Shaking his head, Aaron said, "I've heard of incidences in the old country, where, if that were to happen, which is extremely rare, the mother is charged with infidelity, and she and the child are divorced from the husband."

"Divorced?"

"Middle eastern men are very proud of their reputation, and are very displeased if anyone, or anything brings it into question."

Taking a bite of salad, Christina chewed, and swallowed before asking, "What happens to the woman and child?"

Sighing heavily, Aaron said, "Because of strict rules about women working, or being seen in public, many go back to their parents homes, if they'll allow it, or often times they just disappear."

"Disappear?"

"It's a very harsh world over in the middle east. Their laws are very different than here in America. That's why my parents left. They didn't want to raise me in such an environment."

Holding her glass of tea up in a salute, she said, "Well, I for one, am glad they moved here."

Aaron cocked his head, and smiled. "Thank you. I too am thankful."

The remaining dinner time was spent in light conversation about work, and family events.

Dr. Dawson purchased his dinner, and carrying his tray, walked over to where Aaron and Christina were sitting. Laying his hand on Christina's shoulder, he said, "Hey, you two. Mind if I join you?"

Christina smiled broadly. "Of course not! Aaron and I have been enjoying a nice dinner, and discussion about work and kids."

Pulling a chair from a nearby table, Steven sat, and arranged his food.

Before he took a bite of salad, he said, "So, Aaron, I haven't talked to you in a while. How was your holiday?"

Aaron wiped his mouth with a napkin, and gave a condensed version of what he had shared with Christina.

"How about you?"

Swallowing, Steven placed his hand over Christina's and said, "I was fortunate enough to be invited over to Christina's on New Year's Eve, and had a great time with her and the kids."

Christina, feeling a bit awkward, and conscious of her face and neck blushing, said, "Yeah. It was fun." *Do I hear a hint of jealousy in Steven's voice?* She wondered, as she began gathering her tray items together for disposal.

Cocking his head, Aaron asked, "What did y'all do to occupy your time, before the new year rang in?"

Glancing at Steven, who was adding butter to his roll, she said, "We played table games, and filled up on junk food, until around one the next morning."

Shaking his head, Aaron said, "My folks weren't the table game type. Instead, we spent our spare time reading."

"Interesting how different our childhoods were. My parents weren't readers, but they loved playing games."

"What kind of games?" Aaron asked, leaning forward, and resting his hands on the table.

"Cards, dominoes, board games. Just about any kind that involved a few people. I remember having my girlfriends over, and we'd just sit and play card games for hours, with or without my folks. We didn't have cellphones, and nothing of interest was on television, so we had to make our own entertainment."

"Sounds like fun." Aaron said. Looking at Steven, he asked, "Did you play table games when you were young?"

Swallowing, Steven wiped his mouth, then answered, "Yes. My parents had a group of friends who would get together each Saturday night, and play dominoes or card games." Smiling at the memory, he added, "Sometimes, they'd invite me to join them when one of the other players was absent."

Nodding, Aaron said, "I wish I had known you back then." Looking at Christina, who was pushing her chair away from the table, Aaron asked, "Maybe y'all could teach me how to play some of these card games?"

Standing, Christina smiled. "Of course. Maybe a Sunday afternoon, after lunch and church?"

Nodding, and grinning, Aaron said, "Is it okay to bring Sammie?"

Placing her hand on Aaron's shoulder, Christina said, "Of course! My kids think she is adorable."

Steven watched the exchange, and felt his heart quicken, and his jaw clench. *Am I jealous*? He wondered, as he unclenched his jaw. As Christina and Aaron said their good-byes, he had a mental argument with himself.

Why in the world would I be jealous? Of Aaron? I don't have any rightful claim to Christina. We've only been seeing each other for a few months. I'm not one-hundred-percent sure of her feelings for me. She seems to like me, and enjoys my company, but would she even be interested in a long term relationship with me? Maybe I should back off, and let her explore her feelings for Aaron. Or, should I just keep pursuing her, and see where it leads?

Shaking his head to bring his mind back to the moment, he heard Christina say his name.

"Steven?" She said, laying a hand on his shoulder.

"Oh, yes. I was just thinking about something. Sorry."

"It's okay. I was just letting you know that I'll be heading back upstairs. Will you be coming up to check on your patients?"

Nodding, he said, "Yes. Soon as I'm finished eating."

Lifting her tray, she headed towards the exit. Both men watched her depart. Stepping onto the elevator, Christina blew out a sigh of relief. *That was awkward*, she thought, as she pushed the third floor button.

When Steven had walked in, and joined them, she could feel the atmosphere change, as tension began to build. She sensed...what? *Jealousy? Competition? There was nothing evident in their behavior, so maybe it was just my imagination. But then again...*

Exiting the elevator, she almost ran into Libby.

"Hey, Girl!" Libby said, as she put her hand up.

"Oh, sorry." Christina said sheepishly. I was thinking about something, and obviously not looking where I was going."

Cocking her head, and grinning conspiratorially Libby asked, "Anything you want to share with me?"

Grinning, Christina said, "No."

"Hmm. Right." Entering the elevator, Libby turned, and said, "Well, if you ever need an ear, I've got two."

"Yep. I'll remember that."

Instead of heading directly to the Med-Surg unit, Christina turned, and headed towards the CCU. She wanted to see how far along the workers had gotten since she'd been there last. Opening one of the double doors, she peeked in. Gasping, she was amazed at how clean, and pristine everything looked. Stepping into the hallway, she looked around. She could hear male voices, but didn't see anyone. *Dare I go any further?* Walking quietly, she ventured further in. Feeling like a child sneaking down the stairs on Christmas day, she found herself almost tiptoeing up to the nurses' station. Running her fingertips over the new counter tops, she felt an excitement building in her. *This is amazing! I can hardly wait to return.*

She saw movement in her peripheral vision, and turned to see the Fire Chief, Jesse McCoy approaching.

He looked surprised to see her. "Mrs. Sanders." He said in greeting, as he removed his hard hat and gloves.

Nodding, she said, "I know I probably shouldn't be here, but I just wanted to see how far along y'all had come. Someone said we should be moved in, and up and running in another week."

Nodding, and leaning against the counter, he said, "Yes, Ma'am. No later than Wednesday. It depends on when some of the new equipment arrives."

"New equipment?"

Smiling, he said, "The hospital board agreed to two new crash carts, cardiac monitors, and a whole slew of other things, that I have no idea what they are, or what they're called."

"Nice."

"Hey, would you like to look around more?"

Glancing at her watch, and seeing she had another ten minutes on her break, she said, "As long as I'm not in your way."

Shaking his head, he said, "No way. I'm due for a break anyway. The electrician and I have been going over all the wiring, plugs, connectors and such to insure there aren't any potential fire risks. He had to run out to his truck for something, so actually, this is a perfect time to take you on a tour."

As they walked down the hallway, Jesse pointed out the new equipment, curtains, and other miscellaneous items that had been replaced or revamped. He seemed animated, as if he were showing off his new baby. *Baby. Just yesterday they had buried his baby. How can he be back to work and so chipper? Drugs? Denial? Acceptance?*

Halfway through the tour, he stopped, and leaned against a door jamb.

His voice hitched a bit when he said, "Mrs. Sanders, I just want to tell you again how much I appreciate everything your family did for Jimmy's funeral. Brad did such a nice job on the epitaph, and that young one of yours, well, that was a surprise for sure. I felt God was speaking directly to me."

Christina walked over, and placed a hand on his arm. She wasn't sure what to say.

Smiling, and nodding, she said, "Yes, Nicky surprised us all. I'm glad we were able to help. I can't begin to imagine how difficult this has been for you. As my friend Libby is so fond of saying, "If you need an ear, I've got two."

Jesse smiled, and wiped his eyes. "Thanks, Mrs. Sanders."

"Christina. Please call me Christina."

Tipping his head, he said, "Yes, Ma'am. Christina, it is. You may call me Jesse."

Checking her watch once again, she said, "I have to get back to work."

Nodding, he said, "Yeah. Me too. I'll walk back with you."

When they reached the double doors, he stepped in front, and held one open for her.

"Thanks again, Jesse. The whole CCU staff is anxious to get back to our familiar surroundings. It's been quite a challenge for the Med-Surg staff, and ours, to work out a feasible routine."

"I imagine so. We'll do our best to get y'all back, and operational as soon as possible."

Smiling, Christina said, "By the way, I'm glad we met. I've heard so many good things about you. It's nice to finally get to know the man behind the rumors."

Jesse chuckled. Extending his hand, he said, "It's been a pleasure meeting you as well."

His hand seemed to swallow hers. Looking up into his large frame, and gentle face, she thought, *Wow! He is quite the giant of a man! Put fur on him, and he could pass as a bear.* The only large man she could compare him to was Ed, but Jesse was at least several inches taller, and pounds heavier than Ed. *If I'm ever in a fire, or accident, I would like to have Jesse McCoy rescue me.* Feeling a blush make its way to her face, she turned quickly, and headed to the Med-Surg unit.

Her mind wandered to thoughts of Steven and Aaron. Mumbling to herself, she pushed on the door to the nurse's lounge, and bumped into Sally Jean, the young aid from the CCU.

"Sally Jean!" She exclaimed. "I'm so sorry. Did I hurt you?"

Sally giggled. "No! The door hit my shoe."

"Whew! It sounded like the door hit your head, or some other body part."

Sally waved a hand. "Nope. So, how was your dinner?" Grinning slyly, she said, "I saw you with Dr. Carmichael."

Pretending to be nonplussed, Christina said, "It was nice."

Fanning her face, Sally said, "He is so hot!"

Christina put her hand over her heart, and said, "Sally Jean!"

Both women laughed out loud.

"C'mon Christina, you have to admit he's the best looking doctor around here."

Rolling her eyes, Christina said, "Yeah. He is quite handsome, but so is Dr. Dawson, and several other doctors on staff."

"True." Grinning slyly, Sally asked, "Anything going on with you two?"

Pretending ignorance, Christina asked, "Who two?"

Sally said, "You and Dr. C."

Shaking her head, Christina said, "Nope. Just friends."

Sally looked unconvinced. "Right."

"Hey, don't you have patients to look after?" Christina asked, opening her locker, and returning her purse.

Sally Jean did a thumbs up, and said, "Later."

Before returning to the desk, Christina made a quick phone call home, to check on the kids.

All was well on the home front.

Jesse McCoy watched Christina's retreating back, and thought, *I really like her.*

"Hey, Jess." Called the electrician, as he exited the elevator.

Jesse held the CCU door open as Paul headed his way.

"Did you find what your needed?" Jesse asked, as Paul entered the unit.

Paul held up a coiled cable, and a metal box. Nodding, he said, "Yep. Let's finish this job. I promised my wife we'd go out to dinner."

Jesse patted his back. "I'd like to call it a day as well. I'm still tired from the past several days. I think I could sleep through the whole weekend."

Paul gave him a serious look, and said, "Maybe you should. You've been through a lot these past several weeks."

"Thanks, Man." Releasing a sigh, Jesse said, "Let's get this done."

The two men headed in the direction of the nurses' station, where they needed to tweak a few wires, and make one final inspection.

Janet began her day like the previous few. Waking to a cacophony of noises, she opened her eyes when an aid came in, threw open the window curtain, and with a perky lilt to her voice, said, "Good morning Mrs. Washburn! As you can see, it is a beautiful, sunny day."

Janet moaned. The sunlight hurt her eyes, and the sing-song chatter raked her nerves.

She didn't want to be rude, so she managed a glum, "Morning."

The aid, whose name tag read, Iris, continued to chatter about the weather, her holiday, and would occasionally throw out a question to Janet, who, much to her chagrin felt compelled to answer.

"You're the first patient on my list, so I'm gonna get you all cleaned up, and ready for the day, before your breakfast tray arrives." Patting Janet's hand, she smiled and said, "A cold breakfast is not a good way to start your day!"

Janet, managed a forced smile. "Right."

Holding up the bedpan, she said, "So, first things first. Do you need to use this?"

Janet shook her head. "Not yet."

Setting it down, she said, "Alrighty, then. Let's get started with the bath."

"Iris?" Janet called to the aide, who was in the bathroom, gathering the necessary items to help bathe her. Bringing in the washbasin, towel and washcloths, she sat them down on the bedside tray, and said, "Yes, Mrs. Washburn?" Iris closed the door to the hallway, pulled the curtain for privacy, and donned a pair of latex gloves.

"Try as I might, I can't seem to remember anything before waking up here a few days ago. You said I'd start regaining my memory. Do you know how long that will take?"

Shaking her head, Iris said, "I wish I knew. Everyone is different." Patting Janet's arm, she added, "I know this must be very frustrating for you, but I can almost assure you that your memory will return."

"Almost assure me?"

Smiling, Iris said, "I'm not gonna lie to you, Mrs. Washburn. There are no guarantees about anything in life. Sometimes things go as planned, and other times, they don't."

Helping Janet remove her gown, Iris continued, "One good thing in your favor, is that you didn't suffer any permanent brain damage. All your x-rays, CT scans and MRI's, show a normal brain. So, even though the rest of your body was bruised and battered, your brain miraculously stayed unscathed."

Nodding, Janet said, "Well, I must have a pretty hard head."

Iris chuckled. "Maybe so."

As she washed Janet from face to feet, she chatted on. Janet was informed that she was twenty-two, in her second year of nursing school, had a steady boyfriend, two cats, and still lived with her parents. She is the youngest of five kids, and the only girl. Her brothers all work in the medical field. Two are married, and two are not. She has a niece and nephew, who are totally adorable, that she gets to babysit at least once a month, so their parents can have a date night.

By the time Iris finished with the bath, and linen change, Janet was exhausted. Her ears were tired of the incessant banter, and her body ached from the moving back and forth, and up and down, as Iris removed her gown and bedding, then redressed both. She felt she didn't need any physical therapy if she continued being cared for by Iris. When the aide finally left, Janet closed her eyes for a few minutes, enjoying the peace and quiet.

As she was dropping off into a pleasant dream, there was a knock at her door. Her breakfast tray had arrived.

Lifting the plate cover, expecting to see oatmeal, she was pleased to see two strips of crispy bacon, scrambled eggs, and a slice of white toast. She was finally being served something besides oatmeal and jello. Her mouth watered, as she spread butter and jelly on the toasted bread. The tray also contained a cup of coffee, a small glass of apple juice, and a small container of milk. She prepared the coffee with two packets of cream and sugar, drank the apple juice, and set the milk aside for later. Moaning in delight, she consumed the rest of the food and beverage. Pushing the tray table aside, and lowering the head of the bed, she pulled the sheet and blankets up around her neck, turned her head away from the window, and promptly fell into a deep sleep.

Two hours later, she was roused awake by Iris, calling her name, and patting her arm.

Raising the head of the bed, Iris said, "Mrs. Washburn, the doctor will be here in a few minutes to speak to you."

Shifting her body, as the bed moved, Janet mumbled, "Okay."

"Would you like a drink of water, or something?"

Shaking her head, to clear the fuzziness residing there, Janet said, "Yes, please."

Once Janet was settled, Dr. Knorr walked in.

"How is my patient today?" He asked, as he handed the chart to Iris, crossed the room, to take Janet's hand, and held his fingertips over the artery in her wrist. After a moment, he released it, then removed the stethoscope from around his neck, and proceeded to check her heart and lungs.

Smiling, he said, "Everything sounds normal."

Janet breathed a sigh of relief.

"So, when can I get out of this contraption?" She asked, pointing to the metal unit holding her legs and hips, at a forty-five degree angle.

Patting her leg, he said, "Probably in another week or two."

Janet felt tears sting her eyes. "Another week or two? I figured you'd want me up, and moving about sooner than that."

Nodding, he sat in a chair next to her bed. "I understand that you're tired of all this." Pointing around the hospital room, "But, because of the severity of your injuries, it will take quite a while for all the bones, tendons, and muscles to heal, and reconnect."

He watched as a tear escaped down her cheek. Iris handed her a tissue. Wiping her eyes, and blowing her nose, Janet said, "I understand what you're saying, but my body is screaming to get moving."

"I'm sure it is." Pulling a notepad and pen from his lab coat pocket, he said, "Tell you what, I'll have physical therapy come, and begin a few stretching movements with you. In fact, I'll request that they lower your legs for a few minutes three times a day. I know it doesn't sound like much, but we're going to ease into this. As I said earlier, your body has been severely traumatized."

Wiping her eyes again, Janet nodded, and said, "Okay. Thanks Dr. Knorr."

Standing, Dr. Knorr patted her arm. "Hang in there, Janet. You'll be up and out of here before you know it, and all this will be a distant memory."

Stopping in the doorway, he turned, and said, "Oh, by the way, your friend, Christina, will be bringing your daughter to visit you tomorrow."

"What? Who?"

"The lady taking care of your daughter while you're here, will be coming for a visit tomorrow."

Janet tried not to look confused as she said, "Oh. Okay." She had no idea what he was talking about. *A friend named Christina? A daughter? That's the second or third time someone has mentioned that I have a daughter. How come I don't remember that?*

Try as she might, she could not remember anything prior to waking up in this hospital. *How is that possible?*

After checking in on all of his patients, Dr. Knorr headed to his office in the building adjacent to the hospital. Sitting at his large Mahogany desk, he opened his desk calendar, and perused the page, noting he had a light schedule for the day. Only five pre-op consultations, and two exams. He was thankful for the lighter load. Glancing at the pile of magazines, journals and charts he needed to read, he let out a large sigh. *Will I ever get caught up?*

Running his hand through his ever graying, thinning hair, he leaned back in his chair, and thought about Janet. He was concerned that her memory hadn't returned. There was no physical reason as far as he could see. All her tests were normal. *Could it be psychological? Maybe I should have our Psychologist speak to her.*

He was pleased that her body was healing nicely. The x-rays of her bones showed they were mending well, and her bruising was fading to a pale yellow. From the moment he saw her, he had been captivated by her beautiful face. Sure, she had a few cuts and bruises, but all in all, they had been quite minor.

I wonder what kind of person she was before the accident.

As he pondered this, the phone rang, making him jump.

"Dr. Knorr." He answered.

"Doctor. This is Sheriff Clifton from Alva. How are you today?"

"Hello, Sheriff. I'm well. How are you?"

"Good. Good. Thanks for asking. Hey, I was wondering if you could tell me how Janet Washburn is doing?"

"Interesting you should ask that. I just came back from visiting her. She's slowly improving."

Nodding, Larry said, "That's good to hear."

Leaning forward to rest his elbows on the desk, Dr. Knorr asked, "So, if you don't mind me asking, why are you inquiring about her?"

"I was hoping I could come see her. I have a few questions that need answers."

"Well, Sheriff, I'm not sure if she would be of much help."

"How come?"

"She seems to be suffering from amnesia. Can't remember anything from before she woke up here."

"Amnesia, huh? Well, that's convenient."

"Convenient?"

Shaking his head in disappointment, the sheriff explained why he needed to talk to Janet so he could discern her involvement in a few open cases.

"So," Larry asked, "You think this amnesia is permanent?"

Shaking his head, Dr. Knorr said, "I don't think so. There was no trauma to the brain, so hopefully, when she's off the pain meds, and begins to move around more, her memory will kick back in. In the meantime, we'll just have to wait."

"I see." Larry said, pressing the bridge of his nose with his thumb and forefinger. Sighing heavily, he said, "Will you please let me know as soon as her memory returns?"

"Sure thing, Sheriff. Is there anything else I can help you with?"

"No. Thanks. I'll be in touch."

Larry leaned back in his chair, and wondered aloud, "Is this ever going to end?"

CHAPTER 12

After a non-eventful Friday, Saturday arrived with a beautiful sunrise, and promise of a warmer, brighter day.

Linda woke with sunlight filtering through the thin gauzy curtains in her new room. She rubbed her sleep encrusted eyes. Today was the day she would be able to see her mom. It felt like months since they had taken her by helicopter to Dallas, but in reality only a few days. Linda rolled on her back, placed her hands behind her head, and fantasized how the meeting would go. Her mom would be so happy to see her, and that would boost her morale, and would make her heal faster.

Smiling, she stood, grabbed her robe, and tiptoeing through Stacy's room, headed to the bathroom. Listening to the quiet house, she surmised that no one else was up. Donning her robe, she made her way to the kitchen, and poured a bowl of cereal. She felt weird, being the only one up in the big house. Surely someone would join her in a little while. She curled up on the couch, and finding the remote, brought the TV to life with the press of a button.

Halfway through a cartoon episode, she heard footsteps on the stairs, both human and canine.

She heard Christina tell the dog that she'd let him out once the coffee was brewing. Rising from the couch, Linda said, "Mrs. Sanders, I can let Benji out."

Surprised, Christina nearly dropped the measuring spoon for the coffee.

"Linda! I didn't know anyone was up. And, yes, you may let him out. I'll join you in a moment."

Christina, with a fresh mug of coffee, joined Linda and Benji, in the family room.

"So, how come you're up so early?"

Linda shrugged. "Not sure. Just woke up. I'm excited about seeing my mom today."

Nodding, Christina said, "Ah, yes. That is on the agenda for the day." Setting the cup down, she asked, "When would you like to go?"

"I guess when everyone else is ready. Personally, I would have like to have gone an hour ago."

Christina smiled. "I can understand that. If I were in your shoes, I'm sure I'd feel the same way."

Glancing at her watch, Christina said, "Why don't you go wake Stacey, while I get dressed?"

Groaning, and holding her stomach, Linda stood. "Yes, Ma'am. Are they boys going with us?"

Shaking her head, Christina said, "Not this time. I thought it would be nice to have a girl's day out."

Standing in the doorway, Linda asked, "What are the boy's going to do?"

"Well, Nicky is going to Danny's, and Brad will go to Eric's. I figured after we see your mom, we could do lunch somewhere, and go shopping, if you're up to it."

Linda's face lit up. "That sounds like fun! Maybe we can find me a pair of boots."

Nodding, and disengaging herself from the chair, Christina said, "I bet we could find a whole lot of things we could use."

She listened as Linda slowly, and with a few grunts, made her way up the stairs. The girl still had a ways to go, before returning to her regular life. She wasn't sure how much shopping they'd actually be doing, but she was determined to give the girl as good a day as possible. She hoped Janet was alert, and up to visitors. It would be devastating for Linda, if her mother showed any signs of rejection.

As Christina made it to the top of the stairs, she heard Linda and Stacey whispering, and giggling.

Entering her room to dress for the day, Christina whispered a short prayer. "Please God, let this be a good day for Linda."

"Mrs. Washburn?"

Janet was vaguely aware of her name being called, and she began drifting towards consciousness.

"Mrs. Washburn, it's time to rise and shine!"

"What?" Janet managed to mumble.

"It's time to rise and shine!" Repeated the voice.

Janet moaned. She wasn't ready to rise or shine. *Why can't I just be left alone*, she wondered.

She felt a patting sensation on her arm, and heard the annoying voice again.

"Alright!" She responded grumpily. "I'm awake."

The woman standing next to her bed seemed nonplussed by Janet's apparent grumpiness.

"Aren't you excited about your daughter coming to visit you today?" The aide asked as she began stripping the linen off the bed.

"How can I be excited, when I don't even remember having a daughter?" Janet asked, as she tried to adjust her body to a more comfortable position.

The aide stopped pulling the top sheet and blanket off the bed, and looked at Janet.

"How can you not remember having a daughter?"

Janet shook her head, "Honestly, I don't know. I find I can't remember anything after waking up here. When I try to remember, it's like looking at a blank screen. Nothing."

Laying a hand on Janet's arm, the aide, said, "Oh, that's so sad."

Janet sighed, and said, "It's not so sad, if I can't remember anything to be sad about."

Nodding, the girl said, "I guess so. Do you know if you'll ever get your memory back?"

Shaking her head, Janet said, "No. The Doc isn't even sure why I have amnesia in the first place. He said none of my brain scans show any abnormalities."

Putting a fresh pillowcase on one of Janet's pillows, the girl said, "Well, maybe having your daughter here might jog something in your brain."

Janet nodded, and said, "Maybe."

Watching the girl gather the dirty linen, and place them in a receptacle, Janet asked, "What's your name?"

Pointing to her name-tag, the girl said, "Cassie."

"Cassie." Janet repeated. "Is that short for something?"

Shaking her head, the girl said, "No. I wish it was. I would love to be called Cassandra. It sounds so...magical."

Janet raised her eyebrows. "Magical?"

"I read a book once that had a character named Cassandra, and she could read minds, and predict the future for people."

"Interesting." Janet said.

As Cassie moved Janet around to change the bottom sheet, Janet asked, "How old are you?'

"I'm sixteen."

"They let you be an aide at sixteen?"

Nodding, Cassie said, "Yeah. I can drive, so I guess the powers that be, figure I can handle caring for people."

Janet moaned as Cassie struggled with the bottom sheet. Finding it difficult to do by herself, she apologized to Janet and said, "I'll be right back. I'm going to get help."

Janet sighed. As far as she knew, the other aides never had a problem with changing her linen.

Cassie returned a few minutes later with another, more mature aide. Janet recognized her.

Smiling, she greeted her. "Hi Iris."

"Hi Janet. Cassie is new here, and has never changed a bed with someone in it, so I'm going to show her how it's done. Is that okay with you?"

Nodding, Janet said, "Of course."

The two aides stood on each side of the bed, and worked the sheet under Janet, who clenched her teeth, and tried not to moan, as they lifted, and tugged on her, and the sheet.

Once the sheet was situated, Iris said, "Thank you, Janet. I have to go take care of my other patients now, but I'll come back for a visit when I can."

Janet smiled. "Thank you."

Turning toward Cassie, Janet said, "The first couple of times are challenging, but the more you do it, the easier it'll be."

Nodding, as she straightened the bed sheets, Cassie said, "I hope so. I'd like to be an RN someday, so I hope to work as an aide, and learn as much as I can before going off to college."

Janet smiled. "That's a great plan you have."

"I noticed on your chart that you're an RN."

Janet looked confused for a moment. *Am I?* For the life of her, she couldn't remember.

Noticing Janet's bewildered look, Cassie said, "You don't remember that, either?"

Janet shook her head. "Try as I might, I don't remember anything before yesterday."

Cassie nodded, and patted Janet's hand. "Hopefully, your memories will come back."

Janet nodded, feeling tears burning the back of her eyes. *I sure hope you're right*, she thought, as Cassie finished her care.

Once the girl was gone, Janet lay with her eyes open, staring at the ceiling, and pleading with the powers that be, to please restore her memory. When nothing seemed to be forthcoming, she fell asleep.

Sending Nicky out the door to Danny's with a hug and a kiss, Christina yelled up the stairs to the girls and Brad, "C'mon y'all! Let's hit the road."

The girls bounded down the stairs, and headed out to the van, as Brad, on the phone with Eric, took his sweet time.

Closing and locking the kitchen door, Christina said, "Tell Eric, we'll be there in about five minutes."

Christina let out a sigh, as she brought the engine to life. Backing out, she noticed the front screen door was ajar—as if something was wedged between it, and the front door. Fear gripped her heart, as she remembered a previous package that had contained a fake rat, and threatening note. Stopping the van, she asked Brad to go see what was there. He returned a moment later holding a box that was addressed to Christina. She took it, and looked at the return address. She let out a sigh of relief. It was from her friend, Linda, in Michigan.

Completing her exit from the driveway, she asked Brad, "Could you please open it for me?"

Digging the pocket knife out of his pocket, he cut the tape, and removed the outer wrapping.

The girls leaned forward, anxious to see what the box contained.

Brad removed the tissue paper, and brought out a framed picture of Linda, and her family. There was an envelope taped to the backside.

"Do you want me to read the note?" Brad asked, holding it up for his mother to see.

Nodding, she said, "Sure."

Clearing his voice, he read: "Dear Christina and kids, here's the photo I promised you in my Christmas letter. I personally prefer candid shots as opposed to this posed version, but it's been years since we've had a good family portrait, so here we are, all spiffed up, and polished for the camera!

Now you owe me a picture of you, and your kids! Honestly, it doesn't have to be a posed portrait. I'd be happy with a silly, candid one. When are you guys planning on coming up north? We miss you, and I have to show off our remodeled kitchen! I'm still working crazy hours at the hospital, but I'll always make time to chat, if you give me a call. If you remember, I hardly ever call anyone, so don't hold your breath waiting for me to call you! We love you! God bless you all! Linda and gang."

Folding the note, and returning it to the envelope, Brad said, "So, are we still planning on going for a visit in February?"

"Oh, yeah. I almost forgot about that! Are we still going, Mom?" Stacey asked.

Christina nodded. "Yes. Your grandparents have promised to get us tickets to fly up when y'all have your mid-winter break."

Brad smiled, and nodded. Stacey giggled, and said, "Maybe Linda can go with us."

Christina said, "Maybe. We'll have to see how she, and her mom are doing then."

A minute or so later, Christina pulled into Eric's driveway. Before she could put the van in park, Brad was out, and running up to the door. Eric's mom, Erica, waved from the front door, as she opened it for Brad.

"See you later, Brad." She said to his retreating back.

"Alright, Girls. You ready to head to Dallas?"

She received a resounding "Yes!"

Stopping at the gift shop before heading upstairs to see Janet, Christina took the time to call the nurse's station to check in.

"Mrs. Sanders, I'm so glad you called," said the Nurse who answered the phone. "I wanted to give you a heads up about Janet. It seems she has developed amnesia and says she doesn't recall anything prior to waking up here."

"What does that mean, exactly?" Christina asked, concern filling her voice.

"Well, she doesn't remember you, or her daughter. She says she'll be glad to see y'all, in hopes of jump-starting her memory, but I want you to be prepared if the visit is a bit awkward."

"Should I tell her daughter?" Christina whispered, as she turned away from the girls who were picking out a bouquet of flowers.

"I don't think so. Janet said she would try to act as if she remembered her. No use disappointing the child. From what I hear, she's been through enough trauma herself."

Nodding, Christina said, "Yes, she has. This news would devastate her." Pausing a beat, she asked, "Does she know you're informing me of the situation?"

"Yes, Ma'am."

"Good. I'll pretend everything is okay as well. Let Janet know we'll be up in a few moments."

"I sure will. Thank you."

Placing the phone back in her purse, and putting a smile on her face, Christina turned to face the girls. "Y'all ready to head up?"

Linda grinned, and said, "Yes! Do you like the flowers I picked?"

Nodding, Christina said, "They are beautiful. I'm sure your mom will love them."

CHAPTER 13

Monday morning, after dropping Samara off at school, Cindy pointed her car towards Dallas. She had an appointment to meet with an internist Dr. Harrison had recommended. She was anxious, but hopeful that he would be able to pinpoint the reason for her anemia. As she pulled her car into the parking garage next to the medical facility, she felt her heart-beat kick up a notch, and her palms begin to sweat. She took a few cleansing breaths to calm her nerves, before exiting her vehicle.

Walking into the glass enclosed reception area, she was impressed with the aesthetically pleasing décor. There seemed to be just the right balance between leather, wood, chrome, glass, and plants, to emit a comfortable, non-sterile, non-threatening vibe. After signing in, the receptionist handed her a clipboard containing several papers to be read, answered, and signed. *It's a good thing I came in a half-hour early. The only questions missing are my IQ, and shoe size*, she thought, as she returned the clipboard to the receptionist. Returning to her seat, she grabbed a magazine from a nearby rack. Glancing at the front cover, she was pleased it was a current edition. *I wonder what Brad, Angelina, and Jen are up to this week?* She had just began to peruse the article about the love triangle, when she heard her name called. Returning the magazine to the rack, she followed the heavy set, middle aged, aide to a nearby room.

Pointing to a scale, the aide said, "If you could please step on there, I'll get your weight and height." Writing the numbers down, she motioned for Cindy to follow her to an examination room.

"I'll need to get your blood pressure, and temperature." As Cindy observed the woman's demeanor, she concluded that this wasn't the type of lady interested in small talk, so Cindy kept her questions, and comments, to herself.

Nodding, Cindy removed her sweater, and held out her arm. A thermometer was placed under her tongue, as an oxygen indicator was placed on her finger. Once those numbers were recorded, the aide said, "The Doctor will be in shortly."

Hearing her phone ding, indicating a text message was received, she dug it out of her purse, flipped it open, read the text—from Christina, asking if she could pick the kids up from school around noon, as they had a half day. She turned off the ringer, and placed it back in her purse, just as the Doctor entered the room.

Holding out his hand, he introduced himself.

"Hello Mrs. Murray. I'm Doctor Anthony Kavanaugh." She liked his genuine smile, complete with a dimple on his right cheek, and gentle touch, as she took his hand. His coloring, and body size and shape, reminded her of Steven Dawson. He had sandy blond hair, with streaks of gray, and intense blue eyes, like Steven. He was tall, and she couldn't tell how muscular he was under his lab coat, but, he looked fit and trim—like he rode a bike, or swam frequently.

Clearing her throat, she said, "Hi."

Sitting across from her, he said, "Before I do any exam, I want to go over your paperwork, and ask you a few questions."

Cindy nodded. "Okay."

After questioning her about her family history, and such, poking and prodding her abdomen, and listening to her bowels with his stethoscope, Dr. Kavanaugh wrote out orders for Cindy to have upper, and lower scopes, full body scan to rule out any tumors, and more blood work.

"We'll start with these preliminaries, then go from there, depending on what they show."

Nodding, Cindy took the papers. "Thanks. I hope that whatever shows up will be treatable."

Reaching out for her hand, and smiling, he said, "Most things are."

Walking with her to the door, he said, "Take these papers to the gals at the desk, and they'll get you scheduled."

Cindy thanked him once again, and walked over to the receptionist. Once everything had been scheduled, she headed to the parking garage. Even though the day was beginning to warm up, the air in the garage was quite chilly. She pulled on her gloves, and adjusted the scarf, that was wrapped around her neck, to also encompass her head.

Shivering, she entered her vehicle, turned on the engine, adjusted the heater to full blast, and keeping her promise to Ed, called him.

He answered on the second ring, and listened patiently as she explained the doctor's recommendations.

"Have you set any dates for these tests?" He asked, concern filling his voice.

Shaking her head, she said, "I have the upper and lower x-rays scheduled for next Tuesday. I won't be sedated for those, so you needn't come, but when I have the scopes, I'll need someone to drive me. They'll call me later today, to schedule those."

"Okay. Let me know when they're set, so I can check my schedule as well." Sensing her apprehension, he said, "Honey, it's going to be alright. We'll get through this together."

Sighing heavily, she said, "I know. It's just the not knowing the cause, that is so disconcerting."

"Well, we'll know soon enough, and can take the appropriate steps."

"Yes. You're right. Thanks for reminding me."

After a pause, he said, "I have a ton of paperwork to fill out, so I probably won't be back in Alva for a few days. If you need me, however, I can be there in a snap."

Smiling, she said, "A snap? So you're not only an amazing human being, you've taken on Superman qualities as well?"

He chuckled, and playing along, said, "As a matter of fact, I've had them all along. I've just never had to resort to them, but...I can if I need to."

Cindy laughed out loud. "Okay, Superman. I'll keep that in mind, if or when, I need you to be here in a snap."

"Just doing my best to serve Humankind, Ma'am."

Still chuckling, she said, "I love you, Ed."

"Love you too, Babe."

They disconnected, and Cindy sat in her car a few more minutes before heading towards home.

She and Ed had met under unusual circumstances, soon after Christina and the kids had moved into her parent's house. Christina had said, it must have been divine providence. Cindy had never been "religious," but even she had a difficult time explaining the timing. Maybe God had intervened on her behalf.

As she pulled into traffic on I35 south, she said, "Well, God, if You did have a hand in all this...thank You."

God smiled, and said, "You're welcome."

Lisa and her family began preparing for the welcome home party several weeks before their two Guatemalan children had even been released for adoption by the Guatemalan government. They had prayed long and hard about taking the leap into adoption, and felt a peace to follow through, despite several set-backs along the way. Now, here it was, a few days before the big event. The two children, Rico and Elliana, four and six, had seemed to adjust to their new surroundings, and were picking up English, like little sponges.

Sarah, their fourteen year old daughter, loved dressing Elliana in pretty dresses, and braiding her long black hair.

The twins, Aaron and Alex enjoyed their little brother, and were generous in sharing their time, and possessions with him. Jesse, who had just turned eleven, wasn't as keen on the interruptions in their household. He would often snap at his siblings, and storm off to his room, slamming the door, and refusing entrance by anyone—only venturing out to eat, or hang out with his friends. This behavior concerned Lisa and Tom, and try as they might, could not get their son to explain his behavior. They decided to give him his space, and monitor his moods. If there was no improvement in the next couple of weeks, they would seek a counselor.

"Maybe it's a combination of puberty, and disruption in the family dynamics," suggested Tom, one evening, as he and Lisa prepared for bed.

"Maybe." She sighed. "I just hope we can get to the root of the issue. I'm concerned these negative feelings will continue to fester, and he'll lash out at one of us."

Taking his wife in his arms, Tom kissed the top of her head, and suggested they pray.

Driving to work Monday morning, Christina thought about Saturday's visit to Janet. She was thankful to have been forewarned about Janet's amnesia, or it would have been quite an awkward visit.

It was evident to her that Janet was struggling to keep up the charade of recognizing her child. Linda was so excited to see her mom, that she seemed oblivious to the conflict Janet was experiencing.

Christina had stood in the doorway, as she watched and listened to the interchange between mother and daughter. At one point, Christina thought she saw a flicker of recognition dart across Janet's face, but she wasn't sure. As quickly as it appeared, it disappeared, and Janet's eyes returned to their panicked, and confused look, which she desperately tried to hide from Linda.

They had to keep their visit short, as Janet had an appointment with a physical therapist. Hugging her child one last time, she asked the girls to wait in the hallway, as she spoke to Chrisitna. They obliged, and exited the room. Christina walked over to the bed, and took Janet's hand.

Janet's eyes filled with tears. "I'm so sorry I don't recognize you, or my child. I hope and pray this isn't a permanent situation. Linda seems like such a sweet thing, and I wouldn't want to hurt her."

Chrisitna nodded, and reached for a tissue, which Janet took, and dabbed her eyes with.

"Linda is a wonderful girl. You've done a great job of raising her to be thoughtful, and considerate. I believe that once your body is healed, and you're off all the pain meds and such, your memory will return. In the meantime, we'll continue coming to visit, and play the game of charades, because we both agree that it will be in Linda's best interest, to believe that her mom will be completely healed, and will return to her soon."

Janet nodded, as she blew her nose. "Thank you for taking her in. I have no idea how long I'll be here, but I have a feeling it will be a few more weeks. Hopefully, I'll have my memory back by then."

Just then, Stacey poked her head in the doorway. "Excuse me, Mom, but we're starving!"

Giving Janet a quick hug, Christina said, "I promised that I'd take them out to a fancy restaurant for lunch, so I'd better get going. I'll be praying for your memory to return."

Janet smiled, and waved. "I'll look forward to seeing y'all again."

Christina did a finger wave, and left the room. The girls were waiting at the elevator, anxious to eat at the Japanese restaurant close by.

True to her word, Christina had prayed off and on all weekend for Janet's complete recovery. She was so thankful that Linda had seemed unfazed by her mother's amnesia. Janet had played her role so well, that neither girl had picked up on the awkwardness of the situation.

Janet remembered the events after Saturday's visit, and replayed them in her mind. When the room had once again returned to its tomb-like quietness, after Christina and the girls had left, Janet lay on her back, staring up at the ceiling, willing her mind to remember something—anything, prior to her admittance to this hospital. According to the doctors and nurses, her memory was in tact when she arrived, but had just recently vanished. *Why?* She wondered. *Why now, when my body is finally healing enough to begin physical therapy? Is it a physical condition, or a psychological one? Will I ever regain all my faculties, or will I be stuck in some kind of limbo? Healed, but having residual malfunctions.*

She felt a headache coming on, and called for the nurse.

Entering the room, Iris asked, "What can I do for you Mrs. Washburn?"

"I'd like something for this headache."

Grabbing the pitcher of water, Iris said, "Sure thing. I'll get you some fresh water as well."

Janet nodded. "Thanks."

A couple of minutes later, Iris returned with a medicine cup containing two Tylenol, and a fresh pitcher of ice water. Handing the cup to Janet, she poured out a glass of water. "So how was your visit with your daughter, and your friend?"

Swallowing, Janet said, "Awkward."

Cocking her head, Iris asked, "How so?"

"Try as I might, I couldn't remember them. I had to fake my excitement, and pretend I knew the girl."

"Well, there's no denying she's your girl. She looks just like you."

Janet smiled. She had thought so too. "I really hope my memory returns. She seems like such a sweet child. I'd love to be her mom."

Iris reached out, and patted Janet's arm. "I believe it will return, but it may take a while."

Nodding, Janet sighed. "Yeah. Guess I'll just have to be patient."

"On the bright side, you haven't forgotten everything. We had a guy in here some time ago that had a head trauma, and had to relearn everything. It was like teaching an infant. He had to relearn how to toilet himself, talk, write, walk. Everything we take for granted. He would get so frustrated at times, he'd just sit down and cry."

"Did he regain everything?"

Nodding, and smiling, Iris said, "Yes! But it took a good two years of intensive therapy."

"Goodness, I hope it doesn't take that long for me!"

"I doubt it. Remember, he had to start completely over. You, on the other hand, are half way there already."

Janet yawned. "Excuse me. I think that visit wore me out."

"Is there anything else I can get you?" Iris asked, as she headed for the door.

Shaking her head, Janet said, "No. I think I'll just nap a while. Hopefully this headache will be gone when I wake up."

When Janet had woken from the nap, her headache was gone. She was frustrated to realize her memory hadn't returned either. Sunday was just like every other day, except, the food was getting more palatable, and her pain wasn't as intense.

Heading to the conference room, Christina was joined by Libby, who reached out for a hug.

After greetings, Libby asked, about the meeting with Janet.

Christina recapped the story, to which Libby asked, "And Linda didn't pick up on that?"

Shaking her head, Christina said, "There was no indication. She was so happy to see her mom, I don't think she would have noticed if Janet had sprouted horns on her head."

"Kids can be so unpredictable. Oblivious one minute, and super tuned in the next."

Chuckling, Christina nodded. "That is so true."

Before taking a seat at the conference table, Libby asked, "Has Dr. Carmichael said when Linda can go back to school?"

Pulling a chair out next to Libby, Christina said, "I let her go today. It's only a half-day, because of some teacher conference thing. Hopefully, she'll do okay."

"Knowing Stacey, she'll keep an eye on her."

Smiling, Christina said, "True. She can be quite protective of those she cares about."

"How are they getting home?"

"Cindy said she'd swing by and pick them up. Which reminds me, she had an appointment with the gastroenterologist in Dallas this morning. When we're finished here, I'll give her a call."

Both women looked up, when the previous shifts nurses walked in.

Libby leaned over, and whispered, "Anything happening with you and Steven?"

Christina smiled, and whispered back, "I'll tell you later."

Libby raised her eyebrows, and said, "Ooh. I can hardly wait."

Christina shook her head. *There really wasn't much to tell, but who knew, maybe by the time she got around to talking to Libby, something would happen.*

Cindy drove into town, just in time to swing by the schools to pick up her daughter, and the Sander's kids. Parking in front of the middle-school first, she was surprised to see Linda making her way down the steps with Stacey's help. Christina failed to mention she'd be picking up Linda as well. It would be a crowded ride home with all the kids, and Linda's cumbersome cast.

Linda was still walking slowly and deliberately, and clutching her abdomen, as if she were afraid her insides would fall out. Cindy tooted her horn to get the girl's attention. They both waved, and headed in her direction. She jumped out of the car, opened the trunk, then took the few items in the back seat and threw them in. By the time she had finished the task, the girls had arrived at her vehicle. They hopped in, and she drove a few more yards, and parked in front of the high-school. As she and the girls waited for Brad and Samara, Cindy turned in her seat, and asked how their day went.

"Fine." They said simultaneously, then giggled.

Stacey said, "Everyone was so happy to see Linda. I had to practically fight off the crowd where ever we went."

"It wasn't that bad, Mrs. Murray." Linda said defensively.

Cindy smiled. "It has been a while since you've seen everyone. I'm sure they were happy to see you. Did you get your cast signed?"

Holding it up, for Cindy to see, Linda said, "Yeah. There's hardly a blank spot on it."

Cindy said, "When I broke my arm in elementary school, I kept the cast for several years. It reminded me of all the friends I had."

"Do you still have it?" Stacey asked.

Shaking her head, Cindy said, "No. After taking it with me on a few moves, it lost it's value. I soon forgot the kids the names belonged to, and it looked, and smelled awful."

Rotating the cast so she could read the names, Linda said, "I don't think I'll keep this cast either."

Sniffing it, and making a face, she added, "It already smells kinda bad. Plus, I don't want to be constantly reminded of how I ended up with it."

Cindy nodded, then said, "Oh, I just remembered, how was your trip to Dallas?"

Linda and Stacey recapped the visit with Janet, then went on to describe the Japanese restaurant, and subsequent shopping they did at a couple of the boutiques next to the hospital.

"Sounds like y'all had a great time." She was about to say more, when the front passenger side door opened, and Samara climbed in.

"Hey, Babe." Cindy said, patting Samara's knee.

"Hey, Mom." Looking in the backseat, she said, "Linda! I wasn't expecting to see you here."

Linda smiled, and said, "I decided to try going today, since it was only a half day."

Raising her eyebrows, Samara asked, "So how was it?"

"It was fun, but I'm so ready for a nap. It was a lot more exhausting than I thought it would be."

Stacey said, "She was bombarded with questions where ever she went. I had to act as her body guard."

Samara laughed. "I can only imagine that! I bet you were a good guard."

Stacey grinned, and raised her arms, flexing her biceps. Linda and Samara both burst out laughing. Lowering her arms, Stacey said, "Hey, my muscles might not be so big, but I can pack a punch if I need to!"

Cindy said, "I hope you didn't need to."

"Nah. Not this time."

Brad opened the back door, and climbed in.

Closing the door, he said, "Sorry for the delay. I had to talk to Eric about this weekend."

With a grin, Samara said, "That's fine. We were having quite a discussion about how Stacey was Linda's bodyguard today."

Brad looked at his sister. "What?"

Shrugging, she said, "Well, someone needed to protect her from the hoards of people wanting to autograph her cast."

Everyone chuckled. Cindy thought, *I love these kids!*

Pulling away from the curb, Cindy asked, "Do I need to get Nicky?"

Brad said, "No. He has a full day. He can walk home."

Turning left, Cindy said, "Okay. I was wondering how we would fit him in here. It's a good thing y'all live so close to his school, and he can walk home. Of course next year he'll be in middle school with you, Stacey."

"Yes Ma'am," Stacey answered.

Brad had a flashback of Nicky's kidnapping. Being close to home hadn't mattered then. *Had it been only a few months back? It seemed so long ago.* Brad knew Nicky was still feeling traumatized by the incident, even though he said he was over it. The farthest Nicky ventured, was down five houses to Danny's. He always walked with Danny, or other kids, and stayed on the sidewalk, never walking the back way through the alley, even though it was a shorter distance.

Poor Kid, Brad thought. He then remembered the boldness Nicky exhibited, when he stood in front of the huge crowd at the funeral, and gave his speech. That act had so astounded Brad, he had been speechless for a moment. Thinking along those lines, he felt a deeper love and respect for his younger brother. It started in his heart, and flowed outward, making him feel warm, and tearful. He heard the familiar voice speak in his mind.

"*I want you to be Nicky's protector, and encourager. I have great plans for him as well, and the Prince of Alva wants to destroy him. I need you in the physical realm, and the combination of yours, and his guardian angels in the spiritual realm, to keep him safe.*"

"*For how long?*" Brad thought, wondering if this would be a life-long assignment.

Not hearing a reply, he sighed, and said in his mind, "*Okay, then. I'll do my best to protect him. Hear that Argus? We have a new assignment.*"

"Brad?"

Shaking his head to clear his mind, he said, "Huh? What?"

Stacey frowned at her brother. "You okay?"

"Yeah. Why?"

"It looked like your were asleep or something. Your eyes were closed, and you didn't answer Mrs. Murray's question."

Brad sat up straighter in his seat. "Sorry, Mrs. Murray, what did you ask?"

Concern flitting across her face, she glanced in the rear-view mirror, and said, "I was wondering if you'd talked to Mr. McCoy, since the funeral."

"Not yet. I was planning on calling him this afternoon. See if he needed anything."

She added, "He was so distraught at the funeral, I was concerned for his well-being."

Brad nodded. He knew what she meant.

Brad felt concern for the man clench his heart. He felt an urgency to check on him sooner, rather than later.

The rest of the ride home, Brad bombarded heaven with prayers of protection for Jesse McCoy.

Jesse McCoy sat in his recliner, dozing off and on, his 9mm Glock resting on his chest. He'd been up most of the night, drinking beers, and contemplating ending his life. An overwhelming feeling of despondency had enveloped his whole being, and the only way he could think of ending it, was to end himself.

Every time he put the gun up to his head, or in his mouth, he heard his son's voice screaming at him to stop, then he'd either pass out, or fall asleep.

Pulling himself out of the alcohol induced stupor, he sat up, put the gun on the table beside his chair, and stumbled to the bathroom, where he promptly vomited into the toilet. Retching, until there was nothing but bile, he sat on the cold tiled floor, put his head in his hands, and cried like a baby. *Is this feeling ever going to end?* He wondered. Hearing his cell phone ring, he forced himself to stand, and stumbling to where his phone lay, he reached for it on the last ring. Feeling sweat-drenched, and nauseous, he sat in the nearby chair.

"Hello?" He mumbled.

"Mr. McCoy?" A boy's voice asked.

Still not totally lucid, he asked, "Jimmy?"

Taken aback, Brad said, "No, Mr. McCoy. It's Brad Sanders."

Rubbing his face with a sweaty palm, Jesse said, "Oh, yeah. Sorry. You sounded like Jimmy for an instant there."

Brad wasn't sure how to respond to that. "Mr. McCoy, I just called to see how you're doing."

Looking over at his gun, Jesse decided he wasn't going to burden this kid with his true feelings and thoughts. In reality, he wanted to yell, *"How the heck to do you think I'm doing? I just lost my son, for Pete's sake! I want to die, because I'm so stinkin' miserable!"*

Instead, he said, "I'm taking it a day at a time. It's still hard. This place is so quiet."

Brad, sensing there was more than Jesse was letting on, said, "Mr. McCoy, I'd like to stop by today if that's okay. I have some chocolate chip cookies, that I'd like to share with you."

Jesse felt a knot in his throat, and couldn't speak for a moment.

"Mr. McCoy?" Brad said.

Clearing his throat, Jesse said, "Sure, Brad. What time are you thinking?"

"How about in the next hour or so?"

Jesse glanced at the clock. "Shouldn't you be in school?"

"We had half a day, Sir, so I'm home."

"Do you know where I live?"

"No, Sir. I was just going to ask you that."

"I live out on old Brandon road, right before the split. Do you know where that is?"

"Yes, Sir. What is your house number?"

"There's no number. Mine is the last white house on your left, before the split. There's a mailbox out front with the name McCoy painted on it. You can't miss it."

"Yes, Sir. Thanks. I'll be there soon."

After disconnecting, Jesse looked around, and decided he'd better dispose of the beer cans, and return the gun to it's case. He didn't want to have to explain any of it to the sixteen-year-old.

Brad returned the phone to his pocket, and stood for a moment. He hadn't intended on going to visit Mr. McCoy today, and certainly not in the next hour or so, but the words had flowed out of his mouth, without him even thinking about them. Definitely had to be a God thing. Sighing heavily, he went to the den, where the girls were watching TV, and told them his plans.

"How are you going to get there?" Stacey asked.

Shrugging, Brad said, "I'll ride my bike."

Linda asked, "Where does he live?"

Brad told her, adding, "It's only a couple of miles. Not so far."

Stacey said, "You'd better call Mom, and let her know."

Nodding, Brad said, "I will. Nicky should be home soon, so y'all make sure you lock up, and stay home until I return, or Mom gets home."

Scrunching her face, Stacey asked, "So how long do you think you'll be?"

"I'm not sure. It'll take at least half an hour to get there, then if I sit and talk a while, another half hour or so, then a half hour home. Maybe a couple of hours or so."

Nodding, Stacey said, "Okay." Taking Linda's hand, added, "We'll be fine. Might even take a nap. Right, Linda?"

Linda nodded, and said, "I could definitely use a nap."

Brad said, "Allrighty then, I'll go get the cookies, and be off in a few minutes."

"Don't forget to call Mom!" Stacey called to his retreating back.

"I won't!" He called back.

Brad dressed in his heavy sweatpants, sweatshirt with a hood, winter coat, and gloves. It was sunny, but the temperature was hovering in the mid forties. It would be a chilly ride, for sure.

Christina received the call from Brad as she was heading to the break room for a cup of coffee.

He explained his plans, and she agreed that it would be a nice gesture on his part to visit Jesse, and take him the cookies.

Sighing, Christina said, "Poor Man probably hasn't had any visitors, or decent food since the funeral. I remember when your dad died, I didn't want to eat or socialize for quite a while."

Brad said, "Yeah, I remember. That was a pretty scary time for us."

Christina felt a tinge of guilt rise up. "I know, and I still feel bad about that. I'm just so thankful Aunt Linda came to our rescue."

"Me too. I hope Mr. McCoy doesn't get too depressed. He has no one there with him. I feel a strong concern in my spirit. As if God is urging me to go check on him."

"Well, that's possible. You and God seem to have a pretty close relationship. It's best to listen to that urging."

"Yes. I believe you're right. Well, I'd better head on out. I want to be home before the sun goes down."

"Be careful, and I'll see you later."

When Christina disconnected, she said a quick prayer of protection and wisdom for Brad, and peace for Jesse. Her mind traveled back to the first time she had met Jesse McCoy. It was right after the fire in the Cardiac Care Unit. She had been impressed with his kind, and humble demeanor. For such a large man—his hands reminding her of bear paws—his touch was gentle. She had like him instantly. Her heart ached for him. *He must feel so alone, and lost right now*, she thought. *That's how I felt after David died. I'm not sure how well I'd be doing if I had not only lost David, but one of our children as well.*

As much as she loved, and respected God, and His sovereignty, she would never understand why He allowed some of the things He did. Sometimes, it seemed as if His actions, or inactions, were cruel, unjust, and unwarranted. When she found herself feeling this way, she had to remember that God is outside of time, and He knows far more than we do, or can. He is in ultimate control of everything, and we may never know why things happen the way they do. At least until we cross over to His realm, and by then, it probably won't matter. *This is what faith, and trust are all about—taking a step even when the next one can't be seen.*

Soon after she had talked to Brad, Cindy called to inform her that the kids had been safely delivered home. Christina asked about the Doctor's visit, and Cindy gave her a condensed version.

Christina said, "I asked Steven if he knew Dr. Kavanaugh, and even though he doesn't know him personally, he has heard only good things about him. He was in the top five of his graduating class from Texas A & M."

Christina heard papers rustling in the background, and assumed Cindy must be sorting through her mail as she talked. Cindy said, "Dr. Harrison had positive remarks about him as well. I liked his personality, and he reminded me of Steven."

Taking a sip of coffee, Christina asked, "He did? How so?"

Leaning against her kitchen counter, Cindy said, "His body build, and coloring, mostly. He also has the same intense blue eyes as Steven, and similar mannerisms. His touch was gentle, and he just seemed to have a compassionate spirit. You sure Steven doesn't have brothers?"

"Well, according to Steven, he only has one sister." Standing to walk her empty mug back to the break room, Christina added, "I'm glad you like him. Having a doctor you can relate to, is such an important factor in the healing process."

"I agree. I've only had one doctor that I didn't like, and I only went to him once. He was arrogant, and rough, and had not one iota of compassion. I still get shivers when I think of him."

Christina sighed, "Unfortunately, there are those kind of medical professionals. All brain, and no heart."

Removing a package of frozen hamburger from the freezer, and placing it in the sink, Cindy sighed, "I'd better let you go. I need to get supper started. I'll either talk to you later, or tomorrow."

"Thanks again for getting the kids."

"No problem." Cindy said, as she disconnected.

Returning her phone to her pocket, Chrisitna turned, and almost bumped into a man in a hard hat—one of the construction workers from the CCU.

"Sorry, Ma'am."

Christina took a step back. "It's okay. May I help you?"

Removing his hat, he said, "I wanted you to know that the CCU staff can begin moving back into the unit this Wednesday."

"What?" Christina asked, hardly believing what she was hearing. "This Wednesday? As in day after tomorrow?"

Smiling, and showing a top row of crooked teeth, he said, "Yes, Ma'am. We're basically finished, but the Chief wants everything up and running for the next 24 hours to make sure there are no electrical or plumbing problems.

Assuming everything runs well, y'all can start moving everything back in after that."

Christina put her hand to her mouth. "Oh, that is such good news! I will be sure to inform the staff, but you need to let Mrs. Ferguson, the nursing supervisor know as well."

"Yes, Ma'am. The Chief is talking to her now."

Christina wanted to reach out and hug the man, but put her hand out instead.

Removing a work glove, and taking her hand into his large, rough one, he nodded, and gently shook it.

"Thank you so much for all your hard work. We couldn't help but hear all the banging and whirring of tools. It was quite the disaster in there."

Grinning, he said, "Yes, it was. It's amazing how much damage can be done, in such a short time."

"I'm so glad we caught it when we did. It could have been so much worse."

Nodding, he said, "Yes, Ma'am. A fire like that..." He let his voice trail off. Christina knew what he meant. *A fire like that, left unchecked, could have been tragic for both staff and patients, as well as irreparably damaging the building, making a reality of the nightmare, one of Lisa's children had a few weeks earlier.*

Releasing her hand, the young man said, "Well, I gotta get back to work."

"Thanks again!" Christina called to his retreating back. He gave her a salute, and kept walking towards the double doors across the hallway.

When Libby returned from checking on one of the patients, Christina shared the good news.

Unable to contain her excitement, Libby squealed, and said, "Oh my gosh, Christina! That is so awesome!"

Grinning, and giggling, Christina said, "I know! Right?"

Libby said, "We'll need to tell everyone, and possibly call for more staff. There's quite a bit of equipment, files, medication, and such to organize and move."

Christina paused a moment, then said, "Mrs. Ferguson will probably handle that on her end. We, however, will have to make sure everything returns to its proper place."

"Do you work tomorrow?" Libby asked, leaning on the counter.

Shaking her head, Christina said, "No, but I can come in if I'm needed. I do work Wednesday, however."

Nodding, and chewing on her thumbnail, Libby said, "If Mrs. Ferguson can call in a couple of aides, and another nurse or two, you and I could oversee the transfer of everything."

Tapping her fingernails on the counter, Christina nodded, and said, "That would be fine with me. That way, I'll know where everything is."

After discussing finer details, the two women went their separate ways, agreeing that it would be nice to get back to a normal routine.

As Christina turned to enter her patient's room, she nearly collided with Dr. Dawson.

"Steven!" She said in surprise.

Smiling, he said, "Christina."

Stammering, she said, "Sorry. I didn't expect to see you here. I thought I saw you downstairs."

Nodding, he gently took her arm, and whispered, "Let's go down the hall a bit."

"Okay." She whispered, a bit confused.

Stopping two doors down, in a voice a little above a whisper, he said, "After lunch, I was heading to my office when I got a call from Mr. Turner's wife. She said he was anxious about the upcoming valve replacement tomorrow, and wondered if I could come talk to him again."

Christina frowned. Speaking in hushed tones as well, she said, "I thought you went over all that information this morning."

"I did, but after he thought about it a while, he had a few more questions."

Nodding, Christina said, "Oh. I see. Why didn't you let me know you'd be up here?"

"I would have, but I noticed you and Libby were talking, and I didn't want to interrupt your conversation."

Grinning, she said, "Speaking of that. I nearly bumped into one of the workers, who said we could start moving back into the CCU on Wednesday."

Leaning against the wall, and folding his arms across his chest, Steven said, "That's great news! It's been frustrating not having our own equipment, or having to wait for the new ones to arrive."

Nodding in agreement, Christina added, "As nice as the Med-Surg staff has been, it has been a bit crowded, and difficult, to find some of our supplies. Libby and I are planning on sorting and organizing on Thursday, and I'll ask if the nurses on the afternoon, and night shifts, can come in to help. That way, we'll all know where everything is."

"That sounds like a good plan. Let me know if I can help."

Christina cocked her head. "Don't you have a few major surgeries planned for the next couple of days?"

Nodding, he said, "Yes, but each one will only take a couple of hours or so. I'll be free after that." Grinning slyly, he said, "Besides, I'd love to spend any extra time with you I can. We haven't had any alone time in a while."

Christina said, "Well, I can't guarantee we'd be alone. But if you're asking me out on a date, I might be able to work that into my schedule."

Looking down the hall in both directions, and seeing no one, he stood straight, and took her hands. "Christina Sanders, will you go out on a date with me? Say Friday evening after work?"

Feeling a blush creep up her neck to her cheeks, she said, in a mock Southern drawl, "Why, Dr. Dawson, I'd be honored to go on a date with you. What time would you like me to be ready? And, may I ask, where we would be going?"

Looking like a deer caught in the headlights, he said, "To be honest, I haven't thought that far ahead. May I get back to you on that?"

She giggled, and nodded. "Of course. Keep in mind that we don't have to go anywhere fancy. I'm okay with a pizza, and a movie, or something simple like that."

He pulled her into a quick hug, and said, "I have to go. I'll talk to you before Friday."

Grinning, and shaking her head, she entered Mr. Turner's room.

Completing their eight hour shift, and turning their patients over to the next shift of nurses and aides, Christina and Libby boarded the elevator discussing the ways in which they planned to relax for the remainder of the day.

Libby closed her eyes, and leaned her back against the elevator wall, saying, "First, I'm going to stop and pick up some fried chicken and fixin's, so I don't have to cook, then after the clean up, I'm gonna take a long hot shower. Once the kids are down for the night, I'm gonna ask my sweet hubby for a foot rub." Winking at Christina, she added, "And maybe a back rub."

Christina grinned, and sighed. "I remember back rubs."

Giggling, the two women parted company when they entered the parking lot.

So focused was she on stopping to get fried chicken, she barely had time to react when a car came barreling into the side of the van. She was able to turn the wheel just at the right moment, and avoid a full on collision. The car did, however, clip the area just above the left driver's side wheel area, causing a great deal of damage to the wheel and bumper. She slammed on the brakes, and brought the vehicle to a stop. A second later, a young man came running up to the van to see if she was okay. She was. Just shaken up. The young man, around the same age as Brad, kept apologizing. He said he had hit an icy spot, and couldn't stop his car. He tried to swerve, but the wheels wouldn't cooperate. Christina assured him all was fine, but she ended up calling the sheriff, and Steven. She would need a ride home, because her van would be out of commission for a while.

Brad wasn't sure wearing an extra layer of long-johns under his sweatpants was such a good idea. The ride out to Mr. McCoy's had been chilly in the beginning, but the sun was shining, causing sweat to collect around his waist. By the time he reached the highway on the edge of town, he had stripped off his hat and scarf, and unzipped his hooded sweatshirt.

He passed by the Black-eyed-Pea Restaurant, and the Second Baptist Church, on the right side of the road, and the college on the left. He almost missed the mailbox with Mr. McCoy's name on it, and had to slam on his breaks. *When the man said he lived right before the split in the road, he wasn't kidding. A few more feet, and there it was.*

Dismounting his bike, he leaned it against the porch, and before he could mount the steps, Mr. McCoy opened the screen door.

He looked pretty rough. Normally, his hair was neat, and his whiskers trimmed, but he looked like neither had had a comb or razor for a day or so, and his eyes looked bloodshot. When he reached out his hand, Brad noticed it had a slight tremor as he took it.

"Mr. McCoy." He said in greeting.

"Brad. It's nice to see you made it out here. How was the ride?"

"A little cool in the beginning, but I warmed up pretty quick."

Nodding, Jesse said, "Well, come on in."

Brad walked through the open door into a room that looked as bleak as the man. Even though the curtains had been pulled back to let in as much light as was available, it looked unkempt and disheveled.

Reaching into his backpack, Brad pulled out the Zip-locked plate of cookies.

Mr. McCoy's eyes lit up. "Hey, those look good. How about I pour us each a glass of milk?"

Brad nodded, as he set the plate on a nearby end table, removed his jacket, and placed it and his backpack on a nearby chair.

"Chocolate chip cookies just scream for ice-cold milk." He said, taking a seat on a near by chair.

Jesse returned a moment later with two full glasses of milk, and a couple of napkins.

They ate in silence for a few moments—the only sound being the crunching of cookies, and the occasional groan of delight from Jesse. It made Brad smile.

Jesse broke the silence by saying, "I can't tell you the last time I had homemade chocolate chip cookies. These are amazing." Taking a sip of milk, he asked, "Did you say you made these?"

Brad nodded, and said. "Well, with my brother and sister's help."

Jesse held one up and examined it. "What kind of nuts are in them?"

"Pecans."

Nodding, and popping the cookie in his mouth, he said, "I like pecans."

When the bag was empty, Jesse sat back, and patted his stomach. "That was awesome!"

"Thank you." Brad took the plate, and returned it to his backpack.

"So, Brad, why are you here?"

"First, I wanted to check up on you, and second, I wanted to bring you those cookies."

Jesse couldn't help but smile. He nodded, and said, "Thanks. For both."

"So, Mr. McCoy, how are you, really? I'd like your genuine honesty, if you don't mind."

Jesse rubbed his eyes with the heels of his hands. "Not so good, Brad. I'm really struggling to keep on going, when I'd much rather curl up and die."

Brad nodded.

"When my dad died, my mom went through a severe depression. I was so scared she was going to die too. Stacey and Nicky knew mom was not well, but they had no idea how bad she really was. In the beginning, she would get us up and off to school, and be awake when we got home, but after a week or so, she wouldn't even get up. She lost so much weight, and she smelled awful."

Jesse was leaning forward with his elbows resting on his knees, immersed in the story.

"How did she pull out of it, for obviously, she did."

Brad nodded, and sighed. "Yeah, but it wasn't an easy task. I ended up calling mom's best friend, Linda. We called her Aunt Linda. Anyway, she came over, and literally yanked my mom out of bed." Smiling, he added, "At least that's what my mom said. We had already gone to school by then."

"I was kind of like that when my wife died. In fact, I've been in a kind of emotional fog since then. It's just been in the last couple of months, that I began feeling that fog lift."

Brad sat back, and looking at the man, who was still leaning forward, asked "Anything in particular happen that may have caused the breakthrough?"

Sitting back, and rubbing his eyes, Jesse nodded, and said, "Actually, there was.

"A couple of guys and I went to an event called Promise Keepers, in Dallas. There were thousands of men gathered in the Convention Center, in downtown Dallas."

Brad nodded. His dad had attended a meeting like that in Detroit, the summer before he died.

"Anyway, there were some great speakers, and praise music." Smiling, he added, "I didn't know very many of the songs, except 'The Old Rugged Cross.' I remember singing that at my grandmothers church. It made me think what Heaven must sound like when so many voices blend together to sing praise to God." Pausing, he smiled and shook his head. "I was totally blown away by the whole experience, and prayed that God would forgive me, and be my Savior." Looking at Brad, he added, "It was as if a ton of bricks had been lifted off my shoulders. I pledged that I would turn my life around, and be a better dad to Jimmy." Sighing heavily, he whispered, "Then He betrayed me, and took my son."

Brad frowned. "Why do you think He betrayed you?"

Anger and bitterness filling his voice, Jesse said through clenched teeth, "Because He took my son!"

Brad sighed. He knew that feeling of betrayal all too well, as he had felt the same way when his dad died. Nodding, he said, "I can see how you'd feel that way."

"What? You're not going to tell me I shouldn't feel this way? It's God's will, and I have to just accept it? I can't get mad at God?"

Shaking his head, Brad said, "No. Your feelings are your feelings. There are a lot of things we don't understand about God, and why He does the things He does, or allows things to happen a certain way. When He created us, He gave us all of our emotions. He didn't want us to be robots, never expressing our feelings. He knew some of us would get so caught up in our anger and bitterness, that we'd turn our backs on Him, but it was a chance He was willing to take. He wants us to love Him because we want to, not because we have to." Pausing, he asked, "Does that make sense?"

Jesse nodded. "I understand this in my head, but my emotions, and..." tapping his chest, continued, "my heart don't want to accept it."

"Mr. McCoy, it's okay to grieve. Everyone grieves in their own way, and timetable. I don't think there's a special time limit that the grieving process has to end. Everyone is different, and every circumstance is different. Even Jesus is said to have cried when one of His best friends died. God recognizes that death is an inevitable part of life, and He doesn't like it either. That's why He's given us the gift of eternal life—a new kind of body, that will never die." Pointing to his body, Brad said, "This old body will decay, but our new one will be more awesome than we can even imagine."

Jessie sighed, and placing a hand on Brad's back, said, "I appreciate those words of wisdom from someone as young as yourself. It's like you have a direct line to God, and He's speaking through you."

Nodding, Brad said, "Mr. McCoy, can I tell you about my trip to Heaven?"

Raising his eyebrows in surprise, Jesse asked, "You went to Heaven?"

"Yep. A couple of months ago."

Sitting back, crossing his arms over his chest, and stretching his legs out, Jesse said, "By all means, tell me."

Brad recounted his bout with meningitis, and out of body experience when his heart stopped. Jesse sat in stunned silence. In his line of work as a fireman, he'd heard stories of people seeing angels, and claiming they'd gone to Heaven, and talked to God, but he'd never truly believed them, until now. Here was a young man, whom he knew, and trusted, and he was relating a similar experience. Jesse felt tears sting his eyes as he listened. Hope began to fill his soul, as the heaviness of grief began to dissipate. If Brad was right, and he believed he was, he would see his wife and son again.

When Brad finished with his story, he leaned back and sighed.

All Jesse could say was "Wow!"

Nodding, and smiling, Brad said, "I know. Right?"

Leaning forward, and exhaling air through his lips, Jesse said, "Well, that pretty much solidifies my belief in the after life." Laying a hand on Brad's shoulder, he said, "Brad, I truly believe that our encounter was orchestrated by the Almighty." Shaking his head, he added, "How else can any of this be explained?"

Nodding in agreement, Brad said, "Yeah, me too. Glancing at his watch, he said, "Mr. McCoy, I hate to cut this short but I need to head out before it gets dark."

Standing, Jesse said, "Oh, of course. I didn't realize how much time had passed."

Standing, and putting out his hand, Brad said, "It's been an honor, and pleasure, to have spent this time with you Mr. McCoy. I hope we can continue to meet every now and then. I'd like to know more about you, and your job."

Jesse took Brad's hand, and pulled him into a hug. With a catch in his voice, he said, "I too enjoyed our visit. And, yes, let's meet again, real soon. I can show you, and your family around the fire station."

Pulling free, Brad said, "I'm sure they'd like that." Grabbing his coat, hat, and gloves off the back of the chair, he dressed, as he headed for the door.

"Thanks again for the cookies!" Jesse yelled, as he waved a final goodbye to Brad's retreating back.

Brad waved in acknowledgment, as he turned at the end of the driveway.

Jesse stood on the porch, and watched Brad disappear behind a tall pine. Blowing out a sigh, he whispered, "Thank You, God. I needed that visit."

God whispered, "You're welcome. I'm not finished with either of you, yet."

Even though he had a walking cast on his foot and ankle, Jamie had difficulty maneuvering through the crowded hallways, and up and down the stairs of the school building. Standing in front of his locker, he felt eyes watching him, and could hear whispering as students passed by. He felt lost, and alone. Avoiding eye contact, he walked with his eyes downcast, to his next class.

As he took a seat in the back of the room, the English teacher began roll call. He glanced over at the empty desk his best friend had occupied just a couple of weeks ago. He felt a burning in the back of his eyes, and a lump form in his throat. When his name was called, he raised his hand, and could barely whisper, "here." Before looking back down, he made eye contact with Sylvia. She gave him a smile, and finger wave. He nodded, and gave her a finger wave back.

He thought back to the funeral, and how she had been so instrumental in organizing, and guaranteeing the whole event would run smoothly. He could barely function, and was no help at all, and Jimmy had been his best friend, but she, almost a stranger, had stepped in, and taken charge. He hadn't talked to her, or anyone for that matter, since the funeral. He decided, after class, he'd try to pull her aside, and thank her for being such a huge help.

As the teacher droned on about the different styles of prose and poetry, he laid his head down, and let his mind wander to thoughts of Mr. McCoy. *I wonder how he's doing? I haven't talked to him in a few days. I should give him a call, and see if I can help clean out Jimmy's room.*

His thoughts were interrupted, by a warm hand on his shoulder.

"Jamie?"

Opening his eyes, and raising his head, he looked up, into the face of Sylvia.

Shaking his head, he said, "Uh. Oh hi." Looking around the empty classroom, he said, "Guess class is over?"

Smiling, she said, "Yeah. A few minutes ago." Taking a seat on the desktop across from his, she asked, "You okay?"

Sighing heavily, he said, "No. Not really."

Nodding, and laying a hand on his arm, she said, "I didn't think so. I can't even imagine what you're going through. I've never lost anyone close to me."

Jamie raised his eyebrows. "Really? No one?"

Shaking her head, she said, "Nope. My grandparents are all alive, and as far as I know, the rest of the family. I still have all my close friends as well." Scrunching her face, she said, "I did have a pet goldfish that died, but that really doesn't count, does it?"

He chuckled. "No. Not really."

"Have you had anyone else that you're close to, die?" She asked.

Nodding, and sighing, Jamie leaned back in his chair, and told about his mom's passing.

Putting her hand to her chest, Sylvia said "Oh, Jamie. I'm so sorry to hear that. I can't begin to imagine what I'd do without my mom. Or dad. Bless your heart! Can I give you a hug?"

Shocked, Jamie said, "I guess so."

She leaned down, and wrapped her arms around his shoulders. She smelled faintly of honeysuckle, and her embrace felt genuine. It took a strong act of willpower for Jamie not to stand, and pull her in for a full-body hug. The last female he had hugged, had been his mom.

She released him, and stood, "I hope we can talk more later, but we need to get to our next class."

Jamie stood, and gathered his books. "Right. Where are you going next?"

"I have calculus."

Jamie thought, *pretty and smart.*

Heading out the door, and turning right, she asked, "Where are you headed?"

"Shop class. Gonna learn how to operate a band saw."

"Well, watch out for your fingers. I heard a guy lost a couple last year."

Making a face, Jamie said, "I'll keep that in mind."

They waved, as they parted company, and Jamie realized that he felt better. Almost happy...until he remembered that Jimmy had looked forward to being in the shop class with him. They had planned on working together. Jamie's spirits fell, as he made his way to a workstation. The stool next to him, which should have been occupied by Jimmy, was soon occupied by another senior student Jamie didn't know.

Leaning over, the boy whispered, "Hey. I'm Jeff."

Jamie nodded, and introduced himself. Jeff was big, fair-skinned, blonde, and had sky-blue eyes—nothing like Jimmy. He concluded that the difference was probably a good thing. If he had had any features like Jimmy, it would be a constant reminder of his absence.

The shop teacher, Mr. Bower, droned on about the tools and safety protocols, emphasizing the danger of cutting off one's fingers. He seemed to enjoy telling—in vivid detail—the story of the student who zipped off two of his fingers while using the band saw.

Jeff leaned over, and whispered, "My brother was in this class a couple of years ago, and he said Mr. Bower tells the same story every year. I think it's just a fabricated story to scare the jeepers out of everyone."

Jamie nodded. Even if it was a fabricated story, it was still a good idea to keep ones fingers out of the blades path.

After class, Jeff asked, "Hey, wanna hang out sometime?"

Jamie shrugged. "Sure."

Noticing the cast on Jamie's leg, he asked, "Hey Man. What happened to your leg?"

Sighing, as he slung his backpack over his shoulder, Jamie said, "I tripped, and broke my ankle."

"Ouch! How long do you have to be in the cast?"

"A few more weeks."

Shaking his head, Jeff said, "Man, that's gotta be tough. I've never had a broken bone, so I don't know what you're going through, but if you need help with anything..." He let the offer hang.

Nodding, Jamie said, "Thanks, Jeff. I'll keep that in mind."

"Well, I gotta go. My brother is picking me up out front, and we're gonna go look at a motorcycle he wants to buy."

"Yeah. My dad's meeting me out front too." Heading to his locker, Jamie turned, and said, "Jeff, want to meet over at the Eagle's nest for lunch tomorrow?"

Nodding, and smiling, Jeff said, "Yeah! See you there."

The two teens parted company, and Jamie thought, *Two new friends in one day. Not bad. Maybe the Universe is going to smile on me after all.*

David looked at Jarrod and said, "The Universe?"

Jarrod shook his head. "Silly Human." Looking at Jamie's Guardian Angel, Zephran, he said, "You need to set him straight on Who is in charge of the Universe."

Zephran shrugged. "I will when it's the right moment." When the boy disappeared down the hall, so did Zephran.

David turned to Jarrod, and said, "This new guy, Jeff, will be a positive influence in that area as well."

"Yes. I'm glad Father has brought him into Jamie's life at this time. Your son will also play an important role in Jamie's life."

David cocked his head, "Really? Brad? How so?"

Jarrod said, "Father hasn't been forthcoming on what exactly that role is, because I'm not directly involved in either boy's life. He did say that there'll be some significant events occurring in Alva. Very soon."

Nodding, and watching as students passed around and through them, David said, "Interesting. As if there hasn't already been a few significant events."

After the sheriff had taken down the information from Christina and the boy, a tow truck was called, and Christina's van was taken to Simmon's garage. Steven came to her rescue, and took her home. They made a quick stop at the repair shop. Jack Simmons showed her the van, and she was surprised at the amount of damage done.

Jack said, "It looks a lot worse than it is. We'll just need to replace the front panel, the headlight, and possibly the door, if we can't pull the dents out. Your insurance should pay most of the cost."

Shaking her head, Christina said, "How long before this is ready?"

Rubbing his chin, Jack said, "A couple of weeks at most."

"Do you have a car, or van I can use, or rent, until this one is finished?"

Nodding, Jack pointed towards the office, "We do. Jean, in the office, can help you pick one out. There is a small fee, however."

"That's fine. I just know I can't be without some sort of vehicle for two weeks."

"Right."

Steven and Christina went to the office, then followed Jean out to the lot to pick out a vehicle. There were no vans to choose from, so she chose a gray, four-door, Impala.

Steven asked, "Do you feel up to driving it home?"

Nodding slightly, she said, "Sure. It's not that far."

Jean said, "Come on back to the office, and I'll get the keys for you."

Arriving back at Christina's house, Steven helped her settle in on the couch.

"Thanks, Steven. I'd like to take a little nap. I didn't sleep all that well last night, and that little bit of activity tuckered me out. My body feels like it is beginning to stiffen up."

Entering the quiet house, she assumed the kids were sleeping. She asked Steven to check on them as she settled herself on the couch. He returned a few minutes later, reporting that all three kids were asleep.

She closed her eyes, and was instantly asleep. herself. Once the animals were cared for with fresh food and water, Steven walked back in the den to check on Christina. Finding her sleeping, he bent over, and kissed her forehead, whispering, "Sleep well, Sweetheart."

Two hours later, Christina woke from her nap, refreshed, and ready to take on the rest of the day. Benji was curled up at her feet, and Chloe was on her chest. Both raised their heads, when they felt her stir.

She heard the sounds of feet walking around upstairs. The kids are up, she thought.

Brad walked in the back door, put his backpack and outerwear on the table in the breakfast nook. He need to use the restroom. On his way there, he almost bumped into his mom.

"Sorry!" He said. "I need to go to the bathroom, then I'll come back and put all my stuff away."

Her nodded in understanding, then immediately regretted that movement. Her neck felt tender and the muscles felt tight. *Probably whip lash*, she thought.

Grabbing a glass of ice-tea before heading upstairs, she decided a long, hot soak in the tub, would feel nice. She knocked on Stacey's door.

Her daughter opened the door. Surprise registering on her face. "Mom! I didn't know you were home."

"It is almost six o'clock. Y'all have been sleeping for quite some time."

Stacey said, "Goodness! We must have been super tired!"

Christina smiled, and pulled her daughter into a hug. "Hey, I'm going to take a hot bath, so why don't y'all go get the food ready. I stopped and got fried chicken." *Well, Steven took me, but they didn't have to know that.*

Soaking in the tub, she planned out the rest of her week. Her accident wasn't as bad as it could have been. The van hadn't had irreparable damage, and she had a temporary replacement. The young man who had hit her with his car, had walked away unscathed, and ended up with minor damage to his car. All in all, even though it was a minor set-back, it wasn't devastating.

She thought back to the encounter with Jack Simmons at the garage. When she and Steven had walked in, the man had his back turned to them, and was barking orders at one of the mechanics. When he turned, and saw them, his whole countenance changed. As he approached, he seemed to visibly shrink. His shoulders slumped, and he seemed to look everywhere but into her eyes. She was sure it had to do with his son's breaking and entering involvement. It was obvious he was feeling guilty, and embarrassed. *I wish I had told him not to worry. I don't hold him accountable for his son's poor choices. I hope the kid is doing alright. Hopefully, getting caught red-handed, scared him enough to set him back on the right track.* She thought about the uncanny resemblance between her son, Brad, and Jamie. *What if Brad had done the things Jamie had done? How would I feel about that? Disappointed, for sure, but also sad to think he would resort to such behavior. That's probably what Jack Simmons is feeling.* She thanked God, once again, for keeping His hand of protection on her kids.

I need to call Libby. I told her I'd help her begin packing things up to move to the CCU. I guess I'll just have to work on that tomorrow when we have some down time. Hopefully, there won't be very many patients to care for.

I also need to call Lisa, and ask how she wants me to help with Elliana's and Rico's welcome home party on Saturday. She said they're expecting about a hundred people, give or take a few. It's an open house affair, so hopefully they won't all be there at once.

Realizing the water was beginning to cool, she stood, and reached for a towel, just as her phone buzzed on the toilet seat. Wrapping the towel snugly around her, she grabbed the phone.

"Hello?"

"Hey, Christina, it's Steven."

"Hey, yourself." Wrapping another towel around her dripping hair, she said, "Steven, can I call you right back? I just got out of the tub, and need to get dressed."

"Sure, talk to you then."

She quickly dressed, and sat on the side of the bed, as she reconnected with Steven.

"I was heading to the store, and wanted to see if you needed anything."

"As a matter of fact, I do." She gave him a short shopping list of items, and added, "Steven, I really appreciate your stepping in to help."

He was silent for a moment, and as if weighing each word carefully, said, "Christina, you know there isn't anything I wouldn't do for you, and the kids."

Sensing there was more to his statement, than merely a nice reply, she said, "Thank you, Steven. That means a lot to me...to us."

Silence reigned for a moment, then he said, "Well, alrighty then. Guess I'd better head out. I'll see you in a little while."

Placing the phone next to her, she laid back on the bed, and let her mind play with the idea of having Steven be a permanent part of her and her kid's lives. *Is that where this is headed? Is that what you want for us, Lord? Yes, I have feelings for him, but are they enough? Can he fill that David shaped hole in my heart? Should I give him a chance, or should I continue to keep my options open? It's not like I have to make any immediate decisions. We haven't even dated for that long. What if he wants some kind of commitment, or answer from me?*

Rubbing he eyes, she let those thoughts continue to rattle around in her mind, until the phone rang. Sitting up, she glanced at the ID, and realized it was Cindy.

"Hey, Girlfriend! I was just going to call you."

After a few moments of chatting, Christina invited Cindy, and Samara, over for dinner the next evening.

"We'll keep it simple," Christina said. "I'll pick up some bar-b-q on my way home from work."

"Sounds great! We need to do some catching up."

Steven walked up and down the aisles, retrieving the items on his and Christina's lists. He was enjoying this task, and smiled as he fantasized about doing this kind of thing on a regular basis. *I am so ready to settle down*, he thought.

As he turned onto the bakery aisle, he heard a male voice call his name.

"Steven?"

Turning, he saw Aaron Carmichael, holding on to his little girl's hand, approaching at a leisurely pace.

He stopped, and waited.

Reaching out his hand, Aaron said, "How are you?"

Steven said, "I'm doing well. You?"

Looking down at Sammie, he said, "We're doing great. You've met my daughter, Sammie?"

Nodding, and smiling, Steven squatted, so he could look the girl in the eyes, and said, as he reached out his hand, "Yes. A few Sundays ago at church."

Sammie smiled, and held out her hand, which Steven took and kissed.

"You look pretty as a princess."

Smiling shyly, she looked up to her daddy's encouraging nod.

Barely audible, she said, "Thank you. I dressed myself."

Steven stood, and touched the top of her head. "You did an awesome job. I especially like your sparkly shoes."

Looking down at the red glittered shoes, she giggled. "My Grandma gave me these. She said they look like the ones Dorothy wore in the Wizard of Oz."

Steven nodded. "Well, indeed they do."

Shrugging, she said, "I've never seen the whole movie because I keep falling asleep! Someday, I will see it all."

Chuckling, Aaron said, "Yes, Honey. Someday you will see the whole thing."

Clearing his throat, Steven said, "Well, I need to finish up. I need to drop a few things off at Christina's."

Aaron cocked his head. "Is Christina okay?"

Steven told him about the accident.

Aaron looked shocked. "I had no idea she'd been involved in an accident. You sure she's okay?"

Nodding, Steven said, "Just a minor bump on the head. Her van was pretty damaged though. I'm thinking she'd do well to get a new one. Fortunately, the repair shop guy gave her a car to drive until her van is repaired."

Shaking his head, Aaron said, "That poor lady. Seems like her life is one crisis after another."

Steven agreed. "It's like that whole family has a cloud of misfortune hanging over it."

Sammie tugged on her daddy's arm. Indicating for him to lean down, she whispered in his ear, "Daddy, I have to go potty."

Aaron nodded. Reaching out to shake Steven's hand again, he said, "Daddy duty calls."

Steven smiled, and nodded. "I'll see you at the hospital tomorrow."

Watching the two depart, and wishing for the millionth time that his own daughter had survived, Steven turned, and refocused on the task at hand. *Which Italian bread would Christina want?*

After chatting with Cindy, Christina finished dressing, then headed downstairs. The food items were lined up on the counter, and the kids were eating in the breakfast nook. Pouring a glass of iced tea, she joined them. They all recapped their day. When Christina shared about the accident, the kids were shocked, but relieved. When Brad shared about his visit with Mr. McCoy, they all agreed that they would continue to pray for him. When the meal was finished, and all was cleaned up and put away, Christina went to the den to call Lisa.

After introductions, Christina asked, "Can I get anything from the store before I head over on Saturday?"

Lisa thought for a moment, then said, "Ah, yes. Can you pick up at least three or four large bags of ice? I have a couple in the freezer, but it's supposed to warm up a bit on Saturday, and I'd hate to run out of ice. I'll have a couple of large ice chests full of water, and Cokes, and two three gallon containers of sweet tea, and lemonade. Do you think that'll be enough?"

"I would imagine so. You said you're having some food catered in, but would you like me to bring a tray of cheese and crackers, or better yet, some Texas caviar and chips?"

Christina could hear the excitement in her friend's voice. "That would be awesome! I love your Texas caviar!"

"How much should I make?"

Lisa thought a moment, "Well, however much you normally make. I'll have other snack type food as well, so there should be a good variety, and plenty to go around."

Christina said, "Well, you know how we Texans can eat! Besides, if we run out of food or drinks, I can always make a run to the store."

Lisa giggled. "True on both accounts. The kids and I are so excited about Saturday. Tom, not so much. He's been working hard at getting the inside, and outside, ready, and I think he'll be happy when it's all over!"

Christina sighed. "I remember when we'd have big get-togethers, David would complain about all the preparations, but in the end, would really enjoy the festivities."

"I'm sure Tom will too. We haven't seen some of our friends and family in a long time, so he'll enjoy catching up with them. I just hope I can find time to visit with folks as well."

"Lisa, you won't have to worry about a thing. Donna, Cindy, and I will keep things running smoothly. You can focus on your family, and enjoying all the company."

"Aww. Y'all are such good friends. I'll try not to worry."

"So, if it starts at one, would you want us there around ten?"

"That sounds good. The kids should have their rooms, and bathrooms, cleaned up, but their idea of clean and neat, aren't necessarily the same as mine."

"We'll do whatever you assign us to do. No job too big, or too small, that we can't handle!"

Lisa giggled. "Even toilets?"

"Even toilets."

After disconnecting, Christina called Libby, and explained her inability to help that afternoon,

"I'll be there bright and early tomorrow, though." She said, adding, "And I can stay later if need be. I'm so anxious to move back into our unit."

Libby said, "Bless your heart! I totally understand. Sally Jean, and Sarah, have volunteered to stay after work, and help pack up the meds, and such."

Nodding, Christina said, "That's good. They're hard workers. Knowing them, there may not be any work for me to do tomorrow!"

Libby chuckled. "That's possible. However, you're the one who'll decide where everything will end up. We'll probably just box everything up, and leave them on the counter. It'll be up to you, and the other nurses to sort, and store it."

Christina sighed. "Yeah. You're right. I'm okay with that."

Libby said, "We were invited to Lisa's party on Saturday. What time should we come?"

"It's an all day open house affair, so anytime would be fine. There will be more food in the beginning, however."

Libby giggled, "Then by all means, we'll get there early!"

As she disconnected, she heard a car door slam, followed by a knock on the back door. Steven had arrived with the groceries. Sorting through the items, Christina said, "Thank you, Steven for getting all these things."

As they sorted through the groceries, and put them away, they chatted about their days activities.

Christina said, "I talked to Libby. We're going to start moving everything back into the CCU tomorrow evening, after work. Want to come help?"

Nodding, Steven said, "Yeah. I want to look over some of the new equipment, and familiarize myself with the new monitors and such."

Clapping her hands together like an excited child on Christmas morning, Christina said, "I'm so happy we're finally moving back in! It's almost like moving into a new house!"

Steven chuckled. "I never thought of it like that, but I guess you're right. Everything will be new...well, except for the beds. Those, they were able to salvage.

"I know! It'll be fun organizing the medication room, and getting everything ready for the new influx of patients."

Steven couldn't help but be amused by her excitement. He loved her enthusiasm. He loved her.

What? Really? Yes, you idiot. Admit it. You love her. He felt his heart quicken. Pulling her into an embrace, he had to bite his tongue to keep from letting those words slip past. *I will tell her soon, but not right now.*

"Mom?" She heard Brad call, as he bounded down the stairs. She and Steven disengaged.

"Yes? In the kitchen."

"I just talked to Eric. He invited me over for tomorrow night. Can I go?"

"Sure. Just remember the party on Saturday. I'd at least like you to make an appearance."

"Oh yeah. What time does it end?"

"It's from one to six. The girls and Nicky can go with me in the morning, but if you come later, you can walk them home. I'll be helping with clean up, so I won't be home 'till after dark."

Nodding, Brad said, "Sure. That'll work. Can I show up around five?"

"How about four. It gets dark around five-ish, and I'd like y'all home before then."

Shrugging, Brad said, "Okay. I'll call Eric back." He ran back up the stairs.

Linda and Stacey came down next, dressed in pajamas. Stacey said, "Mom, Linda wants to ask you something."

Turning to face Linda, Christina said, "What is it, Honey?"

Linda pushed a stand of hair behind her ear. "I was wondering, since we can't go see my mom on Saturday, if maybe we could go after church on Sunday?"

Christina thought for a moment, then said, "I don't see why not. I'll call the hospital, and ask if it's okay for us to come."

Turning to Steven, Christina asked, "You want to take a drive up to Dallas with us Sunday afternoon?"

Shrugging, he said, "If the hospital says it's okay, then sure. I'd love to see Janet. See how she's doing."

Christina had told him of Janet's memory loss, and he was curious to see if any of her memory had returned.

Linda walked over, and hugged Christina. "Thanks, Mrs. Sanders."

Christina rubbed Linda's back, and kissed the top of her head. "I'm sure it'll be fine with the hospital. I'm sure your mom will be so happy to see you." *If she even remembers who you are*, she thought.

"Do you girls have homework?" Christina asked, as she released Linda.

"No, Ma'am." Stacey said, as she and Linda did a high five.

Steven said, "I'd best get going. I have two heart catheterizations, and a valve replacement tomorrow, plus two consultations in the afternoon.

Looking surprised, Nicky said, "Wow! That is a lot."

Brad asked, "How long does a catheterization take?"

"About an hour. Sometimes longer, sometimes less. Depends on what we find."

"We?" Stacey asked.

"My associate, Dr. Meils."

"Oh, yeah." Stacey said, "I kinda forgot about him. I keep thinking you're the only cardiologist there."

Steven shrugged, "Well, for a while I was. That was exhausting. I'm so thankful to have Dr. Meils on staff."

Linda said, "I met Dr. Meils when my mom was in the hospital. He's very nice. And cute."

Stacey gave her a surprised look. "Cute? Isn't he old?"

Steven bit his lip to keep from laughing.

Christina said, "We are the same age, so he's not old. Just mature. And I agree with Linda. He is cute, for a mature man."

Everyone laughed. Steven said, "I'm sure he'd appreciate the compliment."

Linda blushed. "Oh, don't tell him I said that!"

Steven reached over, and patted her hand. "Don't worry, Honey. I won't tell him. He's already got an ego the size of Mount Everest!"

Linda giggled.

Steven turned, and headed to the door.

"Well, it's been fun as always." Reaching out, he shook Brad's and Nicky's hands, then gave each girl a quick hug.

The kids headed up to their rooms, as Christina walked him to the door. After donning his hat, gloves and coat, he pulled her into a hug, then bent down, and lightly kissed her lips.

Taking his hands in hers, she looked into his intense blue eyes. "Steven, I really enjoy being with you, and I hope we can continue seeing each other."

Shaking his head, he said, "I sense there's a 'but' coming."

Looking down, then back up, she said with a nod, "But, I can't think about getting serious right now. My heart, and mind, aren't in a stable place, and it wouldn't be fair to you to pretend they are."

Nodding in understanding, he said, "It's okay. I want you to know that I care deeply for you, and the kids, and I would like to continue seeing y'all."

She opened her mouth to speak, but he put his finger up, "With the understanding that this may not lead anywhere." Shrugging, he added, "If it doesn't, then we can continue being good friends, if it does..." He let the sentence dangle.

She smiled, and nodded. "Got it. Let's just continue enjoying each others company, and see what happens."

He pulled her into another hug. "Agreed." He said into her hair.

CHAPTER 14

Friday was a slow day at the hospital, as Christina had one cardiac patient, and Libby was in charge of two. The two women were able to finish packing up, and moving the medicines and supplies, over to the cardiac care unit, while the aides cared for the three residents. Christina was happy to transfer the items, and prepare the unit for Monday, when they could officially move the patient, or patients, over to their new rooms. Sarah and Sally Jean had put clean linens on the beds, and made sure everything was where it should be: water pitchers, cups, tissues, bath linens, and toiletries. The patients coming in, would be made as comfortable as possible.

Christina arrived home with the bar-b-q, and had put the meat, and side dishes on serving platters when she heard a knock on the door. Cindy, and Samara, had arrived.

Everyone, except Brad, who was at Eric's house, grabbed their plates, and filled them with the variety of meats and veggies, before heading into the dining room. There was a cacophony of noise, as everyone vied for the food, and a place to sit. Nicky had to bring a couple more chairs in from the breakfast nook, to accommodate the two extra guests. Once settled, and grace was said, everyone began eating like starving coyotes. Christina looked around, and smiled. It was satisfying to see everyone enjoying the food before them.

"If anyone wants more, feel free to go get it. I put the food in the oven to keep warm."

Everyone smiled, and nodded. Nicky said, "I'll probably get more. This is so good! It's been a while since we've had bar-b-q."

Linda said, "I can't even remember the last time I had bar-b-q."

Scrunching her face, she added, "Maybe at the beginning of summer."

Wiping her mouth on a napkin, Cindy said, "This was a good choice of food, Christina. We had bar-b-q when we were out in LaMesa, and this is as good, if not better, than that."

Christina nodded. "Yeah. I'm glad I got this. It really hit my hungry spot."

When they had finished devouring the food, Stacey said, "Can we have Root beer floats for desert?"

"Ooh, that sounds yummy!" Samara said, as she took her dishes to the kitchen.

Christina looked around the room. "Who else would like a float?"

"I do!" Nicky said, raising his hand.

Linda, Stacey, and Samara, all raised their hands and said, "Me too!"

Christina looked at Cindy with raised eyebrows. "You?"

Cindy put her hand up. "No thanks! I'm too full. I'll help with the preparations though."

"Actually, I think I'll let the kids take care of that. You and I can go in the front room, and chat."

Glancing at her kids, Christina said, "Y'all know where everything is. Just clean up when you're done."

Stacey rolled her eyes, and sighed heavily. "Alright. I'll scoop the ice-cream. Linda, you want to pour the Root beer?"

Linda shrugged, and said, "Sure."

Nicky said, "Why don't we all just fix our own? Linda, you get the glasses, I'll get the ice-cream and Root beer. That way, you can put as much, or as little stuff as you want."

Everyone nodded. Samara patted Nicky on the shoulder and said, "Good idea."

Cindy and Christina enjoyed their time together. They caught up on the latest news, and planned their agenda for helping Lisa the following day.

Setting her empty ice-tea glass on the coffee table, Christina said, "I haven't seen Ed around much lately. Are y'all doing okay?"

Cindy smiled. "Oh yes. We're fine. He's just had a lot of things to do in Dallas. Seems like terrorists never take a break."

Christina nodded. "Have y'all set a date for the wedding?"

Shaking her head, Cindy said, "As far as I'm concerned, the sooner the better! I'm thinking sometime in April. I thought I wanted a big church wedding, but I think I'd love to have the ceremony in a field of bluebonnets, instead."

Clasping her hands together, Christina said, "Ooh! I love bluebonnets! I could never get them to grow up in Michigan."

"Why?" Cindy asked.

Shaking her head, Christina said, "Not sure. Maybe it was just too cold, or the seeds were old. Anyway, I only tried a couple of times."

"Well, now you can enjoy them again, for real."

"I know! I can hardly wait!"

They talked for another hour or so, when Cindy said, "I need to get home so I can be ready for tomorrow. I tire so easily. I'll be glad when we can figure out what's going on."

Nodding, and patting Cindy's hand, Christina said, "Me too. It's awful not knowing the reason behind one's sickness."

Standing, Cindy said, "Hopefully it's something that can be corrected easily."

Christina reached out, and pulled Cindy into a hug. "Yes. Hopefully."

After Cindy and Samara left, Christina gathered the rest of the dishes, and loaded the dishwasher.

Leaning on the door jamb to the den, Christina said, "I'm heading upstairs. Don't stay up too much later. We have a busy day tomorrow."

Grabbing the stack of mail from the kitchen counter, Christina ascended the stairs, with Benji on her heels. After a hot shower, she sat on her bed, and went through the mail: bills, fliers advertising sales, postcards asking for donations, and a letter sized envelope addressed to her.

She was surprised, and pleased, to see it was from her friend, Linda. Lifting the flap, she pulled out a card and note. The card had a picture of a vase full of daisies, her favorite flowers, with "Thinking of you" printed across the bottom. She pulled out the enclosed note and found a gift card for Nicky's birthday, tucked inside. Folding the letter, and stuffing it back in the envelope, Christina felt tears filling her eyes, as she felt a wave of home-sickness wash over her. She missed her Michigan friends, and family, but knew, except by God's hand, she'd never return there. She was where she was supposed to be.

Even if David had survived, and they had lived their remaining lives in Michigan, there would have always been that longing to go "home." Her Texas roots grew deep, and ensnared her heart, soul, and mind. When David died, and she wondered what she should do, she had felt the tug on her heart, and had heard the Siren Song in her spirit, to return to her beloved Texas. Even though it had been difficult to pack up, and leave their home that David had so lovingly prepared for them, she knew, without a doubt, that Texas was to be their final destination.

Smiling, as she looked around the room, that had been her childhood sanctuary, she thought, *And here we are.*

Closing her eyes, she whispered a prayer.

"I don't understand why we're being tested, but I know this is where You want us. In spite of all the drama and trauma, I know You have a plan. Your ways are not our ways, and Your thoughts are not our thoughts, but I sure wish You'd be a little clearer on the direction You want us to go." She continued praying a while longer, asking for mercy, wisdom, and healing for her friends, and family, as well as thanking Him for every provision. Ending her prayer, she heard the children making their way up the stairs. Sighing, she turned off the bedside lamp, scooted under the covers, and was asleep soon after the last bedroom door shut.

Tom, Ed, and Bill exited the ATO office complex in Dallas, and headed to their cars in the outside parking lot, discussing the day's events. The parking garage was still in shambles, following the last terrorist attack by a group claiming responsibility: "WOA—or Wipe out America."

After a few anonymous tips, and further investigation, the ATO found the group's headquarters in a small apartment complex, in the southern district of Dallas. Between the ATO tactical team, and the Dallas SWAT team, they were able to surprise, and subsequently capture the ten members of the WOA team, with a few minor injuries, and no loss of lives. The timing had been perfect, as the gang was gearing up for more attacks, on more parking structures in the Dallas area.

When asked why they were targeting parking garages, the leader, who called himself, "M. J." or Mohammed James, just grinned, displaying a gold tooth, and said, "We get all y'all focused on the parking garages, then we can hit our primary target."

The police chief, Alan Jackson, had asked, "Which would be?"

M. J. just shook his head, smiled, and said, "For us to know, and you to find out...after the boom."

Laughing, he made a hand gesture of a bomb exploding.

M. J. was a tall, thin, African American man, with thick black hair that hung in braids, around his face, a thick black beard, and a gold-plated front tooth, which seemed to sparkle when he smiled. He was dressed in a long tan colored linen-like tunic with matching pants, and sandals. He would have fit in with the inhabitants of a middle-eastern country, but was ill-suited for the Texas winter weather. After an hour or so of interrogation, he was led to a cell-block, occupied by the other gang members. He began to shiver, as he sat on the metal cot, hanging from the wall.

"Hey, can y'all turn up the heat in here?" He shouted at the officer, who had opened one of the other cell doors, and was escorting another WOA gang member to the interrogation room.

Shaking his head, the officer smiled, and said, "Yeah, I'll get right on that."

"Hey, D!" M. J. shouted, "Don't tell them nothin'!"

D nodded.

The officer thought, *This is going to be a long day, and night.*

Ed and Tom rode together to the Dallas police station, to speak to the gang members. They hoped there would be a tidbit of information they could use to squelch any further attacks.

Bill declined riding with the two men, as he had plans with his wife and kids.

Ed and Tom nodded in understanding.

"We've got this covered." Ed said, as he reached out his hand.

"Yeah." Tom agreed, "We'll let you know if there's any further developments."

The drive from the ATO office to the police precinct was a short, eight blocks.

Entering the red brick building, which was bustling with activity, and a cacophony of noise, Ed made a bee line to the front desk. Both men produced their badges, as Ed asked the middle-aged woman behind the counter, where the gang members were being held.

Glancing at the badges, then up to the two men, she said, "They are in the back. You want me to call the Chief?"

"Sure. We'd like to speak to him first."

A few minutes later, Alan Jackson arrived, and shook hands with the two agents.

"Come into my office, where we can talk without shouting."

The two agents followed the man down a narrow hallway.

After a long, and monotonous time of questioning each gang member, they finally got a break when the youngest member, who was fourteen, and little brother to M. J., told them that the next bomb would go off in the parking garage, on the campus of the University of Texas.

As soon as the officers who were standing behind the observation window heard this, they went into action—including the Police Chief.

Ed got an uneasy vibe from the young man, and didn't trust him. He was watching the kids facial expressions, and could have sworn he saw the tiniest of smiles when he gave the information to Tom. Even though the kid said he was fourteen, and had never done anything like this, but agreed to it because of his big brother, and even produced tears, Ed just couldn't buy it. It was too easy.

Tom looked up at Ed, who tilted his head in the direction of the door. Tom stood, and both men exited the room.

Shaking his head, Ed said, "I don't think there's a bomb at the UT. The kid is acting."

Tom said, "You sure?"

Ed and Tom stood outside the room, and watched through the window. The kid grinned, then laid his head down on his crossed arms, and appeared to fall asleep.

Ed pointed a finger at the kid. "See that? He's too calm. He thinks he's pulled one over on us."

After a few more minutes passed, and the kid continued to sleep, Tom said, "I think you're right. Now what?"

Ed shook his head. "I'm not sure. We need to talk to the Chief again."

CHAPTER 15

Lisa and her family were up early, ready to prepare for the big day. "The Gotcha! Celebration."

Beds were made—without complaint—bathrooms made spotless, and floors and tables de-cluttered. Lisa busied herself with the food and drink preparations, while Tom, and the boys set up tables and chairs. Sarah, their oldest child, helped dress the honorees, and then helped her mother finish the meal preparations.

Around ten-o'clock, Cindy and Christina entered, carrying four bags of ice, a huge bowl of Texas caviar, and sever bags of chips. After putting the items in their appropriate places, they lent a hand where needed.

Donna arrived within the hour, bringing bags of gifts, and trays of homemade chocolate chip cookies.

The guests began arriving around twelve-thirty, and soon the house was filled with bodies, laughter, and conversations. The two little ones; Elliana and Rico, enjoyed the attention, but were mostly excited about the gifts—as most children would be.

The day ended too quickly, and as the last attendee pulled out of the driveway, Lisa let out a huge sigh of relief. Heading to the couch with a glass of wine in her hand, Lisa said, "Christina, Cindy, and Donna, get yourselves over here. We need to have a quiet minute before we start dismantling everything."

They each grabbed a beverage of some sort, and joined Lisa on the sectional.

Kicking off her shoes, and raising the foot of the seat she was occupying, Lisa said, "Ah! This feels so good!"

The other three ladies, mimicked her actions. They could hear Tom and Sarah putting food away, as the other kids dismantled tables and chairs.

Feeling a bit guilty, Christina asked, "Shouldn't we be helping?"

They all looked at each other, and broke into laughter.

Holding up her nearly empty glass, Lisa said, "Yeah, right after we finish our drinks."

Tom yelled from the kitchen, "I heard that!"

"Me too!" Said Sarah.

The four ladies on the couch put their hands to their mouths, and stifled a giggle.

"It was an amazing day, right?" Lisa asked, pouring more dark red wine in her glass.

"It truly was." Christina answered, taking a sip of her own wine. She had never liked the taste of wine, but felt she should try once more, because the "Fab Four" were once again reunited.

"Did you see the two little ones snuggled up together on the sofa?" Donna asked.

Christina and Lisa shook their heads. Donna said, "I did. They were so precious. I'm sure this day wore them out."

"They've had a pretty much non-stop week. They've got to be exhausted. I'm glad Tom took them up to bed." Lisa said, on a giggle, "They'll probably sleep through tomorrow. I'm pretty sure I will!"

"Hey, Mom?" Sarah called from the kitchen.

"Yeah?"

"Is this red ceramic tray ours?"

"No. It's Donna's. Just rinse it off, and dry it. Okay?"

"Sure. It'll be on the table by the front door."

Donna asked, "Were there any cookies left?"

"Nope." Sarah said, as she popped the remaining one in her mouth.

Pulling herself off the couch, Lisa said, "I guess I'd better make sure everything is put in its appropriate place."

"I'll go check the bathrooms," Cindy said. "Actually, I need to use one, so I'll make sure it's clean."

Smiling, and nodding, Lisa said, "Thanks."

When the sun was well past setting, the four friends parted company, with plans to get together again soon.

As Christina drove Cindy home, Cindy sighed, and said, "I wish Ed could have come. He would like Tom."

She giggled, and Christina asked, "What?"

"I just realized that Ed's co-worker is named Tom."

Nodding, Christina said, "What are the odds of having two Toms as friends? It would be weird to have two friends named Cindy."

Cindy said, "Yeah. Or two Christinas. Personally, I'm glad to have just one of you."

Christina reached over, and patted Cindy's hand. "I too am glad there's just one of you. I don't think I could handle another Cindy—especially if she's as crazy as you!"

Surprised, Cindy said, "Well, I'm not sure I could handle another me either."

Both friends chuckled.

"Hey, guess who I saw at Wal-Mart this week?"

Shaking her head, Christina said, "I have no idea."

"Janet Blair."

"Who?"

"You know. Bonnie and Janet who were best friends in high-school." She put her fingers up making imaginary quotation marks. "The Witches." "We talked about them a few weeks ago."

Christina nodded. "I remember."

"Janet looks totally different than she did in high-school. Remember, she always wore black clothing, and outlined her eyes with a black pencil."

Nodding, Christina said, "Yeah. She and Bonnie both did that. So, how is she now?"

"Beautiful, and classy.' Christina raised here eyebrows. "Classy?"

Cindy nodded, and continued, "She has aged well. I wouldn't have recognized her, if she hadn't introduced herself."

"Did you talk to her?" Christina asked, as she turned the car into Cindy's driveway.

"For a few minutes. She's married to a Lawyer, and lives in Dallas. She's a stay at home mom, and does a lot of volunteer work at her children's schools, and their church. They have two girls, and a son, who is—get this—going to be a pastor."

Christina gave her a shocked expression. "A pastor?"

"I know! Right?"

Christina shook her head in disbelief, then asked, "Did you ask her about Bonnie?"

"She said Bonnie is a legal secretary for the law firm her husband works in. She's married to a dentist. They have twin boys in high-school."

"Wow! I would have never guessed them to be so successful. They seemed like lost souls in high-school."

"I know! It's nice to hear happy ending stories."

Christina nodded. "Yes, it is. Do you know which law firm Bonnie works with?"

Biting her lower lip, Cindy thought for a moment. "There were three names, but the only one I remember is Marshall. I remember wondering if he was related to the Marshalls who live here in Alva."

"Could it be, Taylor, Marshall, and Campbell?" Christina asked.

Cindy grinned and nodded. "Yeah. That sounds right."

Shaking her head, Christina said, "Oh my goodness! That's the law office I go to. Mark Taylor is the lawyer who is handling David's financial stuff."

Cindy raised her eyebrows in surprise. "What a small world! Maybe you saw Bonnie, and didn't even know it."

"Maybe. It's a large office complex, with a lot of women milling about, so it's possible. What's Bonnie's last name?"

Shaking her head, Cindy said, "I don't know. I never asked."

Sighing, Christina said, "Well, I guess it doesn't really matter."

"Yeah. We didn't travel in the same circles in high-school, so I can't see us establishing a relationship now."

"Right." Christina said. "It's just an interesting bit of information. If I go back to the lawyer's office, I will look her up."

Grabbing the door handle, Cindy said, "Thanks for the ride. It was a fun, but exhausting day."

Nodding, Christina said, "Yes, it was. But it was worth every bit of our time, and energy."

Nodding, Cindy said, "Yep." Then turned, and headed up the sidewalk.

As she drove home, Christina brought up the memories of Bonnie and Janet. The girls' transformation from being shy, plain, and unnoticeable happened rather quickly. It seemed that one week, they were almost invisible, and the next week, they were the talk of the school. They both walked in wearing all black clothing, hair, nails, and heavy black eye make up. By the end of their freshman year in high-school, they had quite a few followers, who also began wearing the same kind of attire. Their behavior stirred quite a mixture of feelings from the teachers, parents, and other students. Thoughts ranged from: *It's just a phase*, to: *We need to nip this in the bud.*

The final consensus was to just let it play out. Those students who joined the group kept to themselves, and caused no harm. Everyone kept close tabs on them, and if there had been questionable, harmful activity, then the school board, and police, would have gotten involved. As it was, by their senior year, many of the followers had outgrown that phase, and only a handful graduated in their full black regalia. Because they were never friends, Christina hardly ever thought about them, except when a class reunion was planned, and some of them would show up. Most had matured past that era, and became clean-cut members of society.

Funny how we all go through different phases in our lives. While we're in the middle of said phase, it seems so important. Only looking back, can we see how foolish we were. I believe God allows those times to help us become better adults: more sympathetic, and empathic, and hopefully wiser in our decision making.

Pulling into the garage, Christina felt a twinge of a headache beginning. Touching the tender area on the back of her head, she thought, *my poor noggin' has had a couple of bad bumps these past few weeks. No wonder I'm getting headaches more often.*

Opening the back door, she was greeted by Benji, who's whole body moved in rhythm with his tail. She could always count on him being excited to see her.

Scratching behind his ears, she pushed passed him into the kitchen.

"Kids! I'm home!" She called, removing her coat, and setting her purse on the counter.

She heard the sound of feet running down the stairs, then Nicky jumping off the last couple of steps, and landing with a loud "boom" on the floor. He entered the kitchen, followed closely by Danny.

"Hey, Mom! Glad you're home."

"Hi Mrs. Sanders." Danny said, lifting his hand in a wave.

"Hi boys. Did y'all eat yet?"

Shaking his head, Nicky said, "No. We were waiting for you to get home."

"Okay. Where's Brad and the girls?"

"Brad's in his room, and the girls are in Stacey's room."

Nodding, Christina said, "Alright. Let's see what they'd like to eat. I'm tired of pizza. Maybe I can find something in the freezer."

She stood at the bottom of the stairs, calling for Brad, and the girls to come down. The vote for pizza was unanimous. She moaned, and said, "Alright. I think I'll just get a salad."

Jamie answered the phone at Pizza Hut. When he heard the name, Sanders, his heart began to race. He still felt embarrassed, and ashamed of his actions concerning them. Even though Mrs. Sanders had not pressed charges, he couldn't help but feel remorse. *Will I ever get past this?*

Because of his broken ankle, his boss wouldn't let him deliver pizzas, even though it was his left one, and he had been driving to school and work. Something about liability. He was thankful he wouldn't have to face the

Sanders at this time, because he wasn't sure he would be able to look them in the eyes, without coming unglued. He had avoided bumping into Brad at school since the incident, but even though they were in different grades, knew it was inevitable, as the high school building wasn't all that large. Sighing heavily, he entered the order into the computer, adding an order of bread-sticks as a token of his remorse.

The Sanders family enjoyed the pizza, salad, and bread-sticks, wondering who had put them in without adding them on the bill. They hadn't realized Jamie was back to work, and had tried to assuage some of his guilt, by adding this gift.

As they ate, they discussed the day's activities, and how well the party for Rico and Elliana went.

"Mrs. Sanders?"

"Yes, Linda?"

"Can we see my mom again soon?"

"Oh yes, Honey. I called the hospital, and they said it would be fine to come by tomorrow afternoon.

Linda's face lit up with excitement. "Really?"

Nodding, and smiling, Christina said, "Really. I figured we'd head up to Dallas after church. We can either grab lunch on the way, or we can eat first."

Linda said, "Whatever you want to do. I'm just excited we're going!"

Christina asked her boys, "Do y'all want to go too, or would you rather stay home?"

Brad said, "Personally, I'd rather stay home. I have some reading to catch up on." Looking at Linda, he said, "Not that I don't want to see your mom, it's just that I really need to get caught up."

Linda shook her head, and said, "It's fine. I understand. I'll have Stacey with me."

Nicky said, "I'd like to stay home too. If it's okay?"

Linda reached over, and patted Nicky's hand. "It's fine." Looking over at Stacey, she grinned and said, "We'll just have a girl's day, again."

Christina said, "Since the boys aren't going, why don't we grab a quick lunch, then I'll drop them off at home, then we can head on up to Dallas?"

Looking around the table, everyone nodded in agreement.

Danny, who had been busy filling his mouth with pizza asked, "Mrs. Sanders, can Nicky come to my house tomorrow, while you're gone? I have a new game I want to show him."

Christina nodded. Looking over to Nicky, she said, "I'll let you know when we get back home."

Standing, she said, "Now that that's all settled, let's get this mess cleaned up. I want to go up to my room, and make a few phone calls before it gets any later."

Everyone stood, and began cleaning up their area. "Oh, and Danny. You should head on home before it gets any later. Brad, can you and Nicky walk him home since it's so dark out?"

"Sure," the boy's said in unison. The three boys donned their coats, and headed out the door, while the girls finished clearing the table, and put the remaining food away.

Christina headed upstairs, and once in her room, called her friend Linda, from Michigan. After catching up on their family news, she called her mother-in-law, Ruth.

They discussed Nicky's upcoming birthday, and the trip they had planned in February during the kid's mid-winter break.

"I'm having difficulty wrapping my head around the fact that my "baby" is going to be eleven! It just hardly seems possible!"

Ruth giggled. "I know! Time just keeps ticking away. You blink and your kids are having kids of their own."

"Goodness! I hope that doesn't happen any time soon!"

Still chuckling, Ruth said, "I don't think you'll have to cross that bridge into grand mothering for several more years!"

Sighing, Christina said, "Well, when that time comes, I'm sure I'll be ready."

After s few more minutes of chatting, they said their "good-byes" with the expectation of talking again next week.

Christina leaned back on the headboard, and let her mind wander. She was looking forward to moving back into the CCU, and getting back into a normal routine. She was thankful the patients were able to be cared for on the medical-surgical unit, but because that unit wasn't well equipped with the cardiac medication, and paraphernalia that went along with cardiac care, it was inconvenient, and time consuming to locate, and carry out said care. Fortunately, most of the patients who had been admitted weren't at a high risk of complications.

Thoughts of the cardiac unit, led to thoughts of Steven. Sighing heavily, she let her thoughts dwell there for a while, as she explored her feelings, and what direction she would like her relationship to head. Their relationship had blossomed in the past few months, and she had certainly developed feelings of intense like for Steven, but was it developing into love?

All through high-school I wanted Steven's attention, and love, and now that it's so close, I can almost touch it, I'm not sure that's what I want. I would like to explore my feelings for Aaron, and possibly other men.

As her mind jumped from one subject to another, she let it pause on thoughts of Janet. *I hope her memory has returned. Linda's feelings will be hurt if she thinks her mom doesn't remember her. I hope this amnesia is a temporary thing.*

Glancing at the clock, she stood, stretched, and decided to head downstairs, and check on the kids.

Tom and Ed entered the Police Chief's office, and Ed told him of his suspicions.

"I don't think the kid is being honest. Either he doesn't know, and is buying time, or he does know, and is sending our guys on a wild goose chase. Either way, time is ticking, and so is the bomb."

Holding his fingertips together as if he were planning to pray, Alan Jackson let out a sigh.

"Did any of those kids give any indication of when the next bomb would go off?"

Shaking his head, Ed said, "We got different answers from each one. So, basically, any time in the next twenty-four hours."

"I see." Placing his hands on his desk, the Police Chief stood.

"I'm going to make their stay here as unpleasant as possible. The only bargaining chip we have is their comfort."

Calling a few of his deputies in, Alan instructed them to separate the boys, turn the heat off, remove the mattresses and blankets, deny them food and water, and give them a bucket to put their waste in.

Turning to Ed and Tom, the Chief said, "If we make them very uncomfortable, maybe they'll be more willing to cooperate to get a blanket, or have the heat turned up, or to go to the bathroom."

Ed smiled, and nodded. "I've seen it work on some of the most avid criminals. It should work on these young'uns."

Tom said, "They'll pretend it doesn't bother them for the first couple of hours, then when they begin to feel the cold, and can't get warm, they'll be crying for their mommies."

Nodding, Alan said, "That's what I'm counting on. Hopefully, they'll give us the info before the next bomb goes off."

The officers, Ed, and Tom, hung around the building, waiting for a break in the case. They ordered pizza, and played poker until they heard the young men begin complaining about the cold. Smiling, Ed said, "Now, maybe we can begin negotiations."

After another hour or so of banter back and forth between the officers and detainees, they were able to get the information they had longed for. Turns out, the young men weren't the only ones behind the bombings. They were working for another group of men—which Ed suspected at the onset. The target was to be the parking structure at the Bluebonnet Mall in Fort Worth. There was to be a grand opening of the ice-skating rink, along with a few new stores, over the weekend, and thousands were predicted to be in attendance. It would be difficult to evacuate the place, but with enough officers and agents, it could be done—hopefully in an orderly fashion. They hoped to find the bomb before the attack was to take place.

Ed and Tom headed back to their office to discuss the proposed procedure with their boss, leaving the sheriff, and his crew, to contact the Fort Worth police, and SWAT department.

As Ed pulled up the information about the suspected culprits behind the plan, he was surprised to see a familiar face. Turning the computer towards Tom and his boss, he asked, "Isn't this the guy who was a suspect up in Detroit?"

Pulling up the file from the Detroit terrorist list, Henry said, "He does look like that guy. Different name, though." Perusing through other files, he said, "I think this is the same guy who was in the ambulance with Christina's husband, David. Even though he kept avoiding a full on facial view in the ambulance camera, there was a pretty good shot of him from the ambulance bay, when he fled the scene. Cameras are everywhere, now days. Lucky for us, he was unaware of that one."

Studying the photo, he said, "I'll have to say, it sure looks like him."

Ed stood over Henry's shoulder, looking at the two pictures.

"I think you may be right! What are the odds of him turning up here?"

Tom said, "Let me see." Enlarging the pictures, he said, "Same face shape. Same eyes."

"Can we do a face recognition comparison?" Ed asked, as he returned to his chair.

Henry said, "Of course." Within a few minutes, they received the results they were hoping for.

"Well, what do you know? It's a match by ninety-eight percent."

Shaking his head, Tom said, "Can't get much closer than that. Now all we have to do is find him."

Nodding, and closing his computer, Ed said, "Yep. The sheriff said, he'd be working on getting more information from the young men. I just hope it will be reliable, and in a timely manner."

Henry leaned back in his chair, which groaned in protest. "I know the sheriff personally, and he always gets the information he needs."

Tom stood and stretched. "If that leader is really the one from Detroit, Christina will be happy to know he's been caught."

"Yeah," agreed Ed. "She'll be happy to close that chapter in her life."

As events were unfolding in Dallas and Fort Worth, the residents of Alva were enjoying a peaceful, uneventful Sunday, blissfully unaware of the events unfolding a few miles away. The sun was shining in a clear blue sky, and the temperatures had risen a few degrees, dispelling some of the frigidly cold air. Families were up, and heading out to their various places of worship, or work, or enjoying a leisurely morning in the comfort of their homes. Restaurants were gearing up for the influx of early morning, and afternoon diners.

Christina, and the kids were on their way to church, when they heard a newscaster report that the new Bluebonnet Mall in Fort Worth, would be closed for the day, and the grand opening would be delayed until further notice.

They didn't think much of the announcement, as it didn't involve them.

Stacey asked, "That's not anywhere near the hospital Mrs. Washburn is in, is it?"

Shaking her head, Christina said, "Nope. It's a long way from there."

"I wonder what's going on that they'd close it?" Linda asked, concern filling her voice.

Shrugging, Christina said, "I guess we'll find out sometime this week. It's probably some maintenance thing."

"We're still planning to go see my mom, right?" Linda asked.

Nodding, Christina said, "Of course! Like I said, that mall is a long way from the hospital your mom's in. It's in Fort Worth, and your mom is in Dallas. We'll be fine."

Sighing, Linda said, "Thanks."

During the first praise and worship song, Christina caught movement in her peripheral vision, and turned to see Aaron and Sammie scooch in the row behind her and the kids. During the meet and greet time, after the second hymn, everyone turned, and welcomed each other, with a promise to talk after the service.

Christina had a difficult time focusing on the sermon, as her mind kept returning to thoughts of Aaron. Even though he looked handsome in his black suit, pale blue shirt, and striped tie, and his smile was readily available, and dazzling, there was a reserve about him which seemed to indicate something was missing. She would notice sometimes, his smile didn't reach his eyes. *Perhaps he had fleeting thoughts of his deceased wife, and would feel a pang of sadness. I know I must look like that on occasion when thoughts of David float past my mind's eye.*

She and Aaron had never been on a formal date. It seemed every time they'd planned to go out, something would happen, and they'd have to cancel. Sure, they'd had lunch together after church and at the hospital, and she was thankful for that, but a one on one date just hadn't happened yet. *Is God keeping us apart? Are we destined to be just co-workers?* As her mind wandered from thought to thought, the sermon ended, and people began to stir. As they stood for the final song, she could feel Aaron's eyes boring a hole in her head, *or is it just my imagination?* She fought the urge to turn and look, until it was time to gather her belongings. By then, he was engaged with Sammie. *Guess I'll never know if he was staring or not,* she thought, as she turned to speak to other congregants. Heading towards the exit, she felt a hand grab hers. Looking down, she saw Sammie's beaming face.

"Mrs. Sanders, Daddy and I would like y'all to join us for lunch, if you can." She grinned, and looked up at her daddy, who was also smiling, and nodding.

Resting his hand on his daughter's shoulder, he asked, "How about it? Y'all want to meet at The Black-eyed Pea?"

Nodding, Christina said, "Sounds good to me. I could go for some chicken-fried steak. Let me check with the kids."

Unbuckling his daughter from her car seat, Aaron was surprised when she threw her arms around his neck and said, "I love you Daddy!"

"I love you too, Honey."

"I miss Mommy, but I'm ready for a new mommy."

Aaron felt his breath catch. Lifting her out of the car, he said, "What brought that on?"

Shrugging, she said, "I just want a mommy with skin on. I like when Mommy visits me, but she hasn't been coming around so much, and she never stays."

Aaron felt tears sting his eyes.

Sighing, and taking his hand, she added, "I want a mommy to fix my hair, and take me shopping."

As he opened the door to the restaurant, she looked up, and asked, "Is it okay if I ask God for a new mommy?"

Speechless, Aaron nodded. During lunch, his mind kept returning to what his daughter had said. The only woman he was remotely interested in, was sitting across from him. *Could she be the one Sammie had in mind, when she thought of a new mommy? Coincidence?*

When Christina looked up, after stuffing a forkful of mashed potatoes in her mouth, and realized Aaron was staring at her, she blushed, and asked, "You okay, Aaron?"

Shaking his head, he said, "Sorry. You just look so happy chowing down that steak, and potatoes."

She chuckled. "It does make me happy. I try to limit my indulgence to about once a month. Otherwise, I'd be big as a house! I can almost feel the gravy clogging my arteries!"

He smiled, and nodded. "I feel the same way about a good T-bone steak. If I didn't have to worry about my cholesterol, I'd be eating one at least once a week."

Wiping her lips with a napkin, she said, "I remember when I was young, and could eat anything without any worries. Now, however, I have to think twice about what goes in my mouth, or it may end up on my hips!"

Nodding, he said, "I've noticed that in the past year or so, my metabolism has slowed. It's like I have to walk, or work out, twice as long to feel any results."

Grinning, she said, "Yep. Getting older isn't always fun."

Glancing over at the kids, at the table across from them, Christina said, "Soon as we're finished, the girls and I are heading up to Dallas to visit Janet."

Nodding, Aaron asked, "How is she doing?"

Lowering her voice so Linda couldn't hear, Chrisitna told of her last visit, and of her concern over Janet's memory loss.

"I don't think Linda picked up on it, but I could tell Janet was struggling, as she tried to put the pieces together. I can't imagine not remembering my children."

"Does the Doctor think it's permanent?"

Shaking her head, Christina said, "No. He seems to think once all the pain meds are out of her system, her mind will begin to clear. She's been on a steady influx of them since the accident."

Glancing over at his daughter, who seemed to be enjoying the attention of the "big kids" as she liked to call them, he said, "Sammie said a most unusual thing today."

Leaning forward, Christina asked, "What did she say?"

"She said she was ready for a new mommy."

Christina sat back, and said, "Has she ever said anything like that before?"

Shaking his head, Aaron said, "No. She tells me that her mom comes to visit her every now and then, but she wants a mommy with skin on. One that will do her hair, and take her shopping."

"Aww. That's so sweet! Kids say the cutest things."

"She then asked if it was okay to ask God for a new mommy."

"Well, I do believe that God hears, and honors the prayers of little kids."

Sighing, and nodding, Aaron said, "Yeah. It'll be interesting to see who God brings into our lives."

Christina smiled, and wiped her mouth. "It will indeed."

Glancing at her watch, she said, "I need to get going. I have to drop the boys off at home, then the girls and I will change clothes, and head on up to Dallas. Hopefully, the traffic won't be too bad."

"At least the weather is nice. You won't have to worry about ice on the roads."

Touching the bruised area on her forehead, that showed up the day after the accident, she chuckled, and said, "Yeah. I could do without ice for a while."

"How is your head doing? And, how are the repairs on your van coming along?"

"My head's fine, and I should have the van back sometime next week. I'll have to admit that I've enjoyed driving the rental. Brad and I have been talking about getting him a car soon. Maybe when we get back from our trip to Michigan."

"Michigan? When are you going there?"

"Oh, I forgot to tell you. We're going over the kid's mid-winter break in February. My in-laws have already reserved the tickets for us."

Smiling, Aaron said, "That's great! I'm sure the kids will enjoy that. Will you be taking Linda as well?"

Christina bit her bottom lip. "I guess if she's still with us, we'll have to take her along. I can't very well leave her home alone. I'll need to ask my in-laws to get her a ticket as well."

After a long night involving the police, SWAT, military, and fire-rescue units, Ed, Tom, and the others, were finally able to head home. They had successfully thwarted the threatened bombing of the mall, and nearby parking garage, capturing not only the perpetrators, but the men behind the plans. The man who had ties to the incidents in Detroit, was found and captured in a nearby apartment complex, along with a couple of other accomplices. The agents found computers, papers, maps, and bomb-making paraphernalia in the main room, tying them all together. They had hit the jack-pot so to speak.

It was nearly six the next morning when Ed and Tom headed out to Ed's van.

"Hey, you want to stop for breakfast at IHOP before heading home?" Tom asked, opening the door of the van.

"Yeah." Ed said, climbing onto the driver's side seat. "I'm still pretty wired about everything."

Nodding, as he fastened his seat belt, Tom said, "Yeah. Me too. You gonna tell Christina about the guy from Detroit?"

Nodding, and looking at his friend, he said, "I think so. What do you think?"

Shrugging, Tom said, "Well, I think she'd like to know that the man who killed her husband is off the streets. I think she deserves that peace of mind."

Turning the key in the ignition, bringing the van to life, Ed said, "My thoughts exactly."

Henry Steil leaned back in his desk chair, resting his hands on his expansive belly. Sighing heavily, he smiled, as he closed his eyes, and watched the days events play like a video across his mind's eye. He hadn't slept in about thirty-six hours, and even though his mind and body ached for sleep, his mind wouldn't rest—yet. He wanted to make absolutely sure his agency hadn't left anything undone. There was no guarantee there wouldn't be another terrorist attempt, or attack, but every cell that was knocked out, and every plan that was thwarted, made the likelihood of imminent danger less likely. The government, and its anti-terrorist agencies, were becoming more diligent with their monitoring devices, and training of personnel. He had been encouraged to hear that all across the nation, the number of graduates from law-enforcement academies had been steadily increasing over the past several years. He reasoned the numbers would continue to rise each year following the 9-11 attack. Many young Americans wouldn't be content to sit on the sidelines as their country became a target for terrorists, and would want to join in the battle. Many would lose their lives, but many would succeed in their mission of protecting America. It would be interesting to see what America would be like in a few years. Hopefully safer.

Stretching, and yawning, he opened his eyes, and stood. He needed to get home, and get some rest. Even though the workday had begun, he felt confident the office could run without his presence—at least for the next eight or so hours. He had competent staff, and if anything extraordinary happened, they'd let him know.

CHAPTER 16

Monday morning. A new beginning of a new week. Christina lay in bed after hitting the alarm button—thinking. She had a few minutes before her feet had to hit the floor. Today would be her first day back on the cardiac unit. She had helped Libby set up the unit on Friday afternoon, in preparation for the weekend arrival of the staff and patients. Everything had been organized, and the unit looked pristine, and ready to handle any cardiac emergency by the time they had left. *I wonder who'll be there today? Sally Jean? Hannah? Sarah? Well, it doesn't matter. I like them all.* Her thoughts about the hospital went on for a few more minutes, then she began to think about yesterday afternoon, and their visit with Janet.

When they walked in the room at the Dallas trauma center, Janet was sitting up in bed. She was smiling, and seemed happy to see them. Linda walked over, put her arms around her mother's neck, then climbed on the bed next to her, and remained there the rest of the visit. Janet, looking less battered and bruised on the outside, still had an air of confusion about her. She kept looking at the three of them—Christina, Linda, and Stacey—like she still couldn't remember who they were, and why they were there visiting. When it was time to leave, Christina sent the girls out first, and stayed behind to talk with Janet.

"Thank you for coming to visit, and bringing Linda, even though I still don't remember her."

Christina nodded, and patted Janet's arm. "You're welcome. I'm glad we can come visit. Has the Doctor given any indication as to when your memory may return?"

Shaking her head slightly, then wincing in pain, Janet said, "No. It's still a mystery. I keep trying to remember things before the accident, and it's like there's a black wall I can't get past."

Sighing, Christina said, "I'll keep praying for complete healing, and resolution to this."

Nodding, Janet said, "Yeah. I'm tired of being in this bed, even though I can now sit on the side. Sometime this week, I'll be standing, and possibly using a bedside toilet." Smiling, she added, "That's at least some progress."

Christina smiled, and nodded. "Yes it is. Oh yes, I almost forgot. The kids and I will be flying up to Michigan in a few weeks over mid-winter break, and I was wondering if we could take Linda with us."

"Sure." Janet said. "Who would she stay with, if you didn't take her with you?"

Nodding, Christina said, "I'd have to give that some thought. I'm not sure she'd feel comfortable staying with any one else."

"That's what I think. She seems to have adjusted quite well into your family."

Smiling, Christina said, "Well, we all love her, and feel like she is one of the family."

Nodding, Janet said, "Good. Even though I don't remember her being my daughter, I still care about her."

Patting Janet's arm, Christina said, "Of course you do. Your memory of her will return before you know it, and everything will fall into place."

"I hope so."

"May I pray with you?"

When she had said "Amen," the girls returned, and asked when they could leave.

After another round of "good-byes," the Sanders group left the hospital.

"Lord, please return Janet's memory of Linda. That young girl needs her momma, and Janet needs her. If there's anything else we can do to help, please let us know.

Pushing thoughts of Janet aside, Christina dressed for the day, and headed downstairs. There were so many items vying for her attention, she had to stop, and take a calming breath.

Along with her cup of coffee, she grabbed a pen and pad of paper. Making a list would be a good place to start. She divided her page into three columns, and began listing items that needed to be taken care of immediately, in the next couple of months, and in the future.

One item that was moving up on her priority list, was deciding what she was going to do about a vehicle. Even though Jack had said she could keep the rental indefinitely, she knew that wasn't practical. *Should I go ahead and get the van repaired, and squeeze a couple more years out of it, or should I just get a new one? I need a guy's opinion on this.* Because David had always taken care of those kind of things, she often found herself baffled, and perplexed, when it came to making certain decisions. Thankfully, God had always provided friends or family, who could walk her through the decision process.

As she sipped her coffee in the easy chair, she let her mind continue to wander. She soon heard footfalls on the stairs, signaling another busy day ahead. Setting the pen and pad down, she stood and stretched.

Cindy woke with the simultaneous ringing of her phone, and the buzzing of her alarm clock. She reached for her cell-phone, while turning off the alarm.

"Hello?" She answered sleepily, as she rubbed her eyes, and yawned.

"Good morning, Beautiful!" Answered Ed's cheery voice.

"Hey, Handsome." She said, stretching.

"Did I wake you?"

"Nah. My alarm, and phone rang at the same time. Perfect timing."

Sitting up, she asked, "Where are you?"

"Still in Dallas. We had a crisis we had to deal with yesterday, and last night."

"What kind of crisis?"

He talked her through the previous day and evenings events.

"Oh my goodness! I'm so glad no one was hurt!"

"Us too. It could have escalated into something horrific."

After a moment's silence, Cindy asked, "Are you coming to Alva tonight?"

"I am, but not 'till later. I need to rest up a bit, then head back to the office. I have a lot of paperwork to fill out."

"Okay. Should we expect you for dinner?"

She could sense him nodding. "Yeah. I should be available then. I need to talk to Christina either this evening or tomorrow. I won't be able to spend the night, as I have an early morning conference meeting tomorrow." Pausing, he added, "I miss my girls, and need to see you both."

"Aww. We miss you too. I'm so glad you'll be here, even for a short time. Why do you need to talk to Christina?"

"Do you remember how I said that we believed there was a connection between the Detroit, and Dallas terrorists cells?"

"Yes."

"Well, turns out, we were right." He proceeded to tell her about capturing the man they believe to be responsible for giving David the lethal injection of Heparin in the ambulance, which led to his death.

Cindy couldn't hide her shock. "Oh my goodness! That's like a miracle! What are the odds that you'd find him down here in Dallas? As Christina would say, that's definitely a God thing!"

"Yes. I'd have to agree. What are the odds of finding that particular man at all? Definitely a God thing."

"She'll be so happy to know that all the loose ends are finally tied up, and she can put all her concerns to rest."

Sighing, Ed said, "Her family has been through enough these past two years. I'm thankful this chapter is finished."

"Me too."

"Hey, Babe, I gotta go. I'll see y'all around six tonight. Love you!"

"Love you too. Rest up, and we'll see you soon."

Stretching, as she replaced the phone on the nightstand, Cindy heard a light tapping on her door.

"Mom?"

"Yes, Samara. Come on in."

Samara entered, rubbing her eyes. "Was that Ed on the phone?"

Patting a spot on the bed next to her, Cindy said, "Yeah. He'll be here later."

"Good. I've missed him. I'll be glad when he's here permanently."

Cindy pulled her daughter into a hug. "Yeah. Me too."

After a moment, Samara pulled away, and said, "I've gotta go get dressed." At the door, she asked, "Don't you have that scope-thing sometime this week?"

Nodding, Cindy said, "Yes. On Thursday. If Ed can't take me, Christina said she could, being it's her day off."

Nodding, Samara said, "Okay. Do you know what time?"

Standing, and pulling the covers up on the bed, Cindy said, "Nine-thirty. I have to be there an hour earlier though."

"So you'll be leaving before I do. What if it's raining? Will I still have to walk to school?"

Cindy shook her head. "If it's raining, I'm sure you can call one of your friends to come by and get you."

Shaking her head, Samara said, "Yeah. Of course. I guess my brain's not quite awake yet."

Cindy was dressed for the day, and having her first cup of coffee, when Samara entered the kitchen.

Watching her daughter pour a cup of coffee, and add add enough sugar and cream to mask any coffee flavor, she said, "It looks like a beautiful, but chilly morning. Do you want me to drive you to school, or do you want to walk?"

Glancing outside, Samara made a face and said, "Can you drive me? I want to hang out with my friends, before we have to go in."

Nodding, Cindy said, "Sure. I'll be heading into work anyway. We should be out of here in the next half hour."

"I'll be ready!" Samara called after her mom.

Sheriff Larry Clifton stretched, and sat on the side of the makeshift bed in his office at the police station. Yawning, he stood, and promptly folded the blankets, and stacked them on the pillow, before heading to the restroom, at the back of the building. Washing his hands, he heard the front door open. Sticking his head out to see who had come in, he smiled when he saw his deputy remove his coat, and hang it on the rack.

"Sheriff?" He called, as he headed towards Larry's office.

"Here!" Larry called, as he exited the bathroom.

After greetings, Mike said, "Did you sleep here again?"

Walking over to the coffee maker, Larry nodded, and said, "Yeah. I was finishing up some paperwork."

Pointing to the couch, Mike asked, "How's that on your back?"

Sighing, Larry said, "Not as bad as one would think."

Nodding, Mike asked, "So what's on the agenda today?"

Pouring coffee into a mug, and holding it up, Larry said, "First, I need to drink this."

Mike nodded in understanding. "I think I need one of those too."

After a few minutes of chatting, and drinking their coffees, the men set their mugs down, and began discussing the town's activities.

"All in all, it's been a pretty quiet week," Mike said, running his hand through his hair. "So, what paperwork were you doing last night?"

Sighing, and leaning back in his chair, Larry said, "I was working on closing out the whole Janet Washburn case."

Mike raised his eyebrows in surprise. "Close it out?"

"After visiting her up in Dallas, and speaking with her doctors, it seems pretty evident that she isn't going to be remembering anything, anytime soon. And, since Christina Sanders isn't going to press charges on the Simmons boy, my hands are tied. I might as well close this, and let everyone move on."

Nodding in understanding, Mike said, "I agree." Running his hand over his face, he said, "This has been rough few months, that's for sure."

"Yep. I'm ready for some quiet time. You know, like traffic violations, and domestic disputes."

Grinning, Mike said, "That sounds good."

Just then, Loraine, the sheriff's secretary, walked in.

"Good morning, Boys." She said, removing her coat, and hanging it on the rack.

"Mornin' Loraine." They said in unison.

"Anything exciting on the agenda for today?" She asked, heading to her desk.

"Nope. Not yet." The sheriff said, as he stood.

Walking across the room, he asked, "Can I get you a cup of coffee?"

"That'd be nice. Thanks."

Pulling her chair out to sit, the phone rang. She glanced at the two men before answering the call.

"Sheriff's office. How may I help you?"

Larry and Mike listened, as she took down the information.

Before disconnecting, she said, "I'll send the sheriff, and call for an ambulance."

Grabbing their coats, the men asked, "What's going on?"

"A lady at Wal-Mart said some guy knocked her down in the parking lot, causing her to hit her head, and hurt her arm. He then stole her purse, and a bag of groceries she was carrying. She said, he jumped in a white car with a female driver, and sped away."

Nodding, the sheriff said, "I don't suppose she got a license plate number?"

"No." Loraine said, handing him a piece of paper with pertinent information. "She did apologize for not being more help."

Nodding, the sheriff said, "Come on Mike, let's go catch some bad guys!"

Christina inhaled deeply, as she entered the newly re-furbished Cardiac Care Unit. The smell of fresh paint, disinfectant, and clean linens assailed her senses. She was surprised, that under all the freshness, there was still a lingering smoky odor. Heading to the nurses' lounge to exchange her winter coat for her lab coat, she passed the desk area, and waved at a couple of the aides.

"Hi Christina." One of the gals said in greeting. "What's the weather like?"

Christina stopped, and said, "It's pretty cold, but no precipitation. I heard it's supposed to get up in the forties today."

Nodding, the aide said, "Good. I was hoping I wouldn't have to scrape my windows off."

Because there were only two cardiac patients, the morning report, and rounds with Dr. Dawson were completed within the first hour of her arrival.

Standing at the desk, Dr. Dawson said, "Christina, I have a light schedule today. You want to meet for lunch?"

Smiling, and nodding, she said, "Sure. Twelve-thirty?"

Closing the chart he had been writing in, he returned her smile and said, "Sounds good. See you then."

She watched as he walked through the double doors, and disappeared around the corner.

She hadn't noticed Sally-Jean's approach until the young woman spoke.

"Y'all still dating?"

Christina jumped. "What?"

Giggling, Sally-Jean repeated her question.

"Yeah. Off and on."

"I'm glad. Y'all make a cute couple."

Nodding, Christina said, "Thanks. I think." Returning the chart to the rack, Christina turned, and said, "Come walk with me." As the ladies walked towards the patient's rooms, they talked about their families, and holiday events. After checking in on the two residents, Christina and Sally-Jean continued their conversation in the break room, over a cup of coffee. Christina brought the aide up to date on Janet's condition.

Shaking her head, Sally-Jean said, "Do you think her memory will ever return?"

Shrugging, Christina said, "Only time will tell. The good news is that her body is recovering well. The bones are mending, and she's able to get out of bed."

"She had a lot of broken bones, didn't she?"

Nodding, Christina said, "From what the Doctor said, pretty much every bone in her body was broken or bruised. It was touch and go for a while."

"I remember how bad she was in the beginning." Biting her bottom lip, she asked, "How's the little girl doing?"

Christina smiled. "She's doing well. You know she's living with us?"

Sally-Jean nodded.

"Her cast should be coming off in another week. She'll be so glad to get back to normal."

Sipping the coffee, Sally-Jean asked, "How are your kids adjusting to having a "new sister?"

"I'm so proud of them. They've all taken her presence in stride. I was concerned about jealousy, especially with Stacey." Crossing her fingers, she added, "But so far, so good."

Standing to rinse her cup, and return it to the rack, Sally-Jean said, "Your kids are pretty amazing, considering everything they've been through these past couple of years."

Rinsing, and returning her mug as well, Christina smiled and nodded. "I agree. Their strength, resilience, attitude, and faith, just blow me away. In some ways, they're a lot stronger than I am."

Shaking her head, Sally-Jean said, "I think you're a pretty tough nut too. Not like you haven't had your share of trials."

Christina chuckled. "Someone once said, 'What doesn't kill us makes us stronger!'"

Sally-Jean laughed out loud. "Well, then you should be able to leap tall buildings in a single bound!"

Shaking her head, Christina reached out, and pulled Sally-Jean into a hug. "Not leaping yet, but I can walk on a sidewalk without stepping on a crack!"

"That's a start!" The young woman said, as she stepped out of the break room, and onto the CCU floor.

After filling his lunch tray, Brad looked around the cafeteria for a place to sit. Spotting Jamie Simmons at a table by himself, Brad headed in his direction.

Jamie was hunched over his food, and eating like it was his last meal. Brad pulled the chair out across from him, and sat. Jamie looked up, surprise registering on his face.

Looking around, he mumbled, "Uh, are you sure you want to sit there?"

Brad, smiled, and said, "Yeah. Is there a problem?"

Shaking his head, Jamie said, "No. Just wondering why you'd want to sit across from me."

Looking around the room, Brad shrugged. "Looked like a good place. Besides, I wanted to talk to you."

Jamie's eyes widened. Blushing, and feeling defensive, he sat up, and asked, "About what?"

Opening his milk carton, and taking a sip before speaking, Brad said, "I wanted to see how you're doing. You've had a tough month, and believe it or not, my family does care about you."

"Really? Why? Not like I did y'all any favors."

Brad took a bite of salad. Swallowing, and sighing, he said, "Look Jamie. What you did was a little weird, but everyone does weird things now and then." Shrugging, he added, "You have your reasons. I just want to assure you that my family doesn't hold grudges. We aren't mad at you, or wish any bad karma on you. We just want bygones to be bygones. We want you, and your dad, to get any help you need, or to just be okay, and move on."

Jamie lowered his head, and bit his bottom lip. Feeling a lump form in his throat, he couldn't speak right away.

Brad continued eating his lunch, aware that Jamie was having an internal struggle. He felt Jarrod's hand on his shoulder, and heard God's voice in his head. *"Just wait, Brad."*

Brad watched as emotions played across Jamie's face, before he finally spoke.

Holding his hands up as if in surrender, Jamie said, "Brad, I'm so sorry for breaking into your house."

Nodding, Brad said, "I know."

"It's just that I..." He paused, rubbing his eyes, as he gathered his words. "I wanted to be close to your family." Placing his hands on the table, he continued. "My mom left when I was young, and my dad sorta went into a depression, and almost forgot I was his son." Wiping his eyes, he continued. "Anyway, I just wanted a family, and yours seemed so perfect." Holding his hands up, he said, "I know, breaking into your house was a stupid way to achieve that goal."

Pushing his tray aside, Brad leaned forward, and said, "Jamie, I'm not here to judge you. You already explained yourself, and your actions, and we have forgiven you. What you need to do now, is decide what you're going to do with this second chance. Are you going to continue in this weird and eventually destructive behavior? Or, are you going to make a choice to be a better person, and reach for another, more prosperous goal?"

Looking directly into Brad's eyes, Jamie said, "I do want to do better. I just haven't got a clue as to what I want to do, or which direction to take."

Brad nodded. "I struggle with that myself. At this point in my life, I know God has something big planned for me, but I haven't a clue as to what the plan is, or how to get there."

Jamie gave a crooked smile. "So, what do we do until we know for sure what we're supposed to do?"

Brad shrugged. "I guess, just do our best at whatever we're doing, and keep praying, and asking God which direction He wants us to take."

Jamie leaned back in his chair, crossing his arms across his chest. Shaking his head, he said, "I don't think God is going to listen to me, much less talk to me."

Jamie smiled, "Oh, but that's not true, Jamie. God is so ready for you to acknowledge Him. He wants to have a relationship with you."

Leaning forward, and resting his arms on the table, Jamie asked, "And how do you know this?"

Brad smiled and said, "Let me tell you a story about when I died."

Jamie's eyes grew wide. "You died?"

Brad nodded, then began telling Jamie about his near-death-experience, or NDE as some people call it.

Jamie sat in captivated silence, as Brad went into detail about his encounter with God, and heaven. The two boys were unaware of the clatter, chatter, and chaos going on around them. It was as if they were in an invisible dome, so focused were they on the story. They had no idea that the angels were protecting them from human, and demonic, interference.

When Brad finished his monologue, he asked, "So Jamie, have you ever asked God to be Lord of your life?"

Jamie looked confused. "Lord of what?"

"Your life. If you want to have a relationship with God, you need to invite Him into your life."

"Isn't He already in my life?"

Brad sighed. "In a sense, He is. We live in His world, and He controls what takes place, but for Him to be in control of *your* life, you have to relinquish it to Him."

Jamie pinched the bridge of his nose, and was silent for a moment, as he contemplated all that Brad had said. *I've certainly made a mess of my life, so far. I could use some divine guidance.* Brad could sense the battle going on in Jamie's mind, and he prayed for the Holy Spirit's intervention.

Looking up, with resolve in his voice, Jamie asked, "How do I do that?"

Smiling, Brad said, "It's easy." After explaining the way to redemption, he led Jamie in a simple prayer.

When finished, Jamie said, "Wow! It feels like a ton of bricks have been lifted off my back!"

Brad nodded. Chuckling, he said, "I've heard other people say things like that."

Cocking his head, Jamie asked, "How does that work? One minute I feel like I've got an elephant on my back, then I pray, and poof, it's gone!" He made a hand gesture of a bomb exploding.

"I know! God is pretty amazing!"

"Yes, but how does He do it?"

Nodding, Brad said, "I think there are evil entities—which we can't see—that attach themselves to us, and influence how we feel, and what we say and do."

"Like demons?"

Nodding, Brad continued. "When we ask God to be our Savior, He sends His Holy Spirit to live in us, which help us control the evil ones. They can't occupy our mind, or body, when the Holy Spirit lives in us."

"Who is Satan, and what role does he play?"

"Satan, or Lucifer, or any other names he's given, was once an angel, but he led a rebellion in Heaven against God, and was cast down to Earth."

The bell rang, causing both boys to look at the clock on the wall.

"Do you need to get to class?" Brad asked Jamie.

"I could, but I'd rather stay, and continue our discussion."

Nodding, Brad said, "Yeah, me too. I don't want either of us to get into trouble for skipping classes though. Why don't we pick up where we left off, either after school today, or lunchtime tomorrow?"

Sighing heavily, Jamie said, "Alright. I really want to learn more about this whole God-thing. I feel so different. Energetic. Happy. It's been a long time since I've felt this way."

Brad gathered his books, and stood. As they left the cafeteria, Brad reached out for a handshake, and Jamie pulled him in for a hug.

"Thanks, Man. See you after school?"

Brad said, "Yeah. You're welcome to walk home with us, and we can talk more."

"You have to walk home?"

"I have to get Stacey and Linda first, but yeah. It's nice out."

"Hey, I have a car. Why don't I take y'all home? It's a nice day and all, but it is chilly."

Nodding, Brad said, "That'll work. We'll meet you in the back lot?"

"Sounds good! See you later!"

Brad watched Jamie limp off to his classroom, then turned to go to his. Looking up, and doing a fist pump, he said, "Thanks God. That was awesome!"

CHAPTER 17

Thursday morning, Cindy's alarm rang at four o'clock. She felt as if she had just drifted off, and moaned as she reached over to hit the button. She heard the toilet flush, and surmised it was Ed. Ed. Her future husband. She stretched, and smiled, as images of him crossed her mind's eye.

He had arrived the previous evening, bringing pastries from a Czech bakery near Dallas. Being on a liquid diet for the endoscopy, and colonoscopy, she was unable to eat one. She sipped her hot tea while Ed and Samara enjoyed their treats.

When Ed realized she couldn't eat one, he apologized, promising he'd buy her a whole box of them after her procedure.

She laughed. "Yeah. I'll be ravenous by then!"

When she heard him head for the kitchen, she grabbed her clothes, and crept to the bathroom. After dressing, she joined him. He was sitting at the table sipping a cup of coffee.

"Hey, Beautiful." He said in greeting.

She leaned down, and planted a kiss on his lips. He grabbed her, and pulled her onto his lap. They both giggled. She rested her head on his shoulder.

After a moment of silence, he asked, "So, are you ready for your tests?"

Nodding, she said, "As ready as I'll ever be. I just hope the Doc finds something to explain this anemia."

"Yeah. That would be nice." They held each other a few more minutes, then Cindy stood, to announced it was time to go. Ed finished his coffee, as Cindy donned her outerwear. The weather man on the previous night's news said the day was supposed to be clear, and a few degrees above freezing. Samara had clapped her hands in relief. She was happy there wouldn't be any kind of precipitation she'd have to deal with on her way to and from school.

Ed went out to start the car, while Cindy tiptoed into her daughter's room, and gently kissed her forehead. Samara barely stirred.

The drive to Dallas was uneventful, and Cindy was checked in and prepped within an hour of arriving. Ed stayed with her until she was wheeled into the procedure room. He had brought some reading material, but ended up leaning his head back, and dozing. It had been a busy and difficult week, and he was mentally, and physically beat. He was dreaming of riding a horse through a field when he heard his name called.

"Mr. Florres?"

He was instantly awake.

"Yes?"

"You may go back to your wife's room. She's just coming out of the anesthesia."

He almost said, "She's not my wife," but decided it wouldn't matter. Standing, he gathered his belongings, and followed the nurse. Walking into the curtained area, he saw Cindy sitting up, with her eyes closed. She looked so angelic. Walking over, he took her hand, and whispered, "Time to wake up, Sleepy Head."

Cindy coughed, and opened unfocused eyes.

Ed patted her hand, and said, "Hey, Babe."

She closed her eyes, and was back to sleep. The nurse came in to check her vital signs, and encouraged Cindy to wake up. She increased the IV flow to help wash out the anesthesia still floating around in her blood. After a half-hour, Cindy was fully awake, and ready to use the restroom. When she returned to her bed, the Doctor walked in.

"Mrs. Murray." Glancing at Ed, he asked, "And you are?"

Ed reached out his hand. "I'm Ed Florres. Her fiance."

Nodding, the Doctor said, "I'm Doctor Kavanaugh. I did Cindy's procedure."

Signaling for Ed to follow, he approached Cindy's bed, and handed her a stack of photos.

Confusion registering on her face, she asked, "What are these pictures of?"

Dr. Kavanaugh chuckled. "Those are pictures of your stomach, and bowel." He went over each picture, explaining what he saw, and answering their questions.

Pulling up the last photo, he said, "This is the one that causes concern."

"Why?" Cindy asked.

Pointing to a spot at the bottom of the page, he said, "That black spot right there, is where I believe your bleeding is originating from."

Ed picked up the photo for a closer look.

"What is that?"

"That, is a duodenal ulcer. It was difficult to find, as it is right below the junction of the stomach, and small intestine."

Cindy made a face. "So what can be done about it?"

"I cauterized it, but you'll have to go on medication, and a special diet until it heals."

"How do I know when it's healed?"

"I'll check your blood-work, and if it hasn't improved, I'll schedule another endoscopy in about six weeks." Clearing his throat, he said, "That spot is not my only concern." He pulled one of the photos from the stack.

"This is my other concern."

Ed and Cindy looked at the picture, then up to the doctor, confusion etched on their faces.

"This is a picture of your large bowel. See those little dark spots?"

Cindy nodded.

"Those are diverticulum. Are you familiar with the term diverticulitis?"

Cindy and Ed both nodded.

"Well, these are what causes that. Diverticuli are little pouches in the large bowels, that can easily get inflamed, clogged, infected, and sometimes even bleed. I noticed some bleeding from one of these."

Biting her bottom lip, Cindy asked, "What can be done about that?"

Sighing, the doctor said, "Unfortunately, not much. Usually these heal on their own, otherwise, I have to go in and remove the damaged area. Hopefully, it won't come to that, but that too can explain your anemia." Ed took Cindy's hand.

"The good news is that there is no cancer, or any other disease that I can see. The two spots can be treated, and in time, will heal. In the meantime, take your medicine, and watch your diet."

Cindy and Ed both nodded.

"Oh, and I'd like you to make an appointment with Dr. Harrison to get blood-work done in two weeks. If there's any improvement, then I'll have you continue on the medicine and diet, and I'll see you in about six weeks. If there's still anemia, I'll schedule another scope." He patted Cindy's hand, then reached out to shake Ed's.

Cindy nodded, and said, "Thank you Dr. Kavanaugh."

"I'm just glad it's nothing more serious." He said, before exiting the room.

Cindy and Ed both exhaled audibly.

Ed bent down, and kissed Cindy's forehead. The nurse came in, removed the IV, and gave Cindy instructions on what she should and shouldn't do, as well as what to expect in the next 24 hours. As she handed Cindy the pamphlet outlining a diet plan, she said, "One of the main things you need to do, is avoid anything with tiny seeds. They can get caught in the diverticuli, and cause problems."

Cindy nodded. "Got it."

The nurse patted Cindy's arm, and said, "Mrs. Murray, you may get dressed, and I'll call for a wheelchair. Mr. Murray, you can bring the car up to the entrance."

Ed almost corrected the young nurse, but decided to let it go. When she left the room, Cindy giggled and said, "Mr. Murray?"

Smiling, he shrugged and said, "It kinda has a nice ring to it. Maybe I should take your last name, instead of you taking mine."

Cindy shook her head, and asked him for her bag of clothes under the bed.

He said, "I'll be waiting for you with a nice warm car."

When they were on the road toward Alva, Cindy called Christina to inform her of the doctor's findings, then fell asleep, and had to be roused when Ed pulled into the driveway.

Walking to the door, he said, "Babe, why don't you go to bed, and I'll do some computer work?"

Yawning, she said, "That sounds like an excellent idea. Please let Sasha out, and make sure she has food and water."

"Will do." Unlocking the front door, he walked in first to grab Sasha before she jumped on Cindy.

The little dog wiggled, and whimpered, and tried to jump out of Ed's strong hands. It was obvious she wanted to greet her mistress. Cindy reached out, and let Sasha lick her hand.

Scratching behind the ears of the wriggling bundle of energy, Cindy said, "It's okay, Baby. I'll pet you later."

Ed said, "You go to bed. I've got this."

She nodded, and yawning, made a bee line to her room.

Brad met the girls at the middle-school, and together they walked to the parking lot behind the high school, to meet Jamie. Brad saw Samara walk past, and called out to her.

"Hey, Samara!"

Turning, she smiled, and waved, then headed in the group's direction.

"What are y'all doing out here?" She asked, looking around the lot.

Brad answered, "We're waiting for a ride."

Arching her eyebrows, she asked, "Who with?"

Stacey said, "Jamie Simmons."

Cocking her head, Samara asked, "Isn't he the guy who broke into your house?"

Nodding, Brad said, "Yes."

Looking confused, Samara asked, "Why in the world would you be getting a ride with him?"

Brad shrugged. "He offered."

Making a face, she said, "I don't get it."

"I talked to Jamie at lunch today, and we have some unfinished talking to do, so he offered to take us home, and continue our conversation."

Nodding, and shrugging, Samara said, "Oh. Okay." Pulling her scarf tighter, she asked, "Do you think he could drop me off at home too. It's a lot colder than I expected."

Looking past her shoulder, Brad said, "He's coming now. We can ask him."

Jamie walked up, and greeted everyone. Samara asked about a ride, and he said "Sure."

Looking at Brad, then Jamie, Samara said, "Man, you two could be brothers, or twins."

Nodding, Brad said, "Yeah. I hear that a lot."

Jamie chuckled. "Weird, huh?"

The ride to Samara's house was short, but noisy, as everyone had stories to tell.

After dropping her off, Jamie asked, "How old is Samara?"

Brad said, "She's fourteen."

Jamie nodded. "She's pretty."

Brad furrowed his brows. "You can't date her."

Jamie blushed. "I know!" Looking at Brad, he said, "I'm just stating an observation."

Brad nodded. "You're right. She is pretty."

The girls giggled.

As Jamie drove past the elementary school, Brad noticed Nicky, and asked if they could stop and get him.

Jamie said, "Sure." He did a double tap on the horn. Nicky, not recognizing the car, kept walking. Brad stepped out, and waved, and Nicky came running over.

Nicky greeted everyone, as he climbed into the car. "You didn't have to stop. It's only a few more steps to our house."

Jamie said, "Yeah, but we were headed that way anyway."

Nicky shrugged, and made a face. "Okay."

Stacey said, "Jamie and Brad have some unfinished business to talk about. That's why we're here."

Nodding in understanding, Nicky asked, "What kind of business?"

Brad turned to look at his little brother. "None of *your* business."

Nicky rolled his eyes and said, "Whatever."

Pulling into the driveway of the Sanders house, Jamie felt his heart accelerate as adrenalin pumped through his body. The last time he was here, it had not ended well.

When they entered the back door, Benji greeted them with a wagging tail, and busy nose and tongue, as he sniffed, and licked each hand that reached out to pet him. Nicky filled the food and water bowl, and grabbed an apple, before heading upstairs to his room.

Stacey and Linda grabbed a bag of chips, and two sodas, then followed Nicky up the stairs. Brad offered Jamie a cold drink, and stuck a bag of popcorn in the microwave. Both boys headed to the den, where they sat at opposite ends of the couch.

Brad asked, "Do you remember what we were talking about when we were so rudely interrupted by the bell?

Jamie scratched his head, as he thought back to their previous conversation.

"We were talking about the devil and his role in our lives."

Nodding, Brad said, "Ah, yes. Lucifer. Did you know his name means "Light Bearer?"

Shaking his head, Jamie said, "I never heard of that. Seems like he's more of a darkness bearer."

"I agree. His deeds are certainly dark and evil. He used to be one of God's favorite angels, until he decided he wanted to kick God off the throne. He led a rebellion among the angels, and he, and his followers were cast down to earth."

"If God created all the universes out there, why did He cast Satan down to our earth? Why not put him and his angels onto another planet far away, so they couldn't bother us?"

"That's a good question." Massaging his forehead in thought, he said, "I have no answer. There are some things God doesn't reveal to us humans. Maybe when we get to heaven, we can ask."

Smiling, Jamie said, "Well, if He decides to take you on another tour, you can ask Him then."

Brad chuckled. "Yeah."

Pausing a moment, Brad asked, "Do you have any other questions? I may not have the answers, but I'll share what I know."

"The main one I have is, where do I go from here? I asked God to forgive me, and I feel like He did, now what?"

Benji came running in, and jumped on the couch between the boys, going from one to the other for a pat, and a scratch before settling in, next to Brad.

"First off, do you have a Bible?"

Nodding, Jamie said, "I do. My mom gave it to me when I turned ten."

"Do you know what version it is?"

"Version?"

"You know. King James, NIV, New King James?"

Shrugging, Jamie said, "I'm not sure."

"Well, it doesn't really matter. My Bible is the NIV translation. I find it easier to read and understand, because it is in modern English as opposed to Old English in the King James Version."

Nodding, Jamie said, "I'll find it, and bring it to school tomorrow. We can compare it then."

Brad nodded. "That'll work. We can meet at lunch again. Besides reading the Bible, attending a good Bible believing church is a good start as well."

"Why? I already attend the Enlightened Ones church."

Brad sighed. He didn't want to push too hard, but he had a feeling the Enlightened Ones didn't use the Bible as a reference. "I know. But, do they use the Bible as their main reference book, or do they use something different?"

Jamie thought for a moment. "I've never seen or heard them speak about the Bible. They do use some kind of reference book, however."

"Tell me about their meetings, and what they discuss."

Jamie took a sip of his drink, sat it on the end table, and began explaining the Enlightened Ones beliefs and practices.

Brad sat in silence, occasionally sipping his drink, or taking a bite of popcorn from the bowl between them.

When Jamie finished, Brad said, "That's interesting. It seems to me, they are worshiping the created things, and giving them power, instead of worshiping the Creator of those things."

Jamie frowned, "I never thought of that, but yeah. You're right."

"It's like thanking the parts of a watch, instead of the person who put the parts together to make it work."

Grabbing a handful of popcorn, Jamie said, "I guess it would be smarter to give God the credit, instead of the things He created. Those things, only have power if He says they do, right?"

Nodding, Brad said, "Yes. God has been known to speak through animals, and burning bushes, so I'm pretty sure, He can speak or direct anything in His creation, to do His bidding."

Looking puzzled, Jamie asked, "Animals? Burning bushes?"

Brad chuckled. "You'll read about those in the Bible. I think you'll find them quite interesting."

Jamie grinned. "I can hardly wait! Do I start at the beginning of the Bible, or somewhere in the middle?"

Brad thought for a moment. "Since you have very limited Biblical background, why don't you start in Genesis. That'll give you the background, and foundation for you to grow on."

Nodding, Jamie said, "Okay, but can you help me? Could we do some kind of study together?"

Brad considered this. "I have a pretty busy schedule with school and work, but we might be able to work something in."

Grinning, Jamie said, "That'd be great!"

Brad said, "How would you feel about meeting me at church this Sunday? I'll introduce you to the youth pastor."

Nodding, Jamie said, "That sounds good. What time?"

"Sunday School starts at nine-thirty, and church service at eleven."

Raising his hand for a high-five, Jamie said, "I'll be there at nine-thirty. You want to meet out front?"

Nodding, and grinning, Brad said, "Yep."

The two boys continued talking, until Jamie looked at his watch, and said, "I have to get going. I promised my dad I'd stop by the shop, and we could go to dinner together."

Both boys stood. Jamie reached out his hand, and Brad pulled him into a hug.

"Thanks, Man." Jamie said, wiping his eyes as he turned to go.

Brad walked him to the door. Jamie walked to his car, and Brad shouted, "See you tomorrow in the cafeteria!"

Jamie waved, and did a thumbs up sign.

Brad leaned against the front door, and let his mind wander through all that had transpired that day. *I might not know exactly what God wants me to do, but in the meantime, I'm gonna do my best to shine for Him, and point people in His direction. As mom always says, "Be salty and bright!"*

He felt a familiar warmth, and knew he was on the right track.

As Jamie drove to the repair shop, his mind revisited the events of the day. He found it interesting that he had formed a bond with Brad in the same location as he and Jimmy had formed theirs. *Jimmy. I sure miss you, Buddy.* He felt his eyes burn, as they filled with tears. He wondered if Jimmy was having a great time in Heaven. *Is he even in Heaven? Of course he's in Heaven. Surely God wouldn't send him to hell. He was a good person. No, a great person. Guess I won't know, 'till I get there.*

His thoughts went to his dad. The biopsy came back negative for cancer, but he had something called emphysema. From what his dad said, he could live another twenty or so years, but he'd get winded easily. *I guess thirty years of smoking did a job on his lungs. I'm so glad he finally quit.*

Pulling into the driveway of the shop, he cut the motor, and exited the car. Grabbing the crutches from the back seat, he hobbled up to the entrance.

The guys stopped what they were doing, and greeted him.

"Hey, where's my dad?" He asked the nearest mechanic.

"He's out back. Digging around for a bumper to match this car."

Jamie looked through the back door, and decided he'd just wait in the office. It was cold, and his ankle ached.

"Tell my dad I'll be in the office."

"Sure thing."

When Jack Simmons returned from the back lot, the mechanic pointed to his office. He could see his son sitting behind the desk, with his foot propped up. Handing the bumper off to the mechanic, he entered the office.

"Hey, Son." He said in greeting.

Jamie sat up. "Hi, Dad. How are you feeling?"

Jack smiled. His son hadn't asked him that in quite a while.

"I'm doing okay. Just glad to be alive."

Jamie smiled. "Me too."

Jack felt a tightness in his chest, as surprise, and joy, filled him. Clearing his throat, he asked, "How was your day?"

Before answering the question, Jamie said, "Dad, do you have a few minutes? I have something to tell you, and a few questions to ask."

Jack nodded, and pulled a chair up in front of the desk. Jamie stood.

"You want to sit here?"

Jack shook his head. "Nah. You sit there. Some day, you might be sitting there all the time."

Jamie nodded. He knew what his dad meant, but wasn't sure he wanted the life of an auto mechanic. He sat, and leaned forward with his elbows on the desk.

He told his dad about his meeting with Brad, then asked him about his own spiritual encounter with God. After about an hour of dialogue, both Simmons men were bowing their heads, and asking for a deeper relationship, with each other, as well as God.

Once done, they both stood, and embraced. Both men fought back tears of joy, and sadness. Joy that their relationship had finally been healed, but sadness at all the lost time, and lost lives in the process.

Jamie pulled away, and said, "This is gonna sound weird, but I wonder if Jimmy had to die so our relationship with each other, and with God, could be healed?"

Jack nodded slightly, and said, "I've wondered that myself. I'm not sure God works that way, but He can take a bad situation, and work it for His glory. We just have to be willing to let Him, and trust that He has our best interest at heart. It's an act of our will. We can give our hearts and lives to Him, or we can turn our backs and walk away. Kinda like I did so many years ago."

Jamie nodded in understanding. "Brad said kinda the same thing in his eulogy for Jimmy."

Jack said, "Yes. I'm so thankful God gives us more chances to turn around, and come back to Him. That was one of the talking points at Promise Keepers. No matter where you are, or what you've done, God is big enough to forgive and forget, and make you brand new."

"From what you've said, that was an amazing event. Can we go this year? Maybe take Brad?"

Jack nodded, and pulled his son into another hug. "That would be great!"

They heard a knock at the door.

"Sorry to bother you Boss, but there's someone here to see you."

Jack left Jamie in the office, and went to take care of business.

Jamie could hardly believe how amazing he felt. Sure his ankle was still broken, and throbbed with each movement, but the rest of him felt as if he was buzzing with electric energy. He felt as if he could leap tall buildings in a single bound. Of course he knew he wasn't Superman, and couldn't defy gravity, but the heaviness he had carried with him the past five years since his mother had disappeared, was gone. He could think of her, and not feel anger, sadness, or abandonment. He was so thankful her body had been found, and that chapter of his life could be finished. Yes, he was sad she had died, but at least she hadn't abandoned him, and his dad. Smiling, he thought, *I am indeed, a new person.*

Janet opened her eyes when she heard a familiar voice call her name. Standing next to her bed was the day shift nurse, Charlotte, and the aide, Iris.

In a perky voice, as she raised the head of the bed, Charlotte said, "Good morning, Sleepy Head. I have some good news for you!"

Janet stretched, and moaned, as pain shot through her limbs.

Yawning, she asked, "What's the good news?"

"We're moving you out of the ICU, to a bed on the second floor."

"What's on the second floor?"

Iris began gathering the bathing paraphernalia, as Charlotte spoke. "Your room will be closer to the rehabilitation center."

"Why there?" Janet asked, as she leaned forward, so Iris could remove her gown.

Grinning, the nurse said, "Because, my dear, the doctor is planning on removing at least two of your casts, or maybe all four today."

Janet gave her a shocked look. "What?"

Charlotte continued, "You will be scheduled to do rehab at least once a day in the beginning, then he'll increase it to two or three times a day, until you are able to function on your own."

Janet raised her eyebrows in disbelief. "He thinks I'm ready to have these casts removed?"

Filling the wash basin with warm water, and wetting the wash cloth, Iris said, "That's what he told us."

Taking the warm cloth, Janet began washing her face, and asked, "How long has it been since the accident?"

Iris took the washcloth, and handed Janet a towel, as Charlotte removed the blanket and sheets from the bed.

"It's been a couple of months."

Janet sighed. "I wish I could remember."

Nodding, the nurse said, "You will, eventually."

Shaking her head, Janet said, "You think so?"

Charlotte stood out of the way, as the aide continued bathing Janet. When it was time to change the bottom sheet, she helped roll Janet onto one side, as she pushed the sheet under, then rolled her to the other side to continue the process. Soon, Janet and her bed were clean. New sheets and blankets were placed on, and around her.

Smiling, Iris said, "Just think, you will be able to take a shower, and won't have to use a bedpan anymore."

"That will be awesome!" Janet said, when they had finished. "I'm gonna miss y'all. You've taken such good care of me these past few weeks."

Both ladies nodded, and smiled. Iris spoke first. "We'll miss you too, but are happy you're progressing."

Charlotte said, "I agree with Iris. Someone will be here in an hour or so, to get you checked in downstairs."

"Will y'all come visit me sometime?"

Charlotte smiled. "Of course." Patting Janet's hand, she said, "Why don't you rest? The doctor will be in before you head downstairs." Janet yawned, and said, "Sure."

Iris lowered the head of the bed, and put pillows under Janet's arms, before exiting the room.

Janet closed her eyes, and was asleep within minutes. She dreamed about the young girl who claimed to be her daughter.

She woke with a start, when she felt someone's hand on her arm. Opening her eyes, she was pleased to see it was Dr. Knorr, and Charlotte.

"Hello Janet."

Swallowing, and clearing her throat, she said, "Hello Dr. Knorr. How are you today?"

Smiling, he said, "I'm doing well. I assume the nurse told you that I'll be removing your casts today?"

Janet motioned for the nurse to raise the head of the bed. Once in a sitting position, she said, "That's what she said, but I have to ask. All of them?"

Chuckling, he said, "Yes. I've looked at your x-rays, and they show that all the bones have healed nicely."

Shaking her head, she said, "I've gotten so used to them, I'm almost afraid."

"Afraid? Why?"

Biting her bottom lip, she said, "I know this sounds silly, but I guess I'll feel naked, and insecure without them."

Smiling, and nodding, he said, "I understand. They've been on a long time. It's only natural to think of them as part of your anatomy. It will feel so good to have them off though. We'll start slow on the rehab, as your arms and legs will be very weak from lack of motion." Donning a pair of gloves, he added,

"If I let you continue wearing the casts, your muscles will continue to atrophy, and you'll have to work harder, to get them back in shape."

Janet nodded. "I know. I'll cooperate."

He patted Janet's hand, and reached for the cast saw.

"As you know, this will not cut you." She nodded.

"Also, it will be noisy, and you'll feel the vibrations." She nodded again.

Thirty minutes later, all four casts were disassembled, and piled onto the bedside tray table.

Janet looked down at her arms and legs, and inhaled sharply. They looked more like twigs than arms and legs. It was definitely going to take a while to get them back to normal.

"I must have lost a lot of weight while here."

Charlotte looked at her chart. "It says here that you've lost at least twenty-five pounds since you've been here. You may have lost some at the other hospital as well."

Janet looked surprised. "Well, I bet once my appetite kicks in, that weight will start adding up."

Dr. Knorr said, "Plus, building up muscle mass will bring your weight up as well. You're thin, but not at a dangerous level. Once you're moved downstairs, I'll ask the kitchen to increase you calorie intake. Since you're more alert, and able to eat and drink, I'll have that IV removed as well."

Nodding, and trying to lift her arms, which felt like a baby elephant was attached to each, she said, "Speaking of food, I think I slept through breakfast, is it time for lunch yet?"

Charlotte chuckled, and nodded. "It is. They should be bringing you food in a few minutes."

Patting her arm once again, Dr. Knorr said, "All in all Janet, you are progressing well. Do you have any questions?"

"Just one."

"Yes?"

"When will my memory return? I'd like to at least remember my daughter."

Shaking his head, the doctor said, "That, I'm not sure of. I will schedule you a neurological consultation. Since the amnesia came on suddenly, it may be related to the medication you've been on. If that's the case, I'll have to figure out which med is causing it."

Nodding, Janet said, "If that's not the case?"

Shrugging, he said, "Well, then we'll just have to rely on time to heal whatever is broken in your brain, or you will have to adjust, and make new memories."

Shaking her head, Janet said, "Hopefully, it's just caused by all the meds I've been on."

"That's what I hope. The neurologists name is Dr. Kennedy. He'll either see you today or tomorrow."

"Okay."

"Any other questions?"

Biting her bottom lip, Janet shook her head.

"Well, I'll see you tomorrow, downstairs." He turned, and left the room, leaving Janet and Charlotte.

Charlotte said, "I'll be right back. I have to go get a couple of things so I can remove the IV."

Once the IV was removed, and lunch was consumed, Janet asked to have her head lowered, and settled in for a nap. Her arms and legs felt weirdly light. She was able to curl up on her side, with the help of extra pillows to support her arm and leg. As she slept, a man in a white tunic came to her, and said, "Most of your memory will return." She asked him why only a portion would return. He had smiled, and said, "Some memories are best left behind."

CHAPTER 18

Nicky's eleventh birthday fell on Monday, January 14th, so Christina planned his party for the Saturday before, on the 12th. He, and three of his friends, wanted to see the new Spiderman movie, showing at the Texas theater in Alva. Christina called the other mothers, and agreed get the boys. They would see the movie, then come back to her house to have cake, ice cream, and play games.

Before the celebration was to take place in the afternoon, Christina took Linda to have her cast removed.

Linda's appointment with Dr. Seltzer, the second pediatrician in Alva, was at ten-o'clock. Linda was excited, and nervous, at the same time. Having never had a cast removed before, she was skeptical when Dr. Seltzer brought the saw out. Her eyes grew big.

"Where's Dr. Carmichael?" She asked.

Sensing her fear, he said, "It's his day off." Scrunching his face, he added, "Sorry. You get me today."

Pointing to the saw, she asked, "Is that even safe? Are you gonna cut the cast with that? Is it gonna hurt?"

Holding the saw up for her to examine, he said, "This saw looks dangerous, but it will only cut the cast, and not your skin." He demonstrated this by running it over his arm. She and Stacey gasped in surprise.

"See. No harm."

Looking skeptical, she held out her arm, saying, "Okay. If you say so."

He smiled, and proceeded to remove the cast.

Linda gasped when she saw her arm. "Oh my goodness! It's all wrinkly and thin!"

"That's because it's been in a cast for six weeks. Don't worry, the color will come back, and once you start using it more, the shape will also return."

Shaking her head in disbelief, she said, "Are you sure?"

Nodding, smiling, and holding up his fingers in a Boy Scout salute, he said, "Absolutely." After checking her arm thoroughly, he asked, "Do you want to keep the cast?"

Shaking her head, she said, "No way! That thing stinks!"

"I would imagine so, but it's got a lot of neat art work and names on it. Maybe you could spray it with Lysol and keep it for a while?" Scrunching her face, she said, "No thanks."

Shrugging, he said, "Okay, as he threw the cast, and other items, in the trash can.

"I want you to start rehab on Monday. In the next couple of days, however, I want you to do a few exercises. They will help strengthen the arm and wrist. It will feel pretty weird at first, because your arm has been resting, and it won't want to cooperate, but you'll need to push through, and keep working it. Once you start rehab, you'll be surprised at how fast you'll get back to normal."

Nodding, then looking over at Christina and Stacey, she said, "Okay."

Stacey said, "We'll help remind you to use that arm."

With a lopsided smile, Linda sighed, and said, "Thanks."

The Dr. patted her shoulder, and said, "I need you to make an appointment for six weeks with either Dr. Carmichael, or myself. We'll want to see how you're progressing."

On the way home, Linda asked if she could call her mother, and tell her about the removal of the cast. Christina said, "Why don't we wait until we get back from the movie, or maybe even tomorrow, after church?"

Sighing, Linda said, "Okay. Tonight or tomorrow will be fine."

When Christina and the girls returned home, she sorted through the mail, finding a card from Lula. She called Nicky into the kitchen, and handed it to him. He ripped it open, and found a birthday card, and picture of Lula and her guinea pig, Sweet Pea. The card had a picture of a boy on a skateboard and said, "Happy Birthday to a boy who's going places!"

Inside, she had written, "*Nicky, I hope you have a wonderful birthday. Sweet Pea and I are doing well. We're both getting fat! I'm starting a Zumba—exercise class—next week. I wonder if they'll let Sweet Pea come with me? We'd sure love it, if you could come for a visit sometime. Take care of yourself, and tell your family hi for me. I hope your mom isn't still mad at me.*" She signed it, "*Love, Lula aka Ruby, and Sweet Pea.*"

Nicky looked up at his mom. "Are you still mad at Ruby?"

Christina sighed, and pulled Nicky into a hug. "No. I was at the time of the abduction, because I was so afraid for you, but I have forgiven her, and only feel sad for her."

Nicky sighed, and said, "Yeah. Me too." Stepping back, he asked, "Do you think we could go visit her sometime?"

Christina cocked her head. "Maybe. Let me think about that."

Looking up at the clock, she said, "We need to leave in the next half hour to go pick up the boys."

Nicky grinned. "I hear the Spider man move is awesome!" Running up the stairs to retrieve his backpack, he almost collided with the girls who were heading downstairs.

"Hey, Linda. How's your arm?"

"It's sore." She replied as he ran past her.

Stopping at the top of the stairs, he said, "Danny says it feels weird, and rubbery at first, but it gets better."

"Yeah. It does feel weird, and rubbery. When did he have a cast?"

"A couple of years ago." Shrugging, he added, "Can't even tell he broke his arm."

Nodding, and shrugging, Linda said, "Okay." The girls continued down, as he headed to his room.

Brad exited his room, and almost collided with Nicky.

"Whoa! Where are you going in such a hurry?"

"We're going to see the Spiderman movie."

"Oh, yeah. I almost forgot. What time does it start?"

Nicky hollered down the stairs, "Mom, what time does the movie start?"

She came to the bottom of the stairs, and said, "At one. We need to hustle if we're going to pick up the other boys, and arrive on time."

Brad leaned over the rail, and asked, "Can you drop me off at work? I forgot I had to go in."

Christina looked at her watch, and frowned. "Can you be ready in about five minutes."

"I can in ten."

She sighed heavily. "Okay. Please hurry."

Brad was true to his word. Christina, and the two boys were in the van in record time. The girls opted to stay home, and watch a movie they had rented from the library.

When Christina, Nicky, and his three friends returned home, cake and ice-cream were served, and Nicky opened his presents. His three friends had pooled their money, and bought him a new game for his Nintendo. All four boys disappeared upstairs.

Linda entered the den, and said, "Mrs. Sanders, is it okay to call my mom now?"

Christina gritted her teeth, but managed a smile, and a nod.

"Sure. Let me get my phone."

She glanced at the clock. Seven fifteen. Still early enough to call. She looked up the number, dialed it, then handed the phone to Linda, who walked into the next room.

She came back in almost immediately. "They've moved my mom to a different room on a different floor." Handing a piece of paper to Christina, she said, "Here's the new number."

Christina dialed the number, and was greeted by a familiar voice.

"Janet?" She asked.

"Yes?"

"This is Christina Sanders. There's a young girl here, who would like to talk to you."

Janet hesitated for a moment before consenting.

"Sure."

Christina handed the phone to Linda, and listened as she recapped her experience with the cast removal. Then, Linda disappeared into the front room, and Christina couldn't hear anything else except muffled mumbling.

About fifteen minutes later, Linda returned to the family room, and handed the phone to Christina.

"My mom got all four of her casts removed today as well. I can't imagine having that many casts removed. I know how rubbery this arm feels, can you imagine both arms and both legs feeling like that?"

Christina shook her head. "Where did they move your mom? And why?"

Linda relayed the information she had been given. "When can we go visit her again?"

Christina thought for a moment, before replying. "How about tomorrow afternoon, after church?"

Linda giggled with joy. "Really? That'd be awesome!" She hugged Christina. "Thank you so much!"

Stacey forced a smile. She was happy for Linda, but she didn't want to go to Dallas. She wanted to stay home, and finish reading a novel she had started. She needed some alone time, away from Linda. *How can I say that without hurting her feelings? I love her, but being with her 24/7 is a bit much. She could probably use a break from me as well. I'll ask Mom if I can stay home tomorrow.*

When it was time for Christina and Linda to leave for Dallas, Stacey hugged them both, and thanked them for understanding her need to stay home.

"Brad and Nicky are here, so I won't be totally alone. I'll be praying everything goes well."

Linda hugged her friend, and said, "I'll miss you, but I understand you need to be alone for a while. I'll tell my mom 'hi' for you."

Stacey waved, as the van pulled out of the driveway.

Alone at last! She did a little happy dance, before going to the kitchen for a soda, and a bag of chips. Heading up the stairs, she could hear the muffled noise of Brad's stereo, and Nicky's Nintendo game. She entered her room, set the snacks down on the bedside table, closed the door, picked up her book, and crawled in bed under the covers. A minute later, Chloe jumped on the bed, purring and kneading the pillow next to Stacey's head.

Reaching out, Stacey scratched behind the cat's ears. Chloe laid across Stacey's belly as she continued to purr, enjoying the extra attention.

Stacey began reading where she had left off, and after an hour or so, laid the book down, slid down under the covers, and fell asleep. She was awakened a couple of hours later by a knocking on her door.

She called out, "Who's there?"

Nicky said, "It's me. Do you want anything to eat? Brad is making mac and cheese and hot dogs."

Stacey yawned, and stretched. "Sure. I'll be down in a few minutes."

While the Sanders kids were enjoying a quiet afternoon, Christina and Linda visited with Janet in her new room.

"I like your new room, Mom." Linda said, as she looked at the Dallas skyline through the large window. "The view is much better."

Janet smiled. "Yeah. Beats the brick wall I had in the last room."

Christina smiled, as she watched mother and daughter interact. Janet seemed happy, and less uncomfortable around her, and Linda. When it was time to leave, Janet said, "Christina, could I please talk to you in private?"

Christina nodded, and looked at Linda.

Linda shrugged, and said, "I'll wait in the hallway, Mrs. Sanders."

"Thanks. I'll be out in a minute."

Janet told Christina about her dream, and said, "I began remembering a few more things today."

Christina smiled, "Like what?"

"I remembered what our house looks like, and what kind of car I used to drive."

"Well, that's a start." Christina said, as she patted Janet's arm.

"In case I haven't said it before, I want to thank you again for taking care of my girl. I'm trying really hard to get better, so I can come home."

"How much longer do you have to be here?" Christina asked, looking around the room.

Janet sighed heavily. "At least six more weeks. Depends on how quickly my limbs regain their strength."

Nodding, Christina said, "I see. We'll continue to pray for a quick healing. Do you remember me asking about taking Linda with us to Michigan next month?"

Smiling, Janet nodded. "I do! I gave you permission to do so, didn't I?"

Christina nodded.

"Do I need to sign anything?"

Christina chuckled. "No. If we were going out of the country, then probably so."

After giving Janet a good bye hug, Christina walked down the hallway, and found Linda by the vending machine, retrieving a package of peanuts.

Linda pointed to the drink machine. "Is it okay if I get a drink too?"

"Of course. I'll get one as well."

The sun had set, by the time Christina and Linda exited the hospital.

When they arrived home, Christina received a call from Cindy, asking if she and Ed could come by for a visit. She said, "Of course!"

Stacey, and the boys, came bounding down the stairs, when they heard Christina and Linda enter the house. It was a pleasant reunion as everyone told of their day.

Christina pulled Stacey into a hug, and whispered in her ear.

"Did you enjoy your alone time?"

Stacey grinned, and nodded. "Thanks. I needed that. I even took a nap."

Christina smiled, and nodded. "Good." Removing her outerwear, she said, "Cindy and Ed are coming by in a few minutes. I'm not sure what they want to discuss, but I'd appreciate if we can have some privacy."

Stacey said, "There's a National Geographic special on tonight we're supposed to watch for our science class."

"What's it about?" Asked Nicky.

"Penguins." Linda said. Making a disgusted face, she added, "We have to write a paper about their life cycles."

"I want to watch it too." Nicky said.

The girls shrugged, and said, "Okay."

Christina said, "Good." She looked at Brad who held up his hands.

"I'll be up in my room studying for a history exam tomorrow."

Cindy and Ed arrived within the next half hour. After preparing coffee, they sat around the dining room table, and Cindy went into more detail about her scopes, showing the pictures of her stomach and bowel.

Christina smiled, and nodded. "I'm so glad it's nothing more serious."

"Like cancer?" Cindy asked.

"Well, yeah. I'll have to admit, I was worried that's what it would be."

"I know." Taking Ed's hand, Cindy added, "It was on our minds as well. Thank God, it wasn't!"

Nodding, Christina agreed. "Yes, thank God."

Cindy set her mug down, and said, "Ed has something to tell you."

Christina cocked her head, and looked at Ed expectantly. "Okay."

"Remember a few months back I told you we were investigating a terrorist cell in Dallas?"

Christina nodded.

"Well, this past week, we were able to infiltrate, and eliminate one in the downtown area."

Christina raised her eyebrows in shock. "Really? That's amazing!"

Ed nodded.

"So, why are you telling me this?"

Ed grinned. "Let me back this story up a bit."

He went into great detail about the tracking down of the terrorist group, and apprehension of the man responsible for David's death, as well as other attacks.

Christina brought her hand to her mouth.

"So what you're saying, is that the man who killed David is now in custody?"

Ed placed his hand over Christina's other hand, which was resting on the table. Smiling, he nodded, and said, "Yes. The same man. What are the odds that we'd capture him here?"

Shaking her head, Christina said, "Only God could orchestrate something like that."

Cindy said, "That is so true."

The three adults sat silently for a few moments, processing the information. Christina broke the silence. "So, what is the next step?"

"He'll be in jail until his court appearance, then he'll be tried as a terrorist, and live out his days in prison."

Sighing, Christina said, "I'm glad that loose end is finally tied up!"

Nodding, Ed said, "Yes. We at the agency are relieved as well. It would be nice if *all* the terrorist cells could be so easily located and destroyed, but it seems for everyone that is eliminated, two more pop up. Sure keeps us busy."

Cindy said, "Evil seems to raise its ugly head, no matter how many times it's chopped off."

Ed and Christina nodded in agreement.

Massaging her forehead, Christina said, "Until Christ returns, or we're called home, the enemy will continue to dispense his evil, and terror."

Ed patted Christina's hand. "You're right. Our job, while we're here, is to thwart as many of his plans as we possibly can."

After a moment of silence, Cindy asked, "Can we change the subject?"

Ed and Christina nodded.

Looking at Christina, Cindy said, "I see you got your van back."

Smiling, Christina said, "Yes. Friday afternoon. I can't even see where the damage was. Mr. Simmons, and his crew, did a great job on the repairs."

Cindy said, "I've heard nothing but good reports about their work."

"How was your trip to Dallas to see Janet?" Cindy asked, as she drank the last few drops of her coffee.

"It went well." Christina expounded on the details of her visit.

"Her memory is still a bit patchy, but she told me she had a dream, where an angel, or Jesus, said she'd get most of her memory back."

"Why not all of her memory?" Cindy asked.

Shaking her head, Christina said, "The person, whom she believed to be Jesus, told her 'some memories are best left behind.'"

Nodding, Cindy said, "That's interesting."

Ed asked, "Have y'all moved back to the CCU?"

Nodding, Christina said, "Yes! It is better than it was before the fire. Everything, from the equipment to the sheets, is new. The whole area looks, and smells, clean and fresh."

Cindy said, "I bet the patients, and staff are enjoying it."

Christina chuckled. "Well, we've only had two patients so far, and they didn't know what it looked like before the fire. The staff, however, is loving it!"

Cindy smiled. "So, Christina, it sounds as if things in your life are heading in the right direction."

Nodding, Christina said, "Seems that way, so far." Crossing her fingers, she added, "I'm hoping, and praying, that this new year will be awesome for everyone I know."

Cindy reached out, and patted Christina's hand. "I hope so too."

Christina asked, "Do y'all want more coffee, or something cold to drink."

Shaking their heads, Cindy and Ed said, "No thanks."

Looking at her watch, Cindy said, "We need to get going."

All three adults stood at the same time. Christina gave hugs to Cindy and Ed. "Thanks so much for coming by, and telling me about that terrorist. I hope this is the end of all the turmoil. At least around here."

Cindy said, "Amen to that!"

"I agree. I don't like those life and death situations, even though that's pretty much what my job is about." Ed said, as he helped Cindy with her coat.

Cindy punched his arm playfully. "Maybe you should consider a different line of work?"

"I said I didn't like those situations, but I do love my job. Any time we can get bad guys off the street, that's a victory I want to be part of."

Putting her arm around his waist, she said, "That's what I love about you. Always looking out for the under dog."

He pulled her close, and did a little growl, then kissed the top of her head.

Christina chuckled. "You two are so cute!"

When they left, Christina said goodnight to the kids, who were watching a movie, and headed upstairs to prepare for bed.

Once settled, she picked up a novel she had started a few weeks ago, and began reading. She heard the kids coming up the stairs, knowing they'd be heading to their own rooms and beds. She was surprised when she heard a knock on her door.

"Come in." She said, wondering who would walk through the door.

Stacey poked her head in, and whispered, "Mom, is it okay if I come in?"

Christina sat up, leaning her back on the headboard. She patted the space beside her and Stacey sat. Putting her arm around her daughter, she asked, "What's going on?"

Stacey sighed. "I wanted to thank you for not making me go to Dallas." Lowering her voice to a whisper, she said, "I feel guilty about not wanting to go, but I really needed some alone time. I love Linda, but..." Her voice trailed off.

Christina pulled her daughter close, kissing the side of her forehead. "It's okay. I understand completely. Sometimes being around someone twenty-four hours a day can get a little wearing. You and Linda haven't been apart since she moved in. She probably appreciated some time alone as well."

"How was your trip to Dallas? How is Mrs. Washburn doing? Linda said she's in a different room on a different floor."

Christina filled her in on the details of the visit, adding, "We need to continue praying for complete healing for her. She's struggling with her memory. The Dr. thinks it'll return, but he doesn't know when, or if all of her memories will resurface."

Stacey nodded in understanding. "Linda and I pray together every night. She really misses her mom."

Christina was surprised. "I didn't know you two prayed together. That's awesome!"

"Actually, it was Linda's idea. I think being here with us has helped her have a better understanding of Christianity."

Christina smiled and nodded, as Stacey continued. "She asked a lot of questions in the beginning, but lately, not so much."

Pulling Stacey into a hug, Christina said, "I'm so proud of you for sharing your faith, but also for sharing everything...including me. You and the boys have done so well in accepting her as one of us. Your daddy would be so proud of each of you."

Stacey was silent for a moment, then asked, "Did you and dad ever get tired of each other?"

Christina thought for a moment. "I remember when we were first married, and we decided to go camping together for a week. After about the fifth day, I was ready to pack up, and go home."

"Why?"

"Don't get me wrong, I loved your dad immensely, but he had a certain way of doing things, which didn't always coincide with mine. We had a few heated disagreements. I decided then and there, that camping was not something I enjoyed. Or something we could do together." Smiling, as she remembered the time, she added, "I loved the hiking, and exploring, I just didn't like the whole campsite thing. We were literally together for twenty-four-seven. I never told him, but I was so happy to get home, and sleep in a real bed, and cook on a real stove. I think he was glad to get back to work."

Stacey smiled. "What did y'all fight about?"

Shaking her head, Christina said, "You know, I'm not sure. Probably something stupid, like how to start a campfire."

"I can't imagine you and dad fighting. Y'all never fought in front of us, and I never heard dad raise his voice to you. You and dad were like Mr. and Mrs. Brady on the Brady Bunch."

Christina gave her daughter a shocked expression. "What? The Brady's? Honey, we disagreed, and even argued. You're right, though, your dad never raised his voice, or threatened me in any way. He was a perfect gentleman. Sometimes we had to agree to disagree, and let the anger go. Whatever it was that we didn't agree on, it wasn't worth damaging our relationship."

Stacey snuggled in closer, and laid her arm across her mothers waist, and her head on her mother's chest. "When I grow up, I want to marry a guy just like daddy."

Christina felt tears sting the back of her eyes. "I hope you do."

Mother and daughter talked for an hour more, until Stacey yawned, and said, "I need to go to bed." She leaned over, and kissed her mom on the cheek, then stood and stretched. A minute later, Christina heard muffled voices, as the bedroom door shut.

Yawning, she thought, *so much for getting any reading done.* After turning off the light, she turned on her side, and was asleep within minutes. She dreamed of sitting on a beach beside very still water. The sky, and surrounding plants were reflected in the mirror-like surface. The atmosphere around her seemed to be holding its breath. No breeze. No sound...not even the chirp, and call of birds, or buzzing of insects. As she sat, she felt a presence, and turned to see who had tip-toed up behind her. No one. She turned back to face the still water, remembering the verse that says, "He leads me beside still waters. He restores my soul." She felt an overwhelming sense of peace wash over her. Closing her eyes, she breathed in the clean air, savoring the sweet aroma of flowers growing nearby. She felt a presence sit next to her. Opening her eyes, she was surprised to see David, staring at the distant shore.

"Hi Christina," He said matter-of-factually. Not looking at her, he added, "It's very peaceful here. It reminds me of the verse that says, "Be still, and know that I am God."

She couldn't take her eyes off him. *How can he be here? How can I be here? Am I in heaven?*

She whispered, "David?"

He turned to look at her, and brought his hand to her face, gently touching her cheek. Smiling and nodding, he said, "I'm here."

"How?"

"You're dreaming, and I'm present in your dream. Father allowed me to come visit you here."

Looking around, she asked, "Where is here?"

He chuckled. "Doesn't it look familiar?"

She looked around once again, and remembered. "This is where we had our first camp out."

Nodding, and grinning, he said, "Yes! Even though it wasn't the best camping experience, there were some special times. Remember how we'd come out here, and sip our coffee, and watch the sunrise, and then in the evening, the sunset?"

Nodding, she whispered, "Yes. Those were the highlights of each day. We'd sit for hours, talking, praying, and planning." Sighing heavily, she added, "We were so young and naive back then. Sometimes, I wish I could go back to those days."

"Ah, yes. If only we could go back with all our knowledge and experience in tact, we could make better choices."

"Exactly!" She said.

Giving her a serious look, he said, "Everyone wants that, but Father only gives us one chance for a reason. Unfortunately, most of us would end up making many of the same mistakes, or choices. God has a perfect plan for every single person, but because of our stubborn nature, and our free will, we don't always ask Him what He wants us to do. Instead, many of us plow through a situation, then pray that He fixes our mistakes."

Christina nodded. "More times than not, I do that very thing."

Looking over the water, David said, "All humans do. Jesus was the only perfect One who did everything right, because He was God, and knew the plan. Fortunately, because Jesus chose to be obedient, we have the ability to ask for wisdom, and forgiveness. Just like we love, teach, and forgive our kids, when they make a wrong choice, our Father loves, teaches, and forgives us. He knows our flesh is weak, and our wills are stubborn, but He is patient. He desires fellowship with every one of His creations, but not everyone desires fellowship with Him."

Placing her hand in his, and laying her head on his shoulder, she said, "I miss you. I wish we could stay here forever."

He squeezed her hand, and kissed her forehead. "I know, but that is not in Father's plan for you or I. Some day when your time on Earth is finished, we will have eternity together." Smiling, he added, "And I can guarantee we won't grow tired of each others company."

Putting her hand over her moth, she whispered, "Did you hear me talking to Stacey?"

Nodding slightly, he said, "It's okay, because it was the truth."

He stood, and reached out to take her hand. He then helped her stand, and pulled her into an embrace. "I love you Christina. You are doing an amazing job raising our children. I will continue watching over you, but I will not visit you as often. Father wants you to move on in your life, as He has another mate picked out for you."

She shook her head. "I don't want anyone else!"

"This person will not be who you think. Father wants to surprise you and the kids with the gift of a new love."

"Who will it be?"

Shaking his head, he said, "I don't know. I just know if he's Father's choice, he'll be perfect for you and the kids."

He pulled away, and began to fade.

"No, David! Don't leave!"

She then heard a different voice. Gentle, but firm. "Be still, Christina, and know that I Am God."

The dream ended, and Christina woke with a start. The clock read 3:33. Rubbing her eyes, she threw the covers off, and headed to the bathroom. The dream, still fresh in her mind, kept playing over and over, like a stuck DVD. *I hope I can continue the dream,* she thought, crawling under the covers.

Instead, she went into a deep, restful sleep, and woke a minute before her alarm went off.

EPILOGUE

Five Years Later

Christina stood in front of her bedroom mirror, staring trance-like, at the woman reflected there.

Am I really doing this? How can this be possible?

Hearing a knock on her door, she answered, "Come in."

Cindy walked in, followed by Stacey and Linda, all wearing dresses in different shades of aqua.

Stacey inhaled sharply. "Mom! You look beautiful! That dark aqua makes your blue eyes glow!"

Linda grinned, and nodded in agreement.

Cindy walked over, and gave her best friend a hug, whispering, "Are you ready?"

Christina returned the hug, and letting out a sigh, said, "As ready as I'll ever be!"

The three females exited the bedroom, and made their way down the stairs. Brad was waiting at the bottom, and reached out to take his mother's hand. He had grown, and matured, into such a handsome young man. Brad was in his second year at Alva Community College, with plans to transfer to Baylor University, majoring in computer technology. Pride filled her being, as she reached out, and let him place her hand in the crook of his arm. He whispered, "You look amazing, Mom. I am so happy for you."

The music, a trio of violins, began playing Canon in D, as she, Brad, Cindy, and the girls, entered the dining room, where the pastor, Ed, and her future husband, stood. Her heart fluttered in her chest, like a bird trying to escape a cage. She glanced into the adjoining living room at the attendees. She saw family, and close friends, gathered to celebrate this momentous occasion.

So much had transpired over the past five years: Cindy and Ed had married, and moved into a bigger home north of Alva, closer to the ATO office in Dallas. Cindy's health improved, and she began teaching a Zumba class every week, in a building next to Mary's Clothes Garden, where she continued to work, part time. Samara was in her first year at Abilene University—half-way between Dallas, and LaMesa, where Ed's family lived. She hoped to be a District Attorney some day, and was majoring in law.

Tom and Eleanor had remarried, and were expecting a baby girl in a couple of months. Tommy was an energetic ten-year-old, looking forward to being a big brother. Eleanor's father passed two years earlier, and she, Tom and Tommy, moved into the family farm house with her mother, on the outskirts of Alva.

Lisa and Donna had kids in every school, from elementary to college, which kept them busy. The four ladies had remained close friends during the years, and once a month, would spend a day or weekend together.

Dr. Carmichael transferred to the Dallas Children's Hospital, and he and Sammie, along with his parents, moved there as well. Christina smiled, as Sammie blew her a kiss. Dr. Carmichael, handsome as ever, gave her a smile, and head nod. She smiled at him, wondering who the blond was, sitting on the other side of Sammie.

Janet regained most of her memory, and came out of the experience with a totally different personality. Gone were the anger, and bitterness. She smiled, and laughed easily, and was gracious and generous. She and Dr. Dawson reconciled their differences, and began dating steadily a year or so after she had fully recovered. Christina wouldn't be surprised if they too tied the knot in the near future. Janet reconnected with her brothers, and their families, which brought much joy to them all.

Jamie went to a trade school in Waco, to learn more about auto mechanics, and business. He had dreams of having his own repair shop some day, but until that time, was content working with his dad. The father, and son, continued to grow in their faith-walk, and were involved in the Promise Keepers movement. Jamie and Brad became close friends, and began a community cupboard to help the needy in their community. When they both left for college, the ministry was handed off to other youth in the area.

Stacey and Linda, both seniors, with plans of going to Mary-Hardin-Baylor College of Nursing in Belton, were still the best of friends, and spent the past four summers attending camp, or going on mission trips together. They both were beautiful inside and out, and were quite involved in community events. They both smiled, and blew her a kiss, before taking their seats in the front row.

Nicky, her "baby" was a sophomore in high-school, and still wanted to be a missionary pilot. He and Danny were thick as thieves, and spent most of their spare time defeating the enemy, via video games. They had just recently begun to show an interest in girls. Nicky and Lula kept in touch over the years, and Christina took him to visit her, on her birthday, for the past few. Nicky, sitting on the first row of seats, gave her a finger wave. She winked at him.

Glancing around the crowded room, of forty or so people, she made eye contact with her friends from the hospital: Sally-Jean, Hannah, Libby, Mrs. Ferguson, and Sarah. She'd talk to them all after the ceremony. Sally-Jean had married a nice young man from Waco, and they were expecting their first child in the next few weeks. Sarah had married Harold, and they lived on his spacious ranch near Dallas. The other women appeared to be happy, and healthy, and between work, and family life, were quite busy.

She was amazed, and pleased, at how beautifully decorated the two rooms were. Thanks to her friends, their spouses, and children, the rooms looked like something out of a Martha Stewart magazine. The chairs all had white covers on them, and there was tulle, ivy, and flowers, placed in, and around the rooms. All the extra furniture had been moved to other areas of the house to make room for all the guests. Not as big and fancy as the church, but it was cozy. Exactly what she was going for.

With the extra money from David's death benefits, she had been able to bring the old house back to life, with all new windows, wiring, plumbing, and central heating, and cooling. She also had new dry wall, moldings, light fixtures, and an expanded kitchen, with a laundry room off the back. One of the things they had enjoyed during the cold winters, had been the new gas fireplace in the family room. She truly loved the old house, and her future husband had agreed to make this their home once they were married.

Releasing the breath she had been holding, she straightened her back, and took the last couple of steps to her man. He looked so handsome in his suit and tie, as he looked down at her, and grinned. Never in a thousand years, would she have predicted this moment. Ready to commit the rest of her life to him. Feeling tears sting her eyes, she batted her lashes to keep them at bay.

The pastor began the ceremony. After welcoming everyone, and giving a brief history of the couple's lives, he gave a short sermon about marriage, and commitment. Then he came to the most important part.

The couple faced each other, held hands, and spoke their prepared vows. When they were finished, the pastor said, "You may kiss your bride." The newly married couple then turned to face the audience as the pastor introduced them.

"I would like to introduce Mr. and Mrs. Jesse McCoy." Everyone stood, cheered, and clapped their approval.

Once all the handshaking, hugging, and congratulations, were finished, Christina encouraged everyone to head to the breakfast nook, and grab a snack, provided by a catering business in downtown Alva. If they wanted, the back yard, and patios, were open as well. It was a perfectly, beautiful June day.

Christina, and Jesse, walked around, and spoke to all the guests. Her friends helped with the serving of the food, and beverages, as well as clean up. She was so thankful for them.

Her Aunt, Uncle, and cousin, from Milford, whom she hadn't seen in a few years, even though they only lived twenty minutes away, came for the ceremony, but left soon after. Her aunt had been ill with pneumonia recently, and hadn't fully recovered her strength.

David's parents were present, and were thankful Christina had chosen such a fine man. They planned to stay with the kids while Christina and Jesse went on their honeymoon. Even though they were getting on in years, they had enough spark, and spunk, to travel not only to Texas, but around the world as well.

The sheriff was there with his new wife, Lucy, who was pregnant with their first child. They appeared to be happy, as they held hands, while chatting with the other guests.

Christina was so overwhelmed with the generosity of her family, and dear friends, she had to take a moment to regain control of her emotions. She wanted to laugh, and cry, at the same time. After a great time of eating, and partying, everyone left a few hours later. Christina walked around the quiet house. All the chairs had been folded, and stood in a corner to be returned to the church the next day. The food had been put away, the garbage collected, and taken to the garage, and most of the tulle, and ivy had been removed. The remaining flowers would stay a while longer. Her in-laws, children, and husband were no where to be seen or heard in the spacious house. Christina walked to the back patio door, and found them sitting around the table, talking, and drinking iced-tea. She stood, silently watching the interaction. Jesse's parents had both passed, and he had been an only child, so he had no one to share his new family with. She was thankful David's parents were willing to fill that gap. They had accepted Jesse with open arms.

Jesse, noticing her standing by the door, stood and walked over to her. He pulled her into a hug, resting his chin on the top of her head.

"Well, Darlin'. We did it. We're officially hitched."

She giggled. She loved when he talked with a twang. Nodding, she looked up into his beautiful blue eyes. "Yep."

Looking at his watch, he said, "Our plane leaves for Florida in about four hours. Then off to the Bahamas tomorrow morning. Why don't you go get your stuff together, and we'll say good-bye to the kids before we head out?"

Standing on her tiptoes to kiss him on the mouth, she said, "That's a great plan, Sir." Giggling, she turned, and sprinted up the stairs.

Jesse wished for the millionth time that his son could be there to participate in this momentous occasion. It hardly seemed possible that five years had passed since he said good-bye to his son. So much had happened since then. Lost in thought, he hadn't heard Nicky approach, until he cleared his throat.

Opening his eyes, he saw Nicky standing in front of him.

Smiling, he said, "Yes, Son?"

Biting his bottom lip, Nicky said, "I just want you to know that I'll try to be a good son. I know I'll never replace Jimmy, but I'd like to just...you know... hang out with you every now and then."

Jesse reached out, and pulled Nicky into a hug. "I'd like that. Maybe you can teach me how to play some of those combat games, on your PlayStation."

Nicky pulled away, and grinned. "I'd love to. When y'all get back from your trip."